HIGH

LONESOME

New & Selected Stories

1966–2006

STORY COLLECTIONS BY
JOYCE CAROL OATES

By the North Gate (1963)
Upon the Sweeping Flood and Other Stories (1966)
The Wheel of Love (1970)
Marriages and Infidelities (1972)
The Goddess and Other Women (1974)
The Poisoned Kiss (1975)
Crossing the Border (1976)
Night-Side (1977)
A Sentimental Education (1980)
Last Days (1984)
Raven's Wing (1986)
The Assignation (1988)
Heat and Other Stories (1991)
Where Is Here? (1992)
Where Are You Going, Where Have You Been?:
Selected Early Stories (1993)
Haunted: Tales of the Grotesque (1994)
Will You Always Love Me? (1996)
The Collector of Hearts: New Tales of the Grotesque (1998)
Faithless: Tales of Transgression (2001)

Joyce Carol Oates

HIGH

LONESOME

New & Selected Stories

1 9 6 6 – 2 0 0 6

FIRST EDITION

Designed by Kate Nichols

Library of Congress Cataloging-in-Publication Data

Oates, Joyce Carol
High lonesome : new & selected stories, 1966–2006 / Joyce Carol Oates.—1st ed.
p. cm.
ISBN-10: 0-06-050119-7 (alk. paper)
ISBN-13: 978-0-06-050119-8
1. United States—Social life and customs—Fiction. I. Title.
PS3565.A8H54 2006
813'.54—dc22

2005051147

06   07   :08   09   10   BVG/QBF   10   9   8   7   6   5   4   3   2   1

for Kristina and Richard Ford

CONTENTS

THE 1970S

THE 1980S

THE 1990S

NEW STORIES

SPIDER BOY

———

"THERE ARE PLACES in the world where people vanish."
His father had said this. His father had spoken flatly, without
an air of mystery or threat. It was not a statement to be challenged and it
was not a statement to be explained. Later, when his father had vanished
out of his life, he would summon back the words as a kind of explanation
and in anxious moments he would mis-hear the words as *There are places
in the world where people can vanish.*

Still later, when he had not seen his father in a long time, or what
seemed to him a long time, months, or maybe just weeks, he would try
to summon the words again, exactly as his father had uttered them, but
by this time he'd become uncertain, anxious. *Where people can vanish,*
or *where people vanish?*

It was such a crucial distinction!

"REMEMBER your new name. Think before you answer. Not just,
'What's your name?' but any question. It helps to lick your lips. That will
give you time not to make a mistake you can't unmake."

Yet not his name but his surname was the issue. For his surname had been so disgraced there had come to be a fascination in its forbidden sound. The elided consonants and vowels, the lift of its final syllable, an expression of (possibly mocking) surprise like an arched eyebrow. In private, in his secret places, he spoke the forbidden name aloud in mimicry of newscasters who gave to it an air of intrigue and reproach. Sometimes in his bed at night in his new room in his grandparents' house he pressed his face deeply into the pillow and spoke the forbidden name, each syllable equally and defiantly stressed—*Szaa ra*. He spoke the name until his breath ran out and his lungs ached and through his body raced a half-pleasurable panic that he would smother.

A pillow. Where his mouth was, wet with saliva. Where his teeth gnawed. A pillow is a comforting thing when your head rests on it, but if a pillow is pressed against your face, if you are lying on your back and a pillow is pressed against your face, you could not summon the strength to push it away and save yourself.

"YES. We've moved out of state."

Before even the impeachment hearings his mother had filed for divorce from their father. But before even she'd filed for divorce she'd moved them—Emily, Philip, herself—into her parents' big stone house overlooking the Hudson River at Nyack, New York.

Now it was a drive of several hours to the old house in Trenton, overlooking the Delaware River. On the map, it was really not very far but there was an air of distance and finality in his mother's frequently repeated words: "Out of state."

Out of state caught in Philip's mind, uttered in his mother's breathless yet adamant voice. As you might say *out of space, out of time.*

Out of danger, out of harm.

Out of toxic contagion.

In this new state it was essential to have a new name. To replace and nullify the old, disgraced name. Quickly!—before Emily and Philip were enrolled in their new schools.

"Yes, we think it's best. Separate schools."

Private day schools. Nyack Academy for Emily, who was fifteen and in her second year of high school, Edgerstoune School for Philip, who would be thirteen in August, and would enter eighth grade. In New Jersey both children had gone to the Pennington Academy, in a northern Trenton suburb. Sometimes their mother drove them to school, sometimes one of their father's assistants. There was a private bus provided by the school, of the identical bright-pumpkin hue of public school buses but only one-third the size. Riding on this bus, they'd never sat together and acknowledged each other only politely, with diffident smiles.

For a few weeks during the impeachment hearings they'd continued to attend the Pennington Academy, but when criminal charges were brought against their father and the impeachment hearings ceased, their mother had removed them from school.

"It has to be done. They can't be made to suffer for him. They are only children."

In Nyack, it soon became official: they had a new name.

Where *Szaara* had been, now there was *Hudgkins*.

Where *Philip Szaara* had been, now there was *Philip Hudgkins*.

Where *Emily Szaara* had been, now there was *Emily Hudgkins*.

For this wasn't a "new" new name, of course. It was their Nyack grandparents' name which they'd long known and with which they had, their mother insisted, only happy associations. Their mother would take up again her old, "maiden" name with relief. During the sixteen years of her marriage to the New Jersey politician Roy Szaara she had retained Hudgkins as her middle name, she'd continued to be known by certain of her women friends, with whom she'd gone to Bryn Mawr, as Miriam Hudgkins. And so: "It isn't a great change. It's more like coming back home." She smiled bravely. She smiled defiantly. She had had her hair cut and restyled and she had a new way of clasping, at waist level, her shaky left hand in her more forceful right hand, as a practiced tennis player might clasp a racket.

"I mean, it is coming home. Where we belong."

"'SPIDER BOY.'"

You might have thought that "Spider Boy" was in playful reference to the comic strip/movie superhero "Spider-man" but in fact Philip had no interest in Spider-man as he had no interest in the comics, action films and video games that so captivated other boys.

" 'Spider Boy.' "

It was a way of evoking the haunting and powerful presence that existed now entirely in memory. Except for a single memento (smelly, ugly, of a clumsy size and in no way to be mistaken for something of Philip's own) kept in a secret place in his room, Philip might begin to consider whether Spider Boy had ever existed. For he understood *He has vanished* without having needed to be told.

And if vanished, all memory of him should vanish. He knew.

Yet vividly he remembered: the effort of smiling. A strange sensation in his jaws. And his voice a girl's voice, weak and disappointing, he'd had to repeat his words so that Spider Boy could hear amid the traffic noises. He remembered: jamming both hands into the pockets of his Pennington Academy jacket. For Spider Boy, panhandling in front of the Camden train station, was standing in an odd posture, sexy-swaggering you might say, one hand brashly extended palm up and the other, as if for ballast, clenched and jammed in a pocket of his filthy jeans.

Spider Boy was older than Philip by several years. He was taller than Philip by several inches. He had a shaved head and deep-set glassy-dark eyes. His jaws were covered in a darkish ghost-beard. There was something twitchy/spidery about his arms jutting from bony shoulders and his restless lanky legs. He wore a grungy black T-shirt and jeans torn at the knees. On his feet, splayed sneakers crudely mended with tape. The smallest toe of his left foot protruded through the rotted sneaker fabric like a wayward tongue.

" 'Spider Boy.' "

Not at the time had Philip said such a thing, of course. At the time he had not been capable of thought. Excited and anxious and taken by surprise when, murmuring *Excuse me?* he'd seen with what eagerness the boy turned to him, a sudden flaring in the sunken eyes of something like hope.

" 'Spider Boy.' " Philip wanted to feel revulsion for him. For then he would not feel a more tender emotion.

"BUT WHY would they 'know who you are'?"

His mother laughed at him, not cruelly but in the way of a mother who loves her child no matter how silly, how mistaken, how annoying he is.

"Why, if you are exactly who you are, 'Philip Hudgkins,' would anyone at your new school think that you are *not*?"

Philip hesitated. Philip frowned. It was *squiggling up your face* in a way to exasperate his mother so quickly he murmured yes, he guessed she was right, he was sorry.

His mother would relent now. If you submitted quickly. If you acknowledged your weakness and wrong. For Mom (Philip's mother wished to be called "Mom" as his father wished to be called "Dad") was not one to persevere after a victory, however justified. Her eyes brimming with the pain of their mutual hurt: "Oh, I know you don't mean it, honey. It's your nerves."

He supposed, yes. All their nerves.

NERVES! A way of allowing Philip to know that he was sensitive, like his mother. Not crude and cruel, manipulative and maneuvering, like his father.

Moreover, *nerves* were not your fault but the fault of others' behavior. The fault of *the circumstances of our lives.*

Yet it was *honey* that most reverberated in his ears. This, too, was a signal that he was loved, as a child is loved; he was not an adolescent boy but a child-boy, his mother's baby. He felt a half-pleasurable guilt, that he didn't deserve *honey* as he didn't deserve his mother's love. Soon he would outgrow *honey*, even his mother would acknowledge. When she learned of the secrets Philip shared with his father.

His father hadn't called Philip *honey* in a long time. Such baby names for a boy offended his father's sense of manly propriety. Instead, his father called him by his full, formal name "Philip" when it was necessary to call him by name. Mostly when they were alone together or in the presence of a hitch-hiker ("hitch-hiker" was the term by which the boys were known) his father called him only just *you.*

In the presence of hitch-hikers his father had a way of speaking exuberantly yet guardedly. A way of laughing that made you want to laugh with him. He was likely to tousle Philip's hair and tease him the way you'd tease a younger child. And touching him, as if to display his affection for his son. Squeezing Philip's arm at the elbow as he let him out of the car at the corner of State Street and Mercer, to return to the twelfth-floor apartment alone. "You've got a key, let yourself in. If I'm not back by twelve, don't wait up. I'll see you in the morning."

You, your. And never *Philip.*

Sometimes, an impulsive kiss on the side of Philip's head.

"Hey you: be good."

. . . THE SWIPE of his father's mouth against Philip's left temple where a thin blue vein beat tremulously. As if at that juncture in his skull the bones had failed to meld properly and the slightest blow might cause irreparable harm.

"FINE, SIR. We are all fine. Thanks for asking."

It was the headmaster Dr. Simmons who made it a point to say hello to the new transfer student from Jersey whom most of his classmates ignored. Hello and how are your mother and her family, tactfully making no mention of any father living or dead, free on $300,000 bail bond or already beginning to serve his twelve-to-fifteen-year sentence at the New Jersey Men's Facility at Rahway. How are you, with a smile warm and encouraging in the way of one greeting a convalescent. And Philip did his best to smile and reply in emulation of his mother's telephone voice, never failing to include *sir.*

In the first terrible days at the Edgerstoune School Philip had believed that the other students must know who he was: whose son. He'd imagined covert looks, stares. He'd imagined suppressed smiles. But with the passage of months it seemed painfully clear to him that Philip wasn't only not "known" but invisible in the eyes of his classmates. If he was jostled by bigger boys it was only that he was there, a diminutive physical presence, to be jostled. He, Philip Hudgkins, a transfer student with a way of retreating even as he moved forward, held little appeal for those who might have wished, in other circumstances, to be cruel.

His teachers knew, Philip supposed. Though Dr. Simmons had promised not to tell anyone (so Philip's mother insisted), still it seemed likely to Philip that they knew. In Nyack, in certain circles, there had to be a residue of the long linkage between "Hudgkins" and "Szaara." Philip's mother wished not to recall that she'd been married in Nyack and through sixteen years she'd brought her gregarious and attractive rising-Republican husband home to visit with her parents and to be introduced to their friends. How could this be nullified by his mother's frantic efforts now? Worse yet, in mid-winter, after months of quiet, *Szaara* headlines were re-emerging, no longer confined to New Jersey media but beginning to appear in the Metro section of the *New York Times*. For the news had catapulted beyond charges of misconduct in political office, misuse of public funds, bribe-taking and deal-making and such into far more serious criminal charges of statutory rape, sexual assault upon a minor, abduction of a minor, and conspiracy to commit these crimes. Investigators for the state attorney general's office wiretapping Roy Szaara's phones to gather evidence for his political misconduct were astonished to discover evidence for another category of misconduct.

Still, Philip's mother insisted. "I've told you! No one knows. Almost no one. We can escape the taint of that name."

"ONLY JUST TELL HER what we did. If she asks. 'Camping.' She won't ask much."

Several times that summer they'd gone "camping" at the Delaware Water Gap State Park in northern New Jersey. That is, the intention had been to go camping there. In the backseat of his father's car were newly purchased sleeping bags, hiking boots, plastic bottles of Evian water and packages of granola. A lightweight blanket from L.L. Bean, a pillow. A single heavy, hefty pillow.

It was so, Philip's mother rarely asked about his weekends with his father. His sister never asked.

"Your mother doesn't really give a damn about you any more than she does about me. It's only pride with her, see. Her wounded class-pride, her wish to scrape me off her shoes. We'll see!" His father laughed and leaned over suddenly to kiss the soft vulnerable spot at the side of Philip's head.

Roy Szaara had a large solid face burnished like a coin. He had the face of a man much-photographed. Laugh lines radiated from the corners of his eyes and his eyes were clear, frank, and engaging. When he laughed you wanted to laugh with him in the way that fallen leaves are drawn in the wake of a speeding vehicle.

Here was a man to be trusted. Here was a man with a handshake. A man who parted his graying dark hair razor-sharp on the left side of his scalp. For certain of his public appearances he wore makeup including inky-black mascara lightly brushed against his eyelashes. For their trips to Chester, Pennsylvania, to South Philly and Camden, New Jersey, he wore tinted glasses in stylish metal frames. He whistled, he was in good spirits. He rarely spoke of his week at the state capitol except to tell Philip that things were going very well. He did not inquire after Philip's mother or sister. He would have shaved just before picking Philip up at the Pennington Academy, Friday afternoon at 3:20 P.M. He smelled of after-shave and something sweet like vanilla.

"Go over there. Poor kid ask him if he wants a ride. If he's hungry."

It was the bus station at Chester. It was the 30th Street Railway Station in Philadelphia. It was the Camden train station. Philip's father urged him from the car with a gentle nudge against his shoulder. Like a sleepwalker with unnaturally widened and alert eyes he made his way past a noisy family loading their minivan to the boy in grungy black T-shirt and jeans panhandling listlessly at the curb. People pushed past him, mostly blacks. He was a lone white-boy panhandler at whom no one gave more than a cursory glance. He stood with one hand extended palm up, listless and yet stubborn, unmoving. The other hand was a fist jammed into a pocket. His face was dirty. His jaws were covered in shadowy fuzz. His eyes were glassy and deep-set with fatigue. There was something both childlike and feral about him that made Philip shy to approach him and so he was surprised when the boy looked at him eagerly as if hoping he might know him.

"Excuse me? My dad and me, we're going to McDonald's for some hamburgers. You could come with us. Dad says."

These words had been programmed for Philip. Except for *Dad says* which was his own invention.

Later, after they'd eaten, his father drove to Trenton to let Philip off at the apartment. It was late now, nearing 10 P.M. and Philip's head ached with exhaustion. He was in the backseat of the car and the boy, the hitch-hiker, who'd said his name was Reuben but who'd been coy about providing a last name, was in the passenger's seat beside Philip's father. Reuben was smoking a cigarette Philip's father had given him and he was talking loudly, boastfully. His speech was interlarded with *shit, suck, fuck.* In McDonald's Reuben had wolfed down three Tex-Mex burgers, two orders of french fries and a Giant Pepsi. He had shocked Philip by belching loudly and without apology as if making a witticism. The conversation had been mostly between Reuben and Philip's father and Philip had felt himself excluded but he had not been hurt or anyway not much hurt for something similar had happened twice before in his father's company in other McDonald's restaurants with other starving hitch-hikers and each time Philip had consoled himself thinking *Dad wants him to feel special. He is someone to be pitied.*

It came out that Reuben was from Tom's River, South Jersey. He'd "hung out" at Atlantic City for a while then caught a ride to Philly where he had contacts. He was headed for New York, as he said, "eventually." When, at the corner of State Street and Mercer, Philip moved to climb out of the car, Reuben had looked surprised asking wasn't he coming with them?—but Philip's father explained that Philip was too young for this place he wanted to take Reuben, the Café à Go-Go Bar & Lounge, Philip was much too young. And Philip's father laughed and Reuben laughed with him, exhaling a mouthful of smoke.

"You've got the key. Don't wait up. Good night!"

Philip hid inside the vestibule and watched his father drive away with Reuben. Now he was hurt, he felt a stab of jealousy, but he knew that, next day, Reuben would be gone and he would have his father to himself. It was the new Acura his father was driving, a sedan with a beautiful pale bronze finish. Roy Szaara always drove new cars which he leased. He did not buy cars, but leased them. Philip had seen the admiration in the boy's eyes as they'd approached his father's car. Now he watched as the Acura moved back into State Street traffic. Soon it disappeared in a stream of glittering cars headed for the bridge over the Delaware River.

Next day, the pillow would be gone from the backseat of the car, though the rest of the camping gear remained. Philip would wonder if it was in the trunk of the car. Or if his father had thrown it away.

THERE WAS FAT BOY, and there was Baldie. There was Luis, and there was Smoke. And there was Spider Boy.

When Philip asked his father where the hitch-hikers had gone, his father laughed and tousled his hair and said, "There are places in the world where people vanish." It was a blunt statement of fact and seemed to carry no further meaning.

Later, Philip's father explained that the hitch-hikers were a secret between him and Philip that no one must ever know. Did Philip promise to keep this secret?

Yes. Philip promised.

Because the hitch-hikers were boys who'd broken the law. They were boys "wanted" by the law for juvenile crimes and very likely they would be sent to juvenile detention facilities—"juvie hall" as it was called—and Philip's father had acted to prevent this. He'd convinced them to return to their homes. He'd given them money to return by bus. He'd listened as they called their parents and he insisted upon speaking with their parents to explain who he was, and what the situation was. "These are lost boys needing to be found."

Sometimes when his father brought Philip to his apartment for a weekend, Philip discovered things the hitch-hikers had left behind: soiled socks and underwear, crumpled cigarette packages, a single sneaker mended with duct tape. A plastic belt patterned to resemble crocodile skin. A sweat-stained baseball cap. A part-eaten slice of pizza hardened to something mineral with the imprint of a stranger's teeth perfectly preserved. Once, his father came up behind him to snatch a filthy undershirt from Philip's fingers. Harshly he laughed, "For shame. Your mother should keep you cleaner."

FOR A LONG TIME then *Your mother should keep you cleaner* reverberated in his ears with a ring of playful reproach. He was a fastidious boy who washed his hands often and kept his fingernails clean and had a compulsion to brush his teeth immediately after eating for he could not bear the sensation of food particles between his teeth. He would come to remember that the filthy undershirt had in fact been his and a deep shame came over him for his father had seen, and his father, too, would remember.

———

" 'SPIDER BOY.' "

It was a secret and would remain a secret. He had promised.

Oh but he'd done a bad thing, a thing his father would not have liked. For his father trusted him and Philip had (maybe) violated that trust. He'd taken with him, wrapped in his own underwear in the rucksack he brought his things in, the single sneaker mended with duct tape, a badly torn, stained and filthy and foul-smelling gun-metal gray sneaker of a size he'd have said was twice that of his own. If he'd been asked why, why bring such a filthy thing home with him, he could not have said why except it would have been lost otherwise.

As if in punishment for what he'd done, the weekends in Trenton ended abruptly. Not for some time would Philip learn why.

AND THEN, ten months later the call came.

Philip's mother was summoned back to Trenton, that despised city. The former Mrs. Miriam Szaara was ordered to bring her thirteen-year-old son Philip to Trenton police headquarters to be questioned by detectives involved in the "continuing investigation" into former New Jersey Republican state senator Roy Szaara.

"He's in prison. He's pleaded guilty. His career is finished. His life is finished. What more do they want from us!"

It was so, Philip's father had begun serving his twelve-to-fifteen-year sentence at the New Jersey Men's Facility at Rahway. He'd changed his initial plea of not guilty to a plea of guilty to assorted charges in order to avoid a protracted and lurid trial and to avoid further legal costs, for he'd declared bankruptcy. By early April of the new year the ugly *Szaara* headlines had disappeared from the *New York Times* to be replaced by other lurid headlines pertaining to strangers. Philip's mother remained unshaken in her belief that, by changing their accursed surname, she had severed all links with her former husband and no one dared suggest otherwise.

Now, she was furious! Yet even more incensed when the detective who'd called her offered to "provide transportation" for her and her son to Trenton police headquarters. "As if I can't drive by myself. As if I don't know the way. As if I might get lost. As if I might disappear."

It was a drive of several hours to Trenton. Philip's mother insisted she wanted no one with them. Philip had to be excused from school and brought with him several textbooks in which he might hide from his mother's rambling quavering voice that was alternately furious and despairing, mocking and pleading.

"But why, why! *Why!* Why would they want to involve *you.*"

He had not seen his father since the mandated weekends had come to an abrupt end. At the time of the impeachment hearings, and before his father's resignation played and replayed on New Jersey Network TV. How many weeks after the night of Spider Boy, he'd have had to calculate. The stolen sneaker was safely hidden in his room behind a row of old videos: *Fly Away Home, Winged Migration, When Dinosaurs Reigned.* The Guatemalan woman who cleaned house for Philip's grandparents knew not to touch Philip's videos or anything on his shelves or desk.

He hadn't been questioned about his father before. Not even by his mother except with a forced smile when she inquired about his weekends in Trenton, had things been "all right," and Philip had said yes and that was all.

Yet it seemed, since his father's departure from his life, and his new name, that Philip thought of his father more frequently. He had not dared to suggest even to his grandparents that he be allowed to visit his father in prison for such a request would dismay and infuriate them and there was no thought, not the faintest glimmer of a thought, that he might say such a thing to his mother.

Though, seeing signs for the Rahway exit on the turnpike, Philip's mother said suddenly, with a breathless laugh, "There! We could stop. You'd like that, wouldn't you."

Philip shook his head. No.

For he'd known that his father would not have wanted to be seen in such a place. Recalling how his father had dressed so stylishly. His father's expensive clothes, haircuts. His fingernails manicured and clean and the cuffs of his trademark white silk dress shirts always spotless and there was a comfort in this, or had been. His father's heavy, handsome watch with its platinum gold stretch band. An expensive watch with a famous brand name, received as a gift. His father had joked that the damned watch was so heavy he couldn't wear it in bed. Damned watch didn't keep time as well as the cheap Timex watches he'd bought in drugstores when he'd been a kid.

Not only in Philip's secret places and in his bed at night but it seemed now everywhere, in the company even of his mother, and in his classes at the Edgerstoune School, Philip thought of his father and heard his father's teasing and admonishing voice. *Your mother should keep you cleaner, secret between us, promise?* Repeatedly he heard *There are places in the world where people vanish* or was it *There are places in the world where people can vanish.* He saw again the beautiful pale bronze Acura cruising the streets of Chester, South Philly, Camden. He saw again the view of glittering lights from his father's twelfth-floor Trenton apartment. He seemed to know that at the Camden train station the ghost-figure of Spider Boy might be sighted and the brightly lighted booth in the McDonald's restaurant would retain the ghost-figures of the three of them and if he could return he would discover them.

On the drive to Trenton he was beset by such memories. As if returning to the city so despised by his mother and invariably described in the *New York Times* as a "decaying city on the Delaware River" he was drawing nearer to their source. He felt a strange excitement, a thrill of apprehension. They had exited the turnpike and were driving south on

Route 1 toward Trenton and the Delaware River and always there was the small thrill of EXIT ONLY and LAST EXIT BEFORE BRIDGE TO PA. Here was a mostly abandoned industrial landscape of smokestacks and refineries, factories and warehouses marooned within acres of cracked and crumbling pavement, overgrown vacant lots, oily ponds, billboards of tattered yet smiling faces, tenement buildings with broken and boarded-up windows. Philip's mother shuddered at such ugliness as if it were a personal affront. Philip smiled as if wishing to believe that he was coming home, though the house on the Delaware River had been sold and his father's twelfth-floor apartment had been vacated and he had no home any longer, not anywhere.

"Just tell them the truth, Philip. You know nothing. How could you, a child, know anything! And remember you new name: 'Hudgkins.' I have the documents."

"EVER SEEN HIM BEFORE, Philip? Take your time."

Spread across the table in the windowless interview room were a half-dozen snapshots of a thin dark-haired boy not much older than Philip. The snapshots were creased. The boy was frowning at the camera in the way of one who is being teased into smiling and doesn't want to smile. His arms seemed to jut from his bony shoulders. His head was not shaved but covered in lustrous dark curls and his eyes were clear and not shadowed like a skull's eyes yet you could see that this was Spider Boy, younger than Philip had seen him.

Quickly Philip shook his head, no. He'd never seen this boy before.

"This is a missing boy, Philip. He's fourteen in these pictures. He's older now, and he's been missing since last May. Any information you can provide."

Philip sat silent, staring. In two of the snapshots the boy was wearing a white T-shirt and smoking a cigarette. In one snapshot he was wearing what appeared to be a rumpled pajama top, partly opened to show a pale sunken chest and a single berry-colored nipple.

No. Philip had no information to provide. His mother stood close behind him with her hand on his shoulder and he could feel the tremor in her hand.

No! He didn't think so.

"Take your time, Philip. There's no hurry."

There were two detectives. Philip knew that they were watching him closely and that they were aware of his mother's hand on his shoulder and his mother's quickened breathing. They had surprised Philip by shaking hands with him as if he were an adult as they shook hands with his mother whom they took care to call "Ms. Hudgkins." In the confusion of the moment Philip had not heard their names. In the dread and excitement of the moment Philip had not heard most of what the detectives had said. He understood that his mother was annoying the detectives by speaking to them in a rapid fretful way insisting that her son was only a child who knew nothing about his father's private life. He had not seen his father in months. He had rarely seen his father during the last several years for his father had lived apart from the family since Philip had been ten. Now he was only thirteen and he was trying to adjust to a new home and a new school . . . The detectives listened politely. They did not interrupt, they appeared to be agreeing with Philip's mother. Philip felt a pang of embarrassment, his mother had become a woman to be pitied and humored. She was wearing dark clothing and her hair was pulled back into a chignon yet her mouth flashed red with lipstick and her eyes were unnaturally bright.

It had been suggested to Philip's mother that she wait outside while the detectives spoke with Philip but of course she refused. She had not brought her son all the way to Trenton, she said, to abandon him to strangers.

"Any of these? Look familiar?"

There were folders of such photographs. All were of teenaged boys. Philip was smiling, and shaking his head no. His eyes were filling with moisture, he was having difficulty seeing. He did not want to wipe his eyes on his sleeve for the gesture would be a sign of weakness and he knew that adult men are contemptuous of weakness in boys.

"Take your time, Philip. We understand."

The hand on Philip's shoulder was urgent, he could feel nails like claws.

Suddenly, Philip had to use a restroom. The need came upon him quick as pain.

But no: Philip's mother insisted upon accompanying him.

"I don't want him alone for a moment. Not in this place."

Philip resented his mother speaking of him in the third person, as if he were a very young child. When he moved toward the door as if to elude her, she seized his arm tightly and walked with him, holding him captive. The detectives behaved as if nothing was unusual. Philip saw their eyes on his mother in the way he'd sometimes seen, years ago, his father's eyes on his mother, detached and calculating.

At the men's room close by (they were on the second floor of the Trenton police headquarters in an old, partly renovated building on Broad Street), Philip's mother balked at allowing him to go inside alone. Nor did she want one of the detectives to accompany him. Oh, Philip hated this woman! He dreaded her entering the men's room with him, he was becoming excited, agitated. One of the detectives suggested a compromise: he would look into the restroom to make sure that no one was inside, then Philip's mother could check to see that this was so, and then Philip could use the restroom undisturbed. No one would be allowed to enter so long as Philip was inside and Philip's mother could wait immediately outside the door to accompany him back to the interview room. In that way, Ms. Hudgkins could be assured that no one would approach her son without her permission.

Reluctantly, as if suspecting a trick, Philip's mother agreed. Philip would long recall this shameful episode in his life, when his mother, doubting the word of the Trenton police officer, insisted upon entering the men's room to determine that, yes, it was empty and no one was waiting inside to accost her son.

It was empty, and Philip was able to use the restroom undisturbed. How like kindergarten this was, his mother anxiously overseeing his first days! He could not bear to see his reflection in the mirror. He could not bear to see his weak frightened soul glittering like tears in his eyes. It was difficult for him to pee, he wondered if a surveillance camera was trained on him. When he emerged from the restroom he was trembling with indignation and trying not to cry and his mother said quickly that this was too upsetting for him, she was taking him back to Nyack immediately, and in a rage Philip threw off her hand and told the detectives, "I saw him. The first one. His name was Reuben."

WAS HE'D SAID without thinking. He had not meant *was*. He had no reason to think *was*. But all that he would tell the detectives that day, that he had not intended to tell, he had been determined not to tell and yet suddenly he would tell in a rush of words his mother could not prevent, would be recorded on tape and could not be unsaid and there was a comfort in this.

"STILL DAYLIGHT! You'd think it would be night."

It was so, they'd been in police headquarters for what seemed like a full day and yet when they emerged the sun was still well above the horizon and the sky was hazy with light. Philip's mother was shaken and dazed and moved like an elderly woman peering at her surroundings as if she had no idea where she was.

At the car, Philip's mother seemed to rouse herself. She turned the key in the ignition briskly and gunned the motor. She'd rejected with contempt the offer of the detectives to provide transportation for her and Philip back to Nyack. "As if I'm helpless. I've been driving since the age of sixteen."

In Trenton traffic, Philip's mother impulsively turned west, in the direction of the river. She couldn't bear Route 1, not for the second time that day. She would take the River Road north to I–95, and avoid most of Trenton altogether. It was out of their way, she said excitedly, but the detour was worth it.

"We'll pass the old house. But we won't drop in. Strangers live there now. Good luck to them!"

At police headquarters, Philip's mother had become too upset to listen to his interview with the detectives and had to be escorted from the room but she hadn't insisted that Philip come with her for she'd known that he would oppose her. She had seen the hatred in his face, she had flinched from it, the sudden rage with which her son had flung off her hand. And afterward when he'd emerged from the interview room she had hurried to embrace him wordlessly. He'd been crying, but he had ceased crying, and she hugged him so tightly they trembled together as the detectives looked on, embarrassed.

Now she said, driving along the River Road, as if thinking aloud, "It had to be. I know."

Running parallel to the River Road was a narrow canal of muddy water and beyond the canal was the wide, windy Delaware River. On the other side of the highway were small suburban houses that, within a few miles, gave way to larger and more imposing houses on hills above the river. There was the mailbox for 992, and there at the top of a landscaped hill was the sprawling glass-and-stucco "contemporary" in which, long ago it now seemed, the Szaara family had lived.

"I was never happy in that house. That style of architecture has no soul."

Philip squinted at the house just barely visible behind a scrim of juniper pines. His eyes flooded with moisture, he couldn't see.

He hated it that strangers lived there now. Another child had appropriated his room. A boy his age or younger for whom the future held no dread.

Philip expected his mother to turn onto the entrance ramp of I–95 at Titusville but without slowing down she drove past. He dared not say anything to her. She was driving beyond the speed limit for the narrow river road, clenching the steering wheel tight. They were veering ever farther from the turnpike and the Garden State Parkway that would return them to Nyack. They were miles beyond suburban Trenton in a sparsely populated area of western New Jersey bounded on their right by densely wooded hills. Philip's mother was breathing quickly. "I am so angry with you, Philip. I am so angry my heart hurts from beating hard. I think I need to stop this car. I think you should get out of this car and leave me alone for a while."

Philip was stunned by these words. He was unable to speak, to defend himself. At police headquarters he'd tried to explain to her, he'd tried to say he was sorry, but his mother had hugged him warmly, gripping him so tight he could scarcely breathe. She had seemed to forgive him.

Yet now she was saying vehemently, "This shame you've brought us.

This new shame. 'Hitch-hikers'! It will be in the newspapers, it will be on television, where can we hide! I can't move us another time. This terrible shame like something foul and rotten in the mouth. You could have let it go, Philip. That boy, that missing boy, you could have let him go."

Her voice lifted in fury. She was braking the car, skidding and sliding from the roadway into a deserted rest stop. They were at the edge of Washington's Crossing State Park. Wordless, Philip yanked the car door open and jumped out. His mother remained in the car with the motor running as Philip charged blindly away. He was trembling with hurt, indignation. He was aware of picnic tables, benches. Shuttered restrooms in a fake-log cabin. An overturned trash can that reeked of garbage.

Philip ran stumbling from the car. Pulses beat in his head. That frail, frantic pulse at his temple, his father had kissed. He wasn't going to cry for he was furious. His mother had no right to punish him at such a time. He had told only the truth of what he knew and he would not have wished the truth untold if it brought shame to them all for it had to be told. He knew, if he pleaded with his mother, if he returned to her tearful and craven, she would relent and love him again, but he'd had enough of her love, he'd had enough of his father's love, he hoped never to see either of them again.

At the edge of the rest stop was a sodden wood chip trail leading into a hilly wooded area. A sign read MOUNTAIN MEADOW 3 MILES. Philip began to hike the trail, breaking into a run from time to time. He had no idea where he was, what he was doing. He wanted only to run! In Trenton in the interview room he'd been exhausted and had wanted to lay his head down on his arms and shut his eyes but now in this new place his strength had returned. There was a smell here of rich damp earth and awakening vegetation. The day had been prematurely warm for early April, already small insects, gnats and flies, brushed against his face. He began to perspire. His mother had made him wear a lined jacket which he removed and dropped onto the trail. He was hiking uphill, always uphill. All that summer, that previous summer, his father had promised to take him camping at the Delaware Water Gap but always something had prevented it, always something had "come up." Now he would never see his father again for he'd broken his promise to his father, all that was finished. His mother would be waiting for him at the car taking for granted that Philip would return to her like a kicked dog after she'd sent him away. But he wasn't going to return.

He passed the one-mile marker, and he passed the two-mile marker. His feet were wet, the trail had become overgrown. He was breathing quickly, still excited. By this time more than forty minutes had passed. By now his mother would be wandering forlorn and fretful among the picnic tables and the reeking garbage calling *Philip? Phil-ip? Where are you?* uncertain if she should be angry, or alarmed. He could see her tugging at the (padlocked) door of the men's restroom. Her red mouth glaring in her face as she called his name, called and called his name and there came, in rebuke, only silence.

THE SUN had descended in the sky, pale and sickle-like just above the treeline. Philip was on high ground, hiking along a ridge above a swift-flowing stream. The wood chip trail had long since vanished. This trail was sometimes so faint as to be indistinct from the underbrush surrounding it. Philip began to hear voices. For a terrible moment he thought he might have hiked in an ellipsis, returning to his mother, but that was impossible, he was making his way trying not to lose his balance along the edge of a hill, and below the hill was the creek, and on the far side of the creek were several adults and children. A man was casting a fishing line into the dark glittering water. A boy crouched beside him. Philip halted, not wanting to be seen. He was about thirty feet above the creek, panting. He squatted amid boulders. He leaned his elbows on his knees, trying to catch his breath. Close around him were rocks, the slightest pressure might release to roll down the hill. He was very still. He saw the boy on the creek bank glance up at him, and wave. He saw the man with the fishing pole look toward him. He had not meant to be seen but he had been seen. Impulsively he raised his arm to wave back.

Maybe they would call to him? Maybe they would invite him to join them? Maybe that was how this long day would end, somewhere in western New Jersey in Washington's Crossing State Park?

THE FISH FACTORY

B ACK OF THE OLD FISH FACTORY on the river is where they saw her.

Boys bicycling home from school. Taking a shortcut along a rutted weedy lane.

It's wrong to say *Three boys saw Tanya: our daughter*. The correct way of saying it is *Three boys saw Tanya's body*. There is a subtle distinction. Yet it is a profound distinction. If you misspeak, even in grief and confusion, you make people uncomfortable. My husband is embarrassed by my emotion sometimes and squeezes my arm just above the elbow as a way of consoling me (you would think) that is actually a way of silencing me when I misspeak.

The reddened impress of a man's fingers on my upper arm, I stroke afterward. *Her body* is the correct way of saying it. *They saw our daughter's body*. On a dirty tarpaulin in the weeds.

SOMETIMES it's better to say nothing. Especially if what you say will be repeated, quoted. I have learned.

NOBODY HERE would call the fish factory by its old name *Neptune Seafood, Inc.* In the papers and on TV it was identified in this way *Neptune Seafood, Inc.* though the canning factory had been shut down since 1982. Nobody goes out there except kids on bicycles and sometimes hikers and joggers. Fishermen. There are NO TRESPASSING signs and rusted wire fences and the riverbank is impassable with overgrown saplings, underbrush. It's a dumping ground, too.

There's still the fishy smell but it's a smell tempered by time. Like the smell of skunk, that fades with distance and time, until it's more the memory of a smell than an actual smell.

She was sixteen when she left us.

When she was taken from us.

Those boys, sighting the body. They were young boys, brothers of ten and eleven, and another boy of eleven, in fact a neighbor of ours. This boy knew Tanya and could have identified her yet was too frightened or confused to say her name to his parents. Only just that they'd seen a girl's body behind the fish factory. What they believed to be a body. From TV and movies they might have been prepared for such a discovery yet it was shocking to them. They almost crashed their bikes. One of them shouted and was pointing and the others almost crashed into him. The youngest boy began crying. He didn't want to look.

None of them came very near the body. It would be estimated that they hadn't come closer than ten or twelve feet. They straddled bikes on the rutted lane and stared.

A girl? A dead girl? A *body*?

It's this moment I see clearly. The young, frightened boys straddling their bicycles, staring. It's possible that the neighbor boy recognized Tanya instantly but he did not say that that was Tanya Roscrae and so for this long shocked moment the body, the girl's body, dumped amid trash behind the old fish factory, was no one's body.

This moment. And this place: about a mile from our house.

And what was I doing at that moment, what was the mother of sixteen-year-old Tanya Roscrae doing at that moment, in her house on Skillman Street, East Trenton, in the kitchen at the rear of that "modest two-bedroom ranch house" on Skillman at approximately 3:50 P.M. of that weekday I was on the phone, and I was calling those girlfriends of my daughter's whose names I knew, or believed I knew. Speaking not with the girls who weren't home and in all cases but one were not my daughter's friends any longer but with their mothers who happened to be home and happened to pick up the phone. For there was the mother of Tanya Roscrae asking, pleading, not for the first time *I'm so sorry to bother you but have you seen Tanya? She was away overnight—they called me from school to say she hadn't been in school yesterday or today—*

No. No one had seen Tanya. Not recently.

They were embarrassed, the mothers of these girls. Of course we all knew one another, to a degree. They all knew me.

They were embarrassed, and concerned for me, and they felt sorry for me, though one or two of them were annoyed by me, exasperated by the plaintive sound of my voice which possibly they'd heard more often than they wished to have heard. The mother of the girl who was still a friend of Tanya's saying *Look, I have no idea where your daughter is. You'd be better off calling her boyfriend's house if you know his name.*

This moment. And behind the fish factory, the boys straddling their bicycles, staring. And the youngest beginning to cry.

A girl in the weeds. Flat on her back. Like she'd been carried inside the tarpaulin and dumped in the weeds and her head was fallen to one side as if it had been kicked and her hair that was dirty-blond and long was spread out around her head like it had been arranged that way deliberately. Her hands were crossed on her chest. Her legs were straight. She was barefoot. On her face there was something greasy and red, and her clothes were soaked with it. Her green T-shirt bunched up at the waist was soaked with it. Her denim cutoffs.

JUICE was the word on Tanya's ugly green T-shirt. Front and back. JUICE in black gothic letters. The name of a rock band, I guess. The T-shirt was an electric green to hurt your eyes and the word JUICE was in six-inch letters and there could be no mistake, the T-shirt was our daughter's. None of the boys was close enough to see JUICE and anyway it might have been blood-soaked, and not visible.

The boys backed their bicycles hastily away. They had no wish to come closer. The youngest had begun to cry. They would have difficulty bicycling out to the street, on the rutted old lane. It took them what seemed like a very long time. As if they'd forgotten how to ride their bicycles, they'd lost that skill. It was as if they'd been struck on the head. They were slow-thinking, groggy. Everywhere they looked things appeared underwater. Pulses beat in their heads. Their mouths tasted of sand. The youngest was crying so, his breath was coming strangely. He could hardly see. He nearly fell from his bicycle. He walked his bicycle home in clumsy strides. By the time he arrived at his home his brother and the other boy were already there and his brother was telling their mother what they had seen behind the fish factory and their mother listened in horror and went to the phone and dialed 911 and reported *A body behind the fish factory.*

It would have been twenty minutes since the boys saw the body on the tarpaulin, before the Trenton police arrived at the fish factory. By which time the body was gone.

WHOEVER DID IT must've panicked. Must've been right there, dragging the body into the weeds and the boys came along and he hid somewhere close by and he panicked and decided to take the body away again.

Probably the river. He'd dump it in the river.

Not by day, though. He'd have to wait for night.

WE MOVED to East Trenton in 1985. Tanya was born the following year. I had prayed for a daughter, I had not truly wanted a son.

Why? I think because I did not feel that a son could be controlled so readily as a daughter. Everyone tells you this, and this was my personal observation.

I think I would have been fearful of a son. Boys and men judge you in ways you don't always comprehend.

My husband, when he loved me, even then he was judging me at all times and especially in public. It was nothing he could help: it was his nature. Yet also it seemed to me a man's nature. *They see you through the eyes mainly. Either they like what they see, or they don't.* I think it was my older sister who told me this.

When Tanya was gone from us, her very body missing, we wanted to believe that she might be alive, especially I wanted to believe that she might be alive but the sight the boys described was that of a body, they did not say it looked like the girl in the green T-shirt was asleep, not once did they utter those words. Because sometimes it is said of a deceased person, in a coffin for instance, that he looks like he is asleep. Looks like he's just sleeping.

So peaceful, it looks like she only just fell asleep.

But the boys did not say that about Tanya Roscrae. Because of the blood. And the way her head was twisted to the side as if it had been kicked. And her snarled hair outspread, and her hands crossed on her chest, on the bloody T-shirt, like someone had done it for a mocking purpose.

Why? Why would anyone want to hurt our daughter?

Who has done such a thing to Tanya?

Yet we did not wish to believe this. That Tanya had been hurt, and was dead. And her body dragged away to be further desecrated. We refused to believe, at the start. And many who spoke with us, neighbors, relatives, even strangers, to our faces at least, told us that, yes Tanya might still be alive. There was no proof that Tanya was dead. The reasons the police gave for the killer or killers taking the body away made no sense, if you thought about it. Why dump a body, and then remove it? What logic was there to this? Yet the police proceeded as if their version must be correct: as if they had knowledge of which we were unaware. (But what knowledge?) They had not found the tarpaulin or any trace of human blood behind the fish factory where they searched for days but they found where the body had been placed, which was where the boys led them; there, there was the "impress" of an object of the size and weight of an adolescent female. Behind the fish factory in the overgrown dumping ground there were many footprints old and new as well as tire tracks and bicycle tracks. And there was a path to the river used by fishermen.

Why, if the killer dumped the body, would he take it away again?

What sense does that make? Where's the logic?

I had never seen my husband so forceful in his speech. So adamant.

Always David has been one to see the illogic in another's position and to expose it. Other parents of other victims, you would suppose, would believe what the police told them, or wished them to know; but not David Roscrae. That was not his nature. So the police assured us yes of course there was the possibility that our daughter was still alive, of course there was this possibility and we should not give up hope. It might even be a coincidence (how calmly they uttered these words!) that Tanya was missing at the very time that the boys claimed to have seen a body resembling her body. Their investigation would continue as if Tanya were alive, they wanted us to know.

Yet one of the older detectives said in an undertone *Anybody who does things like this, you don't expect to make sense.*

This was a rebuke to my husband, I think. But if David heard, he gave no sign.

BECAUSE A GIRL is easier to love, I think. And a girl will love you.

WHEN WE MOVED to East Trenton we knew nothing of *Neptune Seafood, Inc.* as we knew nothing of other shut-down, boarded-up, bankrupt and abandoned factories, mills, and warehouses on the river. The industrial riverfront was a mile away and in our self-contained cul-de-sac neighborhood known as Beechwood Acres there was no direct access to it.

Except footpaths, bicycle trails through vacant lots. Scrubby fields where developers had razed trees and gouged out the earth for the foundations of "custom-built" houses never built.

As a child Tanya had played in such places, with other children in the neighborhood. In those years these were known to be, or believed to be, safe places for children. Always there were adults near. There were mothers near. And there was a neighborhood playground, a small park near the elementary school. Nearly every day in good weather I took Tanya to the park as a baby in her stroller and later we walked hand in hand and still later Tanya would run ahead of me flailing her pudgy little arms in excitement or she would pedal frantically on her tricycle. *Mommy c'mon! Oh Mommy c'mon!*

I had to laugh at my daughter, so determined. My heart swelled with love of her, sometimes it frightened me.

As a small child she had pale fluffy-floating blond hair. Very fine, like gossamer. Her eyes were a mysterious dark blue and were always in motion, hungrily taking in information. Before she could speak she babbled and squealed bursting with information to impart. As an infant she never slept more than two or three hours at a time and as a young child she could not be put to bed before nine o'clock and she could not be kept in bed beyond six o'clock in the morning. Her father and I fell into the habit of boasting that our daughter had more energy than the two of us put together and she was going to be smart, too.

Her father knew. He knew the signs.

Yes she was difficult to handle, yes she was willful, stubborn, petulant, quick-tempered, though also affectionate, loving. Your heart just melted, when Tanya (who'd been naughty, maybe!) climbed into your lap and hugged you around the neck and nibble-kissed your cheek, and collapsed in giggles if she was tickled in just the right way.

Our daughter is special, I know the signs.

Tanya was perceived to be an unusual name, and a fitting name, for this special child. *Tanya* was David's choice.

David Roscrae was the kind of man, called to jury duty in downtown Trenton, selected for a jury, he'd be voted foreman by the other jurors unanimously. He had a master's degree in science education from Rutgers-Newark. In his mid-twenties he was hired as an instructor at Mercer County Community College where he taught physics and computer technology. At the time of Tanya's disappearance he was acting dean of the science division of the college. His salary was higher than if he'd taught in the public school system and he belonged to an aggressive teachers' union that won reasonably good contracts for its members in a time of economic crisis and budget cuts through the state and so he tried never to reveal his disappointment with his life.

I was his wife, and I knew. I would come to see that I was part of his disappointment.

He'd loved science as a kid, David said. And for a while he'd been obsessed with computers.

In his late twenties these passions began to fade. Whatever it was, the mysterious hunger some individuals have for pure knowledge. *Feeding my rat* David called it. He'd been a jogger too, for a while. He'd run in marathons in the early years of our marriage. *Feeding my rat* David spoke of his jogging fondly and I stiffened hearing the ugly expression for the first time and ever after when David uttered the words *Feeding my rat* I wanted to turn away from him in disgust, I wanted to run out of the room and away from him, the man who was the father of the only child I would ever have.

DON'T STOP *loving me, please.*
    Oh God I am so lonely. Please.
    I can't bear to be touched, forgive me.
    Do you think she hated us? And that was why it happened?

I TRY NOT to hate them. The boys who saw Tanya on the dirty tarpaulin behind the fish factory.

I have talked to them, or tried to. Until their parents refused to allow me. Until police officers spoke to "dissuade" me. I know, the boys have suffered, too. I am a mother, I understand.

Through their lives they will remember. Not a day will pass when they will not remember. If they become fathers, seeing their children they will remember. Their names I have memorized. Their first words I did not hear spoken aloud to the police but of course I have memorized these words as they were recounted later. The boys who claimed to have seen not *Tanya Roscrae* but *Tanya Roscrae's body* on a dirty piece of tarpaulin discarded like trash behind the fish factory.

She was sixteen. We loved her. We ask ourselves what did we do wrong. We wait for her abductor/killer to be arrested. We wait for her living/injured/dead body to be returned to us. These pleas I have made on TV, until my husband and my family forbade it.

The boys did not appear on our local TV. Their parents were wise to shield them. Yet everyone in the neighborhood knew who they were and you had to acknowledge that one day they would take pride in their specialness. The older boys especially, once they enter junior high. I am determined not to hate them for this.

Seeing my daughter discarded like trash behind the fish factory where on even the breeziest days a faint stink of fish prevails.

I AM THINKING of Tanya at the age of three. Running through the water spout fountains at Memorial Park. On a square of vivid green grass approximately half the size of a tennis court there were water spouts timed to erupt at intervals: the spouts were five inches high for several seconds and then suddenly they leapt up to five feet as children ran squealing and giggling through them. It was comical how the smaller children (like Tanya) seemed always to be taken by surprise when the tiny spouts leapt up about them, over their heads. Wide-eyed in wonder and excitement Tanya dashed through the spouts making paddling motions with her hands—"swimming" she called it. You had to laugh at her, Tanya was so adamant that this was swimming.

The water spouts were so placed in the grass that, if you were careful, you could walk between them and not get wet. Unless the wind blew spray onto you. And so adults would walk between the water spouts while their children ran frantic and squealing through them, splashing like demented fish. Once when David accompanied us, perhaps the single time David accompanied us to Memorial Park, on a Sunday it must have been, I overheard him speaking with a woman standing at the edge of the green, the woman's intention seemed to be a harmless sort of flirtation asking David which of the children was his and David pointed proudly at the little blond girl in the puckered-pink bathing suit rushing through the steeply rising water spouts squealing and thrashing her arms *That one. That little beauty running her heart out.*

THE CHANGE came upon her suddenly. You ask if you are to blame.

You always ask. For others are asking, with their eyes.

A window opened and something flew inside. Out of the humid dark something flew inside our house, I am thinking of the kitchen at the rear of our "modest two-bedroom ranch" on Skillman Street in East Trenton, and nothing was ever the same again.

Neutrinos David spoke of. *Black matter. Black holes.*

Ninety percent of the universe.

Laws of physics. Who can understand?

He was her father. He had not much wished (before she was born) to be a father but now he was thrilled to be a father, you could see the pride and love in his face. Speaking of science things. His paradoxical science things. On a sheet of paper he would draw with boyish eagerness to make our daughter's eyes widen in wonder.

See? A man is standing on the edge of a black hole, like this. He appears to an onlooker in our world as frozen in time. Yet, in the same instant we see him, this man is sucked into the black hole and disappears. Literally disappears into nothingness.

David snaps his fingers dramatically. He has folded the sheet of paper over, the figure of the man has vanished.

I shook my head, I conceded I could not understand.

David ignored me. It was to Tanya he was speaking and to Tanya he was demonstrating his paradox.

As a young girl Tanya was infinitely curious. She was her daddy's little girl you could see. Asking how could there be a black hole if you couldn't see it? Asking in her urgent childish way how could a man be on the edge of a black hole and *at the same time* inside the black hole? And what was a black hole—why was it *black*?

David loved these impromptu sessions. Smiling as swiftly he drew /0000000/ in a tornado-funnel shape down a sheet of paper, saying *The laws of physics are a mystery, we human beings can only stand on the rim and try to look inside.*

It worried me that my husband should say such things, fatalistic things they seemed to me, to a child so young. In David's universe there was no God of course nor even a mention of God.

Tanya took the sheet of paper as a gift. Her daddy's gift. Taped it to her bedroom wall with other drawings of his, and crayon drawings of her own: planets, stars, suns. Tanya had taped up drawings of animals, too, and brightly colored posters. And two years later when she was twelve and in seventh grade these were abruptly removed and would be replaced with psychedelic posters of rock stars viewed at crotch level, bizarrely made-up and costumed Caucasian males in their twenties, part-naked, luridly tattooed, with pierced tongues, nipples, belly but-

tons. To enter Tanya's room from that time onward was to risk assault
by these strangers. To enter Tanya's room was now to risk Tanya's wrath
at an invasion of her privacy.

Our daughter had begun her journey.

YES she had always been a brash child. Restless, lively. She had a
bright happy smile. Sometimes an impudent smile. And she could be
an impudent girl. Playing tricks on her parents. Hiding, and we didn't
know where she was. *Tanya? Tanya?* I would call trying not to sound
upset because it was a game probably, I knew it was a game, but at a
point I would become frightened and cry *Tanya! Tanya!* hurrying and
stumbling through the house, and there was Tanya crouched behind the
laundry hamper or beneath a chair or squeezed between my husband's
desk and a wall giggling through her fingers.

When she was a little older, too old for such games, hiding in the
carport behind the trash cans. On her face a lurid Indian-mask of
fluorescent-red Mercurochrome.

Seeing my distress she squealed in delight then in the next instant
became repentant. *Oh Mommy! Silly Mommy I'm sor-ry.*

A more serious episode in sixth grade when a call came from the
principal of her school informing us that our daughter had "threatened"
another sixth grader, saying she had a knife and would cut off the girl's
hair, nose, ears. I had to come to the school, where Tanya was being held
in the principal's office. She was suspended from school for several days
protesting to David and me she was only kidding, everybody knew she
was only kidding, the other girl had wanted to get her in trouble, that
was all.

Bitch Tanya called the other eleven-year-old. *Bitch* did it on purpose
to get her into trouble.

BY FIFTEEN Tanya had older friends who were out of high school,
I don't mean graduates but dropouts. Maybe I don't mean friends ex-
actly. Tanya had become a skinny sexy girl of the kind you see hanging
out front of the 7-Eleven with her friends. At the diner by the Sunoco
station flirting with the big-rig truck drivers. In a tank top, bare midriff,

tight jeans or cutoffs, a glittering bit of colored glass in her belly button.
Or her nose is pierced, or her tongue. Tanya's hair had darkened and
was no longer pale blond and gossamer fine. Her face had coarsened.
She smoked, she was loud-talking and loud-laughing and her speech
had become an American-adolescent language of a very limited vocabu-
lary laced with profanities.

David would say of her quietly to hide his shock and disbelief *You
can't tell her from the others, can you. So many others.*

IT WOULD BE SPECULATED by the police that whoever had taken
Tanya away, or whoever had killed Tanya and taken her body away, was
someone who knew her. Someone Tanya "trusted."

At first she'd been evasive about having a boyfriend. Though we saw
her with friends who were boys, that was obvious.

Boys with scruffy beards and goatees. Boys who were sometimes
shirtless.

Boys who drove rust-bucket cars. Motorcycles.

Boys who weren't boys when you looked closely but young men in
their twenties.

Condoms in Tanya's bureau drawer hidden beneath her underwear.

(I never told David. How could I tell David who would have
blamed me.)

*They were negligent parents, what can you expect. Allowed their
daughter to run wild.*

*Couldn't control their daughter, you have to wonder how hard they
tried.*

I tried to explain to the Trenton police. I tried to explain to so many
people until David forbade me.

The change came so suddenly. We were not prepared.

A sixteen-year-old girl is not a child nor can you say that a sixteen-
year-old girl is an adult. Legally, Tanya was a minor. In her behavior
and moods she was a child while in her manipulation of her parents she
was adult.

You ask yourself *Why.* So many times, alone, my fists jammed into
my eyes. *Why!*

The condoms were our secret. I found them immediately after the police searched for Tanya's body behind the fish factory. Before they could make their request to search her room. Ugly pearl-colored things that would be Tanya's and my secret forever.

WHY WAS OUR DAUGHTER taken from us: I have said this to the police and to anyone who will listen and always they agree with me, I am certain that I am right.

The city of Trenton has been shrinking for years. There are abandoned houses, blocks of rubble-strewn vacant lots as after a bombing. There are boarded-up office buildings and factories. The walls of the old state prison you see driving on Route 1 are ugly and weatherworn as ancient stone. The school-age population has so declined, a number of schools have been closed. Tanya had to travel by bus to a high school miles away and she was gone from home so much, so many hours, we began to lose her, couldn't know with certainty where she was. We bought her a cell phone so that we could call her but even then, how do you know where a child *is*? In her voice that could be innocent-sounding— *Oh hi Mom sure I'm O.K.*—and at other times impatient, sneering—*Oh Christ Mom I'm fine, I'll be home soon, can't talk right now.*

After Tanya disappeared the cell phone disappeared, too. Many times I have dialed Tanya's number and there is no ring, there is nothing except a message on the little plastic screen NUMBER INOPERATIVE.

After Tanya disappeared we would learn certain facts about our daughter that shocked us, and shamed us. For instance she rarely took the school bus but rode with "friends" and we had no knowledge of who these "friends" were. Of course we'd been informed by the school that Tanya often cut classes but not that, in school, Tanya was sulky and bored, sometimes so sleepy she could barely keep her eyes open.

When Tanya first started high school her teachers spoke of how she was working below her potential, what a bright intelligent girl she seemed to be and how disappointing it was, her low grades, but during the past year no teacher spoke of Tanya in that way. Her grades were C's, D's.

To our shame we learned that Tanya had had a boyfriend and that this boyfriend was missing, too. He'd disappeared at exactly the time Tanya had disappeared. He was twenty-three years old and had spent time in the Trenton detention center for such crimes as burglary, assault, drug-dealing. His photograph in the Trenton *Times* was of a shaved-head ferret-faced boy with a scruffy goatee and an insolent smile. *Wanted for questioning in a case of possible abduction, homicide.* Rick Traynor's family acknowledged to police that he was a "troubled kid"—"hard to get along with"—but he wouldn't hurt anyone seriously, would never kill a girl they were certain.

The Traynors had "no idea" where Rick was. Often he disappeared from Trenton for weeks, months. He had not lived at home for years. It was true he had a "history of violence" but not against females, they were certain.

The name *Tanya Roscrae* meant nothing to them, they insisted.

Girls chased after Rick, they said. Called him on the phone all the time.

On TV some of the Traynors were interviewed. Staring into the camera and speaking their carefully prepared words and there was the unspoken message *Any girl who fucks a guy like Rick, any girl that cheap and desperate and sluttish, you have to figure she got what she deserved.*

MANY QUESTIONS the police asked of us. With me especially they behaved as if we were invalids. Always it seemed that there was something they were asking that was not said in words. Almost I could hear it the way on the telephone you sometimes hear strangers' voices in the distance.

My husband took a leave from the college. He had a sabbatical due, he said.

Sometimes he spent the night away from home. To *clear my head* he explained. He would check into a hotel on Route 1 and order room service and watch TV, I think. He was not seeing another woman, or women. He had lost all sexual interest, he said. I saw no reason to disbelieve him.

Asked about Tanya we had to concede we knew little about her.

Many times saying, faltering *Not exactly. No.*

Because Tanya didn't share that information with us.

Because we had no way. We had no way of.

We wept often. David's face was drawn and haggard and his eyes seemed protuberant in their sockets as if something was pushing them out. What I looked like, I don't recall. I may not have known. I rarely looked at myself in the mirror if I could avoid it.

We told the police the truth but it was not entirely the truth. There were omissions. Nor did David know of my last conversation with Tanya which had been six days before she disappeared. She had slammed out of the kitchen cursing and I followed her on the stairs and I was shocked to hear myself begging, you don't expect to hear yourself begging anyone when you are forty-one years old. And Tanya relented in embarrassment perhaps. Almost she pleaded with me fixing her smeared eyes on me *Jesus, Mom, hey c'mon. I'm not that important, see? This is no big deal.*

It was then I broke down. Shouting such things I had never said before to Tanya. Into her shocked face I cried how dare she say she was not important, how dare she say this is no big deal, are our lives no big deal? was her life no big deal? Didn't she know she was our daughter, we loved her and wanted to protect her from all harm? and Tanya backed away making a face like something was hurting her head, couldn't bring herself to look at me panting and swiping at her nose saying *I'm not your daughter then. Don't cry over me.*

Those terrible words, I never told another person.

IN MY KHAKI SLACKS too big for me, in the purple canvas jacket that had been Tanya's, and in rubber boots from JC Penney that Tanya would have scorned, I often hike over to the fish factory in the late afternoon. Now David is living elsewhere I am freed from preparing meals and freed from the strain of having to select food my husband would wish to eat. I love the quiet of our house, and I love the quiet at the river.

I pass by the fish factory. The debris-strewn weeds. I don't linger, I know there is nothing to be seen. Police thoroughly investigated the dump and there was nothing to be seen.

I take a path to the riverbank and stand staring at the mist rising

from the river. You catch yourself waiting for the mist to define itself
more clearly, to take shape. As a child playing with neighbor children
Tanya had surely explored this stretch of riverbank, years ago. She'd
surely thrown stones into the river. The Delaware is a broad wide river
that is sometimes swollen and fast-moving after rains and dangerous at
such times but often it looks languid, opaque. In a certain light—our
rainy steel-colored New Jersey winter light—the river looks like dense
lava flowing. You lapse into a dream, you forget that you could drown in
that water. Half-shut your eyes, smiling. It's a time of secrecy, consola-
tion. You see yourself walking on the steely river in a dream that, if you
wake out of, you will drown.

Why'd I leave you, I had to.

Look, I was never dead. You know I was never dead.

Why'd Rick kill me? Rick is crazy for me.

See, I wanted to spare you. And Dad.

*It was a trick, see. Rick and me thought it up. I laid down on the
tarpaulin and he arranged me like he did. It was cranberry juice we used.
We figured I would be seen by some kids after school and we figured they
wouldn't come too close. They'd run away and by the time the police came
I would be gone.*

Where? Just drove away.

Because it was the only way, Mom. The only way to escape you.

*Because I couldn't love you the way you wanted. And I didn't want
you to love me. All that crap, I just didn't want.*

There's lots of us feel this way. No big deal.

THE COUSINS

Lake Worth, Florida
September 14, 1998

Dear Professor Morgenstern,

How badly I wish that I could address you as "Freyda"! But I don't have the right to such familiarity.

I have just read your memoir. I have reason to believe that we are cousins. My maiden name is "Schwart" (not my father's actual name, I think it was changed at Ellis Island in 1936), but my mother's maiden name was "Morgenstern" and all her family was from Kaufbeuren as yours were. We were to meet in 1941 when we were small children, you and your parents and sister and brother were coming to live with my parents, my two brothers and me in Milburn, New York. But the boat that was carrying you and other refugees, the <u>Marea</u>, was turned back by U.S. Immigration at New York Harbor.

(In your memoir you speak so briefly of this. You seem to recall a name other than <u>Marea</u>. But I am sure that <u>Marea</u> was the name, for it seemed so beautiful to me like music. You were so young of course. So much would happen afterward, you would not remember this. By my calculation you were 6, and I was 5.)

All these years I had not known that you were living! I had not known that there were survivors in your family. It was told to us by my father that there were not. I am so happy for you and your success. To think that you were living in the U.S. since 1956 is a shock to me. That you were a college student in New York City while I was living (my first marriage, not a happy one) in upstate New York! Forgive me, I did not know of your previous books, though I would be intrigued by "biological anthropology," I think! (I have nothing of your academic education, I'm so ashamed. Not only not college but I did not graduate from high school.)

Well, I am writing in the hope that we might meet. Oh very soon, Freyda! Before it's too late.

I am no longer your 5-year-old cousin dreaming of a new "sister" (as my mother promised) who would sleep with me in my bed and be with me always.

Your "lost" cousin
Rebecca

Lake Worth, Florida
September 15, 1998

Dear Professor Morgenstern,

I wrote to you just the other day. Now I see to my embarrassment that I may have sent the letter to a wrong address. If you are "on sabbatical leave" from the University of Chicago as it says on the dust jacket of your memoir. I will try again with this, care of your publisher.

I will enclose the same letter. Though I feel it is not adequate, to express what is in my heart.

Your "lost" cousin
Rebecca

P.S. Of course I will come to you, wherever & whenever you wish, Freyda!

Lake Worth, Florida
October 2, 1998

Dear Professor Morgenstern,

I wrote to you last month but I'm afraid that my letters were mis-addressed. I will enclose these letters here, now that I know you are at the "Institute for Advanced Research" at Stanford University, Palo Alto, California.

It's possible that you have read my letters and were offended by them. I know, I am not a very good writer. I should not have said what I did about the Atlantic crossing in 1941, as if you would not know these facts for yourself. I did not mean to correct you, Professor Morgenstern, regarding the name of the very boat you and your family were on in that nightmare time!

In an interview with you reprinted in the Miami newspaper I was embarrassed to read that you have received so much mail from "relatives" since the memoir. I smiled to read where you said, "Where were all these relatives in America when they were needed?"

Truly we were here, Freyda! In Milburn, New York, on the Erie Canal.

Your cousin
Rebecca

Palo Alto, CA
1 November 1998

Dear Rebecca Schwart,

Thank you for your letter and for your response to my memoir. I have been deeply moved by the numerous letters I've received since the publication of <u>Back from the Dead: A Girlhood</u> both in the United

States and abroad, and truly wish that I had time to reply to each of these individually and at length.

Sincerely,

F.M.

Freyda Morgenstern
Julius K. Tracey
Distinguished Professor of Anthropology,
University of Chicago

Lake Worth, Florida
November 5, 1998

Dear Professor Morgenstern,

I'm very relieved now, I have the correct address! I hope that you will read this letter. I think you must have a secretary who opens your mail and sends back replies. I know, you are amused (annoyed?) by so many now claiming to be relatives of "Freyda Morgenstern." Especially since your television interviews. But I feel very strongly, I am your true cousin. For I was the (only) daughter of Anna Morgenstern. I believe that Anna Morgenstern was the (only) sister of your mother, Sara, a younger sister. For many weeks my mother spoke of her sister, Sara, coming to live with us, your father and your Elzbieta, who was older than you by 3 or 4 years, and your brother, Leon, who was also older than you, not by so much. We had photographs of you. I remember so clearly how your hair was so neatly plaited and how pretty you were, a "frowning girl" my mother said of you, like me. We did look alike then, Freyda, though you were much prettier of course. Elzbieta was blonde with a plump face. Leon was looking happy in the photograph, a sweet-seeming boy of maybe 8. To read that your sister and brother died in such a terrible way in "Theresienstadt" was so sad. My mother never recovered from the shock of that time, I think. She was so hoping to see her sister again. When the <u>Marea</u> was turned back in the harbor, she gave up hope. My father did not allow her to speak German, only

English, but she could not speak English well, if anyone came to the house she would hide. She did not speak much afterward to any of us and was often sick. She died in May 1949.

Reading this letter I see that I am giving a wrong emphasis, really! I never think of these long-ago things.

It was seeing your picture in the newspaper, Freyda! My husband was reading the <u>New York Times</u> & called me to him saying wasn't it strange, here was a woman looking enough like his wife to be a sister, though in fact you & I do not look so much alike, in my opinion, not any longer, but it was a shock to see your face, which is very like my mother's face as I remember it.

And then your name, <u>Freyda Morgenstern</u>.

At once I went out & purchased <u>Back from the Dead: A Girlhood</u>. I have not read any Holocaust memoirs out of a dread of what I would learn. Your memoir I read sitting in the car in the parking lot of the bookstore not knowing the time, how late it was, until my eyes could not see the pages. I thought, "It's Freyda! It's her! My sister I was promised." Now I am 62 years old, and so lonely in this place of retired wealthy people who look at me & think that I am one of them.

I am not one to cry. But I wept on many pages of your memoir though I know (from your interviews) you wish not to hear such reports from readers & have only contempt for "cheap American pity." I know, I would feel the same way. You are right to feel that way. In Milburn I resented the people who felt sorry for me as the "gravedigger's daughter" (my father's employment) more than the others who did not give a damn if the Schwarts lived or died.

I am enclosing my picture, taken when I was a girl of 16. It is all I have of those years. (I look very different now, I'm afraid!) How badly I wish I could send you a picture of my mother, Anna Morgenstern, but all were destroyed in 1949.

Your cousin

Rebecca

Palo Alto, CA
16 November 1998

Dear Rebecca Schwart,

Sorry not to have replied earlier. I think yes it is quite possible that we are "cousins" but at such a remove it's really an abstraction, isn't it?

I am not traveling much this year, trying to complete a new book before my sabbatical ends. I am giving fewer "talks" and my book tour is over, thank God. (The venture into memoir was my first and will be my last effort at non-academic writing. It was far too easy, like opening a vein.) So I don't quite see how it would be feasible for us to meet at the present time.

Thank you for sending your photograph. I am returning it.

Sincerely,

F·M

Lake Worth, Florida
November 20, 1998

Dear Freyda,

Yes, I am sure we are "cousins"! Though like you I don't know what "cousins" can mean.

I have no living relatives, I believe. My parents have been dead since 1949 & I know nothing of my brothers, whom I have not glimpsed in many years.

I think you despise me as your "American cousin." I wish you could forgive me for that. I am not sure how "American" I am though I was not born in Kaufbeuren as you were but in New York Harbor in May 1936. (The exact day is lost. There was no birth certificate or it was lost.) I mean, I was born on the refugee boat! In a place of terrible filth, I was told.

It was a different time then, 1936. The war had not begun & people of our kind were allowed to "emigrate" if they had money.

My brothers, Herschel & Augustus, were born in Kaufbeuren & of course both our parents. My father called himself "Jacob Schwart" in this country. (This is a name I have never spoken to anyone who knows me now. Not to my husband of course.) I knew little of my father except he had been a printer in the old world (as he called it with scorn) and at one time a math teacher in a boys' school. Until the Nazis forbade such people to teach. My mother, Anna Morgenstern, was married very young. She played piano, as a girl. We would listen to music on the radio sometime if Pa was not home. (The radio was Pa's.)

Forgive me, I know you are not interested in any of this. In your memoir you spoke of your mother as a record keeper for the Nazis, one of those Jewish "administrators" helping in the transport of Jews. You are not sentimental about family. There is something so craven to it, isn't there. I respect the wishes of one who wrote <u>Back from the Dead</u>, which is so critical of your relatives & Jews & Jewish history & beliefs as of postwar "amnesia." I would not wish to dissuard you of such a true feeling, Freyda!

I have no true feelings myself, I mean that others can know.

Pa said you were all gone. Like cattle sent back to Hitler, Pa said. I remember his voice lifting, NINE HUNDRED SEVENTY-SIX REFU-GEES, I am sick still hearing that voice.

Pa said for me to stop thinking about my cousins! They were not coming. They were <u>gone</u>.

Many pages of your memoir I have memorized, Freyda. And your letters to me. In your words, I can hear your voice. I love this voice so like my own. My secret voice I mean, that no one knows.

I will fly to California, Freyda. Will you give me permission? "Only say the word & my soul shall be healed."

Your cousin

Rebecca

Lake Worth, Florida
November 21, 1998

Dear Freyda,

I am so ashamed, I mailed you a letter yesterday with a word misspelled: "dissuade." And I spoke of no living relatives, I meant no one remaining from the Schwart family. (I have a son from my first marriage, he is married with two children.)

I have bought other books of yours. <u>Biology: A History, Race and Racism: A History</u>. How impressed Jacob Schwart would be, the little girl in the photographs was never *gone* but has so very far surpassed him!

Will you let me come to see you in Palo Alto, Freyda? I could arrive for one day, we might have a meal together & I would depart the next morning. This is a promise.

Your (lonely) cousin
Rebecca

Lake Worth, Florida
November 24, 1998

Dear Freyda,

An evening of your time is too much to ask, I think. An hour? An hour would not be too much, would it? Maybe you could talk to me of your work, anything in your voice would be precious to me. I would not wish to drag you into the cesspool of the past, as you speak of it so strongly. A woman like yourself capable of such intellectual work & so highly regarded in your field has no time for maudlin sentiment, I agree.

I have been reading your books. Underlining & looking up words in the dictionary. (I love the dictionary, it's my friend.) So exciting to consider <u>How does science demonstrate the genetic basis of behavior?</u>

I have enclosed a card here for your reply. Forgive me I did not think of this earlier.

Your cousin
Rebecca

Palo Alto, CA
24 November 1998

Dear Rebecca Schwart,

Your letters of Nov. 20 & 21 are interesting. But the name "Jacob Schwart" means nothing to me, I'm afraid. There are numerous "Morgensterns" surviving. Perhaps some of these are your cousins, too. You might seek them out if you are lonely.

As I believe I have explained, this is a very busy time for me. I work much of the day and am not feeling very sociable in the evening. "Loneliness" is a problem engendered primarily by the too-close proximity of others. One excellent remedy is work.

Sincerely,

F.M.

P.S. I believe you have left phone messages for me at the Institute. As my assistant has explained to you, I have no time to answer such calls.

Lake Worth, Florida
November 27, 1998

Dear Freyda,

Our letters crossed! We both wrote on Nov. 24, maybe it's a sign.

It was on impulse I telephoned. "If I could hear her voice"—the thought came to me.

You have hardened your heart against your "American cousin." It was courageous in the memoir to state so clearly how you had to harden your heart against so much, to survive. Americans believe that suffering makes saints of us, which is a joke. Still I realize you have no time for me in your life now. There is no "purpose" to me.

Even if you won't meet me at this time, will you allow me to write to you? I will accept it if you do not reply. I would only wish that you might read what I write, it would make me so happy (yes, less lonely!), for then I could speak to you in my thoughts as I did when we were girls.

Your cousin

Rebecca

P.S. In your academic writing you refer so often to "adaptation of species to environment." If you saw me, your cousin, in Lake Worth, Florida, on the ocean just south of Palm Beach, so very far from Milburn, N.Y., and from the "old world," you would laugh.

Palo Alto, CA
1 December 1998

Dear Rebecca Schwart,

My tenacious American cousin! I'm afraid it is no sign of anything, not even "coincidence," that our letters were written on the same day and that they "crossed."

This card. I admit I am curious at the choice. It happens this is a card on my study wall. (Did I speak of this in the memoir? I don't think so.) How do you happen to come into possession of this reproduction of Caspar David Friedrich's "Sturzacker"—you have not been to the museum in Hamburg, have you? It's rare that any American even knows the name of this artist much esteemed in Germany.

Sincerely,

F. M.

Lake Worth, Florida
December 4, 1998

Dear Freyda,

The postcard of Caspar David Friedrich was given to me, with other cards from the Hamburg museum, by someone who traveled there. (In fact my son, who is a pianist. His name would be known to you, it's nothing like my own.)

I chose a card to reflect your soul. As I perceive it in your words. Maybe it reflects mine also. I wonder what you will think of this new card, which is German also but uglier.

Your cousin

Rebecca

Palo Alto, CA
10 December 1998

Dear Rebecca,

Yes I like this ugly Nolde. Smoke black as pitch and the Elbe like
molten lava. You see into my soul, don't you! Not that I have wished to
disguise myself.

So I return "Towboat on the Elbe" to my tenacious American
cousin. THANK YOU but please do not write again. And do not call. I
have had enough of you.

F.M.

Palo Alto, CA
11 December 1998/2 A.M.

Dear "Cousin"!

Your 16-yr-old photo I made a copy of. I like that coarse mane of
hair and the jaws so solid. Maybe the eyes were scared, but we know
how to hide that, don't we cousin.

In the camp I learned to stand tall. I learned to be big. As animals
make themselves bigger, it can be a trick to the eye that comes true. I
guess you were a "big" girl, too.

I have always told the truth. I see no reason for subterfuge. I despise
fantasizing. I have made enemies "among my kind" you can be sure.
When you are "back from the dead" you do not give a damn for oth-
ers' opinions & believe me, that has cost me in this so-called profession
where advancement depends upon ass-kissing and its sexual variants not
unlike the activities of our kindred primates.

Bad enough my failure to behave as a suppliant female through my
career. In the memoir I take a laughing tone speaking of graduate stud-
ies at Columbia in the late 1950s. I did not laugh much then. Meeting
my old enemies, who had wished to crush an impious female at the start
of her career, not only female but a Jew & a refugee Jew from one of the
camps, I looked them in the eye, I never flinched, but they flinched, the

bastards. I took my revenge where & when I could. Now those genera-
tions are dying out, I am not pious about their memories. At conferences
organized to revere them, Freyda Morgenstern is the "savagely witty"
truth-teller.

In Germany, where history was so long denied, <u>Back from the Dead</u>
has been a bestseller for five months. Already it has been nominated for
two major awards. Here is a joke, and a good one, yes?

In this country, no such reception. Maybe you saw the "good"
reviews. Maybe you saw the one full-page ad my cheapskate publisher
finally ran in the <u>New York Review of Books</u>. There have been plenty
of attacks. Worse even than the stupid attacks to which I have become
accustomed in my "profession."

In the Jewish publications, & in Jewish-slanted publications, such
shock/dismay/disgust. A Jewish woman who writes so without senti-
ment of mother & other relatives who "perished" in Theresienstadt. A
Jewish woman who speaks so coldly & "scientifically" of her "heritage."
As if the so-called Holocaust is a "heritage." As if I have not earned my
right to speak the truth as I see it and will continue to speak the truth,
for I have no plans to retire from research, writing, teaching & directing
doctoral students for a long time. (I will take early retirement at Chi-
cago, these very nice benefits, & set up shop elsewhere.)

This piety of the Holocaust! I laughed, you used that word so rev-
erentially in one of your letters. I never use this word that slides off
American tongues now like grease. One of the hatchet-reviewers called
Morgenstern a traitor giving solace to the enemy (which enemy? there
are many) by simply stating & restating, as I will each time I am asked,
that the "holocaust" was an accident in history as all events in history are
accidents. There is no purpose to history as to evolution, there is no goal
or progress. Evolution is the term given to what <u>is</u>. The pious fantasizers
wish to claim that the Nazis' genocidal campaign was a singular event
in history, that it has elevated us above history. This is bullshit, I have
said so & will continue to say so. There are many genocides, as long as
there has been mankind. History is an invention of books. In biological
anthropology we note that the wish to perceive "meaning" is one trait
of our species among many. But that does not posit "meaning" in the

world. If history did exist it is a great river/cesspool into which count-
less small streams & tributaries flow. In one direction. Unlike sewage it
cannot back up. It cannot be "tested"—"demonstrated." It simply is. If
the individual streams dry up, the river disappears. There is no "river-
destiny." There are merely accidents in time. The scientist notes that
without sentiment or regret.

Maybe I will send you these ravings, my tenacious American cousin.
I'm drunk enough, in a festive mood!

Your (traitor) cousin

F.M.

Lake Worth, Florida
December 15, 1998

Dear Freyda,

How I loved your letter, that made my hands shake. I have not
laughed in so long. I mean, in our special way.

It's the way of hatred. I love it. Though it eats you from the inside
out. (I guess.)

It's a cold night here, a wind off the Atlantic. Florida is often wet-
cold. Lake Worth/Palm Beach are very beautiful & very boring. I wish
you might come here & visit, you could spend the rest of the winter, for
it's often sunny of course.

I take your precious letters with me in the early morning walking
on the beach. Though I have memorized your words. Until a year ago I
would run, run, run for miles! At the rain-whipped edge of a hurricane
I ran. To see me, my hard-muscled legs & straight backbone, you would
never guess I was not a young woman.

So strange that we are in our sixties, Freyda! Our baby-girl dolls
have not aged a day.

(Do you hate it, growing old? Your photographs show such a vigor-
ous woman. You tell yourself, "Every day I live was not meant to be" &
there's happiness in this.)

Freyda, in our house of mostly glass facing the ocean you would have
your own "wing." We have several cars, you would have your own car.

No questions asked where you went. You would not have to meet my husband, you would be my precious secret.

Tell me you will come, Freyda! After the New Year would be a good time. When you finish your work each day we will go walking on the beach together. I promise we would not have to speak.

Your loving cousin
Rebecca

Lake Worth, Florida
December 17, 1998

Dear Freyda,

Forgive my letter of the other day, so pushy & familiar. Of course you would not wish to visit a stranger.

I must make myself remember: though we are cousins, we are strangers.

I was reading again <u>Back from the Dead</u>. The last section, in America. Your three marriages—"ill-advised experiments in intimacy/lunacy." You are very harsh & very funny, Freyda! Unsparing to others as to yourself.

My first marriage too was blind in love & I suppose "lunacy." Yet without it, I would not have my son.

In the memoir you have no regret for your "misbegotten fetuses" though for the "pain and humiliation" of the abortions illegal at the time. Poor Freyda! In 1957 in a filthy room in Manhattan you nearly bled to death, at that time I was a young mother so in love with my life. Yet I would have come to you, if I had known.

Though I know that you will not come here, yet I hold out hope that, suddenly yes you might! To visit, to stay as long as you wish. Your privacy would be protected.

I remain the tenacious cousin
Rebecca

Lake Worth, Florida
New Year's Day 1999

Dear Freyda,

I don't hear from you, I wonder if you have gone away? But maybe you will see this. "If Freyda sees this even to toss away . . ."

I am feeling happy & hopeful. You are a scientist & of course you are right to scorn such feelings as "magical" & "primitive," but I think there can be a newness in the New Year. I am hoping this is so.

My father, Jacob Schwart, believed that in animal life the weak are quickly disposed of, we must hide our weakness always. You & I knew that as children. But there is so much more to us than just the animal, we know that, too.

Your loving cousin
Rebecca

Palo Alto, CA
19 January 1999

Rebecca,

Yes I have been away. And I am going away again. What business is it of yours?

I was coming to think you must be an invention of mine. My worst weakness. But here on my windowsill propped up to stare at me is "Rebecca, 1952." The horse-mane hair & hungry eyes.

Cousin, you are so faithful! It makes me tired. I know I should be flattered, few others would wish to pursue "difficult" Professor Morgenstern now I'm an old woman. I toss your letters into a drawer, then in my weakness I open them. Once, rummaging through Dumpster trash I retrieved a letter of yours. Then in my weakness I opened it. You know how I hate weakness!

Cousin, no more.
F.M.

Lake Worth, Florida
January 23, 1999

Dear Freyda,

I know! I am sorry.

I shouldn't be so greedy. I have no right. When I first discovered that you were living, last September, my thought was only "My cousin Freyda Morgenstern, my lost sister, she is alive! She doesn't need to love me or even know me or give a thought to me. It's enough to know that she did not perish and has lived her life."

Your loving cousin

Rebecca

Palo Alto, CA
30 January 1999

Dear Rebecca,

We make ourselves ridiculous with emotions at our age, like showing our breasts. Spare us, please!

No more would I wish to meet you than I would wish to meet myself. Why would you imagine I might want a "cousin"—"sister"—at my age? I would like it that I have no living relatives any longer, for there is no obligation to think Is he/she still living?

Anyway, I'm going away. I will be traveling all spring. I hate it here. California suburban boring & without a soul. My "colleagues/friends" are shallow opportunists to whom I appear to be an opportunity.

I hate such words as "perish." Does a fly "perish," do rotting things "perish," does your enemy "perish"? Such exalted speech makes me tired.

Nobody "perished" in the camps. Many "died"—"were killed." That's all.

I wish I could forbid you to revere me. For your own good, dear cousin. I see that I am your weakness, too. Maybe I want to spare you.

If you were a graduate student of mine, though! I would set you right with a swift kick in the rear.

Suddenly there are awards & honors for Freyda Morgenstern. Not only the memoirist but the "distinguished anthropologist" too. So I will travel to receive them. All this comes too late of course. Yet like you I am a greedy person, Rebecca. Sometimes I think my soul is in my gut! I am one who stuffs herself without pleasure, to take food from others. Spare yourself. No more emotion. No more letters!

F.M.

Chicago, IL
29 March 1999

Dear Rebecca Schwart,

Have been thinking of you lately. It has been a while since I've heard from you. Unpacking things here & came across your letters & photograph. How stark-eyed we all looked in black-and-white! Like X rays of the soul. My hair was never so thick & splendid as yours, my American cousin.

I think I must have discouraged you. Now, to be frank, I miss you. It has been two months nearly since you wrote. These honors & awards are not so precious if no one cares. If no one hugs you in congratulations. Modesty is beside the point & I have too much pride to boast to strangers.

Of course, I should be pleased with myself: I sent you away. I know, I am a "difficult" woman. I would not like myself for a moment. I would not tolerate myself. I seem to have lost one or two of your letters, I'm not sure how many, vaguely I remember you saying you & your family lived in upstate New York, my parents had arranged to come stay with you? This was in 1941? You provided facts not in my memoir. But I do remember my mother speaking with such love of her younger sister, Anna. Your father changed his name to "Schwart" from—what? He was a math teacher in Kaufbeuren? My father was an esteemed doctor. He had many non-Jewish patients who revered him. As a young man he had served in the German army in the first war, he'd been awarded a Gold Medal for Bravery & it was promised that such a distinction would protect him while other Jews were being transported. My father disappeared so abruptly from our lives, immediately we were transported to that place, for years I believed he must have escaped & was alive somewhere & would contact us. I thought my mother had information she kept from me. She was not quite the Amazon-mother of <u>Back from the Dead</u> . . . Well, enough of this! Though evolutionary anthropology must scour the past relentlessly, human beings are not obliged to do so.

It's a blinding-bright day here in Chicago, from my aerie on the 52nd floor of my grand new apartment building I look out upon the vast inland sea Lake Michigan. Royalties from the memoir have helped me pay for this, a less "controversial" book would not have earned. Nothing more is needed, yes?

Your cousin,

Freyda

Lake Worth, Florida
April 3, 1999

Dear Freyda,

Your letter meant much to me. I'm so sorry not to answer sooner. I make no excuses. Seeing this card I thought, "For Freyda!"

Next time I will write more. Soon I promise.

Your cousin

Rebecca

Chicago, IL
22 April 1999

Dear Rebecca,

Rec'd your card. Am not sure what I think of it. Americans are ga-ga for Joseph Cornell as they are for Edward Hopper. What is "Lanner Waltzes"? Two little-girl doll figures riding the crest of a wave & in the background an old-fashioned sailing ship with sails billowing? "Collage"? I hate riddle-art. Art is to <u>see</u>, not to <u>think</u>.

Is something wrong, Rebecca? The tone of your writing is altered, I think. I hope you are not playing coy, to take revenge for my chiding letter of January. I have a doctoral student, a bright young woman not quite so bright as she fancies herself, who plays such games with me at the present time, at her own risk! I hate games, too.

(Unless they are my own.)

Your cousin,

Freyda

Chicago, IL

6 May 1999

Dear Cousin:

Yes, I think you must be angry with me! Or you are not well.

I prefer to think that you are angry. That I did insult you in your American soft heart. If so, I am sorry. I have no copies of my letters to you & don't recall what I said. Maybe I was wrong. When I am coldly sober, I am likely to be wrong. When drunk, I am likely to be less wrong.

Enclosed here is a stamped addressed card. You need only check one of the boxes: [ ] angry [ ] not well.

Your cousin,

Freyda

P.S. This Joseph Cornell "Pond" reminded me of you, Rebecca. A doll-girl playing her fiddle beside a murky inlet.

Lake Worth, Florida

September 19, 1999

Dear Freyda,

How strong & beautiful you were, at the awards ceremony in Washington! I was there, in the audience at the Folger Library. I made the trip just for you.

All of the writers honored spoke very well. But none so witty & unexpected as "Freyda Morgenstern," who caused quite a stir.

I'm ashamed to say, I could not bring myself to speak to you. I waited in line with so many others for you to sign <u>Back from the Dead</u> & when my turn came you were beginning to tire. You hardly glanced at me, you were vexed at the girl assistant fumbling the book. I did no more than mumble, "Thank you," & hurried away.

I stayed just one night in Washington, then flew home. I tire easily now, it was a mad thing to do. My husband would have prevented me if he'd known where I was headed.

During the speeches you were restless onstage, I saw your eyes wandering. I saw your eyes on me. I was sitting in the third row of the theater. Such an old, beautiful little theater in the Folger Library. I think there must be so much beauty in the world we haven't seen. Now it is almost too late we yearn for it.

I was the gaunt-skull woman with the buzz cut. The heavy dark glasses covering half my face. Others in my condition wear gaudy turbans or gleaming wigs. Their faces are bravely made up. In Lake Worth/Palm Beach there are many of us. I don't mind my baldie head in warm weather & among strangers, for their eyes look through me as if I am invisible. You stared at me at first & then looked quickly away & afterward I could not bring myself to address you. It wasn't the right time, I had not prepared you for the sight of me. I shrink from pity & even sympathy is a burden. I had not known that I would make the reckless trip until that morning, for so much depends upon how I feel each morning, it's not predictable.

I had a present to give to you, I changed my mind & took it away again feeling like a fool. Yet the trip was wonderful for me, I saw my cousin so close! Of course I regret my cowardice now it's too late.

You asked about my father. I will tell you no more than that I do not know my father's true name. "Jacob Schwart" was what he called himself & so I was "Rebecca Schwart," but that name was lost long ago. I have another more fitting American name, & I have also my husband's last name, only to you, my cousin, am I identified as "Rebecca Schwart."

Well, I will tell you one more thing: in May 1949 my father who was the gravedigger murdered your aunt Anna and wished to murder me but failed, he turned the shotgun onto himself & killed himself when I was

13 struggling with him for the gun & my strongest memory of that time was his face in the last seconds & what remained of his face, his skull & brains & the warmth of his blood splattered onto me.

I have never told anyone this, Freyda. Please do not speak of it to me, if you write again.

Your cousin

Rebecca

(I did not intend to write such an ugly thing, when I began this letter.)

Chicago, IL

23 September 1999

Dear Rebecca,

I'm stunned. That you were so close to me—and didn't speak.

And what you tell me of—. What happened to you at age 13.

I don't know what to say. Except yes I am stunned. I am angry, & hurt. Not at you, I don't think I am angry at you but at myself.

I've tried to call you. There is no "Rebecca Schwart" in the Lake Worth phone directory. Of course, you've told me there is no "Rebecca Schwart." Why in hell have you never told me your married name? Why are you so coy? I hate games, I don't have time for games.

Yes I am angry with you. I am upset & angry you are not well. (You never returned my card. I waited & waited & you did not.)

Can I believe you about "Jacob Schwart"! We conclude that the ugliest things are likely to be true.

In my memoir that isn't so. When I wrote it, 50 yrs later it was a text I composed of words chosen for "effect." Yes there are true facts in <u>Back from the Dead</u>. But facts are not "true" unless explained. My memoir had to compete with other memoirs of its type & so had to be "original." I am accustomed to controversy, I know how to tweak noses. The memoir makes light of the narrator's pain & humiliation. It's true, I did not feel that I would be one of those to die; I was too young, & ignorant, & compared to others I was healthy. My big blonde sister Elzbieta the relatives so admired, looking like a German girl-doll, soon lost all that hair & her bowels turned to bloody suet. Leon died trampled to death, I would learn afterward. What I say of my mother, Sara Morgenstern, is truthful only at the start. She was not a kapo but one hoping to cooperate with the Nazis to help her family (of course) & other Jews. She was a good organizer & much trusted but never so strong as the memoir has her. She did not say those cruel things, I have no memory of anything anyone said to me except orders shouted by authorities. All the quiet spoken words, the very breath of our lives together, was lost. But a memoir must have spoken words, & a memoir must breathe life.

I am so famous now—infamous! In France this month I am a new bestseller. In the U.K. (where they are outspoken anti-Semites, which is refreshing!) my word is naturally doubted yet still the book sells.

Rebecca, I must speak with you. I will enclose my number here. I will wait for a call. Past 10 P.M. of any night is best, I am not so cold-sober & nasty.

Your cousin,

Freyda

P.S. Are you taking chemotherapy now? What is the status of your condition? Please answer.

Lake Worth, Florida
October 8

Dear Freyda,

Don't be angry with me, I have wanted to call you. There are reasons I could not but maybe I will be stronger soon & I promise, I will call.

It was important for me to see you, and hear you. I am so proud of you. It hurts me when you say harsh things about yourself, I wish you would not. "Spare us"—yes?

Half the time I am dreaming & very happy. Just now I was smelling snakeroot. Maybe you don't know what snakeroot is, you have lived always in cities. Behind the gravedigger's stone cottage in Milburn there was a marshy place where this tall plant grew. The wildflowers were as tall as five feet. They had many small white flowers that look like frost. Very powdery, with a strange strong smell. The flowers were alive with bees humming so loudly it seemed like a living thing. I was remembering how waiting for you to come from over the ocean I had two dolls—Maggie, who was the prettiest doll, for you, and my doll, Minnie, who was plain & battered but I loved her very much. (My brother Herschel found the dolls at the Milburn dump. We found many useful things at the dump!) For hours I played with Maggie & Minnie & you, Freyda. All of us chattering away. My brothers laughed at me. Last night I dreamt of the dolls that were so vivid to me I had not glimpsed in 57 yrs. But it was strange, Freyda, you were not in the dream. I was not, either.

I will write some other time. I love you.

Your cousin

Rebecca

Chicago, IL

12 October

Dear Rebecca,

Now I am angry! You have not called me & you have not given me your telephone number & how can I reach you? I have your street address but only the name "Rebecca Schwart." I am so busy, this is a terrible time. I feel as if my head is being broken by a mallet. Oh I am very angry at you, cousin!

Yet I think I should come to Lake Worth, to see you.

Should I?

F.

SOFT-CORE

———

"WHY ARE YOU showing me these?"
                "I thought you should know."
    " 'Should know'—what?"

They were two sisters of youthful middle age with three breasts be-tween them and a history that might be summed up as *much left unsaid.* Maggie, the elder, who'd had a mastectomy eighteen months before, rarely alluded to the fact in her younger sister's company and spoke with an air of startled reproach if Esther brought up the subject of her health; as if Maggie's breast cancer were a symptom of a moral weakness, a defi-ciency of character, about which Esther had no right to know.

Eighteen months before, after the removal of Maggie's left breast, Esther had driven three hundred seventy miles to see her sister and was immediately rebuffed by Maggie's steely good humor as, as girls, she'd been outplayed on the tennis court by Maggie's remarkable cannonball serves and vicious returns. In her very hospital bed, in the presence of Maggie's husband Dwight, Maggie had assured Esther, indicating the bulky-bandaged left side of her chest, "Hey, sweetie, don't look like a funeral. It's no great loss, I wasn't planning on using it again."

Was this funny? Esther had managed to smile, weakly.

Wanting to slap Maggie's face.

Now it was late spring of another year. The day following their elderly father's funeral. Four days after their elderly father's death. Esther had returned to Strykersville too late by forty-five minutes to see Dr. Hewart before he died: of a heart attack, after a long, deteriorating illness.

Esther had returned to Strykersville hurriedly. Esther had returned, it had to be admitted, reluctantly. For twenty years, in fact for more than twenty years, Esther had avoided Strykersville as much as possible for no reason she could name not wanting to concede even to herself *It's Maggie's territory. I hate Maggie.*

Of course, Esther didn't hate her sister. Esther was in terror that her sister would die and leave her, the surviving Hewart sister. About whom people would say *Oh but Maggie was the one we all loved. That Maggie!* In Maggie's presence Esther felt undefined as a tissue soaked in water, yet, when she was summoned into Maggie's presence she understood that there was something crucial at stake, and so she would shortly be defined, her role would become clear to her; her aimless tissue-thin life would acquire a new significance. When Maggie called Esther to say, in her mildly scolding/bemused elder-sister way, that drew upon their shared girlhood, yet resounded with the authority Maggie had acquired as head librarian of a dozen regional public libraries addressing her intimidated staff, "Esther, it's time to be responsible. It's time for you to come back to Strykersville, to make the effort to be an adult," it was Esther's cue to say quickly, "Maggie, I know. It's . . . time."

Cryptically Maggie had said, "More than time."

In middle age we discover that our parents have become, as if overnight, elderly. It's a discovery like sprouting hair and emerging breasts at puberty. It's a discovery that signals *A new era, ready or not.* Because Maggie had never left Strykersville, and lived with her family just across town from their parents, Esther had managed to avoid this new era for a long time. Though of course she'd felt guilty, all those years. Her visits to her former hometown were infrequent and often painful. Pilgrimages fueled by the tepid oxygen of family duty, unease, guilt. The more Esther loved her parents, the more helpless she felt, as they aged, to protect them from harm. A moral coward, she kept her distance.

When Mrs. Hewart began to fall sick in her mid-seventies, Esther had shuttled back and forth between New York and Strykersville for months, feeling herself a puppet cruelly jerked about, exhausted, and demoralized, for she was no longer a young woman and her life was careening past her and when her father was diagnosed with cancer and began his inevitable descent into weakness, dying, death Esther had wanted to scream at Maggie that she'd had enough of Strykersville as you might have enough of a recurring flu—*No more! I've had it.*

Except of course Esther hadn't had it, entirely. There was more.

She'd returned, and when she had expressed a wish to leave the day after the funeral, Maggie had stared at her with a look almost of derision. "Esther, really! We're not contagious."

Half-consciously Maggie had stroked her left breast. What was now, foam rubber inserted into a specially equipped bra, Maggie's left breast.

Seeing this gesture, Esther blushed. She'd wanted to protest *Maggie, I didn't mean you.*

Since Dr. Hewart had moved into a nursing home the previous year, the Hewarts' house had stood empty. It was made of sandstone and red brick in a dignified Queen Anne style but it was old, and in visible need of repair. Before the property could be put on the market it had to be cleared of household furnishings and the accumulation of decades. Esther felt faint at the prospect. So soon after her father's death she couldn't bear to help Maggie, she'd told her sister, she just couldn't. "But why, exactly? Why, if I can bear it?" Maggie had reasonably asked. That reproachful smile, the calm assessing eyes, the voice that, when required, cut through another's voice like a wire cutter cutting wire.

To this, Esther had no reply. It would not have been possible to say *But I'm the lesser Hewart sister. Everyone knows that.*

Sharp-nosed as vultures, local developers had been calling Maggie for months to ask about the untenanted old house. It came with seven acres of prime real estate, extending into Strykersville's most fashionable suburb and bordering a golf course. Each time, Maggie called Esther to gloat: "Can you believe, they're offering two million dollars?"—"Can you believe, they're offering *two point five million*?" Esther gripped the phone receiver tight against her ear and waited to feel some emotion. Was she elated, like Maggie? Was she sick with guilt, to profit from the collapse of her parents' lives, that seemed to her such good, decent, kindly lives? Or had she so long steeled herself against any emotion generated by news out of Strykersville, she was unmoved?

Anesthetized, that was it. The wisest strategy.

She objected, "Dad wouldn't want the property broken up. If that's what the developer is planning. He always said—"

In her wire-cutter voice Maggie interrupted, "Sweetie. This is us now, not Dad. We make the decisions now."

Sobering to concede, this was so. Maggie was fifty-two years old, Esther was forty-nine.

At the old house, Maggie briskly led Esther through familiar rooms that had become subtly unfamiliar since Esther's last visit the previous spring. Maggie's heels rang against the hardwood floors, where carpets had been removed. Esther, fending off a migraine headache, had an impulse to press her hands over her ears.

Making her way through the house she'd always believed to be so imposing, so dignified among its neighbors, now she saw how small and cluttered the rooms, how dated the design, the narrow windows emitting a stingy sort of light. To be the daughter of a highly respected general practitioner in Strykersville, New York, in the 1950s and 1960s was to be respected, too; in some quarters, envied. But all that was past, and could not be retrieved. Returning to this house was like descending in a bathysphere into a region of undersea shadows and darting shapes in which Maggie, the elder sister, always the wisest and certainly the most pragmatic sister, knew her way blind. In this fairy tale the elder, good sister leads the younger through a labyrinth of rooms crammed with elegant but old, fading furniture, chintz draw-curtains, dust-heavy rolled-up carpets. Quilts handmade by their mother. Cracked and chipped Wedgwood china. Stained-glass objects, the most beautiful a Tiffany-style lamp in rich blues and greens made by their restless father in the stained-glass phase of his retirement. Seeing it, Esther looked quickly away. *There: something I could take back with me.* She hated the sudden greed, the desperation. She hated Maggie for bringing her here. She hated Maggie for being so brave about her cancer, not collapsing into a rag doll as Esther would have done.

"Maggie? I can't breathe here . . ."

Maggie heard nothing for Maggie was talking continuously. At the funeral home, close by their father's open, gleaming casket and his wonderfully composed if rather shriveled monkey-face, Maggie had chattered. The good news was, two Buffalo-area developers were now in the bidding, which would drive the price up even higher. And where they could rent a U-Haul for Esther to attach to her car. Dwight would help them load it, Maggie promised.

Esther wondered what Maggie, who'd rarely visited her in New York, imagined of the brownstone into which Esther had recently moved: five rooms in fashionable Chelsea on West Twenty-second near a welfare hotel whose dazed residents sprawled on the front steps even in the rain. Esther's apartment was chic and spare, mostly neutral colors, her living room/dining room scarcely as large as the kitchen in this house. Esther said, pleading, "I don't have space for heirlooms, Maggie. Clutter makes me anxious."

It was true, her breathing had become labored. Possibly the air was rife with pollen. As Maggie tugged a shroud off a sofa, dust lifted. Esther stared at a massive piece of Victorian furniture with claw feet, a scalloped back, a wine-colored velvet fabric that, as a teenager, she'd compulsively stroked, like fur. Reversing the motion, running her hand over it backward, had made Esther shudder, and she shuddered now, recalling. Maggie said, rapidly, "Things you like, that you don't have room for now, you can store. Someday you might want them. And if they're gone, they're gone forever." She paused as if waiting for Esther to object. "I'm going to be storing lots of things."

Maggie too seemed out of breath. Her eyes glistened. Her tone was argumentative, yet shaky. Esther had no intention of arguing with her sister face-to-face.

"ESTHER, look here."

They were in their father's office at the rear of the house. Dr. Hewart had had his professional office in downtown Strykersville, where he saw patients, but he had a work-related office at home, to be distinguished from his book-lined study off the living room. The home office was comfortably cluttered with an old roll-top desk, a much-worn leather chair and hassock, several filing cabinets. Maggie and Esther were forbidden to enter this room as children unless Dr. Hewart was in it, and unless he invited them; the door was always shut. To push the door open so brashly, as Maggie had just done, seemed to Esther an insolent gesture, so soon after their father's death.

"These were in the bottom desk drawer. I think he must have forgotten them. I can't think he'd have wanted . . ." Maggie paused, unconsciously bringing the back of her hand against the left side of her chest. Esther stared at the faded Polaroids on the desk top, at first uncomprehending. Were these old pictures of her and Maggie? Why was Maggie behaving so strangely?

She saw, then. She gave a little cry and pushed the Polaroids away.

"Did you see who it is?"

"Maggie, I don't want to see."

But Esther had seen: Elvira Sanchez.

Elvira!—Elvira she'd always been to them, not Mrs. Sanchez—a woman who'd "helped out" Mrs. Hewart with housework—a former nurse's aide at Strykersville General—Esther seemed to recall this background, though not clearly. This was sometime in the late 1970s when Esther was in high school, and Elvira's daughter Maria was in Esther's class, and so there was an awkwardness between them, an air as of sisters who had no way of speaking to each other and who, you might have thought if you'd seen them unavoidably forced together, didn't know each other's name. Elvira had been a familiar household presence at the Hewarts for a few years, then abruptly she'd disappeared, as often cleaning women, handymen, lawn crews, snow-removal crews appeared

and disappeared in the mysterious life of the dignified old sandstone and
red brick house on East Avenue, and none of this was questioned by the
children of the house, nor even much noticed.

"It must have been an oversight. He was forgetting so much. He did
destroy lots of 'old boring things' he called them, in the fireplace. I was
afraid he'd burnt legal documents, financial records . . ."

It angered Esther that Maggie was speaking like this. In a rapid
voice, with an air of being bemused.

Esther took up the Polaroids to look at them more closely. There
were about a dozen of them, and all were faded. Yet you could see who
it was, unmistakably. Elvira Sanchez: naked. A stocky but good-looking
woman in her mid-forties with enormous breasts, berry-colored nipples
big as coat buttons, a bristling black pelt of pubic hair. Elvira was lying
lazily back, legs spread, on the leather chair in this room; in another
more extravagant pose, tongue protruding between fleshy lipsticked
lips as she fingered the fleshy cleft between her legs, Elvira sprawled
on the wine-colored velvet sofa in the living room. *In that part of the
house?*—Esther was wounded, stunned. As if such behavior in the living
room was more shocking than in Dr. Hewart's office.

Esther fumbled the Polaroids, not wanting to see more.

"This one"—Maggie snatched it from Esther's fingers, to shove into
her face—"it's their bed, see? Mom and Dad's. That's the ivory quilt
Mom sewed."

Esther slapped Maggie's hand away. The Polaroids went flying.

"Why are you showing me these?"

"I thought you should know."

" 'Should know'—what?"

Maggie stooped to pick up the Polaroids. Her breath was agitated
Her face was warm, flushed. Yet she was trying to behave normally, con-
sidering Esther's question as if she might not have thought of it herself.

"Should know what Dad was. What Dad wasn't. I thought you
might like to know, Esther."

Tactfully not adding *Since you avoided knowing so much, all these
years.*

"Did you think it would make me happy to know, Maggie?"

"I wasn't thinking of your happiness, Esther. Believe me, not everyone spends twenty-four hours a day thinking of your happiness, Esther."

There, it was uttered. Esther recoiled in hurt, that her sister hated her, too.

Maggie held the Polaroids like a hand of cards she'd been dealt. She seemed tired. She seemed, in this moment, not-young and possibly ill. "Maybe I didn't want to be the only one to know, Esther. Maybe I felt lonely."

"Lonely! You."

"Why not me? I'm lonely."

Maggie spoke flatly as if daring Esther to believe her.

"You with your family. Your 'good works.'"

"Nothing is more lonely than fucking 'good works.'"

Esther laughed. Though she was shocked, disoriented. Maggie wasn't one to use profanities lightly, still less obscenities. There was something very wrong here.

She's sick Esther thought. *The cancer has come back.*

Maggie said matter-of-factly, "We'll burn them. In the fireplace. Dad would approve. That seems right."

Esther would afterward recall: Maggie had matches in her handbag. Maggie, who didn't smoke. She'd been prepared for this scene, and she'd needed Esther as a witness.

In the fireplace in Dr. Hewart's book-lined study, which was already messy with ashes, Maggie burnt the Polaroids.

Hesitantly Esther asked, picking at a thumbnail, "Do you think Mom knew? About Elvira . . ."

Maggie shrugged. Maggie wasn't going to speculate.

Esther was thinking of Maria Sanchez. The shame of it, if Maria had known! That would explain . . . No, Esther couldn't bear to think so.

Maggie laughed. "Remember we'd find Dad's magazines, sometimes? Those pulpy things like movie magazines, mostly pictures. The shock of it, in bright colors. Once I found, I guess it was only just *Playboy*, under the front seat of Dad's car."

Esther shook her head, no. She didn't remember.

" 'Soft-core porn' it's called now. Nothing worse than what you see in movies now, or on TV, but it seemed shocking then."

They were watching the Polaroids flare up, wan bluish flames tinged with orange. How curious fire is. How quickly evidence disappears, anonymous soot remaining.

With schoolgirl obstinacy Esther objected, "Some of those were Dad's medical magazines. I used to look through those."

Maggie snorted in derision. "Not these, sweetie. These were not the *New England Journal of Medicine*, I assure you."

"No, but there were others, with pictures. Like—" Esther was confused: medical magazines with lurid juicy close-ups of surgical procedures? Childbirth? A bared, red-muscled heart, no more mysterious than meat in a butcher's display case? Was she remembering these, or imagining them?

They waited until the Polaroids were destroyed utterly.

Esther said, "Now you tell me about you, Maggie. I deserve to know."

Maggie turned a startled face toward her. Esther saw what looked like a glimmer of resentment, and guilt.

Here was a fact: Esther had been waiting, since the night of their father's death, for Maggie to confide in her. The claim of one sister upon another. *I knew you before your husband knew you. Long before your children knew you.* As in a nightmare scenario Esther waited for Maggie to confess to her what she hadn't yet been able to tell her husband and children: she was going to die. The cancer had returned. The cancer had—Esther hated this word, familiar from their parents' ordeals—*metastasized*. And how would Esther react? She wondered if she would begin to shake, as she sometimes shook in the cold of the mammography examination room, and Maggie herself would have to console her. *Oh sweetie! C'mon.* Or would she stare at Maggie, who'd been mysterious to her all their lives, as she was staring now, and feel nothing, nothing at all?

" 'Deserve to know'—what?"

"Your health. You never tell me . . ."

"My health." Maggie ran her fingers through her short, springy

talcum-colored hair, that had grown back sparsely after her chemo-
therapy. She smiled roguishly at Esther. "Strong as an ox. Ask my en-
emies."

"Oh, Maggie. Don't be like that."

"Like what? I don't have enemies?"

Esther pleaded, "You would tell me if—wouldn't you?"

" 'If-if'—what?"

Maggie was mocking her but Esther couldn't retreat. She made a
clumsy gesture with her arm, against her left breast.

"*That?* Oh, certainly. You'd be the first to know, Esther. As soon as
my oncologist tells me, and before I tell Dwight."

Maggie spoke sneeringly. Evidently she was angry.

Esther wanted to say *Fuck you, then. I don't need you.*

Esther apologized. She was sorry, she said.

"Maggie, forgive me? I'm only thinking of you."

"Think of yourself, sweetie. I'm fine."

They'd returned to the living room. Esther followed Maggie in a
haze, stumbling into things. By this time her ice pick headache was
causing her eyes to lose focus. The chemical stink of the Polaroids! She
wanted desperately to leave this place but she understood that Maggie
wouldn't allow it, not quite yet. She would have to be punished further.
She'd been summoned back home to be a witness, and to be punished.
The dining room table looked like a table in a yard sale, upon which
items were spread in the forlorn hope of attracting buyers. Tarnished sil-
verware and candlestick holders, woven place mats with shadowy stains,
more of Mrs. Hewart's finery, that had been overlooked, apparently,
after her death. Maggie nudged Esther to "take something, for Christ's
sake," but Esther stood numbed, unable to move. That boxy handbag:
alligator hide? Esther shuddered at the thought of touching such a thing.
She couldn't remember her mother carrying that bag.

Maggie said, annoyed, "The lamp, at least. You can take that, can't
you?"

Maggie meant their father's stained-glass Tiffany-style lamp. She
pointed out the painstaking craftsmanship that had gone into it: the
triangular pieces of glass, blues, greens, pale red and russet-red. "It's

beautiful. Your New York friends will admire it." Again Maggie was sneering, but less angrily than before. "It has nothing to do with—you know. That other."

That other. Esther foresaw that, after today, neither she nor Maggie would allude to what they'd seen in their father's office, and burned together in his fireplace. Not even elliptically as Maggie was doing now, with the mildest embarrassment. *That other.*

They would not utter the name Sanchez.

Esther said, "It is beautiful, Maggie. But . . ." She was groping through the pain in her head. She might have said nothing further but heard her voice continue. "I don't like beautiful things."

Maggie said sharply, "Don't like beautiful things?"

"I mean—beautiful breakable things."

As if to prove her point Esther made a sudden gesture toward the Tiffany lamp. Perhaps it was involuntary, like a tremor. Perhaps Maggie overreacted, shoving at Esther's arm. The Tiffany lamp fell from the end table, slipped through both the sisters' fingers and toppled over onto the floor. *Shattered into a thousand pieces!* But when Esther opened her eyes she saw no broken glass. The lampshade was wrenched around like a head on a broken neck, but the lamp had fallen against a rolled-up carpet. Maggie, trembling with indignation, picked it up and placed it back on the table, exactly where it had been, in a square clear of surrounding dust. "You're right, Esther. You shouldn't take this lamp, or anything. You'd better go back home."

Esther wanted to protest *But I am home!*

Instead she said, wiping at her eyes with a wadded tissue she'd found in her pocket, "Well, Maggie. Now you know my heart."

It wasn't true. But she hoped Maggie would think so, from now on.

THE GATHERING SQUALL

SHE KNEW: HER mother was terribly upset. Because her mother was asking, "Are you going to tell us who it was?" and there was no *us* in the Uhlmanns' household any longer.

"Momma, I said, I didn't see."

"Of course you saw. You're not blind."

"I didn't. I did not."

"But you know. You know who did this to you."

She said nothing. She was lying where she'd crawled the night before, so tired. On her bed atop the rumpled rust-colored corduroy spread her mother had sewn for her when she'd been in seventh grade. How long ago, her brain was too fatigued to calculate. Oh, her sunburnt arms, shoulders! Her face burning as if someone had tossed acid onto it. This was punishment enough for the night before.

Her mother leaned over her, so close Lisellen could feel her warm ragged breath, yet Mrs. Uhlmann was hesitant to touch her, just yet. In another minute she would, Lisellen knew. Lisellen was lying in a tight little pretzel knot, knees drawn up to her chest. Face turned to the wall like they say dying people do. Was it shame, you wanted to hide your face? Or, dying, did you feel you'd had enough of the world, its busyness, its annoying attentions? Needing to hide her bruised and banged-up face from Mrs. Uhlmann's laser eyes. Her older sister Tracy used to say their mother could tell by looking at Tracy's mouth how much she'd been kissed by her boyfriend, kissing left an unmistakable look if you knew how to identify it, but Lisellen had not been kissed. Duncan Baitz had not even tried to kiss her. Not a one of those guys had tried to kiss her.

"God damn, girl, I'm losing my patience."

"Momma, I said I don't know."

Losing patience. Lisellen had to smile, the strangeness of how people talked. Like *patience* was something that could be *lost*, like loose coins.

The night before, staggering into the bathroom to stare at herself in the mirror, Lisellen had been more astonished than shocked. What a freak she'd looked! Her upper lip was swollen to three times its normal size, there was a crust of red (blood? had her nose been bleeding?) around both her nostrils, her hair looked as if an eggbeater had gotten into it. Now, hours later, her lip throbbed as if a wasp had stung it, the delicate skin pulled tight to bursting. The sunburn would cause her fair, freckled skin to peel, maybe to blister. And there were the hot dark eyes she'd had to acknowledge in the mirror, brimming with hurt and disbelief. *I thought you were my friends! I thought you liked me.*

She was of an age, oh God it had seemed to be going on forever, this age when all things were in reference to others. The opinions of others. When she could not have a private thought except somehow it was directed toward staring witnesses whose judgment of her was ceaseless and harsh, but might be amended by an appeal of hers, a helpless smile, a childish disarming gesture.

She must have been whimpering in her sleep. A feverish half-sleep in which she couldn't find a comfortable position. She hadn't removed her clothes, only just kicked off her sandals. She hadn't had the energy. Like a sudden summer squall out of a cloud there'd come Lisellen's mother into her room slamming the door with the flat of her hand—"Lisellen! Good Christ, what is it?" For just that moment, Mrs. Uhlmann had been more frightened than angry. The hour was very early: just after 6 A.M.

Already a hot-acid splotch of sunshine was moving across the plaster wall above Lisellen's head. Mrs. Uhlmann woke early, nerved-up and ready to begin the day, needing to fill the house, emptier since the departure of two of its inhabitants, with purposeful activity, a smell of brewing coffee and the cheering noise of the kitchen radio. And so, waking, she'd heard the whimpering from Lisellen's bedroom; unless it had been the whimpering that had wakened her. And the shock of seeing her daughter lying in that contorted posture, face almost touching the wall, not in bed but on top of it, still in her clothes from the previous day—this had caused Lisellen's mother to cry out, and go in stumbling haste to fetch ice cubes, thinking at first the problem was only just sunburn.

Well, sunburn. Fair freckled thin skin like Lisellen's, if you had sense you kept out of the sun. It was Mrs. Uhlmann's side of the family, not Mr. Uhlmann's. Lisellen knew better than to risk sunburn. Sunstroke. On the wide glaring-sandy beach at Olcott. Where sunshine broke and rippled in the choppy lake in an infinity of laser-like rays. Where there was always wind, so you were deceived the sun wasn't so hot as it was. And the partly clouded, veiled sky so you might think the sun's rays would be diluted. Though Lisellen knew better of course. Only she'd had to take a chance. *Didn't want to miss out. Any of it.* She wasn't of a legal age to drink but there were ways of beating that, if you had older friends. If you hung out in the parking lot, not inside the tavern.

What Lisellen had been wild not to miss, not a minute of it, what she could not bear to confess to her mother, was the partying. At the Summit, above the dunes. Swarms of young people were everywhere inside the mustard-colored stucco building, on the outdoor terrace where there was dancing, in the asphalt parking lot and on the beach and amid the dunes. Deafening rock music was played by a local band that called itself Big Bang, six or seven zoned-out guys of whom Lisellen could claim she knew the straggly-haired drummer, sort of, the older brother of a girl in Lisellen's tenth-grade homeroom last year. And there was Duncan Baitz, the misunderstanding between them . . .

Thought you were my friend. Thought you liked me.

In her upset Mrs. Uhlmann hadn't been able to locate the rubber ice bag. So she'd wrapped ice cubes in a kitchen towel for Lisellen to press against her swollen face. But the ice cubes soon melted from the heat of Lisellen's throbbing skin, dripped and ran and wetted her making her recall the sticky mucus-moisture rubbed and smeared on her legs. On even her belly where her white cotton panties had been yanked down, torn but (at least, she had this to be grateful for, she clung to this small vestige of dignity as one might cling to a barnacle-encrusted rock in terror of drowning in the surf) not torn off.

She knew: word would spread all through Olcott of what had been done to her. But what had not been done to her was more crucial.

She was making a sick-puppy sound. She was shivering. Wanting to evoke her mother's sympathy, but not her mother's alarm. Wanting her mother to know *Yes I've been hurt, your daughter has been hurt Mommy take care of me*. But not wanting her mother to drive her to a doctor. Not wanting her mother to dial 911, to summon police.

Lisellen made an effort to sit up. Pretending to be weaker than she really was except as she tried to raise her head a wave of dizziness weakened her. Like an energy outage, the TV screen suddenly wavering on the brink of collapse.

Honors student they'd teased. She had believed there was affection in their teasing.

That she was smart, that she did well in school, performing easily on tests the others struggled with, disfigured her like acne. She knew, and she knew that the resentment and even the dislike of her classmates was warranted. At Olcott High she had a cerain aura, outside school very little. Not-pretty, and not-sexy. There were many other girls like Lisellen, most of the girls in her class in fact, but Lisellen wasn't patient with her lot. She yearned to be one of the summer girls blossoming like hills of dandelion and tiger lilies, overnight bobbing bright colors in the wind. So fast. It could happen so fast. With some girls, as young as thirteen. Lisellen was sixteen but looked like fourteen. Other girls were sixteen looking like eighteen. She didn't disdain them, nor even yearned to be one of them; she yearned only not to be left behind by them.

She'd crept into the house the night before, praying her mother would be asleep and would not hear her. It was nearly 1 A.M., she'd promised to be home by 11 P.M. Calculating that probably her mother wouldn't wait up for her. Mrs. Uhlmann trusted her younger, honors-student daughter, as she had not trusted Tracy. Tracy who'd been a little wild. Rebellious. Tracy who was nineteen now, a nursing student in Rochester, working this summer as a nurse's aide in the hospital. Tracy had moved out in the season their parents' marriage had finally broken up. Twenty-six years!—Lisellen had thought, with the heartlessness of youth, that the elder Uhlmanns' love had only just worn out. Like a roller-towel in a public restroom, eventually the contraption breaks and the towel becomes filthy, hanging in tatters.

She'd hated her sister. *Good timing, Trace. Thanks for leaving me behind.*

Tracy said, *Every daughter for herself, man.*

Tracy had meant to be funny. She hadn't been.

At the Summit Tavern, in the asphalt parking lot and on the beach, in the slovenly dunes there was an atmosphere of high-decibel festivity. On the terrace the deafening music of Big Bang made thinking more trouble than it was worth, like trying to run in loose sand. Like wading in rough surf. For a brief tormented while Lisellen had believed she'd been left behind by the people who had brought her: the hike back home was three miles, unless she dared telephone her mother to come get her (she wouldn't have dared), or begged a ride with someone going in that direction (maybe, she might've dared). She was hurt to have been left behind by Duncan Baitz in whose car she'd been brought to Olcott but determined to have a good time anyway. In fact, Lisellen's friends (she wanted to think they were more than just stray people she knew from school) hadn't left the Summit just yet. The crowd was so large, she'd lost them. Baitz was a vivid presence in Lisellen's life though she had to suppose she wasn't much of a presence in his. He was older, a year ahead at school. But he looked and behaved as if he were older still. Once, he'd asked Lisellen out. She'd stammered yes, yes she'd like that, but somehow, it was never clear to her how and why and had become the subject of obsessive hours of pondering, Baitz had never called her, he'd been politely indifferent to her ever since. Why?

He must have interpreted her remarks as negative, somehow. Oh, but why?

True, Baitz had stopped at her house to pick Lisellen up to take her to Olcott, but someone else had made the arrangements. Lisellen had crammed herself into the back seat of Baitz's car, one of several passengers shrieking with laughter, sitting on one another's laps, while in front beside Baitz was a male friend of his, a stranger to Lisellen. She was conscious, in Baitz's presence, of a certain degree of tension that remained mysterious, heartrending. Not that Lisellen was one to brood *Why don't you like me anymore, Duncan, what has gone wrong?* She didn't think that Baitz was even attractive, with his odd blunt head like a bucket and his prematurely creased forehead; the Baitzes lived in a ramshackle house on the weedy edge of Strykersville, Mr. Baitz was an auto mechanic. Lisellen had a vague idea that their fathers knew and disliked each other but not why. Lisellen's father was a man of smoldering hurts and grievances that sometimes flared into alarming emotions, like brushfires, you didn't try to comprehend their source, only how to extinguish them; Lisellen guessed that Mr. Baitz might be of the same type, being of the same generation. Her father had done better than Mr. Baitz, though—he'd been a trucker as a young man, bought his own truck, bought several trucks, was now in business for himself, as he liked to define it. Since he'd moved out of the house, leaving just Lisellen and her mother behind, Lisellen had begun to think of her father as she thought uneasily of Duncan Baitz. *You can't make them like you. You can't even make them see you.* When Baitz glanced at Lisellen, if only by accident, and unsmiling, a sensation like a machete lashed through her body leaving her weak, stunned.

Sixteen, Lisellen was too young to be served what's quaintly called *alcoholic beverages* at the Summit. Still she was drinking beer supplied by others. As the manic notes of the Big Bang hammered at her head from all directions Lisellen discovered that, despite its repellent taste, she could swallow mouthfuls of beer. Though sometimes coughing, choking, causing the stinging liquid to drip from her nose in a way some observers found funny: as if Lisellen were doing it on purpose to amuse. (Oh, God! She would recall this with mortification. At the time, it had seemed hilarious to her, too.) The Summit on a Saturday night in midsummer was the place to be, at Olcott Beach. Jammed with people, most of them young. Mrs. Uhlmann had only grudgingly allowed Lisellen to go to the beach; she had not known about the Summit, which had a certain reputation. Mrs. Uhlmann, grimly predicting that Lisellen might get caught up in a wrong crowd, as if *caught up* in a fisherman's net, would have seen her worst suspicions confirmed. For here were loud men in T-shirts that exposed their corded, oily muscles, their lurid tattoos. (Some of these were bikers from Niagara Falls.) There were "older" men in their thirties and perhaps beyond—some as old as Lisellen's father, though far more youthful in dress, hair style, behavior. And girls and young women: not behaving very soberly. Where couples were dancing on the terrace, almost you could see minuscule haloes of perspiration in the air like dust motes. Strobe lighting from a long-ago era. Lisellen was impressed that certain of her friends were high on drugs even as a part of her stood aside in disdain thinking *Not me! Not me like you, not ever.*

Yet somehow there was Lisellen in a rowdy group in the dunes. Running and stumbling along the pebbly beach. By this time her skin was beginning to burn in alarming patches on her face, her shoulders and arms. The tender exposed skin of her upper chest. It was fully night now, the slow-sinking sun had finally disappeared, yet still the air was warm and muggy with gnats. Lisellen understood that things were swerving out of control. Her sandals were sinking into the sand as she ran, and the sand itself appeared to be sinking, tilting at a drunken angle. On the immense lake waves slopped and sloshed. There was a sound of laughter mixed with the relentless downbeat of the Big Bang. Mixed too with a faint stink of dead things: rotting fish strewn on the beach, clam shells, vegetation in long snaky clumps. By day, flies buzzed; by night, gnats got into your hair, eyes, mouth. Lisellen realized she was the only girl in the dunes. There had been one or two others, they must have turned back. The guys were teasing Lisellen by chanting her name—*Lis-el-len Uhl-mann*—in a way that was meant to make her laugh, the name sounded so pretentious, so somehow complicated and silly. *Honors student honors student!*—a loud boisterous singsong chant, Lisellen wanted to interpret it as affectionate, not malicious. And the hands grabbing at her, affectionate and not malicious. A rough kind of flirting. More like grade school than high school. And some of these guys were older, and not known to Lisellen. She was being pulled laughing into the water. A lukewarm sudsy surf it was, like water in a washing machine. Someone was splashing water onto her, Lisellen sputtered with laughter. Her bare shoulders, breasts. Wetting the dress her mother had sewed for her, gorgeous orange poppies on a white background, flaring skirt, a beautiful dress, a dress to make you smile, a dress Lisellen had wanted her father to see but he had not, a dress to flatter her pale freckled skin and boyish body. She'd been disappointed, most of the girls at the Summit were wearing just tank tops, cutoffs, jeans that fitted tight as if they'd been poured into them, the more glamorous wore clingy sexy shifts, miniskirts that bared their gleaming thighs. These were girls with boyfriends. These were girls who were dancing on the terrace, or sitting with their dates inside, in booths. Not girls racing along the beach shrieking with laughter as if being tickled to death.

The boys were so much taller than Lisellen, and bigger. Panting like dogs they formed a circle around her. They were only playing, she knew. She slapped at their bold hands, their quick-darting hands, the pinching fingers, she saw their grinning mouths and eager eyes, the sweat gleaming on their faces. And some yards away there was Duncan Baitz, staring at her. He wasn't in the circle of guys, he was standing on one of the dunes, as if he'd been approaching them but had paused, and stood now irresolute and frowning, his expression unreadable. Was he smiling? Grinning? Or was it a look of alarm—*See? See what you've brought on yourself?*

"Was it that Baitz boy?" Mrs. Uhlmann's guess was sudden, as if she'd been reading Lisellen's mind.

Lisellen stammered no. No it was not. No she didn't remember who it had been, she hadn't seen his face.

ALWAYS Lisellen had had a sense of something in her mother gathering, tightening with tension. The sensation was almost unbearable and yet thrilling. *The Gathering Squall* was the title of a nineteenth-century watercolor Lisellen had seen in a Port Oriskany art gallery, and the feeling she had about her mother was like the feeling generated by that watercolor in which the sky was dense with clouds, near-black, though riddled with rays of sunshine like rents in fabric, and a lone fisherman stood at the edge of a lake, a lake reflecting black, so intent upon the fishing line he'd cast into the eerily glassy water that he was oblivious of the gathering squall. *Run! run for your life!* you wanted to shout at this fool. For in another minute lightning would erupt. The squall would hit in wind and biting raindrops and a smell of sulphur.

In Mrs. Uhlmann, Lisellen had a sense of a gathering squall. Fierce, explosive, pitiless. Yet thrilling. You were frightened of the squall, yet you wanted it. You craved it. There was raw emotion here, needing no story to explain it. *You married beneath yourself* was a remark that might actually have been made to Lisellen's mother by one or another of her female relatives. *You made your bed now lie in it.* These were not subtle women. These were good Christian women with a genuine sympathy for one another, including Mrs. Uhlmann whose name among them was Florrie, and who'd married Lisellen's father instead of staying in school to graduate with her class. (And she hadn't even been pregnant with Tracy, Lisellen had calculated the dates.) Today you could no more believe in a stone speaking than you could believe in Florrie Uhlmann behaving recklessly in love but, presumably, that was what it had been: reckless behavior, love.

Lisellen loved her father, too. Still, she was afraid of him. His moods. His sarcasm. His air of reproach, obscure hurt. The way he spoke over the phone, to someone who owed him money or who had crossed him somehow. The way sometimes he looked at his youngest daughter, as if he hadn't any idea who the hell she was, except something to do with him, a responsibility of his, a blame of his, yes but he could be proud of her too, he could be affectionate and teasing in the right mood, and it was this mood you hoped for, like switching on the radio in the hope of hearing music you liked, though knowing probably you would not, the odds were against it. When Uhlmann Trucking wasn't going well, you could be sure that Clarence Uhlmann's mood would follow, but when things went well, as sometimes they did, you couldn't be sure that Clarence Uhlmann's mood would follow, because—you just couldn't. Uhlmann was a man to drive a hard bargain, it was said. Lisellen smiled, thinking of her father *driving a hard bargain* as he drove one of his trucks.

In April, Lisellen had returned home from school late one afternoon, and there was Mrs. Uhlmann, vacuuming the living room, her face glowing as if she'd polished it with steel wool. In a state of euphoria she shouted at Lisellen over the noise of the cleaner, which she didn't trouble to switch off, "He's gone." Lisellen shouted back, "Who?" Mrs. Uhlmann shouted, "Your father." Lisellen was stunned. She'd known there was trouble, that ever-tightening tension, but they'd lived with it for so long, why now? "*Gone*—where?" she'd asked. But Mrs. Uhlmann ignored her, hauling the vacuum cleaner into another room.

NOW, Mrs. Uhlmann's attention was fierce upon Lisellen, like a blinding light. She was handling Lisellen, using her hands on her, as you might handle a small child. Not wanting to hurt the child, but not indulging the child, either. Firmly turning Lisellen from the wall she'd practically crawled into, turning Lisellen onto her back. Lisellen didn't resist. No point in resisting. Thinking *I was not raped, she won't find evidence.* With a familiarity that startled Lisellen, for mother and daughter were naturally reticent with each other, inclined to physical shyness, Mrs. Uhlmann lifted the badly rumpled skirt of Lisellen's orange-poppy dress, that was stained with beer and a dried snot-substance you didn't require much imagination to guess might be semen. Mrs. Uhlmann saw the torn panties. The panties stained like the dress. These she pulled down, more hesitantly now, as Lisellen shut her eyes. The lower part of her body had been insulted but had not been injured. The boys had hardly touched her there. The most they'd done was rub themselves against her, like boys wrestling together. They'd careened and crashed against her as in a game of bumper cars at the Olcott Amusement Park. Lisellen's pale fuzzy pubic hair, that seemed to her so comical, and sad. Her flat girl's stomach. Hips narrow as a boy's. And her legs too thin, though hard with muscle. *Lis-el-len! Uhl-mann!*

"Was it that Baitz boy, that bastard, was it him? It was, wasn't it?"

"Nobody did anything, Momma . . ."

"Somebody did something! I can see it, and I can smell it. He hit you, your face. Look at you! And your clothes ripped, and—*disgusting.*"

Mrs. Uhlmann gave a choked little cry, yanking down Lisellen's skirt. Lisellen said, pleading, "I wasn't hurt, Momma, really. It wasn't Duncan. Not what you think . . ."

"You're lying. You want to protect him."

Lisellen lay with her eyes tightly shut, seeing him there at the edge of the jeering circle. He'd said something to them. She hadn't heard his words but she'd heard his voice. They paid no attention. They were pinching her nipples through her dress, snatching between her legs, one of them dared to jam his thumb into the crack of her ass. The more Lisellen pleaded for them to stop, the more excited they were becoming. Like dogs she'd once seen cavorting crazily over the part-decayed corpse of a groundhog. Who was the first to unzip his pants, Lisellen wouldn't know, and would not want to know. And where Baitz was by this time, she wouldn't know. The nightmare ended when someone shouted at them from one of the dunes. A stranger, thank God no one who knew her. A young man, with one of the glamorous miniskirted girls. Both were shouting at Lisellen's assailants, and so the guys broke and ran along the beach laughing and stumbling as they zipped themselves up. Lisellen was crying by now, thoroughly ashamed. The girl in the miniskirt comforted her and led her back through the dunes to the parking lot and the couple drove Lisellen home insisting it was no trouble, it wasn't out of their way. "If it was me," the girl said, incensed, "I'd call the police. Somebody'd be arrested." Her companion said, "Well, it isn't you. So let it go."

SHE WOULD NOT accuse him, she had no need. All that had ever passed between them of significance had not required speech. And so this morning, driving to her estranged husband's new living quarters, a rented duplex in Strykersville near the trucking yard, Mrs. Uhlmann rehearsed only the words she would greet him with: "Something has happened to your daughter."

They had not communicated in ten days.

It was not yet 7 A.M. Uhlmann would be awake and up, but still in the duplex. Mrs. Uhlmann struck the door with her fist as if bitterly resenting it, that the door was locked against her. Though she was the one to have banished Uhlmann from her life yet she thought *If he has a woman with him, I will spit in both their faces.*

There appeared to be no woman. Uhlmann was startled to see her, blinking as if she'd wakened him from sleep. Yet he'd shaven, he was nearly dressed. He had no need to ask her if something was wrong, only to listen to what she would say and, once she'd said it, to ask, as she knew he would, "Who?"

"She won't say."

"Won't *say*? She *won't say*?"

Florrie felt now the injustice of it, too. That their younger daughter who had always been the good daughter, the obedient and docile-seeming daughter, the one used as a rebuke to the headstrong elder, should behave now so mutinously.

"Won't say who it was—did what to her?"

Uhlmann was a man not hard of hearing but requiring words to be repeated so that they might not be misunderstood. For words, speech, speaking with others was not a strength of his; if asked, he might have disdained such strength, as over-fastidious, effeminate. But he wanted now to know. He was taller than Florrie by several inches, and heavier by fifty pounds, yet he moved with the wary alacrity of an ex–high school athlete. Even in sleep his body was restless, his muscles twitched and clenched. When upset, or confused, he had a way of smiling savagely with half his mouth, the effect like a razor slash. He was smiling now, waiting for Florrie to reply.

"Abused. Did things to." Florrie gestured vaguely, very much embarrassed, in the direction of her lower body. "Not—not the worst. But her face has been struck by him, it's swollen and bruised and she's just lying there in her bed, crying." Florrie paused. For perhaps this wasn't true, exactly. What had happened to her daughter, beyond the range of Florrie's knowledge, was beginning already to fade. "She has been shamed."

Again Uhlmann asked, staring at her, "Who?"

Meaning: who has done this, who is to blame.

This moment Florrie would long recall as, in the moment preceding an accident, even as the wheels of your vehicle begin their helpless skid, belatedly you think it has not happened yet, you can prevent it.

"She's protecting him but it's that Baitz boy. The one who's always hanging around."

"Is he? Is he hanging around?"

Seeing, but not wishing to fully see, the sick dazed look in her husband's face as she told him, "He drove her to Olcott last night. He came by to pick her up, just sat out in the car and she ran to him. There's been something between them . . . She refuses to say what."

Uhlmann nodded, as if what Florrie was telling him was a fact he knew, a fact he'd always known, or, as the father of the shamed girl, should have known. A father knows such things, by instinct. He had failed his family by not-knowing. His soul was sick with grief, shame of his failure, shame of being publicly expelled from his family. In that instant Florrie understood: lifting her eyes to the face of her repudiated, disdained and humiliated husband of twenty-six years, who was looking stunned as if he'd been kicked in the stomach. His face had become haggard, all the blood had drained out. A clay mask it seemed suddenly to Florrie, about to shatter.

She was in his arms suddenly, sobbing. She was not a woman to weep easily, or with pleasure. Uhlmann's response was immediate, instinctive: he held her, had no choice but to hold her. In his ropey-muscled arms she shut her eyes smelling the rank tobacco odor, the smell of the previous night's whiskey, all that she had come to loathe in him. Florrie had married beneath her, people said. Married for love and made a terrible mistake, maybe.

But there was Tracy, and there was Lisellen. She had her daughters, no one could take them from her. In her husband's arms she was weak as she had not been in a long time. A sick, sliding-down sensation that shocked her, it came so powerfully. As in the first acquiescence to physical love. That moment at which you pass from the merely emotional to the physical: knowing there will be no return.

Would it begin again, her love for this man? She could not bear it.

She was too old, she could not bear it. These emotions she had passed through, and had come to detest.

"I don't want you to—" She paused, trying to think: didn't want him to do what, exactly? "Hurt anyone. No."

Uhlmann made a sound of assent. It was hardly more than a grunt, or might have been muffled laughter.

"No. Promise me, you must not."

Yet Florrie foresaw: she would defend this man, she would support him. She would not lie for him if she was questioned by police, for she was not a woman to lie, her soul abhorred any kind of moral weakness, but she would say, choosing her words with care, that her husband had acted as a father must act, in such circumstances; that was Uhlmann's way, that was his nature, and so she would support him through whatever would come of this moment.

The arrest, the trial.

The aftermath of the trial.

IT WAS STILL EARLY when Uhlmann arrived at the Baitz house: approximately 8:20 A.M.

The Baitzes lived on the scrubby outskirts of Strykersville, about two miles from the place Uhlmann was renting. An old wood-frame house it was, once painted eggshell blue and long since weatherworn and faded, Baitz Gas & Auto Service close by. The garage may have been open for business, a single dim light within. No one was visible behind the front door, the gas pumps were unattended. Uhlmann parked his truck in the driveway of the house. His twelve-gauge double-barreled shotgun he hadn't fired in years, since duck-hunting with his cousins in the Adirondacks, lay on the seat beside him. It would not be clear afterward whether Uhlmann had intended to use the gun. His intention might have been simply to protect himself. Possibly he'd meant to talk with Ed Baitz, the boy's father. More and more it would come to seem to him, afterward, that that was what he'd intended: just to talk. He and Baitz were of the same age, and of the same background, Baitz would understand his agitation, Baitz would know what had to be done. Except it was the boy who appeared in the driveway. Not Ed but the boy, Duncan: unmistakably this was the son, Uhlmann recognized him at once, though Duncan Baitz was looking older than Uhlmann would have believed him, hardly a kid any longer but someone out of high school, too old to be hanging out with high school kids; and unshaven; in jeans, a soiled T-shirt, some kind of asshole flip-flops on his bare feet.

The bare bony white feet, the flip-flops: the way Duncan Baitz was staring at him, that sick scared look: that did it.

The kid saw UHLMANN in white letters on the side of the truck, at once he began to back off. Here was his mistake: even as Uhlmann was getting out of the truck and speaking to him, he turned and began to run. When Uhlmann shouted after him, he began to run faster. It was the kid's mistake and not Uhlmann's. This was not the behavior of an innocent person. It was panicked behavior, and very stupid. For Duncan Baitz had at least thirty yards before he would have reached the barn he meant to hide inside, when Uhlmann lifted the shotgun and aimed for the moving target of the T-shirt, not a moving target shrewd enough to zigzag but simply to run in a single direction, away from the line of fire, and pulled the first of the triggers.

SO TIRED! Lisellen felt as if she had not slept for days.

Drifting to sleep in the bathtub. Warm sudsy soothing water. Her mother had rubbed Noxzema into her sunburnt face, on her smarting shoulders and arms, and these she kept clear of the water. She understood how lucky she was: that worse hadn't happened to her, and known throughout Strykersville to have happened to her. She was grateful that her mother hadn't insisted upon taking her to the doctor, or called the police. Above all grateful to be alone.

The sticky residue of whatever had happened to her was washed away. She seemed to know that her mother would throw away the orange-poppy dress, neither of them need see it again.

Neither of them need speak of it again.

This bathroom, upstairs beneath the sloping roof. The hook-latch on the door. This was one of Lisellen's safe places. Her father had torn out the old stained tiles and replaced them with shiny buttercup-yellow tiles from Sears, the floor was a smart rust-red linoleum. Through her life Lisellen would recall this bathroom, the sloping ceiling above the tub, the myriad cracks in the plaster that resembled a mad scribbling in a foreign language, and most of all the big old stained-white tub that fitted into the small space like a hand in a tight-fitting glove.

Shutting her eyes she saw the rapt grinning faces as they moved upon her. At the edge of their hilarity, the boy she had wanted so badly to care for her, backing away.

He had left her to them, had he? For that, he must be punished.

Again she felt the quick-snatching hands that seemed to her disembodied hands, as her assailed and demeaned body would come to seem depersonalized to her, a female body lacking an identity, the body of any adolescent girl and not her own. They would not have wished to hurt *her*. She would come to interpret the episode as embarrassing, awkward, bad luck. Bad judgment on everyone's part. Too much beer, excitement. The beat-beat-beat of the rock band. They had not meant to hurt her, had they? In a way it had been flattering. A kind of flirtation gone wild. Almost a kind of love. Maybe. Duncan Baitz would have to consider her in a new way, now.

Lisellen rubbed her fingers over her pear-sized little breasts, feeling the nipples harden.

THE LOST BROTHER

—

"ALONE."

She was forty-one. She was unmarried, childless. She was living in a house north of Farmington, Connecticut (whitewashed brick colonial, twenty rooms, original foundation built in 1768), where in fact she'd grown up and had continued to live as an adult. When finally her mother died after a lengthy, wasting illness she felt the terrible isolation of her life like a blow to the back of her head that left her stunned. *If I am being punished, I must deserve it.* This was the voice of the house but it was not her own voice. She did not accept it as her own voice. Why should she deserve to be punished, and why now?

Then it came to her, of course she wasn't alone: she had a brother.

A "lost" brother believed to be living as a recluse in northern Maine, whom she hadn't seen or spoken with in twenty-two years.

HIS NAME was Hayden, he was her senior by six years. In childhood, six years is a lifetime.

And so, Hayden had been, at the time of her growing-up, a kind of adult. So much taller than she, so much absorbed in his own, mostly mental life. So mysterious.

She had adored him, though at a distance. Closer up, she had feared him.

Hayden had left home abruptly, aged twenty-one. He had not been "well" at the time. His parting words had been sharp as a bat's cry, both wounded and jubilant: "All you to the hell!"

All you to the hell. This curse, if it was a curse, was also a riddle. For normally, no one said "the" hell, only just "hell." And "all you" was puzzling as well. For Hayden had hated only their father, not their mother. And he could hardly have hated her, at the time a shy girl of fifteen of whom he'd taken little notice.

In fact, when they'd been younger, before Hayden's illness had worsened, he'd seemed to like her, sometimes. "Sis-ter" he would call her, as if the word was new and special to him, a kind of secret name, melodic, mysterious. "Sis-ter Car-ole. For you."

He'd given her things. What their mother called Hayden's "special, magical things." For it was believed that Hayden would be an artist, someday. One of these was a miniature birdcage made of the bones of actual birds, braided with vividly colored feathers. Another was a jar of dark green wavy glass Hayden had found in a landfill, and filled with mica-glittering pebbles. Most memorably there was a mummified baby rabbit, its soft furry body perfectly preserved by some sort of chemical treatment Hayden had subjected it to, and its tiny pink eyes half-shut. Hayden had whispered for Carole, seven or eight at the time, to put out her hand palm up to receive something special and she'd obeyed without hesitation and tried not to flinch when she saw what the something-special was.

"Sis-ter Car-ole. For you."

Later, their mother had taken the baby rabbit away. She'd been shocked, disapproving. Such a sad little creature, and who knew what germs it carried!

"IT COULD BE the single good thing I do with my life. Bringing my 'lost' brother home."

Buttrick Farm
3 February 2004

Dear Hayden,

It has been so long! If only I had happier news to share with you.

And I wish that I'd found this address for you, and/or a telephone number, last week before Mother's funeral.

I think you must have known, Mother was suffering from Parkinson's? (I'm sure you were informed that Father died four years ago last December.)

I should identify myself: I am your sister Carole. Your younger sister whom possibly/probably you scarcely remember. I was a very young fifteen when you last saw me (September 1982) though very likely you didn't "see" me then, in the sense of registering my existence.

Please call me, Hayden. My number is the family number, unchanged: (860) 919-2746. We have much to discuss, for instance Mother's will.

Your long-ago sister

Carole

This letter (so rapidly written her heart began to beat faster than she could bear like something loose clanging and clattering in the wind) she put into an envelope, addressed and stamped and carried out to the mailbox at the end of the driveway and then, next morning, retrieved from the mailbox just as the postal truck was approaching. "Forgot to put a stamp on this! Sorry." She crumpled the lavender-scented stationery in her hand. She returned to the house, to her own room and not her mother's, to compose, on her computer, a second letter to her brother in Kennebago, Maine.

February 4, 2004

Dear Hayden,

It has been so long! I wish that I had happier news to share with you.

Mother died last Thursday, January 29, and was buried in St. Luke's cemetery on Saturday. I think you knew, that she'd been suffering from Parkinson's for some time. There were numerous complications but at the end her discomfort was eased by morphine, for which I'm so grateful! I arranged for 24-hour hospice care here at the house and Mother slept much of the time, passing away so gradually it was indeed a "peaceful" death. I miss her very much, and I think that you must miss Mother, too, though circumstances kept you from seeing her for so many years.

(You know, I think, that Dad died, four years ago last December? I believe that Mother wrote to you at that time though, I guess, you never answered.)

While Mother was still lucid she spoke often of you, it was as if the past two decades had vanished. The Westinghouse prize you won in seventh grade for a physics project, the comic-book "novels" you painted on construction paper, the ant farm in Dad's old aquarium, the injured squirrel you nursed and tamed, etc.—Mother remembered as if it was yesterday. I found some of your old report cards, and the few pictures of you remaining in the album, what a beautiful child you were, Hayden! Here is a snapshot dated July 1961, you were an infant of only three months in Mother's arms, Mother is *so young* it seems unbelievable and makes me sad.

I wonder if your hair is still so blond as it was, when you left us. You wore your hair shoulder-length, you looked like a Nordic Jesus Christ!

I am so sorry, Hayden. That you were lost to us.

It is sad to tell you, half of our parents' estate was left to non-profit institutions (Farmington College, the Hartford art museum, St. Luke's, the Humane Society), and most of the remainder, I'm embarrassed to say, to me. Mother's will has yet to be probated but we know that the estate is considerable. You have been receiving checks from our grandparents' trust, like me, but Mother said that you haven't been cashing yours (since 1985?) so I suppose that financial matters don't interest you. I remember that your ideal was "non-attachment" to material things and one of your heroes was Henry David Thoreau so I'm afraid that this letter of mine isn't very welcome, either.

Still, I must write it. I hope you have continued to read this far!

You see, I have come to the conclusion that it is unjust for me to have inherited so much, while you have been left nothing. I believe that Mother would have wished to include you in her will but was reluctant to name you because Dad had his strong wishes, as you know, that Mother could not defy even after his death. It was an extreme decision of Dad's to "disown" you and make no effort to find you but Mother could not oppose him, you know what he was like. And I was too young, and too weak. But this morning I woke at dawn my face wet with tears and my heart pounding strangely. A voice urged me *You must share with someone, who is more deserving than your brother?*

Hayden, we have to much to discuss! Please will you call me? Or write to me? Or, will you allow me to visit you? (Since you're not likely to visit me!) I have located Kennebago Lake, Maine, on a map and now I would need your address since I have only the post office box number.

You are my only true "family" remaining, Hayden, and I wonder if I am your only "family," too?

Love from your sister

Carole

The check was for $12,000. It was never cashed.

NEVER CASHED! And her letter that was so warmly confiding, so sisterly and generous, unanswered.

"But why? Does he hate *me*?"

Each day she checked the mailbox, each day she was disappointed.

She waited a week, two weeks. She knew, when he had not answered by the end of the first week, it wasn't likely that he would. Yet she forced herself to wait a full month, before writing again: a shorter letter than the first, not so confiding, not so raw with sisterly yearning. This time, she didn't include a check.

"That might have been the mistake. An insult to him."

Yet, this time too, her letter went unanswered.

"But I could love him. I would be his friend. He must be lonely, too."

It wasn't like her to talk to herself. It wasn't like her to wander the house dazed as a sleepwalker, barefoot and disheveled in a way that would have shocked the Farmington circle to whom her primary identity was *Buttrick, heiress*.

It was distressing to her, to seem to be losing her confidence in herself. To be so weak, vulnerable. So suspended. In a perpetual state of anticipation.

Each time the telephone rang, and the telephone rang often, she hurried to answer breathlessly. Her vision filmed over with moisture, she wasn't able to read the digital caller I.D. and so her anticipation might be extended for another second or two: "Hel*lo*—?"

She knew herself to be a woman without fantasies. She had very little interest in sex, for instance.

Of course, she had expected to marry. All the Buttricks were expected to marry. And there had been men, a few. But the men had not been so very aggressive, and Carole had not been so very approachable. In appearance she was small-boned, straight-backed, with something taut and tight and quivering about her, like an arrow poised to fly. Her hair had both darkened and faded with age, though, as a child, she'd been nearly as blond as her older brother. Her eyes were of no distinct color, pale-blue, pale-gray, alert and watchful, not inclined to easy sympathy. Because she was the daughter of socially prominent parents and her name was Buttrick—a New England name that predated the Revolution—she'd been protected from a need for love of that kind bound up with, usually indistinguishable from, a need for economic security, protection. She was not a woman obliged to marry for financial reasons, as she was not a woman obliged to work to support herself. Her involvements with men began as experiments *I will make love with this man, I will be a woman who has a lover* that played themselves out as experiments and left her confirmed in her sense of self-sufficiency, stoicism. None of her lovers—and they had been few, and select—had ever seen her fully unclothed. The very word *naked* was faintly repellent to her: comic and repellent. In this, in her essentially asexual nature, she resembled her brother, Hayden, who had shrunk from being touched and who'd had (so the family believed, for any other thought was ludicrous) no physical relations with anyone, female or male, in his life.

Carole was struck by a memory of how one day she'd blundered into her brother's room mistaking his slurred mumble for an invitation to enter and not a command to go away, and there, to her astonishment, was Hayden crouched barefoot on the floor of the room in just his dingy Jockey shorts, a painfully thin sunken-chested boy of fifteen, rocking on his heels before a display of what appeared to be photographs (naked bodies? corpses?) torn from magazines.

He'd screamed at her: "Go away go away GO AWAY ALL OF YOU."

In his glaring eyes was a look of shame, fury, hatred.

She was shaken now, remembering. This memory she'd kept at bay for more than twenty years.

"BUT HE NEVER hated *me*. I was his ally."

IN THE SPRING of the year following her mother's death. When she was alone in the old house. When she had difficulty sleeping at night and, during the day, lapsed into waking dreams that cast a seductive, dark-netted vision over her brain. Sometimes, these visions swept over her even when she was in the company of others. *The dream of Hayden* in which her lost brother returned home radiant and smiling and no longer angry, his face smooth and unblemished, his voice warm in greeting her: "Sis-ter." In the dream, their parents had not yet died. And so the Buttricks were a family again.

This dream! It made tears spring into her eyes.

If she was in the company of others (at dinner parties, at bright-buzzing receptions in Farmington and Hartford, even at meetings of the board of trustees of Farmington College for Women where, an alumna of the class of 1988, she'd been named the youngest trustee on the board) friends might mistake her change of mood for a stab of remembered grief, and might take her hands in theirs to console her. "If there is anything we can do for you . . ." She roused herself from her waking trance. She was embarrassed, slightly annoyed. Politely she thanked them, for they meant only to be kind.

"I'm fine! I've been thinking of driving to northern Maine sometime this summer, to see my brother."

"Your brother? Is that—"

"Hayden. You probably don't remember him. He was a bright, precocious boy until he became ill, and quarreled with our father, and left home."

So succinctly narrated: *ill, quarreled, left.*

"We're in communication, finally. Though I wasn't able to notify him about my mother's death in time, that's why he wasn't at the funeral." She paused, frowning. There was a way she'd cultivated of smiling, though also frowning. As always in her outer life, her life performed in the presence of others, she was beautifully groomed, poised. Taut and quivering as an arrow she was, almost you could feel the nerved-up energy lifting from her skin. "He's become something of a recluse, in Maine. I think he's writing some sort of magnum opus about ecology, the environment. But he's lonely, too. He's been away so long."

The dream of Hayden. It was so plausible, really!

Except, in the dream, Carole couldn't "see" faces clearly. She couldn't determine how old anyone was. There was her father, and there was her mother, and there was Hayden, and there was "Carole" . . . If, in the dream, Hayden was twenty-one as he'd been at the time he'd walked out of their lives with a curse, then Carole would have to be fifteen again. (But she would never be fifteen again.) And, if Hayden was younger, before the mysterious illness that came upon him at about the age of seventeen, Carole had to be a younger child still, and she had difficulty remembering herself in those years for Hayden, like a blazing fire, had consumed everyone's attention.

As if, in the Buttrick family, there had been only Hayden.

Among friends and neighbors in Farmington, who'd known the elder Buttricks for decades, memories of the afflicted son Hayden were tactfully vague. Carole recalled that, with friends, and not within her father's hearing, her mother had spoken wistfully of her "lost" son and so she supposed that, generally, in local legend, Hayden Buttrick was recalled as an exceptionally bright boy who had somehow lost his way, and was "lost."

It was a very American story, somehow. "Lost." Each community had such stories. Possibly, each family.

"Kennebago Lake. Just south of the Quebec border. Far inland, nowhere near the seacoast."

So the subject naturally shifted to the geography of Maine. If there seemed little to say about the prospect of locating the lost brother, there was much to say about the seacoast of Maine. The litany of place-names was Bar Harbor, Boothbay Harbor, Brunswick, Portland, Prouts Neck, Kennebunkport and Rockport and Blue Hill. She could smile, and seem to be listening, as *the dream of Hayden* returned to her, to console.

SOMETIMES, she was angry. He hadn't replied to her letters!

"He has to be alive. Of course he's alive. *I know he's alive.*"

He would be forty-seven years old. He would be a middle-aged man, she had to expect he would be much changed from the always so young-looking boy she'd known.

She'd telephoned the Kennebago, Maine, post office. Since her letters hadn't been returned to her, this meant that the address was still a valid one, but was there a "Hayden Buttrick" who actually came in to pick up his mail?

Whoever spoke to her, after a long hold, informed her politely that such information wasn't available.

She asked if there was an address for "Hayden Buttrick" apart from the post office box and was told, politely, that such information wasn't available.

"But why! Why would my brother distrust *me.*"

She'd been his friend, his ally. Though mostly the rapport between them had been unspoken. *Sis-ter. Car-ole.* He'd smiled his beautiful dreamy smile at her, she had to hope that he was seeing her. Those several times, cherished in memory like the glass jar filled with colorful pebbles she still had on a windowsill in her bedroom, he'd helped her with her math homework. His unnerving, yet beautiful eyes that so fiercely stared. The maze of fine white furrow marks imprinted in his forehead, from frowning. A scent that lifted off him, a faint acrid singed smell.

"If only."

It had been their father whom Hayden had feared, and hated. If only Mr. Buttrick had let Hayden alone when he'd wished to be alone.

Their mother had learned to respect Hayden's "sensitive" moods as she called them. But their father had felt the need to make himself known to Hayden as if it were an insult that his son wasn't at all times alert and aware of his presence when they were in the same room together. "Wake up. Look at me. I've been speaking to you. Don't play these games with me." Mr. Buttrick could not bear it, that Hayden had a way of gliding about the house like a sleepwalker with opened eyes. He had a way of not-hearing unless you shouted at him. He had a way of unexpectedly laughing, or scowling; turning away indifferent, or overreacting like a startled infant. Most distracting, his mouth had sometimes worked agitatedly as if he was talking to himself. Such intensity, such concentration!—nothing in the actual world could so fascinate him. And if you dared to touch Hayden at such a time he would recoil with a stricken look, a look of revulsion, as if he'd been touched by a snake.

Recognition returned to his eyes, slowly. Reluctantly.

"God damn you! I said, don't play those games with me."

It would be rare that Mr. Buttrick spoke harshly to Carole, for the game she'd learned to play was a very different game from her brother's. Half-consciously she'd learned this game, and was (maybe) grateful for it.

John Buttrick was a genial, gregarious personality bluntly defined and solid as a boulder. You could not blame him for being disturbed by a son like Hayden. You could not blame him for being threatened by even the semblance of resistance, let alone rebellion, in his household. He'd been proud of the son who'd been initially praised as "gifted"—"a prodigy"—"a boy genius"—but he soon became demoralized and exasperated by the older boy who began to be labeled "difficult"—"uncooperative"—"antisocial." Years of child therapists, psychologists and psychiatrists! Years of prescription drugs, which Hayden refused to take as bidden. By the time Hayden was fifteen, he'd been in several private New England schools, and by the time he was seventeen, a senior at the

Concord Academy with near-perfect SAT scores, such alarming clinical terms as *autistic, manic-depressive, borderline personality* had begun to appear in his files.

Still, Hayden graduated from the Concord Academy with honors. He had been awarded several senior prizes and had been admitted to Harvard. Yet it had begun to happen more frequently during his senior year at the prestigious prep school that he was stricken with bouts of panic and paralysis, refusing to leave his room; refusing sometimes to unlock his door, even to communicate through the door. He went for days without eating. He went for nights without sleeping. He spoke of being "smothered"—"choked." So many people were clamoring at him, staring at him. So many people were wanting to humiliate him. On commencement day at the Concord Academy his panic was so overwhelming he'd had a kind of asthmatic attack and had had to be removed from the school by his distraught parents. As if they'd anticipated a crisis, the elder Buttricks hadn't brought Carole with them. She'd had to remain behind in Farmington with relatives, anxious and resentful.

Over the summer, a powerful medication had seemed to stabilize Hayden's nerves. But then came Harvard, the disaster from which he was never to recover.

Carole was never to know exactly what happened to her brother at Harvard. She began to hear her parents speaking worriedly together behind doors shut to her and she had no contact with Hayden at all. When she asked her mother, Mrs. Buttrick said only, with a brave smile, that Hayden was going through a "period of adjustment" and when she dared to ask her father, Mr. Buttrick said curtly that Hayden's situation was "his business, not yours." Later, she would learn that Hayden was convinced he was being "spied on" by certain of his classmates and professors; he was being "stalked," "persecuted." He'd become involved with militant environmental-activist causes, though he had never showed the slightest interest previously in any sort of collective political effort. Evidently, his attacks of panic and paralysis now alternated with interludes of manic belligerence. He who'd been compulsively fastidious about personal grooming began to go for days, possibly weeks, without changing his clothes or bathing. His room in a university residence hall became filthy, littered with food packages that attracted ants and roaches. Several times, university proctors had had to be summoned by Hayden's suite mates to "calm" him. When at last the Buttricks were summoned to Cambridge to see him, for a day and a half Hayden hid from them in the furnace room of his residence.

It wasn't clear whether Hayden was expelled from Harvard or whether he simply dropped out, sometime in the late winter of 1980. In those classes he'd attended, he had earned high grades. He cut off all relations with his family and lived, evidently, in a succession of furnished rooms in Cambridge. During his lucid periods he worked at minimum-wage jobs (dishwasher, janitor) where he had little need to engage with others. He spent time in video game arcades and in secondhand bookstores specializing in science fiction and comic books. He quarreled with employers, landlords. He was fired, he was evicted. He panhandled, he slept in doorways. Frequently he was beaten and robbed. He scavenged food from Dumpsters. His skin erupted in pimples, boils. His hair was a sight that, on the street, drew startled attention: ashy blond threaded with silver, immense and matted like dreadlocks falling in a tangle past his bony shoulders. He had a look of an Old Testament prophet, unless it was the look of a mad street person. Yet when a private investigator hired by Mr. Buttrick looked for him, Hayden disappeared.

Only when he was arrested by Cambridge police in the fall of 1981 for creating a public disturbance and committed to a psychiatric facility did his parents learn where he was.

Mr. Buttrick drove to Cambridge to arrange for Hayden to be transported by private ambulance to a Hartford clinic. There, Hayden's condition gradually "stabilized" with medication and, after six months, he was released into the custody of his parents. By this time, when Carole at last saw her brother, he'd become so thin he appeared ethereal. He carried himself tentatively, like one walking on very thin ice. Yet his eyes seemed unchanged, moist, staring, with an ironic glisten. Teasing he murmured, "Sis-ter! Here *all this time.*"

It was a rebuke, Carole knew. For when awkwardly she moved to touch her brother, to welcome him home, he turned stiffly from her.

Among her friends at Farmington Day School, Carole never spoke of her family situation. She never spoke of her brother, nor did anyone ask. It was as if Hayden Buttrick had ceased to exist. Carole loved her brother yet came to wish that he would die. *For his own good, dear God.*

But Hayden didn't die, for now he was "stabilized." He was often withdrawn, lethargic and sulky, but rarely belligerent. He went for days without speaking to anyone in the family. He insisted upon eating meals locked away in his room where no one could "stare" at him and "memorize" him. Through the mail he received books with such titles as *Prophet of the Apocalypse*, *The Survivor's 12-Step Handbook*, *Galaxies Beyond*. It was rare for him to initiate a conversation unless he was excited by a subject like time travel, extra-terrestrial life, the "redemption" of the world after *Homo sapiens* becomes extinct. Alone of the family Carole was allowed to see parts of his mammoth illustrated novel *The Lost Galaxy*: elaborate, labyrinthine watercolors in the style of M. C. Escher, on sheets of construction paper. When, at a loss for words, Carole tried to stammer some sort of response, Hayden cut her off curtly: "No."

No! It was the one clear signal Hayden wished to send to his family, if not the world.

All but a few of the watercolors were destroyed by Hayden before he left home. Carole salvaged just one from the trash, a vivid swirl of colors like flames, an exploding sunflower sun, tower-like figures (extra-terrestrials?) stamping out squat, semi-transparent sack-creatures (humans?). She would keep the painting for years, until the stiff, dry construction paper began to crack. As an adult, she would regret she hadn't had it treated somehow, and preserved. For perhaps her brother was a visionary artist/prophet, in the Escher tradition.

One day in September 1982, Carole had only just returned home from school when she heard raised voices in the upstairs hall. There was a sound of struggle and of someone falling, hard. And there came Hayden lurching down the stairs, fierce-eyed, smiling and muttering to himself. Carole backed away into the dining room, frightened. Her brother had slung a duffel bag over his shoulder, crammed with possessions. He'd tied his hair into a ponytail and was wearing, despite the warm day, a sheepskin vest over a turtleneck sweater, neatly pressed trousers and aged, water-stained leather boots. Carole would think afterward that he looked dangerous, that was why she shrank from him. But perhaps he'd seen her. Somewhere upstairs, Mrs. Buttrick was screaming. Hayden ran to the front door and called back over his shoulder those mysterious words to lodge deep in his sister's memory.

"All you to the hell!"

AND SO it had been, a kind of prophecy: Hayden's parents would never fully recover from that curse. Carole wasn't sure, even as an adult, that she had, either.

"ONE MORE TIME. Then I'll give up."

Dated May 29, 2004, this was a politely impersonal letter to Hayden Buttrick, P.O. Box 199, Kennebago Lake, Maine. It made no reference to previous letters. It contained no check. Carole was asking her brother to contact her, please. *I really must insist. Mother would wish it. The interest alone on eight million dollars is too much for one person to spend. Already I am a trustee/donor of Farmington College. I give money to the usual Hartford causes. I am considering establishing the Buttrick Foundation to give money to appropriate institutions and individuals and I am wondering if you would be willing to advise me.* For she recalled how for a brief, combative period during Hayden's freshman year at Harvard he'd been in activist environmental demonstrations. He had been arrested picketing a nuclear power plant outside Boston, and Mr. Buttrick had had to post $5,000 bail for him. He'd been injured in a similar demonstration in New Hampshire, arrested for creating a public disturbance. When he'd lived in a furnished room in Cambridge he'd once been evicted for bringing "hazardous materials" (chemicals? gunpowder?) into the building and creating a "terrible stench." (This, from the report of the private investigator Mr. Buttrick had hired to track Hayden down.)

This time, Carole included a stamped self-addressed postcard with her letter.

SIX DAYS LATER, there was the card in her mailbox.

H WISHES YOU TO KNOW HE IS NOT <u>YOUR</u>
<u>BROTHER</u> DO NOT ATTEMPT TO CONTRACT FURTHER
E

Walking up the driveway to the house, Carole read and reread these enigmatic words. They were block-printed in inch-high letters of the kind a small child might make, who was only just learning to write. The slightly leftward slant of the inked letters reminded her of Hayden's way of writing, toward the left. And the tone, the taut angry tone, would seem to be Hayden's, too.

She wondered why he'd signed the message *E*. And if the mistake in spelling, *r* in what was meant to be "contact," had been deliberate for some reason.

Her hand shook, holding the card. She saw that the postmark was Kennebago Lake, Maine. Her eyes flooded with moisture.

"He's answered. He acknowledges that I am alive, and his sister."

Immediately, in a state of rapture laced with dread, for she so dreaded making a mistake, Carole wrote to Hayden:

June 8, 2004

Dear E,

Thank you so much. I am grateful for your response. I will drive to Kennebago Lake. If my brother will not see me I ask if you will? Thank you!

Carole Buttrick

Another time she enclosed a stamped self-addressed postcard.

Anxiously she waited. Days passed. She began to see, yes she'd made a blunder. Another time she wrote: *May I know if my brother is well? I will not try to contact him if he does not wish to see me. Thank you!* She enclosed another postcard, which appeared in her mailbox after eleven days.

H IS NOT THE <u>BROTHER</u>
    E

This was disappointing! This was not what she'd expected.

She'd begun to think, possibly there was an "E." A companion of some kind. A protector. She hoped, not a woman.

June 23, 2004

Dear E,

Thank you for replying. I am grateful to you. I will not make claims of "brother"—"sister." Only of the welfare of "Hayden Buttrick." Thank you!

Carole Buttrick

This time, her stamped self-addressed postcard wasn't returned.

She was being rebuked. Another time. It was one of those old legends or fairy tales in which an individual embarked upon a quest is faced with challenges. To turn in the wrong direction, to make a mistake, might be fatal. Yet to make no further effort would be shame.

Yet she considered: if she wrote again, "E" would probably not reply. If there was an "E" he might be jealous of her relationship with Hayden; if Hayden himself was "E," he might be offended by her pushy behavior. And if she wrote to tell him she'd decided to drive to Kennebago Lake, Hayden might disappear from the region. She would never locate him.

"I will go in person. If he sees me . . ."

He will know me, acknowledge me. His sister.

SHE HAD NEVER DRIVEN into the interior of Maine before. It was a wild, desolate landscape of densely wooded hills, swift-running streams, lakes. It had an air of romance heightened by a sky of continuous and brooding thunderhead clouds through which an acid-bright sun shone in sudden crevices. She wore dark-tinted glasses, the sun was making her eyes smart. She had not been able to sleep for more than a few hours in the hotel in Portland, now she was edgy, impatient. She had a vision of her brother awaiting her yet holding himself from her, in opposition. " 'Hayden! Hello. I am your sister Carole, I hope you remember me . . .' " Or: " 'Hayden? I hope you won't be angry with me, I had to see you.' " She was an actress memorizing her lines, becoming increasingly apprehensive yet excited, hopeful. " 'Hayden. Hello. I'm your sister Carole. I . . .' " It was a long drive north on I-95 before she exited south of Skowhegan and on secondary, winding roads drove through sparsely populated towns with such names as Norridgewock, New Sharon, Paris and West Paris, Republic, Madrid. There were signs leading to Oquossoc, Umbagog Lake, Mooselookmeguntic Lake. Frequently there were signs warning MOOSE CROSSING NEXT 5 MI.

She felt as if she was entering a region utterly foreign to her. Vehicles came up rudely close behind her car. Several times she pulled off the roadway, to allow them to pass: campers, minivans, pickups, loggers' rattling rigs. She resented being made to feel that she was in danger, a woman driving by herself. But even at rest stops she was hesitant to leave her car. If another vehicle slowed near her, even one identified as MAINE STATE POLICE, she drove hurriedly on.

She arrived in Rangeley in the early evening, too late to drive to Kennebago Lake. Her room, at the rear of an "inn" of shellacked-looking logs, overlooked a landscape of mysteriously broken and denuded pine trees. There were few other guests. The restaurant began to close shortly after nine. In her lumpy bed, that vibrated with the passing of thunderous trucks on the highway not visible from her window, she managed to sleep a thin, erratic sleep in which, near morning, in a voice startlingly close, her mother appealed to her *He has been lost all these years. Promise!*

THE TOWN of Kennebago Lake, at the southeastern point of the long, serpentine lake, was so small that its post office shared quarters with a convenience store. There was a single wall of post office boxes. Carole stooped to peer into the clouded plastic window of box 199, that appeared to be empty. She felt a stab of panic, that Hayden had departed.

Another wall, plasterboard and cork, was covered in post office flyers and WANTED F.B.I. posters. Rapidly her eye scanned the photographs of wanted men, as if seeking Hayden among them.

"Ma'am? Can I assist you?"

The postal clerk was a swarthy-skinned man in his thirties with a scar in his left cheek that gave him a permanent scowl. He was pear-shaped, fattish. His eyes glided onto Carole with a look of detached interest and she'd noticed that he had glanced out the window to see, perhaps to admire, the expensive foreign-built car she was driving. When she asked him if he knew a man named "Hayden Buttrick," a local resident who rented box 199, the clerk's scowl deepened. When she showed him a creased snapshot of Hayden taken at eighteen, explaining that she was looking for her brother whom she had not seen in more than twenty years, he shook his head curtly and told her sorry he didn't know, couldn't help her.

"But he must come in here, to pick up his mail? You must see him. He would be forty-seven now. He would probably be heavier. He might have a beard. He might be bald. He . . ."

Another customer came in, whom the clerk waited on. Carole stood by anxiously. The swarthy-skinned postal clerk was, she felt, her only hope: of course he had to know her brother, in a community small as Kennebago Lake. Only a few post office boxes in the wall of boxes appeared to be in use.

When the customer left, Carole returned to the counter. She was wearing a long-sleeved white shirt with a pleated front, classically tailored trousers in dove-gray flannel. She had removed her dark-tinted glasses and her manner was polite yet assertive in the way of Farmington, Connecticut. She showed the clerk her brother's name and address which she'd typed onto a sheet of paper, as if the formality might impress him. "So? That's here." He swiped quizzically at his nose.

"I was wondering, if you could provide me with Hayden Buttrick's home address?"

"Ma'am, I don't have it."

"But you must! It must be in your records somewhere . . ."

"Ma'am, no."

"But—"

"People who rent these boxes, ma'am, sometimes they don't have permanent addresses. That's why they rent them."

The clerk spoke flatly, without looking at her. In the way you might point out the obvious to a slow-witted individual.

"How can I locate my brother, then? I've driven such a long distance."

How plaintive she was sounding, and how absurd. She felt her face flush. The clerk turned his attention to sorting mail on a nearby table, as if dismissing her. She heard herself say, "My brother has come into an inheritance. He needs to be informed, immediately."

She'd thought that might make an impression on the clerk. But he said only, in his maddeningly flat, neutral voice, "Ma'am, you can write to him. You have the address."

"I have! I have written to him. My letters to him have come through your hands, probably." Carole paused, her heart beating quickly. She had no idea why she was saying such things to a stiff-backed stranger who seemed to resent her. "But I need to speak to him, in person. There are things I must explain."

"You can put a message right there in Mr. Buttrick's box, ma'am. I've have to sell you a stamp, though."

She wondered if the man was laughing at her. She had to concede, yes she was probably amusing. A middle-aged woman from Connecticut pleading with a post office clerk in Kennebago Lake, Maine. A woman who appeared well-to-do, if naive. Driving a new-model foreign-made car with a list price of, at minimum, sixty thousand dollars and yet her voice was quavering, close to pleading. "I need to see my brother immediately, to see if . . ." Carole paused, her words trailed off into silence. She'd been about to say *to see if it's really him.*

The postal clerk continued with his mail-sorting. His black, thinning hair had been slicked back with what smelled like motor oil, from a clay-colored acne-scarred face. He wore a black T-shirt embossed with the faded logo of a rock music band, that swelled outward with the bulge of his stomach.

Carole explained, she'd looked for her brother's name in the local phone directory but of course it wasn't listed. She had thought, if she came here in person, someone could help her. "Do you have a supervisor? A manager?"

The clerk grunted as if bemused. It sounded as if he'd said *That's me*. Or, *Ma'am, me*. He had not troubled to look at her.

This should have ended the exchange. Carole understood that she'd been rebuked. She'd been snubbed. Kennebago Lake, Maine, had snubbed Farmington, Connecticut. From the postal clerk's perspective, she was no more than an annoyance. Yet she persisted, "When does Hayden Buttrick pick up his mail, usually? Is there any particular day of the week, any time?"

To this, the clerk made no response at all. He was sorting mail, breathing audibly. Carole saw that his trousers, that must have been extra-large, were made of some stiff cheap khaki-colored material.

"I—I could wait for him. If I knew. Outside in my car? If I had an idea which day of the week . . ."

The clerk expelled a long hissing breath. When he turned, glaring at her with a look of exasperation edged with pity, she saw that his swarthy, pitted skin had darkened. There was a glisten of sweat on his forehead. "Ma'am, let me see that picture again."

Quickly Carole showed the snapshot of Hayden to him. She had not returned it to her handbag, but had continued to hold it in her slightly trembling fingers. The clerk took it from her and lifted it to the light, squinting. "Yah. Maybe. Saturday morning, sometimes, he might come in. Every two–three weeks." He paused, swiping at his nose. "Or maybe there's more than one of him."

Carole wasn't sure if she'd heard correctly. " 'More than one of'—?"

"Ma'am, I don't know." The clerk passed the snapshot back to her, as if eager to get rid of it.

She would think afterward *He doesn't want to be involved, whatever comes of this*. She thanked him for helping her. As he'd suggested, she left a message for Hayden in his mailbox: she purchased from the clerk a first-class stamp. In the message she explained only that she'd decided to come to see him, and was staying at the Rangeley Inn. She left the address and telephone number of the inn.

She left the same information with the postal clerk. Also her name, Farmington address and telephone number. "If he happens to come in. If you speak with him."

SATURDAY MORNING, sometimes.

She went away, shaken and excited. She would begin to forget *sometimes* and perhaps she had not exactly heard *every two–three weeks*. Obsessively she would think *Saturday morning. Saturday morning.* She would wait in her car in front of the Kennebago Lake Post Office and when Hayden arrived, she would know him at once.

Saturday. Saturday morning. Except it was only Tuesday now. She had four days to wait.

Four days! A lifetime.

"I can't. I can't stay here. What will I do here! I will go mad here." She was in her car, fumbling the key in the ignition. The blinding sunshine rushed upon her like a mirage. She fumbled for her dark glasses. "But I have no choice. I can't give up. I've come so far . . ."

She drove through the small town of Kennebago Lake. To her disappointment she saw that access to the lake was limited. There seemed to be no road that led beside the lake. Beyond the meager town, all was dense woods, underbrush. You could say that it was "beautiful" but it was hardly a region for tourists. North of Kennebago Lake was the Kennebago River descending from Quebec, through a mountainous region in which, so far as Carole's map indicated, there were no settlements, no roads, at all. The highest peaks of the oddly named Longfellow Mountain Range had been designated Mt. Snow, Eustis Ridge, West Kennebago Peak, Tumbledown Mountain—but such names, attached to such a wilderness, seemed more than ordinarily useless.

She wondered if Hayden lived in that impenetrable region, north of the town of Kennebago Lake. A region in which, unless a man wanted to be found, he could not be found.

Yet, perversely, he might be living close by the town of Kennebago Lake. For all she knew, he might be driving a rattletrap pickup along the single main street, approaching her vehicle, passing her oblivious of her.

She wondered if back in the post office the clerk was making a telephone call. Certainly, he'd known Hayden.

Though maybe, no. Maybe he had not. She had to think clearly, she had to guard against becoming emotional.

For that had been her brother's sickness. Certainties based upon no clear evidence. That people were spying on him, "memorizing" him. That strangers could peer into his skull. They could read his thoughts, and they could control his thoughts. They could force him to commit extreme acts against himself and others he had not wished to commit.

It would be reported how, at the convenience store, at the Gulf service station, at the local café, restaurant, package liquor store as well as at the Kennebago County sheriff's office the woman from Connecticut would leave the name of the long-lost older brother she was seeking as well as her own carefully printed name and the address and telephone number of her motel in Rangeley. She would explain that she was the sister of a Kennebago Lake resident whom she hadn't seen in twenty-two years and now that their parents had died she was anxious to contact him for he'd "come into" an inheritance. Most of the individuals to whom she spoke weren't certain if they had ever heard of Hayden Buttrick—"He might use another name, or names. There's people here who are very private persons." No one appeared to recognize Hayden Buttrick's eighteen-year-old likeness but everyone appeared sympathetic with her quest. In the sheriff's office, one of the deputies volunteered to do a quick search for *Hayden Buttrick* in the computer, but came up with nothing.

"Seems he isn't in our system, ma'am. Which, if you're family, is good news."

———

"MA'AM."

The voice was so soft, so tentative, she wasn't sure she'd heard anything.

She'd fallen asleep from nervous exhaustion, in a patch of hot sunshine behind the Rangeley Inn. Gnats had brushed against her face and in the scrubby pine woods beyond the clearing jays were emitting fierce sharp cries. Yet somehow, she'd fallen asleep. She had had to change her room at the motel because she'd discovered roaches in the bathroom and now she had a new room with a screen door that opened out onto the cinder parking lot behind the motel. Beyond the lot was a weedy "picnic" area where she could drag a bedraggled lawn chair, to lie in the sun and turn the pages of several paperback books she'd brought with her to Maine. Normally she was so careful a reader she underlined as she read, and made notations in the margins of pages, but now she found it difficult to concentrate. She was thinking that it wasn't very likely that Hayden would seek her out at the motel and yet she couldn't be certain that he would not. She was thinking that Saturday morning was more likely, if she waited for him at the Kennebago post office. By this time it was Thursday. It was Thursday afternoon. She had only two more nights to get through, then it would be Saturday morning. The post office opened at 8 A.M. and closed at 1 P.M., Saturdays.

Yet she was thinking that, if another individual came to pick up her brother's mail, the mysterious "E": what then? She would not recognize "E." If there was an "E." And if there was an "E," he might be sharp-eyed enough to notice the Connecticut license plate on her car. He might then quickly depart without entering the post office. In any case she had to allow for the possibility of "E" instead of Hayden. In fact, she had to allow for the possibility of "E" in the company of Hayden: two individuals. (Oh, she was hoping that, if "E" existed, "E" was not a woman! For she could not bear a rival for her brother's attention.) Hayden she believed she would recognize after even so many years but "E" would be a total stranger and so, to be certain she wouldn't miss him, if "E" came alone to the post office on Saturday morning, she would have to wait inside for whoever arrived to unlock mailbox 199, and not in the privacy of her car. And she would have to park her car, this ill-chosen luxury vehicle sporting Connecticut plates, somewhere else. Where no one parking at the post office would notice it. The thought of passing five possibly futile hours in the airless quarters of the Kennebago post office under the disdainful scrutiny of the postal clerk filled her with anxiety and dismay in equal measure. "I can't! How can I." These thoughts came frantic and rushing like wheels spinning in sand, ever faster and yet ever more helplessly.

She opened her eyes, startled. She sat up quickly. For there was a man standing at the edge of the cinder parking lot about ten feet away, looking at her.

"Yes? What do you . . ."

A man in baggy khaki work clothes, a mud-colored cap pulled down low on his forehead. A man of no clear age: not young, yet not old. He was round-shouldered, diminutive like one who has been ill and lost weight, and his manner was hesitant, uneasy as if he'd been about to turn away from Carole, before she'd seen him. He had a creased face, clay-colored as if it had been baked, with a surface of fine meshed cracks like glaze. What Carole could see of his head had been shaved up the sides. His jaws were sparsely covered in a wispy steel-colored beard. His nose looked as if it had been broken and had mended asymmetrically. And his eyes!—but his eyes were hidden from her behind clunky black plastic glasses with thick lenses. More disconcerting, the left lens was blackened as if that eye was blind or in some way disfigured.

"Hayden? Is it—you?"

Clumsily she was trying to disentangle herself from the rotted lawn chair. She was barefoot, dazed and groggy from the sun. Her heart beat so quickly she could not breathe.

Vehemently the man was shaking his head, no. He seemed shocked by her question. "Ma'am, I am Elisha. I wrote to you, to tell you. He says to you, 'Go away.' "

In the grass she stood barefoot, blinking. For a moment she could not speak. The man's thin, reedy-whiny voice, just perceptibly inflected with a French-Canadian accent, did not seem to be Hayden's voice and yet his stance, the way in which his mouth worked as if he was trying not to stammer, or to shout, reminded her of Hayden as a boy. And the way in which the man stood with his shoulders rounded and braced and quivering with tension, like a whip about to uncoil and strike. *If he will let me touch him, I will know.*

"Elisha? You are my brother's—friend?"

She came forward as if to shake his hand. She'd managed to kick on her sandals, so clumsily. Her face throbbed with heat. She saw that the man wasn't going to extend his hand to her, that his expression was wary, alarmed.

"He says to tell you 'go away.' See, he doesn't want your money."

"But—how is he? Is he well?"

She was speaking desperately, concerned that the man would turn away and leave her. He must have parked in front of the motel and come to look for her. He was Hayden's age, and his face was one of those old-young faces prematurely weathered by the sun, or negligence, or excessive grimacing, exactly the face you would expect in Hayden Buttrick at that age. And yet, was this Hayden? Carole stared and stared. The man was wearing khaki-colored work clothes that resembled army camouflage fatigues, on even this warm June afternoon a khaki vest with numerous pockets and zippers over a dingy red-and-black-checked long-sleeved flannel shirt. On his feet were mud-splattered work boots. He held his arms stiffly at his sides, his fingers twitching. If this was Hayden, wouldn't his hands be clenched into fists?

"Ma'am, I have to leave now. Good-bye."

"But—wait! I could follow you back, couldn't I? Will you allow me? And Hayden could decide then, if he sees me, I mean, he could see me at a distance and then, he could decide if—"

"Ma'am, no. He told me to tell you no."

"But Hayden has come into an inheritance, as I have. Our parents' estate is worth—"

Elisha said sharply, "He don't want your money, ma'am."

A kind of shudder as of repugnance passed through the man's wiry body. He seemed fearful of Carole, the woman: one who might rush at him impulsively and grip his hand, or worse.

"If Hayden doesn't want his share of the estate, he could give it away. He could give it to you, Elisha! But that should be his personal decision, don't you think?"

Elisha she'd called him. The shudder passed through him again, as if she'd touched him.

In a kind of triumph she thought *He is my ally. He will bring me to my brother.*

By this time they stood in the cinder parking lot behind the motel. In shuffling steps Elisha was backing away as Carole, determined not to lose him, pressed forward. She was a small-boned woman, and intense. She saw something reluctant and yielding in the man's face where in Hayden's she knew there would have been only obduracy, opposition. "Elisha, I could follow you back to him, couldn't I? In my car? I promise that I won't stay long. If Hayden refuses to see me even then, I will leave. Please, Elisha!"

How like a child she was sounding, so vulnerable in appeal! She had never before in her life so opened herself to rejection, repudiation. Yet there was her powerful will beneath.

"It looks as if I won't be having children of my own, Elisha. And I assume, Hayden won't either. And so we should be reunited, our family. We are all that is left of our family."

Carole was moved by her own heedless words. And her listener stood stricken, staring glumly at the ground. For a long moment he said nothing, made no motion, though she could see his mouth twitching silently. Then abruptly, he seemed to have changed his mind. He muttered what sounded like *Yah ma'am O.K.* and turned to walk away, indicating to Carole to follow.

She had triumphed! She'd convinced him.

At the front of the shiny-logged Rangeley Inn he had parked a battered-looking Chevy pickup with rust-pocked Maine plates. At the farther end of the narrow strip of cinders was Carole's leased foreign-built vehicle, gleaming metallic-green and splendid in the sun.

" 'HAYDEN, I hope you remember me? Your sister . . .' "

They drove in a procession of two. In a state of nervous exhilaration she followed the battered pickup, whose paint had oxidized to a frosty no-color, north along the state highway in the direction of Kennebago Lake. About one mile before the lake, Elisha turned onto a two-lane blacktop road called Mink Farm that led into a scrubby pine woods interspersed with an open, hilly landscape of broken trees and scattered

boulders. From time to time they passed small wood-frame houses, trail-
ers on cement blocks, tarpaper shanties. The pickup braked suddenly in
the road, Carole close behind, to allow three Labrador-mix dogs, one of
them burly and limping, to sidle slowly across, indifferent to them; in a
grassy ditch, a dozen tiny-headed guinea hens picked and tittered noisily.
Here was a small, not very prosperous farm, a single-story wood-frame
house and ramshackle outbuildings. Suffused with happiness suddenly
Carole thought *There is so much beauty everywhere.*

She would look for, but would fail to find, any evidence of the mink
farm for which the road had been named.

From Mink Farm Road, Elisha turned onto a narrow nameless gravel
road and continued driving in a gradually ascending, increasingly rocky
terrain. In this way they drove miles. In this way they passed into a kind
of trance, of slow dogged jolting motion. She refused to concern herself
with how she would find her way back to the motel, if Elisha didn't
guide her. She refused to think *I will be lost* but instead exulted *I have
found my brother!* Her only regret was, she would not be able to tell
their mother.

By this time the back of her head was aching. She was not accus-
tomed to driving a vehicle in such conditions, that required intense
concentration yet were numbing, monotonous. Where Elisha's pickup
slowed to a crawl, Carole braced herself for potholes. Some of these
were small crevices in the road, into which a wheel of her car might
pitch, and be trapped. Her spine was beginning to throb from strain,
and her neck. She had to hunch over the steering wheel and grip it tight.
Lapsing into an unwise sleep in the sun, back at the motel, she'd made
herself dazed, groggy; her skin smarted with sunburn. She had a fair,
fine, sensitive skin that could not tolerate much sun, as her nerves could
not tolerate much strain. In her mounting excitement, which might have
been indistinguishable from panic, she was thinking that her brother had
sent Elisha as an emissary to her, not an enemy: some sort of test had
been put to her at the motel, that she had passed. For Elisha had seemed
prepared to give in, to allow her to follow him. At first he'd opposed her,
but then abruptly he had given in. She thought *Elisha is Hayden's good
self. He is Hayden's soul.*

At last, after what seemed like hours but must have been not much more than a single hour, Elisha turned onto a rutted lane leading off the gravel road, and Carole understood that they were approaching Hayden's property. Here was a barbed-wire fence, here were NO TRES-PASSING signs in abundance. It had not occurred to Carole that her recluse brother might actually own property: in her imagination, she'd been thinking of him as homeless, deprived. But Elisha was leading her into a property of at least several acres. The lane passed through a wooded area of tall deciduous trees, a good number of which seemed to be mysteriously broken and fallen. Here too were outcroppings of shale and massive boulders looking like contorted life-forms. They passed over a transparent rippling stream on a crude plank bridge, and entered a clearing. Here was a cabin made of the same crude, unpainted planks, with a steep tarpaper roof and a tilted tin stovepipe. Scattered about the clearing were several sheds, and what looked like an outdoor lavatory. In a corner of the clearing was a six-foot pyramid of glittering bottles. By this time Carole's heart was pounding with apprehension. Why, she was frightened of meeting Hayden! She had been frightened of him as a girl and her last, unnerving memory of him was the occasion when he'd knocked their father down in the upstairs hall of their house, breaking the older man's left wrist and precipitating a minor cardiac episode from which Mr. Buttrick would never fully recover. She had hidden from her raging brother in the dining room, as he'd lurched down the stairs. *All you to the hell!* reverberated still in her memory.

But they were adults now. Now, they were equals.

Carole braked her car behind Elisha's pickup. Frantic relief washed over her, she saw no other vehicle in the clearing.

In the opened doorway of the cabin, no one had appeared to stare angrily at her.

Dazed and shaken from the drive, Carole climbed out of her car slowly. She saw how, only a few yards away, Elisha wasn't glancing back at her as if, in this isolated setting, he'd become shy of her. She heard him mutter almost inaudibly what sounded like *He's away right now.* Again without glancing at her he indicated with an embarrassed motion of his head that she should follow him into the cabin. Close beside the door a shovel rested against the wall, and on the ground, looking like a dissected body, was a partly dismantled and rusted chain saw.

Inside the cabin, Carole's nostrils pinched against commingled odors: dirt, kerosene, coffee grounds, grease and decaying garbage and human sweat, unlaundered clothes and something cloying-sweet like syrup. On a makeshift counter beside a hand-pump sink was a plastic bottle of maple syrup and a box of Wheat-Chex. On shelves were canned goods, boxes of sugar, flour, macaroni. She was thinking of how, as a boy, Hayden had soaked pancakes with maple syrup until they became sodden, liquefied. He'd had a compulsion to devour sweet things until, unexpectedly, he became nauseated by them, as by many foods.

"So this is where Hayden lives! So many times I've imagined . . ."

In fact, Carole had not been able to imagine where her brother might be living. She had never envisioned him in any specific place, even in any specific time.

Her voice sounded awkward, insincere. There was Elisha with both hands thrust into his pockets, wheezing as if he'd been running. How ill at ease he'd become, acutely self-conscious in her presence. In the meager light from the cabin's few windows not only the left lens of his clunky glasses but the right also looked opaque, blind. The wisp of a beard, that was both comical and touching, an old-man beard attached to a wizened-boy face, quivered with his breath. She thought *He's afraid of me. That I might touch him.* She saw that the cabin was a single square room of about the size of her living room in the Farmington house, with a curtained-off area that contained a cot or cots and clothes on hangers, on a clothesline. On the plank ceiling, that was uncomfortably low, were cloud-smudges of wood smoke and grease. In each wall there was a single square window that opened outward with a crank. On the floorboards were filthy carpet remnants. There appeared to be no electricity, only just kerosene lamps. There was a woodstove, there were cardboard boxes stacked with kindling and scrap lumber. There were sagging chairs, a Formica-topped kitchen table that looked as if it had been scavenged from a dump, stacks and shelves of books, magazines, newspapers. In her nerved-up state Carole examined the books that were both hardcover and paperback and appeared to be secondhand. On several were yellow stickers HARVARD CO-OP USED. *A Short History of the Environmental Sciences. Worlds in Collision. Upanishad. A Sufi Way of Life. Autopsy of a Revolution. Gulliver's Travels. The Secret Agent. Revolt of the Masses. Crime and Punishment. Notes from Underground. The End of Nature. The Closing Circle. Travelers Among Us: Extra-Terrestrial Life Since Hiroshima. Walden. Civil Disobedience. American Sociology: A History. The Shame of the Cities. Anarchist Manifesto. The War of the Worlds. The Island of Dr. Moreau. Civilization and Its Discontents. Psychiatry, Neurology, Politics and the Law.* And there were stacks of paintings of the kind Hayden had executed as a boy, on sheets of white construction paper now stiffly dried and warped. "These paintings! I would recognize Hayden's work anywhere." She thought she might put Elisha more at his ease, telling him how gifted and promising an artist her brother had been, as a child. How well he'd done at school, much of the time. Until his "illness" interfered. Yet even in his difficult moods he'd been able to create his illustrated fantasy-sagas. "Hayden had a genuine vision. We were all so amazed by him. I mean our family, and our relatives. And Hayden's teachers. There was this extraordinary continuous saga he was painting, what was the title—*The Galaxy Beyond.* I kept one of the paintings for years, it was my most cherished memory of . . ."

But Elisha was distracted and fidgety, not listening. Since entering the cabin he'd seemed even more ill at ease with Carole than he'd been at the motel. She wondered how Hayden could bear to be around him. As Carole advanced into the interior of the cluttered cabin, making her way around items on the floor (snowshoes, boots, dirt-stiffened socks, a battery-operated radio, parts of a dismantled rifle or shotgun), peering at the titles of Hayden's books, Elisha had been edging his way in front of her as if to block her off. (From what? The makeshift sink, the ancient woodstove? The curtained-off corner of the room where clothes hung on hangers, on a tautly tied clothesline?) Always he managed to remain in front of her, round-shouldered, impassive. In a gesture of clumsy courtesy he'd removed his grimy cap. His head was something of a shock to Carole: near-bald, bumpy as if the scalp were diseased, with a scaly rash, prominent veins and wisps of gunmetal-gray hair growing in patches like lichen. Her sense of him as a prematurely aged man, youth long faded, partly blind and emotionally stunted, roused her to a wave of sudden pity. She wondered if, like Hayden, Elisha had had a promising childhood: had been called a "prodigy."

She was saying, as if to mollify him, quell some of his nervousness, "Elisha, if you're worried that Hayden will be angry at you for bringing me here, I can tell him that it was my idea. I'll tell him immediately. I can tell him that I followed you in my car without your permission." She smiled, she was jubilant suddenly, reckless. "Or—*are* you Hayden? Please tell me! I'm your sister but also—"

Elisha's guarded expression had become a look of alarm and horror. She saw him glance behind her even as she heard a quick stealthy footfall and, turning, felt a blow strike the right side of her head at her temple with enough force to bring her to her knees, and open the floor beneath into an abyss into which she fell, and was weightless in falling.

Meaning to say *your sister but also your friend* but the words were never uttered.

—

AT 7:10 A.M. the next morning a woman would be found naked, unconscious, sticky with blood from a severe head wound, in a marshy ditch at the intersection of Mink Farm Road and the state highway. Ants and other insects were crawling over her, attracted by both the blood and a sweet syrupy liquid that had been dribbled onto her. The woman was alive and breathing, faintly. The young farmer who'd discovered her believed she had to be dead and called 911 to report a "dead body." She was brought by ambulance to Kingfield General Hospital forty miles away where she was eventually identified as *Carole Buttrick, Caucasian female, forty-one, resident of Farmington, Connecticut.* In addition to her physical injuries she would suffer from amnesia, short-term memory loss, and anxiety.

Questioned by Kennebago police officers, Carole Buttrick could not recall what had happened to her. She could not recall even the initial event in an evident sequence of events (making a decision to drive to Maine several days before) that would end with her in critical condition in a hospital hundreds of miles from Farmington, straining to recall why, what, who might have done such a thing to her. Her car, abandoned in underbrush above the Kennebago River, provided no clues. Vaguely she spoke of having been driving on a country highway, a sudden blade of sun reflected on the hood of her car had blinded her—"Beyond that, nothing."

Speaking slowly, with effort. Enunciating each syllable of her words with painstaking care.

Months were required for her to heal, in a rehabilitation clinic in Hartford. And then, she would never walk with her old energy and assurance. She would never play tennis again. She would never approach a horse again. She would never stand casually in a doorway, her back unguarded. Asked about her medical condition she would say she'd had an accident, in Maine. Asked about her family she would say, with a polite smile, "But I have no family. I live alone."

IN HOT MAY

"WHY'S THIS DOOR LOCKED? Mom! Let me in."
It was a hot afternoon in May when the sun-blinding wind swirled with those damned maple seeds that stick in your hair, eyelashes, mouth. Kileen Zaller returned home from school to discover the door to the house locked. She turned the knob, calling "Mom? It's Kileen, let me *in*." She was big-boned impulsive girl who became excited when frightened or confused and she was pounding now at the door with the flat of her hand.

She was stricken with embarrassment, too: if anyone in the school bus was watching!

Kileen was thirteen, physically mature but of that age when being laughed at is the worst thing you can imagine.

But the lumbering old school bus the color of a rotted pumpkin had moved off along the Post Road. And Kileen had to concede: why'd anyone want to watch *her*?

She'd been so happy at school that day. Everyone was complaining of the sudden heat wave, in only mid-May. Teachers threw open windows. Everyone swatted at maple seeds blown inside the classrooms and those tiny quick-darting blackflies that hatch in the spring, suddenly everywhere. But Kileen had not complained. Kileen had scarcely noticed. Perspiration beaded her fair, flushed skin like miniature jewels, and in the girls' lavatory mirror she smiled at her almost-pretty face, breathing *ONE two three ONE two three.*

After school was Kileen's happiest time—at her music lesson and at band practice.

But now.

She'd never been locked out of the house before. She stood baffled on the concrete stoop not knowing what to do. Later she would recall not having been frightened, yet. It was more the surprise of being locked out. Turning a familiar doorknob that turns suddenly unfamiliar. She was trying to think if Erma, her mother, had reason to be angry with her. If that was why. She'd been a mommy's girl for many years, but not recently. Since about her twelfth birthday, it seemed that anything she said, did, left undone, Erma found fault with. And she, Kileen, had to concede she'd acquired bad habits: rolling her eyes, sighing loudly, turning her fleshy lips inside out in a look calculated to infuriate her mother.

Now Erma was punishing her, maybe. That the door might be locked for some other reason would not have occurred to her.

Yet there was another not-exactly-right thing which Kileen had noted from the school bus: both her mother's car and her father's pickup were in the mud-puddled driveway. This meant that Rick Zaller was home at a time when he should have been working, but it also meant that he was back from wherever-he'd-been, someplace Kileen had not been allowed to know. These past few weeks Zaller had been living somewhere in the city, in what Kileen's mother called a new arrangement.

New arrangement! Erma spoke with such a bemused, bitter twist of her mouth, Kileen knew better than to ask for details.

Rick Zaller was a foreman at Strykersville Pipe, where Kileen's older half-brother Lloyd also worked. Zaller drove a mud-splattered Chevy pickup and allowed Erma to drive the newer model Pontiac most of the time. He was a generous man, though unpredictable, especially when he drank. Since Christmas, he'd been away from the house so frequently that Kileen had steeled her heart against him. One of her friends had asked if Kileen's parents were separated, pronouncing *separated* as if it was the name of a repugnant disease, and Kileen had shot back hotly, "Ask them."

She'd dropped her heavy backpack onto the stoop. Pounding on the door so hard her hand stung, she was still thinking that it must be locked against *her.* "Mom? Daddy? It's me, Kileen. . . ."

As if she'd have to identify herself to her parents!

She shaded her eyes and peered through the door pane into the kitchen. No one was in sight. She could see the glass coffee pot that percolated and bubbled for much of the day on the stove, and the avocado-olive refrigerator festooned with comical animal magnets and faded Polaroids; and there was the sink in which breakfast dishes were soaking; and there, slightly out of place, sat the sticky Formica-topped table with its curved tubular legs. One of the matching chairs, the one with the ripped seat, lay overturned on the floor beside it.

Kileen thought *Oh.* This was wrong. This was alarming. A chair overturned. And newspaper pages scattered on the linoleum floor.

He has come back to hurt her.

They are both dead.

She'd avoided hearing them. There was a kind of angry pride in not hearing them. She would press her hands over her ears, she would run outside in the snow; she would tramp along the road, a hot-skinned thirteen-year-old. "Hate them! Don't love them. Why should I love them, they don't give a damn about me." No matter what words Kileen uttered, the wind blew them away.

The house had two doors, but the front one was permanently locked, never used. Kileen winced with embarrassment seeing this door that seemed to float in midair about two feet above ground level with no stoop or steps beneath. On the Post Road there were other eyesores: a tin-colored trailer on cement blocks, a falling-down farmhouse in which a family with seven children and numerous dogs lived. But Kileen was convinced that the most ridiculous sight was the Zallers' front-door-without-steps squarely positioned in the center of its crumbly beige brick facade. To make matters worse, this door was painted a glossy red. From the school bus it was so visible! Kileen hated, too, the grassy-weedy front yard where a septic tank had been inlaid years ago and you could still see the ugly scar-trenches.

Wind was whipping Kileen's hair. Damn maple seeds flew into her face. She'd begun whistling, loudly. When she was nervous, she whistled. Her mother disliked this new, annoying habit of Kileen's. She'd picked it up from school—in fact, from Mr. Kowalcyzk, the music teacher. Kileen was thinking the logical thing was to run next door to the neighbors so she could telephone her own house—but did you really want (Kileen could hear her mother's angry voice) the neighbors to know your business? And if the phone wasn't answered, what then? Kileen's mind went blank.

Or maybe the logical thing was to break a windowpane in the door and try to unlock it (it was closed with a simple bolt), or break a window in the basement and crawl inside. "Oh, man. No." She didn't want to think where such desperation might lead her.

Or what she might find inside the house.

It was almost four-thirty. She'd stayed after school for band practice and taken the late bus home. Until eighth grade this year, Kileen Zaller had never been one to participate in any "activities" at Strykersville Middle School. She believed herself clumsy, friendless. The second-tallest girl in eighth grade, she was chunky, with hips, thighs, and more recently breasts, which the boys called titties, and which had to be hidden inside baggy T-shirts, flannel shirts, khaki shirts. She had her father's rat-colored hair and big-boned frame, and her mother's pale-freckly face with fierce eyes. Since grade school Kileen had been one of those shy/sullen children bused into Strykersville public schools from outlying rural districts. Her grades were a little better than average, but rarely had she shown enthusiasm for any subject except, since last September, music.

Weird. Kileen had signed up for band. Weirder yet: for tuba.

Tuba! But all the other instruments were taken; she'd had no choice.

Erma, who played pop music, soft rock, and country-western all day long on the radio, and had a "nice" husky-breathy voice (as a girl she'd sung in church choir, later sporadically in cocktail lounges and taverns) was incensed: "What kind of musical instrument is a tuba, for Christ's sake? I mean for a girl your age. A boy, maybe. A fat boy. But you, it's an insult. This 'marching band'? You're going to actually march, like in public? It's got to be a joke. A joke against our family. They gave you the tuba as a booby prize. *I am your mother and I resent it.*"

Kileen laughed; Erma flared up in such extravagant ways. Like TV. There'd be genuine emotion in her protests, at least initially. Then she'd go off into exaggeration like a burst of wild music. Her hands fluttered and flailed. *Flying off the handle*, Kileen's father described it. Kileen knew not to take more than half of what Erma said seriously.

Kileen's secret was that she'd have signed up for any instrument at school, however ridiculous. For there was Mr. Kowalcyzk, who directed the school band. And actually, the more you practiced the tuba the less ridiculous it became. Clumsy and ugly, and the notes low and growly like a throat needing to be cleared, and the spit accumulating in the mouthpiece that had to be shaken out—but all the horn players, even the pretty-pretty girls playing flute, had to contend with spit. Kileen had strong arms and strong lungs. She was no pretty-pretty girl to be intimidated.

And Mr. Kowalcyzk—at first he'd seemed amused by her struggle with the tuba, but now he was impressed with her, she could see. Mr. Kowalcyzk was older than her father but much better natured. He had a quick smile and heavy jowls and jaws, squinty eyes, wriggly eyebrows, and a way of rubbing his hands zestfully together no matter how badly the band was playing. In eight years of school, Mr. Kowalcyzk was the first teacher who'd ever teased Kileen; he called her *Freckle Frown-Face.*

Kileen had lapsed into one of her open-eyed cow dreams thinking of these things. She'd forgotten the door locked so strangely against her. She'd forgotten her surroundings. For there was something wonderful in the world to which she alone had access. It was her secret she'd have died to reveal. In a bubble on a turbulent stream Mr. Kowalcyzk rode swiftly to her as he often did, smiling and winking. *Freckle Frown-Face! You'll be all right. I promise.*

Suddenly the door opened. Kileen's mother staggered out and clutched at Kileen's arm. Her eyes were wild and dilated and her streaked blond hair was matted with something liquid and dark. She was disheveled as if she'd dressed hurriedly.

"Kileen! Here's the keys. . . ."

Erma thrust car keys into Kileen's hand. What!

"You're driving. You drive. *Move.*"

Kileen stammered, asking what was wrong, but Erma was pushing at her, leaning on her so heavily that they nearly fell down the steps together. It was all happening so quickly and in such confusion. Kileen's bubble-dream of Mr. Kowalcyzk had ended so abruptly it was like waking dazed and terrified in some unknown place where people were shouting *Wake up! Wake up!*

"Mom? What happened? Are you hurt? Did Daddy—hurt you?" Kileen saw how stiffly her mother was walking as if neither of her knees would bend. Erma whimpered with pain and impatience. She wiped away a trickle of blood at her nose with the flat of her hand.

Kileen protested, "I don't know how to drive, I'll crash the car."

Erma said sharply, "You can drive. Get *in.*"

The door to the kitchen had swung open in the wind, but no one was visible in the doorway. Kileen had a dread of her father appearing in pursuit, knocking her out of the way to get to Erma.

IT WAS LIKE SWIMMING: somehow you did it. You'd never been taught, exactly. Kileen would recall with pride how she'd managed to get the Pontiac started. Gun the gas, lurch forward. Erma was giving instructions: "Press down. Gas pedal. Baby, come *on.*" Kileen felt a thrill of terror; she'd crash the car before they even left the driveway, hit the side of the house or her father's pickup which, she saw now, was parked at a strange drunken angle in the driveway, the door on the driver's side swung open.

He'd been in a hurry parking the pickup, in a rush to get inside the house.

Kileen gripped the steering wheel tight and pressed her right foot on the gas pedal, sitting very straight and staring out the windshield. It was a revelation to her, who had so many times ridden in the passenger's seat of this and other vehicles, that when you are driving the view from the windshield is so *vivid*. When you're a passenger, nothing is very important to observe; but when you are the driver, everything is important.

Erma was murmuring, "Baby, *drive*. We need to get out of here." She was both hunched down in her seat and looking out the rear window of the car, anxiously. Kileen saw to her horror that Erma was naked inside her carelessly buttoned flannel shirt. No bra. A large milky-white breast with a wrinkled brown nipple all but peeped out. Kileen wanted to reach over and close her mother's shirt. She had a thirteen-year-old's horror of seeing her mother part-naked. And Erma's nose kept bleeding in a thin trickle, dripping onto her black polyester slacks.

"Baby, I said drive! Don't look at me."

How strange to be called *baby* by Erma. Kileen wasn't sure how she felt about it. She hadn't been called *baby* by her mother in years. In the midst of this confusion and excitement it was consoling.

The Pontiac moved in slow bucking movements along the driveway toward the Post Road. This driveway, in theory gravel, was in fact mostly mud and glistening puddles of varying depths. Kileen was driving partly on the grass beside the driveway, to avoid the worst mudholes. In the rearview mirror she saw that no one was following them. If her father emerged from the doorway, came running after them—if he shouted for her to stop. . . .

When Kileen's parents had one of their disagreements, you might say quarrels, fights, it was always Zaller who left, slamming out of the house and tearing out of the driveway in his pickup with such fury that the spinning tires made deep ruts in the ground. Usually Erma was left behind sobbing and cursing.

"Mom? Are we going into town? To the—hospital?"

For a moment Kileen's mind was so blank that she couldn't think which direction to turn the wheel.

"Hospital? No. Clarice."

Erma's voice was so choked that Kileen wasn't sure what she'd heard. Clarice? Clarice was a friend of Erma's, also a cousin. She lived about two miles away, farther out in the country.

"But Mom, maybe we should go to the hospital? If—"

"God damn *no*. No *hospital*. I said *Clarice*." Erma half sobbed, slapping at Kileen in a sudden temper.

Blindly Kileen turned the steering wheel to the right. She was afraid to turn onto the Post Road so soon. Instead she drove the Pontiac in the weedy field beside the road, as a child might do, blinking back tears. Erma scolded, "What in hell?" Then she broke down laughing. In this peculiar fashion, the Pontiac bumping and bucking through the field, they drove for about a quarter mile, until Kileen had no choice but to turn onto the country highway. Slowly and with a kind of dignity they drove past the Hogans' house, an eyesore worse than the Zallers', with a tarpaper roof and plastic strips still flapping over the window from winter, and there was Mrs. Hogan about twenty feet away in the yard hanging laundry, shading her eyes to stare at Kileen and Erma bumping past. Erma had not fully recovered from her fit of laughing. Unless it was a fit of sobbing. She rolled down her window to yell out "Get an eyeful, you! Nosey bitch." It was like Erma Zaller to flare up with little provocation. There was a history of neighbor-feuding between the Zallers and the Hogans. Mrs. Hogan, a fattish woman in her fifties with white frizzled hair, was so startled she dropped a towel into the grass. Erma was muttering, "Some people! Nothing better to do. *I* mind my damn business."

Kileen looked over at her mother. Erma was leaking blood from both nostrils. She'd been holding a blood-soaked tissue wadded in her hand; she'd let it fall onto her lap. There was a splattering of blood on her slacks and shoes. Her hair she'd had highlighted with shimmering blond streaks looked like a cheap glamour wig askew on her head, and her shirt was gaping open worse than before. Mrs. Hogan had probably been gaping at that big white tit and would tell all the neighborhood what a sight she'd seen.

"Maybe we should go to the hospital, Mom? If—" Kileen began again.

Erma slapped at her, furious. No, no! They were going to Clarice's, goddamn it.

Kileen bit her lower lip, wishing she could drive through fields all the way to Clarice Moix's house, not risking any road. When you're a little kid you go everywhere on foot or on a bicycle, tramping the fields, the woods, along the railroad embankment. Once you learned to drive you took a car everywhere. This was both a freedom and a limitation. Kileen was laughing suddenly. Her mom was crazy, she guessed. Mr. Kowalcyzk would whistle one of his quick-rising comical tunes in that way he had, wriggling his eyebrows. So funny! Kileen's first experience driving a car and it wasn't a lesson but the real thing. She wished she had friends to tell of it. Maybe she would tell it to Mr. Kowalcyzk, who would be impressed. Her fiercest concentration was focused on this act of driving the big powerful machine which seemed to her as profound and privileged an act as her fumbling attempts at the tuba under Mr. Kowalcyzk's tutelage.

Erma was saying she didn't need any damn doctors fussing, didn't want any damn cops nosing into her and her family's business. She would just get through the rest of the day. Clarice would protect her.

"What about Dad? He might come after us."

Erma laughed, shaking her head. For the first time Kileen wondered if something might have happened to her father too.

It was time to turn onto the Post Road; Kileen had run out of field. She waited until a farmer's pickup passed. So many times she'd bicycled on this road; now she would be driving a car. The road was two lanes, blacktop. Dry-mouthed, Kileen half shut her eyes, pressing down hard on the gas pedal, thinking *It's all right. It will be all right. A deep breath and ONE two three.*

"A GOOD-LOOKING MAN can never be trusted. Go for the homely ones, K'leen. Heed my words!"

Erma made such pronouncements. You had to laugh; she meant to be funny-serious. Erma had a radio voice that derived from her experience as a "professional singer." (In fact, Zaller confided with a wink, Erma had been mostly a cocktail waitress—"But damned good-looking.") Kileen seemed to know that her father had been married before he'd married her mother in some long-ago time before she was born. For there was her brother Lloyd, nine years older than Kileen. She adored Lloyd, though he had not ever paid much attention to her. Now he was twenty-two, lived in Strykersville, and rarely visited home. And when he did visit, Kileen's father had a way of querying and bullying him that made for strained mealtimes.

Lloyd did not wish to speak of his actual mother; in fact no one wished to speak of the first Mrs. Zaller. It was from Katie Hogan next door that Kileen learned this woman had died of some quick-acting female-type cancer when Lloyd was six, which was a long time before Kileen was born. She had no reason to think of it. Ever!

Rick Zaller was not a man you could know. He could know you, you were his daughter, but you could not know him, really. He was shorter than Lloyd but heavier in the chest, a wiry-limbed man with bristling dark hair and a quick harsh laugh and a way of crinkling his face so you knew he would say something to abrade your skin like sandpaper. Erma complained that her husband was so good-looking every female in his life had spoiled him rotten, and now she was left with the sorry results.

"A guy everybody forgives, how the hell's he going to learn to *repent?*"

But you learned not to side with Erma, either, because Erma had a softness for Rick Zaller even when she was furious with him—even when he shoved her against a wall, squeezed and shook her arm, leaving bruises; even when he called her ugly names. (Kileen shut her ears in a way she had, like shutting her eyes: hearing yet not hearing so a minute later she'd have forgotten.) Zaller laughed when Erma threatened to kill him, clumsily flailing at him with scissors or a kitchen knife. One memorable time Zaller grabbed the knife only partly by the handle, so he'd cut his hand on the blade, dripping blood even as he was laughing to show how he didn't feel any pain. Erma had to know it wasn't so easy to kill a man like him.

Kileen peeked from behind a chair. Whatever they did, her parents, it was between them and had nothing to do with her. The excitement between them, the way they spoke to each other and leaned close to each other and touched, pummeled, slapped, punched, was hot like fire that had nothing to do with her.

Eventually, Erma would give in. Erma would laugh, wipe away her tears, forgive Zaller. If he'd slammed out of the house, by the time he called next day, or two days later, she'd be ready to forgive. So if Kileen had been made to think her father was the enemy, now she'd have to change her mind and think he was a sweetie-pie after all, and it made her tired.

You could trust neither one of them, Kileen thought, once the door to their bedroom was shut with them inside and you outside.

Maybe she was adopted. That would explain it!

Except she looked like Erma, everybody said. Worse yet she had Rick Zaller's stocky body. Oh, it was a trap. She hated them.

She thought about running away. Except there was school, and the tuba. Her arms ached pleasurably, holding the ugly ungainly thing. Her ears echoed with those wheezy tuba notes. And there was Mr. Kowalcyzk whistling so you'd never know if he felt good about himself or if his heart was broken. Sharp-eyed Mr. Kowalcyzk had noted her look of guarded hurt and frustration, her big-girl look: *I-know-I'm-ugly*. She needed cheering up, teasing, someone to smile at her, encouragement. *Freckle Frown-Face, not bad! Deep breath and try, try again.*

DRIVING ON THE POST ROAD in a sweaty haze of concentration, gripping the steering wheel so tight her knucklebones glared up waxy-white: from somewhere she'd memorized how this is done. She was a smart, shrewd girl, leaning forward, scarcely drawing a deep breath, her breasts in a baggy steel-colored T-shirt nudging the wheel.

It was startling, Erma's sudden voice.

"You love your mother, don't you, baby?"

"Oh, Mom. Sure."

"Your crazy mother."

What was she suppose to say: Mom, you're not crazy? She frowned at the road ahead. Vehicles overtook her in the left lane. She had an instinct to slow, to let them pass as quickly as possible. She drove with excessive caution. The red speedometer needle quavered between eighteen and thirty-two or -three miles per hour.

"You know I do, Mom."

"You do, do you? Really?"

"Oh, Mom."

"Not bullshitting your crazy old mother, are you, baby?"

"Mom . . ."

Kileen was hurt Erma would say such a word. Out of nowhere such a hurtful word seemed to spring in Erma's presence.

"You don't think I'm a bad mother."

Was this a question or a statement? Either way, it had a wrong sound. Kileen didn't like it. She guessed she was a bad girl. Plenty of times she'd been told so; and the fact was she could be a bully on the bus, sullen and pushy so no one dared cross her except older, bigger boys. But it was a new thought to her, any mother as a bad mother. Never once had she though of Erma as a *bad mother*.

She guessed she loved Erma, actually. When Erma called her *baby* all the opposition in her heart melted—and when she'd seen Erma walking so stiff and hurting back at the house, seen Erma's bleeding face.

"Hey, I love you so much, Mom. I love love love you, Mom. I do!"

In her excitement Kileen banged on the steering wheel with both hands. Her words all came out in a hot rush, like tears.

"Now that *is* bullshitting, baby. But I love it."

Erma leaned over to kiss Kileen wetly on the cheek. This was such strange behavior between them. Kileen kept her eyes fixed straight ahead. Erma must have been drinking, or taking her diet pills that juiced her up like a cat. Unselfconscious as a slovenly little boy, Erma laughed, wiping her face on the front of her shirt. There was a flash of breasts three times the size of Kileen's, drooping toward Erma's fleshy waist. A smell lifted from her hot skin that reminded Kileen of her father's smell.

Sex smell. Must've been. The other day on the school bus older boys had been laughing about sex smells, stinks. Kileen had pretended to ignore these jerks, of course.

"Baby, here's your turn."

"Okay, Mom. I know."

"Brake slow. Turn slow."

At County Line Road, Clarice's road, Kileen braked carefully to a stop before turning in a too-wide arc, very slowly. Luckily there was no one behind her.

"Good, baby," Erma said. "Real good." Kileen gunned the motor and the car leapt ahead like an antic beast. "Whoa, whoa horsy!" Erma laughed.

Now that they were nearing Clarice's house, Kileen felt some relief. There was never much traffic on County Line and if something happened they could walk the rest of the way. Still, her fingers gripped the steering wheel like claws.

Erma was saying in a sudden vehement voice, "I'm not going anywhere. Clarice can hide me. Fuckers try to take me! I'd rather die. I don't give a shit. Don't you frown your face at me, baby! I see that snotty look."

Kileen didn't hear this, or wasn't sure what she'd heard. She saw the Moixs' green-painted wood-frame ranch house up ahead at the end of a cinder drive. The front and side yards were scrubby pastures—Clarice kept two droop-backed horses and a foul-smelling, friendly goat. There were no near neighbors. Clarice's former husband lived in Port Oriskany and came out weekends to tend to the animals. Clarice had been divorced forever but was on friendly terms with her former husband, who was much older than Kileen's father, old enough to be Clarice's father. Erma and Clarice had been friends since childhood—grew up together, they said. Girls together, they said. When she'd been little, Kileen had loved to be taken to Clarice's place to play with the animals. For years, Clarice was Auntie Clarice, but Kileen refused to call her that once she'd learned that her mother's cousin was no actual aunt of hers.

Erma was saying, "You better not testify against me. Your own mother. I wonder if I can trust you. You little shit."

Kileen's eyes smarting. Oh, she was hearing none of this! Her heart pounded so it hurt. Her thighs inside the baggy jeans, her buttocks, were damp with nervous sweat. Rivulets of sweat trickled from her armpits where spiky little hairs sprouted. She'd managed to turn the Pontiac into Clarice's driveway, in such a clumsy wide arc the front left wheel nearly slid off into a ditch. Luckily Erma hadn't noticed. But Kileen was all right now. The Pontiac was on course. Cinders crackled beneath the wheels. This driveway too was mud-puddled and they were bump-bump-bumping toward Clarice's house. There was Clarice in the side yard, staring at her visitors. Clarice in a red tank top and khaki shorts, dyed-black hair messy down her back. Clarice was a big busty woman with hips. Her face looked permanently sunburned. She was digging in the earth with a hoe, a cigarette slanted in the corner of her mouth.

"Stop the fucking car! Let me out."

Erma was furious at Kileen. It made no sense. Kileen was already braking the Pontiac to a jarring stop.

The hoe fell from Clarice's hands. She stared in astonishment at them, calling "Erma? What the hell? Kileen drove here? Oh, Jesus."

HAD TO ESCAPE. Had to hide. Behind Clarice's property, where there was a steep embankment and a creek.

Clarice had called after her but Kileen ignored her.

Run, run! Wanting only to get away from the women, like a panicked animal. Erma was all right now. Kileen's responsibility was over.

The creek. She'd played there as a little girl. It was one of her secret places when they visited Clarice; no adult would trouble to come down the embankment dense with underbrush. It was the creek-without-a-name that dried out in summer so you could walk across on stones, but now after so much recent rain was fast-flowing and noisy, mud-colored. Only in the shallow water at the pebbly shore could you see minnows, tadpoles. Kileen squatted on a flat rock, staring.

If someone was calling her name back at Clarice's house, she didn't hear.

She would hide at the creek. For how long she wasn't thinking. Her brain had shut down. She was exhausted. Driving the Pontiac just that short distance had wiped her out—like practicing the tuba for a straight hour. Her strange wild happiness had leaked from her like air from a balloon. She had driven on the Post Road, like any adult—driven an actual car. She understood it had been an *emergency situation*; that was part of how she might tell it to others, if she told, if there was anyone to tell. But maybe no one would believe her. No one had seen her except Mrs. Hogan and Clarice. And now it was over.

She swiped at a cloud of gnats hovering near. Her sweaty face and arms attracted them. In the unexpected May heat, peepers had wakened and were singing frantically.

Clarice would know what to do. It was up to Clarice now. Kileen had no more responsibility. She was in eighth grade; she had school next day. Damn, why should she think about it?

Her father would come to get them, maybe. This seemed logical. He'd come home from work and see the Pontiac gone; he'd drive out to Clarice's. Around suppertime he'd arrive. He would know exactly where Erma was. Erma had fled to Clarice's before. Kileen could imagine the mud-splattered pickup backing out of their driveway, turning onto Post Road in this direction. Maybe they'd eat at Chicken King or McDonald's on the way home. The Zallers never ate out except on these special occasions. These were funny-sweet times, hungry times. Fried chicken, french fries, onion rings, coleslaw and macaroni drippy with white mayonnaise, cherry pie with gelatin thick as glue. Kileen's mouth watered with hunger like pain. Her eyelids were shutting. Her father's pickup would be turning onto Clarice's driveway. He would drive much faster than Kileen, splashing through the shallow puddles.

"Kileen?"

She looked around, frightened. There was Auntie Clarice on the embankment behind her. The sun had shifted in the sky. It was some other time. The light was behind Clarice so Kileen couldn't see her face.

"Kileen? Come up, honey. Come up to the house."

HIGH LONESOME

THE ONLY PEOPLE I still love are the ones I've hurt. I wonder if
it's the same with you?

Only people I'm lonely for. These nights I can't sleep.

See, my heartbeat is fast. It's the damn medication makes me sweat.
Run my fingers over my stub-forefinger—lost most of it in a chain saw
accident a long time ago.

Weird how the finger feels like it's all there, in my head. Hurts, too.

Who I think of a lot, we're the same age now, I mean I'm the age
Pop was when he died, is my mother's step-daddy who wasn't my actual
grandfather. Pop had accidents, too. Farm accidents. Chain saw got
away from Pop, too. Would've sliced his foot off at the ankle, except
Pop was wearing work boots. Bad enough how Pop's leg was sliced.
Dragged himself bleeding like a stuck pig to where somebody could
hear him yelling for help.

I wasn't there. Not that day. Maybe I was in school. Never heard
Pop yelling from out behind the big barn.

Pop Olafsson was this fattish bald guy with a face like a wrinkled dish rag left in the sun to dry. Palest blue eyes and a kind of slow suspicious snaggletooth smile like he was worried people might be laughing at him. Pulling his leg. He'd say, You kids ain't pullin' my leg, are yah? When we were young we'd stare at Pop's leg, both Pop's legs, ham-sized in these old overalls he wore.

Wondering what the hell Pop Olafsson meant. In this weird singsong voice like his nose is stopped up.

We never called him Grandpa, he wasn't our Grandpa. Mom called him Pop. He was a Pop kind of guy. Until the thing in the newspaper, I don't think I knew his first name which was Hendrick. He was a dairy farmer, he smelled of barns. A dairy farm produces milk and manure. What a barn is, is hay, flies, feed, milk (if it's a dairy barn), and manure. It's a mix where you don't get one ingredient without the rest. Hay flies feed manure. You can smell it coming off a farmer at fifty yards. Why I left that place, moved into town and never looked back.

Except for not sleeping at night, and my stub-finger bothering me, I wouldn't be looking back now.

Pop Olafsson spent his days in the dairy barn. He had between fifteen and twenty Guernseys that are the larger ones, their milk is yellowish and rich and the smell of it, the smell of any milk, the smell of any dairy product, doesn't have to be rancid, turns my stomach. Pop loved the cows, he'd sleep out in the barn when the cows were calving. Sometimes they needed help. Pop would cry when a calf was born dead.

Weird to see a man cry. You lose your respect.

Pop wore bib-overalls over a sweat-stained undershirt with long grimy sleeves. Summers, he'd leave off the undershirt. He wasn't a man to spend time washing. He never smelled himself at fifty yards. There was a joke in the family, a cloud of flies followed Pop Olafsson wherever he went. Mom was ashamed of him, when she was in school. Why her mother married the old man, old enough to be her grandfather not her father, nobody knew. Mom said if her mother had waited, hadn't been desperate after her husband died of lung cancer young at thirty-nine, they'd have done a whole lot better.

Mom made her own mistakes with men. That's another story.

Pop didn't care for firearms. Pop wasn't into hunting like his neighbors. He had an old Springfield .22 rifle like everybody had and a double-barrelled Remington 12-gauge shotgun with a cracked wooden stock, heavy and ugly as a shovel. From one year to the next these guns weren't cleaned. When my cousin Drake came to live with us, Drake cleaned the guns. Drake was five years older than me. He had a natural love for guns. Pop was so clumsy with a gun, he'd be breathing through his mouth hard and jerk the trigger so he'd never hit where the hell he was aiming. Always think the damn thing's gonna blow up in my hands, Pop said.

Pop told us he'd seen a gun accident when he was a boy. He'd seen a man blasted in the chest with a 12-gauge. These were duck hunters. This was in Drummond County in the southern edge of the state. It's a sight you don't forget, Pop said.

Still, Pop taught me to shoot the rifle when I was eleven. When I was a little older, how to shoot the shotgun. It's something that has to be learned, you live on a farm. You need to kill vermin—rats, voles, woodchucks. Pop never actually killed any vermin that I witnessed but we gave them a scare. We never went hunting. Once, I went with Drake and some of his friends deer hunting. Drake was all the time telling me get back! get down!

Must've fucked up. I remember crying. It hurt me, my cousin turning on me in front of his friends. I was thirteen, I looked up to Drake like a big brother.

On the veranda, summer nights, Pop sat with his banjo. People laughed at him saying Pop thinks he's Johnny Cash, well Pop wasn't anywhere near trying to sound like Johnny Cash. I don't know who in hell Pop sounded like—nobody, maybe. His own weird self. He's picking at the banjo, he's making this high old lonesome sound like a ghost tramping the hills. It wasn't singing, more like talking, the kind of whiney rambling a man does who's alone a lot, talks to animals in the barn, and to himself. Pop had big-knuckled hands, splayed fingers and cracked dirt-edged nails. Like he said he was accident-prone and his fingers showed it. Pop kept a crock of hard cider at his feet all the hours he'd sit out there on the porch so it didn't matter how alone he was.

We never paid much attention to Pop. My grandma who'd been his wife died when I was little. That was Mom's mother. Mom still missed her. Pop was just Mom's stepfather she made no secret of the fact. It was just that Pop owned the property, why we moved in there when my dad left us. When Mom was drinking and got unhappy she'd tell Pop that. Pop right away said, Oh I know. I know. I appreciate that, honey.

The songs Pop sang, I wish I'd listened to. They had women's names in them, sometimes. One of them was about a cuckoo-bird. One was about a train wreck. These were songs Pop picked up from growing up in Drummond County. He'd got the banjo in a pawnshop. He never had any music lessons. Most of the songs, he didn't know all the words to so he'd hum in his high-pitched way rocking from side to side and a dreamy light coming into his face. A banjo isn't like a guitar, looks like it's made of a tin pie plate. A guy from school came by to pick me up one night, there's the old man out on the veranda with that damn plunky banjo singing some weird whiny song like a sick tomcat so Rory makes some crack about my grandpa and my face goes hot, Fuck you Pop ain't no grandpa of mine, he's what you call *in-law*.

Didn't hardly care if Pop heard me, I was feeling so pissed.

WHY'RE YOU SO ANGRY, Daryl girls would ask sort of shivery and wide-eyed. *Skin's so hot it's like fever*. Like this is a way to worm into my soul. *You ain't going to hurt me, Daryl, are you?* Hell no it ain't in Daryl McCracken's nature to hurt any girl.

No more than I would wish to hurt my mother. Nor anyone in my family that's my blood kin.

By age seventeen I'd shot up tall as my cousin Drake who's six feet three though I would never get so heavy-muscled as Drake you'd turn your head to observe, seeing him pass by. And in his Beechum County sheriff-deputy uniform that's a kind of gray-olive, and dark glasses, and hair shaved military style, and that way of carrying himself like anybody in his way better get out of his way, Drake looks good.

I was never jealous of Drake. I was proud of my cousin who's a Mc-Cracken like me. Went away to the police academy at Port Oriskany and graduated near the top of his class. Came back to Beechum County that's right next to Herkimer so he'd keep his friends and family. A long time Drake would visit us like every week or so, if Mom made supper he'd stay if he hadn't night shift patrolling the highways. Mom teased Drake saying it's God's will Drake turned out a law enforcement officer not one to break the law. Drake would laugh at any remark of Mom's but he'd be pissed at anybody else hinting his cop integrity isn't authentic. You wouldn't want to roil Drake McCracken that way. In school, saluting the American flag felt good to him. Reciting the Pledge of Allegiance. Wearing the Beechum County Sheriff's Department uniform. Keeping his weapon clean. It's a .38-caliber Colt revolver weighing firm and solid in the hand, dismantling the gun and oiling it is some kind of sacred ritual to him Drake says know why? *Your gun is your close friend when you are in desperate need of a friend.*

I have held that gun. Drake allowed me to hold that gun. It was the first handgun I had ever seen close up. Rifles and shotguns everybody has, not little guns you can conceal on your person.

Hey man, I'd like one of these!

Drake scowls at me like this ain't a subject to joke about. You'd have to have a permit, Daryl. Any kind of concealed weapon.

Do you have a permit?

Drake looks as me like old Pop Olafsson, not catching the joke.

Ain't pulling my leg, Daryl, are yah?—I'm a *cop.*

Yah yah asshole, I get it: you're a *cop.* (For sure, I don't say this aloud.)

Drake's .38-caliber Colt pistol didn't help him, though. Drake was killed off-duty at age twenty-nine, in September 1972.

That long ago! Weird to think my big-brother cousin would be young enough to be my son, now.

Sure I miss him. My wife says I am a hard man but there's an ache in me, that's never been eased since Drake passed away.

We did not part on good terms. Nobody knew this.

There was always rumors in Beechum County and in Herkimer, who killed Drake McCracken. It was believed he'd been ambushed by someone seeking revenge. Friends or relatives of someone he'd arrested and helped send to prison. There were plenty of these. By age twenty-nine, Drake had been a deputy for four years. He'd accumulated enemies.

He'd testified as arresting officer in court. Some guys, the sight of a uniform cop makes them sick. Makes them want to inflict injury. Drake was beat to death with a hammer, it was determined. Skull cracked and crushed and his badge and gun taken from him.

That was the cruel thing. That was hurtful to his survivors. Knowing how Drake wouldn't have wished that. Even in death, to know his badge he was so proud of, his gun he took such care of, were taken from him.

They questioned a whole lot of individuals including some at the time incarcerated. No one was ever arrested for my cousin's murder. No weapon was ever found. Nor Drake's badge or gun. The Beechum County sheriff took it pretty hard, one of his own deputies killed. You'd think from TV the sheriff had known Drake McCracken personally but that wasn't really so. It was a hard time then. Drake's photo in the papers in his dress uniform. Looking good. At the funeral everybody was broke up. Guys he'd gone to school with. Girls he'd gone out with. Relatives who'd known him from when he was born. Mom was the most broke up as anybody, cried and cried so I had to hold her and later we got drunk together, Mom and me.

Saying, It's good Pop isn't here for this. It would kill him.

BACK IN JULY, this happens.

On Route 33 north of Herkimer, about six miles from Pop Olafsson's farm, over the county line in Beechum, there's come to be what locals call the Strip—gas stations and fast-food restaurants and discount stores, adult books & videos, Topless Go-Go and Roscoe's Happy Hour Lounge, E-Z Inn Motor Court, etcetera. A few years ago this stretch was farmland and open fields all the fifteen miles to Sparta. Weird how the look of the countryside has changed. There's biker gangs hanging out on the highway, drug dealers, hookers cruising the parking lots, getting cigarettes at the 7-Eleven, using the toilets at McDonald's, standing out on the highway like they're hitch-hiking. Just up the road from King Discount Furniture and Rug Remnant City, that acre-size parking lot between the Sunoco station and the old Sears, you see females in like bikini tops, miniskirts to the crotch, "hot pants," high-heeled boots to the knee. It's like a freak show, Route 33. High school kids are cruising the scene, racing one another and causing trouble. Mostly this is weekends after dark but sometimes during actual daylight so locals are complaining like hell. Unless a hooker is actually caught soliciting a john, cops can't arrest them. Cops patrol the Strip and make the hookers move on but next night they're back. A few hours later they're back. Got to be junkies, strung out on heroin and what all else. Got to be diseased. Why a man would wish to have sex with a pig! My cousin Drake who's on night shift highway patrol says it's like running off any kind of vermin, they come right back. Kill them, next day it's new vermin taking their place.

None of the sheriff deputies care for this assignment. The Strip is the pus wound of Beechum County. Sparta's the only city, population 15,000. Herkimer ain't hardly any city but it's got more people. Rookies are sent out on the Strip. Older cops, still assigned to highway patrol, you know they fucked up somewhere. There's this undercover team, Drake gets assigned to. He's just backup, in an unmarked van. Five male cops, three females. Sometimes the male cops pretend to be johns, picking up hookers and busting them. Sometimes it's the females are hooker decoys. The female deputies are close in age, looks, behavior to the actual hookers. Sometimes a hooker has darkish skin like she's mixed race but usually they're white females like anybody else. Slutty girls you went to school with, dropped out pregnant and got married and divorced and turned up in Sparta, Chautauqua Falls, Port Oriskany living with some guy or guys, and have another kid maybe mixed-race this time, and turn up back home, and get kicked out from home, and move in somewhere else, and pick up a drug habit, hang out at the E-Z Inn or the Go-Go, Roscoe's, hang out on the Strip, get busted, serve thirty days in Beechum Women's Detention, get out and get back on the Strip, got to be pathetic but you can't feel sorry for them, pigs as they are. The female deputies hate undercover. No dignity in undercover. You wear slut clothes, not your uniform. You wear a wire, not your badge. No weapon, if a john is some sicko wants to hurt you, you got to rely on backup.

Or maybe, undercover is kind of fun. Like Halloween.

Sable Drago, a Beechum County second-year deputy (turns out she is an older cousin of Bobbie Lee Drago, the girl I will marry in 1975) is one of the undercover team who defends the operation. Sable was a high school athlete, belonged to the Young Christian League. Sable believes this is work that has to be done, enforcing the prostitution, loitering, public drunkenness and "public nuisance" statutes. The Beechum County sheriff got elected on a clean-up platform. Sable has a missionary fever about undercover also it can be scary, it's a challenge you're not in your uniform almost you are naked, like any civilian. But when things go right it can feel damn good.

On the Strip Sable is a look-alike hooker. One of those fleshy girls looking like grown women when they're fifteen, now at thirty-one Sable is busty and wide-hipped with beet-colored hair frizzed and sprayed to three times its normal size. Her hard-muscled legs thick as a man's she hides in tight black toreador pants. Hot-pink satin froufrou top tied below her breasts to display her fleshy midriff. Peach-colored makeup thick on her face to hide her freckles. Eye makeup to hide the steely cop-look in Sable's eyes and crimson lipstick shiny as grease. Hey mister wanna party?—wanna date? Hey mistah? Sable's cruising the parking lot by the old Sears, calling to guys in slow-moving cars, pickups, vans passing through like they are intending to turn into the Sunoco station to just get gas, or drive on. Sable can't wear high heels, has to wear flip-flops on her size-ten feet but she has polished her toenails, her kid sister gave her some dime store sexy tattoos to press on exposed parts of her body. Sable can't drift too near the other hookers, they'd make her as a cop. Sable's mumbling and laughing into the wire she's wearing down between her sweaty breasts, the guys in the van are her best buddies, hiding around the corner of the empty Sears. It's a hot-humid day. It's dusk. It's a time of quickening pulses, anticipation. If you're a hunter, you know the feeling. Our country cops are into the kind of arrests where a suspect (drunk, stoned, plain stupid) has put up some resistance so you rush to knock them on their ass, flop them over so their face hits the ground, if they don't turn their face fast enough their nose is broke. You are required to place your knee in the small of their back. You push, to restrain. All this while you are yelling, Hands behind your back! Hands behind your back! Required to bring the suspect under immediate control. If you lose control, you may be blown away. First thing you learn at the academy, Drake says, a police officer never loses control of the situation. An officer can lose his gun, he's killed by his own gun, it happens and it's a shameful thing nobody wishes even to speak of, and disgraceful to the family. Better blow away the suspect than get your own brains blown out, Drake says. For sure.

About 9 P.M. Sable is out at the highway thumbing for a ride. Trailer trucks rush past throwing up dirt in her face. There's a smell of diesel fuel, exhaust. Some vehicles, the drivers swerve like they're going to hit her, surprised to see her, or jeering leaning on their horn. Then this mud-splattered pickup comes along at about twenty miles an hour, and slows. Some kind of farm equipment rattling in the rear. Old bald guy at the wheel. The pickup brakes to a clumsy stop on the shoulder of the road and Sable strolls forward calling in a sexy TV voice, Hi there mister! I'm hoping for a ride! And this old guy bald-headed and sweating in dirty bib-overalls, he's peering into the rearview mirror but doesn't say a word. Sable repeats she's hoping for a ride, mistah. Sable perceives this john is old enough to be somebody's granddaddy which is pitiful if it wasn't so disgusting. It takes like three minutes to get the old guy to tell her climb into the cab, he's tongue-tied and stammering and maybe has something wrong with him (speech impediment, hard-of-hearing, drunk), it's going to require Sable's undercover-hooker skill to get his ass busted. (Right! It's Pop Olafsson. But Drake, in the unmarked van, doesn't know this yet.)

Where're yah goin', the old guy asks. He's mumbling, shy of looking at Sable full in the face. Sable says, Where we can party, mister, you'd like that? Huh? There's such smells lifting off this guy, Sable has to fight the impulse to hold her nose. Almost, she's going to have to do this and make a joke of it, manure-smell, barn-feed smell, whiskey-smell, body odor and tobacco and something sweetish like maybe licorice? Oh man! Wishing she could report to the team back in the van, what this scene is.

The old guy has the pickup in gear, doesn't seem to know what to do: drive on? Move onto the shoulder, and off the highway? Sable keeps asking him wanna party mister, wanna date me, hey mistah? but he's too confused. Or maybe just excited and scared, aroused. Not your

his courage to drive out here for months but now he's here, damn if he hasn't forgotten why. HEY MISTAH says the beet-hair woman like waking him from a doze, know what you look like a real sweet guy, I'm into older men, see? leaning forward so he can see the tops of her heavy breasts straining against a black lace brassiere like you'd see in a girly magazine, sweat-drops on her freckled chest he'd like to lick off with his tongue that's so swollen and thirsty. All this while the beet-hair woman is speaking to him in her husky voice trying not to sound impatient, the way his daughter is impatient having to scold him for dirtying the kitchen floor or leaving dishes in the sink not soaking, coming to the table smelling of the barn like he can't help no matter how he washes, actually Glenda (his honey-haired daughter, divorced and with a grown son) isn't his daughter but stepdaughter, all he has in the world having had no daughter or son of his own, he'd like to explain this to the beet-hair woman, maybe after they have a few drinks from the pint of Four Roses, the beet-hair woman is asking in a louder voice does he want to go somewhere with her? somewhere private? cozy? air-conditioned E-Z Inn? get acquainted? want to date? want to party mistah? what's ya lookin' at like that mistah? cat got your tongue mistah? or do you like maybe have to get home mistah, wifey's waiting for you is that it? and the old guy is stricken suddenly fumbling a smile trying to hide the stained snaggle teeth saying fast and hoarse, Ma'am I buried my wife Agnes Barnstead back in '54, and Sable gives a little cry of hurt and disapproval, Ohhh mister that's not a thing to tell me, if we're gonna party and the old guy looks like he's going to cry, can't seem to think what to say, maybe he's drunker than she thought, so Sable says scornfully placing her hand on the car door handle, Damn mister maybe you don't want to party, huh? maybe I'm wasting my time in this crap rust-buckle smells like a barn? and he's fumbling quick to say no, no don't leave ma'am, stammering, I guess—you would want—money? and Sable says sharp and quick, why'd I want money, mister? and he says, blurting the words out, Ma'am if—if—if we could—be together—and Sable says, Have sex, mister? that's what you're trying to say? and the old guy says, winded like he's been climbing a steep stairs, yes ma'am, and Sable says it's thirty for oral, fifty for straight, it's a deal, mister? and the old guy is blinking and staring at her like he can't comprehend her words so she repeats them, deal, mister? is it? and he says, almost inaudible on the tape being recorded in the unmarked van, yes ma'am.

Okay, you're busted.

LIKE THAT it happens. Happens faster than you can figure it out. You're busted, mister. Step out of the truck, mister. Hey mister out of the truck keep your hands in sight mister, we are Beechum County sheriff deputies.

In that instant Sable is vanished. The woman is vanished, it's loud-talking men, men shouting commands, strangers in T-shirts yelling at him, impatient when he doesn't step out of the pickup quick enough, he's dazed, fumbling, confused looking for the beet-hair woman who was smiling at him, saying you ain't kiddin' me are yah? pullin' my leg are yah? blinking at flashlight beams shining into his face confused he's being shown shiny badges, Beechum County sheriff he's hearing, informed he is under arrest for soliciting an act of sex in violation of New York State law, under arrest he's on tape, keep your hands where we can see them mister, spread your legs Pops, y'hear you are UNDER ARREST, you been operatin' that vehicle while drinkin' Pops? He's con-fused thinking his picture is being taken. Flash going off in his face. Hey yah pullin' my leg are yah? he's more confused than frightened, more stunned than smitten with shame, like somebody out of nowhere has rushed up to him to shove him hard in the chest, spit in his face, knock him on his ass, these young T-shirt guys he's thinking might be bikers, doesn't know who in hell they are though they keep telling him he's under arrest there's this weird smile contorting the lower part of Pop's face like this has got to be a joke, nah this ain't real, ain't happening, he's clumsy resisting the officers, gonna have to cuff you Pops, hands behind your back Pops, under arrest Pops, blinking like a blind man staring at a sight he can't take in, tall burly young scruff-jaw guy in a black T-shirt—Drake McCracken?—he'd wanted to think was some nephew of his? in that instant Pop and Drake recognize each other, Drake is stunned like the old guy, sick stunned look in his face his sergeant sees the situation, understands the two are related, tells Drake back off, shift's over he can report back to the station. One of the deputies has cuffed the old man, poor old bastard is pouring sweat moving his head side to side like a panicked cow, his wallet has been taken from his back pocket, driver's license, I.D., name Hendrick Olafsson that's you? Sable is walking away shaking her beet-frizz hair, laughing and shaking her head, the smell in that truck! smell coming off the old man! Sable's undercover-hooker partner is cracking up over the old john, oldest john they've arrested on the Strip, poor bastard. Sable is saying some johns, the guys are psychos you can see. This old guy, he's more like disgusting. There's guys with strangler eyes. Guys with cocks like rubber mallets. Guys into biting. You can tell, there's johns any female would be crazy to climb into any vehicle with, drive off with, shows how desperate they are, junkie-hookers, asking to be murdered and dumped in a ditch and their kids confiscated by the state, Jesus it's hard to be sympathetic you mostly feel disgust.

Well, this old guy! Old-timey farmer. Not a biter for sure, you see those teeth?

POP IS TAKEN INTO CUSTODY, cuffed. Pop is transported in a van to the sheriff's headquarters on Route 29, Beechum County. Pop is booked. Pop's picture is taken. Pop is fingerprinted. Pop is one of seven "johns" arrested by Beechum County deputies on the Strip, night of July 19, 1972. Pop is fifty-seven, Pop is identified as Hendrick Olafsson, R.D.3, Herkimer, New York. Pop is confused and dazed and (maybe) has a minor stroke in the holding cell crowded with strangers. Pop calls my mother on the phone, it's 11:48 P.M. and she can't make sense of what he's saying. Where? Arrested? Pop? Drunk driving, is it? Accident? *Pop?* Pop is wheezing and whimpering begging Mom to come get him, he don't feel too good. (It will turn out, Pop couldn't remember his own telephone number at the farm, he'd had for thirty years. A female officer on duty looked it up for him.) It's a twelve-mile drive to the sheriff's headquarters over in Sparta. Mom calls me (where I'm living in town, now I work at the stone quarry west of Herkimer Falls) but I'm out. So Mom drives alone. Arrives around 1 A.M. Mom is disbelieving when the charge is read to her, soliciting sex, plus a charge of resisting arrest,

Mom insists her stepfather is not a man to solicit prostitutes, he must have thought the officer was hitch-hiking, Pop is the kind of man would give a hitch-hiker a ride, Mom is so agitated she repeats this until the desk sergeant cuts her off saying, Ma'am it's on tape, it's recorded. In the meantime Pop has been taken from the holding cell to rest on a cot. The cuffs are off, his wrists are raw and chafed and he's disoriented but he's okay, Mom is assured he's okay, doesn't want to be taken to a hospital, Mom will be allowed to speak with him and secure a lawyer for him if wished but she can't take him home just yet, bail hasn't been set, bail won't be set until after 9 A.M. next morning when a judge will set bail at the county courthouse and Mom can return then to take her stepfather home. All this, Mom can't take in. Mom is looking for her nephew Drake McCracken who's a Beechum County deputy but she's told Drake is off duty, nowhere on the premises. Mom is beginning to cry like Pop Olafsson is her own father not her stepfather, Mom is wiping tears from her eyes pleading Pop isn't a well man, Pop has high blood pressure, Pop takes heart pills, this will kill him Mom says, there has got to be some mistake let me talk to the arresting officers, my stepfather is not a man who solicits prostitutes! and the desk sergeant says, Ma'am, none of 'em ever are.

EVER AFTER THIS, Pop Olafsson's life is run down like an old truck can't make it uphill.

Nineteen days from the arrest, sixteen days from the front-page story HERKIMER FARMER, 57, ARRESTED IN "VICE" SWEEP ON RT. 33 STRIP and photo of Hendrick Olafsson in the *Herkimer Journal*, Pop's life runs down.

He's so ashamed, he won't show his face. Any vehicle drives up the lane, Pop skulks away like a kicked dog. He's dizzy, limping. Some blackouts he can't remember where in hell he is, wakes up in a mess of hay and manure and the cows bawling to be milked. He's drinking hard cider, whiskey in the morning. Heart pounds so he can't lie flat in bed, has to sit up through the night. Mom is disgusted with him she hardly speaks to him, leaves his meals on the back porch like he's one of the dogs. Other relatives who come around avoid Pop, too. I drove out to the farm, felt sorry for my mother but for the old man also he's so fucking pathetic. He's an embarrassment to me, too. God damn lucky my name is McCracken not Olafsson. At work the guys are ribbing me bad enough. Quarry workers, they're known for this. To a point, I can take it. Then I'll break somebody's face. My fist, somebody's face. Eye socket, cheekbone, nose, teeth. There's a feel when you break the bone, nothing can come near. Out back of the high school I punched out more than one guy's front teeth. Got me expelled, never graduated but it's one good thing I did, I feel good about remembering. Every scar in my face is worth it. At the house I asked Mom how it's going and Mom says see for yourself, he's out in the barn drinking. Mom's the one had to deal with Pop Olafsson at the court hearing over in Sparta, signed a check to the court for $350 fine, the old man pleaded guilty to the sex charge, "resisting arrest" was dropped, now he's on twelve-month probation a man of fifty-seven! Mom is feeling bad we haven't heard from Drake, you'd think Drake would come see us, at least call, say how sorry he is what happened to Pop. Like Drake stabbed us in the back, Mom says. His own family.

My feeling about Drake is so charged, I can't talk about it.

Located Pop out back of the silo looking like some broke-back old sick man trying to hide what he's drinking when he sees me like I don't know Pop drinks? this is news to me, Daryl? Why I'd come was to tell Pop how sorry I am what happened, what a lousy trick the fucking cops played on him, but somehow seeing the old man, that look in his face like somebody who's shit his pants, I hear myself say Hey Pop: don't take it too hard in this sarcastic voice like I'm fifteen not going on twenty-five. A few days later Pop blows off the top of his head with the clumsy old 12-gauge, came near to missing but got enough of his brain matter to kill him. It was like Pop to take himself out in a back pasture not in any inside space that would have to be cleaned afterward, and not near any stream that drained into the cows' drinking pond.

Pop left the dairy farm to my mother who never loved him. She felt real bad about it. I never loved the old guy either I guess but I missed him. For a long time I felt guilty how I'd spoken to him when he'd been in pain.

Soon as she could, Mom sold the property and moved to town.

Drake showed up at Pop's funeral, at least. The church part. At the back of the church where he wouldn't have to meet anybody's eye. He was wearing civilian clothes not the deputy uniform. Soon as the ceremony was ended, Drake was gone.

A WEEK after the funeral I'm at the Water Wheel with some guys from the quarry and there's my cousin Drake at the bar with some off-duty deputies. It's Friday night, crowded. But not so crowded we don't see each other. Two hours I'm waiting for my cousin to come over to say something to me, and he doesn't. And he's going to walk out not acknowledging me. And I'm waiting, it's like my heart is grinding slow and hard in waiting, like a fist getting tighter and tighter. It comes over me, Drake killed Pop Olafsson. Like he lifted the 12-gauge himself, aimed the barrels at Pop's head and fired. Drake and his rotten cop friends they'd sell their blood kin for a fucking paycheck. I'm thinking *He is a guilty man. He deserves some hurt.*

Even then, if Drake had come over to me, lay a hand on my shoulder and called me Daryl, I'd forgive him. For sure.

It's a few weeks later, I make my move. All this while I've been waiting. Past 11 P.M. when I drive to this place my cousin is renting in Sparta. For a while Drake had a girlfriend living there but looks like the girlfriend is moved out, this is what I've heard. Knock on the side door and Drake comes to see who it is, in just boxer shorts and T-shirt, and barefoot. Drake sees it's me, and lets me in. His eyes are wary. Right away he says, I know what you want, Daryl, and I say, Right: a cold beer. And Drake says, You want me to say I'm sorry for Pop, well I am. But nobody made Pop drive out to the Strip, see. I tell Drake, Fuck Pop. I'm thirsty, man. So Drake laughs and goes to the refrigerator and his back's turned and the claw hammer is in my hand, been carrying it in my jacket pocket for five, six days. I come up behind Drake and bring the hammer down hard on his head, must be the damn thing kind of slips my hand is so sweaty, it's just the side of Drake's head the hammer catches, and he's hurt, he's hurt bad, his knees are buckling but he isn't out, he's dangerous grabbing at me, and I'm shoving at him, and it's like we're two kids trying to get wrestling holds, and some damn way Drake is biting me, he's got my left forefinger between his teeth biting down hard as a pit bull. I'm yelling, this pain is so bad. I'm trying to get leverage to swing the hammer again but the pain in my finger is so bad, almost I'm fainting. Drake is bleeding from a deep cut in his head, a stream of bright blood running into his eye, he's panting his hot breath into my face, groaning, whimpering, a big hard-muscle bastard stinking of sweat from the shock of being hit, outweighs me by fifteen pounds, and desperate to save his life but I've got the hammer free to swing again, I manage to hit Drake on the back of his neck, another wide swing and the hammer gets him high on the skull, this time I feel bone crack. Drake's bulldog jaws open, Drake is on the floor and I'm swinging the hammer wild and hard as I can, hitting his face, forehead that's slippery in blood, his cheekbones, eye sockets, I'm walloping him for the evil in him fucking deputy sheriff betraying his own kind *Like this! like this! like this!* so at last his hard skull is broke like a melon, I can feel the hammer sink in to where there's something soft. Such a relief in this, the hammer goes wild swinging and swinging and when I come to, the linoleum floor is slippery in blood. There's blood on me, work trousers, work shoes, both hands wet with it, blood splattered high as the ceiling, and dripping. I'm stumbling over Drake on the floor twitching like there's electric current jolting him but feebler and feebler. Making this high keening sound like Pop Olafsson singing, so weird Drake has got to be about dead but making this high sharp lonesome sound it finally comes to me, is me, myself. Not Drake but me, Daryl, is making this sound.

Then I see, oh man my finger's about bit in two. One half hanging to the other by some gristle. I'm so pumped up I don't hardly feel the pain, what I need to do is yank the damn thing off, shove it in my pocket with the hammer, see I don't want to leave my fucking finger behind. I'm pumped up but I'm thinking, too. Then I want Drake's deputy badge, and his gun. Fucking brass badge my cousin sold his soul for and fucking .38-caliber Colt revolver in its holster, what I'm doing is confiscating the entire belt heavy as a leather harness.

Last thing I tell Drake is, you did this to yourself, man. Not me.

AIN'T PULLIN' my leg are yah?

These nights it's Pop Olafsson I'm missing. Weird how I hear Pop's voice like his nose is stopped up, thinking I am stone cold sober and awake but must've dozed off. Pop would blink them pale-blue pop-eyes at me seeing the age I am, the face I have now.

My left forefinger, ugly stub-finger, it's a reminder. People ask what happened and I tell them chain saw and they never ask further even my wife, she'd used to kiss the damn thing like it's some kind of test to her, can she accept it. A female will do the damnest things for you as long as they love you.

It's a fact there's "phantom pain." Weird but a kind of comfort like your finger is a whole finger, somewhere. Nothing of you is lost.

These nights I can't sleep, I need to prowl the house downstairs get-- ting a beer from the refrigerator, hanging out the back door staring at the sky. There's a moon, you think it's staring back at you. Some nights I can't hold back, like a magnet pulling me over to the garage. And in the garage I'm shining a flashlight into a toolbox under my workbench, rusted old tools and paint rags and at the bottom Drake McCracken's brass badge and .38-caliber Colt pistol that's a comfort, too. The claw hammer (that was Pop's hammer) covered in blood and brains sticking like fish guts I disposed of in the Chautauqua River with the holster belt, driving home that night. My bloody clothes, I buried deep in the marshy pasture where Pop killed himself.

Pop's banjo that came to me, I kept for twenty years then gave to my son Clayton, damn kid rightaway broke like he's broke about every fucking thing in his life.

All this is so long ago now, you'd think it would be forgotten. But people in Herkimer remember, of a certain age. I need to switch off the flashlight and get back to the house, such a mood comes over me here. This lonesome feeling I'd make a song of, if I knew how.

—————

THE STRANGENESS BEGAN shortly after his eighteenth birthday. A time when, he'd wanted to think, his life might be beginning to be more fully his own.

The new, veiled way in which people were looking at him. Or looking away from him.

Got to be imagining it. Weird!

Nothing about him had outwardly changed, he was sure. He'd been growing steadily since the age of twelve and he was now five feet ten, weighed approximately one-thirty-five, had to be normal, average for his age. Sometimes he cut himself shaving out of carelessness, but that didn't seem to be what anyone was looking at, or not-looking at. He wore his usual clothes: baggy khakis, long-sleeved black T-shirt, size eleven running shoes. In cold weather, he wore his purple school jacket emblazoned with bronze letters MT. OLIVE VARSITY TRACK, Army surplus combat boots. Much of the time he wore his Walkman, his mind was totally elsewhere. It came as something of a shock when he removed the headphones and the heavy throbbing music faded, the way the world, which was a world of adults, a world designed and controlled by adults, rolled in over him like an avalanche.

It wasn't Danny's friends and classmates who behaved strangely with him, only just adults. And not all adults, only a few. His foster parents the Stampfels—"Ed" and "Em" they wanted to be called. Two or three of his teachers at Mt. Olive High. The track team coach Hal Diedrich. The principal Mr. Bernard and the faculty advisor to the student newspaper Mr. Fackler. And there was Mrs. Jameson, the guidance counsellor.

He thought he'd known Mrs. Jameson. Thought she'd known him.

Two years before when Danny Neuworth had been a sophomore, a new transfer to Mt. Olive High, he'd had a difficult time adjusting, he'd been lonely yet not very sociable, poorly motivated in his studies yet anxious about grades, and so he'd been referred to Mrs. Jameson who let him talk without interrupting him, asked him questions that showed she was sympathetic, genuinely interested in him, and so he'd come to trust her, she'd given him good advice he'd tried to follow, but now, so strangely, in November of his senior year when Danny was considering where to apply to college, eager for advice and encouragement, Mrs. Jameson answered his questions in a distracted manner, smiling faintly in his direction without seeming to see him. Opened before her on her desk was a manila file inscribed, in stark black ink, NEUWORTH, DANIEL S. '05. "CONFIDENTIAL."

When he'd first entered Mrs. Jameson's office, she'd been frowning at a document in the file. Glancing up at him then with a look—that look—veiled, startled—"Oh, Danny. Come in." Their conversation had been stiff, awkward. If he hadn't known better, Danny would have thought that the guidance counsellor didn't know him at all. Finally he asked if there was something in his file—"I guess you couldn't tell me, huh?" Mrs. Jameson said quickly, "There's nothing wrong, Danny. Of course. What could be wrong." A deep flush rose into her face. Her voice was oddly flat, toneless.

Danny had friends who'd conferred with the guidance counsellor, whose grades were no better than his, and they'd come away with lists of colleges to apply to, even catalogues and brochures, but Mrs. Jameson didn't seem to have any ideas for him. He said he'd like to study mechanical engineering, maybe. His foster father Ed Stampfel had thought that might work for him. Mrs. Jameson said vaguely yes, that might work for him. "If you have the math. It requires math, you know." Repeatedly Mrs. Jameson blew her nose in a tissue, apologizing for "sinus allergies." Out of a crammed bookshelf she pulled dog-eared catalogues for regional New Jersey colleges—Warren County, Cape May, Hunterdon Community, Rutgers-Camden. "Maybe one of these. Let's see."

Strange, Mrs. Jameson wasn't meeting his eye. Wasn't calling him Danny as she'd used to.

Adults! You couldn't figure them.

Since he'd started kindergarten Danny's teachers had encouraged him, presumably knowing of his foster-home background. Pursue your goals, follow your dream, everyone in America is special, you have only to be *you*. Now when he needed encouragement and advice, Mrs. Jameson couldn't seem to think of anything to tell him. Her sleek slender laptop was opened on her desk and in the lenses of her glasses he saw a faint reflection of mysterious darting movements on the screen, like secret thoughts.

Something in my file. That must be it.

Yet, what could it be? He'd never gotten into trouble at school, or anywhere else. He'd been a sulky kid for a while in high school but had come out of it gradually and became an earnest, diligent if not very imaginative student. In easy subjects like communication arts, social studies, health and fitness he'd earned A–'s but mostly his grades hovered at B–/C+ no matter how hard he worked. He had a small circle of friends, mostly guys like himself. In his senior year at last he'd made the varsity track team by driving himself mercilessly and earning the respect of Coach Diedrich for his effort if not for his actual accomplishments ("Not every guy can be a star, Danny. You're a team player"). His only distinction was, since the second semester of his sophomore year, *Neuworth, Daniel* had been listed on the Mt. Olive Good Citizenship Roster, initiated by the school district to boost morale by "honoring" those students who attended classes regularly, did their school work and caused no trouble. Too bad, the distinction had become a joke since so many names were listed.

Belatedly, in the way of a coach giving a pep talk to a paraplegic athlete, Mrs. Jameson had begun to extol the virtues of small colleges, technical schools, how much more suitable for some students than universities let alone the "prestigious" Ivy League universities which in her opinion were "undemocratic and overrated." Mrs. Jameson was speaking now with a strange vehemence as if someone had dared to argue with her, an invisible presence in her office toward whom she felt animosity. Danny listened uneasily. He saw a thin blade of sunshine ease upon the framed diplomas on the wall behind Mrs. Jameson's desk: her master's degree was in education and psychology from Rutgers-Newark.

Rutgers-Newark! No wonder Mrs. Jameson was so contemptuous of "prestigious" schools.

When Mrs. Jameson fell silent, blowing her nose, Danny reverted to the subject of his file: "I guess there must be something bad in it, right?" and Mrs. Jameson said quickly, with a frown, "No, not at all, Danny. Everything is fine."

"Not so great, not outstanding, but 'fine.' " Danny smiled to show that he understood. Mrs. Jameson said, dabbing at her eyes with a tissue, like a mother gently rebuking a child, "Not everyone can be outstanding, Danny. In our American republic everyone is created 'equal' but only politically—as citizens. Not in other respects. At your age, you must know that."

Danny nodded yes, he knew. How could he not know!

"Not many of us in Mt. Olive are 'outstanding,' I can assure you. Or we wouldn't be here, you see." This was meant to be lightly playful, provocative. But something in Mrs. Jameson's face seemed to crack. Clumsily she rose from behind her desk, a fleshy middle-aged woman with a flushed face, saying, "I think I have—in the outer office—a brochure for—I'm not sure. Excuse me."

The guidance counsellor left her office, pointedly shutting the door behind her. Danny was baffled: was she leaving him alone with his file, was she giving him the opportunity to look into it? Or was he misinterpreting the gesture? Was he being videotaped? Was he making a terrible mistake?

He listened for her footsteps, returning. His heart began to pound with excitement as, leaning over Mrs. Jameson's desk, he tried to read upside down the document lying on top of the manila file. Not hearing footsteps, he dared to go behind the desk to peer at an email document with the letterhead *BIOTECHINC* at the top and NEUWORTH, DANIEL S. *BD*11 1 87 heading a page-long column of densely printed information that appeared to be a mix of scientific terms and mathematical symbols, incomprehensible to him. Danny had to suppose that this was codified data having to do with his grades at Mt. Olive High, the results of the numerous tests—I.Q., "cognitive," "psychological"—he'd taken over the years. His ranking in his class, possibly statewide, even nationwide, was probably indicated, too. At the very bottom of the page was a mysterious numeral of a dozen digits followed by a blank space and *BD* 11 1 87–6 21 05.

What "BD" meant, Danny didn't know. But 11/1/87 was his birthday and, it took him a moment to recall, 6/21/05 was the date of his high school graduation.

They expected him to graduate, then. This was good news!

There had to be something more in the file, that had so distracted Mrs. Jameson. Teachers' confidential reports on Danny Neuworth. Information about him he wasn't allowed to know, beyond the blandly positive remarks invariably noted on his report cards: "Danny works hard"—"Danny is cooperative"—"Danny is promising"—"Danny is reliable." But Mrs. Jameson would be returning, Danny couldn't risk looking further.

He was sitting very still in the chair facing Mrs. Jameson's desk when she re-entered the room briskly. She didn't appear so distracted now. Her face wasn't so flushed, as if she'd dabbed cold water onto it. She had catalogues for Danny to take away with him: "Stockton State, Glassboro State, Atlantic Cape College. Tuition is low for state residents and these colleges don't demand high SAT scores." Danny took the catalogues from her, gratefully. Maybe Mrs. Jameson liked him after all.

As he prepared to leave, the guidance counsellor called after him as if this were an old joke between them, "Remember, Danny: you have only to be *you*."

THIS STRANGENESS. Like invisible odorless gas seeping into his life in the fall, winter, spring of his senior year.

When he'd thought that, nearing graduation, he had a right to feel good about the future.

After Mrs. Jameson's perplexing behavior there was Coach Diedrich who became embarrassed and uneasy when Danny asked if he would write letters of recommendation for him, laying a hand on Danny's shoulder with the warning not to be disappointed if he didn't get accepted—" 'The race is not always to the swift.' " (What did that mean? No one had ever suggested that Danny Neuworth was the swiftest runner on the track team.) There was Ms. Beckman, Danny's history teacher, who gazed at him for a long startled moment as if trying to recall who he was, finally agreeing that yes, she would recommend him for college if he applied to regional state schools. There was Mr. Fackler who'd often encouraged Danny as a reporter on the school newspaper, who smiled strangely at Danny, sighed and said yes, he supposed he could recommend him—"If you really want to go to college." (What the hell was the alternative? Danny wondered. A job at McDonald's, Home Depot, Wal-Mart at the minimum wage? Enlisting in the U.S. Army and getting his legs blown off in an Iraqi desert?) And there was Mr. Lasky, Danny's biology teacher, who shut his eyes shaking his head slowly as if Danny's request was beyond him. Lasky was a teacher known for favoring only a few brainy students with what he called "natural genes" for science. "Hey, I know my grades aren't the highest," Danny said, trying to smile, though his heart beat with resentment, "but colleges want to know about other things, too—how hard a person works, 'good citizenship' and like that." In fact, Danny's grades in biology were B-/C+ and he felt that he was learning a lot and that he'd thought that Lasky knew this, and liked him. On a school expedition to BioCorpLabs in Princeton, Danny Neuworth had been one of the few guys who hadn't cracked up at the sight of some of the "donor animals" the class was shown on a guided tour, in their clean, fluorescent-lighted cages: a normal-sized but immobile gray mouse sprouting a human ear out of its back, like a grotesque tumor; a glum-looking baboon sprouting several human noses out of its face; chimpanzees sprouting human fingers and toes instead of chimp-fingers and toes; a dozen sheep genetically altered to allow human embryos to gestate in their wombs, all in their eighth month of pregnancy; enormous hogs altered to grow human hearts, lungs, livers, kidneys, even eyeballs of which they would be "harvested" to benefit needy human beings. Danny had been struck by the sadness in the animals' eyes as if, though lacking language, they did not lack the intelligence to guess at their fates, but he was canny enough not to include such a naive unscientific observation in his report, only to stick to the facts. Lasky had given him a B on the paper and scrawled *Good work!* in red ink but Lasky seemed now to have forgotten, confounded by Danny's request for letters of recommendation. The biology teacher had removed his glasses and was rubbing his watery eyes with the fingers of both hands as if he'd become very tired. Murmuring what sounded like " 'Good citizenship' we can do for you, Danny. The least we can do."

Bastard! Danny thanked him, and went away shaking with anger.

"THEY DON'T HAVE any hope for me. They don't like me."

It couldn't be true. Yet, it seemed to be true.

Danny's friends, with whom he shared some of his misgivings, said he had to be imagining it, why'd anybody turn against *him?*—"You're just not that special, Danny. C'mon." It didn't reassure him that not one of his friends, even the messed-up guys, seemed to be getting such signals from the adults in their lives; he'd have liked it if everyone he knew, everyone his age, every senior in the Mt. Olive Class of 2005, was having the same weird experience with the same weird adults.

All that had happened was, Danny had turned eighteen. But so had half the senior class. And how would most of his teachers have known, or cared? And why? Officially, Daniel Neuworth was no longer a minor; no longer a ward of the State of New Jersey; though provisions had been made by Passaic County Family Services to allow him to continue to live with the Stampfels until he graduated from high school, began his summer job, and was able to support himself. Beyond that, Danny hoped to be going away to college.

Except now, he wasn't so sure. He had to wonder what kind of letters of recommendation his teachers were writing for him. Had to wonder what was in the confidential file locked away in the principal's office.

Even his foster parents Ed and Em Stampfel who'd always seemed to favor Danny over the others in their crowded, noisy household no longer seemed as relaxed with Danny as they'd been. Their smiles were fleeting, their manner with him was jovial but strained. The Stampfels were not individuals of subtlety or sensitivity but a burly ruddy-faced husband-and-wife team who'd been foster parents to generations of luckless parentless children under the auspices of the New Jersey State Children's Welfare Agency; Ed Stampfel was a part-time prison guard at the Passaic County Men's Correctional Facility and Em had been a kitchen worker there before she'd married Ed. Between the Stampfels they weighed in the vicinity of three-fifty to four hundred pounds. Their usual mode of speech was shouting. Yet from time to time Danny caught the Stampfels looking at him in a way difficult to define. *Like they feel sorry for me. Like there's something in my face they see, I can't.* Ed had praised Danny for making the varsity track team but hadn't been very sympathetic with Danny when it soon emerged that Danny wouldn't be one of the team stars. So what if he rarely won a race, there's plenty of other guys slower than you, Ed argued, even if a few are faster. Danny's grades were only just average—well, slightly better than average—and slightly-better-than-average is a hell of a lot better than slightly-lower-than-average let alone flunking. Ed Stampfel's homegrown wisdom was: "There's always plenty sonsabitches worse off than you, kid. Keep in mind you could trade places with them any time."

This was meant to be a cheering thought. Ed Stampfel was what he called a "practicing optimist."

The Stampfels liked kids, most of the time. Different skin colors, races. Different personality types. It had seemed that they'd favored Danny but he had to suppose they'd favored others, numerous others, over the years. On a cork bulletin board in the kitchen were snapshots of boys and girls who'd lived with the Stampfels before being adopted into "real" families or growing up and going out into the world, too many snapshots to count, in layers like rock strata, curling, yellowed like artifacts from a previous century. When Danny graduated out into the world, his snapshot would be tacked on the board, covering an older snapshot. The Stampfels were good-natured and often kind but they weren't sentimental. Processing kids into and out of their lives was like clipping toenails. As soon as a resident left the household, his bed was stripped, any "personal effects" left behind were dumped into the trash. A few days later if you asked Ed or Em about him you'd be likely to be greeted with a blank stare: "Who? Nobody here by that name."

Sometimes Ed winked to signal *Hey: just joking.*

Sometimes, not.

BEFORE THE STAMPFELS in Mt. Olive, New Jersey, Danny had lived in a smaller household with the Hursts, Will and Martine, in Kittitany. He'd been younger then and hadn't yet grown to his current height nor had he acquired his runner's lean hard-muscled physique and "perfect" physical condition. (One thing Danny could be happy for, he was in excellent physical condition: heart, lungs, blood, etc. As a ward of the State of New Jersey, he was examined by a physician for Family Services annually, like clockwork.) He'd been close to Martine Hurst, who'd broken his heart by informing him, just before his sixteenth birthday, that she and Will were "retiring"—leaving New Jersey to live in St. Petersburg, Florida. Seeing the look in Danny's face, Martine quickly assured him that he, like the other foster children in the household, would be provided for, placed with "wonderful, devoted foster parents" in Mt. Olive, less than forty miles away. Of course it would mean transferring to another school, being "temporarily uprooted." When Danny began to cry, Martine drew back. She seemed fearful of touching him or of being touched by him, as if something in Danny had wounded her. *It's me. She can't stand to see me.*

So the strangeness had begun, really. Years before.

He'd been living with the Hursts since the age of eight. He'd been told that the identity of his "birth mother"—his "biological mother"— was unknown. The circumstances of his birth were unknown. As a day-old infant he'd been found in a municipal building in Newark. It was Martine's belief that Danny's mother had been a young, terrified girl who'd left him in a public place in order to be found, and saved. In Martine's voice the account had the air of a fairy tale. Danny said, as if pleading, "I don't care about her, I care about *you*. You're my real mother." It made him anxious to be told about his very young self, before he'd had consciousness or memory. Whoever his parents were, they'd abandoned him. But the Hursts would abandon him, too.

Before the Hursts, he'd lived in a group home in Newark. His memory of those years was clouded. The singular fact of Danny's early life was he hadn't been adopted. Other children in the Newark home were adopted, even children with disabilities, but Danny Neuworth had not been adopted. He seemed to recall that he hadn't even been interviewed by prospective parents. "Why not me? What's wrong with me?" he'd asked repeatedly. No explanation had been given. At the time he'd supposed the reason had to do with him, in subsequent years he would ponder the strangeness of it. There were several other children in the facility who, like Danny, hadn't been available for adoption. These were boys, Danny's age and size. In fact, Danny learned they had one thing in common: their birthdays.

Jimmy, Bobby, Frankie, Mikey. They'd been like brothers to Danny. But long ago, Danny could scarcely remember. After Newark they'd been placed in different foster homes in New Jersey. Danny had rarely given them a thought in the intervening years. Except now, this strangeness entering his life, making him think strange thoughts, he had to wonder where they'd ended up, where they'd gone to school, what their prospects were for the future.

———

"WELL, Danny. Here is good news."

Mr. Bernard's voice quavered with emotion. After months of seeming not to see Danny, staring through Danny with a vague fixed smile if they happened to pass each other in the school corridor, the principal of Mt. Olive High summoned Danny into his office to inform him that he'd been named a recipient of a Good Citizenship Scholarship to enable

him to attend any college to which he'd been admitted, even provision-
ally. "Congratulations, son. You'll be Mt. Olive's only 'Good Citizen
Scholar' at graduation."

" 'Good Citizen Scholar? *Me?*"

Danny stared at the smiling middle-aged man who held out a hand
to him, to be shaken. Weird! This had to be the weirdest development
yet: shaking Mr. Bernard's hand.

Not one of the state colleges and technical schools to which Danny
had applied had accepted him outright but several had granted him
"provisional" status, meaning his application would have to be supple-
mented by an additional transcript listing his grades for the final se-
mester of his senior year. Honors and awards at the time of graduation
would count in his favor, too. Now Mr. Bernard was explaining that
the Good Citizen Scholarship would cover Danny's tuition, room and
board, even travel expenses. "It's a new program, only funded for the
past two years by a private sponsor. The aim is to honor young citizens
like you, Danny, whose school records don't fully represent the 'quality
of spiritual being.' "

Mr. Bernard was speaking rapidly, as if reciting prepared words. He
smiled at Danny in the tense and oddly animated way he smiled into the
audience at school assemblies, calling for attention from three hundred
restless teenagers. His bifocal glasses winked with a kind of febrile
excitement Danny understood he was expected to share. He'd become
breathless with this good news, the very floor seemed to be tilting be-
neath his feet. He, Danny Neuworth, singled out for an honor for the
first time in his life. Such good news! Yet somehow difficult to believe.

As if reading his thoughts, Mr. Bernard said, "I can't give you this
document, Danny, since it's addressed to me as your principal. But I can
allow you to peruse it."

Danny took from him a sheet of stiff cream-colored paper with
the embossed bronze letterhead *BIOTECHINC* informing Henry
Bernard, Principal of Mt. Olive High, Mt. Olive, New Jersey, that NEU-
WORTH, DANIEL S. was one of fifty recipients of the 2005 Good Citizen-
ship Scholarship in New Jersey. "A news release will be made just before
graduation, Danny. But you may inform the college you'd like to attend,

for certainly you'll be accepted now. Such very good news, Danny! Again, congratulations. We are very proud of you, son."

Danny went away stunned. He'd expected a different sort of reception in the principal's office. Since the strangeness had entered his life, the past several months hadn't been very happy. He'd become reconciled to not going to college. He'd drifted away from his small circle of friends, resenting their talk of college acceptances and their ease in contemplating the future. He'd overheard Ed and Em discussing the "new boy" who'd be moving into their household in mid-June, obviously to take Danny's place. Now within the space of a few minutes, like a sudden turn in a fairy tale, everything was changed. Now, he'd been singled out for an honor. Mr. Bernard had shaken his hand. Mr. Bernard had called him *son*.

BIOTECHINC he'd seen somewhere before but where, couldn't remember. *BIOTECHINC* glowing in his brain like the after-image of a very bright star. *BIOTECHINC* powerful as a sonic boom.

Where, couldn't remember.

FOLLOWING MR. BERNARD'S NEWS, things happened swiftly for Danny Neuworth.

He completed his spring courses, took final exams and passed each. His final average was B–/C+. By graduation, he hadn't decided which college to attend: Glassboro State, or Stockton. He'd been accepted at both.

"Danny, sure you're special. *I* knew."

One of the girls in Danny's graduating class, who'd been only casually friendly with him previously. And now!

These final weeks. Anticipating graduation and the start of a new life. Weeks, days, hours passing in a kind of delirium. Time felt accelerated, not entirely real. Continuously Danny stopped short having to realize he'd been singled out for an honor, he'd become privileged. He was still Danny Neuworth but someone more. Needing to see himself not as the sad-hearted boy nobody wanted to adopt but the eighteen-year-old Good Citizen selected for a special destiny.

(Maybe it was a sign of privilege, you didn't really feel very different? Look in the mirror, you're still just *you*?)

Two days before graduation, Danny was required to have another physical examination, in the office of a Mt. Olive internist who was a medical consultant for *BIOTECHINC*. It was the most painstaking exam Danny had ever endured, involving hours of X-rays, cardiology tests, blood-drawing, internal probes of a kind he'd only imagined with a shudder. The doctor seemed impressed. "Doesn't surprise me you're a runner, son. Your heartbeat is slow, and strong. Your lungs are in excellent condition. Your blood pressure." Smiling, the doctor shook hands with Danny: "Your foster parents must have taken good care of you." It seemed an odd thing to say, but Danny thanked the man.

What he liked least about the experience was being photographed in the nude, front, back, sides. "For *BIOTECHINC* archives exclusively, Danny. 'Confidential.' "

" 'NEUWORTH, Daniel S.?' Come with me."

On the morning of graduation, Danny arrived early at the high school as he'd been directed, but, instead of entering the school gymnasium to be given his black cap and gown with his classmates, he was escorted by a uniformed security guard to a small yellow bus waiting in the parking lot. The bus had dark-tinted windows and was marked PRIVATE. A *BIOTECHINC* representative cordially explained that recipients of Good Citizen scholarships were to be honored at a more important ceremony elsewhere, to be televised over public service TV and to involve, in a five-minute taped segment, personal congratulations from the President of the United States whose administration had supported private-factor scientific research efforts likes those of *BIOTECHINC.* Though he supposed it was a foolish question under the circumstances, Danny asked, "But won't I be graduating with everyone else? Won't I get a diploma?" and the *BIOTECHINC* rep, a middle-aged woman with a radiant smile, said, "Why Danny, of course. Everything your classmates will receive you will receive, except more."

The small, smartly gleaming yellow bus, which held seats for only twelve passengers, was already two-thirds filled with Good Citizen recipients from neighboring townships, most of them boys. Danny took a seat beside a boy from Lake Isle High, a school Mt. Olive had competed against in track, sometimes winning, sometimes losing, but the boy admitted to not having paid much attention to sports. Though Danny had never seen the boy before, he was reminded of someone he knew, or had once known: Frankie, from the Newark foster home? Or—had it been Jimmy?

The bus made several more stops on its three-hour journey to central northern New Jersey on route 23, outside Hardyston. Here, in an enormous hilly parkland of hundreds of acres, protected by ten-foot electrified fences, was *BIOTECHINC* headquarters. The bus pulled up behind a building and its occupants filed out. Close by, another small bus was unloading its passengers, and Danny saw one of them, a tall lanky boy with a familiar face, tentatively raising a hand to wave to him—"Hey Danny: is that you?" But *BIOTECHINC* reps, smiling cordially, urged the boys on.

Jimmy! That boy was Jimmy. Danny had had time for only a glimpse, but he was sure it was so.

" 'Neuworth, Daniel S.?' Come with me."

Once inside the chill, air-conditioned building, which had the sterile look and disinfectant-odor of a hospital, Danny was sorry to be separated from his fellow Good Citizen scholars, and brought into a small windowless cubicle with one glass wall, opaque like the lead backing of a mirror; Danny had the uneasy sensation that the glass was one-way, and that he was being observed. Fluorescent tubing cast a strong shadowless light downward. His heart had begun to beat in childish apprehension as it had when he'd been summoned to Mr. Bernard's office the previous month. The cubicle walls were covered in thick spongy squares like soundproofing. In the center of the cell-like space was what appeared to be a physician's examination table, with stirrups, and close by a small aluminum table and a single vinyl chair. The humming of an air ventilator mixed with the beating of pulses in Danny's head. Thoughts came flying at him like alarmed birds: though he'd mailed a card to Martine Hurst notifying her of his good news, he worried that Martine might not receive it, for it was the Stampfels who'd given him Martine's address in

St. Petersburg and could he trust them? For already they were forget-
ting him, he knew. For already another "foster son" was moving into
Danny's room.

Danny was thinking, almost he'd have given up the distinction of
the Good Citizenship Scholarship, if he'd known how homesick he
would be for Mt. Olive. He'd been taken from the high school park-
ing lot only a few hours ago but time was so strangely accelerating in
his life now, it seemed like days. Soon, it would seem like weeks. More
painful yet, Danny had missed his high school graduation. He'd always
felt like something of an outsider at the school yet, in the final weeks
of his senior year, he'd become more popular suddenly, and had been
invited to several graduation parties this weekend. He wondered if
anyone had missed him at commencement. If his name had been called,
and the Good Citizenship award announced. If the audience had burst
into applause.

Abruptly the door to the cubicle opened, and a burly young man in
a white lab coat and cord trousers, a light-skinned black in his late twen-
ties or early thirties with deep-set ironic eyes, stepped inside. He was
taller than Danny and heavier by perhaps thirty pounds. On his lapel
was a plastic I.D. with an unsmiling photo and the single word CALE.
He was carrying a clipboard and his mood was harassed, sullen. "Sooo
'Dennie.' No: 'Danny.' Birth date 11/1/87. Status 'BD.' " These remarks
were uttered in a rapid voice, not questioning but stating. Before Danny
could reply, Cale urged him to sit at the end of the examination table
while he adjusted a stethoscope around his neck and listened to Danny's
heartbeat. Next, he wound a blood-pressure cuff around Danny's upper
left arm, tight. Danny protested faintly, but Cale prevailed. The young
intern or attendant loomed over him breathing huskily through wide,
very dark nostrils in a blunt snubbed nose. On his sturdy left forearm
was a small but striking tattoo in bronze: *BIOTECHINC* 75.

Danny asked, why was he being examined? Where was the TV cer-
emony? He was beginning to be frightened. Cale was making notations
on his clipboard, irritably. It was clear that, whatever Cale's job was, he
wasn't in a good mood.

" 'BD.' 'Body donor.' That's why you've been brought to our Hardyston headquarters."

" 'Body donor'? What's . . . that?"

"A 'body donor' is a specimen who has been conceived, born, and cultivated for harvest. Your body was contracted for by a client of *BIOTECHINC*. Presumably a male, whose brain will be transplanted into your head and attached to, well—the body that comes with it."

Danny smiled uncertainly. What was this? He understood that Cale was joking, the deadpan expression would dissolve with laughter in another moment.

There were guys at Mt. Olive High like Cale. Big guys who said wild things, insulting things, punched you on the upper arm, ran their knuckles over your head and called you dude, only just kidding around, joking. You had to show that you could take it, then they'd accept you. Danny wasn't exactly friends with these guys but they liked him, he thought. In their crude way, they respected him as an athlete.

Cale said carelessly, "This is high-tech science, it won't hurt. You'll be put to sleep by a colorless odorless gas. It's one-hundred-percent humane. It's been tested in *BIOTECHINC* labs globally. I'm not supposed to clue you in but what the hell, why not. The client is on the other side of that glass." With a derisive wave, Cale indicated the plate-glass wall. His dark skin glowed with a fierce smoldering heat. Danny had to wonder if the man was high on a drug: methamphetamine? Danny had seen guys on this drug, the pinprick-pupils in their eyes and their air of pit bull aggression. In proximity to someone on meth you could feel your heartbeat accelerate with his. "You've got a great body, kid. Lean and hard-muscled but no steroids, no bodybuilding, just the classic-American-boy body. Eighteen is the optimum age. There's a great crop of you, born '87. A world-class neurosurgeon will saw open your skull, remove your brain and insert the client's. I'm guessing he's an old fart who claims to feel eighteen 'in his heart.' Or, he's terminally ill in his worn-out crap body. Or, he's just turned fifty, megamillionaire getting paunchy and his reflexes slow, losing his hair, his wind, and can't depend upon his dick. *Your* dick, that's worth the $1.8 million just by itself. Client wants a new body and if he can afford it who can blame him? Hey man, not me."

All this while Cale was standing uncomfortably close to Danny, breathing on him. His dark hair was rough-rippled and nappy as if it had been shellacked. The bones of his large heavy head seemed to push tight against the singed-looking skin, outlining the eye sockets so that the eyes were recessed, glistening with angry mirth. Danny laughed feebly. It was like one of these guys to say outrageous things and push close, in your face practically, daring you to back off. You didn't expect it from an older guy, especially not someone in a position of responsibility. "Know what, Danny: I'm going to take a blood pressure reading again. It was a little high, I'm thinking. You breathe in, breathe out, relax. Like I say, and CALE is programmed not to lie, you will not feel any pain when the procedure begins. Your days of pain are finished. That's good news, eh?"

"You're kidding, right? What's actually happening here? This is some kind of joke?"

"Kind of a joke, yes." Cale squinted at the instruction sheet on his clipboard. "I guess you could say so. 'Good Citizen.' 'Birth mother unknown.' See, it isn't as if your body was ever yours, Danny. You were planned, engineered, copyright *BIOTECHINC* just like me."

Birth mother? What had Cale said?

Danny wasn't comprehending much of this. His face was frozen in a perplexed smile. Though maybe, in a way yes he was comprehending for there was something here that made sense, Mr. Lasky would be nodding and encouraging Danny. Engineering, made-to-be-harvested, "donor." Yet Danny was thinking of course this was a joke, in a minute Cale would relent and tell him what all this was about. (The Good Citizen scholars were being subjected to a kind of initiation rite? Their reactions were being televised by hidden cameras?)

Danny said, "What, you're saying, if it was so, it would be murder. There are laws against murder."

"No. You and your siblings are the property of *BIOTECHINC* and not independent entities. Without *BIOTECHINC* you'd never have been born. You've had eighteen years, Danny, and more. That's a hell of a lot longer than many millions of human beings who've ever lived. Now your brain will be shut down, as planned. Deprived of oxygen, it will simply fade out. I've been promised the same myself, only I don't know when. My contract is renewable. *They* renew me if my services are wanted. But you, Danny, your body will survive for decades. As a body donor, you're one of the elite."

Danny shivered. In the distance, there was a sound as of amplified voices, or muffled thunder. He laughed, this was so weird! His throat was sore with laughing. "O.K., I get it you're joking? This is some kind of weird initiation and people are laughing at me on TV?"

Cale said, relenting, "Sure, Danny. I'm joking. That's my job here, to joke. Prep you for TV. Next thing, you'll want to lie on this table, just relax, stretch your legs and the makeup girl will be coming in. On TV, your natural skin tone bleaches out. Guys don't like makeup on their faces but believe me, you need it. Even you." Cale lay a warm, consoling hand on Danny's shoulder. In that instant Danny felt comforted. *Cale likes me, Cale is my friend.*

It would be that Danny Neuworth was on TV. A taped segment to be broadcast on channel thirteen. Not many people Danny knew watched channel thirteen, the PBS station, and that was disappointing, but the Hursts might catch it, and somebody in Mt. Olive who knew him might watch, and speak of it to Danny's friends, and to the Stampfels. That was one way it might be but a second way, which was beginning to be exciting to contemplate, was that Cale would defy his *BIOTECHINC* employers and help Danny escape from the compound into the hills of north central New Jersey.

In the distance, a sound like a buzzer was ringing. Cale turned to leave. His expression was less belligerent now. His dark glistening eyes skidded onto Danny in a way that reminded Danny of Mrs. Jameson and the other adults looking at him, not-looking-at-him, as if the sight of Danny was searing in their vision and they had to protect themselves from him. "You're a nice kid, Danny. All of you are. Congratulations."

Cale didn't offer a hand to shake. Before Danny could thank him he was gone, the door shut and locked behind him.

Danny cried, "Hey wait! How long . . ."

Danny could hear air hissing into the cubicle. A high thin whistling noise of a different texture than the air-conditioning. He was anxious, shivering. A tinge of nausea of the kind he felt before a race but it was a fact: some of the best runners on the team, like the best swimmers on the swim team, threw up before their races. That was nothing to be ashamed of, Coach said. You could make a joke of it, almost. Danny would make a joke about this experience when he saw his teammates again. When he saw his friends again back in Mt. Olive. He was trembling with cold but beginning to feel less anxious. He sat on the edge of the examination table as Cale had suggested, and stretched out. He had missed his own graduation, that was a loss. But news of his Good Citizenship award would be on TV and in the local papers. And in the St. Petersburg paper. Ed and Em had been proud of him for winning the scholarship, they'd put his picture on the bulletin board.

He wondered how much they'd known about—what was the name?—*BIOTECHINC*. Whether they were contracted, too. And his previous foster parents.

He smiled to think there'd always been a plan, a purpose. He had not known that. Thoughts came now in slow rippling streams. He placed his feet in the stirrups at the end of the table. They were made of sturdy metal, and held when he pushed against them. It was like pushing off when the practice gun was fired. One-two-three: *go*. Coach was smiling at him. It was so, Coach was proud of Danny. His eyelids were heavy. He covered his eyes with his forearm, to shield them from the fluorescent lights. On the far side of the glass wall invisible to him someone was observing him. Someone was waiting for him. He had never been alone, evidently. All his life he'd never been alone. And now he was going to be adopted. This time, someone would choose him. A voice warm and comforting in his ear. *Danny?*

FAT MAN MY LOVE

———

HE WAS OBESE. He was a fantasist. He was a fetishist. He was a perfectionist. He was a prince. He was a toad. He was a prince born mistakenly as a toad. He was in fact born British. He was a very proud Brit. Though, in time, an American citizen, yet a Brit. He was a "devout" Catholic. He was one who wished revenge. He was one who feared Hell. He was a genius. He was a giant fetus. He was a genius in the form of a giant fetus. He was a smirk. He was an appetite. He was a mouth-hole. He was a maze of guts. He was a giant anus. His (hairless) head was Humpty Dumpty's head before the Fall. His head was filled with dreams. His head was filled with such dreams! He was a virgin-boy for a long time. He was his mother's plump-virgin-boy for a long time. His face was a pious face. His face was congealed grease drippings. His face was a droll jowly smile. His skin was toad-belly white. His eyes were toad-eyes. His eyes were shy-boy eyes. He was very ugly. He was very ugly but very dapper. He was one to wear a good Brit suit. He was one to wear a good dark Brit suit, starched white dress shirt, necktie of a conservative type. He was one to sweat inside his clothes. He was one to scratch at his crotch, in furious yearning. Ah, he was angry! He was a Prince of Rage. His eyes were not shy-boy eyes but raptor eyes. His eyes were hooded eyes. His eyes were hypnotist-eyes. His eyes were X-ray eyes. On the film set (utterly silent, by his decree) his eyes were the eyes of God who has seen all, and need now only remember. His peephole eye, too, was the eye of God. *In our love nest (as in his droll Brit way he wished to call it) he preferred to observe me through the peephole than directly, as lost in blond reverie I slowly, very slowly removed my white satin lacy-conical-breasted Maidenform Bra.* He favored strangulation. He favored ice blondes. He knew how to get their attention.

FAT MAN, a quarter-century dead! Yet still I fear the peephole eye.

WAS HE VERY UGLY, yes very ugly but a very dapper ugly man of power. Was he nice, nooooo not very nice but a very dapper very ugly man of power. Was he a zombie Buddha, yes he was a zombie Buddha but a zombie Buddha of power. Was he cruel, yes he was cruel but was he witty in his cruelty, was he inspired in his cruelty, was he selective in his cruelty (his victims subordinates, underlings), yes for he was one who knew the script. Very few of us (Pippi, certainly!) know the script, but he was one who knew the script. He was one who had memorized the script. He was one who had dreamt the script. He was one who directed the script. He was one who cast the movie choosing *You, and you, but not you, and not you.* He was not one who believed in God. He was one who believed in the Holy Roman Catholic Apostolic Church. He was one to believe in evil. He was one to believe in Hell, damnation. He believed in torture. He believed in the (therapeutic) torture of women. He was born in 1899. He was the approximate age of the movie industry. He was a shy man, socially. He was a showy man, socially. He was Fat Man, a joke. He was (he feared he was) a sexual joke. He was a director to cast beautiful faces, bodies. He was one in awe of glamor. He was one to spell the word *glamour.* He was one to inflict torture. He was an upright phallus. He was a very jolly very portly Humpty Dumpty phallus. He was not a penis or a prick or a good-natured cock but a phallus. He was his mother's phallus. He was his mother's phallus and by twenty-seven yet a virgin. He was twenty-seven and yet a good-boy penitent. He was not Jack the Ripper for he had no sins to confess (none!) yet he was required each evening after work (he was a title-card designer for Famous Players-Lasky Films) to approach his mother's bed and tell her, in the halting way of a penitent confessing his sins to a priest, of his day. Thirty years later *In the taxi in full view of any startled observer who wished to peer into the back seat to observe the ravishingly beautiful elegantly coiffed Ice Blonde model and Famed Fat Man Film Director in Dark Brit Suit moving amid early-evening traffic on Hollywood Boulevard where I was poor hypnotized Pippi required to "tear open" the great man's billowing trousers. I was required to "tear open" the great man's billowing trousers if I could but locate with chill fumbling fingers the damned zipper lost within the goiterous crotch and the great man was to shout with surprise and laughter and "fend the wench off"—as Mother would have wished.*

HE HATED SUSPENSE. He hated not-knowing. He hated not-being-the-One-to-know. He hated not-being-the-One-who-has-written-the-script. He hated the suspense of such impotence and so he would make himself the master of suspense. The Jesuits had terrorized him with tales of Hell, now he would terrorize the world with tales of Hell except he would be a practical joker. His movies would be practical jokes. All movies are practical jokes. Fat Man was so funny! You wet your panties laughing at Fat Man's droll Brit witticisms. You crapped your panties laughing at Fat Man's jokes for Fat Man favored practical jokes involving laxatives slipped into drinks. *Will you have a vodka martini my dear. Will you have a manhattan, will you have a Bloody Mary, will you have a sloe gin fizz my dear.* So funny!

WAS HE A FEARFUL FAT MAN, yes of course. All Fat Men are fearful and he was one to choose his victims solely among those who had no power, who could not retaliate for fear of losing all they had accomplished in the "film world." Was he a mean-raging Fat Man, yes of course. All Fat Men are mean-raging and he was one who saw with peephole accuracy how he would himself be cast in one of his own piti-

less movies. Was he an avid lover, yes of course *How can I force you to
love me if you do not love me if I am Fat Man a sexual joke how can I hurt
you most ingeniously my dear you will see!* Was he a quivery Fat Man,
yes of course. All Fat Men are quivery. Did his numerous chins quiver,
did his bloated torso quiver, did the layers and ledges of flesh around
his belly and buttocks quiver, did his fatty-marbled heart quiver, yes for
there was a hole inside him like an open drain and so many years before
he was brought by wheelchair amid deafening applause to accept the
coveted Lifetime Achievement in Motion Pictures Academy Award he
was one to quiver, and to sit.

He was one to sit, and to dream.

In his massive (hairless) head, such dreams!

Elaborate plots like a maze of guts. Chase scenes, suspense scenes,
shock-surprise scenes, deliriously-circling-camera scenes, vertiginous
scenes, aerial scenes, bloody-stabbing scenes, horror scenes, strangu-
lation scenes, sly orgasm scenes, the minuet-orchestrated ecstasy of
revenge.

He was never one to run. He was a pious plump-boy-virgin hiding
his smirk behind clasped prayer-hands. He was not one to walk, much.
As Fat Man he would sit and dine at favored restaurants, often. He was
one to demand "his" table. He was one to sit and dine for a very long
time each evening for he was very hungry. He was a giant gut, eateating.
He favored scatological jokes. He was very courteous, formal in his man-
ner. He was one to drinkdrink to sodden oblivion. He was one to stuff
himself to fill the hole inside him. Flush-faced and panting and wormy
lips quivering as, in later years, the sharply white dentures chewchewed.
He could not eat alone: he had a horror of eating alone. He required
the presence of (admiring, adoring) others when he dined. Though he
would ignore these (admiring, adoring) others as he dined he required
their presence for there was this hole inside his fatty hulk of mysteri-
ous origin. . . . At first only a few inches in diameter in his chest, later a
larger hole of about six inches in diameter in his belly, in the (later) Hol-
lywood years of fame, legend, wealth, the envy of filmmaker rivals and
the fawning awe of countless others an even larger and more alarming
hole in the lower gut. *Pity me! I am a tub of guts but the guts are always*

aching-empty except when stuffed full for a fat man is always empty except when stuffed full, will you fill my hole my dear?

HE WAS A PLAYFUL FAT MAN. His was the (pitiless) accuracy of the peephole eye.

WAS HE ONE TO SIT, yes! Oh yes he was one to sit.

From boyhood he was one to sit calm and impassive as the Buddha, not to meditate but to dream.

He was not Jack the Ripper. Not a sinful loathsome boy. His hands were never busy beneath the bedclothes. His hands, his arms were properly folded across his chest atop the bedclothes like those of a carved funerary figure. As the Jesuits prescribed, and Mother oversaw. Yet in the night his skin was clammy, damp. His (tight-shut) eyes swerved in their sockets. Mad veins pounded at his temples. His mouth was dry as if he'd swallowed sand. *By night I was a captive of that other. I am not to blame.* Yet by day he was a very good boy-student. He was a very good boy-student in his St. Ignatius uniform. Yes he did believe in God the Father, in Jesus Christ His Only Begotten Son, in the Holy Ghost; and in the Virgin Mary. ("Begotten" was not a word he knew. "Virgin" was not a word he knew, exactly.) He was one to recite British Railway timetables to the astonishment of family and relatives. Lurid illustrated magazines and newspapers he read (in secret) and these too (in secret) he memorized.

He was not Jack the Ripper.

HE WAS JACK THE RIPPER. Stab stabbing the nasty naked women. Nasty mocking ice-blond naked women. In the prime of his power and bulk (three hundred sixty-five pounds) he was Jack the Ripper stab stabbing the women though in fact he preferred strangulation to stabbing *Strangulation is more intimate, I've found.* Yet he would not scorn stabbing. Stabbing provides blood, blood is wonderfully "visual." Certainly he scorned guns, noisy guns, no intimacy with guns, guns were a cliché of shoot-'em-up; cowboys-and-Indians B-films naturally one of his sensibility would scorn. He was classy, classic. He was of the priest caste.

His mother would have wished him a priest but that had not happened. He had not the vocation, his was a secular vocation. Yet he would observe ritual, sacrifice. Sacrifice of the ice-blond temptress. Yes, he would have very happy memories of stabbing. The most spectacular of stab-sex-scenes in movie history would be his. So, he would hardly scorn stabbing. Mother would aid him in this as in so many things, Mother gotten up in Whistler's Mother long dowdy black skirt, proper gray (wig) bun. So exact, Mother could be. So prim and so cruel. (So funny!) Yet, he preferred strangulation for the intimacy. He was one to crave intimacy. He was misunderstood as coldhearted, calculating, lacking in charity. (Through his long life, he gave not a penny to "charity." Why should he?) Many have asked *Did the great film director touch you in a lewd way, Pippi? Did Fat Man grow bored with the peephole merely and one day close his hideous fat fingers around your lovely blond neck? Did Fat Man grunt groan wheeze bellow collapse his bulk upon your slender girl-body paralyzed in terror, broken beneath so hellish an assault? Did I die, was I revived? Was I revived by my ardent lover many times? (Fat Man knew the advantage of strangulation, by garrotte for instance: the dying victim can be revived many times.) Am I revived now, decades later in the 21st century?*

HOLLYWOOD TATLER offered me $$$$ for such "confidential" revelations. *National Enquirer, Playboy, Esquire, Reader's Digest* (in abridged form) and countless others. Always, Pippi declined.

I was so very ashamed.

THE GREAT MAN'S SECRET WAS: he feared laughter.

He feared laughter at him. For all his fame, genius, grandeur he was but a (visual) joke. Girls, women giggling at such a lover!

He had not been a joke to his mother. Never a joke to the Virgin Mary. He was happiest when they observed him for then he would not be bad. But it was exciting when they did not observe him for then he would be bad. And his badness took such flights! Observing his pasty-pale impassive good-boy face at (for instance) the communion railing, you could never have guessed how his badness, like exultant predator birds careening into the air to seek their prey, took flight! He was not a very nice young man but he was a very dapper young man and in time he would be a very dapper Fat Man always impeccably dressed Brit style in sun-splotched Los Angeles among beautiful imbecile faces and bodies a Fat Man of habit, order, discipline in dark suit, starched white dress shirt, conservative tie. *Tent-sized dark Brit suit in fact he owned six of them and each was identical to the others. Tent-sized starched white shirts in fact he owned fifteen of them and each was identical to the others. Plus ten identical ties, six identical pairs of custom-made (XXX width) leather dress shoes, numerous pairs of identical black socks.* He was courteous and contemptuous and he was very happy stabbing, for Jack the Ripper was not laughed at by girls and women. Fat Man was a joke to women, was he?—well *he was not.* Fat Man was not a joke *but a joker.* He was not a joke *but a joker* and that is quite a distinction. And that was his career. He was not a joke but Jack the Ripper who was Jack the Joker and the joke was on you, and on you, and on you.

And the joke was on me.

ONE DAY Maman called to me: You have a gentleman caller, Pippi! You will bathe.

It was 1953. I was a girl model known coyly as Pippi. There was Kiki, there was Fifi, there was Mimi, there was Tippi and there was even, for a while, Gigi. I was Pippi. I was one of the Ice Blondes.

May 1953. A time in which, in some quarters even here in sun-splotched Los Angeles mothers still addressed their daughters in formal terms. And daughters obeyed their Mamans.

May 1924. Aged twenty-three he was a heavyset young man not yet Fat Man and not yet famed. He was the hardest of hard workers at the Famous Players-Lasky Studio. It was the Silent Film Era. Aged twenty-three he had never touched a female *in that way.* He was faithful to his mother as to the Virgin Mary. He was not Jack the Ripper. They would know, he could not be Jack the Ripper. Aged twenty-three he did not know what the word *menstruation* might mean. He did not know what the word *ovulation* might mean. He did not know what the ugly words *sexual intercourse* might mean (though he had some idea, he had glimpsed dogs in the street before looking quickly away). He wrote his first screenplay.

PIPPI'S SCREEN TEST! The famous director was fifty-four and in his Fat Man prime. Maman chaperoned.

> *My dear say I love you*
> > *"I love you"*
> *My dear say I love you with feeling*
> > *"I love you"*
> *Again I love you*
> > *"I love you"*
> *Lift your chin my dear I love you*
> > *"I love you"*
> *As if you meant it my dear lift your beautiful eyes I love you*
> > *"I love you"*
> *Ah no! my dear you must try again I love you*
> > . . . .

Until finally Maman fell asleep, exhausted.

ONE DAY I would realize that as soon as the great director saw me it was to discover that I was already "in" his head. I had no knowledge of this fact of course. I was Pippi, only just nineteen and very silly and very vain and very hopeful of her blond "good looks" as it was expressed in that long-ago era. I had no knowledge that when the great director saw me (in a TV ad) it was "in" his head he was seeing me also. Because I was not physically present but only a gliding TV image at that moment I could not yet know the suffocation of being "in" another's head. That knowledge would come later.

I WISH you were the size of my thumb dear Pippi! Know what I would do dear Pippi I would gobble you down in one delicious gulp dear dear Pippi!

SOMEHOW IT HAPPENED, he was married.

Somehow it happened, "his wife" was pregnant.

He was not certain how it had happened. He believed it had happened during the night. He had not seen the (contorted) face of "his wife" nor had he heard her (whimpering, panting) response when he (or someone in his place, in the bed) had touched her. (Or had he touched *her*? It may have been, "his wife" had touched him.)

He could not bear the bloated belly. He could not bear the hideous bloated breasts. He was ill, his appetite was depressed. He drank. He drank to fill the aching cavity within. He saw that the wife's appearance was a mimicry of his own appearance. He saw smiles in the street, rude stares. He saw the bemused glance of beautiful girls and women. He saw their perfect bodies gliding past. He saw the wife's distended belly · in mockery of his distended belly. It was Mother's belly, was it? It was himself in the womb, was it?

Yet the wife adored him, her name was "A." His name, too, was "A." You might laugh, "A" and "A" were twins. He laughed, for he was one with a jocular sense of humor. He laughed at the coincidence for it meant nothing. (Of course, it meant everything. In the script, there are no coincidences.) His mother was ailing but still living when "A" ("Alfred") married "A" ("Alma" who had converted to Catholicism to please the groom and his family). The two women's lives overlapped for some years so it was not likely that "A" was his mother, still less that his mother was "A." It was not likely that "A" was pregnant with "A" when "A" was the father of the unborn child and it was not likely that the wife was deliberately mocking "A's" distended belly. In cinema, yes. In the German Expressionist cinema he admired, yes. In the ordinary world, no.

Not likely. Yet crude sensationalist vulgar minds would go speculate, after the great man's death.

PARTICULARLY the wife's enormous nursing breasts leaking milk repelled him. He could not bear the sucksucking of the baby. He could not bear another baby in the marriage. He was a practical joker whose specialty was laxative jokes but he did not care for baby diapers nor did he care for babyshit.

There was this hole, ever growing, inside him.

PIPPI I have been celibate so long. I have been celibate forty years Pippi. I have no love I have no sex-love I have only my work in which I am a genius but I am so lonely Pippi I have this hole inside me Pippi I adore you Pippi tell me you adore me Pippi even if it is only the script. Pippi I will make you a star!

Maman brought me the contract, breathless. Pippi, sign!

It was an era when if you were Pippi, or Tikki, or Lili, or Bibi, if you were directed by your Maman to sign, you signed.

Signed away my soul. Seven films!

(Of which only two would be made. The first, legendary and acclaimed. The second, a disaster.)

Why did I submit to the tyranny of Fat Man, why did I submit to Maman, you ask from your pinnacle of wisdom in the 21st century. You cannot comprehend. You cannot put yourself in my place. I was Pippi, I was hypnotized by Fat Man. It was not an era in America when Pippi would not be hypnotized by Fat Man. *I will make you a star Pippi I adore you only try to adore me* for Fat Man did not threaten, at first. That would come later.

You have sold your soul for riches, fame it would be accused but I don't believe this was ever true. Immediately Fat Man saw me I was "in" his head and captive. And it was safest there! For in Fat Man's massive head I was without desire. When in the glaring camera lights I was without desire. Fat Man costumed me, Fat Man oversaw makeup, hair, undergarments, hosiery, all footwear. *Shoes! Fat Man was a fetishist of shoes, feet. Black satin high-heeled pumps, stiletto-heeled sandals in the sheerest silk hosiery.* In Fat Man's head I was the Ice Blonde beauty without desire. For to be Ice Blonde is to be free of desire. I was without desire like a flame that has been blown out. I was without desire to be other than Pippi in Fat Man's massive head and it was a holy place, I believed.

FOR HERE WAS a Brit gentleman of impeccable good manners, taste. Here was a gentleman renowned for his wit. Here was a genius of cinema. Here was lofty sorrow. Here was gross appetite. Here was one shamelessly enthralled by glamor. Here was one famously impatient with underlings. Here was one who remained an infant through life. Here was one who had never been young. Here was a fat drooping phallus. Here was a very fat very drooping phallus. Here was a witty phallus! Here was a wise phallus. Here was a haunted phallus, a poet-phallus, a visionary-phallus to instruct us, ice blondes and all others who yearn for redemption *It's only a movie. Let's not go too deeply into these things. It's only a movie.*

I wept, to be so freed of desire. For desire is the flame that dazzles and blinds as it kills.

SEIZING ONE of us in bloated slug fingers, for Fat Man was the greatest filmmaker in all of history, should not Fat Man be rewarded? should not Fat Man be happy, as ordinary swinish folk are happy? where is justice, otherwise?—lifting the squealing thumb-sized flesh doll to the massive hole of his mouth, and eating, chewing, swallowing with a mouthful of his favorite French burgundy.

WE HAD NOT KNOWN! We had not guessed. (Pippi had not even known that she was but one of a succession of Ice Blondes. Pippi in her stupidity and vanity had imagined she was the sole Ice Blonde!) The movie that was to be made, involving "real" actors, in a "real" set amid "real" technicians and assistants, was but the aftermath of the Fat Man's vision. The movie was but the tunnel for what was inside the giant fetus head to come "outside." If what was inside the head was not realized "outside," the head would explode. For the head, though massive, had to be relieved of its contents. As the hundreds of feet of guts had to be relieved of their contents. Or Fat Man in his proper Brit suit, starched white dress shirt would explode. But after the movie was made and released to the public it began at once to lose its lustre. It became banal, boring. *Only a movie. Only a movie. Only a movie.* Like a mysterious light left burning after the sun has risen. Such light enduring into day, now tawdry, pointless. Fat Man was one whose dreams ceased to interest him once others shared them for the eyes of others debased Fat Man's dream. There was this hole inside him.

FAT MAN BECAME IMPATIENT with his Pippi who did not adore him in the way Fat Man wished to be adored and so had to be punished. Birds were sent to peck at my face, hands, arms. I was made to endure the hellish shrieking of birds. I was made to endure Fat Man's rage. I was made to endure Fat Man's madness. I was Pippi, I had wished to believe that I was beloved. I was Pippi, I had been assured that the birds would be mechanical birds. But when I arrived on the set that day there were cages of live birds and they were excited. And they were hungry. And they were angry. They were furious blackbirds, ravens. They were crows. They were Death-Birds. I was made to endure hours, days of these birds. Pecking beaks, flailing black-feathered wings! A sky of birds, an avalanche of birds! Fat Man observed at a distance. Fat Man was impassive, seemingly uninvolved. Fat Man was a zombie Buddha. Fat Man was in command of the Death-Birds. I was made to bleed by the birds' ravenous beaks. I would be badly infected by the birds' ravenous beaks. My left eye was pecked by a frenzied starling. Birds were being flung at me, I could not defend myself. My hair was encrusted with the suety-sticky white of bird shit. Help! Help me! I was panicked, I could not breathe. Yet Fat Man remained seated in his director's chair impervious to my terror as he was impervious to my pleas for mercy. *Only a movie. Yet it must be endured.*

YET: the final scene of the movie was such beauty! Pippi who had been broken, terrorized, humiliated was yet resurrected, on film. I saw, I was made to see, how Fat Man had the power of such resurrection as Fat Man had the power of utter debasement, humiliation. It was the power of God. It was the power of the giant fetus, as God. In that way in which, in the final scene, the Ice Blonde made her cautious way with other survivors through a vast subdued sea of predator birds. Human beings in their vulnerable featherless flesh making a pilgrimage through the devastated world. It was beautiful, we wept to see it. We had not known, in the filming. We had come to loathe and fear Fat Man who had swallowed us whole and digested us and excreted us yet we wept to see such beauty, and ourselves redeemed within it.

(ALL OF HOLLYWOOD talked of it: an experienced actress would not have tolerated such abuse. An experienced actress would not have tolerated such insult. An experienced actress would not have succumbed to Fat Man's entreaties. For never did Pippi recover, entirely. Never Pippi's lacerated and shat-upon soul restored to its virgin purity.)

IN FAT MAN'S MANY MOVIES there would be the fleeting image of Fat Man for Fat Man was a practical joker and what more of a practical joke than to insert Fat Man in the cinema-world of perfect faces, bodies. Fat Man so very ugly. Fat Man smirking, Fat Man with quivery jowls and bleak empty eyes. Now Fat Man was making lesser movies, you could tell because Fat Man was ever more famous. Fat Man was nearing Death, you could tell because Fat Man was winning ever more awards for Lifetime Achievement.

The next, posthumous. Eagerly I await.

A SUMMONS CAME at last. He had been waiting for many years. He was embittered waiting. He would not forgive this long insult. He had won an Oscar! At last. An attendant would accompany him to the ceremony. The studio would provide transportation. Always Fat Man required transportation. Fat Man did not walk, not much. Fat Man was in a wheelchair, was he? (When had this happened?) Fat Man had difficulty breathing. Fat Man had difficulty swallowing his food. Fat Man was not supposed to drink as he'd once done but Fat Man demanded his drink. To what purpose had he labored these many decades, if he was to be denied his drink? The white-jacketed attendant was in the hire of the studio. Fat Man would not pay for his own attendant, the studio must pay. Fat Man was in a sulk, the Oscar had so many times been denied him. *On my count of three, sir!* the attendant murmured heaving Fat Man into his chair. And now wheeled along a crimson carpet, past cheering throngs. Flashbulbs. Fat Man wore evening attire. Fat Man was squeezed into a tux. Fat Man had been shaved, cologne had been rubbed gently into his collapsed skin. Fat Man was very proud. Fat Man was sulky, the Oscar had been denied him so long. His name was being intoned: Lifetime Achievement in Motion Pictures. His name was being chanted by thousands, tens of thousands. To the very horizon, applause. A standing ovation. A wall of deafening sound. The honored one insists upon heaving himself from his wheelchair, of course he can walk if he wishes. Amid warm dazzling lights, the gleaming statuette of Oscar is held aloft. The master of ceremonies is a tux and a black satin bow tie, bald-gleaming skull smiling above. The master of ceremonies is leading the applause that threatens to suffocate Fat Man but the promise shimmers before him, the hole inside him will be filled. At last! With childlike eagerness Fat Man reaches out to receive the Oscar statuette but the statuette hovers out of reach firmly grasped by the smiling skull above the black satin bow tie and (something happens, a mishap, there are gasps from the audience, where is the damned attendant) Fat Man falls in slow motion in what appears to be a staged comic-cruel sequence of the sort for which Fat Man's movies are known, the audience responds with gales of laughter, applause. Yet Fat Man has fallen heavily, fatally. Fat Man has fallen onto his bloated belly, Fat Man's Humpty Dumpty head cracks. His breath has been knocked from him with rude abruptness. In his death throes Fat Man manages to roll onto his side, and onto his back, he is helpless as a gigantic beetle on its back, still the audience shrieks with laughter, applause. Fat Man's fingers are grasping still for the gleaming statuette which hovers out of reach teasing, tantalizing, luminous amid frenzied applause to the very horizon and cries of *Bravo!*

There will be no final credits. There will be no THE END to signal Fat Man's demise, only a slow . . .

———

BUT WHY am I crying, it is many years later. I am an old woman. I am no longer the Ice Blonde. There is no one to "see" me now. There has been no one to "see" me as Fat Man saw me for a very long time. The shrieking birds are gone, their stabbing beaks and cries. There is an emptiness inside me where the flame of my long-ago desire once quivered.

I loved Fat Man, I think. I feared and loathed Fat Man who destroyed my acting career (exactly as he had vowed) and yet I loved Fat Man. I could not bear Fat Man's clammy repulsive touch and yet I loved Fat Man at the peephole. Fat Man was not God, but who among us is God? (At least, Fat Man aspired to be God.) Fat Man was not God but for many years Fat Man possessed the wonder of God. Fat Man yearned to fill the great hole inside him in a way that was God. For God is but emptiness, we must fill God. We are creatures to fill God. I was too young and foolish then to know, when I was "Pippi." Too young to be worthy of Fat Man's peephole eye. In Fat Man's head I was trapped and tortured and yet I was happy there, I believe. I was absolved of all desire, like a saint or a martyr. (In the wake of my disaster and breakdown, I would convert to the Holy Roman Catholic Apostolic Church.) Yes I was very beautiful but beauty is emptiness. Fat Man knew, as few know. Fat Man too was a saint, a martyr. Fat Man suffered the Hell of ceaseless yearning.

Often in my dreams Fat Man appears, not elderly and ravaged as he was in the later years but in his prime, when I knew him. Fat Man takes my hand to lead me through the devastated landscape. I am still frightened of birds (silly Pippi!), Fat Man must lead me through the Valley of Death-Birds.

Pippi, my dear. Never doubt the director!

I wake from such dreams of warmth and love and yet: why am I crying?

I am astonished to see in mirrors this faded old woman! The peephole eye would regard me with disgust, contempt. The peephole eye would be shuttered at once, seeing me. The formerly elegant blond hair is mere filaments, faded wisps. So thin, the shape of the skull is exposed. If the light is bright behind me I can see through bone, brain matter, gristle. For it is only a movie, Fat Man knew. Pippi was never real. None of us was ever real. (You believe that you are real, do you?) Pippi was only inside Fat Man's head, and we know that Fat Man is dead.

("Fat Man My Love" is purely fiction containing, in transmogrified form, factual material from *The Dark Side of Genius: The Life of Alfred Hitchcock* by Donald Spoto and *The Encyclopedia of Alfred Hitchcock* by Gene D. Phillips and Thomas M. Leitch.)

OBJECTS IN
MIRROR ARE CLOSER THAN
THEY APPEAR

———

FIRST TIME YOU drive past my house Tuesday after school my big-boob spike-haired cousin Gwendolyn Barnstead is sitting with me smoking on the front steps, says Man! you are the handsomest man she has ever seen in actual life. My attention is fixed on the awesome vehicle you are driving, some kind of sexy Jeep with big tires and a flat windshield and a military-metallic dark-green glare like a beetle's back. By the time Gwen's remark registers you are already past.

Being that I am a natural-born skeptic, the only rationalist in the family, I ask Gwen why're you so handsome, what's so special about you, and Gwen says, lowering her voice as if there's anybody to hear (there is not, my mom is flat-out in her sick room making a noise like breathing through a clogged hose), "It looked like this really sexy jet-black hair like a 'Native American.' Looked like he was wearing a white shirt, y'know—a real shirt with sleeves. I don't know, he just looked really cool. Not like anybody lives around here."

Gwen and I wait for you to circle the block like sometimes a guy will do. You don't.

(Actually we live outside town, there's no "blocks" here like in a civilized place. You'd have to drive five, six miles on North Fork Road to circle around. But you might've turned your awesome vehicle around and driven right back in our direction, is what I'm thinking.)

Second time you drive past my house, about 6 P.M. next day, it's a slower hour and you are driving slower and I'm alone in the front room where three window panes are greasy from my forehead pressed against them and when I see the awesome military-beetle vehicle my heart starts knocking like crazy in my chest and I'm thinking *Hey I know you! I know you!* but I'm like paralyzed and can't run outside, I just can't. It's about time for me to make supper, bring my mom her supper on a tray, the macaroni-cheese casserole is in the oven and I'm prowling the house nervous like red ants are biting inside my clothes waiting for the phone to ring, it has not rung since I came home from school it's like the phone is dead or disconnected or all of mankind is annihilated except me, and I'm staring through the grease prints seeing the awesome glaring vehicle slowing, a single driver, male, with jet-black hair, pausing to get the number on our house—is that what you're doing?—trying to see the number 249 that used to be glow-in-the-dark but now it's almost invisible—and it flashes over me like something in a movie who you are: the man at Eckerd's!

I mean, I think so. There can be no such coincidence.

For you are not a guy in just his twenties, say. Not some heavy metal guy I'd be scared shitless to climb into that vehicle with but an adult man, an older man of possibly thirty. A pharmacist! Someone to respect and who would respect me. You are some kind of Asian-American, I guess: Chinese, Japanese, Korean? (What other is there? At my high school are a few Asian-Americans, kind of quiet, very smart and popular, elected to class offices, on the yearbook staff with me.)

At Eckerd's I had to get my mom's prescription refilled and a bedpan and other supplies and you waited on me, very polite. Have to say I didn't take notice of you immediately, I am not one to stare at anybody older, mostly. Or anybody like a pharmacist in a white jacket, necktie showing. Except I did notice the sexy black hair worn in a way to capture the attention, a little long past your collar, kind of flaring like wings from your forehead, no part, but the suggestion of a part, in the middle.

This is styled-hair, no mistake. And your profile, I kind of noticed.
'Course I was feeling sorry for myself right then, slouched and chewing
gum like I had a grudge against it, and my eyes mascara-smeared from
rubbing them. Momma used to tease I'd look like a sleepy raccoon star-
ing out from a hole. And my hair, Mr. Ketchum at school ("Catch-Em")
teaches Drivers' Ed and coaches guys' sports says my hair looks like an
eggbeater got into it but I can tell he likes the look. And you were smil-
ing at me, too. I think. Your face is kind of a flat moon face seen from
the front and your eyes are really dark eagle-eyes and your skin has a
golden-lemony-tan look, very smooth, not like some Caucasian where
the beard-stubble on the jaws is always poking through. You were say-
ing something about the prescription renewal, next time the pharmacist
would have to contact my mother's doctor, I wasn't listening to much of
this just standing there one hip higher than the other, chewing my gum.
I'm like always in a hurry though there's no special place I am going. I'm
actually almost eighteen but look like thirteen. No boobs, and a bitty
ass like two half-doughnuts. My skin is so pale you can see weird little
purple veins on my forehead. You are typing in the computer saying,
"'North Fork,' eh? That's north of here, eh?" and it takes me a beat to
catch on you're kind of joking, and with that little smile of yours, and I
almost swallow my gum. Saying, "Yeah. I guess."

Then, buying the freaky bedpan, "adult size" I asked for, I was
kind of embarrassed, and sullen, knowing my fate is not just to bring
the damn bedpan home but to dump its contents out in the bathroom
periodically if/when Momma gets too weak to use the bathroom, and
you didn't act all sappy and somber like people do, they hear about
my mom's next-scheduled surgery, etcetera, you showed what was on
the shelves and made a recommendation and I'm feeling my eyes sting
with tears staring at this really ugly depressing bright-shiny utensil com-
ing into my life and you said, "One size *does not fit all*. Eh?" And you
glanced at my rear, in my tight bleached jeans, and I'm a skinny thing
ninety pounds and five feet two, and a warm happy blush came over my
face and my knees went weak as water.

Meant to look at your left hand, check for a wedding band but I was
so distracted, I forgot.

Now you are driving on North Fork Road. You are the handsomest man ever glimpsed in actual life as opposed to movies/TV and you are driving an awesome upscale vehicle past my fake-asphalt-sided junker-car-in-the-driveway house, and slowing, peering at number 249, and I'm behind the window unable to move beginning to hear a croak-voice calling *Dee-Dee! Dee-Dee!* like something at the bottom of a well.

"Yeah, Mom! I'm coming."

Since then you haven't been back. Three days you have stayed away from North Fork Road. Why?

Gwen came over and did my hair, it's spiked like hers now, jet-black highlighted with maroon, green. We're out on the front steps smoking, bare-legged and barefoot and our toenails painted frosty blue. Every vehicle that appears, especially pickups and vans, my heart gives a lunge.

In three weeks I will be graduated. My grades are fucked but they won't keep a "school diploma" from me. (An actual diploma is issued by the State of New York.) Until senior year I was on the honor roll, I was co-editor of the yearbook, I was president of Hi-Lo's and was almost elected senior class treasurer. Until she got sick Momma had not a clue I was leaving here. Applied to Oregon, Washington State, not Niagara County Community College and now not even there, I guess. Momma always saying when she can talk past a croak she wants me to be happy and I'm saying, more sarcastic than you'd expect from somebody almost-eighteen with an I.Q. said to be 162, "Momma, I am happy. I am so happy I could piss my pants."

Now Gwen looks me over. I can see she's impressed.

"Well, you look O.K. Like for a prom, or something."

Prom! That's a joke.

"You look, like real *happy*."

It's this spike-hair, and the new eye makeup, and toenail glitter. I had a few swallows of Mom's old dago red she'd hidden in the bathroom cabinet and forgot. My premonition is, you will reappear on North Fork Road. Take me by surprise, I won't know when.

"Why shouldn't I be happy, I am happy. I'm waiting."

THE 1960S

UPON THE

SWEEPING FLOOD

———

ONE DAY IN Eden County, in the remote marsh and swamplands to the south, a man named Walter Stuart was stopped in the rain by a sheriff's deputy along a country road. Stuart was in a hurry to get home to his family—his wife and two daughters—after having endured a week at his father's old farm, arranging for his father's funeral, surrounded by aging relatives who had sucked at him for the strength of his youth. He was a stern, quiet man of thirty-nine, beginning now to lose some of the muscular hardness that had always baffled others, masking as it did Stuart's remoteness, his refinement, his faith in discipline and order that seem to have belonged, even in his youth, to a person already grown safely old. He was a district vice-president for one of the gypsum mining plants, a man to whom financial success and success in love had come naturally, without fuss. When only a child he had shifted his faith with little difficulty from the unreliable God of his family's tradition to the things and emotions of this world, which he admired in his thoughtful, rather conservative way, and this faith had given him access, as if by magic, to a communion with persons vastly different from himself—

with someone like the sheriff's deputy, for example, who approached him that day in the hard, cold rain. "Is something wrong?" Stuart said. He rolled down the window and had nearly opened the door when the deputy, an old man with gray eyebrows and a slack, sunburned face, began shouting against the wind. "Just the weather, mister. You plan on going far? How far are you going?"

"Two hundred miles," Stuart said. "What about the weather? Is it a hurricane?"

"A hurricane—yes—a hurricane," the man said, bending to shout at Stuart's face. "You better go back to town and stay put. They're evacuating up there. We're not letting anyone through."

A long line of cars and pickup trucks, tarnished and gloomy in the rain, passed them on the other side of the road. "How bad is it?" said Stuart. "Do you need help?"

"Back at town, maybe, they need help," the man said. "They're putting up folks at the schoolhouse and the churches, and different families—The eye was spost to come by here, but last word we got it's veered further south. Just the same, though—"

"Yes, it's good to evacuate them," Stuart said. At the back window of an automobile passing them two children's faces peered out at the rain, white and blurred. "The last hurricane here—"

"Ah, God, leave off of that!" the old man said, so harshly that Stuart felt, inexplicably, hurt. "You better turn around now and get on back to town. You got money they can put you up somewheres good—not with these folks coming along here."

This was said without contempt, but Stuart flinched at its assumptions and, years afterward, he was to remember the old man's remark as the beginning of his adventure. The man's twisted face and unsteady, jumping eyes, his wind-snatched voice, would reappear to Stuart when he puzzled for reasons—but along with the deputy's face there would be the sad line of cars, the children's faces turned toward him, and, beyond them in his memory, the face of his dead father with skin wrinkled and precise as a withered apple.

"I'm going in to see if anybody needs help," Stuart said. He had the car going again before the deputy could even protest. "I know what I'm doing! I know what I'm doing!" Stuart said.

The car lunged forward into the rain, drowning out the deputy's outraged shouts. The slashing of rain against Stuart's face excited him. Faces staring out of oncoming cars were pale and startled, and Stuart felt rising in him a strange compulsion to grin, to laugh madly at their alarm. . . . He passed cars for some time. Houses looked deserted, yards bare. Things had the look of haste about them, even trees—in haste to rid themselves of their leaves, to be stripped bare. Grass was twisted and wild. A ditch by the road was overflowing and at spots the churning, muddy water stretched across the red clay road. Stuart drove, splashing, through it. After a while his enthusiasm slowed, his foot eased up on the gas pedal. He had not passed any cars or trucks for some time.

The sky had darkened and the storm had increased. Stuart thought of turning back when he saw, a short distance ahead, someone standing in the road. A car approached from the opposite direction. Stuart slowed, bearing to the right. He came upon a farm—a small, run-down one with just a few barns and a small pasture in which a horse stood drooping in the rain. Behind the roofs of the buildings a shifting edge of foliage from the trees beyond curled in the wind, now dark, now silver. In a neat harsh line against the bottom of the buildings the wind had driven up dust and red clay. Rain streamed off roofs, plunged into fat, tilted rain barrels, and exploded back out of them. As Stuart watched, another figure appeared, running out of the house. Both persons—they looked like children—jumped about in the road, waving their arms. A spray of leaves was driven against them and against the muddy windshield of the car that approached and passed them. They turned: a girl and a boy, waving their fists in rage, their faces white and distorted. As the car sped past Stuart, water and mud splashed up in a vicious wave.

When Stuart stopped and opened the door the girl was already there, shouting, "Going the wrong way! Wrong way!" Her face was coarse, pimply about her forehead and chin. The boy pounded up behind her, straining for air. "Where the hell are you going, mister?" the girl cried. "The storm's coming from this way. Did you see that bastard,

going right by us? Did you see him? If I see him when I get to town—"
A wall of rain struck. The girl lunged forward and tried to push her
way into the car; Stuart had to hold her back. "Where are your folks?"
he shouted. "Let me in," cried the girl savagely. "We're getting out of
here!" "Your folks," said Stuart. He had to cup his mouth to make her
hear. "Your folks in there!" "There ain't anybody there—*Goddamn*
you," she said, twisting about to slap her brother, who had been pushing
at her from behind. She whirled upon Stuart again. "You letting us in,
mister? You letting us in?" she screamed, raising her hands as if to claw
him. But Stuart's size must have calmed her, for she shouted hoarsely
and mechanically: "There ain't nobody in there. Our pa's been gone the
last two days. *Last two days.* Gone into town *by himself.* Gone drunk
somewhere. He ain't here. He left us here. LEFT US HERE!" Again she
rushed at Stuart, and he leaned forward against the steering wheel to let
her get in back. The boy was about to follow when something caught his
eye back at the farm. "Get in," said Stuart. "Get in. Please. Get in." "My
horse there," the boy muttered. "You little bastard! You get in here!"
his sister screamed.

But once the boy got in, once the door was closed, Stuart knew that
it was too late. Rain struck the car in solid walls and the road, when he
could see it, had turned to mud. "Let's go! Let's go!" cried the girl,
pounding on the back of the seat. "Turn it around! Go up on our drive
and turn it around!" The engine and the wind roared together. "Turn it!
Get it going!" cried the girl. There was a scuffle and someone fell against
Stuart. "It ain't no good," the boy said. "Let me out." He lunged for the
door and Stuart grabbed him. "I'm going back to the house," the boy
cried, appealing to Stuart with his frightened eyes, and his sister, giving
up suddenly, pushed him violently forward. "It's no use," Stuart said.
"Goddamn fool," the girl screamed, "goddamn fool!"

The water was ankle deep as they ran to the house. The girl splashed
ahead of Stuart, running with her head up and her eyes wide open in
spite of the flying scud. When Stuart shouted to the boy, his voice was
slammed back to him as if he were being mocked. "Where are you go-
ing? Go to the house! Go to the house!" The boy had turned and was
running toward the pasture. His sister took no notice but ran to the

house. "Come back, kid!" Stuart cried. Wind tore at him, pushing him back. "What are you—"

The horse was undersized, skinny and brown. It ran to the boy as if it wanted to run him down but the boy, stooping through the fence, avoided the frightened hoofs and grabbed the rope that dangled from the horse's halter. "That's it! That's it!" Stuart shouted as if the boy could hear. At the gate the boy stopped and looked around wildly, up to the sky—he might have been looking for someone who had just called him; then he shook the gate madly. Stuart reached the gate and opened it, pushing it back against the boy, who now turned to gape at him. "What? What are you doing here?" he said.

The thought crossed Stuart's mind that the child was insane. "Bring the horse through!" he said. "We don't have much time."

"What are you doing here?" the boy shouted. The horse's eyes rolled, its mane lifted and haloed about its head. Suddenly it lunged through the gate and jerked the boy off the ground. The boy ran in the air, his legs kicking. "Hang on and bring him around!" Stuart shouted. "Let me take hold!" He grabbed the boy instead of the rope. They stumbled together against the horse. It had stopped now and was looking intently at something just to the right of Stuart's head. The boy pulled himself along the rope, hand over hand, and Stuart held onto him by the strap of his overalls. "He's scairt of you!" the boy said. "He's scairt of you!" Stuart reached over and took hold of the rope above the boy's fingers and tugged gently at it. His face was about a foot away from the horse's. "Watch out for him," said the boy. The horse reared and broke free, throwing Stuart back against the boy. "Hey, hey," screamed the boy, as if mad. The horse turned in mid-air as if whirled about by the wind, and Stuart looked up through his fingers to see its hoofs and a vicious flicking of its tail, and the face of the boy being yanked past him and away with incredible speed. The boy fell heavily on his side in the mud, arms outstretched above him, hands still gripping the rope with wooden fists. But he scrambled to his feet at once and ran alongside the horse. He flung one arm up around its neck as Stuart shouted, "Let him go! Forget about him!" Horse and boy pivoted together back toward the fence, slashing wildly at the earth, feet and hoofs together. The ground erupted beneath them. But the boy landed upright, still holding the rope, still with his arm about the horse's neck. "Let me help," Stuart said. "No," said the boy, "he's my horse, he knows me—" "Have you got him good?" Stuart shouted. "We got—we got each other here," the boy cried, his eyes shut tight.

Stuart went to the barn to open the door. While he struggled with it, the boy led the horse forward. When the door was open far enough, Stuart threw himself against it and slammed it around to the side of the barn. A cloud of hay and scud filled the air. Stuart stretched out his arms, as if pleading with the boy to hurry, and he murmured, "Come on. Please. Come on." The boy did not hear him or even glance at him: his own lips were moving as he caressed the horse's neck and head. The horse's muddy hoof had just begun to grope about the step before the door when something like an explosion came against the back of Stuart's head, slammed his back, and sent him sprawling out at the horse.

"Damn you! Damn you!" the boy screamed. Stuart saw nothing except rain. Then something struck him, his shoulder and hand, and his fingers were driven down into the mud. Something slammed beside him in the mud and he seized it—the horse's foreleg—and tried to pull himself up, insanely, lurching to his knees. The horse threw him backwards. It seemed to emerge out of the air before and above him, coming into sight as though out of a cloud. The boy he did not see at all—only the hoofs—and then the boy appeared, inexplicably, under the horse, peering intently at Stuart, his face struck completely blank. "Damn you!" Stuart heard, "he's my horse! My horse! I hope he kills you!" Stuart crawled back in the water, crab fashion, watching the horse form and dissolve, hearing its vicious tattoo against the barn. The door, swinging madly back and forth, parodied the horse's rage, seemed to challenge its frenzy; then the door was all Stuart heard, and he got to his feet, gasping, to see that the horse was out of sight.

The boy ran bent against the wind, out toward nowhere, and Stuart ran after him. "Come in the house, kid! Come on! Forget about it, kid!" He grabbed the boy's arm. The boy struck at him with his elbow. "He was my horse!" he cried.

IN THE KITCHEN of the house they pushed furniture against the door. Stuart had to stand between the boy and the girl to keep them from fighting. "Goddamn sniffling fool," said the girl. "So your goddamn horse run off for the night!" The boy crouched down on the floor, crying steadily. He was about thirteen: small for his age, with bony wrists and face. "We're all going to be blownt to hell, let alone your horse," the girl said. She sat with one big thigh and leg outstretched on the table, watching Stuart. He thought her perhaps eighteen. "Glad you come down to get us?" she said. "Where are you from, mister?" Stuart's revulsion surprised him; he had not supposed there was room in his stunned mind for emotion of this sort. If the girl noticed it she gave no sign, but only grinned at him. "I was—I was on my way home," he said. "My wife and daughters—" It occurred to him that he had forgotten about them entirely. He had not thought of them until now and, even now, no image came to his mind: no woman's face, no little girls' faces. Could he have imagined their lives, their love for him? For an instant he doubted everything. "Wife and daughters," said the girl, as if wondering whether to believe him. "Are they in this storm too?" "No—no," Stuart said. To get away from her he went to the window. He could no longer see the road. Something struck the house and he flinched away. "Them trees!" chortled the girl. "I knew it! Pa always said how he ought to cut them down, so close to the house like they are! I knew it! I knew it! And the old bastard off safe now where they can't get him!"

"Trees?" said Stuart slowly.

"Them trees! Old oak trees!" said the girl.

The boy, struck with fear, stopped crying suddenly. He crawled on the floor to a woodbox beside the big old iron stove and got in, patting the disorderly pile of wood as if he were blind. The girl ran to him and pushed him. "What are you doing?" Stuart cried in anguish. The girl took no notice of him. "What am I doing?" he said aloud. "What the hell am I doing here?" It seemed to him that the end would come in a minute or two, that the howling outside could get no louder, that the howling inside his mind could get no more intense, no more accusing. A goddamn fool! A goddamn fool! he thought. The deputy's face came to mind, and Stuart pictured himself groveling before the man, clutching at his knees, asking forgiveness and for time to be turned back. . . . Then he saw himself back at the old farm, the farm of his childhood, listening to tales of his father's agonizing sickness, the old people's heads craning around, seeing how he took it, their eyes charged with horror and delight. . . . "My wife and daughters," Stuart muttered.

The wind made a hollow, drumlike sound. It seemed to be tolling. The boy, crouching back in the woodbox, shouted: "I ain't scairt! I ain't scairt!" The girl gave a shriek. "Our chicken coop, I'll be gahdammed!" she cried. Try as he could, Stuart could see nothing out the window. "Come away from the window," Stuart said, pulling the girl's arm. She whirled upon him. "Watch yourself, mister," she said, "you want to go out to your gahdamn bastardly worthless car?" Her body was strong and big in her men's clothing; her shoulders looked muscular beneath the filthy shirt. Cords in her young neck stood out. Her hair had been cut short and was now wet, plastered about her blemished face. She grinned at Stuart as if she were about to poke him in the stomach, for fun. "I ain't scairt of what God can do!" the boy cried behind them.

When the water began to bubble up through the floor boards they decided to climb to the attic. "There's an ax!" Stuart exclaimed, but the boy got on his hands and knees and crawled to the corner where the ax was propped before Stuart could reach it. The boy cradled it in his arms. "What do you want with that?" Stuart said, and for an instant his heart was pierced with fear. "Let me take it. I'll take it." He grabbed it out of the boy's dazed fingers.

The attic was about half as large as the kitchen and the roof jutted down sharply on either side. Tree limbs rubbed and slammed against the roof on all sides. The three of them crouched on the middle beam, Stuart with the ax tight in his embrace, the boy pushing against him as if for warmth, and the girl kneeling, with her thighs straining her overalls. She watched the little paneless window at one end of the attic without much emotion or interest, like a large, wet turkey. The house trembled beneath them. "I'm going to the window," Stuart said, and was oddly relieved when the girl did not sneer at him. He crawled forward along the dirty beam, dragging the ax with him, and lay full length on the floor about a yard from the window. There was not much to see. At times the rain relaxed, and objects beneath in the water took shape: tree stumps, parts of buildings, junk whirling about in the water. The thumping on the roof was so loud at that end that he had to crawl backwards to the middle again. "I ain't scairt, nothing God can do!" the boy cried. "Listen to the sniveling baby," said the girl. "He thinks God pays him any mind! Hah!" Stuart crouched beside them, waiting for the boy to press against him again. "As if God gives a good damn about him," the girl said. Stuart looked at her. In the near dark her face did not seem so coarse; the set of her eyes was almost attractive. "You don't think God cares about you?" Stuart said slowly. "No, not specially," the girl said, shrugging her shoulders. "The hell with it. You seen the last one of these?" She tugged at Stuart's arm. "Mister? It was something to see. Me an' Jackie was little then—him just a baby. We drove a far ways north to get out of it. When we come back the roads was so thick with sightseers from the cities! They took all the dead ones floating in the water and put them in one place, part of a swamp they cleared out. The families and things—they were mostly fruit pickers—had to come by on rafts and rowboats to look and see could they find the ones they knew. That was there for a day. The bodies would turn round and round in the wash from the boats. Then the faces all got alike and they wouldn't let anyone come any more and put oil on them and set them afire. We stood on top of the car and watched all that day. I wasn't but nine then."

When the house began to shake, some time later, Stuart cried aloud: "This is it!" He stumbled to his feet, waving the ax. He turned around and around as if he were in a daze. "You goin' to chop somethin' with that?" the boy said, pulling at him. "Hey, no, that ain't yours to—it ain't yours to chop—" They struggled for the ax. The boy sobbed, "It ain't yours! It ain't yours!" and Stuart's rage at his own helplessness, at the folly of his being here, for an instant almost made him strike the boy with the ax. But the girl slapped him furiously. "Get away from him! I swear I'll kill you!" she screamed.

Something exploded beneath them. "That's the windows," the girl muttered, clinging to Stuart, "and how am I to clean it again! The old bastard will want it clean, and mud over everything!" Stuart pushed her away so that he could swing the ax. Pieces of soft, rotted wood exploded back onto his face. The boy screamed insanely as the boards gave way to a deluge of wind and water, and even Stuart wondered if he had made a mistake. The three of them fell beneath the onslaught and Stuart lost the ax, felt the handle slam against his leg. "You! You!" Stuart cried, pulling at the girl—for an instant, blinded by pain, he could not think who he was, what he was doing, whether he had any life beyond this moment. The big-faced, husky girl made no effort to hide her fear and cried, "wait, wait!" But he dragged her to the hole and tried to force her out. "My brother—" she gasped. She seized his wrists and tried to get away. "Get out there! There isn't any time!" Stuart muttered. The house seemed about to collapse at any moment. He was pushing her through the hole, against the shattered wood, when she suddenly flinched back against him and he saw that her cheek was cut and she was choking. He snatched her hands away from her mouth as if he wanted to see something secret: blood welled out between her lips. She coughed and spat blood onto him. "You're all right," he said, oddly pleased. "Now get out there and I'll get the kid. I'll take care of him." This time she managed to crawl through the hole, with Stuart pushing her from behind; when he turned to seize the boy, the boy clung to his neck, sobbing something about God. "God loves you!" Stuart yelled. "Loves the least of you! The least of you!" The girl pulled her brother up in her great arms and Stuart was free to climb through himself.

IT WAS ACTUALLY quite a while—perhaps an hour—before the battering of the trees and the wind pushed the house in. The roof fell slowly, and the section to which they clung was washed free. "We're going somewheres!" shouted the girl. "Look at the house! That gahdamn old shanty seen the last storm!"

The boy lay with his legs pushed in under Stuart's and had not spoken for some time. When the girl cried, "Look at that!" he tried to burrow in farther. Stuart wiped his eyes to see the wall of darkness dissolve. The rain took on another look—a smooth, piercing, metallic glint, like nails driving against their faces and bodies. There was no horizon. They could see nothing except the rushing water and a thickening mist that must have been rain, miles and miles of rain, slammed by the wind into one great wall that moved remorselessly upon them. "Hang on," Stuart said, gripping the girl. "Hang on to me."

Waves washed over the roof, pushing objects at them with soft, muted thuds—pieces of fence, boards, branches heavy with foliage. Stuart tried to ward them off with his feet. Water swirled around them, sucking at them, sucking the roof, until they were pushed against one of the farm buildings. Something crashed against the roof—another section of the house—and splintered, flying up against the girl. She was thrown backwards, away from Stuart, who lunged after her. They fell into the water while the boy screamed. The girl's arms threshed wildly against Stuart. The water was cold, and its aliveness, its sinister energy, surprised him more than the thought that he would drown—that he would never endure the night. Struggling with the girl, he forced her back to the roof, pushed her up. Bare, twisted nails raked his hands. "Gahdamn you, Jackie, you give a hand!" the girl said as Stuart crawled back up. He lay, exhausted, flat on his stomach and let the water and debris slosh over him.

His mind was calm beneath the surface buzzing. He liked to think that his mind was a clear, sane circle of quiet carefully preserved inside the chaos of the storm—that the three of them were safe within the sanctity of this circle; this was how man always conquered nature, how he subdued things greater than himself. But whenever he did speak to her it was in short grunts, in her own idiom: "This ain't so bad!" or "It'll let up pretty soon!" Now the girl held him in her arms as if he were a child, and he did not have the strength to pull away. Of his own free will he had given himself to this storm, or to the strange desire to save someone in it—but now he felt grateful for the girl, even for her brother, for they had saved him as much as he had saved them. Stuart thought of his wife at home, walking through the rooms, waiting for him; he thought of his daughters in their twin beds, two glasses of water on their bureau. . . . But these people knew nothing of him: in his experience now he did not belong to them. Perhaps he had misunderstood his role, his life? Perhaps he had blundered out of his way, drawn into the wrong life, surrendered to the wrong role. What had blinded him to the possibility of many lives, many masks, many arms that might so embrace him? A word not heard one day, a gesture misinterpreted, a leveling of someone's eyes in a certain unmistakable manner, which he had mistaken just the same! The consequences of such errors might trail insanely into the future, across miles of land, across worlds. He only now sensed the incompleteness of his former life. . . . "Look! Look!" the girl cried, jostling him out of his stupor. "Take a look at that, mister!"

He raised himself on one elbow. A streak of light broke out of the dark. Lanterns, he thought, a rescue party already. . . . But the rain dissolved the light; then it reappeared with a beauty that startled him. "What is it?" the boy screamed. "How come it's here?" They watched it filter through the rain, rays knifing through and showing, now, how buildings and trees crouched close about them. "It's the sun, the sun going down," the girl said. "The sun!" said Stuart, who had thought it was night. "The sun!" They stared at it until it disappeared.

THE WAVES calmed sometime before dawn. By then the roof had lost its peak and water ran unchecked over it, in generous waves and then in thin waves, alternately, as the roof bobbed up and down. The three huddled together with their backs to the wind. Water came now in slow drifts. "It's just got to spread itself out far enough so's it will be even," said the girl, "then it'll go down." She spoke without sounding tired, only a little disgusted—as if things weren't working fast enough to suit her. "Soon as it goes down we'll start toward town and see if there ain't somebody coming out to get us in a boat," she said, chattily and comfortably, into Stuart's ear. Her manner astonished Stuart, who had been thinking all night of the humiliation and pain he had suffered. "Bet the old bastard will be glad to see us," she said, "even if he did go off like that. Well, he never knew a storm was coming. Me and him get along pretty well—he ain't so bad." She wiped her face; it was filthy with dirt and blood. "He'll buy you a drink, mister, for saving us how you did. That was something to have happen—a man just driving up to get us!" And she poked Stuart in the ribs.

The wind warmed as the sun rose. Rain turned to mist and back to rain again, still falling heavily, and now objects were clear about them. The roof had been shoved against the corner of the barn and a mound of dirt, and eddied there without much trouble. Right about them, in a kind of halo, a thick blanket of vegetation and filth bobbed. The fence had disappeared and the house had collapsed and been driven against a ridge of land. The barn itself had fallen in, but the stone support looked untouched, and it was against this they had been shoved. Stuart thought he could see his car—or something over there where the road used to be.

"I bet it ain't deep. Hell," said the girl, sticking her foot into the water. The boy leaned over the edge and scooped up some of the filth in his hands. "Lookit all the spiders," he said. He wiped his face slowly. "Leave them gahdamn spiders alone," said the girl. "You want me to shove them down your throat?" She slid to the edge and lowered her legs. "Yah, I touched bottom. It ain't bad." But then she began coughing and drew herself back. Her coughing made Stuart cough: his chest and throat were ravaged, shaken. He lay exhausted when the fit left him and realized, suddenly, that they were all sick—that something had happened to them. They had to get off the roof. Now, with the sun up, things did not look so bad: there was a ridge of trees a short distance away on a long, red clay hill. "We'll go over there," Stuart said. "Do you think you can make it?"

The boy played in the filth, without looking up, but the girl gnawed at her lip to show she was thinking. "I spose so," she said. "But him—I don't know about him."

"Your brother? What's wrong?"

"Turn around. Hey, stupid. Turn around." She prodded the boy, who jerked around, terrified, to stare at Stuart. His thin bony face gave way to a drooping mouth. "Gone loony, it looks like," the girl said with a touch of regret. "Oh, he had times like this before. It might go away."

Stuart was transfixed by the boy's stare. The realization of what had happened struck him like a blow, sickening his stomach. "We'll get him over there," he said, making his words sound good. "We can wait there for someone to come. Someone in a boat. He'll be better there."

"I spose so," said the girl vaguely.

Stuart carried the boy while the girl splashed eagerly ahead. The water was sometimes up to his thighs. "Hold on another minute," he pleaded. The boy stared out at the water as if he thought he were being taken somewhere to be drowned. "Put your arms around my neck. Hold on," Stuart said. He shut his eyes and every time he looked up the girl was still a few yards ahead and the hill looked no closer. The boy breathed hollowly, coughing into Stuart's face. His own face and neck were covered with small red bites. Ahead, the girl walked with her shoulders lunged forward as if to hurry her there, her great thighs straining against the water, more than a match for it. As Stuart watched her, something was on the side of his face—in his ear—and with a scream he slapped at it, nearly dropping the boy. The girl whirled around. Stuart slapped at his face and must have knocked it off—probably a spider. The boy, upset by Stuart's outcry, began sucking in air faster and faster as if he were dying. "I'm all right, I'm all right," Stuart whispered, "just hold on another minute. . . ."

When he finally got to the hill the girl helped pull him up. He set the boy down with a grunt, trying to put the boy's legs under him so he could stand. But the boy sank to the ground and turned over and vomited into the water; his body shook as if he were having convulsions. Again the thought that the night had poisoned them, their own breaths had sucked germs into their bodies, struck Stuart with an irresistible force. "Let him lay down and rest," the girl said, pulling tentatively at the back of her brother's belt, as if she were thinking of dragging him farther up the slope. "We sure do thank you, mister," she said.

Stuart climbed to the crest of the hill. His heart pounded madly, blood pounded in his ears. What was going to happen? Was anything going to happen? How disappointing it looked—ridges of land showing through the water and the healthy sunlight pushing back the mist. Who would believe him when he told of the night, of the times when death seemed certain . . . ? Anger welled up in him already as he imagined the tolerant faces of his friends, his children's faces ready to turn to other amusements, other oddities. His wife would believe him; she would shudder, holding him, burying her small face in his neck. But what could she understand of his experience, having had no part in it? . . . Stuart cried out; he had nearly stepped on a tangle of snakes. Were they alive? He backed away in terror. The snakes gleamed wetly in the morning light, heads together as if conspiring. Four . . . five of them—they too had swum for this land, they too had survived the night, they had as much reason to be proud of themselves as Stuart.

He gagged and turned away. Down by the water line the boy lay flat on his stomach and the girl squatted nearby, wringing out her denim jacket. The water behind them caught the sunlight and gleamed might- ily, putting them into silhouette. The girl's arms moved slowly, hard with muscle. The boy lay coughing gently. Watching them, Stuart was beset by a strange desire: he wanted to run at them, demand their gratitude, their love. Why should they not love him, when he had saved their lives? When he had lost what he was just the day before, turned now into a different person, a stranger even to himself? Stuart stooped and picked up a rock. A broad hot hand seemed to press against his chest. He threw the rock out into the water and said, "Hey!"

The girl glanced around but the boy did not move. Stuart sat down on the soggy ground and waited. After a while the girl looked away; she spread the jacket out to dry. Great banked clouds rose into the sky, re- flected in the water—jagged and bent in the waves. Stuart waited as the sun took over the sky. Mist at the horizon glowed, thinned, gave way to solid shapes. Light did not strike cleanly across the land, but was marred by ridges of trees and parts of buildings, and around a corner at any time Stuart expected to see a rescuing party—in a rowboat or something.

"Hey, mister." He woke; he must have been dozing. The girl had called him. "Hey. Whyn't you come down here? There's all them snakes up there."

Stuart scrambled to his feet. When he stumbled downhill, embar- rassed and frightened, the girl said chattily, "The sons of bitches are crawling all over here. He chast some away." The boy was on his feet and looking around with an important air. His coming alive startled Stuart—indeed, the coming alive of the day, of the world, evoked alarm in him. All things came back to what they were. The girl's alert eyes, the firm set of her mouth, had not changed—the sunlight had not changed, or the land, really; only Stuart had been changed. He wondered at it . . . and the girl must have seen something in his face that he himself did not yet know about, for her eyes narrowed, her throat gulped a big swallow, her arms moved slowly up to show her raw elbows. "We'll get rid of them," Stuart said, breaking the silence. "Him and me. We'll do it."

The boy was delighted. "I got a stick," he said, waving a thin whip-like branch. "There's some over here."

"We'll get them," Stuart said. But when he started to walk, a rock slipped loose and he fell back into the mud. He laughed aloud. The girl, squatting a few feet away, watched him silently. Stuart got to his feet, still laughing. "You know much about it, kid?" he said, cupping his hand on the boy's head.

"About what?" said the boy.

"Killing snakes," said Stuart.

"I spose—I spose you just kill them."

The boy hurried alongside Stuart. "I need a stick," Stuart said; they got him one from the water, about the size of an ax. "Go by that bush," Stuart said, "there might be some there."

The boy attacked the bush in a frenzy. He nearly fell into it. His enthusiasm somehow pleased Stuart, but there were no snakes in the bush. "Go down that way," Stuart ordered. He glanced back at the girl: she watched them. Stuart and the boy went on with their sticks held in mid-air. "God put them here to keep us awake," the boy said brightly. "See we don't forget about Him." Mud sucked at their feet. "Last year we couldn't fire the woods on account of it so dry. This year can't either on account of the water. We got to get the snakes like this."

Stuart hurried as if he had somewhere to go. The boy, matching his steps, went faster and faster, panting, waving his stick angrily in the air. The boy complained about snakes and, listening to him, fascinated by him, in that instant Stuart saw everything. He saw the conventional dawn that had mocked the night, had mocked his desire to help people in trouble; he saw, beyond that, his father's home emptied now even of ghosts. He realized that the God of these people had indeed arranged things, had breathed the order of chaos into forms, had animated them, had animated even Stuart himself forty years ago. The knowledge of this fact struck him about the same way as the nest of snakes had struck him—an image leaping right to the eye, pouncing upon the mind, joining itself with the perceiver. "Hey, hey!" cried the boy, who had found a snake: the snake crawled noisily and not very quickly up the slope, a brown-speckled snake. The boy ran clumsily after it. Stuart was astonished at the boy's stupidity, at his inability to see, now, that the snake had vanished. Still he ran along the slope, waving his stick, shouting, "I'll get you! I'll get you!" This must have been the sign Stuart was waiting for. When the boy turned, Stuart was right behind him. "It got away up there," the boy said. "We got to get it." When Stuart lifted his stick the boy fell back a step but went on in mechanical excitement, "It's up there, gotten hid in the weeds. It ain't me," he said, "it ain't me that—" Stuart's blow struck the boy on the side of the head, and the rotted limb shattered into soft wet pieces. The boy stumbled down toward the water. He was coughing when Stuart took hold of him and began shaking him madly, and he did nothing but cough, violently and with all his concentration, even when Stuart bent to grab a rock and brought it down on his head. Stuart let him fall into the water. He could hear him breathing and he could see, about the boy's lips, tiny flecks or bubbles of blood appearing and disappearing with his breath.

When the boy's eyes opened, Stuart fell upon him. They struggled savagely in the water. Again the boy went limp; Stuart stood, panting, and waited. Nothing happened for a minute or so. But then he saw something—the boy's fingers moving up through the water, soaring to the surface! "Will you quit it!" Stuart screamed. He was about to throw himself upon the boy again when the thought of the boy's life, bubbling out between his lips, moving his fingers, filled him with such outraged disgust that he backed away. He threw the rock out into the water and ran back, stumbling, to where the girl stood.

She had nothing to say: her jaw was hard, her mouth a narrow line, her thick nose oddly white against her dirty face. Only her eyes moved, and these were black, lustrous, at once demanding and terrified. She held a board in one hand. Stuart did not have time to think, but, as he lunged toward her, he could already see himself grappling with her in the mud, forcing her down, tearing her ugly clothing from her body—"Lookit!"

AT THE SEMINARY

M R. DOWNEY LEFT the expressway at the right exit, but ten min-
utes later he was lost. His wife was sitting in the back seat of the
car, her round serious face made unfamiliar by the sunglasses she wore,
and when he glanced at her in the rearview mirror she did not seem to
acknowledge him. His daughter, a big girl in a yellow sleeveless dress,
was bent over the map and tracing something with her finger. "Just what
I thought, that turn back there," she said. "That one to the left, by the
hot dog stand. I thought that was the turn."

His stomach was too upset; he could not argue. He did not argue
with his daughter or his wife or his son Peter, though he could remem-
ber a time when he had argued with someone—his father, perhaps. His
daughter, Sally, sat confidently beside him with her fingernail still poised
against a tiny line on the map, as if she feared moving it would precipi-
tate them into the wilderness. "Turn around, Daddy, for heaven's sake,"
she said. "You keep on driving way out of the way."

"Well, I didn't notice any sign," his wife said suddenly.

His daughter turned slowly. She too wore sunglasses, white plastic glasses with ornate frames and dark curved lenses. He could see her eyes close. "You weren't watching, then. I'm the one with the map anyway. I was pretty sure that was the turn, back there, but he went by too fast. I had to look it up on the map."

"Why didn't you say anything before?"

"I don't know." Sally shrugged her shoulders.

"Well, I didn't see any sign back there."

They had argued for the last hundred miles, off and on. Mr. Downey tried to shut out their voices, not looking at them, concentrating now on finding a place to turn the car around before his daughter complained again. They were on a narrow black-top road in the country, with untended fields on either side. Mr. Downey slowed. "There's a big ditch out there," Sally said. She tapped at the window with her nails. "Be careful, Daddy."

"How much room does he have?"

"He's got—oh—some room yet—Keep on going, Daddy. Keep on—Wait. No, Daddy, wait."

He braked the car. He could tell by his daughter's stiff, alert back that they had nearly gone into the ditch. "Okay, Daddy, great. Now pull ahead." Sally began waving her hand toward him, her pink fingernails glistening roguishly. "Pull ahead, Daddy, that's it. That's it."

He had managed to turn around. Now the sun was slanted before them again; they had been driving into it all day. "How far back was that road," he said.

"Oh, a few miles, Daddy. No trouble."

They arrived at the crossroads. "See, there's the sign. There it is," Sally said. She was quite excited. Though she had been overweight by twenty or twenty-five pounds for years, she often bounced about to demonstrate her childish pleasure; she did so now. "See, what did I tell you? Mom? There it is, there's the sign. U.S. 274, going east, and there's the hot dog stand."

"It's closed."

"Yes, it's closed, I can see that, it's boarded up but it's there," Sally said. She had turned slightly to face her mother, the pink flesh creasing along her neck, her eyes again shut in patient exasperation.

They drove east on 274. "It's only thirty more miles," Sally said. "Can I turn on the radio now?" Immediately she snapped it on. In a moment they heard a voice accompanied by guitars and drums. The music made Mr. Downey's stomach cringe. He drove on, his eyes searching the top of the next ridge, as if he expected to see the handsome buildings of the seminary beckoning to him, assuring him. His wife threw down a magazine in the back seat. "Sally, please turn that off. That's too loud. You know you're only pretending to like it and it's giving your father a headache."

"Is it?" Sally said in his ear.

"It's too loud. Turn it off," his wife said.

"Daddy, is it?"

He began to shake his head, began to nod it, said he didn't know. "This business about Pete," he said apologetically.

Sally paused. Then she snapped off the radio briskly. She seemed to throw herself back against the seat, her arms folded so tightly that the thick flesh of her upper arm began to drain white. They drove for a while in silence. "Well, all right, turn it on," Mr. Downey said. He glanced at Sally, who refused to move. She was twenty-three, not what anyone would call fat, yet noticeably plump, her cheeks rounded and generous. Behind the dark glasses her eyes were glittering, threatened by stubborn tears. She wore a bright yellow cotton dress that strained about her, the color made fierce by the sun, as if it would be hot to the touch. "You can turn it on, Sally," Mr. Downey said. "I don't care."

"It gives you a headache," his wife said. She had thrown down the magazine again. "Why do you always give in to her?"

Sally snorted.

"She doesn't care about Peter!" his wife cried. Her anguish was sudden and unfeigned; both Mr. Downey and Sally stiffened. They looked ahead at the signs—advertisements for hotels, motels, service stations, restaurants. "Got to find a motel for tonight," Sally muttered.

"She doesn't care, neither of you cares," Mr. Downey's wife went on. "The burden always falls on me. He wrote the letter to me, I was the one who had to open it—"

"Daddy got a letter too. He got one right after," Sally said sullenly.

"But Peter wrote to me first. He understood."

"He always was a mommy's boy!"

"I don't want to hear that. I never want to hear that."

"Nevertheless," said Sally.

"I said I don't want to hear that again. Ever."

"Okay, you won't. Don't get excited."

Mr. Downey pulled off the road suddenly. He stopped the car and sat with his head bowed; other automobiles rushed past. "I won't be able to go on," he said. "Not if you keep this up."

Embarrassed, wife and daughter said nothing. They stared at nothing. Sally, after a moment, rubbed her nose with her fist. She felt her jaw clench as it did sometimes at night, while she slept, as if she were biting down hard upon something ugly but could not let go. Outside, in a wild field, was a gigantic billboard advertising a motel. From a great height a woman in a red bathing suit was diving into a bright aqua swimming pool. Mrs. Downey, taking her rosary out of her purse, stared out at this sign also, felt her daughter staring at it, thought what her daughter thought. In the awkward silence they felt closer to each other than either did to Mr. Downey. They said nothing, proudly. After a while, getting no answer, Mr. Downey started the car again and drove on.

THE DRIVE UP to the seminary was made of black-top, very smart and precise, turning gently about the hill, back and forth amid cascades of evergreens and nameless trees with rich foliage. It was early September, warm and muggy. The seminary buildings looked sleek and cool. Mr. Downey had the feeling that he could not possibly be going to see anyone he knew or had known, that this trip was a mystery, that the young man who awaited him, related obscurely to him by ties of blood and name, was a mystery that exhausted rather than interested him. Mr. Downey had been no more worried by his wife's hopes that Peter would become a priest than he had by her hopes that Sally would enter a convent; he had supposed both possibilities equally absurd. Yet, now that Peter had made his decision, now that Mr. Downey had grown accustomed to thinking of him in the way one thinks of a child who is somehow maimed and disqualified for life and therefore deserving of love, he felt as disturbed as his wife by Peter's letters. His son's "problem" could not be named, evidently; Peter himself did not understand it, could not explain it: he spoke of "wearing out," of "losing control," of seeing no one in the mirror when he went to look at himself. He complained of grit in his room, of hairs in food, of ballpoint ink he could not wash off his hands. Nothing that made sense. He spoke of not being able to remember his *name*, and this had disturbed Mr. Downey most of all; the hairs reported in his food had disturbed Mrs. Downey most of all. Nowhere had the boy said anything of quitting, however, and they thought that puzzling. If he had spoken in his incoherent letters of wanting to quit, of going to college, of traveling about the country to observe "life," of doing nothing at all, Mr. Downey would not have felt so frightened. He could not parrot, as his wife did, the words of the novice master who had telephoned them that week: Peter was suffering a "spiritual crisis." It was the fact that Peter had suggested no alternatives to his condition that alarmed his father. It might almost have been—and Mr. Downey had not mentioned this to his wife—that the alternative to the religious life had come to Peter to be no less than death.

God knew, Mr. Downey thought, he had wanted something else for Peter. He had wanted something else for them all, but he could not recall what it was. He blamed Peter's condition on his wife; at least Sally had escaped her mother's influence, there was nothing wrong with her. She was a healthy girl, loud and sure of herself, always her father's favorite. But perhaps behind her quick robust laugh there was the same sniveling sensitivity that had ruined Peter's young life for him. Sally had played boisterously with other girls and boys in the neighborhood, a leader in their games, running heavily about the house and through the bushes, while Peter had withdrawn to his solitary occupations, arranging and rearranging dead birds and butterflies in the back yard; but in the end, going up to bed, their slippers scuffing on the floor and their shoulders set as if resigned to the familiar terrors of the night, they had always seemed to Mr. Downey to be truly sister and brother, and related in no way to himself and his wife.

The seminary buildings were only three years old. Magnificently modern, aqua and beige, with great flights of glass and beds of complex plants on both the outside and the inside, huddling together against glass partitions so that the eye, dazed, could not tell where the outside stopped and the inside began: Mr. Downey felt uncertain and overwhelmed. He had not thought convincing the rector's speech, given on the day they had brought Peter up here, about the middle-class temperament that would relegate all religious matters to older forms, forms safely out of date. The rector had spoken passionately of the beauty of contemporary art and its stark contrast with the forms of nature, something Mr. Downey had not understood; nor had he understood what religion had to do with beauty or with art; nor had he understood how the buildings could have cost five million dollars. "Boy, is this place something," Sally said resentfully. "He's nuts if he wants to leave it and come back *home*." "He never said anything about leaving it," her mother said sharply.

They were met by Father Greer, with whom they had talked on the telephone earlier that week and who, standing alone on the evergreen-edged flagstone walk, seemed by his excessive calmness to be obscuring from them the fact of Peter's not being there. He was dark and smiling, taller than Mr. Downey and many years younger. "So very glad to see you," he said. "I hope you had an enjoyable ride? Peter is expected down at any moment." Very enjoyable, they assured him. Sally stood behind her father, as if suddenly shy. Mrs. Downey was touching her hair and nodding anxiously at Father Greer's words. In an awkward group they headed toward the entrance. Mr. Downey was smiling but as the young priest spoke, pointing out buildings and interesting sights, his eyes jumped about as if seeking out his son, expecting him to emerge around the corner of a building, out of an evergreen shrub. "The dormitory," Father Greer said, pointing. A building constructed into a hill, its first story disappearing into a riot of shrubs, much gleaming glass and metal. Beside it was the chapel, with a great brilliant cross that caught the sunlight and reflected it viciously. The light from the buildings, reflected and refracted by their thick glass, blinded Mr. Downey to whatever lay behind them—hills and forests and remote horizons. "No, we don't regret for an instant our having built out here," Father Greer was saying. They were in the lobby now. Mr. Downey looked around for Peter but saw no one. "They told us in the city that we'd go mad out here, but that was just jealousy. This is the ideal location for a college like ours. Absolutely ideal." They agreed. Mr. Downey could not recall just when he had noticed that some priests were younger than he, but he remembered a time when all priests were older, were truly "fathers" to him. "Please sit down here," Father Greer said. "This is a very comfortable spot." He too was looking about. Mr. Downey believed he could see, beyond the priest's cautious diplomatic charm, an expression of irritation. They were in an area blocked off from the rest of the lobby by thick plates of aqua-tinted glass. Great potted plants stood about in stone vases, the floor was tiled in a design of deep maroon and gray, the long low sofa on which they sat curved about a round marble coffee table of a most coldly beautiful, veined, fleshly color. Father Greer did not sit, but stood with his hands slightly extended and raised, as if he were blessing them against his will. "Will you all take martinis?" he said. They smiled self-consciously; Mrs. Downey said that Sally did not drink. "I'll take a martini," Sally said without looking up. Father Greer smiled.

Someone approached them, but it was not Peter. A boy Peter's age, dressed in a novice's outfit but wearing a white apron over it, came shyly to take their orders from Father Greer. "Peter will be down in a minute," Father Greer said. "Then we can all relax and talk and see what has developed. And we'll be having dinner precisely at six-thirty, I hope, in a very pleasant room at the back of this building—a kind of fireside room we use for special banquets and meetings. You didn't see it the last time you were here because it's just been completed this summer. If anyone would like to wash up—" He indicated graciously rest rooms at the far end of the area, GENTLEMEN, LADIES. Mrs. Downey stood, fingering her purse; Sally said crudely, "I'm all right." She had not taken off her sunglasses. Mrs. Downey left; they could smell the faint pleasant odor of her cologne. "He said he would be down promptly," Father Greer said in a slightly different voice, a confidential voice directed toward Mr. Downey, "but he may have forgotten. That's one of the—you know—one of the problems he has been having—he tends to forget things unless he writes them down. We discussed it Tuesday evening." "Yes, yes," Mr. Downey said, reddening. "He was never like that—at home—" "His mind seems somewhere else. He seems lost in contemplation—in another world," Father Greer said, not unkindly. "Sometimes this is a magnificent thing, you know, sometimes it develops into a higher, keener consciousness of one's vocation. . . . Sometimes it's greatly to be desired." He made Peter sound mysterious and talented, in a way, so that Sally found herself looking forward to meeting him. "If you'll excuse me for just a minute," Father Greer said, "I think I'll run over to his room and see how he is. Please excuse me—"

Sally and her father, left alone, had nothing to say to each other. Sally peered over the rims of her glasses at the lobby, but did not take the glasses off. She felt hot, heavy, vaguely sick, a little frightened; but at the thought of being frightened of something so trivial as seeing Peter again her mouth twisted into a smirk. She knew him too well. She knew him better than anyone knew him, and therefore resented the gravity with which he was always discussed, while her "problems" (whatever they were; she knew she was supposed to have some) were discussed by her mother and aunts as if they were immortal, immutable, impersonal problems like death and poverty, unfortunate conditions no one could change, and not very interesting.

Her mother returned, her shoulders bent forward anxiously as if she were straining ahead. "Where did he go?" she said, gazing from Mr. Downey to Sally. "Nothing happened, did it?" "He'll be right back," Sally said. "Sit down. Stop worrying." Her mother sat slowly; Sally could see the little white knobs of vertebrae at the top of her neck, curiously fragile. When the novice returned he was carrying a tray of cocktails. Another boy in an identical outfit appeared with a tray of shrimp and sauce and tiny golden crackers, which he set down on the marble table. Both young men were modest and sly, like magicians appearing and disappearing. "Suppose we better wait," Mr. Downey said regretfully, looking at the drinks.

But when Peter did arrive, with Father Greer just behind him, they were disappointed. He looked the same: a little pale, perhaps thinner, but his complexion seemed blemished in approximately the same way it had been for years, his shoulders were inclined forward, just like his and pleased with their lives they would just as soon spit in your eye when you passed them on the sidewalk, pushing baby buggies along as if that were a noble task! Sally did not approve of people talking in church or looking around, craning their bony old necks, nor did she approve of children—any children—who were noisy and restless and were apt to ask you why you were so fat, in front of everyone; she did not approve of people photographed on society pages or on magazine covers, or houses that were not made of brick or stone but were in poor neighborhoods with scrawny front lawns, but also she did not approve of lower-class white people who hated Negroes, as if they were any better themselves. She did not approve of high school boys and girls who swung along the sidewalks with their arms around each other, laughing vulgarly, and she did not approve of college students who did the same thing. While at college she had been so isolated by the sternness of her disapproval that no roommate had suited her and she had finally moved to a single room, where she had stayed for four years, studying angrily so that she could get good grades (which she did) and eating cookies and cakes and pies her mother sent her every week. She had loved her mother then and knew her mother loved her, since they never saw each other, but now that she was home and waiting for the placement bureau to send her notice of a decent job, something they evidently were not capable of doing, she and her mother hardly spoke and could feel each other's presence in the house as one feels or suspects the presence of an insect nearby. Her mother had wanted her to be pretty, she thought, and deliberately she was not pretty. (And Peter, there, still chewing, was homely too, she had never really noticed that before.) Sometimes she went to bed without washing her face. Certainly she did not wash her hair more than once a week, no matter what was coming up; and she had pretended severely not to care when her mother appropriated for herself the expensive lavender dress she had worn to the important functions at college when she had been twenty or thirty pounds lighter. She wore no make-up except lipstick, a girlish pink, and her shoes were always scuffed and marked by water lines, and she often deliberately bought dresses too large so the shoulders hung down sloppily. Everything angered her: the vanities of the world, the pettiness of most people, the banal luxuries she saw through at once—like this seminary, and the cocktails, when their own priest back home had new missions every week or new approaches to the Bishop's Relief Fund. She picked up the martini and sipped at it; its bitterness angered her. She put it down. She would not drink it and collaborate in this vanity. Even the graceful gleaming glass, finely shaped like a work of art, annoyed her, for beside it her own stumpy fingers and uneven nails looked ugly. What place was there in the real world for such things? She felt the real world to be elsewhere—she did not know where—in the little town they had passed through on the way up to the seminary, perhaps, where the ugly store fronts faced each other across a cobbled main street fifty years old, and where country people dawdled about in new shoes and new clothes, dressed for Saturday, looking on everything with admiration and pleasure. But what were these people talking about? She hunched forward in an exaggerated attitude of listening. Baseball. She was ashamed of her father, who spoke of baseball players familiarly, slowly, choosing his words as if each were important, so making a fool of himself. Father Greer, debonair and charming, was bored of course but would not show it. Mrs. Downey looked puzzled, as if she could not quite keep up with the conversation; the martini had made her dizzy. Peter, beside her, his awkward hands crossed on his knees, stared at something in the air. He was waiting, as they were all waiting, Sally supposed, for this conversation to veer suddenly around to him, confront him in his odd transfixed fear and demand from him some explanation of himself. Sally sipped at the cocktail and felt its bitterness expand to take in all of the scene before her. If Peter glanced at her she would look away; she would not help him. She needed no one herself, and wanted no one to need her. Yet she wondered why he did not look at her—why he sat so stiff, as if frozen, while about him chatter shot this way and that to ricochet harmlessly off surfaces.

The subject had been changed. "Peter made some particularly perceptive remarks on the *Antigone* of Sophocles this summer," Father Greer was saying. He had finished his martini and rolled the glass slowly between his palms, the delicate stem turning and glinting against his tanned skin. "We study a number of Greek tragedies in the original Greek. The boys find them strangely intriguing. Puzzles." Mr. and Mrs.

Downey were both sitting forward a little, listening. "The world view of the Greeks," Father Greer said severely, "is so astonishingly different from our own." Sally drew in her breath suddenly. "I wouldn't say that, precisely," she remarked. Father Greer smiled at her. "Of course there are many aspects of our civilizations that are similar," he said. "What strikes us as most barbaric, however, is their utter denial of the freedom of man's will." He thought her no antagonist, obviously; he spoke with a faintly condescending smile Sally detested because she believed she had been seeing it all her life. "But that might not be so strange, after all," she drawled. Her mother was frowning, picking at something imaginary on the rim of her cocktail glass. Her father was watching her as if she were performing a foolish and dangerous trick, like standing on her head. But Peter, sitting across from her with his long fingers clasped together on his knees, his back not touching the sofa, was staring at her and through her with a queer theatrical look of recognition, as if he had not really noticed her before. "And their violence," Sally said. "The violence of their lives—that might not be so strange to us either." "There is no violence in Greek drama," Father Greer said. Sally felt her face close up, suddenly. Her eyes began to narrow; her lips pursed themselves in a prim little look of defiance; the very contours of her generous face began to hunch themselves inward.

An awkward minute passed. "You still on that diet?" Peter said.

Sally's eyes opened. Peter was looking at her with a little smile. Her face burned. "What? Me? I—"

"Why, Peter," their mother said. "What do you mean?"

Peter's gaze plummeted. He examined his fingers. Sally, more stunned than angry, watched him as if he had become suddenly an antagonist, an open enemy; she saw that his hands were streaked with something—it looked like red ink or blood, something scrubbed into his skin.

"Sorry," Peter muttered.

In this crisis Father Greer seemed to fall back; his spine might have failed him unaccountably. The very light turned harsh and queer; churned about gently in the air-conditioned lounge, it seemed not to be illuminating them but to be pushing them away from each other, emphasizing certain details that were not to be cherished: Peter's acne,

In the chapel they fell silent. Sally frowned. She was going to take off her sunglasses, but stopped. The chapel was gigantic: a ceiling dull and remote as the sky itself, finely lined, veined as if with the chill of distance or time, luring the eye up and forward, relentlessly forward, to the great statue of the crucified Christ behind the altar. There it was. The walls of the buildings might have fallen away, the veneer of words themselves might have been peeled back, to reveal this agonized body nailed to the cross: the contours of the statue so glib, so perfect, that they seemed to Sally to be but the mocking surfaces of another statue, a fossilized creature caught forever within that crust—the human model for it, suffocated and buried. Father Greer chatted excitedly about something: about that sleek white Christ, a perfect immaculate white, the veins of his feet and throat throbbing a frozen immaculate white. About his head drops of white blood had coagulated over the centuries; a hard white crown of thorns pierced his skin lovingly, rendered by art into something fragile and fine. The chapel was empty. No, not empty; at the very front a figure knelt, praying. The air was cold and stagnant. Nothing swirled here; time itself had run out, run down. Sally felt perspiration on her forehead and under her arms. She had begun to ache strangely, her head and her body; she could not locate the dull throbbing pain. Her head craning stupidly, she stared up at the gigantic statue. Yes, yes, she would agree to Father Greer's questioning glance: was it not magnificent? Yes, but what was it that was magnificent? What did they know? What were they looking at? How did they know—and she thought of this for no reason, absolutely no reason—what their names were, their stupid names? How did they know anything? Her glance fell in confusion to her parents' nervous smiles and she felt she did not recognize them. And to Peter's awkward profile, so self-pitying; was it to tell them he could no longer believe in Christ that he had brought them to the seminary? But she understood, staring at her brother's rigid face, that he could no more not believe in Christ than she could: that the great milky statue itself could more easily twitch into life than they could disbelieve the ghostly contours that lay behind that form, lost in history—and that they were doomed, brother and sister, doomed in some obscure inexplicable vexing way neither could understand, and their parents and this priest, whispering rather loudly about "seating capacity," could never understand. The three adults walked toward the front of the chapel, down the side aisle. Peter stumbled as if a rock had rolled suddenly before his feet; Sally could not move. She stared up at the statue with the martini glass in her hand. She and Peter might have been awaiting a vision, patiently as always. Yet it will only end, she thought savagely, in steak for dinner—a delicate tossed salad—wine— And as her body flinched in outrage at this vision (so powerful as to have evoked in her a rush of hunger, in spite of herself) she felt a sudden release of pressure, a gentle aching relaxation she did not at first recognize. A minute flow of blood. She did not move, paralyzed, her mouth slowly opening in an expression of awe that might have been religious, so total and commanding was it. Her entire life, her being, her very soul might have been conjured up and superimposed upon that rigid white statue, so intensely did she stare at it, her horror transformed into a prayer of utter silence, utter wordlessness, as she felt the unmistakable relentless flow of blood begin in her loins. Then her face went slack. She looked at the martini glass, brought it to her mouth, finished the drink. She smirked. She had known this would happen, had thought of it the day before, then had forgotten. She had forgotten. She could not have forgotten but she did, and it was for this reason she grinned at the smudged glass in her hand. Now Peter turned and followed the others; she followed him. Bleeding warmly and secretly. Her gaze was hot upon the backs of her parents, her mother especially, cleanly odored well-dressed woman: what a surprise! What a surprise she had for her! "I'm afraid this is cloistered," Father Greer whispered. He looked sorry. They headed in another direction, through a broad passageway, then out, out and into a spacious foyer; now they could breathe.

"What beauty! Immeasurable beauty!" Father Greer said aloud. His eyes were brittle with awe, an awe perhaps forced from him; he looked quite moved. Yet what was he moved at, Sally thought angrily, what had they been looking at, what did they *know*? Peter wiped at his nose, surreptitiously, but of course everyone saw him. What did they know? What had they seen? What might they ever trust again in a world of closed surfaces, of panels just sliding shut? She was shaken, and only after a moment did she notice her mother glaring at her, at the cocktail glass and the sunglasses. Her mother's face was white and handsome with the splendor of her hatred. Sally smirked. She felt the faithful blood inside her seeping, easing downward. Father Greer pointed out something further—someone agreed—she felt the hot blood on her legs. She was paralyzed, charmed. The others walked on but she did not move. Her mother glanced around. "Sally?" she said. Sally took a step, precariously. Nothing. Perhaps she would be safe. She caught her mother's gaze and held it, as if seeking help, hoping for her mother to draw her safely to her by the sheer force of her impatience. Then, for no reason, she took a hard, brutal step forward, bringing her flat heel down hard on the floor. Then again. She strode forward, brusquely, as if trying to dent the marble floor. The others were waiting for her, not especially watching her. She slammed down her heel so that it stung, and the blood jerked free. It ran instantly down the inside of her leg to her foot. She was breathing hard, excited and terrified and somehow pleased, waiting for her mother to notice. Why didn't she notice? Sally glanced down, was startled to see how big her stomach was, billowing out in the babyish yellow dress she had worn here out of spite, and saw the delicate trickle of blood there—on her calf, her ankle (which was not too clean), inside her scuffed shoe and so out of sight! At the door the others waited: the slim priest in black, who could see everything and nothing, politely, omnipotently; her father and mother, strangers also, who would see and suffer their vision as it swelled deafeningly upon them, their absolute disbelief at what they saw; her brother Peter, who was staring down at the floor just before her robust feet as if he had seen something that had turned him to stone.

Sally smiled angrily. She faced her mother, her father. Nothing. They looked away, they did not look at each other. Father Greer was holding the door open. No one spoke. Sally wanted to say, "That sure must have cost a lot!" but she could not speak. She saw Father Greer's legs hold themselves in stride, she could nearly see his muscles resist the desperate ache they felt to carry him somewhere—the end of this corridor, through one of the mysterious doors, or back to the cloistered sanctuary behind them. "And these, these," he said, "these are tiny

chapels—all along here—Down there the main sacristy—" His words
fell upon them from a distance, entirely without emotion. He showed
nothing. Sally stomped on the floor as if killing insects, yet he did not
look around. She felt blood trickling down her legs, a sensation she
thought somehow quite pleasant, and in her shoes her toes wriggled in
anticipation of the shame soon to befall them. On they walked. At each
of Father Greer's words they leaned forward, anxious not to be denied,
anxious to catch his eye, force upon him the knowledge that they saw
nothing, knew nothing, heard only what he told them. Sally began to
giggle. She wanted to ask Father Greer something, but the rigidity of her
hysteria was too inflexible; she found she could not open her mouth. Her
jaws seemed locked together. But this isn't my fault, she cried mockingly
to their incredulous accusing backs, I never asked for it, I never asked
God to make me a woman! She could not stop grinning. What beauty!
What immeasurable beauty! It was that she grinned at, nothing else.
That immeasurable beauty. Each heavy step, each ponderous straining
of her thick thighs, centuries old, each sigh that swelled up into her chest
and throat, each shy glance from her brother, all these faded into a sen-
sation of overwhelming light or sound, something dazzling and roaring
at once, that seemed to her to make her existence suddenly beautiful:
complete: ended.

Then Peter was upon her. He grabbed for her throat. His face was
anguished, she was able to see that much, and as she screamed and
lunged back against the wall her parents and the priest turned, whirled
back, seemed for an instant to be attacking her as well. "Damn you!
Damn you!" Peter cried. His voice rose to a scream, a girl's scream. He
managed to break away from Father Greer's arms and struck her, his
fists pounding, a child's battle Sally seemed to be watching from across
the corridor, through a door, across a span of years—"Damn you! Now I
can't leave! I can't leave!" he cried. They pulled him back. He had gone
limp. He hid his face and sobbed; she remembered him sobbing that
way, often. Of course. His habitual sob, sheer helplessness before her
strength, her superior age, weight, complacency. She gasped, her body
still shuddering in alarm, ready to fight, to kill, her strong competent
legs spread apart to give her balance. Her heart pounded like a magnifi-

cent angel demanding to be released, to be set upon her enemies. Peter
turned away, into the priest's embrace, still sobbing. He showed nothing
of his face but a patch by his jaw, a splotched patch of adolescent skin.

MR. DOWNEY entered the expressway without slackening speed. It
was late, nearly midnight. He had far to go. Fortified by alcohol, dizzily
confident, he seemed to be driving into a wild darkness made familiar
by concrete, signs, maps, and his own skillful driving. Beside him his
daughter sat with the map in hand again, but they would not need it.
He knew where he was driving them. The expressway was deserted,
held no challenge to him, the sheer depthless dark beyond the range of
his headlights could not touch him, fortified as he was by the knowledge
of precisely where he was going. Signs, illuminated by his headlights,
flashed up clearly and were gone, they were unmistakable, they would
not betray him, just as visions of that evening flashed up to him, without
terror, and were gone. They knew what to do. None of this surprised
them. Nothing surprised them. (He thought of the confessional; that
explained it.) A few weeks of rest, nothing more, the boy would be
safe, there was nothing to worry about. And he felt, numbly, that there
really was nothing to worry about any longer, that everything had been
somehow decided, that it had happened in his presence but he had not
quite seen it. The priests were right: Father Greer and the older priest,
a very kindly Irishman Mr. Downey had trusted at once. Something had
been decided, delivered over. It was all right. In the back seat his wife
sat impassive and mindless, watching the road that led inexorably back
home. Beside him his daughter sat heavily, her arms folded. She yawned.
Then she reached out casually to turn on the radio. "Please, Sally," her
mother said at once, as if stirred to life. The radio clicked on. Static, a
man's voice. Music. "Sally," her mother said. Sally's plump arm waited,
her fingers still on the knob. "It bothers your father," Mrs. Downey said,
"you know it gives him a headache." "I'll turn it down real low," Sally
said. Out of the corner of Mr. Downey's eye her face loomed blank and
milky, like a threatening moon he dared not look upon.

IN THE REGION
OF ICE

———

SISTER IRENE WAS a tall, deft woman in her early thirties. What one could see of her face made a striking impression—serious, hard gray eyes, a long slender nose, a face waxen with thought. Seen at the right time, from the right angle, she was almost handsome. In her past teaching positions she had drawn a little upon the fact of her being young and brilliant and also a nun, but she was beginning to grow out of that.

This was a new university and an entirely new world. She had heard—of course it was true—that the Jesuit administration of this school had hired her at the last moment to save money and to head off the appointment of a man of dubious religious commitment. She had prayed for the necessary energy to get her through this first semester. She had no trouble with teaching itself; once she stood before a classroom she felt herself capable of anything. It was the world immediately outside the classroom that confused and alarmed her, though she let none of this show—the cynicism of her colleagues, the indifference of many of the students, and, above all, the looks she got that told her nothing much would be expected of her because she was a nun. This took energy, strength. At times she had the idea that she was on trial and that the excuses she made to herself about her discomfort were only the common excuses made by guilty people. But in front of a class she had no time to worry about herself or the conflicts in her mind. She became, once and for all, a figure existing only for the benefit of others, an instrument by which facts were communicated.

About two weeks after the semester began, Sister Irene noticed a new student in her class. He was slight and fair-haired, and his face was blank, but not blank by accident, blank on purpose, suppressed and restricted into a dumbness that looked hysterical. She was prepared for him before he raised his hand, and when she saw his arm jerk, as if he had at last lost control of it, she nodded to him without hesitation.

"Sister, how can this be reconciled with Shakespeare's vision in *Hamlet*? How can these opposing views be in the same mind?"

Students glanced at him, mildly surprised. He did not belong in the class, and this was mysterious, but his manner was urgent and blind.

"There is no need to reconcile opposing views," Sister Irene said, leaning forward against the podium. "In one play Shakespeare suggests one vision, in another play another; the plays are not simultaneous creations, and even if they were, we never demand a logical—"

"We must demand a logical consistency," the young man said. "The idea of education is itself predicated upon consistency, order, sanity—"

He had interrupted her, and she hardened her face against him—for his sake, not her own, since she did not really care. But he noticed nothing. "Please see me after class," she said.

After class the young man hurried up to her.

"Sister Irene, I hope you didn't mind my visiting today. I'd heard some things, interesting things," he said. He stared at her, and something in her face allowed him to smile. "I . . . could we talk in your office? Do you have time?"

They walked down to her office. Sister Irene sat at her desk, and the young man sat facing her; for a moment they were self-conscious and silent.

"Well, I suppose you know—I'm a Jew," he said.

Sister Irene stared at him. "Yes?" she said.

"What am I doing at a Catholic university, huh?" He grinned. "That's what you want to know."

She made a vague movement of her hand to show that she had no thoughts on this, nothing at all, but he seemed not to catch it. He was sitting on the edge of the straight-backed chair. She saw that he was young but did not really look young. There were harsh lines on either side of his mouth, as if he had misused that youthful mouth somehow. His skin was almost as pale as hers, his eyes were dark and not quite in focus. He looked at her and through her and around her, as his voice surrounded them both. His voice was a little shrill at times.

"Listen, I did the right thing today—visiting your class! God, what a lucky accident it was; some jerk mentioned you, said you were a good teacher—I thought, what a laugh! These people know about good teachers here? But yes, listen, yes, I'm not kidding—you are good. I mean that."

Sister Irene frowned. "I don't quite understand what all this means."

He smiled and waved aside her formality, as if he knew better. "Listen, I got my B.A. at Columbia, then I came back here to this crappy city. I mean, I did it on purpose, I wanted to come back. I wanted to. I have my reasons for doing things. I'm on a three-thousand-dollar fellowship," he said, and waited for that to impress her. "You know, I could have gone almost anywhere with that fellowship, and I came back home here—my home's in the city—and enrolled here. This was last year. This is my second year. I'm working on a thesis, I mean I was, my master's thesis—but the hell with that. What I want to ask you is this: Can I enroll in your class, is it too late? We have to get special permission if we're late."

Sister Irene felt something nudging her, some uneasiness in him that was pleading with her not to be offended by his abrupt, familiar manner. He seemed to be promising another self, a better self, as if his fair, childish, almost cherubic face were doing tricks to distract her from what his words said.

"Are you in English studies?" she asked.

"I was in history. Listen," he said, and his mouth did something odd, drawing itself down into a smile that made the lines about it deepen like knives, "listen, they kicked me out."

He sat back, watching her. He crossed his legs. He took out a package of cigarettes and offered her one. Sister Irene shook her head, staring at his hands. They were small and stubby and might have belonged to a ten-year-old, and the nails were a strange near-violet color. It took him awhile to extract a cigarette.

"Yeah, kicked me out. What do you think of that?"

"I don't understand."

"My master's thesis was coming along beautifully, and then this bastard—I mean, excuse me, this professor, I won't pollute your office with his name—he started making criticisms, he said some things were unacceptable, he—" The boy leaned forward and hunched his narrow shoulders in a parody of secrecy. "We had an argument. I told him some frank things, things only a broad-minded person could hear about himself. That takes courage, right? He didn't have it! He kicked me out of the master's program, so now I'm coming into English. Literature is greater than history; European history is one big pile of garbage. Sky-high. Filth and rotting corpses, right? Aristotle says that poetry is higher than history; he's right; in your class today I suddenly realized that this is my field, Shakespeare, only Shakespeare is—"

Sister Irene guessed that he was going to say that only Shakespeare was equal to him, and she caught the moment of recognition and hesitation, the half-raised arm, the keen, frowning forehead, the narrowed eyes; then he thought better of it and did not end the sentence. "The students in your class are mainly negligible, I can tell you that. You're new here, and I've been here a year—I would have finished my studies last year but my father got sick, he was hospitalized, I couldn't take exams and it was a mess—but I'll make it through English in one year or drop dead. I can do it, I can do anything. I'll take six courses at once—" He broke off, breathless. Sister Irene tried to smile. "All right then, it's settled? You'll let me in? Have I missed anything so far?"

He had no idea of the rudeness of his question. Sister Irene, feeling suddenly exhausted, said, "I'll give you a syllabus of the course."

"Fine! Wonderful!"

He got to his feet eagerly. He looked through the schedule, muttering to himself, making favorable noises. It struck Sister Irene that she was making a mistake to let him in. There were these moments when one had to make an intelligent decision. . . . But she was sympathetic with him, yes. She was sympathetic with something about him.

She found out his name the next day: Allen Weinstein.

AFTER THIS she came to her Shakespeare class with a sense of excitement. It became clear to her at once that Weinstein was the most intelligent student in the class. Until he had enrolled, she had not understood what was lacking, a mind that could appreciate her own. Within a week his jagged, protean mind had alienated the other students, and though he sat in the center of the class, he seemed totally alone, encased by a miniature world of his own. When he spoke of the "frenetic humanism of the High Renaissance," Sister Irene dreaded the raised eyebrows and mocking smiles of the other students, who no longer bothered to look at Weinstein. She wanted to defend him, but she never did, because there was something rude and dismal about his knowledge; he used it like a weapon, talking passionately of Nietzsche and Goethe and Freud until Sister Irene would be forced to close discussion.

In meditation, alone, she often thought of him. When she tried to talk about him to a young nun, Sister Carlotta, everything sounded gross. "But no, he's an excellent student," she insisted. "I'm very grateful to have him in class. It's just that . . . he thinks ideas are real." Sister Carlotta, who loved literature also, had been forced to teach grade-school arithmetic for the last four years. That might have been why she said, a little sharply, "You don't think ideas are real?"

Sister Irene acquiesced with a smile, but of course she did not think so: only reality is real.

When Weinstein did not show up for class on the day the first paper was due, Sister Irene's heart sank, and the sensation was somehow a familiar one. She began her lecture and kept waiting for the door to open and for him to hurry noisily back to his seat, grinning an apology toward her—but nothing happened.

If she had been deceived by him, she made herself think angrily, it was as a teacher and not as a woman. He had promised her nothing.

Weinstein appeared the next day near the steps of the liberal arts

building. She heard someone running behind her, a breathless exclama-
tion: "Sister Irene!" She turned and saw him, panting and grinning in
embarrassment. He wore a dark-blue suit with a necktie, and he looked,
despite his childish face, like a little old man; there was something oddly
precarious and fragile about him. "Sister Irene, I owe you an apology,
right?" He raised his eyebrows and smiled a sad, forlorn, yet irritatingly
conspiratorial smile. "The first paper—not in on time, and I know what
your rules are. . . . You won't accept late papers, I know—that's good
discipline, I'll do that when I teach too. But, unavoidably, I was unable
to come to school yesterday. There are many—many—" He gulped
for breath, and Sister Irene had the startling sense of seeing the real
Weinstein stare out at her, a terrified prisoner behind the confident
voice. "There are many complications in family life. Perhaps you are
unaware—I mean—"

She did not like him, but she felt this sympathy, something tug-
ging and nagging at her the way her parents had competed for her love
so many years before. They had been whining, weak people, and out
of their wet need for affection, the girl she had been (her name was
Yvonne) had emerged stronger than either of them, contemptuous of
tears because she had seen so many. But Weinstein was different; he
was not simply weak—perhaps he was not weak at all—but his strength
was confused and hysterical. She felt her customary rigidity as a teacher
begin to falter. "You may turn your paper in today if you have it," she
said, frowning.

Weinstein's mouth jerked into an incredulous grin. "Wonderful!
Marvelous!" he said. "You are very understanding, Sister Irene, I must
say. I must say . . . I didn't expect, really . . ." He was fumbling in a
shabby old briefcase for the paper. Sister Irene waited. She was pre-
pared for another of his excuses, certain that he did not have the paper,
when he suddenly straightened up and handed her something. "Here!
I took the liberty of writing thirty pages instead of just fifteen," he said.
He was obviously quite excited; his cheeks were mottled pink and white.
"You may disagree violently with my interpretation—I expect you to,
in fact I'm counting on it—but let me warn you, I have the exact proof,

right here in the play itself!" He was thumping at a book, his voice grow-
ing louder and shriller. Sister Irene, startled, wanted to put her hand
over his mouth and soothe him.

"Look," he said breathlessly, "may I talk with you? I have a class
now I hate, I loathe, I can't bear to sit through! Can I talk with you
instead?"

Because she was nervous, she stared at the title page of the paper:
" 'Erotic Melodies in *Romeo and Juliet*' by Allen Weinstein, Jr."

"All right?" he said. "Can we walk around here? Is it all right? I've
been anxious to talk with you about some things you said in class."

She was reluctant, but he seemed not to notice. They walked slowly
along the shaded campus paths. Weinstein did all the talking, of course,
and Sister Irene recognized nothing in his cascade of words that she had
mentioned in class. "The humanist must be committed to the totality of
life," he said passionately. "This is the failing one finds everywhere in
the academic world! I found it in New York and I found it here and I'm
no ingénu, I don't go around with my mouth hanging open—I'm experi-
enced, look, I've been to Europe, I've lived in Rome! I went everywhere
in Europe except Germany, I don't talk about Germany . . . Sister Irene,
think of the significant men in the last century, the men who've changed
the world! Jews, right? Marx, Freud, Einstein! Not that I believe Marx,
Marx is a madman . . . and Freud, no, my sympathies are with spiritual
humanism. I believe that the Jewish race is the exclusive . . . the exclu-
sive, what's the word, the exclusive means by which humanism will be
extended. . . . Humanism begins by excluding the Jew, and now," he
said with a high, surprised laugh, "the Jew will perfect it. After the Na-
zis, only the Jew is authorized to understand humanism, its limitations
and its possibilities. So, I say that the humanist is committed to life in
its totality and not just to his profession! The religious person is totally
religious, he is his religion! What else? I recognize in you a humanist
and a religious person—"

But he did not seem to be talking to her or even looking at her.

"Here, read this," he said. "I wrote it last night." It was a long free-
verse poem, typed on a typewriter whose ribbon was worn out.

"There's this trouble with my father, a wonderful man, a lovely man, but his health—his strength is fading, do you see? What must it be to him to see his son growing up? I mean, I'm a man now, he's getting old, weak, his health is bad—it's hell, right? I sympathize with him. I'd do anything for him, I'd cut open my veins, anything for a father—right? That's why I wasn't in school yesterday," he said, and his voice dropped for the last sentence, as if he had been dragged back to earth by a fact.

Sister Irene tried to read the poem, then pretended to read it. A jumble of words dealing with "life" and "death" and "darkness" and "love." "What do you think?" Weinstein said nervously, trying to read it over her shoulder and crowding against her.

"It's very . . . passionate," Sister Irene said.

This was the right comment; he took the poem back from her in silence, his face flushed with excitement. "Here, at this school, I have few people to talk with. I haven't shown anyone else that poem." He looked at her with his dark, intense eyes, and Sister Irene felt them focus upon her. She was terrified at what he was trying to do—he was trying to force her into a human relationship.

"Thank you for your paper," she said, turning away.

When he came the next day, ten minutes late, he was haughty and disdainful. He had nothing to say and sat with his arms folded. Sister Irene took back with her to the convent a feeling of betrayal and confusion. She had been hurt. It was absurd, and yet— She spent too much time thinking about him, as if he were somehow a kind of crystallization of her own loneliness; but she had no right to think so much of him. She did not want to think of him or of her loneliness. But Weinstein did so much more than think of his predicament: he embodied it, he acted it out, and that was perhaps why he fascinated her. It was as if he were doing a dance for her, a dance of shame and agony and delight, and so long as he did it, she was safe. She felt embarrassment for him, but also anxiety; she wanted to protect him. When the dean of the graduate school questioned her about Weinstein's work, she insisted that he was an "excellent" student, though she knew the dean had not wanted to hear that.

She prayed for guidance, she spent hours on her devotions, she was closer to her vocation than she had been for some years. Life at the convent became tinged with unreality, a misty distortion that took its tone from the glowering skies of the city at night, identical smokestacks ranged against the clouds and giving to the sky the excrement of the populated and successful earth. This city was not her city, this world was not her world. She felt no pride in knowing this, it was a fact. The little convent was not like an island in the center of this noisy world, but rather a kind of hole or crevice the world did not bother with, something of no interest. The convent's rhythm of life had nothing to do with the world's rhythm, it did not violate or alarm it in any way. Sister Irene tried to draw together the fragments of her life and synthesize them somehow in her vocation as a nun: she was a nun, she was recognized as a nun and had given herself happily to that life, she had a name, a place, she had dedicated her superior intelligence to the Church, she worked without pay and without expecting gratitude, she had given up pride, she did not think of herself but only of her work and her vocation, she did not think of anything external to these, she saturated herself daily in the knowledge that she was involved in the mystery of Christianity.

A daily terror attended this knowledge, however, for she sensed herself being drawn by that student, that Jewish boy, into a relationship she was not ready for. She wanted to cry out in fear that she was being forced into the role of a Christian, and what did that mean? What could her studies tell her? What could the other nuns tell her? She was alone, no one could help; he was making her into a Christian, and to her that was a mystery, a thing of terror, something others slipped on the way they slipped on their clothes, casually and thoughtlessly, but to her a magnificent and terrifying wonder.

For days she carried Weinstein's paper, marked A, around with her; he did not come to class. One day she checked with the graduate office and was told that Weinstein had called in to say his father was ill and that he would not be able to attend classes for a while. "He's strange, I remember him," the secretary said. "He missed all his exams last spring and made a lot of trouble. He was in and out of here every day."

So there was no more of Weinstein for a while, and Sister Irene stopped expecting him to hurry into class. Then, one morning, she found a letter from him in her mailbox.

He had printed it in black ink, very carefully, as if he had not trusted handwriting. The return address was in bold letters that, like his voice, tried to grab onto her: Birchcrest Manor. Somewhere north of the city. "Dear Sister Irene," the block letters said, "I am doing well here and have time for reading and relaxing. The Manor is delightful. My doctor here is an excellent, intelligent man who has time for me, unlike my former doctor. If you have time, you might drop in on my father, who worries about me too much, I think, and explain to him what my condition is. He doesn't seem to understand. I feel about this new life the way that boy, what's his name, in *Measure for Measure*, feels about the prospects of a different life; you remember what he says to his sister when she visits him in prison, how he is looking forward to an escape into another world. Perhaps you could *explain* this to my father and he would stop worrying." The letter ended with the father's name and address, in letters that were just a little too big. Sister Irene, walking slowly down the corridor as she read the letter, felt her eyes cloud over with tears. She was cold with fear, it was something she had never experienced before. She knew what Weinstein was trying to tell her, and the desperation of his attempt made it all the more pathetic; he did not deserve this, why did God allow him to suffer so?

She read through Claudio's speech to his sister, in *Measure for Measure*:

> Ay, but to die, and go we know not where;
> To lie in cold obstruction and to rot;
> This sensible warm motion to become
> A kneaded clod; and the delighted spirit
> To bathe in fiery floods, or to reside
> In thrilling region of thick-ribbed ice,
> To be imprison'd in the viewless winds
> And blown with restless violence round about
> The pendent world; or to be worse than worst

Of those that lawless and incertain thought
Imagines howling! 'Tis too horrible!
The weariest and most loathed worldly life
That age, ache, penury, and imprisonment
Can lay on nature is a paradise
To what we fear of death.

Sister Irene called the father's number that day. "Allen Weinstein residence, who may I say is calling?" a woman said, bored. "May I speak to Mr. Weinstein? It's urgent—about his son," Sister Irene said. There was a pause at the other end. "You want to talk to his mother, maybe?" the woman said. "His mother? Yes, his mother, then. Please. It's very important."

She talked with this strange, unsuspected woman, a disembodied voice that suggested absolutely no face, and insisted upon going over that afternoon. The woman was nervous, but Sister Irene, who was a university professor, after all, knew enough to hide her own nervousness. She kept waiting for the woman to say, "Yes, Allen has mentioned you . . ." but nothing happened.

She persuaded Sister Carlotta to ride over with her. This urgency of hers was something they were all amazed by. They hadn't suspected that the set of her gray eyes could change to this blurred, distracted alarm, this sense of mission that seemed to have come to her from nowhere. Sister Irene drove across the city in the late afternoon traffic, with the high whining noises from residential streets where trees were being sawed down in pieces. She understood now the secret, sweet wildness that Christ must have felt, giving himself for man, dying for the billions of men who would never know of him and never understand the sacrifice. For the first time she approached the realization of that great act. In her troubled mind the city traffic was jumbled and yet oddly coherent, an image of the world that was always out of joint with what was happening in it, its inner history struggling with its external spectacle. This sacrifice of Christ's, so mysterious and legendary now, almost lost in time—it was that by which Christ transcended both God and man at one moment, more than man because of his fate to do what no other man could do, and more than God because no god could suffer as he did. She felt a flicker of something close to madness.

She drove nervously, uncertainly, afraid of missing the street and afraid of finding it too, for while one part of her rushed forward to confront these people who had betrayed their son, another part of her would have liked nothing so much as to be waiting as usual for the summons to dinner, safe in her room. . . . When she found the street and turned onto it, she was in a state of breathless excitement. Here lawns were bright green and marred with only a few leaves, magically clean, and the houses were enormous and pompous, a mixture of styles: ranch houses, colonial houses, French country houses, white-bricked wonders with curving glass and clumps of birch trees somehow encircled by white concrete. Sister Irene stared as if she had blundered into another world. This was a kind of heaven, and she was too shabby for it.

The Weinsteins' house was the strangest one of all: it looked like a small Alpine lodge, with an inverted-V-shaped front entrance. Sister Irene drove up the black-topped driveway and let the car slow to a stop; she told Sister Carlotta she would not be long.

At the door she was met by Weinstein's mother, a small, nervous woman with hands like her son's. "Come in, come in," the woman said. She had once been beautiful, that was clear, but now in missing beauty she was not handsome or even attractive but looked ruined and perplexed, the misshapen swelling of her white-blond professionally set hair like a cap lifting up from her surprised face. "He'll be right in. Allen?" she called, "our visitor is here." They went into the living room. There was a grand piano at one end and an organ at the other. In between were scatterings of brilliant modern furniture in conversational groups, and several puffed-up white rugs on the polished floor. Sister Irene could not stop shivering.

"Professor, it's so strange, but let me say when the phone rang I had a feeling—I had a feeling," the woman said, with damp eyes. Sister Irene sat, and the woman hovered about her. "Should I call you Professor? We don't . . . you know . . . we don't understand the technicalities that go with—Allen, my son, wanted to go here to the Catholic school; I told my husband why not? Why fight? It's the thing these days, they do anything they want for knowledge. And he had to come home, you know. He couldn't take care of himself in New York, that was the beginning of the trouble. . . . Should I call you Professor?"

"You can call me Sister Irene."

"Sister Irene?" the woman said, touching her throat in awe, as if something intimate and unexpected had happened.

Then Weinstein's father appeared, hurrying. He took long, impatient strides. Sister Irene stared at him and in that instant doubted everything—he was in his fifties, a tall, sharply handsome man, heavy but not fat, holding his shoulders back with what looked like an effort, but holding them back just the same. He wore a dark suit and his face was flushed, as if he had run a long distance.

"Now," he said, coming to Sister Irene and with a precise wave of his hand motioning his wife off, "now, let's straighten this out. A lot of confusion over that kid, eh?" He pulled a chair over, scraping it across a rug and pulling one corner over, so that its brown underside was exposed. "I came home early just for this, Libby phoned me. Sister, you got a letter from him, right?"

The wife looked at Sister Irene over her husband's head as if trying somehow to coach her, knowing that this man was so loud and impatient that no one could remember anything in his presence.

"A letter—yes—today—"

"He says what in it? You got the letter, eh? Can I see it?"

She gave it to him and wanted to explain, but he silenced her with a flick of his hand. He read through the letter so quickly that Sister Irene thought perhaps he was trying to impress her with his skill at reading. "So?" he said, raising his eyes, smiling, "so what is this? He's happy out there, he says. He doesn't communicate with us any more, but he writes to you and says he's happy—what's that? I mean, what the hell is that?"

"But he isn't happy. He wants to come home," Sister Irene said. It was so important that she make him understand that she could not trust her voice; goaded by this man, it might suddenly turn shrill, as his son's did. "Someone must read their letters before they're mailed, so he tried to tell me something by making an allusion to—"

"What?"

"—an allusion to a play, so that I would know. He may be thinking suicide, he must be very unhappy—"

She ran out of breath. Weinstein's mother had begun to cry, but the father was shaking his head jerkily back and forth. "Forgive me, Sister, but it's a lot of crap, he needs the hospital, he needs help—right? It costs me fifty a day out there, and they've got the best place in the state, I figure it's worth it. He needs help, that kid, what do I care if he's unhappy? He's unbalanced!" he said angrily. "You want us to get him out again? We argued with the judge for two hours to get him in, an acquaintance of mine. Look, he can't control himself—he was smashing things here, he was hysterical. They need help, lady, and you do something about it fast! You do something! We made up our minds to do something and we did it! This letter—what the hell is this letter? He never talked like that to us!"

"But he means the opposite of what he says—"

"Then he's crazy! I'm the first to admit it." He was perspiring, and his face had darkened. "I've got no pride left this late. He's a little bastard, you want to know? He calls me names, he's filthy, got a filthy mouth—that's being smart, huh? They give him a big scholarship for his filthy mouth? I went to college too, and I got out and knew something, and I for Christ's sake did something with it; my wife is an intelligent woman, a learned woman, would you guess she does book reviews for the little newspaper out here? Intelligent isn't crazy—crazy isn't intelligent. Maybe for you at the school he writes nice papers and gets an A, but out here, around the house, he can't control himself, and we got him committed!"

"But—"

"We're fixing him up, don't worry about it!" He turned to his wife. "Libby, get out of here, I mean it. I'm sorry, but get out of here, you're making a fool of yourself, go stand in the kitchen or something, you and the goddamn maid can cry on each other's shoulders. That one in the kitchen is nuts too, they're all nuts. Sister," he said, his voice lowering, "I thank you immensely for coming out here. This is wonderful, your interest in my son. And I see he admires you—that letter there. But what about that letter? If he did want to get out, which I don't admit—he was willing to be committed, in the end he said okay himself—if he wanted out I wouldn't do it. Why? So what if he wants to come back? The next day he wants something else, what then? He's a sick kid, and I'm the first to admit it."

Sister Irene felt that sickness spread to her. She stood. The room was so big it seemed it must be a public place; there had been nothing personal or private about their conversation. Weinstein's mother was standing by the fireplace, sobbing. The father jumped to his feet and wiped his forehead in a gesture that was meant to help Sister Irene on her way out. "God, what a day," he said, his eyes snatching at hers for understanding, "you know—one of those days all day long? Sister, I thank you a lot. There should be more people in the world who care about others, like you. I mean that."

On the way back to the convent, the man's words returned to her, and she could not get control of them; she could not even feel anger. She had been pressed down, forced back, what could she do? Weinstein might have been watching her somehow from a barred window, and he surely would have understood. The strange idea she had had on the way over, something about understanding Christ, came back to her now and sickened her. But the sickness was small. It could be contained.

About a month after her visit to his father, Weinstein himself showed up. He was dressed in a suit as before, even the necktie was the same. He came right into her office as if he had been pushed and could not stop.

"Sister," he said, and shook her hand. He must have seen fear in her because he smiled ironically. "Look, I'm released. I'm let out of the nut house. Can I sit down?"

He sat. Sister Irene was breathing quickly, as if in the presence of an enemy who does not know he is an enemy.

"So, they finally let me out. I heard what you did. You talked with him, that was all I wanted. You're the only one who gave a damn. Because you're a humanist and a religious person, you respect . . . the individual. Listen," he said, whispering, "it was hell out there! Hell Birchcrest Manor! All fixed up with fancy chairs and *Life* magazines lying around—and what do they do to you? They locked me up, they gave me shock treatments! Shock treatments, how do you like that, it's discredited by everybody now—they're crazy out there themselves, sadists. They locked me up, they gave me hypodermic shots, they didn't treat me like a human being! Do you know what that is," Weinstein demanded savagely, "not to be treated like a human being? They made me an animal—for fifty dollars a day! Dirty filthy swine! Now I'm an outpatient because I stopped swearing at them. I found somebody's bobby pin, and when I wanted to scream I pressed it under my fingernail and it stopped me—the screaming went inside and not out—so they gave me good reports, those sick bastards. Now I'm an outpatient and I can walk along the street and breathe in the same filthy exhaust from the buses like all you normal people! Christ," he said, and threw himself back against the chair.

Sister Irene stared at him. She wanted to take his hand, to make some gesture that would close the aching distance between them. "Mr. Weinstein—"

"Call me Allen!" he said sharply.

"I'm very sorry—I'm terribly sorry—"

"My own parents committed me, but of course they didn't know what it was like. It was hell," he said thickly, "and there isn't any hell except what other people do to you. The psychiatrist out there, the main shrink, he hates Jews too, some of us were positive of that, and he's got a bigger nose than I do, a real beak." He made a noise of disgust. "A dirty bastard, a sick, dirty, pathetic bastard—all of them. Anyway, I'm getting out of here, and I came to ask you a favor."

"What do you mean?"

"I'm getting out. I'm leaving. I'm going up to Canada and lose myself. I'll get a job, I'll forget everything, I'll kill myself maybe—what's the difference? Look, can you lend me some money?"

"Money?"

"Just a little! I have to get to the border, I'm going to take a bus."

"But I don't have any money—"

"No money?" He stared at her. "You mean—you don't have any? Sure you have some!"

She stared at him as if he had asked her to do something obscene. Everything was splotched and uncertain before her eyes.

"You must . . . you must go back," she said, "you're making a—"

"I'll pay it back. Look, I'll pay it back, can you go to where you live or something and get it? I'm in a hurry. My friends are sons of bitches: one of them pretended he didn't see me yesterday—I stood right in the middle of the sidewalk and yelled at him, I called him some appropriate names! So he didn't see me, huh? You're the only one who understands me, you understand me like a poet, you—"

"I can't help you, I'm sorry—I . . ."

He looked to one side of her and flashed his gaze back, as if he could control it. He seemed to be trying to clear his vision.

"You have the soul of a poet," he whispered, "you're the only one. Everybody else is rotten! Can't you lend me some money, ten dollars maybe? I have three thousand in the bank, and I can't touch it! They take everything away from me, they make me into an animal. . . . You know I'm not an animal, don't you? Don't you?"

"Of course," Sister Irene whispered.

"You could get money. Help me. Give me your hand or something, touch me, help me—please. . . ." He reached for her hand and she drew back. He stared at her and his face seemed about to crumble, like a child's. "I want something from you, but I don't know what—I want something!" he cried. "Something real! I want you to look at me like I was a human being, is that too much to ask? I have a brain, I'm alive, I'm suffering—what does that mean? Does that mean nothing? I want something real and not this phony Christian love garbage—it's all in the books, it isn't personal—I want something real—look. . . ."

He tried to take her hand again, and this time she jerked away. She got to her feet. "Mr. Weinstein," she said, "please—"

"You! You nun!" he said scornfully, his mouth twisted into a mock grin. "You nun! There's nothing under that ugly outfit, right? And you're not particularly smart even though you think you are; my father has more brains in his foot than you—"

He got to his feet and kicked the chair.

"You bitch!" he cried.

She shrank back against her desk as if she thought he might hit her, but he only ran out of the office.

WEINSTEIN: the name was to become disembodied from the figure, as time went on. The semester passed, the autumn drizzle turned into snow, Sister Irene rode to school in the morning and left in the afternoon, four days a week, anonymous in her black winter cloak, quiet and stunned. University teaching was an anonymous task, each day dissociated from the rest, with no necessary sense of unity among the teachers: they came and went separately and might for a year just miss a colleague who left his office five minutes before they arrived, and it did not matter.

She heard of Weinstein's death, his suicide by drowning, from the English Department secretary, a handsome white-haired woman who kept a transistor radio on her desk. Sister Irene was not surprised; she had been thinking of him as dead for months. "They identified him by some special television way they have now," the secretary said. "They're shipping the body back. It was up in Quebec. . . ."

Sister Irene could feel a part of herself drifting off, lured by the plains of white snow to the north, the quiet, the emptiness, the sweep of the Great Lakes up to the silence of Canada. But she called that part of herself back. She could only be one person in her lifetime. That was the ugly truth, she thought, that she could not really regret Weinstein's suffering and death; she had only one life and had already given it to someone else. He had come too late to her. Fifteen years ago, perhaps, but not now.

She was only one person, she thought, walking down the corridor in a dream. Was she safe in this single person, or was she trapped? She had only one identity. She could make only one choice. What she had done or hadn't done was the result of that choice, and how was she guilty? If she could have felt guilt, she thought, she might at least have been able to feel something.

WHERE ARE YOU GOING,

WHERE HAVE YOU BEEN?

For Bob Dylan

———

HER NAME WAS CONNIE. She was fifteen and she had a quick, nervous giggling habit of craning her neck to glance into mirrors or checking other people's faces to make sure her own was all right. Her mother, who noticed everything and knew everything and who hadn't much reason any longer to look at her own face, always scolded Connie about it. "Stop gawking at yourself. Who are you? You think you're so pretty?" she would say. Connie would raise her eyebrows at these familiar old complaints and look right through her mother, into a shadowy vision of herself as she was right at that moment: she knew she was pretty and that was everything. Her mother had been pretty once too, if you could believe those old snapshots in the album, but now her looks were gone and that was why she was always after Connie.

"Why don't you keep your room clean like your sister? How've you got your hair fixed—what the hell stinks? Hair spray? You don't see your sister using that junk."

Her sister, June, was twenty-four and still lived at home. She was a secretary in the high school Connie attended, and if that wasn't bad enough—with her in the same building—she was so plain and chunky and steady that Connie had to hear her praised all the time by her mother and her mother's sisters. June did this, June did that, she saved money and helped clean the house and cooked and Connie couldn't do a thing, her mind was all filled with trashy daydreams. Their father was away at work most of the time and when he came home he wanted supper and he read the newspaper at supper and after supper he went to bed. He didn't bother talking much to them, but around his bent head Connie's mother kept picking at her until Connie wished her mother was dead and she herself was dead and it was all over. "She makes me want to throw up sometimes," she complained to her friends. She had a high, breathless, amused voice that made everything she said sound a little forced, whether it was sincere or not.

There was one good thing: June went places with girl friends of hers, girls who were just as plain and steady as she, and so when Connie wanted to do that her mother had no objections. The father of Connie's best girl friend drove the girls the three miles to town and left them at a shopping plaza so they could walk through the stores or go to a movie, and when he came to pick them up again at eleven he never bothered to ask what they had done.

They must have been familiar sights, walking around the shopping plaza in their shorts and flat ballerina slippers that always scuffed on the sidewalk, with charm bracelets jingling on their thin wrists; they would lean together to whisper and laugh secretly if someone passed who amused or interested them. Connie had long dark blond hair that drew anyone's eye to it, and she wore part of it pulled up on her head and puffed out and the rest of it she let fall down her back. She wore a pullover jersey top that looked one way when she was at home and another way when she was away from home. Everything about her had two sides to it, one for home and one for anywhere that was not home: her walk, which could be childlike and bobbing, or languid enough to make anyone think she was hearing music in her head; her mouth, which was pale and smirking most of the time, but bright and pink on these evenings out; her laugh, which was cynical and drawling at home—"Ha, ha, very funny,"—but high-pitched and nervous anywhere else, like the jingling of the charms on her bracelet.

Sometimes they did go shopping or to a movie, but sometimes they went across the highway, ducking fast across the busy road, to a drive-in restaurant where older kids hung out. The restaurant was shaped like a big bottle, though squatter than a real bottle, and on its cap was a revolving figure of a grinning boy holding a hamburger aloft. One night in midsummer they ran across, breathless with daring, and right away someone leaned out a car window and invited them over, but it was just a boy from high school they didn't like. It made them feel good to be able to ignore him. They went up through the maze of parked and cruising cars to the bright-lit, fly-infested restaurant, their faces pleased and expectant as if they were entering a sacred building that loomed up out of the night to give them what haven and blessing they yearned for. They sat at the counter and crossed their legs at the ankles, their thin shoulders rigid with excitement, and listened to the music that made everything so good: the music was always in the background, like music at a church service; it was something to depend upon.

A boy named Eddie came in to talk with them. He sat backward on his stool, turning himself jerkily around in semicircles and then stopping and turning back again, and after a while he asked Connie if she would like something to eat. She said she would so she tapped her friend's arm on her way out—her friend pulled her face up into a brave, droll look—and Connie said she would meet her at eleven across the way. "I just hate to leave her like that," Connie said earnestly, but the boy said that she wouldn't be alone for long. So they went out to his car, and on the way Connie couldn't help but let her eyes wander over the windshields and faces all around her, her face gleaming with a joy that had nothing to do with Eddie or even this place; it might have been the music. She drew her shoulders up and sucked in her breath with the pure pleasure of being alive, and just at that moment she happened to glance at a face just a few feet away from hers. It was a boy with shaggy black hair, in a convertible jalopy painted gold. He stared at her and then his lips widened into a grin. Connie slit her eyes at him and turned away, but she couldn't help glancing back and there he was, still watching her. He wagged a finger and laughed and said, "Gonna get you, baby," and Connie turned away again without Eddie noticing anything.

She spent three hours with him, at the restaurant where they ate hamburgers and drank Cokes in wax cups that were always sweating, and then down an alley a mile or so away, and when he left her off at five to eleven only the movie house was still open at the plaza. Her girl friend was there, talking with a boy. When Connie came up, the two girls smiled at each other and Connie said, "How was the movie?" and the girl said, "*You* should know." They rode off with the girl's father, sleepy and pleased, and Connie couldn't help but look back at the darkened shopping plaza with its big empty parking lot and its signs that were faded and ghostly now, and over at the drive-in restaurant where cars were still circling tirelessly. She couldn't hear the music at this distance.

Next morning June asked her how the movie was and Connie said, "So-so."

She and that girl and occasionally another girl went out several times a week, and the rest of the time Connie spent around the house—it was summer vacation—getting in her mother's way and thinking, dreaming about the boys she met. But all the boys fell back and dissolved into a single face that was not even a face but an idea, a feeling, mixed up with the urgent insistent pounding of the music and the humid night air of July. Connie's mother kept dragging her back to the daylight by finding things for her to do or saying suddenly, "What's this about the Pettinger girl?"

And Connie would say nervously, "Oh, her. That dope." She always drew thick clear lines between herself and such girls, and her mother was simple and kind enough to believe it. Her mother was so simple, Connie thought, that it was maybe cruel to fool her so much. Her mother went scuffling around the house in old bedroom slippers and complained over the telephone to one sister about the other, then the other called up and the two of them complained about the third one. If June's name was mentioned her mother's tone was approving, and if Connie's name was mentioned it was disapproving. This did not really mean she disliked

Connie, and actually Connie thought that her mother preferred her to June just because she was prettier, but the two of them kept up a pretense of exasperation, a sense that they were tugging and struggling over something of little value to either of them. Sometimes, over coffee, they were almost friends, but something would come up—some vexation that was like a fly buzzing suddenly around their heads—and their faces went hard with contempt.

One Sunday Connie got up at eleven—none of them bothered with church—and washed her hair so that it could dry all day long in the sun. Her parents and sister were going to a barbecue at an aunt's house and Connie said no, she wasn't interested, rolling her eyes to let her mother know just what she thought of it. "Stay home alone then," her mother said sharply. Connie sat out back in a lawn chair and watched them drive away, her father quiet and bald, hunched around so that he could back the car out, her mother with a look that was still angry and not at all softened through the windshield, and in the backseat poor old June, all dressed up as if she didn't know what a barbecue was, with all the running yelling kids and the flies. Connie sat with her eyes closed in the sun, dreaming and dazed with the warmth about her as if this were a kind of love, the caresses of love, and her mind slipped over onto thoughts of the boy she had been with the night before and how nice he had been, how sweet it always was, not the way someone like June would suppose but sweet, gentle, the way it was in movies and promised in songs; and when she opened her eyes she hardly knew where she was, the backyard ran off into weeds and a fencelike line of trees and behind it the sky was perfectly blue and still. The asbestos "ranch house" that was now three years old startled her—it looked small. She shook her head as if to get awake.

It was too hot. She went inside the house and turned on the radio to drown out the quiet. She sat on the edge of her bed, barefoot, and listened for an hour and a half to a program called *XYZ Sunday Jamboree*, record after record of hard, fast, shrieking songs she sang along with, interspersed by exclamations from "Bobby King": "An' look here, you girls at Napoleon's—Son and Charley want you to pay real close attention to this song coming up!"

And Connie paid close attention herself, bathed in a glow of slow-pulsed joy that seemed to rise mysteriously out of the music itself and lay languidly about the airless little room, breathed in and breathed out with each gentle rise and fall of her chest.

After a while she heard a car coming up the drive. She sat up at once, startled, because it couldn't be her father so soon. The gravel kept crunching all the way in from the road—the driveway was long—and Connie ran to the window. It was a car she didn't know. It was an open jalopy, painted a bright gold that caught the sunlight opaquely. Her heart began to pound and her fingers snatched at her hair, checking it, and she whispered, "Christ, Christ," wondering how she looked. The car came to a stop at the side door and the horn sounded four short taps, as if this were a signal Connie knew.

She went into the kitchen and approached the door slowly, then hung out the screen door, her bare toes curling down off the step. There were two boys in the car and now she recognized the driver: he had shaggy, shabby black hair that looked crazy as a wig and he was grinning at her.

"I ain't late, am I?" he said.

"Who the hell do you think you are?" Connie said.

"Toldja I'd be out, didn't I?"

"I don't even know who you are."

She spoke sullenly, careful to show no interest or pleasure, and he spoke in a fast, bright monotone. Connie looked past him to the other boy, taking her time. He had fair brown hair, with a lock that fell onto his forehead. His sideburns gave him a fierce, embarrassed look, but so far he hadn't even bothered to glance at her. Both boys wore sunglasses. The driver's glasses were metallic and mirrored everything in miniature.

"You wanta come for a ride?" he said.

Connie smirked and let her hair fall loose over one shoulder.

"Don'tcha like my car? New paint job," he said. "Hey."

"What?"

"You're cute."

She pretended to fidget, chasing flies away from the door.

"Don'tcha believe me, or what?" he said.

"Look, I don't even know who you are," Connie said in disgust.

"Hey, Ellie's got a radio, see. Mine broke down." He lifted his friend's arm and showed her the little transistor radio the boy was holding, and now Connie began to hear the music. It was the same program that was playing inside the house.

"Bobby King?" she said.

"I listen to him all the time. I think he's great."

"He's kind of great," Connie said reluctantly.

"Listen, that guy's *great*. He knows where the action is."

Connie blushed a little, because the glasses made it impossible for her to see just what this boy was looking at. She couldn't decide if she liked him or if he was a jerk, and so she dawdled in the doorway and wouldn't come down or go back inside. She said, "What's all that stuff painted on your car?"

"Can'tcha read it?" He opened the door very carefully, as if he were afraid it might fall off. He slid out just as carefully, planting his feet firmly on the ground, the tiny metallic world in his glasses slowing down like gelatine hardening, and in the midst of it Connie's bright-green blouse. "This here is my name, to begin with," he said. ARNOLD FRIEND was written in tarlike black letters on the side, with a drawing of a round, grinning face that reminded Connie of a pumpkin, except it wore sunglasses. "I wanta introduce myself. I'm Arnold Friend and that's my real name and I'm gonna be your friend, honey, and inside the car's Ellie Oscar, he's kinda shy." Ellie brought his transistor radio up to his shoulder and balanced it there. "Now, these numbers are a secret code, honey," Arnold Friend explained. He read off the numbers 33, 19, 17 and raised his eyebrows at her to see what she thought of that, but she didn't think much of it. The left rear fender had been smashed and around it was written, on the gleaming gold background: DONE BY CRAZY WOMAN DRIVER. Connie had to laugh at that. Arnold Friend was pleased at her laughter and looked up at her. "Around the other side's a lot more—you wanta come and see them?"

"No."

"Why not?"

"Why should I?"

"Don'tcha wanta see what's on the car? Don'tcha wanta go for a ride?"

"I don't know."

"Why not?"

"I got things to do."

"Like what?"

"Things."

He laughed as if she had said something funny. He slapped his thighs. He was standing in a strange way, leaning back against the car as if he were balancing himself. He wasn't tall, only an inch or so taller than she would be if she came down to him. Connie liked the way he was dressed, which was the way all of them dressed: tight faded jeans stuffed into black, scuffed boots, a belt that pulled his waist in and showed how lean he was, and a white pullover shirt that was a little soiled and showed the hard small muscles of his arms and shoulders. He looked as if he probably did hard work, lifting and carrying things. Even his neck looked muscular. And his face was a familiar face, somehow; the jaw and chin and cheeks slightly darkened because he hadn't shaved for a day or two, and the nose long and hawklike, sniffing as if she was a treat he was going to gobble up and it was all a joke.

"Connie, you ain't telling the truth. This is your day set aside for a ride with me and you know it," he said, still laughing. The way he straightened and recovered from his fit of laughing showed that it had been all fake.

"How do you know what my name is?" she said suspiciously.

"It's Connie."

"Maybe and maybe not."

"I know my Connie," he said, wagging his finger. Now she remembered him even better, back at the restaurant, and her cheeks warmed at the thought of how she had sucked in her breath just at the moment she passed him—how she must have looked to him. And he had remembered her. "Ellie and I come out here especially for you," he said. "Ellie can sit in back. How about it?"

"Where?"

"Where what?"

"Where're we going?"

He looked at her. He took off the sunglasses and she saw how pale the skin around his eyes was, like holes that were not in shadow but instead in light. His eyes were like chips of broken glass that catch the light in an amiable way. He smiled. It was as if the idea of going for a ride somewhere, to someplace, was a new idea to him.

"Just for a ride, Connie sweetheart."

"I never said my name was Connie," she said.

"But I know what it is. I know your name and all about you, lots of things," Arnold Friend said. He had not moved yet but stood still leaning back against the side of his jalopy. "I took a special interest in you, such a pretty girl, and found out all about you—like I know your parents and sister are gone somewheres and I know where and how long they're going to be gone, and I know who you were with last night, and your best girl friend's name is Betty. Right?"

He spoke in a simple lilting voice, exactly as if he was reciting the words to a song. His smile assured her that everything was fine. In the car Ellie turned up the volume on his radio and did not bother to look around at them.

"Ellie can sit in the backseat," Arnold Friend said. He indicated his friend with a casual jerk of his chin, as if Ellie did not count and she should not bother with him.

"How'd you find out all that stuff?" Connie said.

"Listen: Betty Schultz and Tony Fitch and Jimmy Pettinger and Nancy Pettinger," he said in a chant. "Raymond Stanley and Bob Hutter—"

"Do you know all those kids?"

"I know everybody."

"Look, you're kidding. You're not from around here."

"Sure."

"But—how come we never saw you before?"

"Sure you saw me before," he said. He looked down at his boots, as if he was a little offended. "You just don't remember."

"I guess I'd remember you," Connie said.

"Yeah?" He looked up at this, beaming. He was pleased. He began to mark time with the music from Ellie's radio, tapping his fists lightly together. Connie looked away from his smile to the car, which was painted so bright it almost hurt her eyes to look at it. She looked at that name, ARNOLD FRIEND. And up at the front fender was an expression that was familiar—MAN THE FLYING SAUCERS. It was an expression kids had used the year before but didn't use this year. She looked at it for a while as if the words meant something to her that she did not yet know.

"What're you thinking about? Huh?" Arnold Friend demanded. "Not worried about your hair blowing around in the car, are you?"

"No."

"Think I maybe can't drive good?"

"How do I know?"

"You're a hard girl to handle. How come?" he said. "Don't you know I'm your friend? Didn't you see me put my sign in the air when you walked by?"

"What sign?"

"My sign." And he drew an X in the air, leaning out toward her. They were maybe ten feet apart. After his hand fell back to his side the X was still in the air, almost visible. Connie let the screen door close and stood perfectly still inside it, listening to the music from her radio and the boy's blend together. She stared at Arnold Friend. He stood there so stiffly relaxed, pretending to be relaxed, with one hand idly on the door handle as if he was keeping himself up that way and had no intention of ever moving again. She recognized most things about him, the tight jeans that showed his thighs and buttocks and the greasy leather boots and the tight shirt, and even that slippery friendly smile of his, that sleepy dreamy smile that all the boys used to get across ideas they didn't want to put into words. She recognized all this and also the singsong way he talked, slightly mocking, kidding, but serious and a little melancholy, and she recognized the way he tapped one fist against the other in homage to the perpetual music behind him. But all these things did not come together.

She said suddenly, "Hey, how old are you?"

His smile faded. She could see then that he wasn't a kid, he was much older—thirty, maybe more. At this knowledge her heart began to pound faster.

"That's a crazy thing to ask. Can'tcha see I'm your own age?"

"Like hell you are."

"Or maybe a coupla years older. I'm eighteen."

"Eighteen?" she said doubtfully.

He grinned to reassure her and lines appeared at the corners of his mouth. His teeth were big and white. He grinned so broadly his eyes became slits and she saw how thick the lashes were, thick and black as if painted with a black tarlike material. Then, abruptly, he seemed to become embarrassed and looked over his shoulder at Ellie. "*Him*, he's crazy," he said. "Ain't he a riot? He's a nut, a real character." Ellie was still listening to the music. His sunglasses told nothing about what he was thinking. He wore a bright-orange shirt unbuttoned halfway to show his chest, which was a pale, bluish chest and not muscular like Arnold Friend's. His shirt collar was turned up all around and the very tips of the collar pointed out past his chin as if they were protecting him. He was pressing the transistor radio up against his ear and sat there in a kind of daze, right in the sun.

"He's kinda strange," Connie said.

"Hey, she says you're kinda strange! Kinda strange!" Arnold Friend cried. He pounded on the car to get Ellie's attention. Ellie turned for the first time and Connie saw with shock that he wasn't a kid either—he had a fair, hairless face, cheeks reddened slightly as if the veins grew too close to the surface of his skin, the face of a forty-year-old baby. Connie felt a wave of dizziness rise in her at this sight and she stared at him as if waiting for something to change the shock of the moment, make it all right again. Ellie's lips kept shaping words, mumbling along with the words blasting in his ear.

"Maybe you two better go away," Connie said faintly.

"What? How come?" Arnold Friend cried. "We come out here to take you for a ride. It's Sunday." He had the voice of the man on the radio now. It was the same voice, Connie thought. "Don'tcha know it's Sunday all day? And honey, no matter who you were with last night, today you're with Arnold Friend and don't you forget it! Maybe you better step out here," he said, and this last was in a different voice. It was a little flatter, as if the heat was finally getting to him.

"No. I got things to do."

"Hey."

"You two better leave."

"We ain't leaving until you come with us."

"Like hell I am—"

"Connie, don't fool around with me. I mean—I mean, don't fool *around*," he said, shaking his head. He laughed incredulously. He placed his sunglasses on top of his head, carefully, as if he was indeed wearing a wig, and brought the stems down behind his ears. Connie stared at him, another wave of dizziness and fear rising in her so that for a moment he wasn't even in focus but was just a blur standing there against his gold car, and she had the idea that he had driven up the driveway all right but had come from nowhere before that and belonged nowhere and that everything about him and even about the music that was so familiar to her was only half real.

"If my father comes and sees you—"

"He ain't coming. He's at a barbecue."

"How do you know that?"

"Aunt Tillie's. Right now they're—uh—they're drinking. Sitting around," he said vaguely, squinting as if he was staring all the way to town and over to Aunt Tillie's backyard. Then the vision seemed to get clear and he nodded energetically. "Yeah. Sitting around. There's your sister in a blue dress, huh? And high heels, the poor sad bitch—nothing like you, sweetheart! And your mother's helping some fat woman with the corn, they're cleaning the corn—husking the corn—"

"What fat woman?" Connie cried.

"How do I know what fat woman, I don't know every goddamn fat woman in the world!" Arnold Friend laughed.

"Oh, that's Mrs. Hornsby. . . . Who invited her?" Connie said. She felt a little light-headed. Her breath was coming quickly.

"She's too fat. I don't like them fat. I like them the way you are, honey," he said, smiling sleepily at her. They stared at each other for a while through the screen door. He said softly, "Now, what you're going to do is this: you're going to come out that door. You're going to sit up front with me and Ellie's going to sit in the back, the hell with Ellie, right? This isn't Ellie's date. You're my date. I'm your lover, honey."

"What? You're crazy—"

"Yes. I'm your lover. You don't know what that is but you will," he said. "I know that too. I know all about you. But look: it's real nice and you couldn't ask for nobody better than me, or more polite. I always keep my word. I'll tell you how it is, I'm always nice at first, the first time. I'll hold you so tight you won't think you have to try to get away or pretend anything because you'll know you can't. And I'll come inside you where it's all secret and you'll give in to me and you'll love me—"

"Shut up! You're crazy!" Connie said. She backed away from the door. She put her hands up against her ears as if she'd heard something terrible, something not meant for her. "People don't talk like that, you're crazy," she muttered. Her heart was almost too big now for her chest and its pumping made sweat break out all over her. She looked out to see Arnold Friend pause and then take a step toward the porch, lurching. He almost fell. But, like a clever drunken man, he managed to catch his balance. He wobbled in his high boots and grabbed hold of one of the porch posts.

"Honey?" he said. "You still listening?"

"Get the hell out of here!"

"Be nice, honey. Listen."

"I'm going to call the police—"

He wobbled again and out of the side of his mouth came a fast spat curse, an aside not meant for her to hear. But even this "Christ!" sounded forced. Then he began to smile again. She watched this smile come, awkward as if he was smiling from inside a mask. His whole face was a mask, she thought wildly, tanned down to his throat but then running out as if he had plastered makeup on his face but had forgotten about his throat.

"Honey—? Listen, here's how it is. I always tell the truth and I promise you this: I ain't coming in that house after you."

"You better not! I'm going to call the police if you—if you don't—"

"Honey," he said, talking right through her voice, "honey. I'm not coming in there but you are coming out here. You know why?"

She was panting. The kitchen looked like a place she had never seen before, some room she had run inside but that wasn't good enough, wasn't going to help her. The kitchen window had never had a curtain, after three years, and there were dishes in the sink for her to do—probably—and if you ran your hand across the table you'd probably feel something sticky there.

"You listening, honey? Hey?"

"—going to call the police—"

"Soon as you touch the phone I don't need to keep my promise and can come inside. You won't want that."

She rushed forward and tried to lock the door. Her fingers were shaking. "But why lock it," Arnold Friend said gently, talking right into her face. "It's just a screen door. It's just nothing." One of his boots was at a strange angle, as if his foot wasn't in it. It pointed out to the left, bent at the ankle. "I mean, anybody can break through a screen door and glass and wood and iron or anything else if he needs to, anybody at all, and specially Arnold Friend. If the place got lit up with a fire, honey, you'd come runnin' out into my arms, right into my arms an' safe at home—like you knew I was your lover and'd stopped fooling around. I don't mind a nice shy girl but I don't like no fooling around." Part of those words were spoken with a slight rhythmic lilt, and Connie somehow recognized them—the echo of a song from last year, about a girl rushing into her boyfriend's arms and coming home again—

Connie stood barefoot on the linoleum floor, staring at him. "What do you want?" she whispered.

"I want you," he said.

"What?"

"Seen you that night and thought, that's the one, yes sir. I never needed to look anymore."

"But my father's coming back. He's coming to get me. I had to wash my hair first—" She spoke in a dry, rapid voice, hardly raising it for him to hear.

"No, your daddy is not coming and yes, you had to wash your hair and you washed it for me. It's nice and shining and all for me. I thank you sweetheart," he said with a mock bow, but again he almost lost his balance. He had to bend and adjust his boots. Evidently his feet did not go all the way down; the boots must have been stuffed with something so that he would seem taller. Connie stared out at him and behind him at Ellie in the car, who seemed to be looking off toward Connie's right, into nothing. Then Ellie said, pulling the words out of the air one after another as if he were just discovering them, "You want me to pull out the phone?"

"Shut your mouth and keep it shut," Arnold Friend said, his face red from bending over or maybe from embarrassment because Connie had seen his boots. "This ain't none of your business."

"What—what are you doing? What do you want?" Connie said. "If I call the police they'll get you, they'll arrest you—"

"Promise was not to come in unless you touch that phone, and I'll keep that promise," he said. He resumed his erect position and tried to force his shoulders back. He sounded like a hero in a movie, declaring something important. But he spoke too loudly and it was as if he was speaking to someone behind Connie. "I ain't made plans for coming in that house where I don't belong but just for you to come out to me, the way you should. Don't you know who I am?"

"You're crazy," she whispered. She backed away from the door but did not want to go into another part of the house, as if this would give him permission to come through the door. "What do you . . . you're crazy, you . . ."

"Huh? What're you saying, honey?"

Her eyes darted everywhere in the kitchen. She could not remember what it was, this room.

"This is how it is, honey: you come out and we'll drive away, have a nice ride. But if you don't come out we're gonna wait till your people come home and then they're all going to get it."

"You want that telephone pulled out?" Ellie said. He held the radio away from his ear and grimaced, as if without the radio the air was too much for him.

"I toldja shut up, Ellie," Arnold Friend said, "you're deaf, get a hearing aid, right? Fix yourself up. This little girl's no trouble and's gonna be nice to me, so Ellie keep to yourself, this ain't your date—right? Don't hem in on me, don't hog, don't crush, don't bird dog, don't trail me," he said in a rapid, meaningless voice, as if he were running through all the expressions he'd learned but was no longer sure which of them was in style, then rushing on to new ones, making them up with his eyes closed. "Don't crawl under my fence, don't squeeze in my chipmunk hole, don't sniff my glue, suck my Popsicle, keep your own greasy fingers on yourself!" He shaded his eyes and peered in at Connie, who was backed against the kitchen table. "Don't mind him, honey, he's just a creep. He's a dope. Right? I'm the boy for you and like I said, you come out here nice like a lady and give me your hand, and nobody else gets hurt, I mean, your nice old bald-headed daddy and your mummy and your sister in her high heels. Because listen: why bring them in this?"

"Leave me alone," Connie whispered.

"Hey, you know that old woman down the road, the one with the chickens and stuff—you know her?"

"She's dead!"

"Dead? What? You know her?" Arnold Friend said.

"She's dead—"

"Don't you like her?"

"She's dead—she's—she isn't here anymore—"

"But don't you like her, I mean, you got something against her? Some grudge or something?" Then his voice dipped as if he was conscious of a rudeness. He touched the sunglasses perched up on top of his head as if to make sure they were still there. "Now, you be a good girl."

"What are you going to do?"

"Just two things, or maybe three," Arnold Friend said. "But I promise it won't last long and you'll like me the way you get to like people you're close to. You will. It's all over for you here, so come on out. You don't want your people in any trouble, do you?"

She turned and bumped against a chair or something, hurting her leg, but she ran into the back room and picked up the telephone. Something roared in her ear, a tiny roaring, and she was so sick with fear that she could do nothing but listen to it—the telephone was clammy and very heavy and her fingers groped down to the dial but were too weak to touch it. She began to scream into the phone, into the roaring. She cried out, she cried for her mother, she felt her breath start jerking back and forth in her lungs as if it was something Arnold Friend was stabbing her with again and again with no tenderness. A noisy sorrowful wailing rose all about her and she was locked inside it the way she was locked inside this house.

After a while she could hear again. She was sitting on the floor with her wet back against the wall.

Arnold Friend was saying from the door, "That's a good girl. Put the phone back."

She kicked the phone away from her.

"No, honey. Pick it up. Put it back right."

She picked it up and put it back. The dial tone stopped.

"That's a good girl. Now, you come outside."

She was hollow with what had been fear but what was now just an emptiness. All that screaming had blasted it out of her. She sat, one leg cramped under her, and deep inside her brain was something like a pinpoint of light that kept going and would not let her relax. She thought, I'm not going to see my mother again. She thought, I'm not going to sleep in my bed again. Her bright-green blouse was all wet.

Arnold Friend said, in a gentle-loud voice that was like a stage voice, "The place where you came from ain't there anymore, and where you had in mind to go is canceled out. This place you are now—inside your daddy's house—is nothing but a cardboard box I can knock down anytime. You know that and always did know it. You hear me?"

She thought, *I have got to think. I have got to know what to do.*

"We'll go out to a nice field, out in the country here where it smells so nice and it's sunny," Arnold Friend said. "I'll have my arms tight around you so you won't need to try to get away and I'll show you what love is like, what it does. The hell with this house! It looks solid all right," he said. He ran his fingernail down the screen and the noise did not make Connie shiver, as it would have the day before. "Now, put your hand on your heart, honey. Feel that? That feels solid too but we know better. Be nice to me, be sweet like you can because what else is there for a girl like you but to be sweet and pretty and give in?—and get away before her people get back?"

She felt her pounding heart. Her hand seemed to enclose it. She thought for the first time in her life that it was nothing that was hers, that belonged to her, but just a pounding, living thing inside this body that wasn't really hers either.

"You don't want them to get hurt," Arnold Friend went on. "Now, get up, honey. Get up all by yourself."

She stood.

"Now, turn this way. That's right. Come over here to me.—Ellie, put that away, didn't I tell you? You dope. You miserable creepy dope," Arnold Friend said. His words were not angry but only part of an incantation. The incantation was kindly. "Now, come out through the kitchen to me, honey, and let's see a smile, try it, you're a brave, sweet little girl and now they're eating corn and hot dogs cooked to bursting over an outdoor fire, and they don't know one thing about you and never did and honey, you're better than them because not a one of them would have done this for you."

Connie felt the linoleum under her feet; it was cool. She brushed her hair back out of her eyes. Arnold Friend let go of the post tentatively and opened his arms for her, his elbows pointing in toward each other and his wrists limp, to show that this was an embarrassed embrace and a little mocking, he didn't want to make her self-conscious.

She put out her hand against the screen. She watched herself push the door slowly open as if she was back safe somewhere in the other doorway, watching this body and this head of long hair moving out into the sunlight where Arnold Friend waited.

"My sweet little blue-eyed girl," he said in a half-sung sigh that had nothing to do with her brown eyes but was taken up just the same by the vast sunlit reaches of the land behind him and on all sides of him—so much land that Connie had never seen before and did not recognize except to know that she was going to it.

HOW I CONTEMPLATED THE WORLD FROM THE DETROIT HOUSE OF CORRECTIONS, AND BEGAN MY LIFE OVER AGAIN

———

Notes for an essay for an English class at Baldwin Country Day School; poking around in debris; disgust and curiosity; a revelation of the meaning of life; a happy ending . . .

I EVENTS

1. The girl (myself) is walking through Branden's, that excellent store. Suburb of a large famous city that is a symbol for large famous American cities. The event sneaks up on the girl, who believes she is herding it along with a small fixed smile, a girl of fifteen, innocently experienced. She dawdles in a certain style by a counter of costume jewelry. Rings, earrings, necklaces. Prices from $5 to $50, all within reach. All ugly. She eases over to the glove counter where everything is ugly too. In her close-fitted coat with its black fur collar she contemplates the luxury of Branden's, which she has known for many years: its many mild pale lights, easy on the eye and the soul, its elaborate tinkly decorations,

its women shoppers with their excellent shoes and coats and hairdos, all dawdling gracefully, in no hurry.

2. The girl seated at home. A very small library, paneled walls of oak. Someone is talking to me. An earnest, husky, female voice drives itself against my ears, nervous, frightened, groping around my heart, saying, "If you wanted gloves, why didn't you say so? Why didn't you ask for them?" That store, Branden's, is owned by Raymond Forrest who lives on Du Maurier Drive. We live on Sioux Drive. Raymond Forrest. A handsome man? An ugly man? A man of fifty or sixty, with gray hair, or a man of forty with earnest, courteous eyes, a good golf game; who is Raymond Forrest, this man who is my salvation? Father has been talking to him. Father is not his physician; Dr. Berg is his physician. Father and Dr. Berg refer patients to each other. There is a connection. Mother plays bridge with . . . On Mondays and Wednesdays our maid Billie works at . . . The strings draw together in a cat's cradle, making a net to save you when you fall. . . .

3. *Harriet Arnold's.* A small shop, better than Branden's. Mother in her black coat, I in my close-fitted blue coat. Shopping. Now look at this, isn't this cute, do you want this, why don't you want this, try this on, take this with you to the fitting room, take this also, what's wrong with you, what can I do for you, why are you so strange . . . ? "I wanted to steal but not to buy," I don't tell her. The girl droops along in her coat and gloves and leather boots, her eyes scan the horizon, which is pastel pink and decorated like Branden's, tasteful walls and modern ceilings with graceful glimmering lights.

4. Weeks later, the girl at a bus stop. Two o'clock in the afternoon, a Tuesday; obviously she has walked out of school.

5. The girl stepping down from a bus. Afternoon, weather changing to colder. Detroit. Pavement and closed-up stores; grillwork over the windows of a pawnshop. What is a pawnshop, exactly?

II CHARACTERS

1. The girl stands five feet five inches tall. An ordinary height. Baldwin Country Day School draws them up to that height. She dreams along the corridors and presses her face against the Thermoplex glass. No frost or steam can ever form on that glass. A smudge of grease from her forehead . . . could she be boiled down to grease? She wears her hair loose and long and straight in suburban teenage style. Eyes smudged with pencil, dark brown. Brown hair. Vague green eyes. A pretty girl? An ugly girl? She sings to herself under her breath, idling in the corridor, thinking of her many secrets (the thirty dollars she once took from the purse of a friend's mother, just for fun, the basement window she smashed in her own house just for fun) and thinking of her brother who is at Susquehanna Boys' Academy, an excellent preparatory school in Maine, remembering him unclearly . . . he has long manic hair and a squeaking voice and he looks like one of the popular teenage singers, one of those in a group, The Splats, Hunger Hunger, Hot Rats. The girl in her turn looks like one of those fieldsful of girls who listen to the boys' singing, dreaming and mooning restlessly, breaking into high sullen laughter, innocently experienced.

2. The mother. A Midwestern woman of Detroit and suburbs. Belongs to the Detroit Athletic Club. Also the Detroit Golf Club. Also the Bloomfield Hills Country Club. The Village Women's Club at which lectures are given each winter on Genet and Sartre and James Baldwin, by the Director of the Adult Education Program at Wayne State University. . . . The Bloomfield Art Association. Also the Founders Society of the Detroit Institute of Arts. Also . . . Oh, she is in perpetual motion, this lady, hair like blown-up gold and finer than gold, hair and fingers and body of inestimable grace. Heavy weighs the gold on the back of her hairbrush and hand mirror. Heavy heavy the candlesticks in the dining room. Very heavy is the big car, a Lincoln, long and black, that on one cool autumn day split a squirrel's body in two unequal parts.

3. The father. Dr.   . He belongs to the same clubs as 2. A player of squash and golf; he has a golfer's umbrella of stripes. Candy stripes. In his mouth nothing turns to sugar, however; saliva works no miracles here. His doctoring is of the slightly sick. The sick are sent elsewhere (to Dr. Berg?), the deathly sick are sent back for more tests and their bills are sent to their homes, the unsick are sent to Dr. Coronet (Isabel, a lady), an excellent psychiatrist for unsick people who angrily believe they are sick and want to do something about it. If they demand a male psychiatrist, the unsick are sent by Dr.   (my father) to Dr. Lowenstein, a male psychiatrist, excellent and expensive, with a limited practice.

4. Clarita. She is twenty, twenty-five, she is thirty or more? Pretty, ugly, what? She is a woman lounging by the side of the road, in jeans and a sweater, hitchhiking, or she is slouched on a stool at a counter in some roadside diner. A hard line of jaw. Curious eyes. Amused eyes. Behind her eyes processions move, funeral pageants, cartoons. She says, "I never can figure out why girls like you bum around down here. What are you looking for anyway?" An odor of tobacco about her. Unwashed underclothes, or no underclothes, unwashed skin, gritty toes, hair long and falling into strands, not recently washed.

5. Simon. In this city the weather changes abruptly, so Simon's weather changes abruptly. He sleeps through the afternoon. He sleeps through the morning. Rising, he gropes around for something to get him going, for a cigarette or a pill to drive him out to the street, where the temperature is hovering around thirty-five degrees. Why doesn't it drop? Why, why doesn't the cold clean air come down from Canada; will he have to go up into Canada to get it? will he have to leave the Country of his Birth and sink into Canada's frosty fields . . . ? Will the F.B.I. (which he dreams about constantly) chase him over the Canadian border on foot, hounded out in a blizzard of broken glass and horns . . . ?

"Once I was Huckleberry Finn," Simon says, "but now I am Roderick Usher." Beset by frenzies and fears, this man who makes my spine go cold, he takes green pills, yellow pills, pills of white and capsules of dark blue and green . . . he takes other things I may not mention, for what if Simon seeks me out and climbs into my girl's bedroom here in Bloomfield Hills and strangles me, what then . . . ? (As I write this I begin to shiver. Why do I shiver? I am now sixteen and sixteen is not an age for shivering. It comes from Simon, who is always cold.)

III WORLD EVENTS

Nothing.

IV PEOPLE AND CIRCUMSTANCES
CONTRIBUTING TO THIS DELINQUENCY

Nothing.

V SIOUX DRIVE

George, Clyde G. 240 Sioux. A manufacturer's representative; children, a dog, a wife. Georgian with the usual columns. You think of the White House, then of Thomas Jefferson, then your mind goes blank on the white pillars and you think of nothing. Norris, Ralph W. 246 Sioux. Public relations. Colonial. Bay window, brick, stone, concrete, wood, green shutters, sidewalk, lantern, grass, trees, blacktop drive, two children, one of them my classmate Esther (Esther Norris) at Baldwin. Wife, cars. Ramsey, Michael D. 250 Sioux, Colonial. Big living room, thirty by twenty-five, fireplaces in living room, library, recreation room, paneled walls wet bar five bathrooms five bedrooms two lavatories central air conditioning automatic sprinkler automatic garage door three children one wife two cars a breakfast room a patio a large fenced lot fourteen trees a front door with a brass knocker never knocked. Next is our house. Classic contemporary. Traditional modern. Attached garage, attached Florida room, attached patio, attached pool and cabana, attached roof. A front-door mail slot through which pour *Time* magazine, *Fortune, Life, Business Week, The Wall Street Journal, The New York Times, The New Yorker*, the *Saturday Review, M.D., Modern Medicine*,

Disease of the Month . . . and also. . . . And in addition to all this, a quiet sealed letter from Baldwin saying: *Your daughter is not doing work compatible with her performance on the Stanford-Binet. . . .* And your son is not doing well, not well at all, very sad. Where is your son anyway? Once he stole trick-or-treat candy from some six-year-old kids, he himself being a robust ten. The beginning. Now your daughter steals. In the Village Pharmacy she made off with, yes she did, don't deny it, she made off with a copy of *Pageant* magazine for no reason, she swiped a roll of Life Savers in a green wrapper and was in no need of saving her life or even in need of sucking candy; when she was no more than eight years old she stole, don't blush, she stole a package of Tums only because it was out on the counter and available, and the nice lady behind the counter (now dead) said nothing. . . . Sioux Drive. Maples, oaks, elms. Diseased elms cut down. Sioux Drive runs into Roosevelt Drive. Slow, turning lanes, not streets, all drives and lanes and ways and passes. A private police force. Quiet private police, in unmarked cars. Cruising on Saturday evenings with paternal smiles for the residents who are streaming in and out of houses, going to and from parties, a thousand parties, slightly staggering, the women in their furs alighting from automobiles bought of Ford and General Motors and Chrysler, very heavy automobiles. No foreign cars. Detroit. In 275 Sioux, down the block in that magnificent French-Normandy mansion, lives X   himself, who has the C   account itself, imagine that! Look at where he lives and look at the enormous trees and chimneys, imagine his many fireplaces, imagine his wife and children, imagine his wife's hair, imagine her fingernails, imagine her bathtub of smooth clean glowing pink, imagine their embraces, his trouser pockets filled with odd coins and keys and dust and peanuts, imagine their ecstasy on Sioux Drive, imagine their income tax returns, imagine their little boy's pride in his experimental car, a scaled-down C   , as he roars around the neighborhood on the sidewalks frightening dogs and maids, oh imagine all these things, imagine everything, let your mind roar out all over Sioux Drive and Du Maurier Drive and Roosevelt Drive and Ticonderoga Pass and Burning Bush Way and Lincolnshire Pass and Lois Lane.

When spring comes, its winds blow nothing to Sioux Drive, no odors of hollyhocks or forsythia, nothing Sioux Drive doesn't already possess, everything is planted and performing. The weather vanes, had they weather vanes, don't have to turn with the wind, don't have to contend with the weather. There is no weather.

VI DETROIT

There is always weather in Detroit. Detroit's temperature is always thirty-two degrees. Fast-falling temperatures. Slow-rising temperatures. Wind from the north-northeast four to forty miles an hour, small-craft warnings, partly cloudy today and Wednesday changing to partly sunny through Thursday . . . small warnings of frost, soot warnings, traffic warnings, hazardous lake conditions for small craft and swimmers, restless black gangs, restless cloud formations, restless temperatures aching to fall out the very bottom of the thermometer or shoot up over the top and boil everything over in red mercury.

Detroit's temperature is thirty-two degrees. Fast-falling temperatures. Slow-rising temperatures. Wind from the north-northeast four to forty miles an hour. . . .

VII EVENTS

1. The girl's heart is pounding. In her pocket is a pair of gloves! In a plastic bag! Airproof breathproof plastic bag, gloves selling for twenty-five dollars on Branden's counter! In her pocket! Shoplifted! . . . In her purse is a blue comb, not very clean. In her purse is a leather billfold (a birthday present from her grandmother in Philadelphia) with snapshots of the family in clean plastic windows, in the billfold are bills, she doesn't know how many bills. . . . In her purse is an ominous note from her friend Tykie *What's this about Joe H. and the kids hanging around at Louise's Sat. night? You heard anything? . . .* passed in French class. In her purse is a lot of dirty yellow Kleenex, her mother's heart would break to see such very dirty Kleenex, and at the bottom of her purse are brown hairpins and safety pins and a broken pencil and a ballpoint pen (blue) stolen from somewhere forgotten and a purse-size compact of

Cover Girl makeup, Ivory Rose. . . . Her lipstick is Broken Heart, a cor-
rupt pink; her fingers are trembling like crazy; her teeth are beginning
to chatter; her insides are alive; her eyes glow in her head; she is saying
to her mother's astonished face *I wanted to steal but not to buy.*

    2. At Clarita's. Day or night? What room is this? A bed, a regular
bed, and a mattress on the floor nearby. Wallpaper hanging in strips.
Clarita says she tore it like that with her teeth. She was fighting a bar-
baric tribe that night, high from some pills; she was battling for her
life with men wearing helmets of heavy iron and their faces no more
than Christian crosses to breathe through, every one of those bastards
looking like her lover Simon, who seems to breathe with great difficulty
through the slits of mouth and nostrils in his face. Clarita has never
heard of Sioux Drive. Raymond Forrest cuts no ice with her, nor does
the C   account and its millions; Harvard Business School could be
at the corner of Vernor and Twelfth Street for all she cares, and Vietnam
might have sunk by now into the Dead Sea under its tons of debris, for
all the amazement she could show . . . her face is overworked, over-
wrought, at the age of twenty (thirty?) it is already exhausted but fanci-
ful and ready for a laugh. Clarita says mournfully to me *Honey somebody
is going to turn you out let me give you warning.* In a movie shown on
late-night television Clarita is not a mess like this but a nurse, with short
neat hair and a dedicated look, in love with her doctor and her doctor's
patients and their diseases, enamored of needles and sponges and rub-
bing alcohol. . . . Or no: she is a private secretary. Robert Cummings is
her boss. She helps him with fantastic plots, the canned audience laughs,
no, the audience doesn't laugh because nothing is funny, instead her
boss is Robert Taylor and they are not boss and secretary but husband
and wife, she is threatened by a young starlet, she is grim, handsome,
wifely, a good companion for a good man. . . . She is Claudette Col-
bert. Her sister too is Claudette Colbert. They are twins, identical. Her
husband Charles Boyer is a very rich handsome man and her sister,
Claudette Colbert, is plotting her death in order to take her place as the
rich man's wife, no one will know because they are *twins*. . . . All these

marvelous lives Clarita might have lived, but she fell out the bottom at the age of thirteen. At the age when I was packing my overnight case for a slumber party at Toni Deshield's she was tearing filthy sheets off a bed and scratching up a rash on her arms. . . . "Thirteen is young for a Caucasian/suburban girl of the Detroit area," Miss Brock of the Detroit House of Corrections said in an interview for the *Detroit News*: fifteen and sixteen are more common. Yet such "young ages" as eleven and twelve are not uncommon in black girls . . . they are "more precocious." What can we do? Whose fault is it? Taxes are rising even as the city's tax base is falling. The temperature rises slowly but falls rapidly. Everything is falling out the bottom, Woodward Avenue is filthy, Livernois Avenue is filthy! Scraps of paper flutter in the air like pigeons, dirt flies up and hits you right in the eye, oh Detroit is breaking up into dangerous bits of newspaper and dirt, watch out. . . .

Clarita's apartment is over a restaurant. Simon her lover emerges from the cracks at dark. Mrs. Olesko, a neighbor of Clarita's, an aged white wisp of a woman, doesn't complain but sniffs with contentment at Clarita's noisy life and doesn't tell the cops, hating cops, when the cops arrive. I should give more fake names, more blanks, instead of telling all these secrets. I myself am a secret; I am a minor.

3. My father reads a paper at a medical convention in Los Ange-. les. There he is, on the edge of the North American continent when the unmarked detective put his hand so gently on my arm in the aisle of Branden's and said, "Miss, would you like to step over here for a minute?"

And where was he when Clarita put her hand on my arm, that wintry dark sulphurous aching day in Detroit, in the company of closed-down barbershops, closed-down diners, closed-down movie houses, homes, windows, basements, faces . . . she put her hand on my arm and said, "Honey, are you looking for somebody down here?"

And was he home worrying about me, gone for two weeks solid, when they carried me off . . . ? It took three of them to get me in the police cruiser, so they said, and they put more than their hands on my arm.

4. I work on this lesson. My English teacher is Mr. Forest, who is from Michigan State. Not handsome, Mr. Forest, and his name is plain, unlike Raymond Forrest's, but he is sweet and rodentlike, he has conferred with the principal and my parents, and everything is fixed . . . treat her as if nothing has happened, a new start, begin again, only sixteen years old, what a shame, how did it happen?—nothing happened, nothing could have happened, a slight physiological modification known only to a gynecologist or to Dr. Coronet. I work on my lesson. I sit in my pink room. I look around the room with my sad pink eyes. I sigh, I dawdle, I pause, I eat up time, I am limp and happy to be home, I am sixteen years old suddenly, my head hangs heavy as a pumpkin on my shoulders, and my hair has just been cut by Mr. Faye at the Crystal Salon and is said to be very becoming.

(Simon too put his hand on my arm and said, "Honey, you have got to come with me," and in his six-by-six room we got to know each other. Would I go back to Simon again? Would I lie down with him in all that filth and craziness? Over and over again

a Clarita is being betrayed as in front of a Cunningham Drug Store she is nervously eying a black man who may or may not have money, or a nervous white boy of twenty with sideburns and an Appalachian look, who may or may not have a knife hidden in his jacket pocket, or a husky red-faced man of friendly countenance who may or may not be a member of the vice squad out for an early twilight walk.)

I work on my lesson for Mr. Forest. I have filled up eleven pages. Words pour out of me and won't stop. I want to tell everything . . . what was the song Simon was always humming, and who was Simon's friend in a very new trench coat with an old high school graduation ring on his finger . . . ? Simon's bearded friend? When I was down too low for him, Simon kicked me out and gave me to him for three days, I think, on Fourteenth Street in Detroit, an airy room of cold cruel drafts with newspapers on the floor. . . . Do I really remember that or am I piecing it together from what they told me? Did they tell the truth? Did they know much of the truth?

VIII CHARACTERS

1. Wednesdays after school, at four; Saturday mornings at ten. Mother drives me to Dr. Coronet. Ferns in the office, plastic or real, they look the same. Dr. Coronet is queenly, an elegant nicotine-stained lady who would have studied with Freud had circumstances not prevented it, a bit of a Catholic, ready to offer you some mystery if your teeth will ache too much without it. Highly recommended by Father! Progress! Looking up! Looking better! That new haircut is so becoming, says Dr. Coronet herself, showing how normal she is for a woman with an I.Q. of 180 and many advanced degrees.

2. Mother. A lady in a brown suede coat. Boots of shiny black material, black gloves, a black fur hat. She would be humiliated could she know that of all the people in the world it is my ex-lover Simon who walks most like her . . . self-conscious and unreal, listening to distant music, a little bowlegged with craftiness. . . .

3. Father. Tying a necktie. In a hurry. On my first evening home he put his hand on my arm and said, "Honey, we're going to forget all about this."

4. Simon. Outside, a plane is crossing the sky, in here we're in a hurry. Morning. It must be morning. The girl is half out of her mind, whimpering and vague; Simon her dear friend is wretched this morning . . . he is wretched with morning itself . . . he forces her to give him an injection with that needle she knows is filthy, she has a dread of needles and surgical instruments and the odor of things that are to be sent into the blood, thinking somehow of her father. . . . This is a bad morning, Simon says that his mind is being twisted out of shape, and so he submits to the needle that he usually scorns and bites his lip with his yellowish teeth, his face going very pale. *Ah baby!* he says in his soft mocking voice, which with all women is a mockery of love, *do it like this—slowly—*and the girl, terrified, almost drops the precious needle but manages to turn it up to the light from the window . . . is it an extension of herself then?

She can give him this gift then? *I wish you wouldn't do this to me*, she says, wise in her terror, because it seems to her that Simon's danger—in a few minutes he may be dead—is a way of pressing her against him that is more powerful than any other embrace. She has to work over his arm, the knotted corded veins of his arm, her forehead wet with perspiration as she pushes and releases the needle, staring at that mixture of liquid now stained with Simon's bright blood. . . . When the drug hits him she can feel it herself, she feels that magic that is more than any woman can give him, striking the back of his head and making his face stretch as if with the impact of a terrible sun. . . . She tries to embrace him but he pushes her aside and stumbles to his feet. *Jesus Christ*, he says. . . .

5. Princess, a black girl of eighteen. What is her charge? She is closemouthed about it, shrewd and silent, you know that no one had to wrestle her to the sidewalk to get her in here; she came with dignity. In the recreation room she sits reading *Nancy Drew and the Jewel Box Mystery*, which inspires in her face tiny wrinkles of alarm and interest: what a face! Light-brown skin, heavy shaded eyes, heavy eyelashes, a serious sinister dark brow, graceful fingers, graceful wristbones, graceful legs, lips, tongue, a sugar-sweet voice, a leggy stride more masculine than Simon's and my mother's, decked out in a dirty white blouse and dirty white slacks; vaguely nautical is Princess's style. . . . At breakfast she is in charge of clearing the table and leans over me, saying, *Honey you sure you ate enough?*

6. The girl lies sleepless, wondering. Why here, why not there? Why Bloomfield Hills and not jail? Why jail and not her pink room? Why downtown Detroit and not Sioux Drive? What is the difference? Is Simon all the difference? The girl's head is a parade of wonders. She is nearly sixteen, her breath is marvelous with wonders, not long ago she was coloring with crayons and now she is smearing the landscape with paints that won't come off and won't come off her fingers either. She says to the matron *I am not talking about anything*, not because everyone has warned her not to talk but because, because she will not talk;

because she won't say anything about Simon, who is her secret. And she says to the matron, *I won't go home*, up until that night in the lavatory when everything was changed. . . . "No, I won't go home I want to stay here," she says, listening to her own words with amazement thinking that weeds might climb everywhere over that marvelous custom-designed house and dinosaurs might return to muddy the beige carpeting, but never never will she reconcile four o'clock in the morning in Detroit with eight-o'clock breakfasts in Bloomfield Hills. . . . oh, she aches still for Simon's hands and his caressing breath, though he gave her little pleasure, he took everything from her (five-dollar bills, ten-dollar bills, passed into her numb hands by men and taken out of her hands by Simon) until she herself was passed into the hands of other men, police, when Simon evidently got tired of her and her hysteria. . . . *No, I won't go home, I don't want to be bailed out*. The girl thinks as a *Stubborn and Wayward Child* (one of several charges lodged against her), and the matron understands her crazy white-rimmed eyes that are seeking out some new violence that will keep her in jail, should someone threaten to let her out. Such children try to strangle the matrons, the attendants, or one another . . . they want the locks locked forever, the doors nailed shut . . . and this girl is no different up until that night her mind is changed for her. . . .

IX THAT NIGHT

Princess and Dolly, a little white girl of maybe fifteen, hardy however as a sergeant and in the House of Corrections for armed robbery, corner her in the lavatory at the farthest sink and the other girls look away and file to bed, leaving her. God, how she is beaten up! Why is she beaten up? Why do they pound her, why such hatred? Princess vents all the hatred of a thousand silent Detroit winters on her body, this girl whose body belongs to me, fiercely she rides across the Midwestern plains on this girl's tender bruised body . . . revenge on the oppressed minorities of America! revenge on the slaughtered Indians! revenge on the female sex, on the male sex, revenge on Bloomfield Hills, revenge revenge. . . .

X DETROIT

In Detroit, weather weighs heavily upon everyone. The sky looms large. The horizon shimmers in smoke. Downtown the buildings are imprecise in the haze. Perpetual haze. Perpetual motion inside the haze. Across the choppy river is the city of Windsor, in Canada. Part of the continent has bunched up here and is bulging outward, at the tip of Detroit; a cold hard rain is forever falling on the expressways. . . . Shoppers shop grimly, their cars are not parked in safe places, their windshields may be smashed and graceful ebony hands may drag them out through their shatterproof smashed windshields, crying, *Revenge for the Indians!* Ah, they all fear leaving Hudson's and being dragged to the very tip of the city and thrown off the parking roof of Cobo Hall, that expensive tomb, into the river. . . .

XI CHARACTERS WE ARE FOREVER ENTWINED WITH

1. Simon drew me into his tender rotting arms and breathed gravity into me. Then I came to earth, weighed down. He said, *You are such a little girl,* and he weighed me down with his delight. In the palms of his hands were teeth marks from his previous life experiences. He was thirty-five, they said. Imagine Simon in this room, in my pink room; he is about six feet tall and stoops slightly, in a feline cautious way, always thinking, always on guard, with his scuffed light suede shoes and his clothes that are anyone's clothes, slightly rumpled ordinary clothes that ordinary men might wear to not-bad jobs. Simon has fair long hair, curly hair, spent languid curls that are like . . . exactly like the curls of wood shavings to the touch, I am trying to be exact . . . and he smells of unheated mornings and coffee and too many pills coating his tongue with a faint green-white scum . . . Dear Simon, who would be panicked in this room and in this house (right now Billie is vacuuming next door in my parents' room; a vacuum cleaner's roar is a sign of all good things), Simon who is said to have come from a home not much different from this, years ago, fleeing all the carpeting and the polished banisters . . . Simon has a deathly face, only desperate people fall in love

with it. His face is bony and cautious, the bones of his cheeks prominent as if with the rigidity of his ceaseless thinking, plotting, for he has to make money out of girls to whom money means nothing, they're so far gone they can hardly count it, and in a sense money means nothing to him either except as a way of keeping on with his life. *Each Day's Proud Struggle*, the title of a novel we could read at jail. . . . Each day he needs a certain amount of money. He devours it. It wasn't love he uncoiled in me with his hollowed-out eyes and his courteous smile, that remnant of a prosperous past, but a dark terror that needed to press itself against him, or against another man . . . but he was the first, he came over to me and took my arm, a claim. We struggled on the stairs and I said, *Let me loose, you're hurting my neck, my face*, it was such a surprise that my skin hurt where he rubbed it, and afterward we lay face to face and he breathed everything into me. In the end I think he turned me in.

2. Raymond Forrest. I just read this morning that Raymond Forrest's father, the chairman of the board at   , died of a heart attack on a plane bound for London. I would like to write Raymond Forrest a note of sympathy. I would like to thank him for not pressing charges against me one hundred years ago, saving me, being so generous . . . well, men like Raymond Forrest are generous men, not like Simon. I would like to write him a letter telling of my love, or of some other emotion that is positive and healthy. Not like Simon and his poetry, which he scrawled down when he was high and never changed a word . . . but when I try to think of something to say, it is Simon's language that comes back to me, caught in my head like a bad song, it is always Simon's language:

> *There is no reality only dreams*
> *Your neck may get snapped when you wake*
> *My love is drawn to some violent end*
> *She keeps wanting to get away*
> *My love is heading downward*
> *And I am heading upward*
> *She is going to crash on the sidewalk*
> *And I am going to dissolve into the clouds*

XII EVENTS

1. Out of the hospital, bruised and saddened and converted, with Princess's grunts still tangled in my hair . . . and Father in his overcoat looking like a prince himself, come to carry me off. Up the expressway and out north to home. Jesus Christ, but the air is thinner and cleaner here. Monumental houses. Heartbreaking sidewalks, so clean.

2. Weeping in the living room. The ceiling is two stories high and two chandeliers hang from it. Weeping, weeping, though Billie the maid is *probably listening.* I will never leave home again. Never. Never leave home. Never leave this home again, never.

3. Sugar doughnuts for breakfast. The toaster is very shiny and my face is distorted in it. Is that my face?

4. The car is turning in the driveway. Father brings me home. Mother embraces me. Sunlight breaks in movieland patches on the roof of our traditional-contemporary home, which was designed for the famous automotive stylist whose identity, if I told you the name of the famous car he designed, you would all know, so I can't tell you because my teeth chatter at the thought of being sued . . . or having someone climb into my bedroom window with a rope to strangle me. . . . The car turns up the blacktop drive. The house opens to me like a doll's house, so lovely in the sunlight, the big living room beckons to me with its walls falling away in a delirium of joy at my return, Billie the maid is *no doubt* listening from the kitchen as I burst into tears and the hysteria Simon got so sick of. Convulsed in Father's arms, I say I will never leave again, never, why did I leave, where did I go, what happened, my mind is gone wrong, my body is one big bruise, my backbone was sucked dry, it wasn't the men who hurt me and Simon never hurt me but only those girls . . . my God, how they hurt me . . . I will never leave home again. . . . The car is perpetually turning up the drive and I am perpetually breaking down in the living room and we are perpetually taking the right exit from the expressway (Lahser Road) and the wall of the rest room is perpetually

banging against my head and perpetually are Simon's hands moving across my body and adding everything up and so too are Father's hands on my shaking bruised back, far from the surface of my skin on the surface of my good blue cashmere coat (dry-cleaned for my release). . . . I weep for all the money here, for God in gold and beige carpeting, for the beauty of chandeliers and the miracle of a clean polished gleaming toaster and faucets that run both hot and cold water, and I tell them, *I will never leave home, this is my home, I love everything here, I am in love with everything here. . . .*

I am home.

FOUR SUMMERS

———

IT IS SOME KIND of special day. "Where's Sissie?" Ma says. Her
face gets sharp, she is frightened. When I run around her chair she
laughs and hugs me. She is pretty when she laughs. Her hair is long
and pretty.

We are sitting at the best table of all, out near the water. The sun is
warm and the air smells nice. Daddy is coming back from the building
with some glasses of beer, held in his arms. He makes a grunting noise
when he sits down.

"Is the lake deep?" I ask them.

They don't hear me, they're talking. A woman and a man are sitting
with us. The man marched in the parade we saw just awhile ago; he is a
volunteer fireman and is wearing a uniform. Now his shirt is pulled open
because it is hot. I can see the dark curly hair way up by his throat; it
looks hot and prickly.

A man in a soldier's uniform comes over to us. They are all friends,
but I can't remember him. We used to live around here, Ma told me,
and then we moved away. The men are laughing. The man in the uni-

form leans back against the railing, laughing, and I am afraid it will break and he will fall into the water.

"Can we go out in a boat, Dad?" says Jerry.

He and Frank keep running back and forth. I don't want to go with them, I want to stay by Ma. She smells nice. Frank's face is dirty with sweat. "Dad," he says, whining, "can't we go out in a boat? Them kids are going out."

A big lake is behind the building and the open part where we are sitting. Some people are rowing on it. This tavern is noisy and everyone is laughing; it is too noisy for Dad to think about what Frank said.

"Harry," says Ma, "the kids want a boat ride. Why don't you leave off drinking and take them?"

"What?" says Dad.

He looks up from laughing with the men. His face is damp with sweat and he is happy. "Yeah, sure, in a few minutes. Go over there and play and I'll take you out in a few minutes."

The boys run out back by the rowboats, and I run after them. I have a bag of potato chips.

An old man with a white hat pulled down over his forehead is sitting by the boats, smoking. "You kids be careful," he says.

Frank is leaning over and looking at one of the boats. "This here is the best one," he says.

"Why's this one got water in it?" says Jerry.

"You kids watch out. Where's your father?" the man says.

"He's gonna take us for a ride," says Frank.

"Where is he?"

The boys run along, looking at the boats that are tied up. They don't bother with me. The boats are all painted dark green, but the paint is peeling off some of them in little pieces. There is water inside some of them. We watch two people come in, a man and a woman. The woman is giggling. She has on a pink dress and she leans over to trail one finger in the water. "What's all this filthy stuff by the shore?" she says. There is some scum in the water. It is colored a light brown, and there are little seeds and twigs and leaves in it.

The man helps the woman out of the boat. They laugh together.

Around their rowboat little waves are still moving; they make a churning noise that I like.

"Where's Dad?" Frank says.

"He ain't coming," says Jerry.

They are tossing pebbles out into the water. Frank throws his sideways, twisting his body. He is ten and very big. "I bet he ain't coming," Jerry says, wiping his nose with the back of his hand.

After awhile we go back to the table. Behind the table is the white railing, and then the water, and then the bank curves out so that the weeping willow trees droop over the water. More men in uniforms, from the parade, are walking by.

"Dad," says Frank, "can't we go out? Can't we? There's a real nice boat there—"

"For Christ's sake, get them off me," Dad says. He is angry with Ma. "Why don't you take them out?"

"Honey, I can't row."

"Should we take out a boat, us two?" the other woman says. She has very short, wet-looking hair. It is curled in tiny little curls close to her head and is very bright. "We'll show them, Lenore. Come on, let's give your kids a ride. Show these guys how strong we are."

"That's all you need, to sink a boat," her husband says.

They all laugh.

The table is filled with brown beer bottles and wrappers of things. I can feel how happy they all are together, drawn together by the round table. I lean against Ma's warm leg and she pats me without looking down. She lunges forward and I can tell even before she says something that she is going to be loud.

"You guys're just jealous! Afraid we'll meet some soldiers!" she says.

"Can't we go out, Dad? Please?" Frank says. "We won't fight. . . ."

"Go and play over there. What're those kids doing—over there?" Dad says, frowning. His face is damp and loose, the way it is sometimes when he drinks. "In a little while, okay? Ask your mother."

"She can't do it," Frank says.

"They're just jealous," Ma says to the other woman, giggling. "They're afraid we might meet somebody somewhere."

"Just who's gonna meet this one here?" the other man says, nodding with his head at his wife.

Frank and Jerry walk away. I stay by Ma. My eyes burn and I want to sleep, but they won't be leaving for a long time. It is still daylight. When we go home from places like this it is always dark and getting chilly and the grass by our house is wet.

"Duane Dorsey's in jail," Dad says. "You guys heard about that?"

"Duane? Yeah, really?"

"It was in the newspaper. His mother-in-law or somebody called the police, he was breaking windows in her house."

"That Duane was always a nut!"

"Is he out now, or what?"

"I don't know, I don't see him these days. We had a fight," Dad says.

The woman with the short hair looks at me. "She's a real cute little thing," she says, stretching her mouth. "She drink beer, Lenore?"

"I don't know."

"Want some of mine?"

She leans toward me and holds the glass by my mouth. I can smell the beer and the warm stale smell of perfume. There are pink lipstick smudges on the glass.

"Hey, what the hell are you doing?" her husband says.

When he talks rough like that I remember him: we were with him once before.

"Are you swearing at me?" the woman says.

"Leave off the kid, you want to make her a drunk like yourself?"

"It don't hurt, one little sip. . . ."

"It's okay," Ma says. She puts her arm around my shoulders and pulls me closer to the table.

"Let's play cards. Who wants to?" Dad says.

"Sissie wants a little sip, don't you?" the woman says. She is smiling at me and I can see that her teeth are darkish, not nice like Ma's.

"Sure, go ahead," says Ma.

"I said leave off that, Sue, for Christ's sake," the man says. He jerks the table. He is a big man with a thick neck; he is bigger than Dad. His eyebrows are blond, lighter than his hair, and are thick and tufted. Dad is staring at something out on the lake without seeing it. "Harry, look, my goddam wife is trying to make your kid drink beer."

"Who's getting hurt?" Ma says angrily.

Pa looks at me all at once and smiles. "Do you want it, baby?"

I have to say yes. The woman grins and holds the glass down to me, and it clicks against my teeth. They laugh. I stop swallowing right away because it is ugly, and some of the beer drips down on me. "Honey, you're so clumsy," Ma says, wiping me with a napkin.

"She's a real cute girl," the woman says, sitting back in her chair. "I wish I had a nice little girl like that."

"Lay off of that," says her husband.

"Hey, did you bring any cards?" Dad says to the soldier.

"They got some inside."

"Look, I'm sick of cards," Ma says.

"Yeah, why don't we all go for a boat ride?" says the woman. "Be real nice, something new. Every time we get together we play cards. How's about a boat ride?"

"It better be a big boat, with you in it," her husband says. He is pleased when everyone laughs, even the woman. The soldier lights a cigarette and laughs. "How come your cousin here's so skinny and you're so fat?"

"She isn't fat," says Ma. "What the hell do you want? Look at yourself."

"Yes, the best days of my life are behind me," the man says. He wipes his face and then presses a beer bottle against it. "Harry, you're lucky you moved out. It's all going downhill, back in the neighborhood."

"You should talk, you let our house look like hell," the woman says. Her face is blotched now, some parts pale and some red. "Harry don't sit out in his back yard all weekend drinking. He gets something done."

"Harry's younger than me."

Ma reaches over and touches Dad's arm. "Harry, why don't you take the kids out? Before it gets dark."

Dad lifts his glass and finishes his beer. "Who else wants more?" he says.

"I'll get them, you went last time," the soldier says.

"Get a chair for yourself," says Dad. "We can play poker."

"I don't want to play poker, I want to play rummy," the woman says.

"At church this morning Father Reilly was real mad," says Ma. "He said some kids or somebody was out in the cemetery and left some beer bottles. Isn't that awful?"

"Duane Dorsey used to do worse than that," the man says, winking.

"Hey, who's that over there?"

"You mean that fat guy?"

"Isn't that the guy at the lumberyard that owes all that money?"

Dad turns around. His chair wobbles and he almost falls; he is angry.

"This goddamn place is too crowded," he says.

"This is a real nice place," the woman says. She is taking something out of her purse. "I always liked it, didn't you, Lenore?"

"Sue and me used to come here a lot," says Ma. "And not just with you two, either."

"Yeah, we're real jealous," the man says.

"You should be," says the woman.

The soldier comes back. Now I can see that he is really a boy. He runs to the table with the beer before he drops anything. He laughs.

"Jimmy, your ma wouldn't like to see you drinking!" the woman says happily.

"Well, she ain't here."

"Are they still living out in the country?" Ma says to the woman.

"Sure. No electricity, no running water, no bathroom—same old thing. What can you do with people like that?"

"She always talks about going back to the Old Country," the soldier says. "Thinks she can save up money and go back."

"Poor old bastards don't know there was a war," Dad says. He looks as if something tasted bad in his mouth. "My old man died thinking he could go back in a year or two. Stupid old bastards!"

"Your father was real nice . . . ," Ma says.

"Yeah, real nice," says Dad. "Better off dead."

Everybody is quiet.

"June Dieter's mother's got the same thing," the woman says in a low voice to Ma. "She's had it a year now and don't weigh a hundred pounds—you remember how big she used to be."

"She was big, all right," Ma says.

"Remember how she ran after June and slapped her? We were there—some guys were driving us home."

"Yeah. So she's got it too."

"Hey," says Dad, "why don't you get a chair, Jimmy? Sit down here."

The soldier looks around. His face is raw in spots, broken out. But his eyes are nice. He never looks at me.

"Get a chair from that table," Dad says.

"Those people might want it."

"Hell, just take it. Nobody's sitting on it."

"They might—"

Dad reaches around and yanks the chair over. The people look at him but don't say anything. Dad is breathing hard. "Here, sit here," he says. The soldier sits down.

Frank and Jerry come back. They stand by Dad, watching him. "Can we go out now?" Frank says.

"What?"

"Out for a boat ride."

"What? No, next week. Do it next week. We're going to play cards."

"You said—"

"Shut up, we'll do it next week." Dad looks up and shades his eyes. "The lake don't look right anyway."

"Lots of people are out there—"

"I said shut up."

"Honey," Ma whispers, "let him alone. Go and play by yourselves."

"Can we sit in the car?"

"Okay, but don't honk the horn."

"Ma, can't we go for a ride?"

"Go and play by yourselves, stop bothering us," she says. "Hey, will you take Sissie?"

They look at me. They don't like me, I can see it, but they take me with them. We run through the crowd and somebody spills a drink—he yells at us. "Oops, got to watch it!" Frank giggles.

We run along the walk by the boat. A woman in a yellow dress is carrying a baby. She looks at us like she doesn't like us.

Down at the far end some kids are standing together.

"Hey, lookit that," Frank says.

A blackbird is caught in the scum, by one of the boats. It can't fly up. One of the kids, a long-legged girl in a dirty dress, is poking at it with a stick.

The bird's wings keep fluttering but it can't get out. If it could get free it would fly and be safe, but the scum holds it down.

One of the kids throws a stone at it. "Stupid old goddamn bird," somebody says. Frank throws a stone. They are all throwing stones. The bird doesn't know enough to turn away. Its feathers are all wet and dirty. One of the stones hits the bird's head.

"Take that!" Frank says, throwing a rock. The water splashes up and some of the girls scream.

I watch them throwing stones. I am standing at the side. If the bird dies, then everything can die, I think. Inside the tavern there is music from the jukebox.

II

We are at the boathouse tavern again. It is a mild day, a Sunday afternoon. Dad is talking with some men; Jerry and I are waiting by the boats. Mommy is at home with the new baby. Frank has gone off with some friends of his, to a stock-car race. There are some people here, sitting out at the tables, but they don't notice us.

"Why doesn't he hurry up?" Jerry says.

Jerry is twelve now. He has pimples on his forehead and chin.

He pushes one of the rowboats with his foot. He is wearing sneak-
ers that are dirty. I wish I could get in that boat and sit down, but I am
afraid. A boy not much older than Jerry is squatting on the boardwalk,
smoking. You can tell he is in charge of the boats.

"Daddy, come on. Come on," Jerry says, whining. Daddy can't hear
him.

I have mosquito bites on my arms and legs. There are mosquitoes
and flies around here; the flies crawl around the sticky mess left on
tables. A car over in the parking lot has its radio on loud. You can hear
the music all this way. "He's coming," I tell Jerry so he won't be mad.
Jerry is like Dad, the way his eyes look.

"Oh, that fat guy keeps talking to him," Jerry says.

The fat man is one of the bartenders; he has on a dirty white apron.
All these men are familiar. We have been seeing them for years. He
punches Dad's arm, up by the shoulder, and Dad pushes him. They are
laughing, though. Nobody is mad.

"I'd sooner let a nigger—" the bartender says. We can't hear any-
thing more, but the men laugh again.

"All he does is drink," Jerry says. "I hate him."

At school, up on the sixth-grade floor, Jerry got in trouble last
month. The principal slapped him. I am afraid to look at Jerry when
he's mad.

"I hate him, I wish he'd die," Jerry says.

Dad is trying to come to us, but every time he takes a step backward
and gets ready to turn, one of the men says something. There are three
men beside him. Their stomachs are big, but Dad's isn't. He is wear-
ing dark pants and a white shirt; his tie is in the car. He wears a tie to
church, then takes it off. He has his shirt sleeves rolled up and you can
see how strong his arms must be.

Two women cross over from the parking lot. They are wearing high-
heeled shoes and hats and bright dresses—orange and yellow—and
when they walk past the men look at them. They go into the tavern. The
men laugh about something. The way they laugh makes my eyes focus
on something away from them—a bird flying in the sky—and it is hard
for me to look anywhere else. I feel as if I'm falling asleep.

"Here he comes!" Jerry says.

Dad walks over to us, with his big steps. He is smiling and carrying a bottle of beer. "Hey, kid," he says to the boy squatting on the walk, "how's about a boat?"

"This one is the best," Jerry says.

"The best, huh? Great." Dad grins at us. "Okay, Sissie, let's get you in. Be careful now." He picks me up even though I am too heavy for it, and sets me in the boat. It hurts a little where he held me, under the arms, but I don't care.

Jerry climbs in. Dad steps and something happens—he almost slips, but he catches himself. With the wet oar he pushes us off from the boardwalk.

Dad can row fast. The sunlight is gleaming on the water. I sit very still, facing him, afraid to move. The boat goes fast, and Dad is leaning back and forth and pulling on the oars, breathing hard, doing everything fast like he always does. He is always in a hurry to get things done. He has set the bottle of beer down by his leg, pressed against the side of the boat so it won't fall.

"There's the guys we saw go out before," Jerry says. Coming around the island is a boat with three boys in it, older than Jerry. "They went on the island. Can we go there too?"

"Sure," says Dad. His eyes squint in the sun. He is suntanned, and there are freckles on his forehead. I am sitting close to him, facing him, and it surprises me what he looks like—he is like a stranger, with his eyes narrowed. The water beneath the boat makes me feel funny. It keeps us up now, but if I fell over the side I would sink and drown.

"Nice out here, huh?" Dad says. He is breathing hard.

"We should go over that way to get on the island," Jerry says.

"This goddamn oar has splinters in it," Dad says. He hooks the oar up and lets us glide. He reaches down to get the bottle of beer. Though the lake and some trees and the buildings back on shore are in front of me, what makes me look at it is my father's throat, the way it bobs when he swallows. He wipes his forehead. "Want to row, Sissie?" he says.

"Can I?"

"Let me do it," says Jerry.

"Naw, I was just kidding," Dad says.

"I can do it. It ain't hard."

"Stay where you are," Dad says.

He starts rowing again, faster. Why does he go so fast? His face is getting red, the way it does at home when he has trouble with Frank. He clears his throat and spits over the side; I don't like to see that but I can't help but watch. The other boat glides past us, heading for shore. The boys don't look over at us.

Jerry and I look to see if anyone else is on the island, but no one is. The island is very small. You can see around it.

"Are you going to land on it, Dad?" Jerry says.

"Sure, okay." Dad's face is flushed and looks angry.

The boat scrapes bottom and bumps. "Jump out and pull it in," Dad says. Jerry jumps out. His shoes and socks are wet now, but Dad doesn't notice. The boat bumps; it hurts me. I am afraid. But then we're up on the land and Dad is out and lifting me. "Nice ride, sugar?" he says.

Jerry and I run around the island. It is different from what we thought, but we don't know why. There are some trees on it, some wild grass, and then bare caked mud that goes down to the water. The water looks dark and deep on the other side, but when we get there it's shallow. Lily pads grow there; everything is thick and tangled. Jerry wades in the water and gets his pants legs wet. "There might be money in the water," he says.

Some napkins and beer cans are nearby. There is part of a hot-dog bun, with flies buzzing around it.

When we go back by Dad, we see him squatting over the water doing something. His back jerks. Then I see that he is being sick. He is throwing up in the water and making a noise like coughing.

Jerry turns around right away and runs back. I follow him, afraid. On the other side we can look back at the boathouse and wish we were there.

III

Marian and Betty went to the show, but I couldn't. She made me come along here with them. "And cut out that snippy face," Ma said, to let me know she's watching. I have to help her take care of Linda—poor fat Linda, with her runny nose! So here we are inside the tavern. There's too much smoke, I hate smoke. Dad is smoking a cigar. I won't drink any more root beer, it's flat, and I'm sick of potato chips. Inside me there is something that wants to run away, that hates them. How loud they are, my parents! My mother spilled something on the front of her dress, but does she notice? And my aunt Lucy and uncle Joe, they're here. Try to avoid them. Lucy has false teeth that make everyone stare at her. I know that everyone is staring at us. I could hide my head in my arms and turn away, I'm so tired and my legs hurt from sunburn and I can't stand them any more.

"So did you ever hear from them? That letter you wrote?" Ma says to Lucy.

"I'm still waiting. Somebody said you got to have connections to get on the show. But I don't believe it. That Howie Masterson that's the emcee, he's a real nice guy. I can tell."

"It's all crap," Dad says. "You women believe anything."

"I don't believe it," I say.

"Phony as hell," says my uncle.

"You do too believe it, Sissie," says my mother. "Sissie thinks he's cute. I know she does."

"I hate that guy!" I tell her, but she and my aunt are laughing. "I said I hate him! He's greasy."

"All that stuff is phony as hell," says my uncle Joe. He is tired all the time, and right now he sits with his head bowed. I hate his bald head with the little fringe of gray hair on it. At least my father is still handsome. His jaws sag and there are lines in his neck—edged with dirt, I can see, embarrassed—and his stomach is bulging a little against the table, but still he is a handsome man. In a place like this women look at him. What's he see in *her?* they think. My mother had her hair cut too short last time; she looks queer. There is a photograph taken of her when she was young, standing by someone's motorcycle, with her hair long. In the photograph she was pretty, almost beautiful, but I don't believe it. Not really. I can't believe it, and I hate her. Her forehead gathers itself up in little wrinkles whenever she glances down at Linda, as if she can't remember who Linda is.

"Well, nobody wanted you, kid," she once said to Linda. Linda was a baby then, one year old. Ma was furious, standing in the kitchen where she was washing the floor, screaming: "Nobody wanted you, it was a goddamn accident! An accident!" That surprised me so I didn't know what to think, and I didn't know if I hated Ma or not; but I kept it all a secret . . . only my girl friends know, and I won't tell the priest either. Nobody can make me tell. I narrow my eyes and watch my mother leaning forward to say something—it's like she's going to toss something out on the table—and think that maybe she isn't my mother after all, and she isn't that pretty girl in the photograph, but someone else.

"A woman was on the show last night that lost two kids in a fire. Her house burned down," my aunt says loudly. "And she answered the questions right off and got a lot of money and the audience went wild. You could see she was a real lady. I love that guy, Howie Masterson. He's real sweet."

"He's a bastard," Dad says.

"Harry, what the hell? You never even seen him," Ma says.

"I sure as hell never did. Got better things to do at night." Dad turns to my uncle and his voice changes. "I'm on the night shift, now."

"Yeah, I hate that, I—"

"I can sleep during the day. What's the difference?"

"I hate those night shifts."

"What's there to do during the day?" Dad says flatly. His eyes scan us at the table as if he doesn't see anything, then they seem to fall off me and go behind me, looking at nothing.

"Not much," says my uncle, and I can see his white scalp beneath his hair. Both men are silent.

Dad pours beer into his glass and spills some of it. I wish I could look away. I love him, I think, but I hate to be here. Where would I rather be? With Marian and Betty at the movies, or in my room, lying on the bed and staring at the photographs of movie stars on my walls—those beautiful people that never say anything—while out in the kitchen my mother is waiting for my father to come home so they can continue their quarrel. It never stops, that quarrel. Sometimes they laugh together, kid around, they kiss. Then the quarrel starts up again in a few minutes.

"Ma, can I go outside and wait in the car?" I say. "Linda's asleep."

"What's so hot about the car?" she says, looking at me.

"I'm tired. My sunburn hurts."

Linda is sleeping in Ma's lap, with her mouth open and drooling on the front of her dress. "Okay, go on," Ma says. "But we're not going to hurry just for you." When she has drunk too much there is a struggle in her between being angry and being affectionate; she fights both of them, as if standing with her legs apart and her hands on her hips, bracing a strong wind.

When I cross through the crowded tavern I'm conscious of people looking at me. My hair lost its curl because it was so humid today, my legs are too thin, my figure is flat and not nice like Marian's—I want to hide somewhere, hide my face from them. I hate this noisy place and these people. Even the music is ugly because it belongs to them. Then, when I'm outside, the music gets faint right away and it doesn't sound so bad. It's cooler out here. No one is around. Out back, the old rowboats are tied up. Nobody's on the lake. There's no moon, the sky is overcast, it was raining earlier.

When I turn around, a man is standing by the door watching me.

"What're you doing?" he says.

"Nothing."

He has dark hair and a tanned face, I think, but everything is confused because the light from the door is pinkish—there's a neon sign there. My heart starts to pound. The man leans forward to stare at me. "Oh, I thought you were somebody else," he says.

I want to show him I'm not afraid. "Yeah, really? Who did you think I was?" When we ride on the school bus we smile out the windows at strange men, just for fun. We do that all the time. I'm not afraid of any of them.

"You're not her," he says.

Some people come out the door and he has to step out of their way. I say to him, "Maybe you seen me around here before. We come here pretty often."

"Who do you come with?" He is smiling as if he thinks I'm funny. "Anybody I know?"

"That's my business."

It's a game. I'm not afraid. When I think of my mother and father inside, something makes me want to step closer to this man—why should I be afraid? I could be wild like some of the other girls. Nothing surprises me.

We keep on talking. At first I can tell he wants me to come inside the tavern with him, but then he forgets about it; he keeps talking. I don't know what we say, but we talk in drawling voices, smiling at each other but in a secret, knowing way, as if each one of us knew more than the other. My cheeks start to burn. I could be wild like Betty is sometimes—like some of the other girls. Why not? Once before I talked with a man like this, on the bus. We were both sitting in the back. I wasn't afraid. This man and I keep talking and we talk about nothing, he wants to know how old I am, but it makes my heart pound so hard that I want to touch my chest to calm it. We are walking along the old boardwalk and I say: "Somebody took me out rowing once here."

"Is that so?" he says. "You want me to take you out?"

He has a hard, handsome face. I like that face. Why is he alone? When he smiles I know he's laughing at me, and this makes me stand taller, walk with my shoulders raised.

"Hey, are you with somebody inside there?" he says.

"I left them."

"Have a fight?"

"A fight, yes."

He looks at me quickly. "How old are you anyway?"

"That's none of your business."

"Girls your age are all alike."

"We're not all alike!" I arch my back and look at him in a way I must have learned somewhere—where?—with my lips not smiling but ready to smile, and my eyes narrowed. One leg is turned as if I'm ready to jump away from him. He sees all this. He smiles.

"Say, you're real cute."

We're walking over by the parking lot now. He touches my arm. Right away my heart trips, but I say nothing, I keep walking. High above us the tree branches are moving in the wind. It's cold for June. It's late—after eleven. The man is wearing a jacket, but I have on a sleeveless dress and there are goose-pimples on my arms.

"Cold, huh?" he says.

He takes hold of my shoulders and leans toward me. This is to show me he's no kid, he's grown-up, this is how they do things; when he kisses me his grip on my shoulders gets tighter. "I better go back," I say to him. My voice is queer.

"What?" he says.

I am wearing a face like one of those faces pinned up in my room, and what if I lose it? This is not my face. I try to turn away from him.

He kisses me again. His breath smells like beer, maybe, it's like my father's breath, and my mind is empty; I can't think what to do. Why am I here? My legs feel numb, my fingers are cold. The man rubs my arms and says, "You should have a sweater or something. . . ."

He is waiting for me to say something, to keep on the way I was before. But I have forgotten how to do it. Before, I was Marian or one of the older girls; now I am just myself. I am fourteen. I think of Linda sleeping in my mother's lap, and something frightens me.

"Hey, what's wrong?" the man says.

He sees I'm afraid but pretends he doesn't. He comes to me again and embraces me, his mouth presses against my neck and shoulder, I feel as if I'm suffocating. "My car's over here," he says, trying to catch his breath. I can't move. Something dazzling and icy rises up in me, an awful fear, but I can't move and can't say anything. He is touching me with his hands. His mouth is soft but wants too much from me. I think, What is he doing? Do they all do this? Do I have to have it done to me too?

"You cut that out," I tell him.

He steps away. His chest is heaving and his eyes look like a dog's eyes, surprised and betrayed. The last thing I see of him is those eyes, before I turn and run back to the tavern.

IV

Jesse says, "Let's stop at this place. I been here a few times before."

It's the Lakeside Bar. That big old building with the grubby siding, and a big pink neon sign in front, and the cinder driveway that's so bumpy. Yes, everything the same. But different too—smaller, dirtier. There is a custard stand nearby with a glaring orange roof, and people are crowded around it. That's new. I haven't been here for years.

"I feel like a beer," he says.

He smiles at me and caresses my arm. He treats me as if I were something that might break; in my cheap linen maternity dress I feel ugly and heavy. My flesh is so soft and thick that nothing could hurt it.

"Sure, honey. Pa used to stop in here too."

We cross through the parking lot to the tavern. Wild grass grows along the sidewalk and in the cracks of the sidewalk. Why is this place so ugly to me? I feel as if a hand were pressing against my chest, shutting off my breath. Is there some secret here? Why am I afraid?

I catch sight of myself in a dusty window as we pass. My hair is long, down to my shoulders. I am pretty, but my secret is that I am pretty like everyone is. My husband loves me for this but doesn't know it. I have a pink mouth and plucked darkened eyebrows and soft bangs over my forehead; I know everything, I have no need to learn from anyone else now. I am one of those girls younger girls study closely, to learn from. On buses, in five-and-tens, thirteen-year-old girls must look at me solemnly, learning, memorizing.

"Pretty Sissie!" my mother likes to say when we visit, though I told her how I hate that name. She is proud of me for being pretty, but thinks I'm too thin. "You'll fill out nice, after the baby," she says. Herself, she is fat and veins have begun to darken on her legs; she scuffs around the house in bedroom slippers. Who is my mother? When I think of her I can't think of anything—do I love her or hate her, or is there nothing there?

Jesse forgets and walks ahead of me, I have to walk fast to catch up. I'm wearing pastel-blue high heels—that must be because I am proud of my legs. I have little else. Then he remembers and turns to put out his hand for me, smiling to show he is sorry. Jesse is the kind of young man thirteen-year-old girls stare at secretly; he is not a man, not old enough, but not a boy either. He is a year older than I am, twenty. When

I met him he was wearing a navy uniform and he was with a girl friend of mine.

Just a few people sitting outside at the tables. They're afraid of rain—the sky doesn't look good. And how bumpy the ground is here, bare spots and little holes and patches of crab grass, and everywhere napkins and junk. Too many flies outside. Has this place changed hands? The screens at the windows don't fit right; you can see why flies get inside. Jesse opens the door for me and I go in. All bars smell alike. There is a damp, dark odor of beer and something indefinable—spilled soft drinks, pretzels getting stale? This bar is just like any other. Before we were married we went to places like this, Jesse and me and other couples. We had to spend a certain amount of time doing things like that—and going to movies, playing miniature golf, bowling, dancing, swimming—then we got married, now we're going to have a baby. I think of the baby all the time, because my life will be changed then; everything will be different. Four months from now. I should be frightened, but a calm laziness has come over me. It was so easy for my mother. . . . But it will be different with me because my life will be changed by it, and nothing ever changed my mother. You couldn't change her! Why should I think? Why should I be afraid? My body is filled with love for this baby, and I will never be the same again.

We sit down at a table near the bar. Jesse is in a good mood. My father would have liked him, I think; when he laughs Jesse reminds me of him. Why is a certain kind of simple, healthy, honest man always destined to lose everything? Their souls are as clean and smooth as the muscular line of their arms. At night I hold Jesse, thinking of my father and what happened to him—all that drinking, then the accident at the factory—and I pray that Jesse will be different. I hope that his quick, open, loud way of talking is just a disguise, that really he is someone else—slower and calculating. That kind of man grows old without jerks and spasms. Why did I marry Jesse?

Someone at the bar turns around, and it's a man I think I know—I have known. Yes. That man outside, the man I met outside. I stare at him, my heart pounding, and he doesn't see me. He is dark, his hair is neatly combed but is thinner than before; he is wearing a cheap gray suit. But is it the same man? He is standing with a friend and looking around, as if he doesn't like what he sees. He is tired too. He has grown years older.

Our eyes meet. He glances away. He doesn't remember—that frightened girl he held in his arms.

I am tempted to put my hand on Jesse's arm and tell him about that man, but how can I? Jesse is talking about trading in our car for a new one. . . . I can't move, my mind seems to be coming to a stop. Is that the man I kissed, or someone else? A feeling of angry loss comes over me. Why should I lose everything? Everything? Is it the same man, and would he remember? My heart bothers me, it's stupid to be like this: here I sit, powdered and sweet, a girl safely married, pregnant and secured to the earth, with my husband beside me. He still loves me. Our love keeps on. Like my parents' love, it will subside someday, but nothing surprises me because I have learned everything.

The man turns away, talking to his friend. They are weary, tired of something. He isn't married yet, I think, and that pleases me. Good. But why are these men always tired? Is it the jobs they hold, the kind of men who stop in at this tavern? Why do they flash their teeth when they smile, but stop smiling so quickly? Why do their children cringe from them sometimes—an innocent upraised arm a frightening thing? Why do they grow old so quickly, sitting at kitchen tables with bottles of beer? They are everywhere, in every house. All the houses in this neighborhood and all neighborhoods around here. Jesse is young, but the outline of what he will be is already in his face; do you think I can't see it? Their lives are like hands dealt out to them in their innumerable card games. You pick up the sticky cards, and there it is: there it is. Can't change anything, all you can do is switch some cards around, stick one in here, one over here . . . pretend there is some sense, a secret scheme.

The man at the bar tosses some coins down and turns to go. I want to cry out to him, "Wait, wait!" But I cannot. I sit helplessly and watch him leave. Is it the same man? If he leaves I will be caught here, what can I do? I can almost hear my mother's shrill laughter coming in from outside, and some drawling remark of my father's—lifting for a moment above the music. Those little explosions of laughter, the slap of someone's hand on the damp table in anger, the clink of bottles accidentally touching—and there, there, my drunken aunt's voice, what is she saying? I am terrified at being left with them. I watch the man at the door and think that I could have loved him. I know it.

He has left, he and his friend. He is nothing to me, but suddenly I feel tears in my eyes. What's wrong with me? I hate everything that springs upon me and seems to draw itself down and oppress me in a way I could never explain to anyone. . . . I am crying because I am pregnant, but not with that man's child. It could have been his child, I could have gone with him to his car; but I did nothing, I ran away, I was afraid, and now I'm sitting here with Jesse, who is picking the label off his beer bottle with his thick squarish fingernails. I did nothing. I was afraid. Now he has left me here and what can I do?

I let my hand fall onto my stomach to remind myself that I am in love: with this baby, with Jesse, with everything. I am in love with our house and our life and the future and even this moment—right now—that I am struggling to live through.

THE 1970S

SMALL AVALANCHES

———

IKEPT BOTHERING MY MOTHER for a dime, so she gave me a dime, and I went down our lane and took the shortcut to the highway, and down to the gas station. My uncle Winfield ran the gas station. There were two machines in the garage and I had to decide between them: the pop machine and the candy bar machine. No, there were three machines, but the other one sold cigarettes and I didn't care about that.

It took me a few minutes to make up my mind, then I bought a bottle of Pepsi-Cola.

Sometimes a man came to unlock the machines and take out the coins, and if I happened to be there it was interesting—the way the machines could be changed so fast if you just had the right key to open them. This man drove up in a white truck with a license plate from Kansas, a different color from our license plates, and he unlocked the machines and took out the money and loaded the machines up again. When we were younger we liked to hang around and watch. There was something strange about it, how the look of the machines could be changed so fast, the fronts swinging open, the insides showing, just because a man with the right keys drove up.

I went out front where my uncle was working on a car. He was under the car, lying on a thing made out of wood that had rollers on it so that he could roll himself under the car; I could just see his feet. He had on big heavy shoes that were all greasy. I asked him if my cousin Georgia was home—they lived about two miles away and I could walk—and he said no, she was baby-sitting in Stratton for three days. I already knew this but I hoped the people might have changed their minds.

"Is that man coming today to take out the money?"

My uncle didn't hear me. I was sucking at the Pepsi-Cola and running my tongue around the rim of the bottle. I always loved the taste of pop, the first two or three swallows. Then I would feel a little filled up and would have to drink it slowly. Sometimes I even poured the last of it out, but not so that anyone saw me.

"That man who takes care of the machines, is he coming today?"

"Who? No. Sometime next week."

My uncle pushed himself out from under the car. He was my mother's brother, a few years older than my mother. He had bushy brown hair and his face was dirty. "Did you call Georgia last night?"

"No. Ma wouldn't let me."

"Well, somebody was on the line because Betty wanted to check on her and the goddam line was busy all night. So Betty wanted to drive in, all the way to Stratton, drive six miles when probably nothing's wrong. You didn't call her, huh?"

"No."

"This morning Betty called her and gave her hell and she tried to say she hadn't been talking all night, that the telephone lines must have gotten mixed up. Georgia is a goddam little liar and if I catch her fooling around . . ."

He was walking away, into the garage. In the back pocket of his overalls was a dirty rag, stuffed there. He always yanked it out and wiped his face with it, not looking at it, even if it was dirty. I watched to see if he would do this and he did.

I almost laughed at this, and at how Georgia got away with murder. I had a good idea who was talking to her on the telephone.

The pop made my tongue tingle, a strong acid-sweet taste that almost hurt. I sat down and looked out at the road. This was in the middle of Colorado, on the road that goes through, east and west. It was a hot day. I drank one, two, three, four small swallows of pop. I pressed the bottle against my knees because I was hot. I tried to balance the bottle on one knee and it fell right over; I watched the pop trickle out onto the concrete.

I was too lazy to move my feet, so my bare toes got wet.

Somebody came along the road in a pickup truck, Mr. Watkins, and he tapped on the horn to say hello to me and my uncle. He was on his way to Stratton. I thought, *Damn it, I could have hitched a ride with him.* I don't know why I bothered to think this because I had to get home pretty soon, anyway, my mother would kill me if I went to town without telling her. Georgia and I did that once, back just after school let out in June, we went down the road a ways and hitched a ride with some guy in a beat-up car we thought looked familiar, but when he stopped to let us in we didn't know him and it was too late. But nothing happened, he was all right. We walked all the way back home again because we were scared to hitch another ride. My parents didn't find out, or Georgia's, but we didn't try it again.

I followed my uncle into the gas station. The building was made of ordinary wood, painted white a few years ago but starting to peel. It was just one room. The floor was concrete, all stained with grease and cracked. I knew the whole place by heart: the ceiling planks, the black rubber things hanging on the wall, looped over big rusty spikes, the Marlboro cigarettes ad that I liked, and the other ads for beer and cigarettes on shiny pieces of cardboard that stood up. To see those things you wouldn't guess how they came all flat, and you could unfold them and fix them yourself, like fancy things for under the Christmas tree. Inside the candy machine, behind the little windows, the candy bars stood up on display: Milky Way, Oh Henry!, Junior Mints, Mallow Cup, Three Musketeers, Hershey's. I liked them all. Sometimes Milky Way was my favorite, other times I only bought Mallow Cup for weeks in a row, trying to get enough of the cardboard letters to spell out Mallow Cup. One letter came with each candy bar, and if you spelled out the whole name you could send away for a prize. But the letter *w* was hard to find. There were lots of *l*'s, it was rotten luck to open the wrapper up and see another *l* when you already had ten of them.

"Could I borrow a nickel?" I asked my uncle.

"I don't have any change."

Like hell, I thought. My uncle was always stingy.

I pressed the "return coin" knob but nothing came out. I pulled the knob out under Mallow Cup but nothing came out.

"Nancy, don't fool around with that thing, okay?"

"I don't have anything to do."

"Yeah, well, your mother can find something for you to do."

"She can do it herself."

"You want me to tell her that?"

"Go right ahead."

"Hey, did your father find out any more about that guy in Polo?"

"What guy?"

"Oh, I don't know, some guy who got into a fight and was arrested—he was in the Navy with your father, I don't remember his name."

"I don't know."

My uncle yawned. I followed him back outside and he stretched his arms and yawned. It was very hot. You could see the fake water puddles on the highway that were so mysterious and always moved back when you approached them. They could hypnotize you. Across from the garage was the mailbox on a post and then just scrub land, nothing to look at, pastureland and big rocky hills.

I thought about going to check to see if my uncle had any mail, but I knew there wouldn't be anything inside. We only got a booklet in the mail that morning, some information about how to make money selling jewelry door-to-door that I had written away for, but now I didn't care about. "Georgia has all the luck," I said. "I could use a few dollars myself."

"Yeah," my uncle said. He wasn't listening.

I looked at myself in the outside mirror of the car he was fixing. I don't know what kind of car it was, I never memorized the makes like the boys did. It was a dark maroon color with big heavy fenders and a bumper that had little bits of rust in it, like sparks. The runningboard had old, dried mud packed down inside its ruts. It was covered with black rubber, a mat. My hair was blown-looking. It was a big heavy mane of hair the color everybody called dishwater blond. My baby pictures showed that it used to be light blond.

"I wish I could get a job like Georgia," I said.

"Georgia's a year older than you."

"Oh hell . . ."

I was thirteen but I was Georgia's size, all over, and I was smarter. We looked alike. We both had long bushy flyaway hair that frizzed up when the air was wet, but kept curls in very well when we set it, like for church. I forgot about my hair and leaned closer to the mirror to look at my face. I made my lips shape a little circle, noticing how wrinkled they got. They could wrinkle up into a small space. I poked the tip of my tongue out.

There was the noise of something on gravel, and I looked around to see a man driving in. Out by the highway my uncle just had gravel, then around the gas pumps he had concrete. This man's car was white, a color you don't see much, and his license plate was from Kansas.

He told my uncle to fill up the gas tank and he got out of the car, stretching his arms.

He looked at me and smiled. "Hi," he said.

"Hi."

He said something to my uncle about how hot it was, and my uncle said it wasn't too bad. Because that's the way he is—always contradicting you. My mother hates him for this. But then he said, "You read about the dry spell coming up?—right into September?" My uncle meant the ranch bureau thing but the man didn't know what he was talking about. He meant the "Bureau News & Forecast." This made me mad, that my uncle was so stupid, thinking that a man from out of state and probably

from a city would know about that, or give a damn. It made me mad. I
saw my pop bottle where it fell and I decided to go home, not to bother
putting it in the case where you were supposed to.

I walked along on the edge of the road, on the pavement, because
there were stones and prickles and weeds with bugs in them off the side
that I didn't like to walk in barefoot. I felt hot and mad about some-
thing. A yawn started in me, and I felt it coming up like a little bubble
of gas from the pop. There was my cousin Georgia in town, and all she
had to do was watch a little girl who wore thick glasses and was sort of
strange, but very nice and quiet and no trouble, and she'd get two dol-
lars. I thought angrily that if anybody came along I'd put out my thumb
and hitch a ride to Stratton, and the hell with my mother.

Then I did hear a car coming but I just got over to the side and
waited for him to pass. I felt stubborn and wouldn't look around to see
who it was, but then the car didn't pass and I looked over my shoul-
der—it was the man in the white car who had stopped for gas. He was
driving very slow. I got farther off the road and waited for him to pass.
But he leaned over to this side and said out the open window, "You
want a ride home? Get in."

"No, that's okay," I said.

"Come on, I'll drive you home. No trouble."

"No, it's okay. I'm almost home," I said.

I was embarrassed and didn't want to look at him. People didn't do
this, a grown-up man in a car wouldn't bother to do this. Either you
hitched for a ride or you didn't, and if you didn't, people would never
slow down to ask you. *This guy is crazy*, I thought. I felt very strange. I
tried to look over into the field but there wasn't anything to look at, not
even any cattle, just land and scrubby trees and a barbed-wire fence half
falling down.

"Your feet will get all sore, walking like that," the man said.

"I'm okay."

"Hey, watch out for the snake!"

There wasn't any snake and I made a noise like a laugh to show that
I knew it was a joke but didn't think it was very funny.

"Aren't there rattlesnakes around here? Rattlers?"

"Oh I don't know," I said.

He was still driving right alongside me, very slow. You are not used to seeing a car slowed-down like that, it seems very strange. I tried not to look at the man. But there was nothing else to look at, just the country and the road and the mountains in the distance and some clouds.

"That man at the gas station was mad, he picked up the bottle you left."

I tried to keep my lips pursed shut, but they were dry and came open again. I wondered if my teeth were too big in front.

"How come you walked away so fast? That wasn't friendly," the man said. "You forgot your pop bottle and the man back there said somebody could drive over it and get a flat tire, he was a little mad."

"He's my uncle," I said.

"What?"

He couldn't hear or was pretending he couldn't hear, so I had to turn toward him. He was all-right-looking, he was smiling. "He's my uncle," I said.

"Oh, is he? You don't look anything like *him*. Is your home nearby?"

"Up ahead." I was embarrassed and started to laugh, I don't know why.

"I don't see any house there."

"You can't see it from here," I said, laughing.

"What's so funny? My face? You know, when you smile you're a very pretty girl. You should smile all the time. . . ." He was paying so much attention to me it made me laugh. "Yes, that's a fact. Why are you blushing?"

I blushed fast, like my mother; we both hated to blush and hated people to tease us. But I couldn't get mad.

"I'm worried about your feet and the rattlers around here. Aren't there rattlers around here?"

"Oh I don't know."

"Where I come from there are streets and sidewalks and no snakes, of course, but it isn't interesting. It isn't dangerous. I think I'd like to live here, even with the snakes—this is very beautiful, hard country, isn't it? Do you like the mountains way over there? Or don't you notice them?"

I didn't pay any attention to where he was pointing, I looked at him and saw that he was smiling. He was my father's age but he wasn't stern like my father, who had a line between his eyebrows like a knife cut, from frowning. This man was wearing a shirt, a regular white shirt, out in the country. His hair was dampened and combed back from his forehead; it was damp right now, as if he had just combed it.

"Yes, I'd like to take a walk out here and get some exercise," he said. His voice sounded very cheerful. "Snakes or no snakes! You turned me down for a free ride so maybe I'll join you in a walk."

That really made me laugh: *join you in a walk.*

"Hey, what's so funny?" he said, laughing himself.

People didn't talk like that, but I didn't say anything. He parked the car on the shoulder of the road and got out and I heard him drop the car keys in his pocket. He was scratching at his jaw. "Well, excellent! This is excellent, healthy, divine country air! Do you like living out here?"

I shook my head, no.

"You wouldn't want to give all this up for a city, would you?"

"Sure. Any day."

I was walking fast to keep ahead of him, I couldn't help but giggle, I was so embarrassed—this man in a white shirt was really walking out on the highway, he was really going to leave his car parked like that! You never saw a car parked on the road around here, unless it was by the creek, fishermen's cars, or unless it was a wreck. All this made my face get hotter.

He walked fast to catch up with me. I could hear coins and things jingling in his pockets.

"You never told me your name," he said. "That isn't friendly."

"It's Nancy."

"Nancy what?"

"Oh I don't know." I laughed.

"Nancy I-Don't-Know?" he said.

I didn't get this. He was smiling hard. He was shorter than my father and now that he was out in the bright sun I could see he was older. His face wasn't tanned, and his mouth kept going into a soft smile. Men like my father and my uncles and other men never bothered to smile like that at me, they never bothered to look at me at all. Some men did, once in a while, in Stratton, strangers waiting for Greyhound buses to Denver or Kansas City, but they weren't friendly like this, they didn't keep on smiling for so long.

When I came to the path I said, "Well, good-bye, I'm going to cut over this way. This is a shortcut."

"A shortcut where?"

"Oh I don't know," I said, embarrassed.

"To your house, Nancy?"

"Yeah. No, it's to our lane, our lane is half a mile long."

"Is it? That's very long. . . ."

He came closer. "Well, good-bye," I said.

"That's a long lane, isn't it?—it must get blocked up with snow in the winter, doesn't it? You people get a lot of snow out here—"

"Yeah."

"So your house must be way back there . . . ?" he said, pointing. He was smiling. When he stood straight like this, looking over my head, he was more like the other men. But then he looked down at me and smiled again, so friendly. I waved good-bye and jumped over the ditch and climbed the fence, clumsy as hell just when somebody was watching me, wouldn't you know it. Some barbed wire caught at my shorts and the man said, "Let me get that loose—" but I jerked away and jumped down again. I waved good-bye again and started up the path. But the man said something and when I looked back he was climbing over the fence himself. I was so surprised that I just stood there.

"I like shortcuts and secret paths," he said. "I'll walk a little way with you."

"What do you—" I started to say. I stopped smiling because something was wrong. I looked around and there was just the path behind me that the kids always took, and some boulders and old dried-up manure from cattle, and some scrubby bushes. At the top of the hill was the big tree that had been struck by lightning so many times. I was looking at all this and couldn't figure out why I was looking at it.

"You're a brave little girl to go around barefoot," the man said, right next to me. "Or are your feet tough on the bottom?"

I didn't know what he was talking about because I was worried; then I heard his question and said vaguely, "I'm all right," and started to walk faster. I felt a tingling all through me like the tingling from the Pepsi-Cola in my mouth.

"Do you always walk so fast?" The man laughed.

"Oh I don't know."

"Is that all you can say? Nancy I-Don't-Know! That's a funny name—is it foreign?"

This made me start to laugh again. I was walking fast, then I began to run a few steps. Right away I was out of breath. That was strange—I was out of breath right away.

"Hey, Nancy, where are you going?" the man cried.

But I kept running, not fast. I ran a few steps and looked back and there he was, smiling and panting, and I happened to see his foot come down on a loose rock. I knew what would happen—the rock rolled off sideways and he almost fell, and I laughed. He glanced up at me with a surprised grin. "This path is a booby trap, huh? Nancy has all sorts of little traps and tricks for me, huh?"

I didn't know what he was talking about. I ran up the side of the hill, careful not to step on the manure or anything sharp, and I was still out of breath but my legs felt good. They felt as if they wanted to run a long distance. "You're going off the path," he said, pretending to be mad. "Hey. That's against the rules. Is that another trick?"

I giggled but couldn't think of any answer.

"Did you make this path up by yourself?" the man asked. But he was breathing hard from the hill. He stared at me, climbing up, with his hands pushing on his knees as if to help him climb. "Little Nancy, you're like a wild colt or a deer, you're so graceful—is this your own private secret path? Or do other people use it?"

"Oh, my brother and some other kids, when they're around," I said vaguely. I was walking backward up the hill now, so that I could look down at him. The top of his hair was thin, you could see the scalp. The very top of his forehead seemed to have two bumps, not big ones, but as if the bone went out a little, and this part was a bright pink, sunburned, but the rest of his face and his scalp were white.

He stepped on another loose rock, and the rock and some stones and mud came loose. He fell hard onto his knee. "Jesus!" he said. The way he stayed down like that looked funny. I had to press my hand over my mouth. When he looked up at me his smile was different. He got up, pushing himself up with his hands, grunting, and then he wiped his hands on his trousers. The dust showed on them. He looked funny.

"Is my face amusing? Is it a good joke?"

I didn't mean to laugh, but now I couldn't stop. I pressed my hand over my mouth hard.

He stared at me. "What do you see in my face, Nancy? What do you see—anything? Do you see my soul, do you see *me*, is that what you're laughing at?" He took a fast step toward me, but I jumped back. It was like a game. "Come on, Nancy, slow down, just slow down," he said. "Come on, Nancy. . . ."

I didn't know what he was talking about. I just had to laugh at his face. It was so tense and strange: it was so *important*.

I noticed a big rock higher up, and I went around behind it and pushed it loose—it rolled right down toward him and he had to scramble to get out of the way. "Hey! Jesus!" he yelled. The rock came loose with some other things and a mud chunk got him in the leg.

I laughed so hard my stomach started to ache.

He laughed too, but a little different from before.

"This is a little trial for me, isn't it?" he said. "A little preliminary contest. Is that how the game goes? Is that your game, Nancy?"

I ran higher up the hill, off to the side where it was steeper. Little rocks and things came loose and rolled back down. My breath was coming so fast it made me wonder if something was wrong. Down behind me the man was following, stooped over, looking at me, and his hand was pressed against the front of his shirt. I could see his hand moving up and down because he was breathing so hard. I could even see his tongue moving around the edge of his dried-out lips. . . . I started to get afraid, and then the tingling came back into me, beginning in my tongue and going out through my whole body, and I couldn't help giggling.

He said something that sounded like "—won't be laughing—" but I couldn't hear the rest of it. My hair was all wet in back where it would be a job for me to unsnarl it with the hairbrush. The man came closer, stumbling, and just for a joke I kicked out at him, to scare him—and he jerked backward and tried to grab onto a branch of a bush, but it slipped through his fingers and he lost his balance and fell. He grunted. He fell so hard that he just lay there for a minute. I wanted to say I was sorry, or ask him if he was all right, but I just stood there grinning.

He got up again; the fleshy part of his hand was bleeding. But he didn't seem to notice it and I turned and ran up the rest of the hill, going almost straight up the last part, my legs were so strong and felt so good. Right at the top I paused, just balanced there, and a gust of wind would have pushed me over—but I was all right. I laughed aloud, my legs felt so springy and strong.

I looked down over the side where he was crawling, down on his hands and knees again. "You better go back to Kansas! Back home to Kansas!" I laughed. He stared up at me and I waited for him to smile again but he didn't. His face was very pale. He was staring at me but he seemed to be seeing something else, his eyes were very serious and strange. I could see his belt creasing his stomach, the bulge of his white shirt. He pressed his hand against his chest again. "Better go home, go home, get in your damn old car and go home," I sang, making a song of it. He looked so serious, staring up at me. I pretended to kick at him again and he flinched, his eyes going small.

"Don't leave me—" he whimpered.

"Oh go on," I said.

"Don't leave—I'm sick—I think I—"

His face seemed to shrivel. He was drawing in his breath very slowly, carefully, as if checking to see how much it hurt, and I waited for this to turn into another joke. Then I got tired of waiting and just rested back on my heels. My smile got smaller and smaller, like his.

"Good-bye, I'm going," I said, waving. I turned and he said something—it was like a cry—but I didn't want to bother going back. The tingling in me was almost noisy.

I walked over to the other side, and slid back down to the path

and went along the path to our lane. I was very hot. I knew my face
was flushed and red. "Damn old nut," I said. But I had to laugh at the
way he had looked, the way he kept scrambling up the hill and was just
crouched there at the end, on his hands and knees. He looked so funny,
bent over and clutching at his chest, pretending to have a heart attack
or maybe having one, a little one, for all I knew. *This will teach you a
lesson*, I thought.

By the time I got home my face had dried off a little, but my hair was
like a haystack. I stopped by the old car parked in the lane, just a junker
on blocks, and looked in the outside rearview mirror—the mirror was
all twisted around because people looked in it all the time. I tried to fix
my hair by rubbing my hands down hard against it, but no luck. "Oh
damn," I said aloud, and went up the steps to the back, and remembered
not to let the screen door slam so my mother wouldn't holler at me.

She was in the kitchen ironing, just sprinkling some clothes on the
ironing board. She used a pop bottle painted blue and fitted out with
a sprinkler top made of rubber, that I fixed for her at grade school a
long time ago for a Christmas present; she shook the bottle over the
clothes and stared at me. "Where have you been? I told you to come
right back."

"I did come right back."

"You're all dirty, you look like hell. What happened to you?"

"Oh I don't know," I said. "Nothing."

She threw something at me—it was my brother's shirt—and I caught
it and pressed it against my hot face.

"You get busy and finish these," my mother said. "It must be ninety-
five in here and I'm fed up. And you do a good job, I'm really fed up.
Are you listening, Nancy? Where the hell is your mind?"

I liked the way the damp shirt felt on my face. "Oh I don't know,"
I said.

CONCERNING THE CASE

OF BOBBY T.

———

B OBBY T. STRUGGLED with Frances Berardi and yanked her to the side as if trying to knock her over. But she twisted her small body to keep from falling. She was screaming. They were near the boarded-up cabin in Reardon Park—a refreshment stand not open this summer, though painted a tart black-green that still smelled fresh—and three friends of Frances, girls her own age, were on the wide dirt path nearby, watching, and other people in the park turned to watch, hearing the noise. Bobby T. noticed nothing. He shook Frances so her head swung forward and back and her long black hair flicked into his face, stinging his eyes.

This seemed to drive him into a frenzy, her hair stinging his eyes.

She fell to her knees. Bobby T. was gripping her by the upper arm, and he yanked her back up onto her feet again and gave her a final shove, back at her friends. She collided with one of the girls. The girls were so surprised by all this that they hadn't had time to cry for help until it was all over and Bobby T. was running. By then people were coming—a man who had been sitting on a blanket nearby, with his wife and baby and a portable radio, and some Negro men who were fishing at the river, and some boys on bicycles, attracted by all the yelling. But by then Bobby T. had run crashing through the bushes and was gone.

That was around seven-thirty on a very hot evening in Seneca, New York.

August 9, 1971

Frances Berardi, thirty-one years old, separated now for nearly two months from her husband, stood behind the counter in her father's music store and thought about Bobby T. Cheatum.

In spite of the airless heat of the store, she was shivering. She stared, fascinated and contemptuous, at the prickly flesh on her bare arms.

She was helping out at Berardi's Music Store, in its "new location"—since 1969—on Drummond Avenue. Her father was giving an organ lesson to a widow named Florence Daley, in the soundproof room at the rear of the store. Twelve free lessons came with each purchase of an organ; Mrs. Daley's son and his wife had bought her an organ for her birthday. From time to time Frances could hear the muffled breathless shrieks of the organ, though maybe she was imagining it. The room was supposed to be soundproof. She inclined her head, listening. Yes, she did hear the shrieks. She heard something.

If Bobby T. walked through the door she would say to him, *I'm not Frances Berardi any longer. I'm Frances Laseck.*

Her father's store was small, only half the size of the shoe store on one side of it and perhaps one-third the size of the drugstore at the corner. He had crowded it with merchandise—pianos and organs lining the walls and out in the middle of the floor. It was hard to walk around in here. There were several counters of smaller musical instruments—accordions and guitars and drums—and racks of sheet music and records, though Frances's father made no effort to compete with the discount department stores that sold popular records so cheaply. He wouldn't compete with them, he said angrily; there, records were stocked "by the foot" according to what sold fast, and nobody cared what kind of music was being sold. He didn't want to compete on that level, he said. But Berardi's Music Store kept going, year after year. Frances liked helping her father because the store was so familiar, so contained, like a box seen from the inside. There were no surprises here. She loved the smell of the clean polished wood, the pianos and organs that looked so perfect, handsome and mute and oiled, with their white and black keys.

If she had to wait for Bobby T., she was safer here than at home.

Her eyes felt bright and glittery, her neck strangely long and thin. She had not slept well for several nights. She knew that her collar bones showed in this dress, and that she looked wispy and shrill in it, like a bird, but she had worn it anyway. If Bobby T. did come to look her up, after so many years, he might take pity on her when he saw how thin she was. After the baby she had never gained weight. After the trouble with her husband she had never gained weight.

Frances checked her watch: four-thirty. A very long, hot, quiet afternoon. She looked at the clock on the wall behind her: four-thirty. Outside, people strolled by on the sidewalk and did not come in, sometimes didn't even glance into the window. Now someone was slowing down, lingering—a middle-aged woman in a housedress, who stared at the small $989 organ for sale there, and at the music books displayed on a velvet cloth, "Gershwin's Finest Hours," "Two on the Aisle," "Songs from South Pacific." The woman's name was Mrs. Fuhr; Frances knew her daughter Maude from high school. She hoped that Mrs. Fuhr wouldn't come in the store.

Only an hour and a half, Frances thought. Then they could close the store.

July 2, 1952

Again and again they asked Frances what had happened. Her face was hot and stiff from crying. If she cried hard enough they might let her alone. Why wouldn't they let her alone? Her mother sat broad and creaking in a cane-backed chair, ashamed, silent. Her father was unable to stay in one place, kept jumping up from his seat and pacing around, making everyone nervous. "Just tell them, Frannie. Tell them again. Speak up nice and tell them, please," he said.

They were in the downtown police station, in one of the back rooms. The police station! Frances knew that Bobby T. was locked up somewhere nearby.

"Repeat, please, what you told us. Then what? Then, after he knocked you down, then what?" a man was asking her.

Frances went through it all again.

Her upper arm was bruised, ugly orange and yellow and purple bruises—look at that, her father said, turning Frances's arm for the man to see. Yes, he saw it. Her knees were scratched bad. The policeman tried not to look at Frances's knees. Anyway the scratches were covered with bandages and adhesive tape her mother changed several times a day.

"She could get infection—bad infection—" her father muttered.

"Yes," said the policeman. He was a sizable man with a gleaming bald head, her father's age. He did not wear a uniform like the other policemen who were listening. As he talked, Frances stared at the grim creases around his mouth. From time to time he rubbed a handkerchief into these sweaty creases because it was so hot, even with the fan going. It had been hot now, up in the nineties, for over a week. Everyone in Seneca was sick of the weather.

"Bobby T. Cheatum was always a wise guy, smart-assing around," the policeman said, "but I never thought he'd go crazy like this."

"You just keep him locked up," Frances's father said loudly. "If he breaks out—"

"He isn't going to break out."

"No? Who says so, a jail like this? I know this town. I know how my kids and my neighbors' kids get chased around—boys or girls, it don't matter—Look, you see this goes to a trial—in a courtroom, with a judge and all that," he stammered, "because there are some things this town should learn—"

"Yes, Mr. Berardi, that's right. I happen to agree with you," the policeman said, wiping his face.

Frances had no more tears left. She wondered if they had come to the end of the questioning. For four days now she had been kept in the house, her father had closed up the store and stayed home, sometimes weeping angrily in the bedroom, sometimes storming out of the house, bypassing Frances, not even looking at her. As if he hated her. Frances had cried until she was worn out. She thought in a flash of anger that Bobby T. was a stupid goddam nigger, though he thought he was smarter than the other niggers, and the next time she saw him she would tell him so.

November 19, 1956

"My name is Herbert Ryder from Legal Aid. I came out here the other time with your sister Bonnie. Do you remember me, Bobby?"

Bobby T. Cheatum sat with his arms listless on his big knees, knees parted and tilting to either side of his body. His face was oily with a peculiar sweatless perspiration, especially the wings of his broad nose. His eyes were yellowed. Sometimes his lips were pursed, sometimes slack. He did not glance at Herbert Ryder.

"Bobby, I want to ask you a few questions. Are you listening, Bobby?"

They were in a visitors' room, an alcove off the veranda used for arts and crafts instructions on certain days of the week. This was a Wednesday evening, the only time Ryder could come to the hospital. The alcove was quite cold. There was no one around except a nurse at the reception desk in the foyer; she was typing in brief, hacking spasms, and listening to music on a small transistor radio.

"As soon as you can be examined again and released from here we'll get you on the court docket. I'm confident the charges will be dismissed. Bobby, are you listening?"

Bobby did not reply.

"Why aren't you listening? Don't you trust me? Your sister Bonnie came to me for help—don't you remember, she introduced me to you? You know who I am. You want to get out of here, don't you?"

Bobby shrugged his shoulders. "Hell," he mumbled.

"What?"

"Hell with it," he said hoarsely.

"What do you mean? Don't you want to get out of here?"

Bobby stared at the floor. His hair was oily and very woolly. The tight, tiny curls gave his face a look of tension that was misleading. Really he was very relaxed, slack, almost unconscious. He sat sunk into himself, his beefy bare arms heavy on his thighs, his big hands loose on his knees. Though it was drafty in the alcove he appeared warm; the large pores of his nose glowed.

"Everything will be cleared up . . . I'm confident the charges will be dismissed. But you have to get well. I mean you have to be declared well. If you would only make an effort. . . ."

Suddenly Bobby appeared to be listening.

"When you're scheduled to be examined, if you would only try to be . . . try to. . . . If you would only make an effort to act normal. . . ."

The nurse in the foyer began typing again, interrupting the music. Bobby T. flinched: it had been the music he was listening to, not Ryder.

"Do you want to rot in here?" Ryder asked impatiently.

Bobby T. did not bother to reply.

July 6, 1952

Bounding on and off the prison cot at the downtown Seneca jail, shouting. On and off the bars, throwing himself against the bars, which he couldn't believe in. They had dragged him here and locked him in! Bobby T. Cheatum himself!

When he got out—

He mashed his sweating face against the iron bars. His eyeballs itched with the heat and this way he could scratch them. Roll them hard against the bars, then harder, and then he knocked his forehead against them—it maddened him to think of how he was locked up while everyone else was loose. Probably laughing at him. Shaking their heads over him. His mother had predicted all this, with her used-up sour laugh. *Bobby T., your troubles and mine are set to begin soon, with that lip of yours.* She wouldn't come visit him. But she sent him a message through his sister: *I give you my undivided love and attention. God bless you always.*

He kept hearing Frances Berardi's scream. Why had that little bitch made so much noise? And when he looked around, sure enough Roosevelt had run, and the girls started to scream for help—Where had those girls come from, anyway? Dawdling on the path, holding back and then walking forward, fast, right up out of the awful waves of heat, heat like air easing out of an oven, and no place to hide from it. He had worked all day at Allied storage, loading and unloading vans, and what he looked forward to was the evening—strolling down to Reardon Park to see who was around.

He could shut his eyes and see everyone there, hanging around the concrete abutment, telling jokes about how Bobby T. had gotten dragged off to jail.

He banged his head against the bars to see what would happen. Suddenly he liked the hard-soft feel of the iron, its cool flatness, the way it pushed back at his hot face. There was something to respect in those bars.

. . . He remembered the little brash-faced Italian girls from when he'd been in school, how they joked with him and didn't even mind sitting next to him on the Uptown bus. He had gotten along with all of them. Everyone liked him. The kids from Lowertown all stuck together, riding the bus three or four miles up to Lawrence Belknap School. Frances Berardi hadn't been on that bus—she was younger than Bobby T. and his friends—he wasn't sure what age she was, but she was young. The little white bitch, with that yell of hers. . . .

His mouth had been cut on the inside and he'd spat out blood, but no doctor would come to see him.

He pressed his face, his cheek, his jaw against the bars. An idea came to him slowly. He could see it, beginning as a pinprick in his head, then swelling. He watched it swell until it was too large to stay inside his head.

"You let me out!" he yelled.

The noise of his voice astonished him. It was the noise he'd heard in the fight with Frances—not really his own voice, but another, that pushed its way out of him. Now that it was free it yelled again: "You're listenin'! You guys're listenin'! You let me out—you—"

He paused, panting. His heart was pounding now as if it had gotten away from him, jubilant and wild. *Yes, yes, Bobby T.,* he thought to himself, a thought that was like a shout, and something seemed to burst in his head. He picked the mattress off his cot and, grunting, threw it against the wall. Then he wheeled around and saw the frame and seized it—it wasn't heavy, it was disappointing, but anyway it was something to grab, a real opponent. Not like little Frances Berardi who turned out to weigh almost nothing, for all her smart-aleck taunts—he could have snapped her neck in a second—

That face of hers froze in his head. He remembered the sudden springing madness he'd felt, Frances's face, how she'd turned against him and slapped him, right for everybody to see— He began slamming the cot against the wall. Again. And again. Beating the cot against the wall and the bars and yelling for them to let him out, until he couldn't stop, didn't want to stop—

"Let me out 'n' I'll kill you—the goddam bunch of you—"

July 9, 1952

Nine-thirty in the morning. He knew that from seeing a clock. All night long Bobby T.'s eyes were rolling like crazy in his head, wanting to get loose. Leather belts kept him in bed. To spite the nurse he wet the bed on purpose—let her clean it up. Sponge it up. She was a claw-handed white bitch, afraid of him, wouldn't come near him if she could help it. He tried to throw up on her but it caught somewhere inside him— wouldn't come up. So he had to taste it, seeping back down his throat. That drove him wild.

A shot in the left buttock and then he was up and into somebody's clothes, not clothes he recognized. Now his head was very heavy, though he knew it was only nine-thirty in the morning and he had a long day ahead. They walked him out to an ambulance and helped him up and closed the door on him, with more leather straps to keep his arms against his sides and an attendant sitting by the door to guard him. A white punk of maybe twenty, staring at Bobby T. as if he expected Bobby T. to leap at him.

So they really thought he was crazy!

He had to laugh, that was such a joke. The white boy by the back door, sitting on a little stool, stared at him and said nothing.

So he was mentally unfit to stand trial—so they said—so he had fooled them, all of them—

Mentally unfit to stand trial! He was fooling them all.

June 28, 1952

Frances Berardi and some friends of her, girls her own age, were cutting through Reardon Park, it was after supper and everyone was out. They talked for a while with some boys they knew, and Frances took a few puffs of a cigarette from one of them—a small, dark, ferret-faced boy named Joe Palisano. She smoked with a squinting, adult detachment, as if assessing the taste of the smoke carefully and finding it not bad. She and Joe were not older than the others but they acted older; but then he started to tease her about certain things, about something that had been written about her on a viaduct nearby, and she told him to go to hell.

She led her friends away, walking stiffly and angrily. "I don't like guys who talk dirty," she said. "I don't have to put up with that crap from anybody's mouth."

She spoke with a tart philosophical air. She and her friends wandered down to the river, where people were fishing—most of them Negroes, boys and older men, even a few heavy black women, sitting on upended boxes and sighing with the heat. There was no one here that Frances was interested in. She and her friends walked along the abutment, kicking Mallow Cup wrappers and Popsicle wrappers into the water. It was a very hot, airless evening.

Frances was wearing jeans cut off high on her thighs and a jersey blouse that pulled tight over her head, pink and white stripes and a white stretch collar; she had bought it just the Saturday before, at an Uptown store. She knew she looked good in 'it. She was twelve years old but mature for her age, her black hair glossy and loose, her bangs falling thick over her forehead so that they brushed the tops of her thick eyebrows. She was short, trim, athletic, with quick eyes and a brief upper lip, a little loud in her laughter and joking. You could always hear Frannie from a distance, one of her sisters complained—at school or hanging around the grocery store or here in the park, always Frannie Berardi with her big mouth, fooling around. Her friends stood around her, envious and uneasy.

There was nothing to do by the river so they headed back up toward Market Street. Joe Palisano and his friends were gone. Frances regretted walking away like that, but she had thought maybe he would follow her. Right now she might be riding on the crossbar of his bicycle, hot-faced and excited. . . . . "The hell with him," she muttered. She and her friends walked slowly, scuffing their feet. They all wore moccasins made of imitation leather, a bright tan, and decorated with small colored beads, bought at the same store Uptown. It was a thing they did, scuff their feet, especially when they walked on the pavement. They scuffed their feet now in the dirt. They all had the same dark-bright faces, dark eyes moving restlessly. Their minds were tipped in one direction by someone honking a horn up ahead—but it was nobody they knew—and then another way by a blast of music from someone's radio—but it was just a married couple with their baby, lying on a blanket nearby, a cousin of Frances's and her husband—and then in another direction by two Negro boys up ahead. Frances knew one of them, Bobby T., a big boy wearing jeans and a buckled belt and a white T-shirt tucked into the belt.

"Look who's hanging around," Frances called out to him in a drawl.

He turned to her with a surprised grin. "I see a cute little fox," he said, raising his hand to sight her through his fingers, a circle made by his thumb and forefinger.

Frances laughed. "That's all you got to do, huh, hang around here? I thought you had a car. How come you're hanging around here?"

"Taking in the sights," Bobby T. said.

Frances looked Bobby T. straight in the eye. He was nineteen and had been in the same class with her brother Salvatore. But he acted younger and was always lots of fun. He was a good-looking black boy.

"Out for any special sight?" Frances said. She was hot-faced and bold. Her friends giggled at the way Frances walked right up to him with her hands on her hips, like someone in a movie.

"Could be we might take a drive Uptown. Want to come along?" Bobby T. said.

"Not tonight." Frances saw that he was barefoot and that his feet were powdery with the dust. She giggled at the size of his feet. "Anyway, I heard your car broke down. That's what I heard."

"How come not tonight? You got some special business?"

Frances shrugged her shoulders. She was very excited, almost giddy. It was as if someone were pushing her from behind, pushing her toward Bobby T. *Come on, don't be afraid! Stand right up to him!*

"Hell, my father would kill me," Frances said.

"Who's gonna tell him?"

"I heard your car broke down and anyway I got better things to do."

"Your father ain't gonna know about it—he never knew about it the other time, did he?"

Frances hoped her friends hadn't heard that. A kind of flame passed over her face and she poked Bobby T. with her forefinger, right in the center of his chest.

"Somebody's got a big mouth," she drawled.

Bobby T. just grinned.

That made Frances mad. Something was beating furiously in her. She had to stand back on her heels, with her head tilted, in order to look up straight into Bobby T.'s face. She wasn't going to back down from him.

"I got better things to do than ram around with you," she said.

"How come you so fussy? That's never what I heard about Frannie Berardi."

She almost laughed. Then, lit by a sudden giddy excitement, a daring she had rehearsed in her imagination many times—slapping Joe Palisano's face in front of everyone—Frances reared back and struck Bobby T. on the side of the face, with the flat of her hand, slapping her palm hard against his cheek—

April 23, 1960

"So I slapped his face. I was just kidding around. And he grabbed my wrist and started shaking me . . . and I tried to kick him . . . and. . . ."

Frances hesitated, staring at Father Luciano as if she expected him to nod, to remember. But he couldn't remember. He couldn't see that summer evening, the park and the wide dirt path and the boarded-up refreshment stand and Bobby T. and her. . . .

"Didn't this all happen a long time ago, Frances? Years ago?" he asked.

"Yes, before we all moved Uptown, a whole lot of us moved," Frances said slowly. "It was like the kids themselves decided to move—you know—kids who were friends with one another—now it's mostly all Negro down there. By the river. Eddie drives me by there sometimes and I look at our old house and it's all colored, a big family. . . . Lowertown used to be all Italian and colored, now it's just colored. . . . It's funny how that changed."

Father Luciano smiled a pursed little smile. His expression looked out of focus, not quite right. Wasn't he listening? Frances sat forward. She had to make him understand. There was something urgent she had to explain, she must ask his forgiveness and his absolution, she must confess it and get it all straightened out so that she could forget about it and get married and pass beyond that part of her life.

"It was a long time ago, yes," she stammered, "and I was a brat, it makes me sick to remember myself! I was such a show-off. . . . We'd go roller-skating on Saturdays, and kid around with the Uptown boys, and ride our bicycles all over. . . . It makes me so ashamed to remember myself," she said. She took a tissue out of her purse and wiped her forehead. "And Bobby T.—Bobby T. Cheatum—he was a neighborhood kid a little older than we were. He went to school with my brother but dropped out. Everybody played together, you know, white and colored, in the park and at school and all over, and Bobby T. was always a nice kid—kind of daring, the way he would climb across the railroad bridge when a train might come at any time, and you know how that thing wobbles—"

Why was she saying all this? Father Luciano didn't know what she was talking about. Probably he had never even driven down to Lowertown. He was new to the city of Seneca itself and his parish was nowhere near the hill. He was from Buffalo, forty miles away. Frances was confused. She wanted to make him understand, she wanted to make him remember—those years in the cinder playgrounds, in the park, at Lawrence Belknap school, she wanted to make him remember again the kids in the neighborhood, who were all grown up now, a lot of them married, some still in the Navy or the Army, a few of them gone on to college; or disappeared, two of them killed in car accidents, and a few of them with crazy bad luck—like Bobby T., locked up in the state hospital all these years.

"Would you like to begin your confession now?" Father Luciano asked.

"No, not yet, no, wait. . . . I want to explain something . . . ," she said slowly, confused. Out in the anteroom Eddie was waiting and she could imagine him smoking a cigarette, frowning. This was taking too long. She knew what was coming: a little lecture on birth control, the paper she would have to sign swearing that she would not use any artificial methods of birth control and that her children would be brought up Catholic. Yes. She was ready for that. But first she had to explain something about those years of her childhood, her young girlhood, when she was twelve years old and had bought that pink and white blouse she liked so much, when she had walked up to Bobby T. Cheatum that night in the park. . . .

"You said that the boy is in the hospital," Father Luciano said, when Frances did not speak for a while. "Don't you think he's in good hands there? He's out of danger and he can't cause danger to others. . . . I'm sure they have an excellent staff there to help him. If he were out on his own he'd just be a threat to himself and to others."

"But I was such a brat, I was always shooting my mouth off. . . ."

"And the court showed the proper wisdom, I believe. I'm sure of it. Does anyone else ever talk about this incident, Frances? Does anyone else ever remember except you?"

"Oh, no. No," Frances said at once. "Not in my family. We stopped talking about it right away. And Eddie used to live outside Seneca, he's from the country where his parents have a farm. . . . The kids are all sort of scattered now, except for some girls I see around, you know, shopping. We all moved Uptown. And Bobby T.'s people, well, I didn't know them . . . his father died a few years ago, I heard . . . but probably people don't remember. . . ."

Father Luciano could see the lawn out front and the grilled iron gates decorated with golden crosses, cross after cross stretching along the sidewalk. She looked down at her hands, at the frayed damp tissue. She couldn't remember having taken it out of her purse.

"If he were out on his own," Father Luciano said gently, "he'd just be a threat to himself and to others. Isn't that so?"

"I thought if I could visit him . . . maybe I could explain it to him. . . . But that would drive my father wild, I couldn't even bring it up. Once some lawyer came to see me, he was from Legal Aid. I think that's what it was called. He was trying to get Bobby T. set for a trial or something. He asked me questions but my father was right there with me, so I had to keep saying the old answers. . . . And . . . Oh, I don't know. That was a long time ago too, three or four years ago. I suppose people don't remember now."

"I'm sure they don't," Father Luciano said.

August 9, 1971

Frances answered the phone on the first ring.

"Frannie? How is it there?"

"What do you mean, how is it?" she said irritably. "The four o'clock lesson came and went—the lady with the organ lessons—and it's dead as hell in here, and hot. Why he wants to stay open till six is beyond me."

"You sure nobody came in?"

"If you mean Bobby T., he's nowhere in sight and what's more no Negro is in sight or has even looked in the window all day. So. How's everything at home?"

"Frannie, I just happened to mention that this colored boy was being released today, you know, I just happened to mention it to Edith

Columbo, and she said maybe we better notify the police. I don't mean to be asking for trouble, Frannie—but just be sensible—to give warning—"

"No."

"You should let Eddie know, anyway. He would want to know. He would be worrying about you right now."

Frances made a despairing droll face that her mother should be so stupid! That her mother should think Eddie gave a damn about her!

"How's Sue Ann?" Frances asked flatly.

"Outside playing with the kid next door. . . . You sure nobody's hanging around there? Out on the sidewalk?"

Frances's father came out of the back room, looking at her. She mouthed the word "Mama" to him and he nodded, his face closing up. He walked to the front of the store and gazed out at the street. Traffic passed slowly. After a few minutes Frances said, "Mama, I got to hang up, a customer is coming in—"

She stared at her father's back, his damp white shirt, and wondered what he was thinking. Not of Bobby T. No. He wouldn't spend five minutes in all these years thinking of him: that black bastard, that maniac, beating his daughter up the way he did, and then running so wild it took three policemen to drag him away. . . . Frances took out her compact and checked her face. It was always a surprise, that she should look so cute. *Cute.* That's all you could say for her face but it was enough—with her short upper lip and her long thin nose and her dark, darting eyes, and the way her hair didn't turn kinky even in this hot weather. Yes, she was cute. Short and cute. What had someone said to her once?—Bobby T. himself?—*The best things come in small packages.*

Once she had been under the awning at the Rexall Drugs on Main Street, waiting for rain to stop, and cruising along the curb in his rattle-trap jalopy was Bobby T. and that friend of his with the funny name— she couldn't remember it now—and Bobby asked her how'd she like a ride home? Because they lived near each other. Frances hesitated only a second, then said Okay. Great. And she had jumped in the back seat. She had always had a lot of nerve. They drove right down the big hill to

Lowertown, Bobby T. showing off a little bit, thumping on the steering wheel as if it were a drum, but putting himself out to be nice to her. Yet he let you know, that Bobby T., that he was always thinking around the edges of what he shouldn't be thinking. That was the day he had said, teasing her, *the best things come in small packages.*

Bobby T.'s friend—his name was Roosevelt—couldn't keep up with her and Bobby T., the way they kidded each other. What a nerve she had! She knew her father would kill her if he saw her in a car with any boys, let alone colored boys. But she had jumped in the car anyway.

Then, as they approached her own neighborhood, she began to wonder if this had been a good idea. Someone on the street might see her and tell her father. So she poked Bobby T. on the shoulder and said, "Hey, maybe you better let me out here."

"In the rain, honey? You'll spoil that high-class outfit of yours!"

She snorted at this—she was wearing shorts and a soiled blouse.

But Bobby T. let her out anyway, near a grocery store so that she could wait for the rain to stop. Nobody had seen her, evidently. Nobody told her father. And yet now, today, so many years later, she wanted to tell her father about that ride. How they had all giggled together. . . .

"I've been thinking about Bobby T. all day . . . ," she said softly.

Her father stood with his back to her, blunt and perspiring. He had grown heavy and bald: once a good-looking man, even when his hair had thinned unevenly, now he sagged with worry and irritability. Frances was a little afraid of him. She feared his peevish scowl, that scowl that had been directed at her over the years—because she was no good at the piano, because her marriage had been bad from the start, most of all because she had a pert, impatient, unserious scowl herself.

"What did you say?" her father said, turning suddenly.

His face warned her: *Better shut up, Fran. Shut your cute little mouth.*

"Nothing," she said.

"It better be nothing," her father said.

August 9, 1971

They had located Bobby T.'s older sister, Bonnie, who was married and living now in Buffalo. At first she had said no, no; she couldn't take him in, she was afraid of him, and her husband was in and out of trouble himself.... What would Bobby T. do around the house? Wouldn't he be dangerous?

A woman social worker told her: "Bobby has ten years' experience working in the hospital laundry. He'll be able to get a good job in a laundry. He only needs to adjust himself to society again. He needs a friendly home for a while, to get him started again."

"How long's that gonna take, to get him started again?" Bonnie asked suspiciously.

She was a grave-faced, thick woman in her mid-forties, with a habit of shaking her head negatively as she thought, as if nothing seemed right to her. But in the end she agreed to take Bobby T. in.

So they brought Bobby T. to her one Monday afternoon. He turned out to be a tall, thin black man with a slight stoop, shy and apologetic. He was carrying a small suitcase. He had five dollars release money.

"Well, Bobby T.," she said awkwardly. "Such a long time...."

They shook hands like people in a movie. Bonnie didn't know what to do: she remembered her brother as taller and heavier, and maybe this man was someone else.

"Hello," he said.

A voice like a whisper, so hoarse! She didn't recognize that either.

She cleared off a place for him to sit on the sofa and he set the suitcase primly at his feet. So this was her crazy put-away brother Bobby Templar, the one nobody in the family liked to talk about.... He had a curious way of ducking his head. He would not meet her gaze, not directly. A tall thin scrawny bird, birdlike in his nervousness, with a glaze to his dark skin that was like permanent sweat, and a smell in his clothes of panic. Bonnie stared at him, her heart sinking. This was a mistake and she couldn't get out of it.

"Been a lot of time since we seen each other," she said slowly. "They treated you okay there, huh?"

"Yes," Bobby said.

"The big trouble—you know—the courtroom and all—I mean the trial—that got all cleared up, huh?"

"The charges were dismissed," Bobby T. said softly.

"Charges were dismissed, oh yes," his sister said seriously, nodding. That was an important fact. That was good news.

She couldn't think what to do—start supper with him sitting here?—so after a while she suggested that they go down to the corner to get some things she needed. "Just a five-minute walk," she said.

Bobby got to his feet self-consciously and followed her out of the building—she had an apartment on the first floor, a good location—and she noticed out of the corner of her eye that he walked in a kind of crouch, leading with his forehead. He didn't look crazy, not the way some people on the street looked, but he didn't look quite right either, with that stiff walk of his, like an old man's walk and not a man of—what was he now?—thirty-eight? He kept staring out at the street, at the buses and trucks.

At the intersection he froze and didn't seem able to move. "It's just across the street, that's the grocery right over there," Bonnie said, panicked herself. *Oh Jesus*, she thought, *they brought him to me still crazy and they drove away again!* "Look, Bobby T., it ain't nothing to get across this street—nobody's going to hurt you—"

What was wrong with him? He stood on the curb, sweating, and wouldn't step off onto the street. He was staring ahead, his eyes wide. He stood in that crouched-over, crazy way, his shoulders hunched as if for battle. Bonnie broke out into a sweat, standing beside him. She didn't know if she should touch his arm, or what. He looked paralyzed. And all around them people were passing, some of them staring at him—didn't he have any shame, to act like this on the street?

"Bobby T., there just *ain't* no trouble getting over there. . . ."

He didn't look at her but he seemed to be listening. After a long wait he took one step forward, off the curb and into the gutter. Bonnie drew in her breath slowly, cautiously.

"See, how there ain't any trouble? It's real easy," she said.

He took another step, slow as hell; at this rate it would take them an hour to cross the street, but anyway it was a start.

She took hold of his arm and led him. "Okay, Bobby T., you see how easy it is, huh . . . ? See how easy . . . ?" He was slow as hell and she was burning hot with the shame of it, but he was her brother, after all. Her baby brother. Anyway, today was a start.

THE TRYST

———

S HE WAS LAUGHING. At first he thought she might be crying, but she was laughing.

Raggedy Ann, she said. You asked about nicknames—I've forgotten about it for years—but Raggedy Ann it was, for a while. They called me Raggedy Ann.

She lay sprawled on her stomach, her face pressed into the damp pillow, one arm loose and gangly, falling over the edge of the bed. Her hair was red-orange and since it had the texture of straw he had thought it was probably dyed. The bed jiggled, she was laughing silently. Her arms and shoulders were freckled and pale, her long legs were unevenly tanned, the flesh of her young body not so soft as it appeared but rather tough, ungiving. She was in an exuberant mood; her laughter was child-like, bright, brittle.

What were you called?—when you were a boy? she asked. Her voice was muffled by the pillow. She did not turn to look at him.

John, he said.

What! John! Never a nickname, never Johnny or Jack or Jackie?

I don't think so, he said.

She found that very funny. She laughed and kicked her legs and gave off an air, an odor, of intense fleshy heat. I won't survive this one, she giggled.

HE WAS ONE of the adults of the world now. He was in charge of the world.

Sometimes he stood at the bedroom window and surveyed the handsome sloping lawn, the houses of his neighbors and their handsome lawns, his eye moving slowly along the memorized street. Day or night it was memorized. He knew it. The Tilsons . . . the Dwyers . . . the Pitkers . . . the Reddingers . . . the Schells. Like beads on a string were the houses, solid and baronial, each inhabited, each protected. Day or night he knew them and the knowledge made him pleasurably intoxicated.

He was Reddinger. Reddinger, John.

Last Saturday night, late, his wife asked: Why are you standing there, why aren't you undressing? It's after two.

He was not thinking of Annie. That long restless rangy body, that rather angular, bony face, her fingers stained with ink, her fingernails never very clean, the throaty mocking voice: he had pushed her out of his mind. He was breathing the night air and the sharp autumnal odor of pine needles stirred him, moved him deeply. He was in charge of the world but why should he not shiver with delight of the world? For he did love it. He loved it.

I loved it—this—all of you—

He spoke impulsively. She did not hear. Advancing upon him, her elbows raised as she labored to unfasten a hook at the back of her neck, she did not look at him; she spoke with a sleepy absentmindedness, as if they had had this conversation before. Were you drunk, when you were laughing so much? she asked. It wasn't like you. Then, at dinner, you were practically mute. Poor Frances Mason, trying to talk to you! That wasn't like you either, John.

There must have been a party at the Buhls', across the way. Voices lifted. Car doors were slammed. John Reddinger felt his spirit stirred by the acrid smell of the pines and the chilly bright-starred night and his wife's warm, perfumed, familiar closeness. His senses leaped, his eyes blinked rapidly as if he might burst into tears. In the autumn of the year he dwelt upon boyhood and death and pleasures of a harsh, sensual nature, the kind that are torn out of human beings, like cries; he dwelt upon the mystery of his own existence, that teasing riddle. The world itself was an intoxicant to him.

Wasn't it like me? he asked seriously. What am I like, then?

I DON'T ASK YOU about your family, the girl pointed out. Why should you ask me about other men?

He admired her brusque, comic manner, the tomboyish wag of her foot.

Natural curiosity, he said.

Your wife! Your children!—I don't ask, do I?

They were silent and he had the idea she was waiting for him to speak, to volunteer information. But he was disingenuous. Her frankness made him uncharacteristically passive; for once he was letting a woman take the lead, never quite prepared for what happened. It was a novelty, a delight. It was sometimes unnerving.

You think I'm too proud to ask for money, I mean for a loan—for my rent, Annie said. I'm not, though. I'm not too proud.

Are you asking for it, then?

No. But not because I'm proud or because I'm afraid of altering our relationship. You understand? Because I want you to know I could have asked and I didn't—you understand?

I think so, John said, though in fact he did not.

AT CHRISTMAS, somehow, they lost contact with each other. Days passed. Twelve days. Fifteen. His widowed mother came to visit them in the big red-brick colonial in Lathrup Park, and his wife's sister and her husband and two young children, and his oldest boy, a freshman at Swarthmore, brought his Japanese roommate home with him; life grew dense, robustly complicated. He telephoned her at the apartment but no one answered. He telephoned the gallery where she worked but the other girl answered and when he said softly and hopefully, Annie? Is that

Annie?, the girl told him that it was *not* Annie; and the gallery owner, Mr. Helnutt, disapproved strongly of personal calls. She was certain Annie knew about this policy and surprised that Annie had not told him about it.

He hung up guiltily, like a boy.

A PREVIOUS AUTUMN, years ago, he had made a terrible mistake. What a blunder!

The worst blunder of my life, he said.

What was it? Annie asked at once.

But his mood changed. A fly was buzzing somewhere in her small, untidy apartment, which smelled of cats. His mood changed. His spirit changed.

He did not reply. After a while Annie yawned. I've never made any really bad mistakes, she said. Unless I've forgotten.

You're perfect, he said.

She laughed, irritated.

. . . Perfect. So beautiful, so confident . . . So much at home in your body. . . .

He caressed her and forced himself to think of her, only of her. It was not true that she was beautiful but she was striking—red hair, brown eyes, a quick tense dancer's body—and he saw how other people looked at her, women as well as men. It was a fact. He loved her, he was silly and dizzy and sickened with love for her, and he did not wish to think of his reckless mistake of that other autumn. It had had its comic aspects, but it had been humiliating. And dangerous. While on a business trip to Atlanta he had strolled downtown and in a dimly lit bar had drifted into a conversation with a girl, a beautiful blonde in her twenties, soft-spoken and sweet and very shy. She agreed to come back with him to his hotel room for a nightcap, but partway back, on the street, John sensed something wrong, something terribly wrong, he heard his voice rattling on about the marvelous view from his room on the twentieth floor of the hotel and about how fine an impression Atlanta was making on him—then in midsentence he stopped, staring at the girl's heavily made-up face and at the blond hair which was certainly a wig—he stammered that he had made a mistake, he would have to say good night now; he couldn't bring her back to the room after all. She stared at him belligerently. She asked what was wrong, just what in hell was wrong?—her voice cracking slightly so that he knew she wasn't a girl, a woman, at all. It was a boy of about twenty-five. He backed away and the creature asked why he had changed his mind, wasn't she good enough for him, who did he think he was? Bastard! Shouting after John as he hurried away: *who did he think he was?*

I never think about the past, Annie said lazily. She was smoking in bed, her long bare legs crossed at the knee. I mean what the hell?—it's all over with.

HE HAD NOT LOVED any of the others as he loved Annie. He was sure of that.

He thought of her, raking leaves. A lawn crew serviced the Reddingers' immense lawn but he sometimes raked leaves on the weekend, for the pleasure of it. He worked until his arm and shoulder muscles ached. Remarkable, he thought. Life, living. In this body. Now.

She crowded out older memories. Ah, she was ruthless! An Amazon, a Valkyrie maiden. Beautiful. Unpredictable. She obliterated other women, other sweetly painful memories of women. That was her power.

Remarkable, he murmured.

Daddy!

He looked around. His eleven-year-old daughter, Sally, was screaming at him.

Daddy, I've been calling and calling you from the porch, couldn't you hear me?—Momma wants you for something! A big grin. Amused, she was, at her father's absentmindedness; and she had a certain sly, knowing look as well, as if she could read his thoughts.

But of course that was only his imagination.

HE'S JUST A FRIEND of mine, an old friend, Annie said vaguely. He doesn't count.

A friend from where?

From around town.

Meaning—?

From around town.

A girl in a raw, unfinished painting. Like the crude canvases on exhibit at the gallery, that day he had drifted by: something vulgar and exciting about the mere droop of a shoulder, the indifference of a strand of hair blown into her eyes. And the dirt-edged fingernails. And the shoes with the run-over heels. She was raw, unfinished, lazy, slangy, vulgar, crude, mouthing in her cheerful insouciant voice certain words and phrases John Reddinger would never have said aloud, in the presence of a member of the opposite sex; but at the same time it excited him to know that she was highly intelligent, and really well-educated, with a master's degree in art history and a studied, if rather flippant, familiarity with the monstrousness of contemporary art. He could not determine whether she was as impoverished as she appeared or whether it was a pose, an act. Certain items of clothing, he knew, were expensive. A suede leather coat, a pair of knee-high boots, a long skirt of black soft wool. And one of her rings might have been genuine. But much of the time she looked shabby—ratty. She nearly fainted once, at the airport; she had confessed she hadn't eaten for a while, had run out of money that week. In San Francisco, where she spent three days with him, she had eaten hungrily enough and it had pleased him to feed her, to nourish her on so elementary a level.

Who bought you this? he asked, fingering the sleeve of her coat.

What? This? I bought it myself.

Who paid for it?

It's a year old, I bought it myself.

It's very beautiful.

Yes?

He supposed, beforehand, that they would lose contact with each other when Christmas approached. The routine of life was upset, schedules were radically altered, obligations increased. He disliked holidays; yet in a way he liked them, craved them. Something wonderful must happen! Something wonderful must happen soon.

He was going to miss her, he knew.

She chattered about something he wasn't following. A sculptor she knew, his odd relationship with his wife. A friend. A former friend. She paused and he realized it was a conversation and he must reply, must take his turn. What was she talking about? Why did these girls talk so, when he wanted nothing so much as to stare at them, in silence, in pained awe? I don't really have friends any longer, he said slowly. It was a topic he and his wife had discussed recently. She had read an article on the subject in a woman's magazine: American men of middle age, especially in the higher income brackets, tended to have very few close friends, very few indeed. It was sad. It was unfortunate. I had friends in high school and college, he said, but I've lost touch . . . we've lost touch. It doesn't seem to happen afterward, after you grow up. Friendship, I mean.

God, that's sad. That's really sad. She shivered, staring at him. Her eyes were darkly brown and lustrous, at times almost too lustrous. They reminded him of a puppy's eyes.

Yes, I suppose it is, he said absently.

ON NEW YEAR'S EVE, driving from a party in Lathrup Park to another party in Wausau Heights, he happened to see a young woman who resembled Annie—in mink to midcalf, her red hair fastened in a bun, being helped out of a sports car by a young man. That girl! Annie! His senses leaped, though he knew it wasn't Annie.

For some reason the connection between them had broken. He didn't know why. He had had to fly to London; and then it was mid-December and the holiday season; then it was early January. He had tried to telephone two or three times, without success. His feeling for her ebbed. It was curious—other faces got in the way of hers, distracting him. Over the holidays there were innumerable parties: brunches and luncheons and cocktail parties and open houses and formal dinner parties and informal evening parties, a press of people, friends and acquaintances and strangers, all demanding his attention. He meant to telephone her, meant to send a small gift, but time passed quickly and he forgot.

After seeing the girl on New Year's Eve, however, he found himself thinking again of Annie. He lay in bed, sleepless, a little feverish, thinking of her. They had done certain things together and now he tried to picture them, from a distance. How he had adored her! Bold, silly, gawky, beautiful, not afraid to sit slumped in a kitchen chair, naked, pale, her uncombed hair in her eyes, drinking coffee with him as he prepared to leave. Not afraid of him—not afraid of anyone. That had been her power.

His imagination dwelt upon her. The close, stale, half-pleasant odor of her apartment, the messy bed, the lipstick- and mascara-smeared pillows, the ghostly presence of other men, strangers to him, and yet brothers of a kind: brothers. He wondered if any of them knew about *him*. (And what would she say?—what might her words be, describing him?) It excited him to imagine her haphazard, promiscuous life; he knew she was entirely without guilt or shame or self-consciousness, as if, born of a different generation, she were of a different species as well.

At the same time, however, he was slightly jealous. When he thought at length about the situation he was slightly jealous. Perhaps, if he returned to her, he would ask her not to see any of the others.

WHAT HAVE YOU been doing? What is your life, now?

Why do you want to know?

I miss you—missed you.

Did you really?

In early March he saw her again, but only for lunch. She insisted he return to the gallery to see their current show—ugly, frantic, oversized hunks of sheet metal and aluminum, seemingly thrown at will onto the floor. She was strident, talkative from the several glasses of wine she had had at lunch, a lovely girl, really, whose nearness seemed to constrict his chest, so that he breathed with difficulty. And so tall—five feet ten, at least. With her long red hair and her dark, intense eyes and her habit of raising her chin, as if in a gesture of hostility, she was wonderfully attractive; and she knew it. But she would not allow him to touch her.

I think this is just something you're doing, she said. I mean—something you're watching yourself do.

When can I see you?

I don't know. I don't want to.

What?

I'm afraid.

They talked for a while, pointlessly. He felt his face redden. She was backing away, with that pose of self-confidence, and he could not stop her. But I love you! I love you! Had he said these words aloud? She looked so frightened, he could not be certain.

Afraid! he laughed. Don't be ridiculous.

ONE DAY, in early summer he came to her, in a new summer suit of pale blue, a lover, his spirit young and gay and light as dandelion seed. She was waiting for him in a downtown square. She rose from the park bench as he appeared, the sun gleaming in her hair, her legs long and elegant in a pair of cream-colored trousers. They smiled. They touched hands. Was it reckless, to meet the girl here, where people might see him?—at midday? He found that he did not care.

We can't go to my apartment.

We can go somewhere else.

He led her to his car. They were both smiling.

Where are we going? she asked.

For the past several weeks a girl cousin of hers had been staying with her in the apartment, so they had been going to motels; the motels around the airport were the most convenient. But today he drove to the expressway and out of the city, out along the lake, through the suburban villages north of the city: Elmwood Farms, Spring Arbor, Wausau Heights, Lathrup Park. He exited at Lathrup Park.

Where are we going? she asked.

He watched her face as he drove along Washburn Lane, which was graveled and tranquil and hilly. Is this—? Do you live—? she asked. He brought her to the big red-brick colonial he had bought nearly fifteen years ago; it seemed to him that the house had never looked more handsome, and the surrounding trees and blossoming shrubs had never looked more beautiful.

Do you like it? he asked.

He watched her face. He was very excited.

But— Where is— Aren't you afraid—?

There's no one home, he said.

He led her through the foyer, into the living room with its thick wine-colored rug, its gleaming furniture, its many windows. He led her through the formal dining room and into the walnut-paneled recreation room where his wife had hung lithographs and had arranged innumerable plants, some of them hanging from the ceiling in clay pots, spidery-leafed, lovely. He saw the girl's eyes dart from place to place.

You live here, she said softly.

In an alcove he kissed her and made them each a drink. He kissed her again. She shook her hair from her eyes and pressed her forehead against his face and made a small convulsive movement—a shudder, or perhaps it was suppressed laughter. He could not tell.

You live here, she said.

What do you mean by that? he asked.

She shrugged her shoulders and moved away. Outside, birds were calling to one another excitedly. It was early summer. It was summer again. The world renewed itself and was beautiful. Annie wore the cream-colored trousers and a red jersey blouse that fitted her tightly and a number of bracelets that jingled as she walked. Her ears were pierced: she wore tiny loop earrings. On her feet, however, were shoes that pleased him less—scruffy sandals, once black, now faded to no color at all.

Give me a little more of this, she said, holding out the glass.

MY BEAUTY, he said. My beautiful girl.

SHE ASKED HIM why he had brought her here and he said he didn't know. Why had he taken the risk?—why was he taking it at this moment, still? He said he didn't know, really; he didn't usually analyze his own motives.

Maybe because it's here in this room, in this bed, that I think about you so much, he said.

She was silent for a while. Then she kicked about, and laughed, and chattered. He was sleepy, pleasantly sleepy. He did not mind her chatter, her high spirits. While she spoke of one thing or another—of childhood memories, of nicknames—Raggedy Ann they had called her, and it fitted her, he thought, bright red hair like straw and a certain ungainly but charming manner—what had been the boy's name, the companion to Raggedy Ann?—Andy?—he watched through half-closed eyes the play of shadows on the ceiling, imagining that he could smell the pines, the sunshine, the rich thick grass, remembering himself at the windows of this room not long ago, staring out into the night, moved almost to tears by an emotion he could not have named. You're beautiful, he told Annie, there's no one like you. No one. He heard his mother's voice: Arthritis, you don't know what it's like—you don't *know*! A woman approached him, both hands held out, palms up, appealing to him, the expanse of bare pale flesh troubling to him because he did not know what it meant. You don't know, don't *know*. He tried to protest but no words came to him. Don't know, don't know. Don't *know*. His snoring disturbed him. For an instant he woke, then sank again into a warm grayish ether. His wife was weeping. The sound of her weeping was angry. You brought that creature here—that filthy sick thing—you brought her to our bed to soil it, to soil me—to kill me— Again he wanted to protest. He raised his hands in a gesture of innocence and helplessness. But instead of speaking he began to laugh. His torso and belly shook with laughter. The bed shook. It was mixed suddenly with a gigantic fly that hovered over the bed, a few inches from his face; then his snoring woke him again and he sat up.

Annie?

Her things were still lying on the floor. The red blouse lay draped across a chintz-covered easy chair whose bright red and orange flowers, glazed, dramatic, seemed to be throbbing with energy. Annie? Are you in the bathroom?

The bathroom door was ajar, the light was not on. He got up. He saw that it was after two. A mild sensation of panic rose in his chest, for no reason. He was safe. They were safe here. No one would be home for hours—the first person to come home, at about three-thirty, would be Sally. His wife had driven with several other women to a bridge luncheon halfway across the state and would not be home, probably, until after six. The house was silent. It was empty.

He thought: What if she steals something?

But that was ridiculous and cruel. Annie would never do anything like that.

No one was in this bathroom, which was his wife's. He went to a closet and got a robe and put it on, and went out into the hallway, call-ing Annie?—Honey?—and knew, before he turned the knob to his own bathroom, that she was in there and that she would not respond. Annie? What's wrong?

The light switch to the bathroom operated a fan; the fan was on; he pressed his ear against the door and listened. Had she taken a shower? He didn't think so. Had not heard any noises. Annie, he said, rattling the knob, are you in there, is anything wrong? He waited. He heard the fan whirring. Annie? His voice was edged with impatience. Annie, will you unlock the door? Is anything wrong?

She said something—the words were sharp and unintelligible.

Annie? What? What did you say?

He rattled the knob again, angrily.

What did you say? I couldn't—

Again her high, sharp voice. It sounded like an animal's shriek. But the words were unintelligible.

Annie? Honey? Is something wrong?

He tried to fight his panic. He knew, he knew. Must get the bitch out of there. Out of the house. He knew. But if he smashed the paneling on the door?—how could he explain it? He began to plead with her, in the voice he used on Sally, asking her to please be good, be good, don't make trouble, don't make a fuss, why did she want to ruin everything? Why did she want to worry him?

He heard the lock being turned, suddenly.

He opened the door.

SHE MUST HAVE TAKEN the razor blade out of his razor, which she had found in the medicine cabinet. Must have leaned over the sink and made one quick, deft, hard slash with it—cutting the fingers of her right hand also. The razor blade slipped from her then and fell into the sink. There was blood on the powder-blue porcelain of the sink and the toilet, and on the fluffy black rug, and on the mirror, and on the blue-and-white tiled walls. When he opened the door and saw her, she screamed, made a move as if to strike him with her bleeding arm, and for an instant he could not think: could not think: what had happened, what was happening, what had this girl done to him? Her face was wet and distorted. Ugly. She was sobbing, whimpering. There was blood, bright blood, smeared on her breasts and belly and thighs: he had never seen anything so repulsive in his life.

My God—

He was paralyzed. Yet, in the next instant, a part of him came to life. He grabbed a towel and wrapped it around her arm, struggling with her. Stop! Stand still! For God's sake! He held her; she went limp; her head fell forward. He wrapped the towel tight around her arm. Tight, tight. They were both panting.

Why did you do it? Why? Why? You're crazy! You're sick! This is a—this is a terrible, terrible—a terrible thing, a crazy thing—

Her teeth were chattering. She had begun to shiver convulsively.

Did you think you could get away with it? With this? he cried.

I hate you—

Stop, be still!

I hate you—I don't want to live—

She pushed past him, she staggered into the bedroom. The towel came loose. He ran after her and grabbed her and held the towel against the wound again, wrapping it tight, so tight she flinched. His brain reeled. He saw blood, splotches of blood, starlike splashes on the carpet, on the yellow satin bedspread that had been pulled onto the floor. Stop. Don't fight. Annie, stop. Goddamn you, stop!

I don't want to live—

You're crazy, you're sick! Shut up!

The towel was soaked. He stooped to get something else—his shirt—he wrapped that around the outside of the towel, trembling so badly himself that he could hardly hold it in place. The girl's teeth were chattering. His own teeth were chattering.

Why did you do it! Oh, you bitch, you bitch!

After some time the bleeding was under control. He got another towel, from his wife's bathroom, and wrapped it around her arm again.

It stained, but not so quickly. The bleeding was under control; she was not going to die.

He had forced her to sit down. He crouched over her, breathing hard, holding her in place. What if she sprang up, what if she ran away?—through the house? He held her still. She was spiritless, weak. Her eyes were closed. In a softer voice he said, as if speaking to a child: Poor Annie, poor sweet girl, why did you do it, why, why did you want to hurt yourself, why did you do something so ugly . . . ? It was an ugly, ugly thing to do. . . .

Her head slumped against his arm.

HE WALKED HER to the cab, holding her steady. She was white-faced, haggard, subdued. Beneath the sleeve of her blouse, wound tightly and expertly, were strips of gauze and adhesive tape. The bleeding had stopped. The wound was probably not too deep—had probably not severed an important vein.

Seeing her, the taxi driver got out and offered to help. But there was no need. John waved him away.

Slide in, he told Annie. Can you make it? Watch out for your head.

He told the driver her address in the city. He gave the man a fifty-dollar bill, folded.

Thanks, the man said gravely.

It was 2:55.

FROM THE LIVING ROOM, behind one of the windows, he watched the cab descend the drive—watched it turn right on Washburn Lane—watched its careful progress along the narrow street. He was still trembling. He watched the blue-and-yellow cab wind its way along Washburn Lane until it was out of sight. Then there was nothing more to see: grass, trees, foliage, blossoms, his neighbors' homes.

Tilsons . . . Dwyers . . . Pitkers . . . Reddingers . . . Schells.

He must have spoken aloud; he heard his own slow dazed voice. But what he had said, what words those were, he did not know.

THE LADY WITH

THE PET DOG

1

STRANGERS PARTED AS if to make way for him.

There he stood. He was there in the aisle, a few yards away, watching her.

She leaned forward at once in her seat, her hand jerked up to her face as if to ward off a blow—but then the crowd in the aisle hid him, he was gone. She pressed both hands against her cheeks. He was not there, she had imagined him.

"My God," she whispered.

She was alone. Her husband had gone out to the foyer to make a telephone call; it was intermission at the concert, a Thursday evening.

Now she saw him again, clearly. He was standing there. He was staring at her. Her blood rocked in her body, draining out of her head . . . she was going to faint. . . . They stared at each other. They gave no sign of recognition. Only when he took a step forward did she shake her head *no—no—keep away*. It was not possible.

When her husband returned, she was staring at the place in the aisle where her lover had been standing. Her husband leaned forward to interrupt that stare.

"What's wrong?" he said. "Are you sick?"

Panic rose in her in long shuddering waves. She tried to get to her feet, panicked at the thought of fainting here, and her husband took hold of her. She stood like an aged woman, clutching the seat before her.

At home he helped her up the stairs and she lay down. Her head was like a large piece of crockery that had to be held still, it was so heavy. She was still panicked. She felt it in the shallows of her face, behind her knees, in the pit of her stomach. It sickened her, it made her think of mucus, of something thick and gray congested inside her, stuck to her, that was herself and yet not herself—a poison.

She lay with her knees drawn up toward her chest, her eyes hotly open, while her husband spoke to her. She imagined that other man saying, *Why did you run away from me?* Her husband was saying other words. She tried to listen to them. He was going to call the doctor, he said, and she tried to sit up. "No, I'm all right now," she said quickly. The panic was like lead inside her, so thickly congested. How slow love was to drain out of her, how fluid and sticky it was inside her head!

Her husband believed her. No doctor. No threat. Grateful, she drew her husband down to her. They embraced, not comfortably. For years now they had not been comfortable together, in their intimacy and at a distance, and now they struggled gently as if the paces of this dance were too rigorous for them. It was something they might have known once, but had now outgrown. The panic in her thickened at this double betrayal: she drew her husband to her, she caressed him wildly, she shut her eyes to think about that other man.

A crowd of men and women, parting, unexpectedly, and there he stood—there he stood—she kept seeing him, and yet her vision blotched at the memory. It had been finished between them, six months before, but he had come out here . . . and she had escaped him, now she was lying in her husband's arms, in his embrace, her face pressed against his. It was a kind of sleep, this love-making. She felt herself falling asleep, her body falling from her. Her eyes shut.

"I love you," her husband said fiercely, angrily.

She shut her eyes and thought of that other man, as if betraying him would give her life a center.

"Did I hurt you? Are you—?" her husband whispered.

Always this hot flashing of shame between them, the shame of her husband's near failure, the clumsiness of his love—

"You didn't hurt me," she said.

2

They had said good-by six months before. He drove her from Nantucket, where they had met, to Albany, New York, where she visited her sister. The hours of intimacy in the car had sealed something between them, a vow of silence and impersonality: she recalled the movement of the highways, the passing of other cars, the natural rhythms of the day hypnotizing her toward sleep while he drove. She trusted him, she could sleep in his presence. Yet she could not really fall asleep in spite of her exhaustion, and she kept jerking awake, frightened, to discover that nothing had changed—still the stranger who was driving her to Albany, still the highway, the sky, the antiseptic odor of the rented car, the sense of a rhythm behind the rhythm of the air that might unleash itself at any second. Everywhere on this highway, at this moment, there were men and women driving together, bonded together—what did that mean, to be together? What did it mean to enter into a bond with another person?

No, she did not really trust him; she did not really trust men. He would glance at her with his small cautious smile and she felt a declaration of shame between them.

Shame.

In her head she rehearsed conversations. She said bitterly, "You'll be relieved when we get to Albany. Relieved to get rid of me." They had spent so many days talking, confessing too much, driven to a pitch of childish excitement, laughing together on the beach, breaking into that pose of laughter that seems to eradicate the soul, so many days of this that the silence of the trip was like the silence of a hospital—all these surface noises, these rattles and hums, but an interior silence, a befuddlement. She said to him in her imagination, "One of us should die." Then she leaned over to touch him. She caressed the back of his neck. She said, aloud, "Would you like me to drive for a while?"

They stopped at a picnic area where other cars were stopped—couples, families—and walked together, smiling at their good luck. He put his arm around her shoulders and she sensed how they were in a posture together, a man and a woman forming a posture, a figure, that someone might sketch and show to them. She said slowly, "I don't want to go back. . . ."

Silence. She looked up at him. His face was heavy with her words, as if she had pulled at his skin with her fingers. Children ran nearby and distracted him—yes, he was a father too, his children ran like that, they tugged at his skin with their light, busy fingers.

"Are you so unhappy?" he said.

"I'm not unhappy, back there. I'm nothing. There's nothing to me," she said.

They stared at each other. The sensation between them was intense, exhausting. She thought that this man was her savior, that he had come to her at a time in her life when her life demanded completion, an end, a permanent fixing of all that was troubled and shifting and deadly. And yet it was absurd to think this. No person could save another. So she drew back from him and released him.

A few hours later they stopped at a gas station in a small city. She went to the women's rest room, having to ask the attendant for a key, and when she came back her eye jumped nervously onto the rented car—why? did she think he might have driven off without her?—onto the man, her friend, standing in conversation with the young attendant. Her friend was as old as her husband, over forty, with lanky, sloping shoulders, a full body, his hair thick, a dark, burnished brown, a festive color that made her eye twitch a little—and his hands were always moving, always those rapid conversational circles, going nowhere, gestures that were at once a little aggressive and apologetic.

She put her hand on his arm, a claim. He turned to her and smiled and she felt that she loved him, that everything in her life had forced her to this moment and that she had no choice about it.

They sat in the car for two hours, in Albany, in the parking lot of a Howard Johnson's restaurant, talking, trying to figure out their past. There was no future. They concentrated on the past, the several days behind them, lit up with a hot, dazzling August sun, like explosions that already belonged to other people, to strangers. Her face was faintly reflected in the green-tinted curve of the windshield, but she could not have recognized that face. She began to cry; she told herself: *I am not here, this will pass, this is nothing.* Still, she could not stop crying. The muscles of her face were springy, like a child's, unpredictable muscles. He stroked her arms, her shoulders, trying to comfort her. "This is so hard . . . this is impossible . . . ," he said. She felt panic for the world outside this car, all that was not herself and this man, and at the same time she understood that she was free of him, as people are free of other people, she would leave him soon, safely, and within a few days he would have fallen into the past, the impersonal past. . . .

"I'm so ashamed of myself!" she said finally.

She returned to her husband and saw that another woman, a shadow-woman, had taken her place—noiseless and convincing, like a dancer performing certain difficult steps. Her husband folded her in his arms and talked to her of his own loneliness, his worries about his business, his health, his mother, kept tranquillized and mute in a nursing home, and her spirit detached itself from her and drifted about the rooms of the large house she lived in with her husband, a shadow-woman delicate and imprecise. There was no boundary to her, no edge. Alone, she took hot baths and sat exhausted in the steaming water, wondering at her perpetual exhaustion. All that winter she noticed the limp, languid weight of her arms, her veins bulging slightly with the pressure of her extreme weariness. *This is fate*, she thought, to be here and not there, to be one person and not another, a certain man's wife and not the wife of another man. The long, slow pain of this certainty rose in her, but it never became clear, it was baffling and imprecise. She could not be serious about it; she kept congratulating herself on her own good luck, to have escaped so easily, to have freed herself. So much love had gone into the first several years of her marriage that there wasn't much left, now, for another man. . . . She was certain of that. But the bath water made her dizzy, all that perpetual heat, and one day in January she drew a razor blade lightly across the inside of her arm, near the elbow, to see what would happen.

Afterward she wrapped a small towel around it, to stop the bleeding. The towel soaked through. She wrapped a bath towel around that and walked through the empty rooms of her home, light-headed, hardly aware of the stubborn seeping of blood. There was no boundary to her in this house, no precise limit. She could flow out like her own blood and come to no end.

She sat for a while on a blue love seat, her mind empty. Her husband telephoned her when he would be staying late at the plant. He talked to her always about his plans, his problems, his business friends, his future. It was obvious that he had a future. As he spoke she nodded to encourage him, and her heartbeat quickened with the memory of her own, personal shame, the shame of this man's particular, private wife. One evening at dinner he leaned forward and put his head in his arms and fell asleep, like a child. She sat at the table with him for a while, watching him. His hair had gone gray, almost white, at the temples—no one would guess that he was so quick, so careful a man, still fairly young about the eyes. She put her hand on his head, lightly, as if to prove to herself that he was real. He slept, exhausted.

One evening they went to a concert and she looked up to see her lover there, in the crowded aisle, in this city, watching her. He was standing there, with his overcoat on, watching her. She went cold. That morning the telephone had rung while her husband was still home, and she had heard him answer it, heard him hang up—it must have been a wrong number—and when the telephone rang again, at 9:30, she had been afraid to answer it. She had left home to be out of the range of that ringing, but now, in this public place, in this busy auditorium, she found herself staring at that man, unable to make any sign to him, any gesture of recognition. . . .

He would have come to her but she shook her head. *No. Stay away.*

Her husband helped her out of the row of seats, saying, "Excuse us, please. Excuse us," so that strangers got to their feet, quickly, alarmed, to let them pass. Was that woman about to faint? What was wrong?

At home she felt the blood drain slowly back into her head. Her husband embraced her hips, pressing his face against her, in that silence that belonged to the earliest days of their marriage. She thought, *He will drive it out of me.* He made love to her and she was back in the auditorium again, sitting alone, now that the concert was over. The stage was empty; the heavy velvet curtains had not been drawn; the musicians' chairs were empty, everything was silent and expectant; in the aisle her lover stood and smiled at her—Her husband was impatient. He was apart from her, working on her, operating on her; and then, stricken, he whispered, "Did I hurt you?"

The telephone rang the next morning. Dully, sluggishly, she answered it. She recognized his voice at once—that "Anna?" with its lifting of the second syllable, questioning and apologetic and making its claim—"Yes, what do you want?" she said.

"Just to see you. Please—"

"I can't."

"Anna, I'm sorry, I didn't mean to upset you—"

"I can't see you."

"Just for a few minutes—I have to talk to you—"

"But why, why now? Why now?" she said.

She heard her voice rising, but she could not stop it. He began to talk again, drowning her out. She remembered his rapid conversation. She remembered his gestures, the witty energetic circling of his hands.

"Please don't hang up!" he cried.

"I can't—I don't want to go through it again—"

"I'm not going to hurt you. Just tell me how you are."

"Everything is the same."

"Everything is the same with me."

She looked up at the ceiling, shyly. "Your wife? Your children?"

"The same."

"Your son?"

"He's fine—"

"I'm so glad to hear that. I—"

"Is it still the same with you, your marriage? Tell me what you feel. What are you thinking?"

"I don't know. . . ."

She remembered his intense, eager words, the movement of his hands, that impatient precise fixing of the air by his hands, the jabbing of his fingers.

"Do you love me?" he said.

She could not answer.

"I'll come over to see you," he said.

"No," she said.

What will come next, what will happen?

Flesh hardening on his body, aging. Shrinking. He will grow old, but not soft like her husband. They are two different types: he is nervous, lean, energetic, wise. She will grow thinner, as the tension radiates out from her backbone, wearing down her flesh. Her collarbones will jut out of her skin. Her husband, caressing her in their bed, will discover that she is another woman—she is not there with him—instead she is rising in an elevator in a downtown hotel, carrying a book as a prop, or walking quickly away from that hotel, her head bent and filled with secrets. Love, what to do with it? . . . Useless as moths' wings, as moths' fluttering. . . . She feels the flutterings of silky, crazy wings in her chest.

He flew out to visit her every several weeks, staying at a different hotel each time. He telephoned her, and she drove down to park in an underground garage at the very center of the city.

She lay in his arms while her husband talked to her, miles away, one body fading into another. He will grow old, his body will change, she thought, pressing her cheek against the back of one of these men. If it was her lover, they were in a hotel room: always the propped-up little booklet describing the hotel's many services, with color photographs of its cocktail lounge and dining room and coffee shop. Grow old, leave me, die, go back to your neurotic wife and your sad, ordinary children, she thought, but still her eyes closed gratefully against his skin and she felt how complete their silence was, how they had come to rest in each other.

"Tell me about your life here. The people who love you," he said, as he always did.

One afternoon they lay together for four hours. It was her birthday

and she was intoxicated with her good fortune, this prize of the after-
noon, this man in her arms! She was a little giddy, she talked too much.
She told him about her parents, about her husband. . . . "They were all
people I believed in, but it turned out wrong. Now, I believe in you. . . ."
He laughed as if shocked by her words. She did not understand. Then
she understood. "But I believe truly in you. I can't think of myself with-
out you," she said. . . . He spoke of his wife, her ambitions, her intel-
ligence, her use of the children against him, her use of his younger son's
blindness, all of his words gentle and hypnotic and convincing in the late
afternoon peace of this hotel room . . . and she felt the terror of laughter,
threatening laughter. Their words, like their bodies, were aging.

She dressed quickly in the bathroom, drawing her long hair up
around the back of her head, fixing it as always, anxious that everything
be the same. Her face was slightly raw, from his face. The rubbing of his
skin. Her eyes were too bright, wearily bright. Her hair was blond but
not so blond as it had been that summer in the white Nantucket air.

She ran water and splashed it on her face. She blinked at the water.
Blind. Drowning. She thought with satisfaction that soon, soon, he
would be back home, in that house on Long Island she had never seen,
with that woman she had never seen, sitting on the edge of another bed,
putting on his shoes. She wanted nothing except to be free of him. Why
not be free? *Oh,* she thought suddenly, *I will follow you back and kill
you. You and her and the little boy. What is there to stop me?*

She left him. Everyone on the street pitied her, that look of absolute
zero.

3

A man and a child, approaching her. The sharp acrid smell of fish.
The crashing of waves. Anna pretended not to notice the father with
his son—there was something strange about them. That frank, silent
intimacy, too gentle, the man's bare feet in the water and the boy a few
feet away, leaning away from his father. He was about nine years old and
still his father held his hand.

A small yipping dog, a golden dog, bounded near them.

Anna turned shyly back to her reading; she did not want to have to speak to these neighbors. She saw the man's shadow falling over her legs, then over the pages of her book, and she had the idea that he wanted to see what she was reading. The dog nuzzled her; the man called him away.

She watched them walk down the beach. She was relieved that the man had not spoken to her.

She saw them in town later that day, the two of them brown-haired and patient, now wearing sandals, walking with that same look of care. The man's white shorts were soiled and a little baggy. His pullover shirt was a faded green. His face was broad, the cheekbones wide, spaced widely apart, the eyes stark in their sockets, as if they fastened onto objects for no reason, ponderous and edgy. The little boy's face was pale and sharp; his lips were perpetually parted.

Anna realized that the child was blind.

The next morning, early, she caught sight of them again. For some reason she went to the back door of her cottage. She faced the sea breeze eagerly. Her heart hammered. . . . She had been here, in her family's old house, for three days, alone, bitterly satisfied at being alone, and now it was a puzzle to her how her soul strained to fly outward, to meet with another person. She watched the man with his son, his cautious, rather stooped shoulders above the child's small shoulders.

The man was carrying something, it looked like a notebook. He sat on the sand, not far from Anna's spot of the day before, and the dog rushed up to them. The child approached the edge of the ocean, timidly. He moved in short jerky steps, his legs stiff. The dog ran around him. Anna heard the child crying out a word that sounded like "Ty"—it must have been the dog's name—and then the man joined in, his voice heavy and firm.

"Ty—"

Anna tied her hair back with a yellow scarf and went down to the beach.

The man glanced around at her. He smiled. She stared past him at the waves. To talk to him or not to talk—she had the freedom of that choice. For a moment she felt that she had made a mistake, that

the child and the dog would not protect her, that behind this man's
ordinary, friendly face there was a certain arrogant maleness—then she
relented, she smiled shyly.

"A nice house you've got there," the man said.

She nodded her thanks.

The man pushed his sunglasses up on his forehead. Yes, she recog-
nized the eyes of the day before—intelligent and nervous, the sockets
pale, untanned.

"Is that your telephone ringing?" he said.

She did not bother to listen. "It's a wrong number," she said.

Her husband calling: she had left home for a few days, to be alone.

But the man, settling himself on the sand, seemed to misinterpret
this. He smiled in surprise, one corner of his mouth higher than the
other. He said nothing. Anna wondered: *What is he thinking?* The dog
was leaping about her, panting against her legs, and she laughed in em-
barrassment. She bent to pet it, grateful for its busyness. "Don't let him
jump up on you," the man said. "He's a nuisance."

The dog was a small golden retriever, a young dog. The blind child,
standing now in the water, turned to call the dog to him. His voice was
shrill and impatient.

"Our house is the third one down—the white one," the man said.

She turned, startled. "Oh, did you buy it from Dr. Patrick? Did
he die?"

"Yes, finally . . ."

Her eyes wandered nervously over the child and the dog. She felt the
nervous beat of her heart out to the very tips of her fingers, the fleshy
tips of her fingers: little hearts were there, pulsing. *What is he thinking?*
The man had opened his notebook. He had a piece of charcoal and he
began to sketch something.

Anna looked down at him. She saw the top of his head, his thick
brown hair, the freckles on his shoulders, the quick, deft movement of his
hand. Upside down, Anna herself being drawn. She smiled in surprise.

"Let me draw you. Sit down," he said.

She knelt awkwardly a few yards away. He turned the page of the
sketch pad. The dog ran to her and she sat, straightening out her skirt

beneath her, flinching from the dog's tongue. "Ty!" cried the child. Anna sat, and slowly the pleasure of the moment began to glow in her; her skin flushed with gratitude.

She sat there for nearly an hour. The man did not talk much. Back and forth the dog bounded, shaking itself. The child came to sit near them, in silence. Anna felt that she was drifting into a kind of trance while the man sketched her, half a dozen rapid sketches, the surface of her face given up to him. "Where are you from?" the man asked.

"Ohio. My husband lives in Ohio."

She wore no wedding band.

"Your wife—" Anna began.

"Yes?"

"Is she here?"

"Not right now."

She was silent, ashamed. She had asked an improper question. But the man did not seem to notice. He continued drawing her, bent over the sketch pad. When Anna said she had to go, he showed her the drawings—one after another of her, Anna, recognizably Anna, a woman in her early thirties, her hair smooth and flat across the top of her head, tied behind by a scarf. "Take the one you like best," he said, and she picked one of her with the dog in her lap, sitting very straight, her brows and eyes clearly defined, her lips girlishly pursed, the dog and her dress suggested by a few quick irregular lines.

"Lady with pet dog," the man said.

She spent the rest of that day reading, nearer her cottage. It was not really a cottage—it was a two-story house, large and ungainly and weathered. It was mixed up in her mind with her family, her own childhood, and she glanced up from her book, perplexed, as if waiting for one of her parents or her sister to come up to her. Then she thought of that man, the man with the blind child, the man with the dog, and she could not concentrate on her reading. Someone—probably her father—had marked a passage that must be important, but she kept reading and rereading it: *We try to discover in things, endeared to us on that account, the spiritual glamour which we ourselves have cast upon them; we are disillusioned, and learn that they are in themselves barren and devoid of the charm that they owed, in our minds, to the association of certain ideas. . . .*

She thought again of the man on the beach. She lay the book aside and thought of him: his eyes, his aloneness, his drawings of her.

They began seeing each other after that. He came to her front door in the evening, without the child; he drove her into town for dinner. She was shy and extremely pleased. The darkness of the expensive restaurant released her; she heard herself chatter; she leaned forward and seemed to be offering her face up to him, listening to him. He talked about his work on a Long Island newspaper and she seemed to be listening to him, as she stared at his face, arranging her own face into the expression she had seen in that charcoal drawing. Did he see her like that, then?—girlish and withdrawn and patrician? She felt the weight of his interest in her, a force that fell upon her like a blow. A repeated blow. Of course he was married, he had children—of course she was married, permanently married. This flight from her husband was not important. She had left him before, to be alone, it was not important. Everything in her was slender and delicate and not important.

They walked for hours after dinner, looking at the other strollers, the weekend visitors, the tourists, the couples like themselves. Surely they were mistaken for a couple, a married couple. *This is the hour in which everything is decided*, Anna thought. They had both had several drinks and they talked a great deal. Anna found herself saying too much, stopping and starting giddily. She put her hand to her forehead, feeling faint.

"It's from the sun—you've had too much sun—" he said.

At the door to her cottage, on the front porch, she heard herself asking him if he would like to come in. She allowed him to lead her inside, to close the door. *This is not important*, she thought clearly, *he doesn't mean it, he doesn't love me, nothing will come of it*. She was frightened, yet it seemed to her necessary to give in; she had to leave Nantucket with that act completed, an act of adultery, an accomplishment she would take back to Ohio and to her marriage.

Later, incredibly, she heard herself asking: "Do you . . . do you love me?"

"You're so beautiful!" he said, amazed.

She felt this beauty, shy and glowing and centered in her eyes. He stared at her. In this large, drafty house, alone together, they were like accomplices, conspirators. She could not think: how old was she? which year was this? They had done something unforgivable together, and the knowledge of it was tugging at their faces. A cloud seemed to pass over her. She felt herself smiling shrilly.

Afterward, a peculiar raspiness, a dryness of breath. He was silent. She felt a strange, idle fear, a sense of the danger outside this room and this old comfortable bed—a danger that would not recognize her as the lady in that drawing, the lady with the pet dog. There was nothing to say to this man, this stranger. She felt the beauty draining out of her face, her eyes fading.

"I've got to be alone," she told him.

He left, and she understood that she would not see him again. She stood by the window of the room, watching the ocean. A sense of shame overpowered her: it was smeared everywhere on her body, the smell of it, the richness of it. She tried to recall him, and his face was confused in her memory: she would have to shout to him across a jumbled space, she would have to wave her arms wildly. *You love me! You must love me!* But she knew he did not love her, and she did not love him; he was a man who drew everything up into himself, like all men, walking away, free to walk away, free to have his own thoughts, free to envision her body, all the secrets of her body. . . . And she lay down again in the bed, feeling how heavy this body had become, her insides heavy with shame, the very backs of her eyelids coated with shame.

"This is the end of one part of my life," she thought.

But in the morning the telephone rang. She answered it. It was her lover: they talked brightly and happily. She could hear the eagerness in his voice, the love in his voice, that same still, sad amazement—she understood how simple life was, there were no problems.

They spent most of their time on the beach, with the child and the dog. He joked and was serious at the same time. He said, once, "You have defined my soul for me," and she laughed to hide her alarm. In a

few days it was time for her to leave. He got a sitter for the boy and took
the ferry with her to the mainland, then rented a car to drive her up to
Albany. She kept thinking: *Now something will happen. It will come to
an end.* But most of the drive was silent and hypnotic. She wanted him
to joke with her, to say again that she had defined his soul for him, but
he drove fast, he was serious, she distrusted the hawkish look of his
profile—she did not know him at all. At a gas station she splashed her
face with cold water. Alone in the grubby little rest room, shaky and very
much alone. In such places are women totally alone with their bodies.
The body grows heavier, more evil, in such silence. . . . On the beach
everything had been noisy with sunlight and gulls and waves; here, as if
run to earth, everything was cramped and silent and dead.

She went outside, squinting. There he was, talking with the station
attendant. She could not think as she returned to him whether she
wanted to live or not.

She stayed in Albany for a few days, then flew home to her husband.
He met her at the airport, near the luggage counter, where her three
pieces of pale-brown luggage were brought to him on a conveyer belt,
to be claimed by him. He kissed her on the cheek. They shook hands, a
little embarrassed. She had come home again.

"How will I live out the rest of my life?" she wondered.

In January her lover spied on her: she glanced up and saw him, in a
public place, in the DeRoy Symphony Hall. She was paralyzed with fear.
She nearly fainted. In this faint she felt her husband's body, loving her,
working its love upon her, and she shut her eyes harder to keep out the
certainty of his love—sometimes he failed at loving her, sometimes he
succeeded, it had nothing to do with her or her pity or her ten years of
love for him, it had nothing to do with a woman at all. It was a private
act accomplished by a man, a husband, or a lover, in communion with
his own soul, his manhood.

Her husband was forty-two years old now, growing slowly into
middle age, getting heavier, softer. Her lover was about the same age,
narrower in the shoulders, with a full, solid chest, yet lean, nervous. She
thought, in her paralysis, of men and how they love freely and eagerly

so long as their bodies are capable of love, love for a woman; and then, as love fades in their bodies, it fades from their souls and they become immune and immortal and ready to die.

Her husband was a little rough with her, as if impatient with himself. "I love you," he said fiercely, angrily. And then, ashamed, he said, "Did I hurt you? . . . "

"You didn't hurt me," she said.

Her voice was too shrill for their embrace.

While he was in the bathroom she went to her closet and took out that drawing of the summer before. There she was, on the beach at Nantucket, a lady with a pet dog, her eyes large and defined, the dog in her lap hardly more than a few snarls, a few coarse soft lines of charcoal . . . her dress smeared, her arms oddly limp . . . her hands not well drawn at all. . . . She tried to think: did she love the man who had drawn this? did he love her? The fever in her husband's body had touched her and driven her temperature up, and now she stared at the drawing with a kind of lust, fearful of seeing an ugly soul in that woman's face, fearful of seeing the face suddenly through her lover's eyes. She breathed quickly and harshly, staring at the drawing.

And so, the next day, she went to him at his hotel. She wept, pressing against him, demanding of him, "What do you want? Why are you here? Why don't you let me alone?" He told her that he wanted nothing. He expected nothing. He would not cause trouble.

"I want to talk about last August," he said.

"Don't—" she said.

She was hypnotized by his gesturing hands, his nervousness, his obvious agitation. He kept saying, "I understand. I'm making no claims upon you."

They became lovers again.

He called room service for something to drink and they sat side by side on his bed, looking through a copy of *The New Yorker*, laughing at the cartoons. It was so peaceful in this room, so complete. They were on a holiday. It was a secret holiday. Four-thirty in the afternoon, on a Friday, an ordinary Friday: a secret holiday.

"I won't bother you again," he said.

He flew back to see her again in March, and in late April. He telephoned her from his hotel—a different hotel each time—and she came down to him at once. She rose to him in various elevators, she knocked on the doors of various rooms, she stepped into his embrace, breathless and guilty and already angry with him, pleading with him. One morning in May, when he telephoned, she pressed her forehead against the doorframe and could not speak. He kept saying, "What's wrong? Can't you talk? Aren't you alone?" She felt that she was going insane. Her head would burst. Why, why did he love her, why did he pursue her? Why did he want her to die?

She went to him in the hotel room. A familiar room: had they been here before? "Everything is repeating itself. Everything is stuck," she said. He framed her face in his hands and said that she looked thinner— was she sick?—what was wrong? She shook herself free. He, her lover, looked about the same. There was a small, angry pimple on his neck. He stared at her, eagerly and suspiciously. Did she bring bad news?

"So you love me? You love me?" she asked.

"Why are you so angry?"

"I want to be free of you. The two of us free of each other."

"That isn't true—you don't want that—"

He embraced her. She was wild with that old, familiar passion for him, her body clinging to his, her arms not strong enough to hold him. Ah, what despair!—what bitter hatred she felt!—she needed this man for her salvation, he was all she had to live for, and yet she could not believe in him. He embraced her thighs, her hips, kissing her, pressing his warm face against her, and yet she could not believe in him, not really. She needed him in order to live, but he was not worth her love, he was not worth her dying. . . . She promised herself this: when she got back home, when she was alone, she would draw the razor more deeply across her arm.

The telephone rang and he answered it: a wrong number.

"Jesus," he said.

They lay together, still. She imagined their posture like this, the two of them one figure, one substance; and outside this room and this bed there was a universe of disjointed, separate things, blank things, that had nothing to do with them. She would not be Anna out there, the lady in the drawing. He would not be her lover.

"I love you so much . . . ," she whispered.

"Please don't cry! We have only a few hours, please. . . ."

It was absurd, their clinging together like this. She saw them as a single figure in a drawing, their arms and legs entwined, their heads pressing mutely together. Helpless substance, so heavy and warm and doomed. It was absurd that any human being should be so important to another human being. She wanted to laugh: a laugh might free them both.

She could not laugh.

Sometime later he said, as if they had been arguing, "Look. It's you. You're the one who doesn't want to get married. You lie to me—"

"Lie to you?"

"You love me but you won't marry me, because you want something left over—Something not finished—All your life you can attribute your misery to me, to our not being married—you are using me—"

"Stop it! You'll make me hate you!" she cried.

"You can say to yourself that you're miserable because of *me*. We will never be married, you will never be happy, neither one of us will ever be happy—"

"I don't want to hear this!" she said.

She pressed her hands flatly against her face.

She went to the bathroom to get dressed. She washed her face and part of her body, quickly. The fever was in her, in the pit of her belly. She would rush home and strike a razor across the inside of her arm and free that pressure, that fever.

The impatient bulging of the veins: an ordeal over.

The demand of the telephone's ringing: that ordeal over.

The nuisance of getting the car and driving home in all that five o'clock traffic: an ordeal too much for a woman.

The movement of this stranger's body in hers: over, finished.

Now, dressed, a little calmer, they held hands and talked. They had to talk swiftly, to get all their news in: he did not trust the people who worked for him, he had faith in no one, his wife had moved to a text-book publishing company and was doing well, she had inherited a Ben Shahn painting from her father and wanted to "touch it up a little"—she was crazy!—his blind son was at another school, doing fairly well, in fact his children were all doing fairly well in spite of the stupid mistake of their parents' marriage—and what about her? what about her life? She told him in a rush the one thing he wanted to hear: that she lived with her husband lovelessly, the two of them polite strangers, sharing a bed, lying side by side in the night in that bed, bodies out of which souls had fled. There was no longer even any shame between them.

"And what about me? Do you feel shame with me still?" he asked.

She did not answer. She moved away from him and prepared to leave.

Then, a minute later, she happened to catch sight of his reflection in the bureau mirror—he was glancing down at himself, checking himself mechanically, impersonally, preparing also to leave. He too would leave this room: he too was headed somewhere else.

She stared at him. It seemed to her that in this instant he was break-ing from her, the image of her lover fell free of her, breaking from her . . . and she realized that he existed in a dimension quite apart from her, a mysterious being. And suddenly, joyfully, she felt a miraculous calm. This man was her husband, truly—they were truly married, here in this room—they had been married haphazardly and accidentally for a long time. In another part of the city she had another husband, a "husband," but she had not betrayed that man, not really. This man, whom she loved above any other person in the world, above even her own self-pitying sorrow and her own life, was her truest lover, her des-tiny. And she did not hate him, she did not hate herself any longer; she did not wish to die; she was flooded with a strange certainty, a sense of gratitude, of pure selfless energy. It was obvious to her that she had, all along, been behaving correctly; out of instinct.

What triumph, to love like this in any room, anywhere, risking even the craziest of accidents!

"Why are you so happy? What's wrong?" he asked, startled. He

THE DEAD

———

U SEFUL IN ACUTE *and chronic depression, where accompanied by
anxiety, insomnia, agitation; psychoneurotic states manifested by
tension, apprehension, fatigue.* ... They were small yellow capsules, very
expensive. She took them along with other capsules, green-and-aqua,
that did not cost quite so much but were weaker. *Caution against hazard-
ous occupations requiring complete mental alertness.* What did that mean,
"complete mental alertness"? Since the decline of her marriage, a few
years ago, Ilena thought it wisest to avoid complete mental alertness.
That was an overrated American virtue.

For the relief of anxiety and the relief of the apprehension of anxiety:
small pink pills. *Advise against ingestion of alcohol.* But she was in the
habit of drinking anyway, always before meeting strangers and often be-
fore meeting friends, sometimes on perfectly ordinary, lonely days when
she expected to meet no one at all. She was fascinated by the possibility
that some of these drugs could cause paradoxical reactions—fatigue
and intense rage, increase and decrease in libido. She liked paradox.
She wondered how the paradoxical reactions could take place in the

same body, at the same time. Or did they alternate days? *For the relief of chronic insomnia:* small harmless white barbiturates. In the morning, hurrying out somewhere, she took a handful of mood-elevating pills, swallowed with some hot water right from the faucet, or coffee, to bring about a curious hollow-headed sensation, exactly as if her head were a kind of drum. Elevation! She felt the very air breathed into her lungs suffused with a peculiar dazzling joy, worth every risk.

Adverse reactions were possible: *confusion, ataxia, skin eruptions, edema, nausea, constipation, blood dyscrasias, jaundice, hepatic dysfunction, hallucinations, tremor, slurred speech, hyperexcitement. . . . But anything was possible, after all!*

A young internist said to her, "These tests show that you are normal," and her heart had fallen, her stomach had sunk, her very intestines yearned downward, stricken with gravity. Normal? Could that be? She had stared at him, unbelieving. "The symptoms you mention—the insomnia, for instance—have no organic basis that we can determine," he said.

Then why the trembling hands, why the glitter to the eyes, why, why the static in the head? She felt that she had been cheated. This was not worth sixty dollars, news like this. As soon as she left the doctor's office she went to a water fountain in the corridor and took a few capsules of whatever was in her coat pocket, loose in the pocket along with tiny pieces of lint and something that looked like the flaky skins of peanuts, though she did not remember having put peanuts in any of her pockets. She swallowed one, two, three green-and-aqua tranquillizers, and a fairly large white pill that she didn't recognize, found in the bottom of her purse with a few stray hairs and paper clips. This helped a little. "So I'm normal!" she said.

She had been living at that time in Buffalo, New York, teaching part-time at the university. Buffalo was a compromise between going to California, as her ex-husband begged, and going to New York, where she was probably headed. Her brain burned dryly, urging her both westward and eastward, so she spent a year in this dismal Midwestern city in upstate New York, all blighted elms and dingy skies and angry politicians. The city was in a turmoil of excitement; daily and nightly the city police prowled the university campus in search of troublesome students, and the troublesome students hid in the bushes alongside buildings, eager to plant their homemade time bombs and run; so the campus was not safe for ordinary students or ordinary people at all. Even the "normal," like Ilena, long wearied of political activism, were in danger.

She taught twice a week and the rest of the time avoided the university. She drove a 1965 Mercedes an uncle had willed her, an uncle rakish and remote and selfish, like Ilena herself, who had taken a kind of proud pity on her because of her failed marriage and her guilty listlessness about family ties. The uncle, a judge, had died in St. Louis; she had had to fly there to get the car. The trip back had taken her nearly a week, she had felt so unaccountably lazy and sullen. But, once back in Buffalo, driving her stodgy silver car, its conservative shape protecting her heavily, she felt safe from the noxious street fumes and the darting excitable eyes of the police and the local Buffalo taxpayers—in spite of her own untidy hair and clothes.

The mood-elevating pills elevated her several feet off the ground and made her stammer rapidly into the near, dim faces of her students, speaking faster and faster in the hope that the class period would end sooner. But the tranquillizers dragged her down, massaged her girlish heart to a dreamy condition, fingered the nerve ends lovingly, soothingly, wanted only to assure her that all was well. In her inherited car she alternately drove too fast, made nervous by the speedier pills, or too slowly, causing warlike sounds from the rear, the honking of other drivers in American cars.

In the last two years Ilena had been moving around constantly: packing up the same clothes and items and unpacking them again, always eager, ready to be surprised, flying from one coast to the other to speak at universities or organizations interested in "literature," hopeful and adventurous as she was met at various windy airports by strangers. Newly divorced, she had felt virginal again, years younger, truly childlike and American. Beginning again. Always beginning. She had written two quiet novels, each politely received and selling under one thousand copies, and then she had written a novel based on an anecdote overheard by her at the University of Michigan, in a girls' rest room in the library, about a suicide club and the "systematic deaths of our most valuable natural resource, our children"—as one national reviewer of the novel said gravely. It was her weakest novel, but it was widely acclaimed and landed her on the cover of a famous magazine, since her *Death Dance* had also coincided with a sudden public interest in the achievement of women in "male-dominated fields." Six magazines came out with cover stories on the women's liberation movement inside a three-month period; Ilena's photograph had been exceptionally good. She found herself famous, and fame made her mouth ironic and dry with a sleeplessness that was worse than ever, in spite of her being "normal."

The pills came and went in cycles—the yellow capsules favored for a while, then dropped for the small pink pills, tranquillizers big enough to nearly knock her out taken with some gin and lemon, late at night. These concoctions were sacred to her, always kept secret. Her eyes grew large with the prospect of all those "adverse reactions" that were threatened but somehow never arrived. She was lucky, she thought. Maybe nothing adverse would ever happen to her. She had been twenty-six years old at the start of the breakup of her marriage; it was then that most of the pills began, though she had always had a problem with insomnia. The only time she had truly passed out, her brain gone absolutely black, was the winter day—very late in the afternoon—when she had been in her office at a university in Detroit, with a man whom she had loved at that time, and a key had been thrust in the lock and the door opened—Ilena had screamed, "No! Go away!" It had been only a cleaning lady, frightened off without seeing anything, or so the man had assured Ilena. But she had fainted. Her skin had gone wet and cold; it had taken the terrified man half an hour to bring her back to normal again. "Ilena, I love you, don't die," he had begged. Finally she was calm enough to return to her own home, an apartment she shared with her husband in the northwestern corner of the city; she went home, fixed herself some gin and bitter lemon, and stood in the kitchen drinking it while her husband yelled questions at her. "Where were you? Why were you gone so long?" She had not answered him. The drink was mixed up in her memory with the intense relief of having escaped some humiliating danger, and the intense terror of the new, immediate danger of her husband's rage. Why

was this man yelling at her? Whom had she married, that he could yell at
her so viciously? The drinking of that gin was a celebration of her evil.

That was back in 1967; their marriage had ended with the school
year; her husband spent three weeks in a hospital half a block from his
mother's house in Oswego, New York, and Ilena had not gone to see
him, not once, being hard of heart, like stone, and terrified of seeing him
again. She feared his mother, too. The marriage had been dwindling all
during the Detroit years—1965–1967—and they both left the city shortly
before the riot, which seemed to Ilena, in her usual poetic, hyperbolic,
pill-sweetened state, a cataclysmic flowering of their own hatred. She
had thought herself good enough at hating, but her husband was much
better. "Die. Why don't you die. *Die*," he had whispered hypnotically to
her once, as she lay in bed weeping very early one morning, before dawn,
too weary to continue their battle. Off and on she had spoken sentimen-
tally about having children, but Bryan was wise enough to dismiss that
scornfully—"You don't bring children into the world to fix up a rotten
marriage," he said. She had not known it was rotten, exactly. She knew
that he was jealous of her. A mutual friend, a psychiatrist, had told her
gently that her having published two novels—unknown as they were,
and financial failures—was "unmanning" to Bryan, who wanted to write
but couldn't. Was that her fault? What could she do? "You could fail at
something yourself," she was advised.

In the end she had fallen in love with another man. She had set out
to love someone in order to punish her husband, to revenge herself upon
him; but the revenge was forgotten, she had really fallen in love in spite
of all her troubles . . . in love with a man who turned out to be a disap-
pointment himself, but another kind of disappointment.

Adverse reactions: *Confusion, ataxia, skin eruptions, edema, nausea,
constipation, blood dyscrasias, jaundice, hepatic dysfunction, hallucina-
tions.* . . . Her eyes filmed over with brief ghostly uninspired hallucina-
tions now and then, but she believed this had nothing to do with the
barbiturates she took to sleep, or the amphetamines she took to speed
herself up. It was love that wore her out. Love, and the air of Detroit, the
gently wafting smoke from the manly smokestacks of factories. Love and
smoke. The precise agitation of love in her body, what her lover and her

husband did to her body; and the imprecise haze of the air, of her vision, filmed-over and hypnotized. She recalled having loved her husband very much at one time. Before their marriage in 1964. His name was Bryan Donohue, and as his wife she had been *Ilena Donohue*, legally; but a kind of maiden cunning had told her to publish her novels as *Ilena Williams*, chaste Ilena, the name musical with *l*'s. Her books were by that Ilena, while her nights of sleeplessness beside a sleeping, twitching, perspiring man were spent by the other Ilena. At that time she was not famous yet and not quite so nervous. A little insomnia, that wasn't so bad. Many people had insomnia. She feared sleep because she often dreamed of the assassination of Kennedy, which was run and rerun in her brain like old newsreels. Years after that November day she was still fresh with sorrow for him, scornful of her own sentimentality but unable to control it. How she had wept! Maybe she had been in love with Kennedy, a little. . . . So, sleeping brought him back to her not as a man: as a corpse. Therefore she feared sleep. She could lie awake beside a breathing, troubled corpse of her own, her partner in this puzzling marriage, and she rehearsed her final speech to him so many times that it became jaded and corny to her, out of date as a monologue in an Ibsen play.

"There is another man, of course," he had said flatly.

"No. No one."

"Yes, another man."

"No."

"Another man, I know, but I'm not interested. Don't tell me his name."

"There is no other man."

"Obviously, there is. Probably a professor at that third-rate school of yours."

"No."

Of course, when she was in the company of the *other man*, it was Bryan who became "the other" to him and Ilena—remote and masculine and dangerous, powerful as a nightmare figure, with every right to embrace Ilena in the domestic quiet of their apartment. He had every right to make love to her, and Gordon did not. They were adulterers, Ilena and Gordon. They lost weight with their guilt, which was finely

wrought in them as music, precious and subtle and prized, talked over
endlessly. Ilena could see Gordon's love for her in his face. She loved
that face, she loved to stroke it, stare at it, trying to imagine it as the face
of a man married to another woman. . . . He was not so handsome as
her own husband, perhaps. She didn't know. She only knew, bewildered
and stunned, that his face was the center of the universe for her, and she
could no more talk herself out of this whimsy than she could talk herself
out of her sorrow for Kennedy.

Her husband, Bryan Donohue: tall, abrupt, self-centered, amusing,
an instructor in radiology at Wayne Medical School, with an interest in
jazz and a desire to write articles on science, science and sociology, jazz,
jazz and sociology, anything. He was very verbal and he talked excel-
lently, expertly. Ilena had always been proud of him in the presence
of other people. He had a sharp, dissatisfied face, with very dark eyes.
He dressed well and criticized Ilena when she let herself go, too rushed
to bother with her appearance. In those days, disappointed by the low
salary and the bad schedule she received as an instructor at a small
university in Detroit, Ilena had arrived for early classes—she was given
eight-o'clock classes every semester—with her hair barely combed, loose
down to her shoulders, snarled and bestial from a night of insomnia,
her stockings marred with snags or long disfiguring runs, her face glossy
with the dry-mouthed euphoria of tranquillizers, so that, pious and sour,
she led her classes in the prescribed ritual prayer—this was a Catholic
university, and Ilena had been brought up as a Catholic—and felt freed,
once the prayer was finished, of all restraint.

Bad as the eight-o'clock classes were, the late-afternoon classes
(4:30–6:00) were worse: the ashes of the day, tired undergraduates
who needed this course to fill out their schedules, high-school teach-
ers—mainly nuns and "brothers"—who needed a few more credits
for their Master's degrees, students who worked, tired unexplained
strangers with rings around their eyes of fatigue and boredom and the
degradation of many semesters as "special students." When she was
fortunate enough to have one or two good students in these classes,
Ilena charged around in excitement, wound up by the pills taken at
noon with black coffee, eager to draw them out into a dialogue with her.

They talked back and forth. They argued. The other students sat docile
and perplexed, waiting for the class to end, glancing from Ilena to one
of her articulate boys, back to Ilena again, taking notes only when Ilena
seemed to be saying something important. What was so exciting about
Conrad's *Heart of Darkness*, they wondered, that Mrs. Donohue could
get this worked up?

Her copper-colored hair fell in a jumble about her face, and her skin
sometimes took a radiant coppery beauty from the late-afternoon sun as
it sheered mistily through the campus trees, or from the excitement of a
rare, good class, or from the thought of her love for Gordon, who would
be waiting to see her after class. One of the boys in this late-afternoon
class—Emmett Norlan—already wore his hair frizzy and long, though
this was 1966 and a few years ahead of the style, and he himself was
only a sophomore, a small precocious irritable argumentative boy with
glasses. He was always charging up to Ilena after class, demanding that
she explain herself—"You use words like 'emotions,' you bully us with
your *emotions*!" he cried. "When I ask you a question in class, you
distort it! You try to make everyone laugh at me! It's a womanly trick,
a *female* trick, not worthy of you!" Emmett took everything seriously,
as seriously as Ilena; he was always hanging around her office, in the
doorway, refusing to come in and sit down because he was "in a hurry"
and yet reluctant to go away, and Ilena could sense by a certain sullen
alteration of his jaw that her lover was coming down the hall to her
office. . . .

"See you," Emmett would say sourly, backing away.

Gordon was a professor in sociology, a decade or more older than
Ilena, gentle and paternal; no match for her cunning. After a particu-
larly ugly quarrel with her husband, one fall day, Ilena had looked upon
this man and decided that he must become her lover. At the time she
had not even known his name. *A lover. She would have a lover.* He was
as tall as her own husband, with a married, uncomfortable look about
his mouth—tense apologetic smiles, creases at the corners of his lips,
bluish-purple veins on his forehead. A handsome man, but somehow
a little gray. His complexion was both boyish and gray. He did not
dress with the self-conscious care of her husband Bryan; his clothes

were tweedy, not very new or very clean, baggy at the knees, smelling of tobacco and unaired closets. Ilena, determined to fall in love with him, had walked by his home near the university—an ordinary brick two-story house with white shutters. Her heart pounded with jealousy. She imagined his domestic life: a wife, four children, a Ford with a dented rear fender, a lawn that was balding, a street that was going bad—one handsome old Tudor home had already been converted into apartments for students, the sign of inevitable disaster. Meeting him, talking shyly with him, loving him at her finger tips was to be one of the gravest events in her life, for, pill-sweetened as she was, she had not seriously believed he might return her interest. He was Catholic. He was supposed to be happily married.

When it was over between them and she was teaching, for two quick, furtive semesters at the University of Buffalo, where most classes were canceled because of rioting and police harassment, Ilena thought back to her Detroit days and wondered how she had survived, even with the help of drugs and gin: the central nervous system could not take much abuse, not for long. She had written a novel out of her misery, her excitement, her guilt, typing ten or fifteen pages an evening until her head throbbed with pain that not even pills could ease. At times, lost in the story she was creating, she had felt an eerie longing to remain there permanently, to simply give up and go mad. *Adverse reactions: confusion, hallucinations, hyperexcitement.* . . . But she had not gone mad. She had kept on typing, working, and when she was finished it was possible to pick up, in her fingers, the essence of that shattering year: one slim book.

Death Dance. *The story of America's alienated youth . . . shocking revelations . . . suicide . . . drugs . . . waste . . . horror . . . $5.98.*

It had been at the top of the *New York Times* best-seller list for fifteen weeks.

Gordon had said to her, often, "I don't want to hurt you, Ilena. I'm afraid of ruining your life." She had assured him that her life was not that delicate. "I could go away if Bryan found out, alone. I could live alone," she had said lightly, airily, knowing by his grimness that he would not let her—surely he would not let her go? Gordon thought more about

her husband than Ilena did, the "husband" he had met only once, at a
large university reception, but with whom he now shared a woman. Two
men, strangers, shared her body. Ilena wandered in a perpetual sodden
daze, thinking of the . . . the madness of loving two men . . . the freak-
ishness of it, which she could never really comprehend, could not assess,
because everything in her recoiled from it: this could not be happening
to her. Yet the fact of it was in her body, carried about in her body. She
could not isolate it, could not comprehend it. Gazing at the girl stu-
dents, at the nuns, she found herself thinking enviously that their lives
were unsoiled and honest and open to any possibility, while hers had
become fouled, complicated, criminal, snagged, somehow completed
without her assent. She felt that she was going crazy.

Her teaching was either sluggish and uninspired, or hysterical. She
was always wound up and ready to let go with a small speech on any
subject—Vietnam, the oppression of blacks, religious hypocrisy, the
censorship haggling over the student newspaper, any subject minor or
massive—and while her few aggressive students appreciated this, the rest
of her students were baffled and unenlightened. She sat in her darkened
office, late in the afternoon, whispering to Gordon about her classes:
"They aren't going well. I'm afraid. I'm not any good as a teacher. My
hands shake when I come into the classroom. . . . The sophomores are
forced to take this course and they hate me, I know they hate me . . ."
Gordon stroked her hands, kissed her face, her uplifted face, and told
her that he heard nothing but good reports about her teaching. He
himself was a comfortable, moderately popular professor; he had been
teaching for fifteen years. "You have some very enthusiastic students,"
he said. "Don't doubt yourself, Ilena, please; if you hear negative things
it might be from other teachers who are jealous. . . ." Ilena pressed
herself gratefully into this good man's embrace, hearing the echo of her
mother's words of years ago, when Ilena would come home hurt from
school for some minor girlish reason: "Don't mind them, they're just
jealous."

A world of jealous people, like her husband: therefore hateful, there-
fore dangerous. Out to destroy her. Therefore the pills, tiny round pills
and large button-sized pills, and the multicolored capsules.

There were few places she and Gordon could meet. Sometimes they walked around the campus, sometimes they met for lunch downtown, but most of the time they simply sat in her office and talked. She told him everything about her life, reviewing all the snarls and joys she had reviewed, years before, with Bryan, noticing that she emphasized the same events and even used the same words to describe them. She told him everything, but she never mentioned the drugs. He would disapprove. Maybe he would be disgusted. Like many Catholic men of his social class, and of his generation, he would be frightened by weakness in women, though by his own admission he drank too much. If he commented on her dazed appearance, if he worried over her fatigue—"Does your husband do this to you? Put you in this state?"—she pretended not to understand. "What, do I look so awful? So ugly?" she would tease. That way she diverted his concern, she bullied him into loving her, because he was a man to whom female beauty was important—his own wife had been a beauty queen many years ago, at a teachers' college in Ohio. "No, you're beautiful. You're beautiful," he would whisper.

They teased each other to a state of anguish on those dark winter afternoons, never really safe in Ilena's office—she shared the office with a nun, who had an early teaching schedule but who might conceivably turn up at any time, and there was always the possibility of the cleaning lady or the janitor unlocking the door with a master key—nightmarish possibility! Gordon kissed her face, her body, she clasped her hands around him and gave herself up to him musically, dreamily, like a rose of rot with only a short while left to bloom, carrying the rot neatly hidden, deeply hidden. She loved him so that her mind went blank even of the euphoria of drugs or the stimulation of a good, exciting day of teaching; she felt herself falling back into a blankness like a white flawless wall, pure material, pure essence, a mysterious essence that was fleshly and spiritual at once. Over and over they declared their love for each other, they promised it, vowed it, repeated it in each other's grave accents, echoing and unconsciously imitating each other, Ilena carrying home to her apartment her lover's gentleness, his paternal listening manner. Maybe Bryan sensed Gordon's presence, his influence on her, long before the breakup. Maybe he could discern, with his scientist's keen heatless eye, the shadow of another personality, powerful and beloved, on the other side of his wife's consciousness.

Ilena vowed to Gordon, "I love you, only you," and she made him believe that she and Bryan no longer slept in the same bed. This was not true: she was so fearful of Bryan, of his guessing her secret, that she imitated with her husband the affection she gave to Gordon, in that way giving herself to two men, uniting them in her body. *Two men. Uniting them in her body.* Her body could not take all this. Her body threatened to break down. She hid from Bryan, spending an hour or more in the bathtub, gazing down through her lashes at her bluish, bruised body, wondering how long this phase of her life could last—the taunting of her sanity, the use of her rather delicate body by two normal men. *This is how a woman becomes prehistoric,* she thought. *Prehistoric. Before all personalized, civilized history. Men make love to her and she is reduced to protoplasm.*

She recalled her girlhood and her fear of men, her fear of someday having to marry—for all her female relatives urged marriage, marriage!—and now it seemed to her puzzling that the physical side of her life should be so trivial. It was not important, finally. She could have taken on any number of lovers, it was like shaking hands at a party, moving idly and absent-mindedly from one man to another; nothing serious about it at all. Why had she feared it so? And that was why the landscape of Detroit took on to her such neutral bleakness, its sidewalks and store windows and streets and trees, its spotted skies, its old people, its children—all uniformed, unpersonalized, unhistoric. Everyone is protoplasm, she thought, easing together and easing apart. Some touch and remain stuck together; others touch and part. . . . But, though she told herself this, she sometimes felt her head weighed down with a terrible depression and she knew she would have to die, would have to kill her consciousness. She could not live with two men.

She could not live with one man.

Heated, hysterical, she allowed Gordon to make love to her in that office. The two of them lay exhausted and stunned on the cold floor—unbelieving lovers. Had this really happened? She felt the back of her mind dissolve. Now she was committed to him, she had been degraded, if anyone still believed in degradation; now something would happen, something must happen. She would divorce Bryan; he would divorce his wife. They must leave Detroit. They must marry. They must change their lives.

Nothing happened.

She sprang back to her feet, assisted by this man who seemed to love her so helplessly, her face framed by his large hands, her hair smoothed, corrected by his hands. She felt only a terrible chilly happiness, an elation that made no sense. And so she would put on her coat and run across the snowy, windswept campus to teach a class in freshman composition, her skin rosy, radiant, her body soiled and reeking beneath her clothes, everything secret and very lovely. Delirious and articulate, she lived out the winter. She thought, eying her students: *If they only knew.* . . . It was all very high, very nervous and close to hysteria; Gordon loved her, undressed her and dressed her, retreated to his home where he undressed and bathed his smallest children, and she carried his human heat with her everywhere on the coldest days, edgy from the pills of that noon and slightly hungover from the barbiturates of the night before, feeling that she was living her female life close to the limits, at the most extreme boundaries of health and reason. Her love for him burned inward, secretly, and she was dismayed to see how very soiled her clothes were, sometimes as if mocking her. Was this love, was it a stain like any other? But her love for him burned outward, making her more confident of herself, so that she did not hesitate to argue with her colleagues. She took part in a feeble anti-Vietnam demonstration on campus, which was jeered at by most of the students who bothered to watch, and which seemed to embarrass Gordon, who was not "political." She did not hesitate to argue with hard-to-manage students during class, sensing herself unladylike and impudent and reckless in their middle-class Catholic eyes, a *woman* who dared to say such things!—"I believe in birth control, obviously, and in death control. Suicide must be recognized as a natural human right." This, at a Catholic school; she had thought herself daring in those days.

Emmett Norlan and his friends, scrawny, intense kids who were probably taking drugs themselves, at least smoking marijuana, clustered around Ilena and tried to draw her into their circle. They complained

that they could not talk to the other professors. They complained about
the "religious chauvinism" of the university, though Ilena asked them
what they expected—it was a Catholic school, wasn't it? "Most profes-
sors here are just closed circuits, they don't create anything, they don't
communicate anything," Emmett declared contemptuously. He was no
taller than Ilena herself, and she was a petite woman. He wore sloppy,
soiled clothes, and even on freezing days he tried to go without a heavy
coat; his perpetual grimy fatigue jacket became so familiar to Ilena that
she was to think of him, sharply and nostalgically, whenever she saw
such a jacket in the years to come. The boy's face was surprisingly hand-
some, in spite of all the frizzy hair and beard and the constant squint-
ing and grimacing; but it was small and boyish. He had to fight that
boyishness by being tough. His glasses were heavy, black-rimmed, and
made marks on either side of his nose—he often snatched them off and
rubbed the bridge of his nose, squinting nearsightedly at Ilena, never
faltering in his argument. Finally Ilena would say, "Emmett, I have to
go home. Can't we talk about this some other time?"—wondering anx-
iously if Gordon had already left school. She was always backing away
from even the students she liked, always edging away from her fellow
teachers; she was always in a hurry, literally running from her office to
a classroom or to the library, her head ducked against the wind and her
eyes narrowed so that she need not see the faces of anyone she knew.
In that university she was friendly with only a few people, among them
the head of her department, a middle-aged priest with a degree from
Harvard. He was neat, graying, gentlemanly, but a little corrupt in his
academic standards: the Harvard years had been eclipsed long ago by
the stern daily realities of Detroit.

The end for Ilena at this school came suddenly, in Father Hoffman's
office.

Flushed with excitement, having spent an hour with Gordon in
which they embraced and exchanged confidences—about his wife's
sourness, her husband's iciness—Ilena had rushed to a committee that
was to examine a Master's degree candidate in English. She had never
sat on one of these committees before. The candidate was a monk,
Brother Ronald, a pale, rather obese, pleasant man in his thirties. His

lips were more womanish than Ilena's. The examination began with a question by a professor named O'Brien: "Please give us a brief outline of English literature." Brother Ronald began slowly, speaking in a gentle, faltering voice—this question was always asked by this particular professor, so the candidate had memorized an answer, perfectly—and O'Brien worked at lighting his pipe, nodding vaguely from time to time. Brother Ronald came to a kind of conclusion some fifteen minutes later, with the "twentieth century," mentioning the names of Joyce, Lawrence, and T. S. Eliot. "Very good," said O'Brien. The second examiner, Mr. Honig, asked nervously: "Will you describe tragedy and give us an example, please?" Brother Ronald frowned. After a moment he said, "There is *Hamlet* . . . and *Macbeth*. . . ." He seemed to panic then. He could think of nothing more to say. Honig, himself an obese good-natured little man of about fifty, with a Master's degree from a local university and no publications, smiled encouragingly at Brother Ronald; but Brother Ronald could only stammer, "Tragedy has a plot . . . a climax and a conclusion. . . . It has a moment of revelation . . . and comic relief. . . ." After several minutes of painful silence, during which the only sounds were of O'Brien's sucking at his pipe, Brother Ronald smiled shakily and said that he did not know any more about tragedy.

Now it was Ilena's turn. She was astonished. She kept glancing at O'Brien and Honig, trying to catch their eyes, but they did not appear to notice. Was it possible that this candidate was considered good enough for an advanced degree, was it possible that anyone would allow him to teach English anywhere? She could not believe it. She said, sitting up very straight, "Brother Ronald, please define the term 'Gothicism' for us." Silence. Brother Ronald stared at his hands. He tried to smile. "Then could you define the term 'heroic couplet' for us," Ilena said. Her heart pounded combatively. The monk gazed at her, sorrowful and soft, his eyes watery; he shook his head *no*, he didn't know. "Have you read any of Shakespeare's sonnets?" Ilena asked. Brother Ronald nodded gravely, *yes*. "Could you discuss one of them?" Ilena asked. Again, silence. Brother Ronald appeared to be thinking. Finally he said, "I guess I don't remember any of them. . . ." "Could you tell us what a sonnet is, then?" Ilena asked. "A short poem," said Brother Ronald uncertainly.

"Could you give us an example of any sonnet?" said Ilena. He stared at his hands, which were now clasped together. They were pudgy and very clean. After a while Ilena saw that he could not think of a sonnet, so she said sharply, having become quite nervous herself, "Could you talk to us about any poem at all? One of your favorite poems?" He sat in silence for several seconds. Finally Ilena said, "Could you give us the *title* of a poem?"

A miserable half minute. But the examination was nearly over: Ilena saw the monk glance at his wrist watch.

"I've been teaching math at St. Rose's for the last five years . . ." Brother Ronald said softly. "It wasn't really my idea to get a Master's degree in English . . . my order sent me out. . . ."

"Don't you know any poems at all? Not even any titles?" Ilena asked.

"Of course he does. We studied Browning last year, didn't we, Brother Ronald?" O'Brien said. "You remember. You received a B in the course. I was quite satisfied with your work. Couldn't you tell us the title of a work of Browning's?"

Brother Ronald stared at his hands and smiled nervously.

"*That's my last duchess up there on the wall . . .*," O'Brien said coaxingly.

Brother Ronald was breathing deeply. After a few seconds he said, in a voice so soft they could almost not hear it, "*My last duchess? . . .*"

"Yes, that is a poem," Ilena said.

"Now it's my turn to ask another question," O'Brien said briskly. He asked the monk a very long, conversational question about the place of literature in education—did it have a place? How would he teach a class of high-school sophomores a Shakespearean play, for instance?

The examination ended before Brother Ronald was able to answer.

They dismissed him. O'Brien, who was the chairman of the examining committee, said without glancing at Ilena, "We will give him a B."

"Yes, a B seems about right," the other professor said quickly.

Ilena, whose head was ringing with outrage and shame, put her hand down flat on the table. "No," she said.

"What do you mean, no?"

"I won't pass him."

They stared at her. O'Brien said irritably, "Then I'll give him an A, to balance out your C."

"But I'm not giving him a C. I'm not giving him anything. How can he receive any other grade than F? I won't sign that paper. I can't sign it," Ilena said.

"I'll give him an A also," the other professor said doubtfully. "Then . . . then maybe he could still pass . . . if we averaged it out. . . ."

"But I won't sign the paper at all," Ilena said.

"You have to sign it."

"I won't sign it."

"It is one of your duties as a member of this examining board to give a grade and to sign your name."

"I won't sign it," Ilena said. She got shakily to her feet and walked out. In the corridor, ghostly and terrified, Brother Ronald hovered. Ilena passed by him in silence.

But the next morning she was summoned to Father Hoffman's office.

The story got out that she had been fired, but really she had had enough sense to resign—to write a quick resignation note on Father Hoffman's memo pad. They did not part friends. The following year, when her best-selling novel was published, Father Hoffman sent her a letter of congratulations on university stationery, charmingly worded: "I wish only the very best for you. We were wrong to lose you. Pity us." By then she had moved out of Detroit, her husband was in San Diego, she was living in a flat in Buffalo, near Delaware Avenue, afraid of being recognized when she went out to the drugstore or the supermarket. *Death Dance* had become a selection of the Book-of-the-Month Club; it had been sold for $150,000 to a movie producer famous for his plodding, "socially significant" films, and for the first time in her life Ilena was sleepless because of money—rabid jangling thoughts about money. She was ashamed of having done so well financially. She was terrified of her ability to survive all this noise, this publicity, this national good fortune. For, truly, *Death Dance* was not her best novel: a hectic narrative about college students and their preoccupation with sex and drugs and death, in a prose she had tried to make "poetic." Her more abrasive colleagues at the University of Buffalo cautioned her against believing the praise that was being heaped upon her, that she would destroy her small but unique talent if she took all this seriously, etc. Even her new lover, a critic, separated from his wife and several children, a fifty-year-old ex–child prodigy, warned her against success: "They want to make you believe you're a genius, so they can draw back and laugh at you. First they hypnotize you, then they destroy you. Believe nothing."

The flow of barbiturates and amphetamines gave her eyes a certain wild sheen, her copper hair a frantic wasteful curl, made her voice go shrill at the many Buffalo parties. She wondered if she did not have the talent, after all, for being a spectacle. Someone to stare at. The magazine cover had flattered her wonderfully: taken by a Greenwich Village photographer as dreamily hungover as Ilena herself, the two of them moving about in slow motion in his studio, adjusting her hair, her lips, her eyelashes, the tip of her chin, adjusting the light, altering the light, bringing out a fantastic ethereal glow in her eyes and cheeks and forehead that Ilena had never seen in herself. The cover had been in full color and Ilena had looked really beautiful, a pre-Raphaelite virgin. Below her photograph was a caption in high alarmed black letters: ARE AMERICAN WOMEN AVENGING CENTURIES OF OPPRESSION?

Revenge!

Death Dance was nominated for a National Book Award, but lost out to a long, tedious, naturalistic novel; someone at Buffalo who knew the judges told Ilena that this was just because the female member of the committee had been jealous of her. Ilena, whose head seemed to be swimming all the time now, and who did not dare to drive around in her Mercedes for fear of having an accident, accepted all opinions, listened desperately to everyone, pressed herself against her lover, and wept at the thought of her disintegrating brain.

This lover wanted to marry her, as soon as his divorce was final; his name was Lyle Myer. He was the author of twelve books of criticism and a columnist for a weekly left-wing magazine; a New Yorker, he had never lived outside New York until coming to Buffalo, which terrified him. He was afraid of being beaten up by militant students on campus, and he was afraid of being beaten up by the police. Hesitant, sweet, and as easily moved to sentimental tears as Ilena herself, he was always telephoning her or dropping in at her flat. Because he was, or had been, an alcoholic, Ilena felt it was safe to tell him about the pills she took. He seemed pleased by this confidence, this admission of her weakness, as if it bound her more hopelessly to him—just as his teenaged daughter, whose snapshot Ilena had seen, was bound to be a perpetual daughter to him because of her acne and rounded shoulders, unable to escape his love. "Drugs are suicidal, yes, but if they forestall the actual act of suicide they are obviously beneficial," he told her.

With him, she felt nothing except a clumsy domestic affection: no physical love at all.

She was so tired most of the time she did not even pretend to feel anything. With Gordon, in those hurried steep moments back in Detroit, the two of them always fearful of being discovered, her body had been keyed up to hysteria and love had made her delirious; with Bryan, near the end of their marriage, she had sometimes felt a tinge of love, a nagging doubtful rush that she often let fade away again, but with Lyle her body was dead, worn out, it could not respond to his most tender caresses. She felt how intellectualized she had become, her entire body passive and observant and cynical.

"Oh, I have to get my head straight. I have to get my head straight," Ilena wept.

Lyle undressed her gently, lovingly. She felt panic, seeing in his eyes that compassionate look that had meant Gordon was thinking of his children: how she had flinched from that look!

The end had come with Gordon just as abruptly as it had come with Father Hoffman, and only a week later. They had met by accident out on the street one day, Gordon with his wife and the two smallest children, Ilena in a trench coat, bareheaded, a leather purse with a frayed strap slung over her shoulder. "Hello, Ilena," Gordon said guiltily. He was really frightened. His wife, still a handsome woman, though looking older than her thirty-seven years, smiled stiffly at Ilena and let her gaze travel down to Ilena's watermarked boots. "How are you, Ilena?" Gordon said. His eyes grabbed at her, blue and intimidated. His wife, tugging at one of the little boys, turned a sour, ironic smile upon Ilena and said, "Are you one of my husband's students?" Ilena guessed that this was meant to insult Gordon, to make him feel old. But she explained politely that she was an instructor in the English Department, "but I'm leaving after this semester," and she noticed covertly that Gordon was not insulted, not irritated by his wife's nastiness, but only watchful, cautious, his smile strained with the fear that Ilena would give him away.

"In fact, I'm leaving in a few weeks," Ilena said.

His wife nodded stiffly, not bothering to show much regret. Gordon smiled nervously, apologetically. With relief, Ilena thought. He was smiling with relief because now he would be rid of her.

And so that had ended.

They met several times after this, but Ilena was now in a constant state of excitement or drowsiness; she was working out the beginning chapters of *Death Dance*—now living alone in the apartment, since her husband had moved out to a hotel. Her life was a confusion of days and nights, sleepless nights, headachey days, classes she taught in a dream and classes she failed to meet; she spent long periods in the bathtub while the hot water turned tepid and finally cold, her mind racing. She thought of her marriage and its failure. Marriage was the deepest, most mysterious, most profound exploration open to man: she had always believed that, and she believed it now. Because she had failed did not change that belief. This plunging into another's soul, this pressure of bodies together, so brutally intimate, was the closest one could come to a sacred adventure; she still believed that. But she had failed. So she forced herself to think of her work. She thought of the novel she was writing—about a "suicide club" that had apparently existed in Ann Arbor, Michigan—projecting her confusion and her misery into the heads of those late-adolescent girls, trying not to think of her own personal misery, the way love had soured in her life. Her husband. Gordon. Well, yes, men failed at being men; but maybe she had failed at being a woman. She had been unfaithful to two men at the same time. She deserved whatever she got.

Still, she found it difficult to resist swallowing a handful of sleeping pills. . . . Why not? Why not empty the whole container? There were moments when she looked at herself in the bathroom mirror and raised one eyebrow flirtatiously. *How about it? . . . Why not die? . . .* Only the empty apartment awaited her.

But she kept living because the novel obsessed her. She had to write it. She had to solve its problems, had to finish it, send it away from her completed. And, anyway, if she had taken sleeping pills and did not wake up, Gordon or Bryan would probably discover her before she had time to die. They often telephoned, and would have been alarmed if she hadn't answered. Gordon called her every evening, usually from a drug-store, always guiltily, so that she began to take pity on his cowardice. Did he fear her committing suicide and leaving a note that would drag him in? Or did he really love her? . . . Ilena kept assuring him that she was all right, that she would be packing soon, yes, yes, she would always remember him with affection; no, she would probably not write to him, it would be better not to write. They talked quickly, sadly. Already the frantic hours of love-making in that office had become history, outlandish and improbable. Sometimes Ilena thought, *My God, I really love this man*, but her voice kept on with the usual conversation—what she had done that day, what he had done, what the state of her relationship with Bryan was, what his children were doing, the plans his wife had for that summer.

So it had ended, feebly; she had not even seen him the last·week she was in Detroit.

Bryan called her too, impulsively. Sometimes to argue, sometimes to check plans, dates. He knew about the pills she took, though not about their quantity, and if she failed to answer the telephone for long he would have come over at once. Ilena would have been revived, wakened by a stomach pump, an ultimate masculine attack upon her body, sucking out her insides in great gasping shuddering gulps. . . . So she took only a double dose of sleeping pills before bed, along with the gin, and most of the time she slept soundly enough, without dreams. The wonderful thing about pills was that dreams were not possible. No dreams. The death of dreams. What could be more lovely than a dreamless sleep? . . .

In late April, Bryan had a collapse of some kind and was admitted to a local clinic; then he flew to his mother's, in Oswego. Ilena learned from a mutual friend at Wayne Medical School that Gordon had had a general nervous collapse, aggravated by a sudden malfunctioning of the liver brought on by malnutrition—he had been starving himself, evidently, to punish Ilena. But she worked on her novel, incorporating this latest catastrophe into the plot; she finished it in January of 1968, in Buffalo, where she was teaching a writing seminar; it was published in early 1969, and changed her life.

Lyle Myer pretended jealousy of her—all this acclaim, all this fuss! He insisted that she agree to marry him. He never mentioned, seemed deliberately to overlook, the embarrassing fact that she could love him only tepidly, that her mind was always elsewhere in their dry, fateful struggles, strung out with drugs or the memory of some other man, someone she half remembered, or the letters she had to answer from her agent and a dozen other people, so many people inviting her to give talks, to accept awards, to teach at their universities, to be interviewed by them, begging and demanding her time, her intense interest, like a hundred lovers tugging and pulling at her body, engaging it in a kind of love-making to which she could make only the feeblest of responses, her face locked now in a perpetual feminine smile. . . . With so much publicity and money, she felt an obligation to be feminine and gracious to everyone; when she was interviewed she spoke enthusiastically of the place of art in life, the place of beauty in this modern technological culture—she seemed to stress, on one national late-night television show, the tragedy of small trees stripped bare by vandals in city parks as much as the tragedy of the country's current foreign policy in Vietnam. At least it turned out that way. It was no wonder people could not take her seriously: one of the other writers at Buffalo, himself famous though more *avant-garde* than Ilena, shrugged her off as that girl who was always "licking her lips to make them glisten."

She did not sign on for another year at Buffalo, partly because of the political strife there and partly because she was restless, agitated, ready to move on. She sold the Mercedes and gave to the Salvation Army the furniture and other possessions Bryan had so cavalierly— indifferently—given her, and took an apartment in New York. She began writing stories that were to appear in fashion magazines, Ilena's slick, graceful prose an easy complement to the dreamlike faces and bodies of models whose photographs appeared in those same magazines, everything muted and slightly distorted as if by a drunken lens, the "very poetry of hallucination"—as one reviewer had said of *Death Dance*. Lyle flew down to see her nearly every weekend; on other weekends he was with his "separated" family. She loved him, yes, and she agreed to marry him, though she felt no hurry—in fact, she felt no real interest in men at all, her body shrinking when it was touched even accidentally, not out of fear but out of a kind of chaste boredom. So much, she had had so much of men, so much loving, so much mauling, so much passion. . . .

What, she was only twenty-nine years old?

She noted, with a small pang of vanity, how surprised audiences were when she rose to speak. *Ilena Williams looks so young!* They could not see the fine vibrations of her knees and hands, already viciously toned down by Librium. They could not see the colorless glop she vomited up in motel bathrooms, or in rest rooms down the hall from the auditorium in which she was speaking—she was always "speaking," invited out all over the country for fees ranging from $500 to a colossal $2000, speaking on "current trends in literature" or "current mores in America" or answering questions about her "writing habits" or reading sections from her latest work, a series of short stories in honor of certain dead writers with whom she felt a kinship. "I don't exist as an individual but only as a completion of a tradition, the end of something, not the best part of it but only the end," she explained, wondering if she was telling the truth or if this was all nonsense, "and I want to honor the dead by reimagining their works, by reimagining their obsessions . . . in a way marrying them, joining them as a woman joins a man . . . spiritually and erotically. . . ." She spoke so softly, so hesitantly, that audiences often could not hear her. Whereupon an energetic young man sitting in the first row, or on-stage with her, would spring to his feet and adjust the microphone. "Is that better? Can you all hear now?" he would ask. Ilena saw the faces in the audience waver and blur and fade away, sheer protoplasm, and panic began in her stomach—what if she should vomit right in front of everyone? on this tidy little lectern propped up on dictionaries for her benefit? But she kept on talking. Sometimes she talked about the future

of the short story, sometimes about the future of civilization—she heard
the familiar, dead, deadened word *Vietnam* uttered often in her own
voice, a word that had once meant something; she heard her voice echo-
ing from the farthest corners of the auditorium as if from the corners of
all those heads, her own head hollow as a drum, occasionally seeing her-
self at a distance—a woman with long but rather listless copper-red hair,
thin cheeks, eyes that looked unnaturally enlarged. *Adverse reactions:
confusion, edema, nausea, constipation, jaundice, hallucinations.* . . . Did
that qualify as a legitimate hallucination, seeing herself from a distance,
hearing herself from a distance? Did that qualify as a sign of madness?

During the fall and winter of 1969 and the spring of 1970 she trav-
eled everywhere, giving talks, being met at airports by interested strang-
ers, driven to neat disinfected motel rooms. She had time to write only
a few stories, which had to be edited with care before they could be
published. Her blood pounded barbarously, while her voice went on
and on in that gentle precise way, her body withdrawing from any man's
touch, demure with a dread that could not show through her clothes.
She had been losing weight gradually for three years, and now she had
the angular, light-boned, but very intense look of a precocious child.
People wanted to protect her. Women mothered her, men were always
taking her arm, helping her through doorways; the editor of a famous
men's magazine took her to lunch and warned her of Lyle Myer's habit
of marrying young, artistic women and then ruining them—after all, he
had been married three times already, and the pattern was established.
Wasn't it? When people were most gentle with her, Ilena thought of
the tough days when she'd run across that wind-tortured campus in
Detroit, her coat flapping about her, her body still dazzled by Gordon's
love, damp and sweaty from him, and she had dared run into the class-
room, five minutes late, had dared to take off her coat and begin the
lesson. . . . The radiators in that old building had knocked as if they
might explode; like colossal arteries, like her thudding arteries, over-
whelmed with life.

In the fall of 1970 she was invited back to Detroit to give a talk
before the local Phi Beta Kappa chapter; she accepted, and a few days
later she received a letter from the new dean of the School of Arts—new

since she had left—of her old university, inviting her to a reception in her honor, as their "most esteemed ex-staff member." It was all very diplomatic, very charming. She had escaped them, they had gotten rid of her, and now they could all meet together for a few hours. . . . Father Hoffman sent a note to her also, underscoring the dean's invitation, hoping that she was well and as attractive as ever. So she accepted.

Father Hoffman and another priest came to pick her up at the Sheraton Cadillac Hotel; she was startled to see that Father Hoffman had let his hair grow a little long, that he had noble, graying sideburns, and that the young priest with him was even shaggier. After the first awkward seconds—Father Hoffman forgot and called her "Mrs. Donohue"—they got along very well. Ilena was optimistic about the evening; her stomach seemed settled. As soon as they arrived at the dean's home she saw that Gordon was not there; she felt immensely relieved, though she had known he would not come, would not want to see her again . . . she felt immensely relieved and accepted a drink at once from Father Hoffman, who was behaving in an exceptionally gallant manner. "Ilena is looking better than ever," he said as people crowded around her, some of them with copies of her novel to sign, "better even than all her photographs. . . . But we don't want to tire her out, you know. We don't want to exhaust her." He kept refreshing her drink, like a lover or a husband. In the old days everyone at this place had ignored Ilena's novels, even the fact of her being a "writer," but now they were all smiles and congratulations—even the wives of her ex-colleagues, sturdy, dowdy women who had never seemed to like her. Ilena was too shaky to make any sarcastic observations about this to Father Hoffman, who might have appreciated them. He did say, "Times have changed, eh, Ilena?" and winked at her roguishly. "For one thing, you're not quite as excitable as you used to be. You were a very *young* woman around here." She could sense, beneath his gallantry, a barely disguised contempt for her—for all women—and this knowledge made her go cold. She mumbled something about fighting off the flu. Time to take a "cold tablet." She fished in her purse and came out with a large yellow capsule, a tranquillizer, and swallowed it down with a mouthful of Scotch.

Father Hoffman and Dr. O'Brien and a new, young assistant professor—a poet whose first book would be published next spring—talked to Ilena in a kind of chorus, telling her about all the changes in the university. It was much more "community-oriented" now. Its buildings—its "physical plant"—were to be open to the neighborhood on certain evenings and on Saturdays. The young poet, whose blond hair was very long and who wore a suede outfit and a black silk turtleneck shirt, kept interrupting the older men with brief explosions of mirth. "Christ, all this is a decade out of date—integration and all that crap—the NAACP and good old Martin Luther King and all that crap—the blacks don't want it and I agree with them one hundred percent! King is dead and so is Civil Rights—just another white middle-class week-night activity the blacks saw through long ago! I agree with them one hundred percent!" He seemed to be trying to make an impression on Ilena, not quite looking at her, but leaning toward her with his knees slightly bent, as if to exaggerate his youth. Ilena sipped at her drink, trying to hide the panic that was beginning. Yes, the NAACP was dead, all that was dead, but she didn't want to think about it—after all, it had been at a civil-rights rally that she and Bryan had met, years ago in Madison, Wisconsin. . . . "I haven't gotten around to reading your novel yet," the poet said, bringing his gaze sideways to Ilena.

Ilena excused herself and searched for a bathroom.

The dean's wife took her upstairs, kindly. Left alone, she waited to be sick, then lost interest in being sick; she had only to get through a few more hours of this and she would be safe. And Gordon wasn't there. She looked at herself in the mirror and should have been pleased to see that she looked so pretty—not beautiful tonight but pretty, delicate—she had worked hard enough at it, spending an hour in the hotel bathroom steaming her face and patting astringent on it, hoping for the best. She dreaded the cracks in her brain somehow working their way out to her skin. What then, what then? . . . But beauty did no good for anyone; it conferred no blessing upon the beautiful woman. Nervously, Ilena opened the medicine cabinet and peered at the array of things inside. She was interested mainly in prescription containers. Here were some small green pills prescribed for the dean's wife, for "tension." Tension, good! She took two of the pills. On another shelf there were some yellow capsules, perhaps the same as her own, though slightly smaller; she checked, yes, hers were 5 mg. and these were only 2. So she didn't bother with them. But she did discover an interesting white pill for "muscular tension," Dean Sprigg's prescription; she took one of these.

She descended the stairs, her hand firm on the bannister.

Before she could return safely to Father Hoffman, she was waylaid by someone's wife—the apple-cheeked Mrs. Honig, a very short woman with white hair who looked older than her husband, who looked, in fact, like Mrs. Santa Claus, motherly and dwarfed; Mrs. Honig asked her to sign a copy of *Death Dance*. "We all think it's so wonderful, just so wonderful for you," she said. Another woman joined them. Ilena had met her once, years before, but she could not remember her name. Mr. Honig hurried over. The conversation seemed to be about the tragedy of America—"All these young people dying in a senseless war," Mrs. Honig said, shaking her white hair; Mr. Honig agreed mournfully. "Vietnam is a shameful tragedy," he said. The dean's wife came by with a tray of cheese and crackers; everyone took something, even Ilena, though she doubted her ability to eat. She doubted everything. It seemed to her that Mrs. Honig and these other people were talking about Vietnam, and about drugs and death—could this be true?—or was it another hallucination? "Why, you know, a young man was killed here last spring, he took part in a demonstration against the Cambodian business," Mrs. Honig said vaguely; "they say a policeman clubbed him to death. . . ." "No, Ida, he had a concussion and died afterward," Mr. Honig said. He wiped his mouth of cracker crumbs and stared sadly at Ilena. "I think you knew him . . . Emmett Norlan?"

Emmett Norlan?

"You mean—Emmett is dead? He died? He died?" Ilena asked shrilly.

The blond poet came over to join their group. He had known Emmett, yes, a brilliant young man, a martyr to the Cause—yes, yes—he knew everything. While Ilena stared into space he told them all about Emmett. *He* had been an intimate friend of Emmett's.

Ilena happened to be staring toward the front of the hall, and she saw Gordon enter. The dean's wife was showing him in. Flakes of snow had

settled upon the shoulders of his gray coat. Ilena started, seeing him so
suddenly. She had forgotten all about him. She stared across the room
in dismay, wondering at his appearance—he wore his hair longer, his
sideburns were long and a little curly, he even had a small wiry brown
beard—But he did not look youthful, he looked weary and drawn.

Now began half an hour of Ilena's awareness of him and his aware-
ness of her. They had lived through events like this in the past, at other
parties, meeting in other groups at the university; a dangerous, nervous
sensation about their playing this game, not wanting to rush together.
Ilena accepted a drink from a forty-year-old who looked zestful and
adolescent, a priest who did not wear his Roman collar but, instead,
a black nylon sweater and a medallion on a leather strap; Ilena's brain
whirled at such surprises. What had happened? In the past there had
been three categories: men, women, and priests. She had known how
to conduct herself discreetly around these priests, who were masculine
but undangerous; now she wasn't so sure. She kept thinking of Emmett
dead. Had Emmett really been killed by the police? Little Emmett? She
kept thinking of Gordon, aware of him circling her at a distance of some
yards. She kept thinking of these people talking so casually of Vietnam,
of drugs, of the death of little Emmett Norlan—these people—the very
words they used turning flat and banal and safe in their mouths. "The
waste of youth in this country is a tragedy," the priest with the sweater
and the medallion said, shaking his head sadly.

Ilena eased away from them to stare at a Chagall lithograph,
"Summer Night." Two lovers embraced, in repose; yet a nightmarish
dream blossomed out of their heads, an intricate maze of dark depth-
less foliage, a lighted window, faces ghastly-white and perhaps a little
grotesque. . . . Staring at these lovers, she sensed Gordon approaching
her. She turned to him, wanting to be casual. But she was shaking. Gor-
don stared at her and she saw that old helplessness in his eyes—what, did
he still love her? Wasn't she free of him yet? She began talking swiftly,
nervously. "Tell me about Emmett. Tell me what happened." Gordon,
who seemed heavier than she recalled, whose tired face disappointed
her sharply, spoke as always in his gentle, rather paternal voice; she tried
to listen. She tried to listen but she kept recalling that office, the two

of them lying on the floor together, helpless in an embrace, so hasty, so reckless, grinding their bodies together in anguish. . . . They had been so close, so intimate, that their blood had flowed freely in each other's veins; on the coldest days they had gone about blood-warmed, love-warmed. Tears filled Ilena's eyes. Gordon was saying, "The story was that he died of a concussion, but actually he died of liver failure. Once he got in the hospital he just disintegrated . . . he had hepatitis . . . he'd been taking heroin. . . . It was a hell of a thing, Ilena. . . ."

She pressed her fingers hard against her eyes.

"Don't cry, please," Gordon said, stricken.

A pause of several seconds: the two of them in a kind of equilibrium, two lovers.

"Would you like me to drive you back to your hotel?" Gordon said.

She went at once to get her coat. Backing away, always backing away . . . stammered a few words to Father Hoffman, to the dean and his wife, words of gratitude, confusion. Good-by to Detroit! *Good-by, good-by.* She shook hands. She finished her drink. Gordon helped her on with her coat—a stylish black coat with a black mink collar, nothing like the clothes she had worn in the old days. Out on the walk, in the soft falling snow, Gordon said nervously: "I know you're going to be married. Lyle Myer. I know all about it. I'm very happy. I'm happy for you. You're looking very well."

Ilena closed her eyes, waiting for her mind to straighten itself out. Yes, she was normal; she had gone to an internist in Buffalo and had been declared normal. *You are too young to be experiencing menopause,* the doctor had said thoughtfully; *the cessation of menstrual periods must be related to the Pill or to an emotional condition.* She thought it better not to tell Gordon all that. "Thank you," she said simply.

"I'm sorry they told you about Emmett," Gordon said. "There was no reason to tell you. He liked you so much, Ilena; he hung around my office after you left and all but confessed he was in love with you . . . he kept asking if you wrote to me and I said no, but he didn't believe me . . . he was always asking about you. . . ."

"When did he die?"

"Last spring. His liver gave out. Evidently it was just shot. Someone said his skin was bright yellow."

"He was taking heroin? . . ."

"God, yes. He was a wreck. The poor kid just disintegrated, it was a hell of a shame. . . ."

He drove her back downtown. They were suddenly very comfortable together, sadly comfortable. Ilena had been in this car only two or three times in the past. "Where is your wife?" she asked shyly. She watched him as he answered—his wife was visiting her mother in Ohio, she'd taken the children—no, things were no better between them—always the same, always the same—Ilena thought in dismay that he was trivialized by these words: men were trivialized by love and by their need for women.

"I've missed you so much . . . ," Gordon said suddenly.

They walked through the tufts of falling snow, to the hotel. A gigantic hotel, all lights and people. Ilena felt brazen and anonymous here. Gordon kept glancing at her, as if unable to believe in her. He was nervous, eager, a little drunk; an uncertain adolescent smile hovered about his face. "I love you, I still love you," he whispered. In the elevator he embraced her. Ilena did not resist. She felt her body warming to him as toward an old friend, a brother. She did love him. Tears of love stung her eyes. If only she could get her head straight, if only she could think of what she was supposed to think of . . . someone she was supposed to remember. . . . In the overheated room they embraced gently. Gently. Ilena did not want to start this love again, it was a mistake, but she caught sight of Gordon's stricken face and could not resist. She began to cry. Gordon clutched her around the hips, kneeling before her. He pressed his hot face against her.

"Ilena, I'm so sorry . . . ," he said.

She thought of planets: sun-warmed planets revolving around a molten star. Revolving around a glob of light. And the planets rotated on their own private axes. But now the planets were accelerating their speed, they wobbled on their axes and the strain of their movement threatened to tear them apart. She began to sob. Ugly, gasping, painful sobs. . . . "Don't cry, please, I'm so sorry," Gordon said. They lay down together. The room was hot, too hot. They had not bothered to put on a light. Only the light from the window, a dull glazed wintry light; Ilena allowed him to kiss her, to undress her, to move his hands wildly about her body as she wept. What should she be thinking of? Whom should she remember? When she was with Lyle she thought back to Gordon . . . now, with Gordon, she thought back to someone else, someone else, half-remembered, indistinct, perhaps dead. . . . He began to make love to her. He was eager, breathing as sharply and as painfully as Ilena herself. She clasped her arms around him. That firm hard back she remembered. Or did she remember? . . . Her mind wandered and she thought suddenly of Bryan, her husband. He was her ex-husband now. She thought of their meeting at that civil-rights rally, introduced by mutual friends, she thought of the little tavern they had gone to, on State Street in Madison, she thought of the first meal she'd made for Bryan and that other couple . . . proud of herself as a cook, baking them an Italian dish with shrimp and crabmeat and mushrooms . . . yes, she had been proud of her cooking, she had loved to cook for years. For years. She had loved Bryan. But suddenly she was not thinking of him; her mind gave way to a sharper thought and she saw Emmett's face: his scorn, his disapproval.

She stifled a scream.

Gordon slid from her, frightened. "Did I hurt you? Ilena?"

She began to weep uncontrollably. Their bodies, so warm, now shivered and seemed to sting each other. Their hairs seemed to catch at each other painfully.

"Did I hurt you? . . ." he whispered.

She remembered the afternoon she had fainted. Passed out cold. And then she had come to her senses and she had cried, like this, hiding her face from her lover because crying made it ugly, so swollen. . . . Gordon tried to comfort her. But the bed was crowded with people. A din of people. A mob. Lovers were kissing her on every inch of her body and trying to suck up her tepid blood, prodding, poking, inspecting her like that doctor in Buffalo—up on the table, naked beneath an oversized white robe, her feet in the stirrups, being examined with a cold sharp metal device and then with the doctor's fingers in his slick rubber gloves—checking her ovaries, so casually—*You are too young for meno-pause*, he had said. Was it the pills, then? The birth-control pills? *This kind of sterility is not necessarily unrelated to the Pill*, the doctor had conceded, and his subtlety of language had enchanted Ilena. . . .

"Don't cry," Gordon begged.

She had frightened him off and he would not make love to her. He only clutched at her, embraced her. She felt that he was heavier, yes, than she remembered. Heavier. Older. But she could not concentrate on him: she kept seeing Emmett's face. His frizzy hair, his big glasses, his continual whine. Far inside her, too deep for any man to reach and stir into sensation, a dull, dim lust began for Emmett, hardly more than a faint throbbing. Emmett, who was dead. She wanted to hold him, now, instead of this man—Emmett in her arms, his irritation calmed, his glasses off and set on the night table beside the bed, everything silent, silent. Gordon was whispering to her. *Love. Love.* She did not remember that short scratchy beard. But she was lying in bed with an anxious, perspiring, bearded man, evidently someone she knew. They were so close that their blood might flow easily back and forth between their bodies, sluggish and warm and loving.

She recalled her husband's face: a look of surprise, shock. She had betrayed him. His face blended with the face of her student, who was dead, and Gordon's face, pressed so close to her in the dark that she could not see it. The bed was crammed with people. Their identities flowed sluggishly, haltingly, from vein to vein. One by one they were all becoming each other. Becoming protoplasm. They were protoplasm that had the sticky pale formlessness of semen. They were all turning into each other, into protoplasm. . . . Ilena was conscious of something fading in her, in the pit of her belly. Fading. Dying. *The central sexual organ is the brain*, she had read, and now her brain was drawing away, fading, dissolving.

"Do you want me to leave?" Gordon asked.

She did not answer. Against the hotel window: soft, shapeless clumps of snow. She must remember something, she must remember someone . . . there was an important truth she must understand. . . . But she could not get it into focus. Her brain seemed to swoon backward in an elation of fatigue, and she heard beyond this man's hoarse, strained breathing the gentle breathing of the snow, falling shapelessly upon them all.

"Do you want me to leave?" Gordon asked.

She could not speak.

THE 1980S

"surreal" images, he has taken to writing poetry feverishly in his last days) to Toledo, to buy a $15 pistol for $78.24 at the Liberty Pawnshop, from a clerk whose gold-rimmed innocently round eyeglasses resemble his own, and whose swarthy good looks (so Saul imagines) mirror his in an *almost* Semitic way. The Ohio laws governing the sale of rifles, handguns, and bullets are much friendlier than the laws of neighboring states. If you are a former convict or a former mental patient, if you are visibly agitated and "in the wings of" the hottest event of your life (so Saul has been gleefully warning his friends for weeks) you will not be turned away. "No doubt about it," says the youngish stoop-shouldered gentleman with the gold-rimmed glasses, Saul's smirking twin, "—a gun is your best friend these days. Of course I am speaking of an emergency. Have you ever found yourself caught up in the confusing flurry of an emergency?" Saul was turning the pistol over and over in his icy fingers. He hadn't counted on the object having such weight; such gravity. ("There is physicality here in all its surprising abruptness," he tells himself. For a brief while Wittgenstein's disciples toyed with the idea of calling his philosophy "physicalism" or a word to that effect: selling it to Stalin perhaps: but Stalin had been unimpressed, probably had his mind on other things.) He hadn't counted on so much reality though he was the proud author of two articles on the subject of current "academic shibboleths" published precociously in *The New Republic*, and a one-hundred-sixty-five-page seminar paper on the subject of Buber, Existentialism, Structuralism, Post-Structuralism, and the Holocaust as Text, a paper generally acclaimed as brilliant among Morgenstern's circle, though intemperately rejected as "unacceptable as either scholarship or poetry" by that Professor W——— who had best remain nameless, as Saul is "contemplating" graphic revenge. Saul's fingers are shaking. He pays no heed. Nor does the pawnbroker's clerk. It is a workday like any other, a Tuesday perhaps. It is ordinary life "sliced" in a perfectly ordinary way. Saul could photograph with his eyes the crowded interior of the Liberty Pawnshop on Seventh Street, downtown Toledo, or is it Dayton?—the affable clerk bent smiling over the badly scarified glass counter, he has an unfailing "photographic memory" ("what a great device for cheating," his envious freshman-dorm roommate little

Sammy Frankel said, Sammy set like a wind-up toy for medical school and a million-dollar practice: contemptible little Jewboy, Saul called him)—but why trouble to immerse himself in what is, after all, only *statistical* reality? (The police report will describe a Colt New Police model .32-caliber revolver, its original five-inch barrel sawed off to two, for pocket convenience; the usual six-shot cylinder. A weapon manufactured twenty-five years ago. Commonly sold over (and under) the counter. So badly in need of oiling, "surprising that it worked at all," one of the police will say.) Saul has been staring for some uncomfortable seconds at the amazing *object* in his hands, and his eyes, though customarily "dark, piercing, or brooding," have gone as blank and round and empty as his glasses. The clerk breathes warmly onto Saul's hands. He squints up companionably at him. "This material is chrome, if you are wondering," he says, "—that, zinc. A fine gun. The very best for emergencies. And if you had maybe a secret pocket sewed into your coat, I don't mean any big deal, or maybe you have one already?—it would be absolutely safe. And the price is right." Saul stares at the gun and the left corner of his mouth begins to twitch. Because he has seen this gun before, he has seen the scratched glass counter before, his own nail-bitten winter-reddened hands, the clerk's amiable ghostly reflection observing him from out of the glass. The forbidden thought arises: the Messiah has come and gone. Saul Morgenstern is too late. But "Right-o," Saul says in his deep bass voice, the most manly of voices, to deflect the clerk from suspicion. It is really a very ordinary very *routine* sort of morning. Rabbi Reuben Engelman is always telling Saul that it is the *routine* of life, the "happy dailiness" in which Faith and Practice are "wed," that constitutes the real challenge. Saul defeats the hypocritical old windbag with one loud slam of his hand on the desk top. And afterward re-enacts the scene for his table of undergraduate disciples in the student union cafeteria. ("I'm the Zen hand, the single Zen hand, that pounds and pounds and pounds my enemies to dust," he shouts. Saul Morgenstern the Scourge of G-d. Saul Morgenstern who rejected a Rhodes Scholarship. So forceful in the smoky interior of the Union, so Biblical, with his deep voice and flashing eyes and lustrous black wiry kinky hairs that curl from out of his clothes . . . no wonder the little WASP girls slit their eyes at him.)

Now he turns the pistol in his fingers. Murmurs. "Right-o," while he tries to remember precisely why he is here. Murmurs, "But can't I 'jew you down' a few bucks, I have doubts that this thing is worth $85. . . ." Several minutes of animated conversation. Saul says laughingly that he doesn't intend to kill his father: Ernest Morgenstern isn't worth killing: that kind of sloppy *personal* behavior ("acting out" the shrinks call it) has no class. The pawnbroker's clerk agrees. Or hasn't precisely heard. Saul turns the empty cylinder, sights along the barrel, licks his numbed lips, asks the clerk if he'd had any member or members of his family lost in the Holocaust, makes the comment (mildly, even sadly, smiling) that the family is a vanishing animal in the United States, doomed to extinction. "That's right," the clerk says agreeably. Saul stares blinking at him and sees that he isn't a twin at all, he's a morose ugly man in his late thirties, going bald, a queer sagging to one eyelid. He's an informant, probably. The pawnshop is monitored. ". . . a target like Kissinger," Saul is saying, ". . . from the point of view of the Jewish community. But of course it's too late. Years too late. I was only a high school kid then, I didn't know shit. Also I've always been a pacifist. Even when my father struck me in the face and cracked my nose—I didn't strike back." "That's right," the clerk says. He is making an unconscious "wringing" gesture with his hands. Pontius Pilate. Naturally. "David Gridlock" (the name on the purchase slip) files the image away for future reference. He has become feverishly interested in poetry lately; he begins to wonder if his real talent doesn't lie in that direction, and not in the direction of somber meticulous mirthless scholarship. . . . Also, he hasn't yet settled upon the absolute sequence of events, to be enacted in the synagogue next Sabbath: whether, after performing the assassination, he will then commit suicide by firing a single bullet, calmly, into the base of his skull; or whether he will allow himself to be captured by his enemies and led away. At the moment he leans toward the former. But, if the latter, he will want to immerse himself in poetry. And certain images are so "haunting," so "clustering." . . . The bargain is made, the price is right, Saul pays in cash, that is, "David Gridlock" pays unhesitatingly in cash, though he wonders if he is being cheated—being so bookish, so obviously not a man of the world. The price of the bullets too is suspiciously high. But what can he do?—he plays it safe, buys three dozen. ·

Freddy C———, Dale S———, Sol M——— discuss the problem of Morgenstern endlessly. "Frankly I'm afraid of him," says Freddy. "Also very exhausted. I wish he'd kill himself soon." But this isn't serious talk, this is sorrow, despair, cowardice. Vera R——— (by simple and insignificant happenstance a niece of Mrs. Morgenstern's oldest sister-in-law) becomes emotional, sometimes very angry, when the others say such things. ". . . how do you think we'll all feel, if . . ." she says in a low trembling voice. Of course they agree. They absolutely agree. And the fact that Saul has been going about claiming his former housemates have cheated him of "six months' rent" and "invaluable rare books" cannot fail to add to their uneasiness. Denise E——— has tried to make contact with Saul's former psychiatrists (Dr. Ritchie at the hospital, Dr. Mermelstein in the city) but since she is afraid of telling the gentlemen who she is, and hasn't been able to finish typing out a fifteen-page letter chronicling Saul's behavior in the past several months, her efforts have been unsuccessful. (Afterward, Denise will tell at least one reporter that Dr. Ritchie was "flippant" and "hurried" on the telephone, and told her that "if Saul's hostility was acted out, it would most likely be directed only against himself." This statement Dr. Ritchie has denied having made.) Dale thinks the police should be called and if Saul shows up at the house again he will call them himself. Sol thinks the parents · should be told ("but they know all about it, don't they"), the hospital's administration should be told ("but they don't give a damn"), Saul's former professors at the university, Saul's former friends. . . . But maybe it's wisest not to get involved. Not to get involved officially. For Saul has already threatened to sue everyone from the Governor of the state on down to his former housemates at 18332 Twenty-third Street if any terminology hinting at his "mental condition" is made public. He has told Rose P——— (herself not altogether stable) that certain betrayers of his trust will soon "regret the day of their birth" as the inhabitants of the cities of Hiroshima, Berlin, and Pompeii regretted theirs. Rose P——— thinks Saul is probably a saint. If he could be rooted in the

earth somehow, brought into contact with his sensual primitive funda-
mental self . . . "It's ideas and thinking and books that have made him
sick," she says in a passionate reedy voice, which makes Dale explode
nervously. "For Christ's sake Saul doesn't think at *all* these days, he's
given up thinking for the past six months, he can't even sit still to *read*
unless he's on medication," and Vera says over and over, ". . . if he's
really dangerous and does something, and . . . how do you think we'll
feel. . . ." However, it *is* a free country. Even if Saul has some sort of
"infectious malaise" as Rose thinks, a "psychic virus" picked up out
of the air of America. Even if he drives without a driving license. (His
license has been suspended for ninety days.) Even if as rumor has it he
has bought a gun. And probably he *is* a saint, Rose says, are there saints
in the Jewish religion . . . ? Rose makes a nuisance of herself hanging out
around school, dropping in at the house on Twenty-third all hours of
the night, hinting clumsily that she and Saul are "devoted lovers." The
others will refute her angrily, saying that Saul hadn't ever made love to
a girl, he basically detested girls, but Rose, ferret-faced little Rose, will
make her grubby claim now and forever. After all she often accompanies
Saul on his nocturnal wanderings about the city and at the Eastland Hills
Shopping Mall where he sings so that his rich vibrating voice (a baritone
voice?) echoes. He sings fearlessly, lustily, even in the library stacks, even
in the Chippewa Tavern where the younger workers from the Chrysler
plant hang out, even in the maze-like undulations of Abbey Farms, the
"luxury custom-homes" development where the Morgensterns bought
a house before the husband divorced the wife—easily worth one-half
million dollars in today's inflated market: he isn't shy. Singing Leporello,
singing Don Giovanni, singing sweet German lyrics by Schubert, shift-
ing raucously into the sleaziest of Janis Joplin, while his spaced-out girl
trots after him clapping until her palms burn. She loves him, she's crazy
about him, why isn't her adoration enough to save him, why didn't he
(if Fate and Karma pulled him in that direction) propose that they die
together, snug in his Volkswagen overlooking the lake, while the snow
dreamily falls and covers them up . . . ? Rose P——— who wants to
convert to Judaism, "the most orthodox kind." Rose P——— who is
the only person, apart from Saul's mother, to notice that his right eye

is just perceptibly darker—a darker greeny-brown—than his left. Rose
P——— at whose tremulous bosom Saul had once cocked and fired a
forefinger, chuckling, in front of five or six embarrassed friends. Rose
P——— whom Saul succeeded in "breaking down" by reading her
harrowing selections from such Holocaust literature as *Survivors of Aus-
chwitz, Voices of the Deathcamp, In the Ghettos of Warsaw and Lodz*, and
After the Apocalypse. Rose P——— to whom he confessed on the eve of
the assassination/suicide, "The real thing is, God's curse on me is, *I was
born too late. All the suffering is over—all the memoirs have been written.
Every breath of Saul's has been breathed by someone else.*"

His senior year, Saul is editor-in-chief of the student newspaper
and works on the average of fifty hours a week. He is known for his
generosity. He is known for his "biting" sarcasm. He is locally famous
for having published articles in *The New Republic* that bravely criticize
the university from which he will graduate. An editorial on academicians
who have "prostituted" themselves for federal grant money appeared
on the Op-Ed page of the *New York Times*, and impressed even Mr.
Morgenstern (at that time living on East Seventy-sixth Street with his
second and very young, or at any rate youthful, wife and her eleven-year-
old son). He discovers that he doesn't require sleep as other people do.
He runs for miles in the still dry winter night (temperatures as low as
5°, breath steaming, heart a wondrous unstoppable fist that opens and
closes, opens and closes, absolutely triumphant—why for Christ's sake
had he ever worried about his health, frightened himself that he had
cancer of the rectum when it was only bleeding hemorrhoids)—he chins
himself on railings, impresses those credulous WASP girls by climb-
ing over walls, not minding the iron spikes and broken glass scattered
about, he *is* invulnerable on certain days, and strong as an ox besides.
He gorges on non-kosher food and never feels a tinge of nausea. He sits
at the rear of the Adath Israel Synagogue, that "eye-stopping eye-sore"
that Rabbi Reuben Engelman dreamt up out of his shameless materi-
alistic dreams, before (and after) the murder/suicide lavishly featured
in national magazines—Saul sits quietly as any sweet little brainwashed
Jew-boy, a yarmulke on his head, taking notes in his loose-leaf journal
on the fixtures, the fur coats, the "masks of cunning and deceit" on all

sides. He even takes notes in a shorthand of his own invention when Rabbi Engelman delivers his rousing patriotic take-pride-in-America-and-don't-look-back sermons. Sometimes he chuckles, but quietly. No one appears to notice.

No psychiatrist can help him because he's too smart—he knows the Freudian crap, the jargon, inside and out. His I.Q. has been measured at 168. Perhaps it is 186. No one at the hospital dares approach him *on his own terms* because his problems aren't trivial and personal: his problems have to do with life and death, G-d and man, the special destiny of the Jews, the contrasting fates of Vessels of Grace and Vessels of Wrath. ("For twenty-two years I was a Vessel of Grace," Saul says with a bitter lopsided grin, "—and then I realized that was the wrong category.") Dr. Ritchie is an idiot, Dr. Mermelstein a homosexual sadist, Professor W——— who handed back his paper covered in red ink is an impostor, a crook. "David Gridlock" was born one drizzly December afternoon while Saul ran panting through the hospital woods, his parrot-green canvas jacket unzipped and his tongue lolling, borne along on waves of elation so powerful, so exquisite, he knew they were the province of G-d: except of course he didn't believe in such superstitious crap. He never had, in fact. Even at his Bar Mitzvah, in fact, reading his prayers and singing his chants with as much solemn assurance as if he'd been doing it all his young life. ("If I were G-d," Saul tells his nervous housemates Freddy and Dale, "I would bless you all and suck away your oxygen and that would be that—before you had a chance to wake up and ruin everything. Of course I mean 'you' in a generic sense," he explains.)

The psychiatrists, the psychologists, the therapists, the self-appointed do-gooders, certain meddlesome members of the Morgenstern family . . . no one is qualified to give advice to *him*. He baffles Mermelstein with a recitation from Kafka which he asks him to identify ("If we are possessed by the Devil it cannot be by one, for then we should live quietly, as with God, in unity, without contradiction . . . always sure of the man behind us"), he shocks a former philosophy professor at Ann Arbor by a late-night visit meant to "hammer out" the problem of Wittgenstein ("Is it true that 'what can be said at all can be said clearly, and what we cannot talk about we must pass over in silence'?—and how is this to be

reconciled with the philosopher's compulsive homosexual promiscu-
ity?" —delivered in a ringing triumphant voice), he dismays his father
with an unannounced appearance in New York during spring break
("Van Gogh cut off his ear with a razor blade for atonement," he tells his
angry bewildered father, "—if I castrated myself would that please you
and the new Mrs. Morgenstern?"), he works long fevered idle hallu-
cinatory hours on a prose-poem tentatively titled "Last Days" ("... At
the age of twenty-three I see that everything is falling in place at last
and that there was no secret to its meaning all along, except that Saul
Morgenstern 'saw through a glass darkly' "). He wakes in alarm, and
sometimes in a sweating rage, with the conviction that he will be, *he
cannot avoid being,* a belated Messiah. It is very late in the twentieth
century. The sacrificial act has already been performed. Every syllable
of his speech has been recorded on tape, even the gunshots, even the
idiot screams of the congregation: and pirated (no doubt) for the local
radio stations.

"I'm starving! Dying of hunger!" Saul accuses his mother when he
chances to appear at the house on Sussex Drive. "I can't breathe," he ac-
cuses his housemates, who foul the air with their cigarettes, their solemn
mirthless clichés, the unwashed heat of their bodies. Dale S——— will
remember an "uncannily lucid" conversation with Saul on the subject
of the Holocaust and its significance for all of human history, past and
future. The face of absolute evil, the anonymity of sin, Hitler as the Anti-
Messiah, the "Final Solution" being the pollution of every cubic foot of
oxygen—hence Saul's choking, his coughing spells. (Which certain of
his acquaintances, grown less indulgent with time, saw as shabbily the-
atrical. "He was faking," they say. "He was always faking. Except—of
course—at the end. But only at the *very* end.")

He graduates with highest honors, he is the only Rhodes Scholar
named this year in the state of Michigan, he will study history, politics,
religion at Oxford: but sickness intervenes. Now he practices firing his
Colt New Police pistol into a pile of stacked newspapers and magazines
in the basement of his mother's (no longer his parents') custom-made
house on Sussex Drive. His mother is away for the afternoon, fortu-
nately. At the Club. At the hospital visiting an aged ailing female rela-

tive. "I cannot understand you, Saul," Mrs. Morgenstern has said many
times. Sometimes she blinks tears out of her eyes, sometimes she stands
somber and stoic, not to be "broken down" (in Saul's own words) by
the non-negotiable presence of her son. Her name is Barbara, she is al-
together American, assimilated. She bears very little resemblance to her
dignified son except for the shade of her eyes—a queer muddy-green—
sometimes enlivened with thought, sometimes merely muddy. Saul loves
her, he readily admits, but he cannot bear her: not her voice which is so
painfully *sympathetic*, not her touch which burns, not the faintest whiff
of her expensive lethal perfume. All this he explains patiently to Rabbi
Engelman in the rabbi's handsome paneled library in his home. All this
he explains to Freddy, to Sol, to Vera, to Dr. Ritchie, to the contempt-
ible Mermelstein, to passengers on the Greyhound bus returning from
Toledo, to anyone who will listen: for, after all, as Saul reasons, isn't it
the story of our (collective) lives? Stunning in its transparency, irrefut-
able as a mathematical equation, how can it be resisted—? Pulling the
trigger, shocked and gratified by the simple loud *noise* of the explosion,
Saul knows for the first time that though everyone is lying to him, every-
one has agreed to "humor" him at least to his face, it no longer matters
to him what they think.

Still, in his last days, he makes many telephone calls. He will become
famous for his telephone calls.

Lying sleepless in his rumpled bed on the third floor (rear) of the
"boarding house" at 3831 Railroad Avenue, a half-mile from the squalid
southerly fringes of the university campus, some eleven miles south and
east of the Adath Israel Synagogue on the Hamilton Expressway . . . Ly-
ing sleepless by day and night, "David Gridlock" plotting his revenge
which will take the form of simple atonement. It isn't the sickish terror
of insomnia that overcomes him. He has long been adjusted to insomnia.
It's the bed rumpled and smelling of someone else's heated thoughts,
someone else's turbulent nights, *before Saul lies in it*. It's the soiled
sheets, the indentation of a stranger's head on the pillow, stray hairs,
curly and dark but not his own. The unflushed toilet in the hall. Waste,
foul and sickening and *not his own*. His fear is of being unoriginal, ac-
cused of plagiarism, exposed, ridiculed, cast aside as ordinary: "What's

so special about *you*, that you have the right to persecute *me?*" Mr.
Morgenstern shouts. As editor-in-chief of the student newspaper he
knocks himself out, rewrites slovenly half-assed copy, his head buzzing
with coffee, cigarettes, amphetamines. Often he hears the half-scolding
half-awed exclamation: "Saul, don't knock yourself out!" And again,
"Saul, why do you knock yourself out over this?—you don't even get
academic credit." It is his responsibility to write three or four editorials
a week. Provocative "controversial" pieces. The undemocratic nature of
fraternities and sororities, discrimination even by self-styled liberals, *de
facto* segregation . . . that sort of thing. One of his editorials is a passion-
ate attack upon prejudice. He is actually moved as he types it out, very
moved, agitated, close to tears. For the principle is—*can* human nature
be changed, after all; what in fact is "human nature," that it might be
"changed"; what hope is there after so many centuries . . . ? A bold edi-
torial, Saul thinks. An attack. A frontal assault. And then comes a prissy
sarcastic letter from a graduate student in engineering, *engineering* of all
contemptible subjects, ignoring the thrust of Saul's editorial and accus-
ing him of plagiarism. Plagiarism!—with reference to a (famous) essay
by Sartre on anti-Semitism which Saul has never read, or cannot remem-
ber having read, G-d as his witness. Fortunately Saul can get rid of the
letter before anyone sees it. . . . Then again, not long ago, in his "Issues
in Contemporary Thought" seminar, for which Saul wrote a fifty-page
paper embellished with clever footnotes, he is accused of "not having ad-
equately acknowledged" his sources: whole paragraphs, it seems, in the
language of Camus, certain insights from Camus's "Reflections on the
Guillotine" ("Capital punishment throughout history has always been a
religious punishment. . . . The real judgment is not pronounced in this
world but in the next. . . . Religious values are the only ones on which
the death penalty can be based. . . ."), turns of phrase appropriated from
Buber and Tillich: *which Saul has never read, or cannot remember having
read.* The mortification, then, of pleading his case with the professor. Of
uttering the truth in so shaky and childish a voice, it is transformed into a
falsehood. I am innocent, Saul says, how can I prove my innocence, have
I been born too late, have all the words been used, has all the oxygen
been breathed . . . ? His heart pounds with the shame of it, the oppres-

sion, the humiliation not to be borne. Better to die, Saul instructs Saul, than to crawl like a dog into someone else's sheets, stare helplessly into the toilet at someone else's shit.

In general, however, he is happy; almost euphoric. He shakes the hands of strangers, helps derelicts across the wide windy streets, helps push a car out of an icy snowbank. He never exaggerates because there isn't the need. "Around me," he boasts, "the world itself exaggerates." In any case he knows the importance of maintaining a certain level of energy in his bloodstream, maintaining a certain gut strength. He's bookish but no fool. He's suffered the ignominy of electro-convulsive shock treatments but he has always bounced back. In his loose-leaf journal he writes as clearly as possible so that, after his death, he won't be misunderstood as he was misunderstood in life. *Around the hero all things turn into tragedy; around the demigod, into a satyr-play; around Morgenstern—clumsy farce.* The freshness of the insight and the vigor of its language excite him. Death promises not to be painful at all.

In the crappy little room on Railroad Avenue he finds himself thinking of Fort Spear and the long dazed fluorescent-lit corridors, the fenced-in woods through which he ran with the intention of making his heart burst; but when he was in the hospital he thought of the house on Sussex Drive, the Abbey Farms sub-division, Rabbi Engelman and his wife Tillie seated in the living room, Mrs. Morgenstern serving them coffee and weeping. In one place he thinks of another. In one time-zone he yearns for another. Hence the frantic letter-writing, the telephone calls. . . . His father in Manhattan, Moses Goldhand at the University of Chicago, Professor Fox at the University of Michigan who had had such "high hopes" for him as a Rhodes Scholar, Vera R——— who "perhaps unconsciously" betrayed him, Dr. Ritchie the homosexual-charlatan, Dr. Mermelstein whom he will soon expose. It is a preposterous and almost unsayable fact that both his parents, united after years of bitter disagreement, conspired to so misrepresent facts to a Probate Court judge that Saul was "committed" to a state hospital: this truth must be acknowledged, turned fearlessly in the fingers like a rare poisonous insect, a lurid glaring jewel of an insect, *this truth the son cannot shirk.*

"Rabbi," Saul says in a boy's abrupt voice, "I think I need help. It isn't that I feel sick or weak or anything . . . I feel too strong."

Saul's clothes don't exactly fit though he dresses with fussy self-consciousness: his Englishy tweed jacket with the leather patches at the elbows and the buttons covered in leather; his handsome silk tie, a taste-ful dark red; his black silk-and-cotton socks, the very best quality. "He took pride in his appearance," says Rose P———, "and why shouldn't he—? He was so beautiful sometimes, you could see his soul shining in his eyes." Vera R——— says, "Well—he was a little vain, I suppose, when I first met him. He said something strange once: that if he'd been able to sing, if he'd gone on the stage, his life would have been peaceful and dedicated to beauty." The girls adore him, his disciples in the coffee shop applaud, Morgenstern the Scourge of G-d with his wiry curly black hair, his Semitic nose and eyes, the gold-rimmed glasses that give him so perplexed and scholarly and teacherly a look—one of those skinny dark-browed anarchists of Old Russia, a student out of Dostoyevsky, prepared to give his life in the rebellion against tyranny. But lately his clothes have grown so baggy he wonders if in fact they are *his*. Perhaps his housemates have hatched a cruel prank, sneaking into his new room, substituting someone else's clothes for his. Suddenly it seems very plausible. A Jew's worst enemy is another Jew, right? The swastikas scrawled on his poster of Freud with cigar (taped to the door of his library carrel) were doubtless the work of other Jews envious of Saul's success at the university and with WASP females in particular. Sol M———, for instance. The Frank kid, what is his name, his physician-father hangs out with Rockefeller. . . .

"Rabbi," Saul says, "I think I need help. People are insulting me be-hind my back. It hasn't been the same since Fort Spear, since my parents turned me in, I mean they gave me the highest dosage of drugs there, the highest legal dosage, and I lost count of how many shock treatments, which I believe are against the state law—I'm seeing a lawyer in the morning—I'm not going to let any of this rest—but from you I need help, they have begun calling me the 'worst kind of Jew,' *will you please tell them to stop?*"

He pays $78 in cash for two weeks in the boarding house (the flophouse) on slummy Railroad Avenue though he knows secretly that he won't be there that long. He won't be anywhere that long. Carefully he arranges a selection of his most cherished books, certain newspaper and magazine clippings, a slightly wrinkled but still dramatic poster-photograph of Ché Guevara ("Ché Guevara!" Freddy C——— will exclaim, "—I mean, since when, Ché Guevara and Saul Morgenstern?"), and the typed and heavily annotated manuscript of "Last Days." But the clean white dime-store envelope containing his denunciation speech is kept in the left pocket of his tweed coat. In the right pocket, the pistol. Its compact weight has become assimilated to his own in recent days: he rarely needs to think of it any longer.

His friends, his former friends, the frightened housemates, certain university acquaintances and gossipers—they debate the existence of the pistol, which no one has ever seen. Some are certain that Saul has a gun ("He keeps his elbow pressed against his pocket in a way, you know there's something dangerous there"), others are equally certain that he is lying ("All he wants is for us to talk about him—always to talk about *him*"), a few believe that his carefully stylized "crazy behavior" is the real thing and that he should be considered dangerous ("Maybe he was kidding around at first but now he's lost control—you can smell a really weird odor on him"). An unidentified young woman tells one of the campus security police that there is going to be trouble unless a certain "graduate student in history" is taken into custody, but she professes not to know his name, and refuses to give any further information. Mrs. Morgenstern telephones her former husband and leaves a message with his maid which is never returned: possibly because (so Mrs. Morgenstern says, she is renowned for always putting the best face on things) the maid spoke with a heavy Hispanic accent, and probably had not understood the message.

Saul aka "David Gridlock" jogs through the Abbey Farms subdivision one chill Sunday morning, wishing to see it with uncontaminated (i.e., an anthropologist's) eyes. Essex Drive, Queens Lane, Drakes Center, Pemberton Circle, Shropshire Way, Sussex Drive. . . . An exemplary Jewish neighborhood, Saul thinks, panting, laughing silently, a real kike fantasy, all these English names, all the undulations of the lanes, ways, roads, drives, not a street among them, not a hint of urban origins. He runs, he swings his arms, he forgets not to breathe through his opened mouth, the fierce sunlight pours into him and swells him with energy, his very brain is tumescent, he realizes suddenly that he will live forever: a bullet from his own gun cannot stop him. Drakes Center and Shropshire and here is Sussex Drive and here is 18 Sussex . . . a custom-made house like all the rest . . . built by the same developer . . . dreamt up by the same architect. Saul "sees" for the first time since the Morgensterns bought the house eleven years before that 18 Sussex is . . . a remodeled barn: that all the houses in Abbey Farms are remodeled barns: made of wood specially treated to look "weathered," even slightly "rotted"; with narrow vertical windows designed to give the illusion of having been "cut out" of obdurate barn walls. He begins to laugh aloud as he runs. Perhaps he will succumb to a fit of laughing, wheezing, asthmatic, choking, he can't help himself, it *is* hilariously funny, he will have to add a footnote to "Last Days," a sly dig at Abbey Farms the "restricted residential community" a few miles from Adath Israel, the private and domestic expression of that Jewish essence of which (he is straining for the most muscular but also the most mocking syntax) Adath Israel is the public and cultural expression. English lanes and circles and ways, gaunt gray-weathered Andrew Wyeth barns, hexagonal and octagonal "classic" shapes, rough unpainted fences, even "split-rail" fences, even mock-silos with orange-red aluminum roofs adjacent to garages. . . . Disneyland! Fantasy land! Kike heaven! Saul jogs along the deserted wintry streets, his breath steaming, his lips and tongue going numb. "I will go until I am stopped," he thinks, elated, "—and I never am stopped. G-d be praised."

The Last Will & Testament of Saul Morgenstern: . . . *as I cannot and will not continue to live in this abomination of hypocrisy I will make you an outright present of my life to satisfy your bloodlust. As for my worldly goods . . . if it should be discovered that the debts lodged against me are fraudulent and I should possess after all some wealth I direct that it be given to the Lubavitcher Hasidim and not a penny to those who have betrayed me. My books, papers, personal possessions etc. to be burnt and scattered with my body.*

Saul's car breaks down en route to Adath Israel but he has learned to be affable (i.e., fatalistic) enough, he doesn't waste precious minutes shaking his fist at the skies, why despair when it's only a few minutes after eleven and in his tweed coat and red necktie and glinting gold-rimmed glasses he's an excellent candidate to be picked up and offered a ride by a passing motorist . . . ? In any case he is only about four miles south of the synagogue, on the Hamilton Expressway. And a weightless sensation pulses through him. *He cannot fail, he has entered History.*

A certain Judge Marvin McL——— of the Probate Court receives a letter from Dr. Harold A———, the Director of the Fort Spear State Hospital, explaining that Mr. Saul Morgenstern, having left the hospital on "unauthorized leave," was now being granted the status of "convalescent" as he had initiated "therapy of a private nature" outside the hospital, with a certain Dr. Aaron Mermelstein, and had made a "reasonable adjustment" there. This, a bitter triumph for the forces of Justice after long haggling, begging, whispered pleading, the defiant restraint of the injured party to scream aloud the circumstances of his degradation. Mrs. Morgenstern is particularly alarmed to see that he's grown so skinny—a weight loss of fifteen pounds in two weeks—does this mean that her boy is *eluding her in the flesh*? Vera R——— is also "alarmed" and "shocked" when by accident she encounters Saul in the university library, he looks so sallow, so "old," "not himself." . . . Speaking idly but lucidly in the coffee shop he reads to her selected passages from "Last Days," explaining the principles of desecration (DE-(reversal) + (CON)SECRATE): these principles necessary in order that G-d be summoned back to the community. First, there is the desecration of the SABBATH, the holiest day of the week; then, the desecration of the SYNAGOGUE, the holiest place; if possible, the desecration of the BIMAH, the most sacred place in the synagogue; the desecration of the HOLINESS OF THE RABBI; the desecration of the PUBLIC RITUAL. . . . ("By which I mean that a 'counter-ritual' is performed not only in view of the members of the congregation, and by extension all the Jews of the world, but *the entire world of non- and anti-Jews itself*," Saul says.) Vera R——— confess that her underlying instinct was simply to escape her old (former) (doomed) (depressing) friend. She "maybe" told three or four people about the conversation. In truth she didn't take it altogether seriously because Saul had been talking along such lines for months and didn't know whether Suicide to him meant an actual act or a metaphor (as in one of his favorite expressions, "the suicidal drift of our generation . . ."), you didn't know whether an elaborate exegesis of the principles of desecration was something he had dreamt up himself or appropriated from one of his masters, Buber, say, or Eliade. And in any case, says Vera R———, he spoke in so calm and low-keyed and even *fatigued* a voice, it didn't seem that anything urgent was being pressed upon her. He said too as she was leaving that he probably wouldn't be seeing her again—he had been accepted as a tutorial student at the Jung Institute in Zurich and would be leaving the first of March.

Saul walks as many as eight or nine miles in the falling snow, in the cruel swirling winds. A "living snowman": hatless, gloveless, wearing only his shoes, lightweight socks. Is he cold? Are his teeth chattering? His skin is so hot that snow melts and runs down his cheeks in rivulets like tears. He arrives as if against his will at his married sister's house in Bay Ridge: ". . . with no explanation, just walking in and announcing he was starving, he hadn't eaten all day, I'd better prepare him something to eat or he'd collapse. Della and I were both terrified, he walked in without knocking or ringing the doorbell, we thought it was a madman at first. . . ." He arrives at the university library from which he has been barred by an "executive order" of the provost: he only wants to test the thoroughness of the security police. (The doors are unguarded. The librarians don't recognize him. No one "sees" him, in fact.) He arrives at Flanagans on Fifteenth Street where he sits with a group of (former) friends and acquaintances, a long rowdy table that shifts as the hours pass (from approximately nine in the evening to one-thirty in the morning), being most crowded and friendly around eleven. In the dim light he insists upon reading passages from an "obscene" and "outrageous" book titled *The Fallacy of the "Final Solution"*—"some book by a writer no one had ever heard of, Saul claimed he'd stolen it from the bookstore, the thesis being that the Holocaust had never occurred, it was only 'public relations' on the part of the Jews. . . . The book *was* fairly outrageous but when I asked Saul why didn't he just throw it away, who gives a damn about a nut like that, he didn't even seem to hear me, he just looked through me, then went back to the book, leafing and paging through it. . . . He said that someone had told him not to pollute his spiritual energy with sick people, it might have been a professor or a rabbi, or his father, Saul was never very clear who it was, only that he'd said in rebuttal, 'but it's *sick people* we have got to help.' " He is radiant with certainty, his eyes shine, his hands no longer shake. He says: "Some of the Holocaust survivors believed that simple survival was resistance but what does that mean for us . . . ? Simple survival is defeat now. It's succumbing to the enemy." No one argues, no one even questions him. Perhaps no one hears.

Saul arrives at the synagogue just as Rabbi Engelman is concluding his sermon. He has been sleeping a stuporous "David Gridlock" sleep for forty-eight hours. Reverently he puts a yarmulke on his head, unobtrusively he enters the sanctuary at the rear (left), makes his way along the aisle at the far left, walking slowly, calling little or no attention to himself. He takes his seat in the same pew with members of his mother's family but doesn't catch sight of his mother or sister at first. He has heard the sermon before and has no need to hear it again. All the words have been spoken, *all* the words, Saul clutches this excruciating truth to his chest and belly, a clawing beast, clawing and tearing and pulling at his guts, and sits slightly hunched over. He is breathing shallowly through his mouth. The pistol is comfortable in his pocket along with five or six Smith & Wesson cartridges. The speech in the envelope has been carefully prepared, typed, proofread. *I make this congregation a present of my life, before you can take it from me.*

The pawnbroker's assistant in Toledo will not remember him.

After the first breakdown in Ann Arbor his father said: You've been poisoned by books. (Saul had just read a passage from Kafka, in a high ringing accusing voice, and thrown the book down on a table.) According to friends who remember Saul's anecdote he shouted triumphantly in the (angry? frightened?) man's face: What should I have been poisoned by—*you?*

The room is dimly and vaguely oval. There are no windows. There are queer and somehow frightening indentations in the walls. . . . When Saul approaches the wall it shrinks away. He knows he must escape because his oxygen supply is diminishing but there are no windows, no doors, no actual walls. . . . Suddenly he sees his own body lying at the front of the synagogue. His arms and legs are outspread, he is vomiting blood. Is he "conscious" or "unconscious," is he "in terrible pain" or "beyond pain" . . . ? The commotion is distracting, the place is a madhouse, screams, wails, a stampede in the aisles, where is his mother . . . ? It is the dying rabbi the congregation mourns but Saul can't see where he has fallen. One shot in the side of the neck, the second in the upper left arm, the third into the left eye and into the brain. . . . Abruptly the image dissolves and Saul finds himself in an unfamiliar dark that isn't dark enough. The ghostly outline of his single window disturbs his sleep, a mottled patch of light from the street that falls slantwise across his ceiling. . . .

Once Saul confided in his closest friend Freddy C——— (who later betrayed him) that he was "afraid." "Afraid of what?" Freddy asked. "Just afraid," said Saul. After a long uneasy moment Freddy said, blinking and staring at his feet, "Well—I guess I am too." But now Saul isn't at all afraid because the Sabbath services are always taped and everything he says will be preserved for the record. His elegant speech of denunciation won't be distorted or mangled or misquoted. And he is well-informed enough to know that the crucial area of the brain is at the base of the skull, he won't fail to fire directly into it, he has always been something of a physical coward but this lies in the province of abstract logic. In "Last Days" he puzzles over the fact that in life *as it is actually lived* we feel very little genuine emotion: it is after an event, perhaps even years afterward, when we "remember," that we imagine we also "feel." *Hence an episode as it is actually lived (performed) may be without any emotion whatsoever.*

The elder of the two cantors has opened a prayerbook at the lectern and Rabbi Engelman has returned to his seat when Saul reasons that it is time to make his move. Lithe and unhesitating, though still somewhat hunched over, he rises and comes forward with the pistol in his hand. If he has worried that his voice won't be forced enough, that it will turn shrill at the climactic moment, he was mistaken—it is vibrant and manly beyond his most intoxicated dreams.

All who are gathered here this morning . . . an outrage and an abomination . . . a betrayal of the sacred heritage of . . . Deceit, worship of false gods, mendacity, hypocrisy . . . I alone raise my voice in protest . . . I alone utter the forbidden thought. . . . Did the Jews of Europe bring upon themselves the cruel justice of the Holocaust. . . . Do the Jews of the "New World" bring upon themselves . . .

He runs in the stinging swirling snow to hail the Greyhound bus as it is pulling away from the curb. He runs through the woods at dawn, in his green Windbreaker, not minding how the branches of trees and bushes claw against his face. ("Don't be so faint-hearted, time is running out," he says when he meets one of his numberless girls in a coffee shop on State Street and she professes shock at his bleeding forehead and cheeks. "Don't you know we're in the *last days* of this era—?") He's exhausted, he wants to press his face against his mother's breasts and burrow in deep, deep. He's exuberant, trotting out to I-95 by way of the back fields of the Fort Spear hospital grounds, an illicit $15 snug in his pocket. Who can stop him? What is the magic word that can stop him?

To the dazed congregation it must look as if Rabbi Engelman is welcoming him on the bimah. As if the performance has been rehearsed. "I know this young man," the rabbi says in a high stern courageous voice. "I know this young man and I trust him," he says, raising his voice to be heard over the murmurs, the isolated screams, the faint falling incredulous cries. Saul bounds up the steps to the bimah, to the sacred place, pistol raised like a scepter. He smiles calmly into a blur of light, a pulsing radiance in which no single face can be discerned. Why had he ever imagined fear, why had he ever imagined failure? He belongs to history now. Every syllable will be taped and preserved. "I know this young man and I trust him," the rabbi is saying, insisting. "I don't fear him. Please do as he says. Please do not anger him. Of course we are willing to listen to him, of course he may have the lectern and the microphone and our undivided attention. . . ."

The surrender of one generation to another, Saul thinks. The aged battered wolf, king of the pack, baring his throat to the fangs of the next king. "Thank you, Rabbi Engelman," he says in a strong formal voice.

He takes his speech of denunciation out of his pocket and begins to read.

Dale S————, though not present at Adath Israel this morning, will write an article called "The Enigma of Saul Morgenstern, Sacrificial Assassin," to be published in late May in the Sunday supplement of the larger of the two newspapers: a controversial piece that draws so much attention Dale is led to think (mistakenly, as it turns out) that he might have a career in journalism of a glamorous sort. Freddy C———— will revise a doctoral dissertation on the subject of "American assassinations" in which Saul Morgenstern is eventually relegated to a lengthy footnote—a reasonably well-received academic study published by Oxford University Press. Sol M———— tries for months to organize his thoughts on the subject of Morgenstern (did he despise Morgenstern from the very first, did he envy him his brash crazy style, did he think that "basically" Morgenstern was correct, did he think that in fact Morgenstern was insane?)—and eventually fails: *there is too much to say.* Denise E————, though on the periphery of Saul's "circle," writes an overlong impressionistic piece for the university paper, "The Tragedy of a Lost Soul." Rose P———— will stubbornly revise a short story over the years, presenting it in various awkward forms to writing workshops in the university's extension school, and rejecting all criticism with the angry rejoinder, "but it happened like this, *it happened exactly like this.*" Saul Morgenstern assassinated Rabbi Engelman of Adath Israel Congregation in full view of eight hundred people by shooting him point blank, three times: the fatal shot entering the brain through the left eye, at a slightly upward angle. Without hesitating he then turned the gun against himself, pressing the barrel just behind his right ear, and pulled the trigger. The impact of the blow sent him staggering backward. His legs spun beneath him, his wet shoes skidded, he fell heavily and never rose again. A witness cited in Rose's story says Saul Morgenstern "stood on tiptoe" when he pulled the trigger. His expression was tight and strained but "radiant." He fell about ten feet from the dying rabbi. His head was nearly touching the base of the Ark. A blood-tinted foam with bits of white matter began to seep from the wound in his head, and, dying, he started helplessly to vomit. At first he vomited bile and blood, and then just blood, a thick flow of blood, a powerful hemorrhage. . . . He was vomiting as he died. (But Rose P——— wasn't a witness. She isn't Jewish, she never was Saul's lover, she must have read about the assassination-suicide in the newspaper, like everyone else.)

Saul Morgenstern, the Scourge of G-d. His style is outrage tinged with irony and humor. "Black Humor" perhaps but humor nonetheless. He is a marvelous talker, a tireless spinner of anecdotes, tall tales, moral parables. With enviable agility he climbs the steps to the "sacred" space before the congregation. With a burst of extraordinary energy he hauls himself over a six-foot wall (littered with broken bottles, it is afterward claimed) while his friends stand gaping and staring. He risks death, he defies death, knowing himself immortal. The entire performance is being taped. Not a syllable, not a wince, will be lost. He has penciled in last-minute corrections in his fastidious hand, the manuscript awaits its public, he can hear beforehand the envious remarks of his friends and acquaintances and professors. Am I the Messiah, he wonders, with so many eyes upon me?—standing erect at the lectern, the pistol in one hand and the microphone in the other.

MY WARSZAWA: 1980

IN ROOM 371 of the Hotel Europejski in Warsaw a bellboy in a tight-fitting uniform is asking Carl Walser a question in English. But it is not an English Carl or Judith can comprehend—like Polish it slips and hisses, plunges too rapidly forward, comes too abruptly to a full stop. Does he want a larger tip? Judith thinks, puzzled, slightly angry (for she has brought to this beleaguered country hazy but stubborn ideas about the "people" and their integrity), is he offering them a service of some dubious sort—? She thinks of, but immediately rejects, two or three unpleasant possibilities.

The bellboy isn't of course a boy, he is perhaps thirty years old, smiling a strained unconvincing smile as if in the presence of fools or children, his nicotine-stained fingers making a prayerlike impatient gesture. As he repeats his question to Carl—only to Carl, he ignores Judith—Judith cannot stop from observing that his skin is remarkably oily, his teeth are gray and crooked, his eyes slightly crossed. (She has been noticing teeth in this part of Europe. East Europe. She suspects that her penchant for noticing details, for being struck in the face by details, will

soon become a curse, and is in any case a symptom of her Western frame
of mind—a hyperesthesia of the soul.)

"Yes? What? I can't quite—" Carl is saying, cupping his ear. His
high spirits at simply being here, in Poland, in Warsaw, in this "rep-
resentative" hotel, in this very room, have become strained by the
bellboy's persistence; Judith notices a slight trembling of his jaw. "If you
could repeat more slowly—"

"—Dollar," says the bellboy, grinning, now looking nervously from
Carl to Judith as if seeking her aid. He has given the word an odd intona-
tion but Judith certainly recognizes it. "Dollar—zloty—change—money
change?" In his outgrown costume—short green jacket, red collar and
cuffs, small tarnished brass buttons—he strikes a note both comic and
sinister.

Finally Carl understands. He says at once: "No thank you. Thank
you but *no*. And please get out of this room."

Judith is surprised at his sudden vehemence but the bellboy, sweat-
ing and smiling, appears not to understand. "Dollar, zloty?" he says,
gesturing with all his fingers, "—please money change?"

"Thank you, no," says Carl. "Will you leave—?"

The bellboy retreats, grinning and twitching, his gaze hopelessly out
of focus. If Judith knew which eye to engage she would signal the poor
man a look of courteous regret, sympathetic disapproval, something
adequate to the occasion; but the exchange has taken place rapidly. And
she is a little intimidated by her lover's high moral tone.

The incident of the "*agent provocateur*"—as they will call it after-
ward—leads at once into their first serious quarrel since leaving New
York. "Why were you so rude," Judith hears herself saying, so upset she
cannot unpack her suitcase, "—why did you treat him like that? You
can imagine how poor, how desperate he was—how we must appear to
them—" So the words spill out, righteous, quavering, though Judith has
vowed not to argue on this trip; though she has promised herself that
her behavior in Carl Walser's presence must accurately represent her
feeling for him.

Carl is hanging things in the closet methodically. Without troubling
to glance at her he says that she's being foolish, sentimental—they've

been warned against money changers a dozen times, *agents provocateurs* who can get them arrested. "You *don't* think that poor silly man was a police agent, do you?" Judith says incredulously. "That's ridiculous." Carl does not reply. (The official rate of exchange is 33 cents American currency to one zloty; on the black market, however, it is $1.50. And the German mark is even stronger.) "You don't *really* think so, you're just being cruel," Judith says.

As he sets his small portable typewriter on the bureau Carl says mildly, in the voice he knows will provoke Judith Horne into an outburst of indignant anger: "For all I know, for all *you* know, everyone we meet on this visit might be working for the police."

FORMIDABLE JUDITH HORNE, enviable, much-photographed: today she is wearing a black suede jump suit with innumerable zippers, slantwise across each breast, at her thighs, at each knee—one horizontal, the other vertical. Kidskin boots, gloves. (Warsaw is cold in May.) She is striking to the eye, aggressively casual; the Poles will not know how to interpret her. A woman, yes—but a *womanly* woman? She is wearing jewelry—three rings on her right hand, two rings on her left; and several necklaces—beautiful sullen-heavy silver that looks, and is, very expensive. Her gray eyes are wide-set in her strong (slightly Slavic?) face, her mouth in repose sometimes appears tremulous; but that, surely, is a misconception since Judith Horne thrives on combat, her profession as writer is almost exclusively combative, analytical, severe, resolutely unsentimental. Or so her reputation would have it.

Olive-dark skin, not yet visibly lined, clean of makeup; strong cheekbones; a strong squarish jaw; dark brown slightly coarse hair worn, for the European tour, in a braid that falls between her thin shoulder blades—a fashion stylish enough in the West but which might strike East European eyes (Judith isn't innocent of the possible confusion) as in some way, well, *peasant*. Her fingers are long and slender and restless; her mannerisms are abrupt. In public her voice is clear and dauntless as a bell. Her intelligence is bright, brittle, rarely in question, and then only by persons—almost always men—bitterly jealous of her reputation. (Judith Horne is clearly the most important member of the American delegation to this First International Conference on American Culture, for instance. Though only a few of her essays have been translated into Polish, and not one of her books is available here, the intellectual Poles seem to be agreeably familiar with her work, or at least with its dominant ideas.) She is a successful American—which is to say, simply, an *American*. With her passport she can travel anywhere. Her curiosity, her blunt questions, her skepticism, will never get her into official trouble: it's sobering to realize that Judith Horne, and Carl Walser, and Robert Sargent, and the other Americans "of literary distinction" who have come to Warsaw for the conference, can *never* get themselves into trouble . . . for anything they might say or write. Their defiance of their government might be published in foot-high headlines, or engraved in stone, and they will never be arrested or imprisoned or executed or even interrogated. So they appear formidable in their brazenness, their eerie invulnerability, like mythic creatures, demi-gods, or golems not quite possessed of souls. It is never clear how they are to be interpreted but it is always a possibility that they can prove helpful.

About Judith Horne there are two mysteries, not related. The first is spurious—*Is* she female in the classic sense of the word? The black jump suit armored with its zippers; the expensive but unpolished boots; the squarish combative jaw and the mouth that tightens rather than relaxes into a smile. . . . And her famous strong will. . . . Yet, there is the journalist Carl Walser, with whom she appears to be traveling. They are lovers, surely; though probably not married. But what precisely *is* the nature of their love?—A trivial mystery but one which engages some murmured speculation. Even in East Europe the private life is hardly over.

The second mystery: her background.

Horne is an English name, a nullity of a name. But Judith. *Judith.* Biblical, Semitic. . . .

And consider the woman's dark somewhat kinky hair, and her dark uneasy eyes; the edginess of her imagination. Her American fame too, with its New York City base. (Her Polish hosts have generously exaggerated all this, but no matter.) All of which suggests—the Biblical Judith, the Hebrew Judith.

(Judith intends to keep her background to herself, which seems to her nothing more than discretion in this part of the world. She sees no reason to burden her well-intentioned hosts with the dreary and possibly too-familiar recitation of facts—another American with Polish-Jewish ancestors, Polish-Jewish victims, come at last to visit Poland. And Judith thinks of herself as only obliquely Jewish anyway: she has some Jewish "blood," no more—remote aunts and uncles, cousins, who lived in a farming village northeast of Warsaw and who were shipped away (yes, all were shipped away) to die at Oświęcim; that is, Auschwitz. But Judith does not care to bring up the subject. Judith is not going to bring up the subject.)

THIRTY-THREE THOUSAND FEET above the earth, traveling east-ward in defiance of the sun, Judith found herself mesmerized by the cloud tundra above which the plane moved with so little apparent effort. In transit, in motion. America behind, Poland ahead. A fictitious sort of balance, Judith thinks: in size America is a continent, a complete world; in size Poland is New Mexico.

Beside her Carl Walser sits comfortably with his lightweight type-writer on his knees, recording notes, ideas, suggestions to himself. He will write—perhaps he has already begun to write—a story on the "atmosphere" of Poland; after Poland he will spend two weeks in West Germany, interviewing German citizens. What are their feelings about the presence of American GI's in their country—how do they feel about the recent arrests of drug dealers, the recent scandal involving so many GI's: heroin, hashish, cocaine, marijuana being sold to Germans, many of them teenagers. It will make a provocative story. It will stir questions, denials, outbursts. So Carl works steadily, with no mind for the extraor-dinary cloud landscape beyond the plane's broad wing. He has seen it all before.

Nor will Judith annoy him by calling his attention to it: they are not newlyweds, after all; they are not obliged to share every sensation.

The Awkward Age lies opened but unread in Judith's lap. A tragedy with the tone and pace of a comedy, or was it a comedy with the preten-sion of tragedy. . . . Since Judith Horne takes her reading very seriously there is a logic to the choice of Henry James vis-à-vis Communist Poland but at the moment she is too distracted to recall her motives. Thirty-three thousand feet above the earth it is sometimes difficult to recall any past intentions, any past self, at all.

Do you think you should risk it? Carl asked some weeks before. Meaning the visit to Warsaw. Of all places, Warsaw.

Judith was offended. You don't know me very well *yet*, do you, she said quietly.

As if she were Jewish—a Jewess!—*she*, Judith Horne.

SHE TAKES CARE not to think about that Jewish "blood" (whatever "blood" means); she takes care not to think, not to brood upon, Carl Walser, whom she loves with an emotion that is incalculable. Perhaps it is humiliating, demeaning, even futile; perhaps it is exhilarating; in any case it seems necessary. Carl Walser who is her friend before he is her lover, Carl Walser who is assuredly not "her" husband. . . . She argues with him about the issue of Jewishness, blood, ancestry, guilt. After all she is more directly, more *significantly*, English: the Hornes are from Manchester, her father and mother married young, it all took place a very long time ago, before 1935. They married in New York City and Judith was born in New York City and has lived there all her life, she isn't religious, she certainly isn't sentimental about the past. . . .

Are we arguing, Carl might ask. And Judith hears herself say—No, of course not. There is no issue about which we might argue.

BOUND FOR POLAND Judith found herself sleepless in the hours after takeoff, as uneasy as if she'd never flown before. She was the plane's only witness (so she imagined) to the 2 A.M. sunrise with its marvels of light. Carl slept heavily beside her and could not be nudged into waking.

One moment there was only dark—that "blackness ten times black"—and then, abruptly, the light appeared. The sun did not rise, it simply appeared, *And then there was light*. A rosy bronze deepening in the plane's massive wing . . . the sea of cloud gradually defining itself. The darkness dissolved, they were being hurtled east, plunging through time. It is an extraordinary experience no matter how often one lives through it. . . . Judith stared at the lunar landscape, the rivulets and gullies, the ravines, the abysses, and felt both elation (for it *was* sunrise, this *was* beauty) and a curious impersonal dread. What did human claims mean, after all, at such a height—what did "time" and "history" mean? The minuteness of personality, wisps of vapor contained precariously in human skulls—? Thirty-three thousand feet in the air it was possible to speculate that neither "Judith Horne" nor "Carl Walser" existed: and that "human love" was sheer vapor, the most illusory of cloud-formations.

Judith's sporadic reading in philosophy and Eastern religion allowed her to know that the very inhumanity of the universe is a consolation. But she felt no consolation, she felt only a bone-chilling loneliness. While her lover slept beside her, his breath arrhythmic and moist, one of his strong hands lying against her thigh. Other passengers, stirring from sleep, must have been annoyed by the dawn—they began to pull down their opaque shades. Of all the consolations, Judith thought, pulling down shades must be the most pragmatic.

SMOKE, coils of smoke, airless air heavy with smoke: in every Pole's fingers a burning cigarette: meeting rooms, restaurants, even on the street. A smoke-haze that stings Judith's eyes, permeates her clothing, makes her hair, her very skin smell. Even Carl, who smokes himself, is annoyed. "No ventilation, that's the problem," he says, "of course they can't afford such luxuries. . . ." Layers of smoke-cloud in the shabby coffee shop of the Europejski Hotel, drifting layers of smoke-cloud at the luncheon hosted by the Polish Writers' Union and *Literatura na Swiecie*. Even at the ambassador's residence, at the jammed cocktail reception. Ten o'clock in the morning, cigarettes and coils of smoke, vodka served in cylindrical glasses, the polished wood of meeting tables, tea served Russian style: a glass set on a silver holder, wedges of lemon; and always, in the background, tiptoeing, old Polish women carrying trays . . . carrying trays . . . meant to be subservient and unobtrusive but in fact extremely obtrusive . . . interrupting the flow of remarks with their profferings of tea and cream and sugar, vodka, cognac, warm mineral water; taking away ashtrays to empty them, bringing ashtrays back, fussy, vaguely maternal, *always* on hand. And in every Pole's fingers a burning cigarette.

"What do you make of it," Judith asks Robert Sargent, an American poet here for the conference, a slight but old acquaintance, sweet and mandarin and ostensibly apolitical (the only other conference Robert has been invited to, he claims, was a "Festival of the Arts" organized by the sister of the Shah of Iran some years ago—Robert accepted the invitation immediately, without question; attended the festival without precisely absorbing the climate of opinion surrounding Iran at that time; came away admirably innocent); "what do you make of the compulsive smoking, the drinking?" Judith asks.

Robert considers her question, frowning. His eyes are a pale frank childlike blue behind the round schoolboyish lenses of his glasses. His expression is contemplative, even fastidious. Then he says, sighing, that since the takeoff from Kennedy he has been in a peculiar state of consciousness and isn't altogether certain *what* he thinks about anything. Flying so terrifies him, Robert says, he takes three or four Valium; and on the plane he quickly has one or two—well, several—drinks; and after that he slides into—a rocky but uninterrupted oblivion. The change of time zones has certainly affected him too, he feels both inappropriately elated and sick, "high" and exhausted. No, he tells Judith, he hasn't been aware of smoke in Warsaw since fresh air, being drafty, often irritates his nostrils and provokes sneezing fits. "In a way I feel I am in my own element here," Robert says. "The delightful hotel like something out of an old film—the secret cocktail bar in the basement—don't you and Carl even *know* about it?—it isn't advertised, of course—and the Stalinist architecture, the shabby people, the long queues—the sense of time having stopped in the early Fifties, or, I suppose, in 1944; something in it appeals to me."

"You don't think the smoke is a political gesture?" Judith asks, nettled by Robert's dreamy calm.

"A political gesture . . . ?" says Robert, blinking, as if he has never heard of such a thing. He gives off an agreeable odor of alcohol and talcum powder. The tiny white lines radiating from his eyes suggest his age—forty-eight, fifty—but do not detract from his rapt boyish air. He repeats, savoring the words: "A *political* gesture . . ."

It is said of Judith Horne by her most severe critics that she lacks consciousness of herself: she pursues intellectual notions to the point of, say, the absurd, without knowing—or is it simply caring?—what she does. In truth Judith long ago decided to be merciless toward what might be called her social, her "womanly," self. She will not be waylaid by Robert Sargent's ingenuousness. "Yes, political," she says. "Smoking and drinking compulsively. In the Soviet Union it's said to be even worse. Here, it's smoking and drinking and religion. Haven't you noticed, Robert, our hosts are all *Catholic*?"

"All Catholic?"

"Catholic."

"Ah—*Roman* Catholic," says Robert. "The religion. Yes—very nice—quaint—I've been attracted to it myself off and on."

Judith waves away a cloud of smoke. Her throat constricts in anger. She says passionately: "The smoke-haze of Warsaw is no less political than the smoke-haze of their religion. This is a *tragic* nation."

"It is?" Robert says, startled.

WEEKS AGO Carl said to Judith in her apartment on Eleventh Street as they sat drinking coffee with their lives in snarls and knots about them, as usual: "Do you really think you should risk it, Judith?"

"Risk what?" Judith asked irritably. "Please don't speak in riddles."

"The Polish tour," he said. "Ten days in Warsaw."

His voice was uncharacteristically light, his manner uncharacteristically gallant. Judith perceived that her lover's normal ironic tone was now in suspension; which meant that he was being careful with her. He was being *nice*. "Yes?" she said. "What about it? Do you prefer to go alone?"

"That isn't what I mean, Judith."

"Then what do you mean?"

Carl was a former foreign service officer—he'd quit both because of the Vietnam War and because the State Department was going to ship him to Reykjavík, Iceland—who knew a great deal about international

politics and had a way, sometimes charming, sometimes not, of hint-
ing that he knew much more. So that his pretense that night of being
vaguely baffled was all the more suspect. "What do I *mean* . . . ? Or
what have I *said*. . . ."

Rain was drumming on Judith's window. *Her* window, *her* apart-
ment—they had experimented with living together on several occasions,
but none had been a success; Judith appeared capable of making the
effort—the sacrifice—of having no real private sanctuary in her life, but
Carl, who had lived alone for too long and who cherished his loneliness,
evidently could not. Though he protested that he loved her—he *really*
did love her. It was invariably Carl who wanted to try again.

Do you think you should risk it, he asks casually. As if he doesn't
know Judith at all.

Because she is silent he continues, as if arguing, quietly, calmly:
"You've sometimes been upset by circumstances, haven't you. And this
Warsaw conference—Poland—your family background—"

"You're provoking me," Judith says carefully.

"I'm preparing you. Preparing us."

She refuses to look at him. At such moments the anxiety of her love
for him—for his remorseless authority—is so keen, she believes that the
slightest touch of his hand would cause her to burst into angry tears.
Rigid she sits apart, rigid she holds her head high. A swan's graceful
neck—so an interviewer once noted, apparently without irony. Does
she compel Carl Walser with her beauty? Or is her beauty entirely ficti-
tious? (Lovers, Judith knows very well, flatter each other innocently and
shamelessly. But when love is withdrawn the flattery too is withdrawn:
You aren't *really* so exceptional. So beautiful, so graceful, so wise. You
aren't *really* going to live forever.)

". . . has a tragic history, I think we can agree on that," Carl is saying
reasonably. "I've been in Warsaw several times—it's a somber place.
Something is clearly going to happen to them soon and whatever it is,
it won't be pleasant, it won't be *Polish* as they might wish it. And over
their shoulders is the Uprising. They can't forget. The wounds are that
fresh. It's all very real—they loathe and are terrified of Germans. To
hear them talk you'd imagine that anti-Semitism is an invention of Ger-

mans and Russians exclusively. Unless of course you know something about Polish history."

"I think you exaggerate my weakness," Judith says.

"You are hardly a weak woman," Carl says.

"My sensitivity, then. My 'femininity.' "

"East Europe is a strain on anyone's nerves," Carl tells her. "The more sensitive you are, the more strain. Furthermore——"

Judith cannot resist interrupting. "Do you know, Carl, there was a pogrom in my family's village outside Warsaw, in 1946."

Carl sips at his coffee, wincing.

"1946," Judith says.

Carl sets down his cup, makes a whistling sound, as if it were expected of him. "In *1946*? For Christ's sake why?"

"Not why—we know why," Judith says. She is trembling with dignity, control. "We always know why. The question here isn't *why* but *how*."

JUDITH, late for a meeting with the Polish Writers' Union, is striding toward a glass door, a double door. In her stylish jump suit, chains about her neck, she is hurrying, staring at the pavement, her brain jammed with shards of thought. And Polish words. Polish syllables. That dizzying cascade of Polish *sounds*—a mountain stream breaking and crashing about her head, scintillating, teasing, utterly unintelligible. Though one of her guides has been trying patiently to teach her a few elementary expressions she seems incapable of remembering from one day to the next. For one who lives so intensely in language, with such customary control, it is unnerving to journey into a country whose language is so very foreign. Not a word, not a phrase, is familiar; even the hand gestures— lavish, stylized—confuse her. If she were in France, or Italy, or Spain—if she were in Germany—she would feel immediately at home.

She strides along the dirty pavement, her leather shoulder bag swinging at her side. The morning is cold; damply cold; melancholy. She is acquiring a reputation for always being late for meetings, luncheons, dinners. Precisely why she cannot say: elsewhere Judith Horne is known for being punctual. But there are so *many* meetings and luncheons and dinners. . . . Always, it seems, she is hurrying; always, she is about to be late. Toweling her long thick hair dry in the hotel room, in the dismal bathroom, dressing hurriedly while Carl waits, rattling the oversized keys to the room. "They're going to misunderstand," he says, "—they'll think you're being disrespectful. Why can't you get ready on time?"—a husbandly question, of course; and quite reasonable.

Judith cannot explain. She does not know why she isn't herself here, in this particular place, when she has traveled widely since the age of twenty—when she has boasted of being most comfortable while traveling, in motion. She doesn't know why she feels so edgy here, so obsessed by melancholy thoughts. The architecture (which should interest her) depresses her; the smoky air (to which she should have become accustomed by now) makes her sick; the odor of fried onions, the sight of Pepsi-Cola bottles everywhere, displayed on banquet tables like bottles of French wine, the half-fearful half-brazen references to Soviet Russia ("The light doesn't always shine from the East!"—the boldest statement she has heard a Pole utter), the shabby hotel room in the shabby hotel, the very look of the overcast sky. . . . Judith cannot tell him that she feels unreal; a fiction; an impostor; shaking so many strangers' hands, smiling and being smiled at in return. She feels weak. She feels Jewish at last. And womanly—in the very worst sense of the word.

A Jew, a woman, a victim—can it be?

"Robert is later than I am most of the time," she says sullenly, as if reporting on a favored brother. "And that woman from the State Department—"

"Marianne Beecher? But I don't think it's the State Department exactly. Some education foundation—"

"She's always late. She's always begging so very prettily to be *forgiven*."

"Judith, the issue isn't Marianne but you," Carl says.

The very equanimity of his remark infuriates her. She tells him she can't help it. She hurries—but she's late. It's like a stereotypical dream situation in which she hurries in order to be late. She can't sleep until four in the morning—is awakened at six—tries to sleep again—falls into a light groggy sleep beset by violent dreams—then he shakes her awake and it's almost nine o'clock and they're late again, late *again*. Yes it's her fault but she doesn't know why unless she is breaking down.

Carl gives her a look both censorious and fearful. For what if she does break down . . . ?

She strides toward the glass door, ten minutes late for whatever has been scheduled for 10:30 A.M. The door is an automatic door which will open, must open, when she breaks a certain invisible force-field. She is late but she means no disrespect (should she apologize?—or maintain her dignity?); she is late but she isn't precisely ill. Impossible to blame her hotel, or Poland itself. . . . Her amiable guides Tadeusz and Miroslav are parking the car up the street. They have just brought her from the modest office of her Polish publishers where she received, with some ceremony, her Polish royalties, held in trust for her in Warsaw these many years. (Several "classic" essays of Judith's have been translated for anthologies of American writing of the Sixties and Seventies.) Six thousand four hundred and twenty-three zlotys!—which must be spent before she leaves Poland.

Judith naively believed that the money was worth far more than it actually was. The senior editor of the publishing house, and an elderly female clerk, and Tadeusz, and Miroslav, and one or two others—all stood watching as she signed papers in triplicate, as if this were a significant (an historic?) moment. Six thousand four hundred and twenty-three zlotys paid to the author Judith Horne: how will she spend it?—what will she do, suddenly wealthy? She must give gifts to them all, she must treat people to dinners, gaily she will spend the zlotys, but how much, precisely, are they worth? Though she knows vaguely of the rate of exchange something childlike and hopeful in her leaps at the very thought of so much . . . cash.

She glances up to see her hurrying reflection in the door. Tadeusz is calling out: "Miss Horne!"

She had been about to walk head-on into the door.

She had been about to walk into it, thinking (but why?) that it is a seeing-eye door, that it would open automatically with her approach.

"Thank you, Tadeusz," she says, her face burning, "I was distracted, I—I wasn't thinking."

She pushes the door open. As if nothing were unusual. As if she hadn't come within a hair's breadth of crashing into plate glass and seriously injuring herself.

A DROLL LITTLE INCIDENT to report to Carl, she thinks.

Unless of course she had better not report it to Carl.

HERE IS the Old Town District, restored since the devastation of 1944; here is Castle Square; Market Square; the Adam Mickiewicz Museum (where Judith and the other smiling Americans are presented with a bilingual edition of Mickiewicz's *Complete Poems*). Weatherstained monuments, churches, cathedrals. Rococo statues of the Virgin, a stone effigy of the head of St. John the Baptist. Medieval alleyways, a Gothic guardhouse, nineteenth-century street lamps, plaster facades, vaulted gates, forged iron doorcases, barrel-organs. All very beautiful, Judith thinks, staring, deeply moved in a way she cannot recall having been moved before; not knowing in which direction her emotions might rush next. Her Polish guides are young and enthusiastic and rather shy; she suspects they feel extremely vulnerable—for what if their "distinguished" American visitors don't praise this rebuilt district?—what if they murmur only a few courteous pleasantries, and move on? Judith reads a plaque aloud, in its heroic entirety: Market Square of the Old Town Monument of National Culture and Revolutionary Struggle of the People of Warsaw Turned to Ruins by Fascist Occupants in 1944 Raised from Ruins and Returned to the Nation by the Government of People's Poland in the Years 1951–1953.

They pass by the Jesuit Church, so jammed with worshippers at this hour of the evening (8 P.M.) that people are standing out on the cobblestone street, in a light cold drizzle. Judith and Carl try to listen to the priest, who is giving an impassioned sermon—in Polish of course—his words amplified by a loudspeaker. How young he sounds, and his voice so melodious, and intelligent, and reasonable!—Judith listens with her head bowed. There is such passion in the young Jesuit's voice, such urgency, she halfway feels that, at any moment, the language will yield its mystery to her: she will understand, and her life will be transformed.

BUT THEIR RELIGION, Judith thinks, what of their religion—the Roman Catholic Church. The Church of bigotry, racism, pogroms.

It puzzles and alarms her that all their guides—these wonderful bright young literary people—declare themselves Catholic. Tadeusz and Miroslav and Andrzej and Jerzy and Maria and Elizbieta. They are proudly, defiantly Catholic.

"Aren't there any Communists in Poland?" Carl joked at a small dinner at the ZZPK Club honoring the Americans. But no one laughed. After a moment Jerzy said, squinting through a cloud of smoke: "No, Mr. Walser, but there are many police."

Tadeusz is working on a doctoral degree in linguistics at Warsaw University; Miroslav, the recent father of a baby girl, does night-school teaching—Polish, English, French—and freelance translations. Andrzej and his wife are both high school teachers who live with Andrzej's parents in one of the crowded high-rise apartment buildings in the suburbs; they have been waiting for an apartment of their own for—eleven years. Jerzy is a junior editor in a textbook publishing house; Maria, one of Judith's favorites, is an American studies scholar, a graduate student who has visited the States (she spent a year at the University of Iowa). Elizbieta, who looks so very young, is married, has a four-year-old son, teaches whenever she can get a course and does freelance translations too; she is highly enthusiastic about a project she hopes to begin as soon as the conference is over—the translation of Jane Austen's *Emma* into Polish. Please don't ask if they would like to study abroad, in the States for instance, the embassy people cautioned Judith and the other delegates, you'll only arouse their hopes . . . of course they would like to leave Poland.

Nevertheless, talk drifts in that direction. Perhaps the young Poles initiate it themselves.

Travel abroad, to United States . . . England . . . Sweden . . . Italy.

To be awarded a fellowship for study abroad, to be invited to the West for a semester or a year—the young people agree quietly that this would be wonderful for them, for their careers and their lives.

But the competition is very strong, Miroslav murmurs. The awards go to professors, important editors. Older men.

Tadeusz agrees that there isn't much chance for people like them. "We must be realistic," he says, sighing, coughing as he smokes, "—my brother, for instance—he defected to Stockholm on *his* year away—so it would be impossible for me to get a visa now; forever, I am afraid, it will be impossible."

Discreetly, the Americans query the Poles about the Communist Party—that is, the Polish United Workers Party—and about the Soviet Union. What of censorship, repression, arrests . . . ? But the Poles are reluctant to speak. And Judith quite understands: Carl has been saying since their arrival that there are certainly police spies involved in the conference, and that their guides, however friendly they appear to be, will be interrogated afterward. "I suppose they might even inform upon one another," Judith said slowly, as if such a thing were really impossible and Carl would refute her at once. But he said nothing. He may have laughed.

No, Judith thinks, watching their faces—Tadeusz, and Miroslav, and Maria, and Andrzej, and Jerzy, and Elizbieta—no, these young people are genuine, these young people are *ours*.

"*AREN'T* THERE ANY COMMUNISTS IN Poland?" Robert Sargent asks, slightly drunk, disappointed, "—I was anticipating all sorts of attacks, like the kind I get back home—you know, that I and my art are degenerate—hermetic—Mannerist. But no one here has read my poetry, it seems. And everyone likes me!" He smiles his marvelous dazed smile and blinks at Judith through his schoolboy lenses. "When I said that the United States is an imperialist nation—we *are*, aren't we?—sweet little Miroslav shrugged his shoulders and said, Who is better? And they are all Catholic, Judith, as you saw—it's so wonderfully *bizarre*."

Judith tells him soberly: "Their religion is all they have, Robert. When one can't move horizontally, one must move vertically."

CHURCH BELLS are forever ringing across the city, young priests stride along the narrow streets, Masses are always overflowing out onto the sidewalks. Judith tries not to think: censorship, repression, contempt for women, anti-Semitism, pogroms. Yes there have always been pogroms and today the nation is (as an official inadvertently bragged) 97% pure.

The young people absorb nothing of their guests' bewilderment at all this religion, this conspicuous faith. In fact they are eager to know—What do Americans think of the Pope? Pretty blond Marianne from the arts foundation in Washington, far more skilled at diplomacy than her face and her clothes and her finishing-school manners suggest, elects to speak quickly for the American contingent, before anyone else can reply. The Pope is very popular of course. Intelligent, remarkable, world leader, international stature, extraordinary. A force for morality and justice and freedom in the world. A force for good.

With a shy smile Jerzy points out that there are millions of Poles in the States, which might account for his popularity there. And Marianne says at once, "Not at all—certainly not—Americans all admire the Pope immensely. He *is* an extraordinary man."

Judith considers saying a few words. She has been uncharacteristically silent for hours. Moody, disoriented, not "quite right"—a consequence perhaps of the transatlantic flight, loss of sleep. But if she begins speaking she might not be able to stop. What of the Church and Polish history, Jews, discrimination, mass graves, death. . . .

(Carl senses her agitation. He has told her, as if she required telling, that religion for the Poles means *Poland. Poland* and not *Russia.* Their own history and their own language—it's as simple as that. "A church of hatred—of rot," Judith says. "Yes," says Carl. "But their own.")

Still, consider the young priests in their ankle-length black skirts, fresh-shaven, handsome, swinging along the streets—isn't there something engaging about them, something fascinating? Judith stares, stares. At one point, in a group including Robert Sargent, the two of them happen to exchange a glance; and she realizes that she has been looking upon these young men with the startled appreciation of a male homosexual.

They are shown madonnas everywhere—in niches, in courtyards, on pedestals. And the Soviet-built Palace of Culture in the center of the city—a rainstreaked monstrosity with Byzantine spires and domes—Stalinist chic—a dingy wedding cake about to collapse. "You can see why people fall in love with East Europe," Carl says expansively, "—everything is so sad here, even the jokes and the laughter are sad, people want *uplifting.* They want us. Westerners on the streets milling about in the lobbies of hotels, eager to change hard currency into zlotys. . . . They like us well-heeled Americans almost as much as they like the well-heeled Germans."

"That's an absurd thing to say," Judith says.

"I thought it was a vicious thing to say," Carl laughs.

The smoke-haze, cigarettes burning in fingers, slanted between lips, everywhere. The odor of fried onions. The tolling church bells, worshippers hurrying again to Mass, in a shabby courtyard off a side street near the University an extraordinary sight: a sooty-skinned madonna and child in a niche about eight feet above the pavement, both plastic flowers and real tulips—red tulips—arranged before it. Elizbieta explains, "The Virgin—she is protecting the people who live here, especially. I mean—they believe in *her,* in her power. To protect them."

"I see," Judith says.

"They are perhaps slightly superstitious," the young woman says, smiling, looking from Judith to Carl as if to gauge their feelings. "I mean—in this district. But it is something they believe strongly in, the statue."

"Yes," says Carl, "but why is the Virgin black?—she *is* black, isn't she?"

Elizbieta considers the question. The Madonna is dusky-skinned but not otherwise Negroid; and the infant in the crook of her arm is clearly a northern European—a Polish?—baby. Judith finds herself moved by the ugly plastic flowers, the red tulips wilted and brown, the shadowy dirt of the little niche, the impoverishment of the tenement building. If she draws a deep breath—which she will not—she will smell the perpetual odors of grease, potatoes, onions, damp. She is moved too by young Elizbieta's shy smile in which there is a margin, however subtle, of pride.

"Oh I would say . . . I would think the people found this statue . . . somewhere or other, like a store with old things, you know . . . maybe in rubble, debris. You question because she is black?—yes, but probably this is the only statue of the Virgin and Child they could get. The people who live here, I mean. They are very specially devoted to her, you see."

"Are they?" Judith says, staring at the Virgin's dark chipped eyes.

"Yes," says Elizbieta. "All of us. For she does protect."

IN THE ELEGANT DRAWING ROOM of the residence of the United States deputy chief of mission the American conferees are being introduced at last to a number of Polish dissident writers. Judith notes that all eight are men—are there no dissident women?

Her question results in a mumbled reply, an air of vague irritation, that does not inspire her to ask it again.

She finds herself in a spirited conversation with a tall sad-eyed man of middle age who publishes translations under a pseudonym. He will not tell her, but she has learned beforehand that he was fired from his teaching position at the University, and can no longer publish under his own name, as a consequence of his criticism of the government. Nor will he tell her that he lives in a single room—a hovel, really—in a crowded tenement building. Instead they talk of the Soviets, the Polish "people," recent events in West Germany.

She is introduced to Wladislaw, Witold, Andrzej. The enormous drawing room has begun to fill up with smoke. There is vodka, there is cognac, there is strong black tea. A servant appears and disappears, discreetly; a man whose expression is totally neutral. Judith, drinking her third cup of tea, notes that her saucer and teacup rattle—are her hands trembling that badly?

She resists watching her lover at such times, in crowded social gatherings. Of course he is eloquent, wise, warm, funny, argumentative, even a little bullying. She loves him and is humiliated by her love for him and will not observe him at such times, any more than he pauses to observe her. Explain to me about Werblan, Judith says to one of the Poles: Werblan, a notorious high-ranking Communist. And what of Khoyetzki. And Konwicki, whose fiction, translated, she has read with great admiration. . . .

Robert Sargent, cheeks flushed with drink, draws Judith over to another corner. He and a young American documentary filmmaker named Brock have become involved in a noisy general conversation with three Poles and a member of the U.S. embassy—the cultural attaché, in fact, who has arranged this important meeting. Unfortunately the Poles know only rudimentary English; everything must be translated. Judith, whose natural speaking voice is rapid, has to force herself to speak slowly . . . slowly. Is the situation worsening, or does it remain static? she asks, squinting against the smoke. Is there any logic to it? Is it true you're forbidden to own duplicating machines?—you can't even print up wedding or funeral announcements without the censor's seal of approval? And will there be—here Judith draws a deep breath, then decides, yes, she will ask—"Will there ever be open rebellion?"

The talk shifts to Brodsky, that envied hero. What of Günter Grass, what of Bienkowski. Judith nods, speaks animatedly, tries to absorb not only all that is being said but all that is being indicated. She shakes hands. She is being touched on the elbow, turned another way, introduced, drawn into another discussion. She tries not to note how, in any conversational group, the dissidents direct their questions primarily to the American men—any men at all—even the junior staff members of the embassy. She will save up for retelling back in the States, when the anger is safely subsided, an anecdote about being questioned by one of the dissidents about her relationship to the conference—she is Mr. Sargent's secretary, perhaps? She is Carl Walser's assistant?

"No," Judith said flatly, and refused to elaborate.

"No? *Not?*"

"No."

A "discharged" editor of a philological journal, a "discharged" professor of economics, a white-haired gentleman (a poet) who has been arrested eleven times in the past several years: the U.S. embassy people seem quite keen on him. Judith is led forward to meet a prominent culture critic, the editor of the country's leading Catholic journal. His handshake is strong, vigorous, and Judith's is no less forthright.

They talk for a while of Miroslav Khoyetzki, who became famous for having been arrested for the twenty-first time a few weeks previously. By applying different articles of the criminal code the police were able to legally take from his apartment: tins of meat, a jar of curry sauce, a pair of scissors, blank paper, a typewriter, jazz recordings, scientific journals. He is charged with publishing illegally—bringing out books banned by the censor. Is he in jail now, Judith asks. What will happen to him?

Judith excuses herself, the smoke is so thick. In the bathroom—which is modern, elegant, very clean, "American"—she studies her face in the mirror without affection and decides that her sallow skin and the shadows beneath her eyes emphasize her Semitic blood. I know your position on censorship by the Communists, she will ask the dissidents—but what is your position on censorship by the Church?

She returns to the room but does not ask the question. Nearby, Carl is talking animatedly with a frizzy-haired youngish Pole, one of the translators, and close beside him stands Marianne Beecher, of whom it is whispered that she is a spy—she travels about East Europe spying on foreign service people for their mutual employer, the State Department. But her official identity has to do with a science foundation—or is it education—or the arts—and Judith must not underestimate the woman's intelligence simply because she is so very beautiful. That madonna's face, that air of half-surprised wonder, that exquisite blond hair. She is wearing a linen suit, deep pink; a pale gray silk blouse; gold earrings; fingernail polish; high heels; her legs are lovely, slender. And it's clear that she has done her homework before attending this party.

Judith observes to an American diplomat that Poland doesn't seem to be a Communist country at all—it's an occupied country.

He agrees. The very air is poisoned, isn't it?

Isn't it!—now Judith knows why she has been feeling ill for days.

They speak together in an undertone, like conspirators. He says: "Even when these people talk openly, as they are now, you can sense the contamination, the fear. They can't really trust anyone—not even one another."

Judith sees the sad pouched eyes, the bracketed mouths. Courageous, stubborn men. But they too can be broken, as history has shown. "Tragic" Poland. The Uprising of 1944, Hitler's command that Warsaw must be completely destroyed, razed to the ground. How could any Pole forget?

How *dare* any Pole forget? Even the younger people—born as late as the very Sixties—refer to 1944 as if it had taken place only a few years ago.

And in our country, Judith thinks, history is something that happened only a few weeks ago—or didn't happen.

THE RECEPTION continues. One reception blends into the next: vodka, cognac, cherry cheesecake, a second trip to the bathroom (Judith's nose is oily, her eyes bloodshot from the smoky air, her nerves strung tight), a convoluted tale about the Polish P.E.N. which "discriminates" against its own young people. The translators, it seems, never cooperate with one another; they're jealous, suspicious, selfish; often they won't even reveal what their projects are. "Sad," agrees Marianne Beecher, glancing at her jeweled little watch.

It is said of Marianne Beecher that she has a Ph.D. in art history, other degrees in psychology and economics, she has traveled virtually everywhere for the State Department. In this room of dour hangdog men in ill-fitting suits the vision of Marianne is almost disconcerting. (That morning in the Europejski coffee shop she entertained a table of fellow Americans with tales of how she is continually mistaken for a Polish prostitute. "It's my hair," she said, laughing irritably, "—and the fact that I'm usually without an escort." She told of a Japanese businessman in the hotel who seated himself near her in the lobby the other morning and pushed a fifty-dollar bill, an American bill, in her direction. When she failed to respond he added another fifty. Finally she got up, walked away, too furious to speak. "What I should have done was take his money," Marianne said, "—just put it in my purse and walk away. That arrogant little bastard!")

Now Marianne and the cultural attaché draw Judith into a conversation about current party leadership in Poland. The word Stalinist is used. Allusions to Czechoslovakia, Hungary . . . remember the uprising of 1956. . . . Judith says impulsively: "Please, is there anything we can do to help? I mean we Americans—could we form a committee, could we write about your situation and publicize it—more than it has been publicized—could we finance trips to the States, or Sweden?—England?"

The cultural attaché is pleased at Judith's remarks but cautions her in an aside: these particular men, after all, cannot get visas to the West.

"Yes," says Judith, embarrassed. "Of course not. I realize that."

The Poles are listening intently, hungrily. It is the first time they have looked at Judith Horne as she is accustomed to being looked at, in her own sphere—as if she had significance, as if she possessed power. The cultural attaché is saying: ". . . anything you might do back home, of course . . . you might work directly with P.E.N. . . . you might donate some money to the Index on Censorship in London, and get your friends to donate too. . . . In fact I can deliver mail to certain individuals if you send it to me in care of the embassy," he says. "Our post office box is New York City. I'll give you my card."

"Yes," says Judith. "Thank you. I want to do whatever I can."

The dissidents continue to stare at her as her words are translated. Judith smiles, smiles. She has never smiled so much. Finally they smile at her in return, offer to shake her hand again. "I want to do whatever I can," she hears herself say.

WAITING FOR CARL, propped up in bed, reading *The Awkward Age*.

Twice this evening the telephone has rung—the bell jingles, twitters, but no one is calling. Carl is away at a meeting of Polish filmmakers which Judith, unsteady on her feet, decided to miss. Now she is alone, and rather lonely. Now she has time in which to contemplate her predicament.

The "awkward age" in James's novel is an entire era, an entire swath of idle English society; it also refers specifically to the age of a young woman—no longer a girl—as she steps into the adult world, not very prepared. She has no vocation, no fate, no life except marriage. Nanda *must* marry.

And must I? Judith thinks.

Except for the fact that she has outlived her girlhood by many years. She has outlived—defiantly, bravely—the period of her availability.

A number of men have loved her and she has loved them, or some of them, in return. (There have even been one or two women—but never mind.) Now, in love with Carl Walser, her vanity is pricked by the fact that she is not loved in return quite so much as she loves: not pound for pound, ounce for ounce. Her passion must be greater than Carl's because her ferocity is far greater. Consequently she hates him and often fantasizes his death.

Lately she thinks of herself as a mourner—lamenting her youth, her nearly forgotten Jewish blood, the sick sad futile sentiment of being *female*. She has wanted only to be a woman of independent means—a woman secure in a public career, a formidable public reputation—a woman whose name is comfortably *known*: and all this she has, and more. Her books and articles bring her a steady income, she tours the United States each spring giving lectures (and her fee is not modest), she has only to pick up a telephone or write a letter or make inquiries and an academic appointment would be offered her at once . . . at least as a visiting professor. She is a thoroughly successful woman in a bitterly competitive field yet now, lately, her thoughts have fastened helplessly upon Carl Walser. Does she want only a life shared with him, *conventional* in every sense of the word . . . ?

Fortunately, she thinks ironically, I'm almost too old to have children. *That* temptation is nearly past.

Again the telephone almost rings, and again no one is on the line.

"Yes? Who is it? What do you want—?" Judith cries.

It is twelve-thirty and Carl is late returning from the meeting.

Carl is very late: hadn't he said he'd be back by eleven?

Earlier today Judith gave a highly successful lecture at the University. Three hundred students had crowded into a tiered auditorium to hear her. There were professors, a gratifying contingent from the U.S. Embassy, there were newspaper and magazine reporters. Judith Horne the distinguished American writer. Judith Horne the distinguished American cultural critic. A handsome dark-haired woman in a gray corduroy jacket and gray slacks, a white turtleneck sweater, hiding her nervousness by walking briskly to the podium, exchanging light laughing remarks with her Polish hosts. She felt exhilarated, elated—a sign of panic, perhaps—and her cheeks were flushed, her eyes bright. She was no longer precisely a beautiful woman but she was certainly striking. *The distinguished American woman of letters Judith Horne . . .*

Carl couldn't attend, he'd been elsewhere, interviewing two Poles involved in the "Flying University"—an informal and indeed illegal organization that offered courses late at night on subjects forbidden by the official universities. These days, in any case, Carl was being patient with her—watchful, cautious.

Having an audience was a marvelous tonic for Judith. She spoke with her customary passion and authority, she knew she was doing well, being admired, her words taking root. The topic was broad enough— Contemporary American Culture—but Judith chose to surprise her listeners by talking about censorship in America, church-inspired, state-inspired, marketplace-inspired. It did not escape her notice that her Polish audience was *very* interested.

Yes, there was censorship in the States. But it was oblique, informal, indirect.

Making her points Judith felt her voice gain strength, she felt how forcefully she was convincing her audience. And afterward the applause was gratifying—really, rather overwhelming. Even the embassy people clapped. (For Judith Horne had the reputation of being quirky, provocative, provoking—there was no telling what she might say. It wasn't until hours later that Judith realized she had totally forgotten to speak of censorship by the Roman Catholic Church. . . .)

"I hear it went beautifully," Carl said, rummaging in his suitcase for something. "I hear everyone was impressed. Why did you worry?"

"Did I worry?—I don't remember worrying," Judith said.

She ran both hands roughly through her hair, which needed shampooing again. The air of Warsaw was so polluted, so filthy . . . but she loathed the shabby little bathroom.

"I hope you weren't disappointed that I couldn't make it," Carl said.

"Of course not."

Idly, Judith took the bouquet of flowers from the bureau—six red roses, baby's breath, daisies, carnations—and dropped it into the wastebasket, container and all.

"Why did you do that?" Carl asked, staring.

"I don't like flowers," Judith said.

"What do you mean?—of course you like them."

"I don't deserve them."

Carl stood with his hands on his hips, staring at Judith as if he'd never seen her before. There was a tiny red nick on the underside of his jaw—he'd shaved for the second time that day.

Judith went on, not quite coherently. "I don't like flowers, I don't like the assumption behind them—a woman is presented publicly with a bouquet—a woman is obliged to be grateful—" She paused and made a wriggling gesture with her fingers. "It's such a masquerade."

After a moment Carl turned back to his suitcase. He rarely troubled to unpack his suitcases of small items—underwear, socks—even when he was staying in one hotel room for a week or more. Consequently he was always rooting about, rummaging impatiently.

". . . I don't feel I deserve them," Judith said.

"Well, all right. But you're being ridiculous."

"I don't *want* them."

Carl found what he was looking for and went into the bathroom and closed the door.

Now the telephone is ringing, full-throated. Judith pushes aside *The Awkward Age*, picks up the receiver, says quickly, "Carl?—hello?" But of course it isn't Carl. A man, a stranger, is speaking in a language she cannot comprehend. She tries to explain that he must have the wrong number but of course he can't understand, he persists, seems to be trying to argue. "You have the wrong number," Judith says, suddenly furious. *"Please leave me alone."*

LONG LINES IN CENTRUM and in the other downtown stores. Futile for Judith to shop there, simply to spend her zlotys, and in any case the goods look second-rate, shoddy. Long queues at fruit stands: withered lemons, small shriveled apples in outdoor bins. The ugly Palace of Culture dominates the skyline. SMAK bars, SPOOTEM restaurants, signs for Pepsi-Cola and Coke and Hot Dogs. Church steeples with graceful Moorish lines. (Which is the church in which Chopin's heart is said to be buried—Judith must visit it.) Red trolley cars, red buses, hurtling along the streets, emitting their poisonous exhaust. Crowds, noise, rain in the morning and sunshine at noon, a pervasive chill. Cobblestone streets. Monuments. The elegant Park Lazienkowski. The Palace Marszatkowska.—How many Jews live in Warsaw at the present time? Judith asks, and her guide Tadeusz replies, There are no statistics.

Driven from place to place, from meeting to meeting, in a handy Boy Scout sort of van owned by the U.S. Embassy, or in Soviet-built Fiats—perky little vehicles possessing the size and grace of tin bathtubs. (Judith's teeth rattle, the cobblestone streets are not easy to navigate.) Where was the Jewish ghetto? Judith asks, and one day, finally, she and Robert Sargent are driven to it—but there's nothing to see except pavement, high-rise apartment buildings, a monument. "When you say that Warsaw was completely rebuilt," Judith tells the Poles, "you don't of course mean *completely*—the ghetto wasn't rebuilt."

The monument to the Warsaw ghetto is rectangular, made of a lightless tearstained stone. Five prominent figures, all male; heroic; "noble"; with muscular chests and arms; *very* male. (A female in the background, emerging feebly from stone. Judith recognizes the figure as female because it is equipped with breasts and carries a terrified baby.) It hardly needs to be pointed out that the heroic stone figures boast a craggy Aryan look—not a Jew in their midst.

Robert Sargent tries, and fails, to take a picture of the monument; but the film is jammed in his camera. Judith can't make it work either. "Mechanical things lose their ability to function in my hands," Robert tells her, "—I don't think it has anything to do with this place."

JUDITH MAKES OTHER, persistent inquiries about the number of Jews in Warsaw, and this time the answer is more helpful: Maybe seven . . . hundred? . . . seven hundred fifty? . . . but very few children. Perhaps no children.

HER TEETH RATTLING in the Soviet-built cars, her senses stung by something acrid in the air. *Is* there a poison here?—but what is it?—where? Judith doesn't care to be morbid or sentimental; she really

isn't the kind of person who feeds personal hungers with grandiose
"historical" notions. That is cheap, that is unworthy of her intelligence.
Warsaw is a city that was destroyed by the Nazis but rebuilt itself—
almost completely. Look at Old Town, they are justified in being proud
of Old Town. Judith and Carl stroll through it in the early evening,
grateful to be alone after a day of meetings, receptions, speeches, hand-
shakes, smoke-filled rooms, cognac, tea with lemon, smiles disclosing sad
stained teeth . . . grateful for the open cobblestone square, the freedom
from traffic and exhaust. The facades of the buildings on the market
square are almost *too* perfect. Less absurdly ostentatious than the Grand
Place of Brussels, but touristy nonetheless—almost "quaint"—hand-
some olive greens and pale russets and gray and brown and subdued red
brick: all very clean, very neat. Too bad the Soviets are bleeding these
people white, Carl observes. They could fix up the rest of Warsaw.

Hills, cobblestone streets. Rozbrat, Krakowskie Przedmieścic,
Wybrzeze, Gdanskie, Bolésce, Rybaki, Kozia. The same damp chill.
Polish spring. Money changers approaching them on the street, quite
openly, even insolently, like panhandlers in New York: "Change—?
Money change—? Dollar, zloty—?" Following after them with hands
extended. No thank you! Judith says angrily. She is ashamed for her
Polish friends.

WARSAW IS AN OCCUPIED CITY, an occupied zone, Judith thinks,
waking, staring at herself in the dim bathroom mirror—and something
is happening to her here. *Is* there a subtle poison in the air? While her
lover dresses in the other room, whistling under his breath. He was
out very late last night. He too has his secrets, his malaise. (Judith has
decided to forgive him his most recent infidelity. She tells herself she
hasn't any curiosity about the woman though she wonders . . . was she
an American, a Pole?)

No time to think, to brood. She has thousands of zlotys to spend,
must buy gifts, books, take everyone out to dinner, perhaps on the last
evening of the conference. If this won't strike the young Poles as too
blatantly "American" a gesture of charity, condescension, good will.

No time to meditate upon subtleties. Not here. Driven about in the embassy van, in one of the Fiats, Robert Sargent jostled against her, smelling of shaving lotion. Judith must fight her almost physical distress at the sound of Polish—the frustrating tumble of words, melodic, inaccessible, the structure of the compound sentence with its many variations: the subordinate clauses, the coordinate clauses: which Judith can hear (or so it seems) without being able to understand.

My Warszawa, she thinks. The place of my undoing.

The language remains inaccessible in its beauty. And Carl, what of Carl?—she forgives him his infidelity (his most recent infidelity) but cannot forgive him the fact that he lied to her and expected her to believe it.

No time to herself, shaking hands, squinting against the smoke, accepting another glass of tea Russian style. No time to brood about that monument to the "martyrs" of the ghetto, the Jewish resistance; it seems curiously beside the point to be bitter or even uncommonly interested at this point in history—for 1944 *was* a long time ago. And should Judith Horne take the entire Polish delegation out to dinner, perhaps at the famous (and expensive) Crocodile Restaurant on the square? Or will they sneer at her behind her back? Or do they genuinely like her, admire her, as they appear to? (There have been several floral bouquets so far. She hasn't been able to bring herself to throw them all away.)

There isn't time, they are being herded into the embassy van, Judith is listening with enormous interest to an anecdote told by the American cultural attaché whose last post, evidently a perversely cherished post, was in Saudi Arabia: 130-degree heat, damp heat, public stonings, yes, but worse, far worse punishments, and sanitary conditions, and sickness, and of course women *there* don't exist—really don't exist. Judith is concerned with her digestion, her bowels. She has come to dread the very look, the odor, of the bathroom in her hotel room. The oilcloth shower curtain with its faded floral design. The stained sink, the stained tile floor. The enormous crazy roaring splash when the toilet is flushed. ("I thought my toilet was attacking me!" Robert Sargent said with a shudder.) Judith's eyes water, her head reels; she must concentrate on a not quite coherent but possibly hostile charge being made by a red-bearded young playwright: they are both on a five-member panel organized by

P.E.N. to discuss the "problem" of translating. The young man's En-
glish has a distinct Scots accent, acquired from his two years abroad.
Other accents are British and Midwestern (the University of Iowa, to be
specific). Judith assiduously inquires after names and addresses, accepts
printed cards, if only there were time to think . . . she wants to help the
Poles get translated into English, published in the States . . . and she
knows of exchange-student programs, she can inquire about grants for
study, Iowa, Columbia, Stanford, Michigan, she will write letters of rec-
ommendation, make telephone calls. Back in New York she intends to
form a committee to help the Polish dissidents who have lost their jobs
and are "nonpersons"—she will make contact with Polish dissidents in
exile in the States—she will donate money to the Index on Censorship
in London. Exhaustion rings her eyes, her hands tremble, she fears she
is losing her energy, her faith in herself. Does anything we say or write or
publish *matter*, she thinks, when we risk nothing?—we who are free.

But there isn't time to puzzle over the situation, the embassy van
is idling at the curb, Tadeusz is waiting, Marianne Beecher is wearing
soft flannel trousers and a casual suede jacket as if in imitation of Judith
Horne's style, there will be a television interview at 2 P.M., Carl has
been attentive all morning, Tadeusz smiles his shy, exquisitely courteous
smile and corrects—but very gently—her pronunciation of Mickiewicz
for the second or third time.

GROGGY WITH SLEEP, leaden-boweled, Judith turns from him as
if to hide in the bedclothes. Carl is trying to wake her. Down on the
street the morning traffic has begun, in the corridor outside the room
workmen are moving furniture, there are maids with vacuum cleaners,
the same chill pale light suffuses the room: *Warszawa*. Judith must wake
once again to her city.

Carl asks is she ill?—otherwise they must hurry.

Perhaps he hasn't been unfaithful to her, she thinks, her eyes shut,
perhaps Carl always tells the truth and it is she who distorts everything.
Quick to see meanings, significance, even in the wallpaper, heraldic
designs too faint to engage a more robust eye.

"That woman journalist who has been asking to interview you, Marta something, she's probably downstairs in the coffee shop waiting," Carl says, stooping to peer at himself in the bureau mirror, combing his hair, "—I think you'll like her: she's quick, sharp, intelligent, knows English quite well."

"Marta who?" Judith says. "I don't remember any Marta."

". . . met her the other evening, she has read most of your essays she *says*, she's of course very eager to meet you. . . . Are you all right, Judith? Why don't you get up?"

"I don't remember any Marta," Judith says. "I don't remember any appointment for an interview."

"I have the woman's card here," Carl says. Judith does not look in his direction. "—You asked me to take it, write down the details, don't you remember?"

Judith does not reply.

Carl goes into the bathroom. Running water, the straining noise of the old plumbing, the roar of the flushed toilet.

Today Judith is going to be taken at last to the Jewish cemetery. She has declined to tell Carl (who is busy with engagements of his own) because she knows that he will disapprove. Do you really think you should . . . ? he will ask. Though perhaps he will say nothing at all.

Carl reappears, Judith is up, brushing her hair impatiently. Stroke after stroke. Curly kinky dark-but-graying hairs in the hairbrush.

He asks her about *The Awkward Age*, and she says it isn't a Polish sort of story, and he says, Yes, but how do you find it? and she says, Very slow, very rich, very dull, very profound—in fact heartbreaking. He says that James always is, if you read him correctly; and Judith says, I make an effort to read most books "correctly."

Carl rummages through his suitcase. He says, as if casually: "Of course you do, Judith. You're the star of the conference, after all. The queen, the A+ student, the one with the most style, the only one the Poles want to interview. . . . What are we arguing about? Are we arguing?"

"I don't know," Judith says evenly, "—are we arguing?"

Carl doesn't reply. Judith continues her rapid compulsive brushing.

After a moment, in a slightly different voice, Carl says: "They were asking me yesterday about the NATO thing."

"The NATO 'thing'—?" Judith asks.

"In Norway. You must have read about it. They've decided to install five hundred seventy-two new missiles, some sort of five-year plan."

"Because of the Soviets?"

Carl lets the lid of his suitcase fall and says irritably: "The joke of it is that NATO is begging the Soviets this week to negotiate an arms control agreement but the Soviets won't negotiate unless NATO abandons its plan. Does that make sense?"

"What has Norway to do with it?"

"The meeting took place there. I don't know. Norway has nothing to do with it—no more than any of these countries."

Judith drops the hairbrush on the bed. "Yes I know about that," she says, the leaden sensation in her bowels growing heavier, "—or something exactly like it. I read it in the embassy bulletin the other day."

"Well—this is newer news."

"It's all the same news."

"Our Poles were asking me about it yesterday at lunch," Carl says. "Not exactly—as you know—*asking*. Because of course they don't really know what's going on in the world. They know that their government censors the news but they don't know if they can trust Western reports and of course we don't either."

"They don't even know their own history," Judith says.

"Does anyone?"

"Don't be flippant: *yes*. Yes, some of us do know."

"We know what we've been told, what we read."

"Yes, and we make it our business to be told and to read a great deal."

Carl says, sighing: "West Germany is quite willing to go along with the NATO plan, for obvious reasons. England and Italy have fallen into line too."

"But the Soviets have missiles too," Judith says, frowning. "Why are we arguing?"

"We're *not* arguing," Carl says. "I agree with you. The Soviets have thousands of missiles—they've been manufacturing one a week. Most are aimed at West Europe but some are aimed at China."

"Yes," says Judith. "We know. And North America."

"It isn't new news, you're right. It's exactly the same old news."

Judith is now hunting through her suitcase, through her leather bag. Passport, notebook, wallet, crumpled Kleenex, a loose ballpoint pen. A much-folded street map of Warsaw. Why am I here, she thinks, staring at something in her hand—why in this room, in this city, with this stranger?

She stares at the item in her hand and eventually it becomes a plastic toiletries case.

Carl says abruptly, touching her arm: "Judith, I feel that I'm confronting an adversary in you. It's gotten much worse this past week. The tension, the continual strain—"

"An adversary in *me*, or an adversary *in* me?" Judith asks absently, not turning. After a moment, when he fails to respond, she says lightly: "Maybe you just feel guilty."

"Why should I feel guilty?" Carl laughs, backing away. "I'll meet you downstairs."

NOW THINGS RUSH HEAD-ON, a cascade of minor epiphanies.

The mystical interpretation of the universe, Judith thinks, is probably correct: each day is precisely *the* day, each hour and each moment is an eternal present, immutable. Thus Pascal might argue, thus Spinoza, and all the Oriental mystics, and . . . The world is awash in visions yes I fully realize. But to explain to melancholy Robert Sargent on the way to the Gezia Cemetery as the poor man recites his litany of bad luck (his malfunctioning camera was "lost" somewhere in the Europejski; this morning he didn't wake until ten-thirty already late for the opening session of the day, lying in a pool of harsh sunlight on the carpet of his room *fully clothed*; he was paralyzed, stricken, unable to remember clearly whether he was back home on Thirteenth Street or still in Warsaw or was it Paris?—how very long he has been traveling! His soul-mate, as he calls him, has surely betrayed him by now, back on Thirteenth Street; surely he has broken into the forbidden liquor cabinet as well, being a creature incapable of delaying gratification, let alone fidelity in the usual sense of the word: so he awoke this morning, did Robert, a vile taste in his mouth, his eyes unfocused, saliva drooling in a thread down his chest, Robert Sargent the unassuming though much-acclaimed post-modernist poet who has quietly confessed in interviews that, yes, he *is* related to John Singer Sargent that extraordinary genius but what good does it do him!—he who is merely *Robert* Sargent!—he awoke to the stench of vomit not his own and the certitude that his traveler's checks were gone and all his zlotys and hard currency as well, and personal papers, notes scribbled over with first drafts of poems; and after ten minutes of this soul-paralysis he managed to crawl to a chair and hoist himself to his feet and yes everything *was* gone—stolen—everything except the notes for poems, and of course the handful of zlotys for who would want *zlotys?*—has Judith ever heard anything so piteous?) . . . sitting beside Judith in a Fiat driven by a young Polish editor named Bruno . . . sitting shivering in a tweedy sports jacket baggy at the shoulders and worn at the elbows, a true poet's costume, appealing to Judith for aid or advice or sympathy or simply shared amusement at his predicament. Is it the human predicament, Robert wonders?

"The cultural attaché has been very kind," Robert says in an undertone to Judith, "I mean he didn't scold. If he felt disgust he was kindly enough not to betray it. He promised to cable home for money for me, thank God he knows exactly what to do, I was sick with dread of going to the police, you know I'd never do such a thing, the young man—a blond, a poet too or so he claimed—the young man was very, very naughty to have run off with my things but I can't really blame him, I mean after all I *am* an American, we're all fair game so to speak, don't you think? In any case I couldn't possibly have described him, my glasses had fallen off . . . my vision has deteriorated badly in my left eye since my arrival in Warsaw, in fact. . . . Oh Judith we've been here so long—away from home so long! You *won't* laugh at me back home, will you, dear, and spread tales . . . ?"

Judith laughs uncomfortably and pats Robert's arm.

The world is awash with visions, she thinks, and today, the day of her

visit to Gezia Cemetery, is the only day that matters; the day of salvation
or damnation; this hour, this very moment. But Judith is not a religious
person. She is not inclined to mysticism, however comforting or terrify-
ing. She cannot really believe in the blood—in the rich dark unconscious
current of being—whatever it might be called—whatever arcane expres-
sion: she cannot believe. And the trouble with epiphanies is that they fall
from the air all too frequently.

Nevertheless Gezia Cemetery affects her profoundly, leaves her
rocky and exhausted and scant of breath. Spring is still withheld, sus-
pended; here birds call to one another with a wintry plaintiveness; the
atmosphere is rural and timeless, distant from the city of Warsaw which
in fact surrounds it on all sides. A chill greeny-damp tranquility, hun-
dreds of startlingly white birch trees, grave after grave. . . . In such places
one realizes that the earth belongs not to the living but the dead, who
populate it in such incalculable numbers.

Robert Sargent is similarly subdued as well, staring, as Judith does,
at the city of graves. His childlike blue eyes are widened, his hands are
thrust into the pockets of his oversized tweed coat.

The elderly caretaker Pinchas leads Judith and Robert and their
tall young Polish guide. A wide pathway of cracked pavement, beneath
overhanging tree branches, between rows of graves. Pinchas is gnome-
like and droll and quietly assured. No American visitors intimidate
him—he has had so many. Ceaselessly, tirelessly he speaks, pointing out
graves, identifying the dead with a careless fond familiarity. Judith notes
his leathery expressionless face, his sunken Slavic eyes, protruding ears.
Kafka in caricature—grown old and sallow. He wears a shirt and tie and
a soiled coat. He appears very much at home in this beautiful desolate
place as if he has lived here all his life. "Is Pinchas a first or a last name?"
Robert inquires, but when Bruno translates the question the caretaker
does not answer. Perhaps he is deaf? His monologue continues almost
uninterrupted—now he is pointing out a ruined mausoleum, speaking
in low rapid Polish.

"A wealthy manufacturer," Bruno translates. "One of the class of
Jews who made Warsaw a center of commerce for all of Europe. . . ."

The little procession continues. Judith is wearing only the suede

jump suit, her head is bare, she is never quite prepared for the chilly
May wind. Robert Sargent stoops to read inscriptions but of course the
inscriptions are unreadable. "It's frightening to realize that Latin too can
be of no help," Robert murmurs. Five hundred thousand graves. Monu-
ments of all sizes: some as high as fifteen feet, some low and squat, some
mere markers half-covered by grass. Judith, always alert to details, asks
about materials: that is Swedish granite (the black stone); Polish granite
(pink-gray); sandstone; marble. Pinchas points out with melancholy
pride a gravesite elaborately ornamental (pansies and petunias in bloom,
protected by iron grillwork), the father of a millionaire now living in Mi-
ami Beach, "the wife sends a check twice a year to cover all expenses,"
Bruno translates, Pinchas leads them on, pointing out a small brick
tower in another large fenced-off plot, "here the great Mendelssohn,
great in his day, secretary to Marx. Very fine people, very wealthy."

Judith and Robert see a swastika scratched on a granite monument
nearby.

The cemetery is actually a forest, Judith thinks, in which graves are
tolerated. Everywhere are lovely trees—birch, maple—just beginning
to leaf. Pale cold green, almost translucent. Now Pinchas is pointing
out the graves of famous Jews—poets, writers, musicians—famous
men—Bruno translates with a quiet courtesy, as if he has been this way
before and has heard Pinchas's monologue many times.

These, after all, are the fortunate Jews—the Jews who died natural
deaths and were buried in their own soil.

Epiphanies cancel one another out, Judith thinks, wiping her eyes
roughly with the back of her hand. Robert notices but discreetly turns
aside. After a moment he says, as if to comfort her: "Once, years ago, I
was fighting my way across a street in Rome, I was a young man then,
and absurdly vulnerable, and something about the crowd of *handsome
people*—for Romans are all handsome, or nearly—something about the
crowd pierced my heart. *This is a lonely predicament*, I thought. I never
understood the sentiment but I think it applies to today."

Judith neither agrees nor disagrees.

At the cemetery gate she gives the caretaker a twenty-dollar bill—
hard currency—and notes how the old man's deep-sunk eyes fairly

glow. He is moved, agitated, repeats his thanks in Polish several times, shakes her hand until Judith, embarrassed, half-ashamed, edges away.

Driving back to the Europejski Judith senses Bruno's disapproval. Robert Sargent says: "You made old Pinchas's day, my dear. In fact you've probably made his year."

CARL SAYS QUIETLY: "It's simply that I feel I am confronting an adversary in you."

Judith says: "I don't understand."

Carl says: "I mean an adversary *in* you—inside you—a rival of mine. He's inside you and the two of us are struggling for you."

Judith laughs sharply. Her lover's tone is so humorless and flat, and his words are so ridiculous. "But is the struggle worth it?" she can't resist asking.

Carl is sitting on the edge of the rumpled bed, a newspaper on his knees, sheets of notebook paper scattered across the bedclothes. His eyes are threaded with blood, his skin sallow. It is past nine o'clock and he hasn't shaved and the lower half of his face looks malevolent. There is something weary and husbandly about him and Judith thinks, He is going to ask for a divorce.

Each woke before dawn. Traffic noises, plumbing. Judith woke to her low-grade Warsaw anxiety as if surfacing through a few feet of gray soapy water—no depth to it, but enough to drown in.

Last night, if she remembers clearly, they had tried to make love for the first time in many days. Carl was tender, desperate. "Is it men you hate," he whispered, "—or the entire species?"

Judith prides herself on being a woman who believes in the body, in the life of the body. "Sensuality"—as a philosophical principle at least—means a great deal to her. So she could not reply. She turned away, sobbing, burying her wet face in the pillow.

Now it is morning and she is in control. She says: "You make such pronouncements as a way of not saying other things."

"Such as—?" Carl asks, watching her.

"*I love you, I hate you,*" Judith says lightly. "The usual things that people say, or so we're led to believe."

"I'm not in the habit of making formal pronouncements regarding my emotions," Carl says. "You must be confusing me with someone else."

"Of course," Judith says. "That must be the problem."

". . . This adversary I spoke of," Carl says, assembling the newspaper, frowning at his ink-stained fingers, "this adversary is *your* emotion. A kind of shadow, a reflection. It isn't precisely you—Judith—but it inhabits you. I can see it dimly at times, at other times it eludes me—it's too cunning. It occupies you and crowds me out, it's a rival, I think it's winning."

Judith says slowly, beginning to be frightened: "I don't understand."

Carl sighs, tosses the newspaper away. "You're not a happy woman," he says.

"Is that an accusation?"

"A man feels a certain challenge with a woman like you—your intelligence, your quality. Your style. There aren't many women I can talk with as an equal—no I *won't* apologize for that remark, I haven't time for hypocrisy right now—and I think you must know how I value our friendship?—of course you know. But this struggle with—with whatever—this adversary—*you* becomes exhausting."

Judith stares at him. For a long moment neither speaks. Then she hears herself say in a soft, rot-soft voice: "But I don't understand, I love you."

"Oh yes, do you?" Carl says at once, as if fearful of allowing the words any resonance. "*Do* you?"

"I love you."

Carl smiles coldly at her, or in her direction. He is sitting, still, on the edge of the bed, his shoulders slightly hunched, a man of young middle age, dark chest hair shadowy inside his white undershirt. Ten years, Judith thinks, panicked. Twelve. My lifetime. And now in Warszawa.

(The other day, walking through Old Town, they stopped to examine a display of "carved" Christs in an outdoor booth. The Christs were all on the cross but there were several close-ups, the head and shoulders, the crown of horns, lurid droplets of paint-bright blood. The figures had the slick stamped-out look of manufactured goods though

they were advertised as handmade, which Judith found both amusing
and depressing. Dying-eyed Jesus Christ in cartoon colors. "Shall I buy
you one, Judith," Carl asked, "as a souvenir of Poland?" Judith drew
away, suddenly angry. Mockery was inappropriate here—mockery was
beside the point. The market square, the cobblestones, horse-drawn
buggies hauling tourists, melodic incomprehensible Polish spoken on all
sides, heavy shutters on the buildings, eighteenth-century facades on all
sides. . . . Except of course they were not legitimately eighteenth-century
because everything was post-war, arisen from rubble. Judith thought: I
never felt Jewish before. Before Warsaw.)

Now Carl is winding his wristwatch, not quite impatiently. In his
weary husband's voice he says: "Well. We should go downstairs, our
guides are waiting."

But Judith stands staring at him. "I don't understand," she repeats
stubbornly. "*You* seem to want nothing I offer. Nothing that's deep,
that's genuine or permanent. When I'm happy, you're indifferent or
jealous. When things go well with my public life, my career—you draw
away, you *are* jealous. *Don't deny it.* Yet you were attracted to me
because I have a public career. Only when I'm miserable are you
sympathetic, only when things go wrong—then you say absurd things,
things I can't understand. The sort of thing you've been saying this
morning."

Carl rises abruptly to his feet, is about to go to the closet, but Judith
grabs hold of his arm. She hears herself saying the most remarkable
words: ". . . You don't love me. You don't give a damn about me. Noth-
ing is genuine or . . ."

Carl tries to quiet her but she cannot be quieted. Now she is half-
whispering, sobbing: "I can't bear this—boxed up in this wretched room
with you—do you think I want to be here, do you think I'm enjoying
this? I hate you! Your cruelty, your condescension—"

"Judith, for Christ's sake—"

"I want a normal life with you!" Judith says, her voice rising. "I be-
lieve in mutual respect—honesty—fidelity—I've been willing to wait—
I've been willing to sacrifice my pride—but I won't demean myself for
nothing!—for you!"

She has become hysterical suddenly. Carl tries to hold her; she pushes him away; she strikes out with her fists, sobbing like a child. It is all very amazing. It is not really happening and Judith cannot accept responsibility.

A hysterical woman, no longer young, screaming with such rage that her face is distorted . . . her throat scraped raw with words she cannot believe she hears: "You don't love me! You never have!"

AFTERWARD, an oasis of calm. Frightened tenderness.

"Of course I'm sorry," Carl says, shaken by the scene. "Of course I love you. But I'm not always certain that . . . that I know you."

"You know me well enough," Judith says.

She is lying on the unmade bed, exhausted. Her voice is flat and dull; her head feels hollow. Loathing for herself, for the absurd creature Judith Horne, has acquired a sharp tangible taste, like vomit.

"It's this place, we've been poisoned by this place," Carl says slowly. He might be echoing Judith's own words, speaking in her own cadences. ". . . An occupied zone after all."

"Yes," says Judith flatly. "An occupied zone."

IS IT NAPOLEON, there in the wall?—in a faded mural of curlicues and clouds? Judith, bored by the soporific ceremony in the museum, no longer quite so fascinated by the sound of Polish and not at all fascinated by the English into which it is being translated, seeks out diversions in the ceiling, in the floor, in the wall. The air is thick with smoke, no windows have been opened, vodka is being served in tiny glasses, tea Russian style, an old woman servant tiptoes officiously about. Judith notes with envy that Carl is writing something quickly in his notebook. A bell is ringing in the steeple of the Jesuit Church, a high cold clear sound. They will be leaving Poland at the end of the week. Soon. But perhaps it is too late.

Judith studies the mural of Napoleon. A portly cherub captured by an adoring painter in the moment of—can it be?—his ascent to Heaven.

(For Napoleon is a savior to the Poles, having promised them "freedom." His armies are consequently awaited with enormous hope.) Judith notes the laurel leaves in his hair, the way in which his eyes turn upward in an ecstasy of heroic innocence. He wears a freshly starched white waistcoat, a short green jacket with red collar and cuffs and smart little brass buttons. It seems to Judith that she has seen this Napoleon somewhere else in Warsaw, but she cannot remember where.

THE AMERICANS are taken to visit a collective farm outside the city, and then to the village of Zelazowa Wola, Chopin's birthplace. Judith tries to read Mickiewicz and decides the translation must be inadequate. She studies publications the Poles have given her and notes the recurring words, the inescapable words—*collapse, subjugated peoples, revolutionary fervor, sacrifice, betrayal, tyrants, annihilation, survival, partition, national independence, clandestine organizations, secret police, Uprising, oppressed peoples, despot, oppressor, suffering, struggle.* It is too painful for her to read again about the Uprising of 1944 and the Nazi attack.

At lunch an earnest young university instructor tells them passionately that Soviet Russia is not a nation like any other. "Democracy is too weak to deal with such people," he says, exhaling a cloud of smoke. "If it was not the case of the many Jews in Washington, in your country, there would be an invasion tomorrow—the next day!—you would see. But their influence is strong, very strong, and never friendly to Poland."

JUDITH TAKES TADEUSZ to dinner, alone. She would prefer to ask him questions about himself but he insists upon asking her questions: in fact he is interviewing her for a Polish literary journal, as it turns out. Her theory of literature . . . her judgment of her contemporaries ("You have formed an opinion of Jerzy Kosinski?") . . . her aspirations for the future. They dine on rump of boar, duck Cracow style with mushrooms, cabbage with nuts, mizeria (cucumber salad), date mazurek, saffron baba. Very sweet wine. Very strong coffee in small cups. Tadeusz is profuse, blushing, in his gratitude.

(Seven months later Judith will receive a translation of the interview, sent to her courtesy the U.S. Embassy. She will be stunned, in fact incredulous, at the hostility of the interviewer and the distortions of her remarks. *Judith Horne pretends a wide awareness of Polish culture but betrays herself by ignorance of . . . Judith Horne like her compatriots boasts smug superiority to U.S. writers like Saroyan, Sinclair Lewis, and Jack London, whose works are prized above hers . . . Judith Horne manifested dislike of her hotel accommodations, Polish food and customs, the busy streets . . . the very air itself which she claimed to find unclean.*)

"WELL—the Jewish ghetto wasn't much of a loss architecturally," Judith hears one of the Poles say to one of the American delegates; but it takes her too long to absorb the meaning—by then the conversation has shifted, moved on. In any case she is too demoralized to speak. In any case she is intent upon threading her way through the crowd and finding the women's restroom.

GOSSIP that might interest Judith and Carl: it was in this very house—the U.S.-owned residence of the deputy chief of mission—that Mary McCarthy wrote *The Group*. Does she, Judith, admire that novel? Is it much read and respected in the States at the present time?

ROBERT SARGENT drifts into the coffee shop forty-five minutes late, so freshly shaven his fair skin gleams, so sleep-befuddled his eyes appear half their normal size. "Judith—Carl—it's the most bizarre thing—my toenails are growing wildly here in East Europe, I've had to clip them back twice this week, is the same thing happening to you?"

Since Gezia Cemetery Robert has been particularly edgy, antic, bright, insouciant in her presence. Judith has stopped smiling at his remarks, which only provokes him all the more.

"*My* toenails," says Carl, yawning, "—have atrophied."

HOPING TO AVOID the furniture-congested corridor that leads to the hotel's central staircase—a kind of grand spiral with a solid crimson carpet—Judith seeks out the back stairs, the fire exit, and descends floor after floor in the half-dark, trying doorknobs (the doors are all locked), her heart in a flurry. Is it possible she'll be trapped in the stairwell?—it isn't possible because she can always scream, pound on the doors, perhaps there is a fire alarm. Unfortunately the floors are not marked. Unfortunately the air is very close and warm, vaguely feculent.

Finally Judith is in the basement—she can go no further—turning a doorknob, throwing herself against the door, hearing a few yards away the voices and laughter of strangers. It is extremely warm here, and quite dark. "Hello," says Judith, "—is someone there? Can you let me out? The door is locked—"

But no one hears. In a panic she runs up to the next floor—which is, perhaps, the ground floor of the hotel—and tries the door but of course the door is locked. "Hello," she calls out calmly, "is anyone there? Can anyone hear me? I seem to be locked in. . . ." An odor of fried onions, grease. No sound. Nothing. So she hurries up to the next floor, her heart now thudding, and then to the next, and the next. . . . But the doors are all locked. The doors are all locked.

Suddenly she is pounding on a door, shouting for help, desperate, shameless. A pulse beats wild in her head. "Help me—please—I'm trapped—please, isn't anyone around?—oh God please—"

Then it happens, marvelously, that a door is opened *on the floor below*, as if in response to Judith's cry. She hurries downstairs, shouting. Two men are backing through the doorway, carrying a stepladder. Judith rushes upon them, manic with relief and gratitude: "Oh for God's sake *thank you*—oh please don't let the door close—"

She hurries past them, past their astonished faces, and finds herself at the far end of the very corridor that leads to room 371.

An amusing anecdote to tell Carl, someday. Or her friends back home.

Then again, perhaps not.

JUDITH JOTS DOWN NAMES, and addresses, in her notebook. Yes she knows someone at the University of Iowa—yes she has a friend at Stanford—certainly she will make inquiries about exchange fellowships. She is introduced to the hearty bearded Secretary of the International Committee for Unification of Terminological Neologisms. He shakes her hand hard, tells her that he is also a translator, under contract to translate one of her books—though he would prefer to do a book not yet published in the States. "Not yet published? But how would that be possible?" Judith asks, puzzled. The young man leans close to her, smiles nervously, insolently, says: "It will be that I must work closely with you, Miss Horne, confer with you over the manuscript itself . . . spend three-four weeks at the least in New York City collaborating. . . ." Judith draws away and says: "I don't think that's feasible." He says, smiling: "Then I must convince you!—only make me the opportunity."

JUDITH IS APPALLED at the tiny worms of dirt that roll beneath her fingertips. Between her breasts, across her thighs, her belly. She has taken only the briefest, most perfunctory showers in Warsaw.

She rubs her skin hard with a washcloth. A white washcloth in which the ubiquitous word *Orbis* is stitched. Layers of grime, flakes, near-invisible bits of dirt. Her feet are especially afflicted. It takes her twenty minutes to get clean; her skin is reddened in ugly swaths, smarting.

I'm turning into mere flesh, Judith thinks. A beast.

TWO MEMBERS of the American delegation are leaving early, having come to Warsaw from Budapest. They are on a six-week tour of East Europe for the State Department, as "cultural emissaries," and Judith admires their stamina. "We've absorbed firsthand the tragic history of Poland," one says, "—and the tragic history of Hungary. Before that—the tragic history of Bulgaria, Yugoslavia, and Czechoslovakia. Do you know where we're headed next?—East Germany."

CARL IS TYPING OUT the first draft of a story on the political atmosphere of Poland that will eventually wind up in the *New York Times Magazine*. In fact Carl Walser will get the cover that week. Now he glances up irritably at Judith who wants his advice: Should she buy gifts for their Polish hosts?—all of them, or only the ones they've become acquainted with? Or should she treat the whole group to a dinner in Old Town? (It falls to Judith Horne to be bountiful because she is the one with all the zlotys—neither Carl nor Robert Sargent received any Polish royalties at all.)

"Or do you think I should give the money in person to one of the dissidents?" she asks. "I mean—the one who needs it most."

"Who the hell would that be?" Carl asks.

"I have his name written down," Judith says, searching through her purse, "—the one with the beard, Wladislaw something. Elizbieta told me about him, he's a member of the Social Defense Committee who's been arrested a dozen times, he's penniless, I remember thinking I felt a particular kinship with him—"

"Who the fuck *is* the man?" Carl asks impatiently. "A face, a hand-shake?—a pair of melancholy watery eyes? Just because the man can't speak English and he's been arrested a few times you want to give him money."

Judith turns her purse upside down. Scraps of paper fall out, much-folded notebook pages. "Elizbieta said he'd been in Sweden for a few years publishing Polish writing but he got so homesick he had to return, despite the danger. Now he can't get a visa and he's unemployed—you must remember him—you and Marianne were talking with him too."

"You've become unbalanced here," Carl says.

"Because I feel sorry for these people? Because I feel sympathy?—I want to help?" Judith says angrily.

"You don't *know* them. A dissident isn't by definition a saint—there are anti-Semites who are dissidents—look at Solzhenitsyn. You're being ridiculous, this is another form of hysteria."

"I don't think of Solzhenitsyn as an anti-Semite," Judith says.

"He's a Russian, isn't he."

"Is he an anti-Semite?" Judith asks, staring at Carl.

"He admires Nixon. He admires stability. What do you think?"

Judith says nothing, staring. She is breathing quickly and shallowly. Carl says, trying to take her hand: "For Christ's sake sit down, you look exhausted. *You can't save the world.*"

Judith draws away. "I'm not at all exhausted," she says. "I feel the strongest I've felt in days."

"Fortunately we're leaving tomorrow."

"I'm not ready to leave, I want to *do something* for these people."

"Sit down. Come here."

Judith has located a scrap of paper, her finger shaking. "Here it is—Barańczak—is that the name? I'm probably not pronouncing it correctly—"

"Barańczak," said Carl doubtfully, "isn't that another man? The philology professor with the bad eyes?"

THE EMBASSY VAN is being routed down a side street. On the boulevard is a royal procession—or what appears to be a royal procession—limousines, army vehicles, police on horseback, many soldiers. The sidewalks, however, are totally empty.

Brezniew, it is explained to the Americans—Brezniew back in town, the Warsaw Pact discussions, twice in a single month.

"Suppose he's assassinated," Robert Sargent says with an exquisite shiver. "Wouldn't we be in a fix then!"

MARTA, her short dark hair frizzed about her face, her dark eyes bright, smoking cigarette after cigarette, flattering Judith Horne with her spirited admiration. Of all the American writers "of the highest rank". . . . Of all the American writers who have visited Poland. . . . "And of course," Marta insists, making an emphatic gesture that Judith has come to recognize as specifically Polish—a kind of restrained jab with the flat of the hand against the air, accompanied by a look of fastidious pain—"of course it is pleasing to me as a woman, I mean that *you* are a woman too, though your writing is superior to—is that the expression?—the feminist ideas of the elementary level—"

Judith murmurs an assent, or a question; but Marta continues speaking. She is pert and argumentative and almost ugly, then again she *is* attractive, her features mobile, her eyes narrowing and widening with intensity. Ah, how delighted she is to be interviewing, at last, the distinguished American writer Judith Horne! For days she has been begging for an interview, leaving messages at the Europejski desk, trying to make requests through the U.S. Embassy people, and now . . . now there is *so much* to ask. . . .

Judith squints against the smoke, begins to gnaw on a sore thumbnail. She always dislikes flatterers, however guileless, but there is something about Marta that offends her in any case.

Marta is Jewish, of course. No doubt about it. The eyes, the nose, the mouth, the frizzy-kinky hair—doesn't she resemble Judith herself, in a smaller pushed-together version? But she is wearing a small gold cross around her neck. Small but prominent. Defiant. It rides the hollow at the base of her throat, moves with her breath, her voice. Judith finds herself staring at it as Marta "interviews" her—fires long paragraphs of questions that contain their own answers; recites critical judgments of Judith's work on which Judith is asked, please, to comment; asks once again, as so many Poles have asked, what are Judith's firsthand impressions of Poland?

Judith interrupts. "That thing you're wearing—are you Catholic?"

Marta draws back. The reaction is almost mechanical; it seems to Judith not quite unpremeditated. Marta says with an air of surprised gravity: "Yes of course I am a Catholic." After a pause she adds: "I am a convert."

"A convert," says Judith. "When were you converted?—is that the correct expression, *were* converted?—how old were you?"

"At the age of sixteen," Marta says uneasily, "—but we have not much time, Miss Horne, we must concentrate on you."

"I asked you to call me Judith."

"Yes—but it is so difficult, you see!—for you are famous—and we have not much time if you must all leave tomorrow—so soon!" Marta tries to smile engagingly. "In fact my next question is, Miss Horne, when will you return to our country?—and stay for a longer time?"

"Was your entire family converted," Judith asks, "or just you?—I'm not clear about these procedures."

"I made my own decision," Marta says, again with that air of dignified surprise, "—my beliefs are my own, you see, coming from within."

"What about your family?"

"My family," Marta says slowly, carefully, "is scattered . . . not in Warsaw." She sucks on her cigarette, exhales smoke. Judith irritably waves it away.

"Scattered—?"

"Scattered, living in different parts," Marta says with a shrug of her shoulders, "some are, you know, dead—missing." After a pause she adds in an undertone: "My family was very wealthy. Aristocrats. My grandfather and his uncles—they had an export firm. They did business, Miss Horne, in London, Paris, Berlin, Vienna—everywhere. Leather exports of the finest quality."

"I see," says Judith. "Aristocrats."

Marta pauses long enough to allow a young waitress to pass by their table, then leans forward, her expression keen, shrewd, her voice lowered. "The Jews—the other Jews—I mean the Jews of Warsaw, of the ghetto—they could have saved themselves if they made the effort," Marta says. "Also the villagers. You see, Miss Horne, they were very slow—very ignorant—filled with superstition—lazy." Marta shakes her head, half-sorrowfully, half-repulsed. That look again of fastidious pain. "They could have saved themselves, the ones who ended up in Oświęcim. But they did not try."

"They did not try," Judith says slowly.

"It is difficult to explain to an American," Marta says, "but you must know—they were peasants—mainly peasants. Very ignorant."

"Mainly peasants," says Judith quietly. "I see."

There is a long uneasy pause. Judith stares at the tea glasses on the table, at the lemon wedges. The coffee shop is noisy, smoky, bustling, cheery even in the dimness, not a place for significant gestures.

"Now, Miss Horne, to continue," says Marta, "—I have here an important question—"

In one version Judith suddenly slaps the cigarette from Marta's fingers: it falls to the table, rolls to the floor. In another version Judith simply rises from her chair so abruptly that her interviewer is startled, jerks back, drops her cigarette. It falls to the table, rolls to the floor. . . .

CARL FOLLOWS JUDITH UPSTAIRS, comes into their room some thirty seconds after her. He appears to be more bewildered than angry. "What the hell happened down there?" he asks.

Judith, trembling, standing at the window, does not reply.

"—I wasn't watching, myself—a few of us happened to be having coffee—I saw you and Marta come in and you seemed to be getting along well—I *told* you she was nice—the next thing I knew you were on your way out and the poor woman was calling after you."

"Was she," Judith says. "I didn't hear."

JUDITH AND CARL excuse themselves from the evening's program to have dinner alone, though both of them—as they explain to the conference director—would have liked very much to see the Poznan Dance Theater at the Opera House. "Next time we visit Warsaw," Carl promises.

They leave the Europejski and cross the wide windy square to the Victoria Hotel, the single "international" hotel, for an expensive meal. Polish cuisine, of course—but in quiet, elegant surroundings. (The table-cloths are white linen, there are single long-stemmed roses at each table, a pretty young woman in a filmy white dress is playing a harp, the lighting is discreet, flattering.) "I don't know why we're doing this," Judith says guiltily. "I really *don't* like pretentious overpriced restaurants."

"Maybe you do," says Carl, "*really*."

Judith hears the mild contempt in his voice but refuses to respond. They have quarreled so much in Warsaw, emotion of any kind now strikes her as futile. Rage and tears and hatred followed by embraces, comforting, forgiveness. The gestures of "love." Even when she is denouncing her lover a part of her stands aside, skeptical, doubting the very authenticity of the moment. Is Judith responding to Carl Walser in himself, or is she only fulfilling a role?—saying lines not her own, lines that belong simply to Woman.

Self-loathing has swollen in her, she thinks, like a fetus.

Carl orders a bottle of wine though Judith isn't drinking. Mineral water with ice will be fine. (*Ice.* Neither of them has had an iced drink for days except at the residence of the deputy chief of mission: what luxury!) Carl decides upon a shrimp cocktail though Judith warns him that the shrimp very likely won't be fresh; after all, Warsaw. He orders the shrimp cocktail anyway and Judith orders borscht. Her choice should have been a wise one but the borscht is simply liquid, very sweet; she takes only a few sips and puts down her spoon. Carl's shrimp are tiny and rubbery. "Maybe they *are* rubber—rubber shrimp for tourists," he says. Judith says: "I told you not to order shrimp."

"Yes," says Carl, "right, you did."

The doomed meal continues. Stringy roast beef, duck roasted so long it has become impossibly dry. Judith watches her lover, thinking, I hate this man—if we were married I would leave him. But she cannot help noticing his handsome flushed face (anger becomes him, even his eyes appear darker, shrewder), his movements which are no less graceful for being irritably self-conscious. If we were married I would leave him, Judith thinks. But we are not married.

The dining room is fairly crowded, unlike the sepulchral dining room of the old Europejski. Here, guests are extremely well dressed, the atmosphere is gracious and restrained, the young woman harpist is really quite talented so far as Judith can judge. (She is playing a dreamy version of "Clair de Lune.") At a table to Judith's right German is being spoken, briskly and loudly; at a smaller table behind Carl two older women sit, talking in what seems to be Swedish. There is a French table, there is another German table. No Polish? Carl's eyes move restlessly about. "What do you think," Judith asks in an undertone, "—the Germans? Surely they aren't East Germans, here?" Carl tries to overhear the conversation, sitting very still. After a minute or so he says: "I think you're right. *West* German."

He and Judith exchange an amused, baffled, startled look. . . . Remarkable that West German tourists should come to Warsaw, of all places: unless of course it isn't at all remarkable, it has become customary, no one except Judith and Carl is surprised.

"Well," says Carl in the flippant tone Judith has come to dread, "—*we're* here, after all."

The statement is illogical, senseless, not even witty; but Judith does not wish to question it. At times there is a childhood spirit between her and Carl, childhood in the least agreeable sense: you said that, I did not, you *said* that and got it wrong, no I did *not*, I hate you, I hate you too, I *hate* you I wish you were dead.

THE CHECK for the meal is slow in coming. Carl drums his fingernails on the table, Judith yawns behind her hand. Such fatigue, she thinks, could crack the high ornate ceiling of the dining room, could crack the very surface of the earth. "I'll wait for you in the lobby," Judith says, "I can't stand your restlessness," and she rises abruptly from the table and strides away, her face flushed, her leather bag swinging. No other woman in the dining room of the Victoria Hotel is wearing trousers tonight, let alone so defiantly sporty a costume as a suede jump suit with a half-dozen oversized zippers. But then no other woman in the room has the presence of the American Judith Horne.

She waits for her lover in the lobby. Examining advertisements for hotels elsewhere in Europe—Prague, Budapest. Handsome high-rise hotels with "every modern convenience." She yawns again. In another day they will be leaving Warsaw—in another day they will be gone. They will fly out of Poland to Frankfurt, to the West; immediately they will recognize their home territory. Posters of left-wing *Terroristen* are prominently displayed in the Frankfurt Airport—sad sullen intelligent faces, the eyes rather like Judith's own—and young German guards stroll about in pairs, their submachine guns cradled casually in their arms. A journalist friend of Judith's who once interviewed West German soldiers reported that the young men had never heard of Auschwitz, Belsen, Dachau . . . they'd never even heard the names.

Along with standard signs for restaurants, restrooms, telephones, and first aid there will be, in the Frankfurt Airport, signs for sex shops: cartoon drawings of the female figure. Home territory, the West.

Judith rouses herself from her reverie to see Carl approaching, through the plate glass door. He is walking quickly as usual; his expression is irritable, sullen, as if he knows she is watching and refuses to raise his eyes to hers. Impatiently he puts bills in his wallet, his head lowered. Judith watches him without love and thinks, I don't know the man who is going to walk head-on into that glass door, I have never seen him before in my life.

And then, incredibly, it does happen: Carl walks into the door: his head, slightly bowed, slams against the glass with a thud that reverberates through the lobby. People glance around. A woman exclaims in English—"Oh that poor man!" And Judith has not moved. She has watched her lover walk into a glass door and she has not moved, she has not spoken, she stands rooted to the spot, staring like any stranger.

BLARING AMERICAN ROCK MUSIC on the plane, announcements in Polish and Russian, box lunches of cheese, cold cuts, rye bread, Pepsi-Cola (warm) in small plastic cups. The stewardesses are Russian but their stylish self-conscious chic is international: blue suits with white turtleneck blouses, very red lips, rouged cheeks, long shining hair braided and fixed at the back of the head with silver barrettes. We have already left Poland, Judith thinks, climbing into the Soviet plane.

"Are you all right . . . ?" she asks Carl hesitantly. The ugly swelling on his forehead doesn't hurt, he has assured her. But she saw him swallowing aspirin back in the hotel, two and three at a time.

"You could have injured yourself seriously," Judith murmurs. Her eyes flood with tears at the memory, the image: Carl walking so confidently into that glass door. Before Judith had time to call out a warning.

"An idiotic accident," Carl says, shrugging. "It serves me right. Expecting a door to open automatically in Warsaw. . . ."

In the hotel room they packed quickly, carelessly. The room was in great disorder. Judith threw things in her suitcase without taking the time to fold them, she made a fumbling attempt to sort through her many papers—the farrago of names and addresses on slips of paper, notes to herself, booklets, maps, pamphlets printed by the state and pamphlets printed by illegal presses—while Carl said, "Never mind all that, come on, the limousine is waiting, throw it all in the suitcase or throw it all in the wastebasket, we're late."

Judith didn't have room for everything in her suitcase yet how could she sort through her things with Carl waiting, watching, pacing about . . . ? "Please don't make me nervous, damn you," she said, and Carl said, "for Christ's sake come *on*," and finally Judith threw nearly everything away—except three or four printed cards; these she secured in one of her pockets. "Here," said Carl, stooping to pick up *The Awkward Age* from the floor, "this too, let's go. We are not going to miss that plane."

Handshakes at the airport, farewells that might have been farewells between old friends, old comrades. All is rushed, precarious, poignant. Judith is touched by Tadeusz's shy smile—that look of genuine loss, of stricken comprehension—the essence, she thinks, of Polish melancholy. "Thank you so much for your kindness, your generosity," Judith says, shaking his hand hard, shaking Miroslav's hand, embracing Elizbieta who is, she discovers, terribly frail, "I have your names and addresses, I will write, we'll see one another again someday, thank you all very much. . . ." Carl too shakes hands, smiling. Judith had noticed that he is blinking frequently and that his right eye is awash with tears. The bump on his forehead is ugly and, even with its ridge of dried blood, slightly comic—a blind but glaring third eye. (The young Poles asked discreetly what had happened and Carl said, embarrassed, trying to laugh, "Nothing, an accident—entirely my fault.")

The plane taxis along the runway, exactly on time. Judith grips her lover's hand for comfort, for strength, thinking as always at such moments *The plane crashed within seconds of takeoff, killing all passengers and crew,* but nothing happens, nothing has ever happened, the plane simply rises, riding the air. Below there are squares and rectangles and long narrow strips of farmland . . . railroad tracks . . . highways . . . the long building of a collective farm. My Warszawa, Judith thinks, blinking tears from her eyes, recognizing nothing.

The plane ascends, banks to the left, moves into a blazing white mist. Now all is routine, mechanical. "There's the collective farm they took us to," Judith tells Carl, who is studying a glossy booklet printed in Cyrillic—he can read Russian, up to a point—and he looks over, peers out the window, frowns, says: "No I don't think so, I think the farm we saw is in another direction, miles away."

OUR WALL

—

L ONG BEFORE MANY of us were born, The Wall *was*.
    It is difficult for even the most imaginative and reckless of us to posit a time when The Wall *was not*.

Of course there are people—older people—who claim to remember not only the construction of The Wall (which, in its earliest stages, was rather primitive: primarily barbed wire, guarded by sentries and dogs) but a time when The Wall did not in any form *exist*.

Could one go freely into the Forbidden Zone then? We children never tire of asking, faintly scandalized and ready to burst into nervous laughter as if in the presence of something obscene. But the elderly tell us that there was no Forbidden Zone then, in the days of their youth.

No Forbidden Zone?—we are incredulous.

No Forbidden Zone?—we are somewhat frightened.

The shrewdest child among us, who is always asking bold, impudent questions, says brightly: If there was no Forbidden Zone then, why was The Wall constructed?

But no one understands his question. He repeats it insolently: *If there was no Forbidden Zone then, why was The Wall constructed?* No one, not even our oldest citizen, understands. Each of the boy's words, taken singly, is comprehensible; but the question in its entirety is incomprehensible. . . . *Why was The Wall constructed?*

It is far easier—most of us find it easier—to assume that The Wall is eternal, that it ever was and ever shall be. And that the Forbidden Zone (which of course none of us has ever seen) is eternal too.

SEVERAL TIMES A YEAR, though never on predictable dates, our leaders declare a Day of Grace. Which means that citizens of our country above the age of eighteen who are free of debt, familial responsibilities, and other private or civic handicaps, may attempt to scale The Wall without fear of punishment or reprisal. On a Day of Grace all explosives buried in the earth are inoperative; the current flowing through the barbed wire is shut off; the watchdogs are tied fast with chains; the sentries in their sentry boxes, hidden from sight, do not poke the muzzles of their submachine guns out and fire. It is said that on each Day of Grace a number of citizens do run across the burnt-out section of earth before The Wall (in some parts of the city it is no more than thirty feet wide, in others it is at least one hundred feet wide and represents, as one can well imagine, a formidable expanse!)—a number of citizens do run to The Wall and scale it and disappear on the other side. And are not stopped, not even scolded. So it is said.

And what becomes of them, on the other side? No one knows.

Of course we are only human, and rumors fly from house to house, wild improbable tales are told and repeated and embellished, no one knows what to believe. It may be claimed that a Day of Grace has been announced for a certain area—a privileged area—and not for another; or that the Day will begin on the first stroke of noon instead of on the last, or on the first stroke of midnight instead of on the last; or that there will be no restrictions at all regarding age, financial status, etc. As one might well imagine such cruel rumors result in butchery: the unstable rush forward too soon, or too late, or on the wrong day entirely, and before the horrified eyes of hundreds of witnesses (for there are always witnesses along The Wall) are shot down, or blown quite literally to bits by landmines, or savagely mauled by dogs. For we are, despite our history, a hopeful people.

Nevertheless each Day of Grace is eagerly awaited. Speculation on the exact date is widespread; we are all acquainted with certain obsessed and rather pathetic individuals who can speak of nothing else (though—of course!—these are the very individuals who would never dream of trying to scale The Wall). Even those who have never in their lifetimes witnessed a single successful escape (for sometimes the slang expression "escape" is used openly)—people who have been passive onlookers, for decades, at many a spectacular and heartrending slaughter—continue to have faith. One would think that their number might gradually dwindle, but the contrary happens to be true. For we are, as our historians have noted, a hopeful people.

THE WALL APPEARS to be about twenty-five feet high, though some theoreticians claim that it is considerably higher, while others believe that it may be lower. Measurements are imprecise since they must be made—if at all—at a distance from The Wall, and under cover of darkness. It is a commonplace belief that The Wall is made of fairly smooth concrete, an ordinary enough material, and in itself not particularly fearful. The top has been rounded for aesthetic and security reasons: it is more attractive that way, and presents more difficulties for those who try to scramble over the wall using their bare hands. (Barbed grappling hooks are said to be necessary for a successful escape, but such grappling hooks are forbidden by law. Indeed, there are those of us who have never seen a grappling hook, not even a picture of one: yet we whisper the words "grappling hook" amongst ourselves quite freely.) Our elders claim that The Wall did not always have a rounded top, but it is difficult for most of the population under a certain age—about forty—to remember any other kind of top.

In heavily populated areas of the city there are two additional "walls" or barriers. One is a wire-mesh fence with barbed wire at the top, which is (evidently) electrified; another is a row of anti-tank obstacles placed at five- or six-foot intervals. The obstacles, like The Wall itself, are painted a uniform dove-gray, and are quite attractive. Beds of yellow and purple pansies lend a cheerful touch: nothing extravagant, but welcome to the eye.

In less populated areas The Wall stands majestically alone, and in the burnt-out space before it landmines have been buried so carefully that (so it is rumored) not even the shrewdest eye can detect them. Nocturnal hares, poor creatures, frequently detonate these explosives. They know no better. We are often awakened from our sleep by the sharp cracking thunder of an explosion: is it near, or far? At such times we lie awake, not caring to speak, for what is there to say?—the hares know no better, they are poor ignorant beasts, and nuisances at that.

Two nights ago there was an explosion. Difficult to judge its distance. To the east, to the west?—difficult to judge. Did you hear that noise, one of us asks another softly, and the other says, Did I hear what? or perhaps does not reply at all. What is there to say? Nocturnal hares, nuisances.

THE WALL IS CONSIDERED a work of art by some citizens, and an abomination by others. The largest percentage of the population, however, does not "see" The Wall at all—that is, literally. Consequently The Wall elicits no emotion and, indeed, the term "The Wall" is rarely used. The expression *over there* is fairly frequent, as in (to a naughty child): If you don't behave I'll send you *over there*. (Over where? I once asked my mother boldly. Over *where*? *Where*?—You'll see over where, my mother said, slapping my face. Her breath came quick and hard; her own cheeks were burning.)

AND DO YOU KNOW that children's bones are buried in The Wall?— in the foundation of The Wall? Children of exceptional beauty or talent—children who were orphans, or in some way unprotected—too high-spirited for their own good and for the good of the community. On dark wet nights when the wind blows from The Wall you can hear their querulous chatter.

Of course these are silly tales, in which none of us believes. In our district we have eradicated superstition. The Wall is The Wall and (so we believe) it is made of ordinary material. It is *not* haunted: its great strength has nothing to do with children's corpses. Sometimes, late at night, you can hear their faint high voices. Where are we, what year is it, what has happened . . . ?

But no: there are no voices: there are no spirits. The Wall is only *(only!)* The Wall.

ONE OF THE VOICES is my brother's voice.

Do you hear him, I asked my parents, but they did not hear a thing. Only the wind, the wind. Rain drumming on the roof, on the windows. Streaming down the windowpanes.

I burrowed beneath the bedclothes to the foot of the bed and lay very still. My thumb and then two fingers stuck in my mouth. The wind, the wind from The Wall, rain drumming on the roof all night, his voice, his crying for help, I could see him dragging himself on the stubbled grass and his uplifted face glistening with blood: and the half-circle of witnesses. For there are always witnesses—silent witnesses—along the many miles of The Wall.

Toward morning, when the wind died down, I fell asleep. And did not dream at all.

IT IS ONLY A COINCIDENCE, but according to reliable sources the next Day of Grace will fall *on my eighteenth birthday.* Which is to say, at the very end of the interminable month of August.

THE WALL: which stretches out forever. Mesmerizing and boring and beautiful, so beautiful! You can't know. You can't know unless you crouch here with me in my secret place, my hiding place; in a stand of scrub birch hundreds of yards from the nearest house. Underfoot are shards of glass, fragments of board, rubble from The War (which took place long before I was born, before even the building of The Wall—if the old people can be trusted to tell the truth). I crouch here for long minutes at a time, staring at The Wall, letting its gray uniformity flood into my brain. Mesmerizing and boring, so boring, and so beautiful, our Wall!—long minutes, long unrecorded hours at a time, my back aching, my face beaded with sweat. I want nothing from The Wall, I am content merely to gaze upon it. Knowing that it is there. That it exists. That one cannot move *in that direction*. That there is a *Forbidden Zone* which has been explicitly marked, and from which we are to be protected forever. How was it possible for human beings in my country to live, to endure their lives, before the construction of The Wall?—when they might have *freely* moved in any direction, even in the direction of that which is forbidden? (The thought fills me with anxiety. Tears begin to sting in my eyes, and threaten to roll down my warm cheeks. To move *freely* in any direction, what horror!)

Gray concrete. Miles. Years. A lifetime. An eternity. So boring. At peace. So beautiful my heart plunges. In the midday sun, in the late afternoon sun, in a fine light drizzle that obliterates all outlines . . . The Wall is absolutely motionless . . . one cannot imagine a time when it was not . . . and the sentries' boxes every two hundred yards or so . . . the border guards (chosen for both their skill as soldiers and their loyalty to the State) hidden from view, even the muzzles of their submachine guns hidden. As a young boy I wanted to be one of them. But then the shame of my brother, the fuss, the black mark. . . . I want to be one of them now. I want to sit for long empty mesmerizing hours inside a sentry box, a submachine gun in my hands, always ready, always ready to fire.

Ugly things are told about some of the border guards.

—They shoot *at will* if they choose. If a face offends them, or a gesture. If they are bored. If nothing exciting has happened in a long time.

—They themselves are frequently defectors. (Which is, of course, logical. For no one has such opportunity to escape as they do. Enviable men! I hate them, as everyone in my district does.)

—They have no more loyalty to the State than the next person, but enjoy the power of the sentry box and the feel, the weight, of the submachine gun in their hands.

I crouch in my hiding place for hours. Sometimes it seems that years have passed. I am not a child now. I am waiting.

Beyond The Wall the sky is a feathery blue, or a turbulent rippled gray. Sometimes it rains. Sometimes the sun glares. I am at peace, gazing at The Wall. Its wonderful sameness, its mysterious strength . . . while human beings change . . . grow old, weak, unreliable. I am at peace here. If I hear gunfire in the distance, or the barking of dogs, I am never agitated. For I do not intend to make a run for it like the others. I am content to live my life *on this side*.

WHAT, precisely, is the Forbidden Zone, from which the citizens of my country must be protected?

Absolute truth is impossible to come by, since anyone who climbs The Wall successfully disappears from our world and never returns; and anyone who climbs The Wall unsuccessfully is killed on the spot. However, here are the most popular theories:

> —There is a paradise beyond The Wall in which men and women live "freely." (Though of course they must be bound—how could they fail to be?—by The Wall, just as we are. Perhaps it is somehow worse for them because our Wall surrounds them.)
> —There are dangerous, diseased, psychotic people beyond The Wall. A race not unlike ours, but degenerate. A brother-race? But degenerate. At one point in history (evidently during the life-spans of some who are still living) all of us constituted a single race, from which the population of the Forbidden Zone fell away.
> —There is nothing but a graveyard beyond The Wall: a mere dumping ground for the dead. The bleak truth of The Wall is that it protects the living from the dead (the noxious gases of the cemetery); or, as the more subtle among us reason, it protects us from our own future.
> —There is an ordinary world beyond The Wall—our own world,

in fact—but it is a mirror-image, a reversal. None of us could survive in it.

My own theory? I have none. I think only of The Wall. The fact of The Wall, which settles so massively in the mind. The Wall exists to be scaled, like all walls: it is the most exquisite of temptations. The Wall poses the question—*How long can you resist?*

I AM A GOOD RUNNER, I can run for miles, my heart beats large and steady in my chest, my pulses race, my muscular body grows sweat-slick, I am pitiless toward my legs and feet; and my hands are strong. These are mere facts. They point toward nothing beyond themselves.

"TRAITORS"—"criminals"—"subversives"—"degenerates"—"enemies of the People"—"victims of aberration": these are the official terms for those who defect from our side of The Wall. A formal death sentence is passed upon them in absentia, and their families are subjected to harsh penalties. (Though in fact it frequently happens that the families, having publicly exhibited their shame and grief, and having publicly vowed their love for and loyalty to the State, escape the most severe penalties and even enjoy a curious sort of celebrity. For humiliation, if it is properly absorbed, can be a sacred experience.)

Yet I would not abandon my family. My mother and father who lie to me, as they lie to each other; but out of necessity; out of love.

I would not abandon them as others have.

I have never seen The Wall desecrated.

I have never been a witness.

Except: I was among that crowd of schoolchildren who gawked at the dying boy at the foot of The Wall one weekday morning. He had tried to escape during the night and had actually scaled The Wall—he was strong and supple, he must have prepared for his "escape" for many months in secret—but of course the guards shot him down, as they always do: who could elude them? They shot him during the night but did not kill him and so he lay for hours, for many hours, into the dawn, the morning, the mid-morning, bleeding to death in a field of stubbled grass, and calling for help. A high faint voice. An incredulous voice. Not a voice I recognized.

SUNDAY, the last Sunday of the month, is to be a Day of Grace. My eighteenth birthday. The official proclamation has not been made but rumors fly freely from house to house.

The Wall, in the midday sun, appears to show a certain *benevolent* aspect. If you stare for a very long time, your eyes held open wide, this *benevolence* becomes obvious. Yet why has no one remarked upon it, to my knowledge?

So few of my fellow citizens "see" The Wall at all.

WASN'T THAT YOUR BROTHER who was shot down in the field, people asked.

I don't have a brother, I said angrily.

Wasn't that your brother?—the one they shot down? schoolchildren teased.

My brother? Whose brother? I don't have a brother.

They jeered and threw stones at me. Chanted: He deserved it, he deserved it, the traitor, he deserved every bullet they gave him! *I don't have any brother*, I shouted.

IT IS SAID, and if you climb high enough you can ascertain for yourself, that The Wall zigzags and curves back upon itself, by no means describing a perfect circle around the Forbidden Zone. Strange. Hard to comprehend. Unless the workers who built it were drunk, or playful. Or subversive.

TO CARESS—just once—the blank face of The Wall. To get that close. To lay your hands upon it. Just once! In dreams, the most shameful and turbulent of dreams, where one is clambering up The Wall—*and* being riddled by the guards' bullets at the same time (for death too, at such a time, in such a manner, would be exquisite): in dreams we scale The Wall nightly, and keep our secrets to ourselves.

THE WALL, where small yellow butterflies impale themselves upon the barbed wire. A great fist in my chest. Broken glass beneath my feet. A delirium that must be love. . . . Of course there are lurid tales: men and even women shot down and dragged away and never heard of again, and never spoken of again. Because they stared too hard at The Wall. Might have seemed to be studying it, memorizing it. Adoring it. (Do I know anyone who has disappeared? I know no one. "Disappearing" carries with it the obliteration of memory, after all. *Everything* connected with a traitor is lost.)

A very strange tale, too wild to be credible, about a family in a balloon who drifted across The Wall. Seven people including a baby. Romantic but implausible. . . . Wouldn't a large balloon make an irresistible target?

(SOMEDAY, it is whispered, we *will* overcome The Wall. And mate with those men and women on the "other side." As we are destined to do. As we had done in history. We will breed a race of giants once again, we will conquer the world. . . . The Wall, one must assume, has been erected solely to prevent this, the fulfillment of our destiny: The Wall is an invention of our enemies and must be surmounted.)

BUT NOW, today, this sunny morning, what of today?—my eighteenth birthday? A helmeted guard has poked his head out of his sentry box and is waving to me in my hiding place. Yes? Yes? Perhaps he knows it is my birthday? I stand slowly, blinking. The sunlight is fierce. The guard has taken pity on me, perhaps, and is waving me forward. Come stand in the shadow of The Wall. Come press your overheated cheek against The Wall's cool side. . . . For the first time I can see fine cracks in The Wall, and weeds growing lavishly at its base. (I have never been so close before.) Come closer, have no fear, long before you were born The Wall was, and forever will The Wall endure.

RAVEN'S WING

———

BILLY WAS AT the Meadowlands track one Saturday when the accident happened to Raven's Wing—a three-year-old silky black colt who was the favorite in the first race, and one of the crowd favorites generally this season. (Though Billy hadn't placed his bet on Raven's Wing. Betting on the 1.06 favorite held no excitement and, in any case, things were going too well for Raven's Wing, his owner's luck would be running out soon.) Telling his wife about the accident the next morning Billy was surprised at how important it came to seem, how intense his voice sounded, as if he were high, or on edge, which he was not; it was just the *telling* that worked him up, and the way Linda looked at him.

"So there he was in the backstretch, looping around one, two, three, four horses to take the lead—he's a hard driver, Raven's Wing, doesn't let himself off easy—a little skittish at the starting gate, but then he got serious—in fact he was maybe running a little faster than he needed to run, once he got out front—then something happened, it looked like he stumbled, his hindquarters went down just a little—but he was going so fast, maybe forty miles an hour, the momentum kept him going—Jesus, it must have been three hundred feet!—the poor bastard, on three legs. Then the jockey jumped off, the other horses ran by, Raven's Wing was just sort of standing there by the rail, his head bobbing up and down. What had happened was he'd broken his left rear leg—came down too hard on it, maybe, or the hoof sunk in the dirt wrong. Just like that," Billy said. He snapped his fingers. "One minute we're looking at a two-million-dollar colt, the next minute—nothing."

"Wait. What do you mean, nothing?" Linda said.

"They put them down if they aren't going to race any more."

" 'Put them down'—you mean they kill them?"

"Sure. Most of the time."

"How do they kill them? Do they shoot them?"

"I doubt it, probably some kind of needle, you know, injection, poison in their bloodstream."

Linda was leaning toward him, her forehead creased. "Okay, then what happened?" she said.

"Well, an ambulance came out to the track and picked him up, there was an announcement about him breaking his leg, everybody in the stands was real quiet when they heard. Not because there was a lot of money on him either but because, you know, here's this first-class colt, a real beauty, a two-million-dollar horse, finished. Just like that."

Linda's eyelids were twitching, her mouth, she might have been going to cry, or maybe, suddenly, laugh, you couldn't predict these days; near as Billy figured she hadn't washed her hair in more than a week and it looked like hell, she hadn't washed herself in all that time either, wore the same plaid shirt and jeans day after day, not that he'd lower himself to bring the subject up. She was staring at him, squinting. Finally she said, "How much did you lose?—you can tell me," in a breathy little voice.

"How much did *I* lose?" Billy asked. He was surprised as hell: they'd covered all this ground, hadn't they, there were certain private matters in his life, things that were none of her business, he'd explained it—her brother had explained it too—things she didn't need to know. And good reasons for her not to know. "How much did *I* lose—?" .

He pushed her aside, lightly, just with the tips of his fingers, and went to the refrigerator to get a beer. It was only ten in the morning but he was thirsty and his head and back teeth ached. "Who says I lost? We were out there for five races. In fact I did pretty well, we all did, what the fuck do you know about it," Billy said. He opened the beer, took his time drinking. He knew that the longer he took the calmer he'd get and it was one of those mornings—Sunday, bells ringing, everybody's schedule off—when he didn't want to get angry. But his hand was trembling when he drew a wad of bills out of his inside coat pocket and let it fall onto the kitchen counter. "Three hundred, go ahead and count it, sweetheart," he said, "you think you're so smart."

Linda stood with her knees slightly apart, her big belly straining at the flannel shirt she wore, her mouth still twitching. Even with her skin grainy and sallow, and pimples across her forehead, she looked good, she was a good-looking girl; hell, thought Billy, it was a shame, a bad deal. She said, so soft he almost couldn't hear, "I don't think I'm so smart."

"Yeah? What?"

"I don't think I'm anything."

She was looking at the money but for some reason, maybe she was afraid, she didn't touch it. Actually Billy had won almost $1,000 but that was his business.

LINDA WAS EIGHT years younger than Billy, just twenty-four though she looked younger, blond, high-strung, skinny except for her belly (she was five, six months pregnant, Billy couldn't remember), with hollowed-out eyes, that sullen mouth. They had been married almost a year and Billy thought privately it was probably a mistake though in fact he loved her, he *liked* her, if only she didn't do so many things to spite him. If she wasn't letting herself go, letting herself get sick, strung-out, weird, just to spite him.

He'd met her through her older brother, a friend of Billy's, more or less, from high school, a guy he'd done business with and could trust. But they had had a misunderstanding the year before and no longer worked together.

Once, in bed, Linda said, "If the man had to have it, boy, then things would be different. Things would be a lot different."

"What? A baby? How do you mean?" Billy asked. He'd been halfway asleep, he wanted to humor her, he didn't want a fight at two in the morning. "Are we talking about a baby?"

"They *wouldn't* have it, that's all."

"What?"

"The baby. Any baby."

"Jesus—that's crazy."

"Yeah? Who? Would you?" Linda said angrily. "What about your own?"

Billy had two children, both boys, from his first marriage; but as things worked out he never saw them and rarely thought about them—his wife had remarried, moved to Tampa. At one time Billy used to say that he and his ex-wife got along all right, they weren't out to slit each other's throat like some people he knew, but in fact when Billy's salary at G-M Radiator had been garnisheed a few years ago he wasn't very happy; he'd gone through a bad time. So he'd quit the job, a good-paying job too, and later, when he tried to get hired back, they were already laying off men, it was rotten luck, his luck had run against him for a long time. One of the things that drove him wild was the fact that his wife, that is his ex-wife, was said to be pregnant again, and he'd maybe be helping to support another man's kid; when he thought of it he wanted to kill somebody, anybody, but then she got married after all and it worked out and now he didn't have to see her or even think of her very much: that was the advantage of distance. But now he said, "Sure," trying to keep it all light, "what the hell, sure, it beats the Army."

"*You'd* have a baby?" Linda said. Now she was sitting up, leaning over him, her hair in her face, her eyes showing a rim of white above the iris. "Oh, don't hand me that. Oh, please."

"Sure. If you wanted me to."

"I'm asking about *you*—would *you* want to?"

They had been out drinking much of the evening and Linda was groggy but skittish, on edge, her face pale and giving off a queer damp heat. The way she was grinning, Billy didn't want to pursue the subject.

"How about *you*, I said," she said, jabbing him with her elbow, "I'm talking about *you*."

"I don't know what the hell we are talking about."

"You do know."

"What?—I don't."

"You do. You do. Don't hand me such crap."

WHEN HE AND LINDA first started going together they'd made love all the time, like crazy, it was such a relief (so Billy told himself) to be out from under that other bitch; but now, married only a year, with Linda dragging around the apartment sick and angry and sometimes talking to herself, pretending she didn't know Billy could hear, now everything had changed, he couldn't predict whether she'd be up or down, high or low, very low, hitting bottom, scaring him with her talk about killing herself (her crazy mother had tried *that* a few times, it probably ran in the family) or getting an abortion (but wasn't it too late, her stomach that size, for an abortion?), he never knew when he opened the door what he'd be walking into. She didn't change her clothes, including her underwear, for a week at a time, she didn't wash her hair, she'd had a tight permanent that sprang out around her head but turned flat, matted, blowsy if it wasn't shampooed, he knew she was ruining her looks to spite him but she claimed (shouting, crying, punching her own thighs with her fists) that she just *forgot* about things like that, she had more important things to think about. (One day Billy caught sight of this great-looking girl out on the street, coat with a fox fur collar like the one he'd bought for Linda, high-heeled boots like Linda's, blond hair, wild springy curls like a model's, frizzed, airy, her head high and her walk fast, almost like strutting—she knew she was being watched, and not just by Billy—and then she turned and it *was* Linda, his own wife, she'd washed her hair and fixed herself up, red lipstick, even eye makeup—he'd just stood there staring, it took him by such surprise. But then the next week she was back to lying around the apartment feeling sorry for herself, sullen and heavy-hearted, sick to her stomach even if she hadn't eaten anything.)

The worst of the deal was, he and her brother had had their misunderstanding and didn't do business any longer. When Billy got drunk he had the vague idea that he was getting stuck again with another guy's baby.

THE RACING NEWS WAS, Raven's Wing hadn't been killed after all. It *was* news, people were talking about it, Billy read about it in the newspaper, an operation on the colt's leg estimated to cost in the six-figure range, a famous veterinary surgeon the owner was flying in from Dallas, and there was a photograph (it somehow frightened Billy, that photograph) of Raven's Wing lying on his side, anesthetized, strapped down, being operated on like a human being. The *size* of a horse—that always impressed Billy.

Other owners had their opinions, was it worth it or not, other trainers, veterinarians, but Raven's Wing's owner wanted to save his life, the colt wasn't just any horse (the owner said), he was the most beautiful horse they'd ever reared on their farm. He was insured for $2,200,000 and the insurance company had granted permission for the horse to be destroyed but still the owner wanted to save his life. "They wouldn't do that for a human being," Linda said when Billy told her.

"Well," Billy said, irritated at her response, "this isn't a human being, it's a first-class horse."

"Jesus, a *horse* operated on," Linda said, laughing, "and he isn't even going to run again, you said? How much is all this going to cost?"

"People like that, they don't care about money. They have it, they spend it on what matters," Billy said. "It's a frame of reference you don't know shit about."

"Then what?"

"What?"

"After the operation?"

"After the operation, if it works, then he's turned out to stud," Billy said. "You know what that is, huh?" he said, poking her in the breast.

"Just a minute. The horse is worth that much?"

"A first-class horse is worth a lot, I told you. Sometimes three, four million—these people take things *seriously*."

"Millions of dollars for an animal?" Linda said slowly. She sounded dazed, disoriented, as if the fact were only now sinking in; but what *was* the fact, what did it mean? "I think that's *sick*."

"I told you, Linda, it's a frame of reference you don't know shit about."

"That's right, I don't."

She was making such an ugly face at him, drawing her lips back from her teeth, Billy lost control and shoved her against the edge of the kitchen table, and she slapped him, hard, on the side of the nose, and it was all Billy could do to stop right there, just *stop*, not give it back to the bitch like she deserved. He knew, once he got started with this one, it might be the end. She might not be able to pick herself up from the floor when he was done.

BILLY ASKED AROUND, and there was this contact of his named Kellerman, and Kellerman was an old friend of Raven's Wing's trainer, and he fixed it up so that he and Billy could drive out to the owner's farm in Pennsylvania, so that Billy could see the horse; Billy just wanted to *see* the horse, it was always at the back of his mind these days.

The weather was cold, the sky a hard icy blue, the kind of day that made Billy feel shaky, things were so bright, so vivid, you could see something weird and beautiful anywhere you looked. His head ached, he was so edgy, his damn back teeth, he chewed on Bufferin, he and Kellerman drank beer out of cans, tossed the cans away on the road. Kellerman said horse people like these were the real thing, the real fucking thing, look at this layout, and not even counting Raven's Wing they had a stable worth millions, a Preakness winner, a second-place Kentucky Derby winner, but was the money even in horses?—hell no, it was in some investments or something. That was how rich people worked.

In the stable, at Raven's Wing's stall, Billy hung over the partition and looked at him for a long time, just looked. Kellerman and the trainer were talking but Billy just looked.

The size of the horse, that was one of the things, and the head, the big rounded eyes, ears pricked forward, tail switching, here was Raven's Wing looking at last at him, did he maybe recognize Billy—no, did he maybe sense who Billy was?—extending a hand to him, whispering his name. Hey, Raven's Wing. Hey.

The size, and the silky sheen of the coat, the jet-black coat, that skittish air, head bobbing, teeth bared, Billy could feel his warm breath, Billy sucked in the strong *smell*—horse manure, horse piss, sweat, hay, mash, and what was he drinking?—apple juice, the trainer said. *Apple juice*, Christ! Gallons and gallons of it. Did he have his appetite back, Billy asked, but it was obvious the colt did, he was eating steadily, chomping hay, eyeing Billy as if Billy was—was what?—just the man he wanted to see. The man who'd driven a hundred miles to see him.

Both his rear legs were in casts, the veterinarian had taken a bone graft from the good leg, and his weight was down—1,130 pounds to 880—his ribs showing through the silky coat, but Jesus did he look good, Jesus this was the real thing wasn't it?—Billy's heart fast as if he'd been popping pills, he wished to hell Linda was here, yeah, the bitch should see *this*, it'd shut her up for a while.

Raven's Wing was getting his temper back, the trainer said, which was a good thing, it showed he was mending, but he still wasn't 99 percent in the clear, maybe they didn't know how easy it was for horses to get sick—colic, pneumonia, all kinds of viruses, infections—even the good leg went bad for a while, paralyzed, they had to have two operations, a six-hour and a four-hour, the owner had to sign a release they'd put him down right on the operating table if things looked too bad. But he pulled through, his muscle tone was improving every day, there he was, fiery little bastard—watch out or he'll nip you—a steel plate, steel wire, a dozen screws in his leg, and him not knowing a thing. The way the bone was broken it wasn't *broken*, the trainer told them, it was smashed, like somebody had gone after it with a sledgehammer.

"So he's going to make it," Billy said, not quite listening. "Hey. Yeah. *You*. You're going to make it, huh."

He and Kellerman were at the stall maybe forty-five minutes, and the place was busy, busier than Billy would have thought, it rubbed him the wrong way that so many people were around when he'd had the idea he and Kellerman would be the only ones. But it turned out that Raven's Wing always had visitors. He even got mail. (This Billy snorted to hear—a horse gets *mail*?) People took away souvenirs if they could, good-luck things, hairs from his mane, his tail, that sort of thing, or else they wanted to feed him by hand: there was a lot of that, they had to be watched.

Before they left Billy leaned over as far as he could, just wanting to stroke Raven's Wing's side, and two things happened fast: the horse snorted, stamped, lunged at his hand; and the trainer pulled Billy back.

"Hey, I told you," he said. "This is a dangerous animal."

"He likes me," Billy said. "He wasn't going to bite hard."

"Yeah?—sometimes he does. They can bite damn hard."

"He wasn't going to bite actually *hard*," Billy said.

THREE DOZEN blue snakeskin wallets (Venezuelan), almost two dozen upscale watches (Swiss, German—chronographs, water-resistant, self-winding, calendar, ultrathin, quartz, and gold tone), and a pair of pierced earrings, gold and pearl, delicate, Billy thought, as a snowflake. He gave the earrings to Linda to surprise her and watched her put them in; it amazed him how quickly she could take out earrings and slip in new ones, position the tiny wires exactly in place, he knew it was a trick he could never do if he was a woman. It made him shiver, it excited him, just to watch.

Linda never said, "Hey, where'd you get *these*," the way his first wife used to, giving him that slow wide wet smile she thought turned him on. (Actually it had turned him on, for a while. Two, three years.)

Linda never said much of anything except thank you in her little-girl breathy voice, if she happened to be in the mood for thanking.

ONE MORNING a few weeks later Linda, in her bathrobe, came slowly out of the bedroom into the kitchen, squinting at something she held in the air, at eye level. "This looks like somebody's hair, what is it, Indian hair?—it's all black and stiff," she said. Billy was on the telephone so he had an excuse not to give her his fullest attention at the moment. He might be getting ready to be angry, he might be embarrassed, his nerves were always bad this time of day. Linda leaned up against him, swaying a little in her preoccupation, exuding heat, her bare feet planted apart on the linoleum floor. She liked to poke at him with her belly, she had a new habit of standing close.

Billy kept on with his conversation, it was in fact an important conversation, and Linda wound the several black hairs around her forearm, making a little bracelet, so tight the flesh started to turn white—didn't it hurt?—her forehead creased in concentration, her breath warm and damp against his neck.

GOLDEN GLOVES

———

HE WAS A premature baby, seven months old, born with deformed feet: the tiny arches twisted, the toes turned inward like fleshly claws. He didn't learn to walk until the age of three; then he tottered and lurched from side to side, his small face contorted with an adult rage, a rim of white showing above the irises of his eyes. His parents watched him in pity and despair—his father with a kind of embarrassment as well. Even at that age he hated to be helped to walk. Sometimes he hated to be touched.

Until the age of eight, when both his feet were finally operated on, he was always stumbling, falling, hurting himself, but he was accustomed to pain, he rarely cried. He wasn't like other children! At school, on the playground, out on the street, the cruelest children mocked him, called him names—Cripple, Freak—sometimes they even tripped him—but as he got older and stronger they learned to keep their distance. If he could grab them he'd hurt them with his hard pummeling fists, he'd make them cry. And even with his handicap he was quick: quick and clever and sinewy as a snake.

After the operation on his feet his father began to take him to boxing matches downtown in the old sports arena. He will remember all his life the excitement of his first Golden Gloves tournament, some of the boxers as young as fifteen, ribs showing, backs raw with acne, hard tight muscles, tiny glinting gold crosses on chains around their necks. He remembers the brick-red leather gloves that looked as if they must be soft to the touch, the bodies hotly gleaming with sweat, white boys, black boys, their amazing agility, the quickness of their feet and hands, high-laced shoes and ribbed socks halfway to their knees. They wore trunks like swimming trunks, they wore robes like bathrobes, and all with such nonchalance, in public. He remembers the dazzling lights focused upon the elevated ring, the shouts of the crowd that came in waves, the warm rippling applause when one boy of a pair was declared the winner of his match, his arm held aloft by the referee. What must it be, to be that boy!—to stand in his place!

He was seated in a child's wheelchair in the aisle, close beside his father's seat. Both legs encased in plaster from hip to toe: and him trapped inside. He was a quiet child, a friendly child, uncomplaining and perhaps even shy, showing none of the emotion that welled up in him—hurt, anger, shame—when people stared. They were curious, mainly—didn't mean to be insulting. Just ignore them, honey, his mother always said. But when he was alone with his father and people looked at him a little too long his father bristled with irritation. If anyone dared ask what had happened to him his father would say, Who wants to know? in a certain voice. And the subject was quickly dropped.

To him his father said, Let the sons of bitches mind their own business and we'll mind ours. Right?

THE OPERATION had lasted nine hours but he remembered little of it afterward except the needle going into his arm, into a vein, the careening lights, then waking alone and frightened in a room so cold his teeth began to chatter. Such cold, and such silence: he thought he must have died. Then the pain began and he knew he was alive, he cried in short breathless incredulous sobs until the first shock was past. A nurse stood over him telling him he'd be all right. He'd been a brave, brave little boy, she said.

The promise all along had been: he'd be able to walk now like any other boy. As soon as the casts were removed.

And: he'd be able to run. (Until now he'd crawled on his hands and knees faster than he'd been able to walk, like something scuttling along a beach.)

In his wheelchair at the Golden Gloves tournament he told himself he would be a boxer: he told himself at the conclusion of the first three-round match when a panting grinning boy was declared the winner of his match, on points, his arm held high, the gleaming brick-red glove raised for all to see. And the applause!—immediate, familial, rising and swelling like a heartbeat gone wild. The boy's father was in the ring with him, other boys who might have been his brothers or cousins—they were hugging one another in their happiness at the victory. Then the ring was emptied except for the referee, and the next young boxers and their seconds appeared.

He knew: he would be up there in the ring one day in the lights, rows of people watching. He would be there in the lighted ring, not in a wheelchair. Not in the audience at all.

AFTER THE CASTS were removed he had to learn to walk again.

They stood him carefully against a wall like a small child and encouraged him, Don't be afraid, take a step, take another step, come to them as best he could. They told him it wouldn't hurt and though it did hurt he didn't care, he plunged out lurching, swaying, falling panicked into his mother's arms. Yes, said his mother. Like that. Come *on*, said his father. Try again.

It was a year before he could walk inside the house without limping or turning his left foot helplessly inward. It was another year before he could run in the yard or in the school playground. By then his father had bought him a pair of child's boxing gloves, soft simulated dark brown leather. The gloves were the size of melons and so beautiful his eyes filled with tears when he first saw them. He would remember their sharp pungent smell through his life.

His father laced on the gloves, crouched to spar with him, taught him a few basic principles—how to hold his guard, how to stand at an angle with his chin tucked against his shoulder (Joe Louis style), how to jab, how to keep moving—later arranged for him to take boxing lessons at the YMCA. His father had wanted to be a boxer himself when he was a boy, he'd fought in a few three-round matches at a local club but had won only the first match; his reflexes, he said, were just slightly off: when his opponent's jab got to him he forgot everything he knew and wanted to slug it out. He'd known enough to quit before he got hurt. Either you have the talent or you don't, his father said. It can't be faked.

He began to train at the Y, he worked out every day after school and on Saturday mornings; by the age of sixteen he'd brought his weight up to 130 pounds standing five foot six, he could run ten, twelve, as many as fifteen miles without tiring. He was quick, light, shrewd, he was good at boxing and he knew he was good, everyone acknowledged it, everyone watched him with interest. When he wasn't at the gym—when he had to be in school, or in church, or at home, even in bed—he was thinking about the gym, the ring, himself in his boxing trunks and leather gloves, Vaseline smeared on his face and his headgear on his head, he was in his crouch but getting ready to move, his knees bent, his hands closed into fists. He was ready! He couldn't be taken unawares! He couldn't be stopped! He became obsessed with some of the boys and young men he knew at the gym, their weights, their heights, the reach of their arms, could they knock him out if he fought them, could he knock them out? What did they think about *him*? There were weeks when he was infatuated with one or another boy who might be a year or two older than he, a better boxer, until it was revealed that he wasn't a better boxer after all: he had his weaknesses, his bad habits, his limitations. He concentrated a good deal on the feel of his own body, building up his muscles, strengthening his stomach, his neck, learning not to wince at pain—not to show pain at all. He loved the sinewy springiness of his legs and feet, the tension in his shoulders; he loved the way his body came to life, moving, it seemed, of its own will, knowing by instinct how to strike his opponent how to get through his opponent's guard how to hurt him and hurt him again and make it last. His clenched fists inside the shining gloves. His teeth in the mouthpiece. Eyes narrowed and shifting behind the hot lids as if they weren't his own eyes merely but those belonging to someone he didn't yet know, an adult man, a man for whom all things were possible.

SOMETIMES on Saturday afternoons the boys were shown film clips and documentaries of the great fighters. Jack Dempsey—Gene Tunney—Benny Leonard—Joe Louis—Billy Conn—Archie Moore—Sandy Saddler—Carmen Basilio—Sugar Ray Robinson—Jersey Joe Walcott—Rocky Marciano. He watched entranced, staring at the flickering images on the screen; some of the films were aged and poorly preserved, the blinds at the windows fitted loosely so that the room wasn't completely darkened, and the boxers took on an odd ghostly insubstantial look as they crouched and darted and lunged at one another. Feinting, clinching, backing off, then the flurry of gloves so swift the eye couldn't follow, one man suddenly down and the other in a neutral corner, the announcer's voice rising in excitement as if it were all happening now right now and not decades ago. More astonishing than the powerful blows dealt were the blows taken, the punishment absorbed as if really finally one could not be hurt by an opponent, only stopped by one's own failure of nerve or judgment. If you're hurt you deserve to be hurt! If you're hurt badly you deserve to be hurt badly! Turning to the referee to protest a low blow, his guard momentarily lowered—there was Jack Sharkey knocked out by Jack Dempsey with a fast left hook. Like that! And the fight was over. And there was aging Archie Moore knocked down repeatedly, savagely, by young Yvon Durrelle, staggering on his feet part-conscious but indomitable—how had he come back to win? how had he done it?—boasting he wasn't tired afterward, he could fight the fight all over again. Young Joe Louis baffled and outboxed by stylish Billy Conn for twelve rounds, then suddenly as Conn swarmed all over him trying to knock him out Louis came alive, turned into a machine for hitting, combinations so rapid the eye couldn't follow, left hooks, right crosses, uppercuts, a dozen punches within seconds and Conn was finished—that was the great Joe Louis in his prime. And here, Jersey Joe Walcott outboxing Rocky Marciano until suddenly Marciano connected with his right, that terrible incalculably powerful right, Let's see the knockout in slow motion, the announcer said, and you could see this time how it happened,

Walcott hit so hard his face so stunned so distorted it was no longer a human face, no longer recognizable. And Rocky Marciano and Ezzard Charles fighting for Marciano's heavyweight title in 1954—after fifteen rounds both men covered in blood from cuts and gashes in their faces but embracing each other like brothers, smiling, laughing it seemed, in mutual respect and admiration and it didn't—almost—seem to matter that one man had to lose and the other had to win: they'd fought one of the great fights of the century and everyone knew it.

And *he* knew he was of their company. If only he might be allowed to show it.

HE WAS SIXTEEN YEARS OLD, he was seventeen years old, boxing in local matches, working his way steadily up into state competitions, finally into the Golden Gloves Tri-State tournament. He had a good trainer, his father had seen to that. He had trophies, plaques, photographs taken at ringside, part of the living room was given over to his boxing as to a shrine. What do your friends think about your boxing? his relatives asked. Isn't it a dangerous sport? But he hadn't any friends that mattered and if his classmates had any opinion about him he couldn't have guessed what it might be, or cared. And, no, it wasn't a dangerous sport. It was only dangerous if you made mistakes.

It was said frequently at the gym that he was "coming along." The sportswriter for the local newspaper did a brief piece on him and a few other "promising" amateurs. He was quick and clever and intuitive, he knew to let a blow slide by his shoulder then to get his own in then to retreat, never to panic, never to shut his eyes, never to breathe through his mouth, it was all a matter of breath you might say, a matter of the most exquisite timing, momentum, a dancer's intelligence in his legs, the instinct to hit, to hit hard, and to hit again. He was a young Sandy Saddler they said—but he didn't fight dirty! No, he was a young Sugar Ray. Styled a bit on that brilliant new heavyweight Cassius Clay, who'd surprised the boxing world by knocking out Sonny Liston. He hadn't a really hard punch but he was working on it, working constantly, in any case he was winning all his matches or fighting to a draw, there's nothing wrong in fighting to a draw his father told him, though he could see his father was disappointed sometimes, there were fights he should have won but just didn't—couldn't. The best times were when he won a match by a knockout, his opponent suddenly falling, and down, not knocked out really, just sitting there on the canvas dazed and frightened, blinking, looking as if he were about to cry but no one ever cried, that never happened.

You have real talent, he was told. Told repeatedly.

You have a future!

The promise was—he seemed to know—that he couldn't lose. He'd understood that years before, watching one or another of the films, young Dempsey fierce as a tiger against the giant Jess Willard, twenty-year-old Joe Louis in action, Sugar Ray Robinson who'd once killed an opponent in the ring with the force of his blows: he was of their company and he knew it and he knew he couldn't lose, he couldn't even be seriously hurt, that seemed to be part of the promise. But sometimes he woke in the night in his bed not knowing at first where he was, was he in the gym, in the ring, staring panicked across the wide lighted canvas to his opponent shadowy in the opposite corner, he lay shivering, his heart racing, the bedclothes damp with sweat. He liked to sweat most of the time, he liked the rank smell of his own body, but this was not one of those times. His fists when he woke would be clenched so hard his fingernails would be cutting into his palms, his toes curled in tight and cramped as if still deformed, secretly deformed. Cripple! Freak! The blow you can't see coming is the blow that knocks you out—the blow out of nowhere. How can you protect yourself against a blow out of nowhere? How can you stop it from happening again? He'd been surprised like that only a few times, sparring, not in real fights. But the surprise had stayed with him.

YET THERE WAS a promise. Going back to when he was very small, before the operation.

And his father adored him, his father was so happy for him, placing bets on him, not telling him until afterward—after he'd won. Just small bets. Just for fun. His father said, I don't want you to feel any pressure, it's just for fun.

THEN of course he was stopped and his "career" ended abruptly and unromantically. As he should have foreseen. Just a few weeks before his eighteenth birthday.

It happened midway in the first round of a Golden Gloves semifinal lightweight match in Buffalo, New York, when a stocky black boy from Trenton, New Jersey, came bounding at him like a killer, pushing and crowding and bulling him back into the ropes, forcing him backward as he'd never been forced; the boy brushed aside his jabs and ignored his feints, popped him with a hard left then landed a blow to his exposed mouth that drove his upper front teeth back through his slack lower lip but somehow at the same time smashed the teeth upward into his palate. He'd lost his mouthpiece in the confusion, he'd never seen the punch coming, he was told afterward it had been a hard straight right like no amateur punch anyone could recall.

He fell dazed into the ropes, he fell to the canvas, he hid his bleeding face with his gloves, gravity pulled him down and his instinct was to submit to curl up into a tight ball to lie very still maybe he wouldn't be hit again maybe it was all over.

And so it happened.

THAT WAS his career as an amateur boxer. Twenty or so serious matches: that was it.

Never again, he told himself. That *was* it.

(THE BLACK BOY from New Jersey—Roland Bush Jr.—was eighteen years old at the time of the fight but had the face of a mature man, heavy-lidded eyes, broad flat nose, scars in his forehead and fanning his eyes. An inch shorter than his white opponent but his shoulder and leg muscles rippled with high-strung nervous strength, he'd thickened his neck muscles to withstand all blows, he was ready, he was hot, he couldn't be stopped. His skin was very dark and the whites of his eyes were an eerie bluish-white, luminous, threaded almost invisibly with blood. He weighed no more than his opponent but he had a skull and a body built to absorb punishment, he was solid, hard, relentless, taking no joy in his performance just doing it, doing it superbly, getting it done, he went on to win the Golden Gloves title in his division with another spectacular knockout and a few months later turned professional and was advanced swiftly through the lightweight ranks then into the junior welterweights where he was ranked number fourteen by *Ring* magazine at the time of his death—he died aged twenty of a cerebral hemorrhage following a ten-round fight in Houston, Texas, which he'd lost in the ninth round by a technical knockout.)

THE FIGHT WAS STOPPED, the career of "promise" was stopped, now he is thirty-four years old and it seems to him his life is passing swiftly. But at a distance. It doesn't seem in fact to belong to him, it might be anybody's life.

In his professional career, in his social life, he is successful, no doubt enviable, but he finds himself dreaming frequently these days of the boy with the crippled feet. Suppose he'd never had the operation: what then! He sees the creature on its hands and knees crawling crablike along the ground, there is a jeering circle of boys, now the terrible blinding lights of the operating room snuff him out and he's gone. And now seated in his aluminum wheelchair staring down helplessly at the white plaster casts: his punishment. Hips to toes, toes to hips. His punishment.

The adults of the world conspire in lies leaning over him smiling into his face. He will be able to walk he will be able to run he won't feel any pain he won't be hurt again doesn't he want to believe?—and of course he does. He does. His wife's name is Annemarie, a name melodic and lovely he sometimes shapes with his lips, in silence: an incantation.

He had fallen in love with Annemarie seeing her for the first time amid a large noisy gathering of relatives and friends. When they were introduced and he was told her name he thought extravagantly, Annemarie, yes—she's the one!

From the first she inspired him to such extravagant fancies, such violations of his own self. Which is why he loves her desperately.

Annemarie is twenty-nine years old but has the lithe small-boned features of a girl. Her hair is light brown, wavy, silvery in sunshine, her eyes wide-set and intelligent, watchful. Most of the time she appears to be wonderfully assured, her center of gravity well inside her, yet in the early weeks of the pregnancy she cried often and asked him half angrily, Do you love me? And he told her, Yes, of course. Of course I love you. But shortly afterward she asked him again, as if she hadn't believed him, Do you love me—*really*? More than before, or less? and he laughed as if she were joking, as if it were one of her jokes, closing his arms around her to comfort her. This was Annemarie's second pregnancy after all: the first had ended in a miscarriage.

Don't be absurd, Annemarie, he tells her.

Most of the time, of course, she is good-natured, sunny, uncomplaining; she loves being pregnant and she is eager to have the baby. She chooses her maternity outfits with care and humor: flowing waistless dresses in colorful fabrics, blouses with foppish ties, shawls, Indian beads, cloth flowers in her hair. Some of the outfits are from secondhand shops in the city, costumes from the forties and fifties, long skirts, culottes, silk pants suits, a straw boater with clusters of artificial berries on the rim: to divert the eye from her prominent belly, she says. But the childlike pleasure Annemarie takes in dressing is genuine and her husband is charmed by it, he adores her for all that is herself, yes, he'd fight to the death to protect her he'd die in her place if required.

Odd how, from the start, she has had the power to inspire him to such melodramatic extravagant claims.

THE MISCARRIAGE took place in the fifth month of the first pregnancy. One night Annemarie woke with mock-labor pains and began to bleed, she bled until nothing remained in her womb of what was to have been their son. And they were helpless, helpless to stop it.

They'd known for weeks that the fetus was impaired, the pregnancy might not go to term; still, the premature labor and the premature death were blows from which each was slow to recover. Annemarie wept in his arms and, he thought, in his place: her angry childish mourning helped purge his soul. And Annemarie was the first to recover from the loss for after all—as her doctor insisted—it wasn't anything personal, *it's just physical*. The second pregnancy has nothing at all to do with the first.

So we'll try again, Annemarie said reasonably.

And he hesitated saying, Not now. Saying, Isn't it too soon? You aren't recovered.

And she said, Of course I'm recovered.

And he said, But I think we should wait.

And she said, chiding, *Now*. When if not *now*?

(Twenty-nine years old isn't young, in fact it is "elderly" in medical terms for a woman pregnant with her first child. And they want more than one child, after all. They want a family.)

So they made love. And they made love. And he gave himself up to her in love, in love, in a drowning despairing hope, it's just physical after all it doesn't mean anything. Such failures of the physical life don't mean anything. You take the blow then get on with living isn't that the history of the world? Of course it is.

He's an adult man now, not a boy any longer. He knows.

He cradles his wife's belly in his hands. Stroking her gently. Kissing her. Fiercely attentive to the baby's secret life, that mysterious interior throb, that ghostly just-perceptible kick. Through the doctor's stethoscope each listened to the baby's heartbeat, a rapid feverish-sounding beat, *I am, I am, I am*. This pregnancy, unlike the first, has been diagnosed as "normal." This fetus unlike the first has been promised as "normal."

Approximately fifteen days yet to go: the baby has begun its descent head first into the pelvic cavity and Annemarie has begun, oddly, to feel more comfortable than she has felt in months. She assures him she is excited—not frightened—and he remembers the excitement of boxing, the excitement of climbing through the ropes knowing he couldn't turn back. Elation or panic? euphoria or terror?—that heartbeat beating everywhere in his body.

For months they have attended natural childbirth classes together and he oversees, genially but scrupulously, her exercises at home: he will be in the delivery room with her, he'll be there all the while.

This time, like last time, the fetus is male, and again they have drawn up a list of names. But the names are entirely different from the first list, Patrick, William, Alan, Seth, Sean, Raymond; sometimes Annemarie favors one and sometimes another but she doesn't want to choose a name until the baby is born. Safely born.

Why hasn't he ever told Annemarie about his amateur boxing, his "career" in the Golden Gloves?—he has told her virtually everything else about his life. But it is a matter of deep shame to him, recalling not only the evening of his public defeat but his hope, his near-lunatic hope that he would be a hero, a star! a great champion! He has told her he'd been a premature baby, born with a "slight deformity" of one foot which was corrected by surgery immediately after his birth: this is as near to the truth as he can manage.

Which foot was it? Annemarie asks sympathetically.

He tells her he doesn't remember which foot, it isn't important.

But one night he asks her to caress his feet. They are in bed, he is feeling melancholy, worried, not wholly himself. He has begun to profoundly dislike his work in proportion to his success at it and this is a secret he can't share with Annemarie; there are other secrets too he can't share, won't share, he fears her ready sympathy, the generosity of her spirit. At such times he feels himself vulnerable to memory, in danger of reliving that last fight, experiencing moments he hadn't in a sense experienced at the time—it had all happened too swiftly. Roland Bush Jr. pressing through his defense, jabbing him with precise machinelike blows, that gleaming black face those narrowed eyes seeking him out. White boy! White boy who are *you*! Bush was the true fighter stalking his prey. Bush was the one.

He hadn't been a fighter at all, merely a victim.

He asks Annemarie to caress his feet. Would she hold them? Warm them? Would she . . . ? It would mean so much, he can't explain.

Perhaps he is jealous of their son so cozy and tight upside down beneath his wife's heart but this is a thought he doesn't quite think.

Of course Annemarie is delighted to massage his feet, it's the sort of impulsive whimsical thing she loves to do, no need for logic, no need for explanations, she has wanted all along to nourish the playful side of his personality. So she takes his feet between her small dry warm hands and gently massages them. She brings to the intimate task a frowning concentration that flatters him, fills him with love. What is she thinking?

he wonders. Then suddenly he is apprehensive: What does she know of me? What can she guess? Annemarie says, smiling, Your feet are so terribly cold! But I'll make them warm.

The incident is brief, silly, loving, quickly forgotten. One of those moments between a husband and a wife not meant to be analyzed, or even remembered. It never occurs a second time, never again does Annemarie offer to caress his feet and out of pride and shame he certainly isn't going to ask.

The days pass, the baby is due in less than a week, he keeps thinking, dreaming, of that blow to his mouth: the terrible power of the punch out of nowhere. His skull shook with a fierce reverberation that ran through his entire body and he'd known then that no one had ever hit him before.

It was his own death that had crashed into him—yet no more than he deserved. He was hit as one is hit only once in a lifetime. He was hit and time stopped. He was hit in the second minute of the first round of a long-forgotten amateur boxing match in Buffalo, New York; he was hit and he died and they carried him along a corridor of blinding lights, strapped to a stretcher, drooling blood and saliva, eyes turned up in his head. Something opened, lifted, a space of some kind clearing for him to enter, his own death but he hadn't had the courage to step forward.

Someone whose face he couldn't see was sinking a needle deep into his forearm, into the fleshy part of his forearm, afterward they spoke calmly and reassuringly saying it isn't really serious, a mild concussion not a serious fracture, his nose wasn't broken, only his mouth and teeth injured, that could be fixed. He flinched remembering the blow flying at him out of nowhere. He flinched, remembering. It happens once in a lifetime after that you're dead white boy but you pick yourself up and keep going.

There followed then the long period—months, years—when his father shrank from looking him fully in the face. Sometimes, however, his father examined his mouth, wasn't entirely pleased with the plastic surgeon's work. It had cost so damned much after all. But the false teeth were lifelike, wonderfully convincing, some consolation at least. Expensive too but everyone in the family was impressed with the white perfect teeth affixed to their lightweight aluminum plate.

ALL THAT THE OLD TALES of pregnancy promise of a female beauty luminous and dewy, lit from within, was true: here is Annemarie with eyes moist and bright as he'd rarely seen them, a skin with a faint rosy bloom, feverish to the touch. Here is the joy of the body as he had known it long ago and had forgotten.

There were days, weeks, when she felt slightly unwell yet the bloom of pregnancy had held and deepened month following month. A woman fully absorbed in herself, suffused with light, heat, radiance, entranced by the plunge into darkness she is to take. Pain—the promised pain of childbirth—frightens yet fascinates her: she means to be equal to it. She doesn't shrink from hearing the most alarming stories, labors of many hours without anesthetic, cesarean deliveries where natural childbirth had been expected, sudden losses of blood. She means to triumph.

Within the family they joke—it's the father-to-be, not Annemarie, who is having difficulty sleeping these past few weeks. But that too is natural, isn't it?

One night very late in her term Annemarie stares down at herself as if she'd never seen herself before—the enormous swollen belly, the blue-veined stretched skin with its uncanny luminous pallor—and because she has been feeling melancholy for days, because she is fatigued, suddenly doubting, not altogether herself, she exclaims with a harsh little laugh, God look at me, at this, how can you love anything like—*this*!

His nerves are torn like silk. He knows she isn't serious, he knows it is the lateness of the hour and the strain of waiting, it can't be Annemarie herself speaking. Quickly he says, Don't be absurd.

BUT THAT NIGHT as he falls slowly asleep he hears himself explaining to Annemarie in a calm measured voice that she will be risking something few men can risk, she should know herself exalted, privileged, in a way invulnerable to hurt even if she is very badly hurt, she'll be risking something he himself cannot risk again in his life. And maybe he never risked it at all.

You'll be going to a place I can't reach, he says.

He would touch her, in wonder, in dread, he would caress her, but his body is heavy with sleep, growing distant from him. He says softly, I'm not sure I'll be here when you come back.

But by now Annemarie's breathing is so deep and rhythmic she must be asleep. In any case she gives no sign of having heard.

MANSLAUGHTER

———

EDDIE FARRELL, TWENTY-SIX, temporarily laid off from Lacka-wanna Steel, had been separated from his wife, Rose Ann, for several months, off and on, when the fatal stabbing occurred. This was on a January afternoon near dusk. Most of the day snow had been falling lightly and the sun appeared at the horizon for only a few minutes, the usual dull red sulfurous glow beyond the steel mills.

According to Eddie's sworn testimony, Rose Ann had telephoned him at his mother's house and demanded he come over, she had something to tell him. So he went over and picked her up—while he was driving his brother's 1977 Falcon—they went to the County Line Tavern for a drink—then drove around, talking, or maybe quarreling. Suddenly Rose Ann took out a knife and went for him—no warning—but he fought her off—he tried to take the knife away—*she* was stabbed by accident—he panicked and drove like crazy for twenty, twenty-five minutes—until he was finally flagged down by a state trooper out on the highway, doing eighty-eight miles an hour in a fifty-five-mile zone. By then Rose Ann had bled to death in the passenger's seat—she'd been stabbed in the throat, chest, belly, thighs, thirty or more times.

"I guess I lost control," Eddie said repeatedly, referring to the drive in the "death car" (as the newspapers called it), not to stabbing his wife: he didn't remember stabbing his wife. It seemed to him he had only defended himself against her attack, somehow she had managed to stab herself. Maybe to punish him. She was always criticizing him, always finding fault. She called up his mother, too, and bitched over the telephone—*that* really got to him.

When asked by police officers how his wife had come into possession of a hunting knife belonging to his brother, Eddie replied at first that he didn't have any idea, then he said she must have stolen it and hidden it away in the apartment. He really didn't know. She did crazy things. She threatened all kinds of crazy things. The knife was German-made, with an eight-inch stainless steel blade and a black sealed wood handle, a beautiful thing, expensive. Lying on a little table at the front of the courtroom, beneath the judge's high bench, it looked like it might be for sale—the last of its kind, after everything else had been bought.

At first Eddie Farrell was booked for second-degree murder, with $45,000 bail (which meant 10 percent bond); then the charges were lowered to third, with $15,000 bail. Midway in the trial the charges would be lowered further to manslaughter, voluntary.

IN WAS BEATRICE GRAZIA'S BAD LUCK to happen to see the death car as it sped along Second Avenue in her direction. She was on her way home from work, crossig the street, when the car approached. She jumped back onto the curb, she said. The driver was a goddamned maniac and she didn't want to get killed.

Sure, she told police, she recognized Eddie Farrell driving—she got a clear view of his face as he drove past. But it all happened so quickly, she just stood on the curb staring after the car. Her coat was splashed with slush and dirt, he'd come that close to running her down.

At the trial five months later Beatrice swore to tell the truth, the whole truth, and nothing but the truth, but it all seemed remote now—insignificant. Her voice was so breathless it could barely be heard by the spectators in the first row. She was the tenth witness for the prosecution, out of twenty-seven, and her testimony seemed to add little to what had already been said. She hadn't wanted to appear—the district attorney's office had issued her a subpoena. Yes, she'd seen Eddie Farrell that day. Yes, he was driving east along Second. Yes, he was speeding. Yes, she had recognized him. Yes, he was in the courtroom today. Yes, she could point him out. Yes, she had seen someone in the passenger's seat beside him. No, she hadn't recognized the person. She believed it was a woman—she was fairly certain it was a woman—but the car passed by so quickly, she couldn't see.

Her voice was low, rapid, sullen, as if she were testifying against her will. Both the district attorney's assistant and the defense lawyer repeatedly asked her to speak up. The defense lawyer grew visibly irritated, his questions were edged with malice: How could she be certain she recognized the driver of the car?—wasn't it almost dark?—did she have *perfect* vision?

Blood rushed into her cheeks; she stammered a few words and went silent.

Eddie Farrell was sitting only a few yards away, staring dully into a corner of the courtroom—he didn't appear to be listening. His hair was slickly combed and parted on the side. He wore a pin-striped suit that fitted his skinny body loosely, as if he had put it on by mistake. His eyes were deep-set, shadowed; there was a queer oily sheen to his skin. Beatrice wasn't sure she would have recognized him, now.

THOUGH EVERYONE WAITED for Eddie to take the stand, to testify for himself, it wasn't his lawyer's strategy to allow him to speak: this disappointed many of the spectators. In all, the defense called only six people, four of them character witnesses. They spoke of Eddie Farrell as if they didn't realize he was in the courtroom with them; they didn't seem to have a great deal to say.

The most articulate witness was a young man named Ron Boci who had known Eddie, he said, for ten, twelve years, since grade school. He spoke rapidly and fluently, with a faint jeering edge to his voice; his swarthy skin had flushed darker. Yeah, he was a friend of Eddie's, they went places together—yeah, Eddie'd told him there was trouble with his wife—but it wasn't ever serious trouble, not from Eddie's side. He loved his wife, Ron Boci said, looking out over the courtroom, he wouldn't ever hurt her, he put up with a lot from her. Rose Ann was the one, he said. Rose Ann was always going on how she'd maybe kill herself, cut her throat, take an overdose or something, just to get back at Eddie, but Eddie never thought she meant it, nobody did—that was just Rose Ann shooting off her mouth. Yeah, Ron Boci said, moving his narrow shoulders, he knew her, kind of. But not like he knew Eddie.

Ron warmed as he spoke; he crossed his legs, resting one high-polished black boot lightly on his knee. He had a handsome beakish face, quick-darting eyes, hair parted in the center of his head so that it could flow thick and wavy to the sides, where it brushed against his collar. His hair was so black it looked polished. He too was wearing a suit—a beige checked suit with brass buttons—but it fitted his slender body snugly. His necktie was a queer part-luminous silver that might have been metallic.

DURING ONE of the recesses, when Beatrice went to the drinking fountain, Ron Boci appeared beside her and offered to turn on the water for her. It was a joke but Beatrice didn't think it was funny. "No thank you," she said, her eyes sliding away from his, struck by how white the whites were, how heavy the eyebrows. "No thank you, I can turn it on myself," Beatrice said, but he didn't seem to hear. She saw, stooping, lowering her pursed lips to the tepid stream of water, that there was a sprinkling of small warts on the back of Ron Boci's big-knuckled hand.

IT WAS SHORTLY after the New Year that Beatrice's husband, Tony, drove down to Port Arthur, Texas, on the Gulf, to work for an offshore oil drilling company. He'd be calling her, he said. He'd write, he'd send back money as soon as he could.

A postcard came in mid-February, another at the end of March. Each showed the same Kodacolor photograph of a brilliant orange-red sunset on the Gulf of Mexico, with palm trees in languid silhouette. Not much news, Tony wrote, things weren't working out quite right, he'd be telephoning soon. No snow down here, he said, all winter. If it snows it melts right away.

Where is Tony? people asked, neighbors in the building, Beatrice's parents, her girlfriends, and she said with a childlike lifting of her chin, "Down in Texas where there's work." Then she tried to change the subject. Sometimes they persisted, asking if she was going to join him, if he had an apartment or anything, what their plans were. "He's supposed to call this weekend," Beatrice said. Her narrow face seemed to thicken in obstinacy; the muscles of her jaws went hard.

He did call, one Sunday night. She had to turn the television volume down but, at the other end of the line, there was a great deal of noise—as if a television were turned up high. A voice that resembled Tony's lifted incoherently. Beatrice said, "Yes? Tony? Is that you? What?" but the line crackled and went dead. She hung up. She waited awhile, then turned the television back up and sat staring at the screen until the phone rang again. This time, she thought, I know better than to answer.

"WHAT ARE YOU DOING about the rent for July?—and you still owe for June, don't you?" Beatrice's father asked.

Beatrice was filing her long angular nails briskly with an emery board. Her face went hot with blood but she didn't look up.

"*I* better pay it," Beatrice's father said. "And you and the baby better move back with us."

"Who told you what we owe?" Beatrice asked.

She spoke in a flat neutral voice though her blood pulsed with anger. People were talking about them—her and Tony—it was an open secret now that Tony seemed to have moved out.

"Tony won't like it if I give this place up," Beatrice said, easing the emery board carefully around her thumbnail, which had grown to an unusual length. To provoke her father a little she said, "He'll maybe be mad if he comes back and somebody else is living here and he's got to go over to our house to find me and Danny. You know how his temper is."

Beatrice's father surprised her by laughing. Or maybe it was a kind of grunt—he rose from his chair, a big fleshy man, hands pushing on his thighs as if he needed extra leverage. "I can take care of your wop husband," he said.

It was a joke—it really *was* a joke because Beatrice's mother was Italian—but Beatrice hunched over the emery board and refused even to smile. "You wouldn't talk like that if Tony was here," she said.

"I wouldn't need to talk like this if Tony was here," her father said. "But the point is, he isn't here. That's what we're talking about."

"That's what you're talking about," Beatrice said.

When her father was leaving Beatrice followed after him on the stairs, pulling at his arm, saying, "Momma wants Danny with her and that's okay, Momma is wonderful with him, but, you know, this was supposed to be . . ." She made a clumsy pleading gesture indicating the stairs, the apartment on the landing, the building itself. She swallowed hard so that she wouldn't start to cry. "This was supposed to be a new place, a different place," she said, "that's why we came here. That's why we got married."

"I already talked to the guy downstairs," her father said, rattling his car keys. "He said you can move any time up to the fifteenth. I'll rent one of them U-Hauls and we'll do it in the morning."

"I don't think I can," Beatrice said, wiping angrily at her eyes. "I'm not going to do that."

"Next time he calls," Beatrice's father said, "tell him the news. Tell him your old man paid the rent for him. Tell him to look me up, he wants to cause trouble."

"I'm not going to do any of that," Beatrice said, starting to cry.

"It's already halfway done," her father said.

ONE NIGHT around ten o'clock Beatrice was leaving the 7-Eleven store up the street when she heard someone approach her. As she glanced back an arm circled her shoulders, which were almost bare—she was wearing a red halter top—and a guy played at hugging her as if they were old pals. She screamed and pushed him away—jabbed at him with her elbow.

It was Ron Boci, Eddie Farrell's friend. He was wearing a T-shirt and jeans, no shoes. No belt, the waist of the jeans was loose and frayed, you could see how lean he was—not skinny exactly but lean, small-hipped. His hair was a little longer than it had been in the courtroom but it was still parted carefully in the center of his head; he had a habit of shaking it back, loosening it, when he knew people were watching.

"Hey, you knew who it was," he said. "Come on."

"You scared the hell out of me," Beatrice said. Her heart was knocking so hard she could feel her entire body rock. But she stooped and picked up the quart of milk she'd dropped, and the carton of cigarettes, and Ron Boci stood there with his knuckles on his hips, watching. He meant to keep the same kidding tone but she heard an edge of apology in his voice, or maybe it was something else.

"You knew who it was," he said, smiling, lifting one corner of his mouth, "you saw me in there but you wouldn't say hello."

"Saw you in where?" Beatrice asked. "There wasn't anybody in there but the salesclerk."

"I was in there, I stood right in the center of the aisle, where the soda pop and stuff is, but you pretended not to see me, you looked right through me," Ron Boci said. "But I bet you remember my name."

"I don't remember any name," Beatrice said. Her voice sounded so harsh and frightened, she added quickly, "It's just a good thing I wasn't carrying any bottles or anything, it'd all be broke now." She said, "Well, I know the name Boci. Your sister Marian."

"Yeah, Marian," Ron Boci said.

Beatrice started to walk away and Ron Boci followed close beside her. He was perhaps six inches taller than Beatrice and walked with his thumbs hooked into the waist of his jeans, an easy sidling walk, self-conscious, springy. His smell was tart and dry like tobacco mixed with something moist: hair oil, shaving lotion. Beatrice knew he was watching her but she pretended not to notice.

He was a little high, elated. He laughed softly to himself.

"Your telephone got disconnected or something," Ron Boci said after a pause. He spoke with an air of slight reproach.

"I don't live there anymore," Beatrice said quickly.

She saw a sprinkling of glass on the sidewalk ahead but she didn't intend to warn him: let him walk through it and slice up his filthy feet.

"Where do you live, then, Beatrice?" he asked casually. "I know Tony is in Texas."

"He's coming back in a few weeks," Beatrice said. "Or I might fly down."

"I used to know Tony," Ron Boci said. "The Grazias over on Market Street—? Mrs. Grazia and my mother used to be good friends."

Beatrice said nothing. Ron Boci's elbow brushed against her bare arm and all the fine brown hairs lifted in goose bumps.

"Where are you living now, if you moved?" Ron Boci asked.

"It doesn't matter where I live," Beatrice said.

"I mean, what's their name? You with somebody, or alone?"

"Why do you want to know?"

"I'm just asking. Where are you headed now?"

"My parents' place, I'm staying overnight. My mother helps out sometimes with the baby," Beatrice said. She heard her voice becoming quick, light, detached, as if it were a stranger's voice, overheard by accident. She was watching as Ron Boci walked through the broken glass—saw his left foot come down hard on a sliver at least four inches long—but he seemed not to notice, didn't even flinch. His elbow brushed against her again.

He was watching her, smiling. He said, in a slow, easy voice, "I didn't know Tony Grazia had a kid, how long ago was that? *You* don't look like you ever had any baby."

Beatrice said stiffly, "There's lots of things you don't know."

"I SAW YOU LAST NIGHT at the Hi-Lo but you sure as hell didn't see me," Beatrice's father told her across the supper table. His face was beefy and damp with perspiration. "Ten, ten-thirty. You sure as hell didn't notice *me*."

It was late July and very hot. They'd had a heat spell for almost a week. Beatrice and her mother had set up a table in the living room, where it was cooler, but the effort hadn't made much difference. Beatrice's arms stuck unpleasantly to the surface of the table and her thighs stuck against her chair. She could see that her father was angry—his face was red and mottled with anger—but he didn't intend to say much in front of Beatrice's mother.

"I wasn't at the Hi-Lo very long," Beatrice said. "I don't even remember."

"Wearing sunglasses in the dark, *dark* glasses," Beatrice's father said with a snort of laughter, "like a movie star or something."

"That was just a joke," Beatrice said. "For five minutes. I had them on for five minutes and then I took them off."

"Okay," her father said, chewing his food. "Just wanted you to know."

"I just went out with some friends," she said.

"Okay," her father said.

After a while Beatrice said, "I don't need anybody spying on me, I'm not a kid. I'm twenty years old."

"You're a married woman," Beatrice's father said.

Beatrice's mother tried to interrupt but neither of them paid her any attention.

"If I want to go out with some friends," Beatrice said, her voice rising, "that's my business."

"I didn't see any *friends*, I saw only that one guy," Beatrice's father said. "As long as you know what you're doing."

Beatrice had stopped eating. She said nothing. She sat with her elbows on the table, staring and staring until her vision slipped out of focus. She could look at something—a glass saltshaker, a jar of mustard—until finally she wasn't seeing it and she wasn't thinking of anything and she wasn't aware of her surroundings either. In the past, when she lived at home, lapsing into one of these spells at the supper table could be dangerous—her father had slapped her awake more than once. But now he wouldn't. Now he probably wouldn't even touch her. "Do you like this?" Ron Boci was saying.

Beatrice woke slowly. "No," she said. "Wait."

"Do you like *this*?" Ron said, laughing.

"No. Please. Wait." Her voice was muffled, groggy, she had dreamed she was suffocating and now she couldn't breathe. "Wait," she said.

After a while he said, "Christ, are you crying?"—and she said no. She was sobbing a little, or maybe laughing. Her head spun, Jesus she was hung over, at first she almost didn't know where she was, only that she didn't ever want to leave.

AT WORK in the post office those long hours—waiting for the Clinton Street bus—changing the baby's diaper, her fingers so swift and practiced my God you'd think she had been doing this all her life—she found herself thinking of him. Of him and of it, what he did to her. That was it. That was the only thing. Sometimes the thought of him hit her so hard she felt a stabbing sensation in the pit of the belly, between her legs. She never thought of her husband, sometimes she went for hours without thinking of her baby. Once, changing his diaper, she pricked him and he began to cry angrily, red-faced, astonished, furious; she picked him up she held him in her arms she buried her face against him begging to be forgiven but the baby just kept crying: hot and wriggling and kicking and crying. Like he doesn't know who I am, Beatrice thought. Like he doesn't trust me.

RON BOCI'S DRIVER'S LICENSE had been suspended for a year but in his line of work, as he explained, he had to use a car fairly often, especially for short distances in the city. He needed to make deliveries and he couldn't always trust his buddies.

He made his deliveries at night, he told Beatrice. During the day there was too much risk, his face was too well known in certain neighborhoods.

He usually borrowed his brother's '84 Dodge. Not in the best condition, it'd been around, Ron said, had taken some hard use. His own car, a new Century, white, red leather inside, wire wheels, vinyl roof, stereo—he'd totaled it last January out on the highway. Hit some ice, went into a skid, it all happened pretty fast. Totaled, Ron said with a soft whistle, smiling at Beatrice. He'd walked away from the crash, though, just a few scratches, bloody nose—"Not like the poor fuckers in the other car."

Beatrice stared. "So you were almost killed," she said.

"Hell no," Ron said, "didn't I just tell you? I walked away on my own two feet."

(ONCE BEATRICE had happened to remark to Tony that he was lucky, real lucky about something. The precise reason for the remark she no longer remembered but she remembered Tony's quick reply: "Shit," he said, "you make your own luck.")

MANSLAUGHTER should have meant—how many years in prison? Not very many compared to a sentence for first-degree murder, or even second-degree murder, but, still, people in the neighborhood were astonished to hear that a governing board called the state appeals court had overturned Eddie Farrell's conviction. Like that!—"overturned" his conviction on a technicality that had to do with the judge's remarks while the jury was in the courtroom!

"Christ, I can't believe it," Beatrice's father said, tapping the newspaper with a forefinger. "I mean—*Jesus*. How do those asshole lawyers do it?"

So Eddie Farrell was free, suddenly. Released from the county house of detention and back home.

It was no secret that Eddie had killed his wife but people had been saying all along she'd asked for it, she'd asked for it for years, knowing Eddie had a nasty temper (like all the Farrells). Beatrice was stunned, didn't know what to think. And didn't want to talk about it. Her father said, laughing angrily, "It says here that Eddie Farrell told a reporter 'I was innocent before, and I'm innocent now.' "

Word got around the neighborhood: Eddie hadn't any hard feelings toward people who'd testified against him at the trial. He guessed they had to tell the truth as they saw it, they'd been subpoenaed and all. He guessed they didn't mean him any personal injury.

Now, he said, he hoped everybody would forget. *He* wasn't the kind of guy to nurse a grudge.

BEATRICE'S MOTHER heard from a woman friend that Tony was back in town—someone had seen him with one of his brothers over on Holland Avenue. One day, pushing Danny in the stroller, Beatrice thought she heard someone come up behind her, she had a feeling it was Tony, but she didn't look around: just kept pushing the stroller. In Woolworth's window she saw the reflection of a young kid in a T-shirt striding past her. It wasn't Tony and she was happy with herself for not being frightened. You don't have any claim on me, she would tell him. I'm twenty years old. I have my own life.

The rumor that Tony Grazia was back in town must have been a lie, because Beatrice received another postcard from him at the beginning of August. He'd written only hello, asked how she and Danny were, how the weather was up north—it was hot as hell, he said, down there. *Hot as hell* was underscored. Since there was no return address Beatrice couldn't reply to the card. I have my own life, she was going to tell him, all her anger gone quiet and smooth.

It was meant to be a joke in the household, Tony's three postcards Scotch-taped on the back of the bathroom door, each the same photo of a Gulf of Mexico sunset.

"You're getting a strange sense of humor," Beatrice's father told her.

"Maybe I always had one," Beatrice said.

LATER THAT WEEK Beatrice was in the shower at Ron Boci's, lathering herself vigorously under her arms, between her legs, between her toes, when she felt a draft of cooler air—she heard the bathroom door open and close. "Hey," she called out, "don't come in here. I don't want you in here."

He'd said he was going out for a pack of cigarettes but now he yanked open the scummy glass door to the stall and stepped inside, naked, grinning. He clapped his hands over his eyes and said, "Don't you look at me, honey, and I won't look at you." Beatrice laughed wildly. They were so close she couldn't see him anyway—the skinny length of him, the hard fleshy rod erect between his legs, the way coarse black hairs grew on his thighs and legs, even on the backs of his pale toes.

They struggled together, they nipped and bit at each other's lips, still a little high from the joint they'd shared, and the bottle of dago wine. Beatrice wanted to work up a soapy lather on Ron Boci's chest but he knocked the bar of soap out of her hands. He gripped her hard by the buttocks, lifted her toward him, pushed and poked against her until he entered her, already thrusting, pumping, hard. Beatrice clutched at him, her arms around his neck, around his shoulders, her eyes shut tight in pain. It was the posture, the angle, that hurt. The rough tile wall of the shower stall against her back. "Hold still," he said, and she did. She locked herself against him in terror of falling. "Hold still," he said, grunting, his voice edged with impatience.

Later they shared another joint, and Beatrice cut slices of a melon, a rich seedy overripe cantaloupe she'd brought him from the open-air market. Though it was on the edge of being rotten it still tasted delicious; juice ran down their chins. Beatrice stared at herself in Ron Boci's bread knife, which must have been newly purchased, it was so sharp, the blade so shiny.

"I can see myself in it," Beatrice said softly, staring. "Like a mirror."

ONE SATURDAY NIGHT in the fall Ron Boci played a sly little trick on Beatrice.

They were going out, they were going on a double date with another couple, and who should come by to Ron's apartment to pick them up but Eddie Farrell? He was driving a new green Chevy Camaro; his girlfriend was a slight acquaintance of Beatrice's from high school, named Iris O'Mara.

Beatrice's expression must have been comical because both Eddie and Ron burst out laughing at her. Eddie stuck out his hand, grinning, and said, "Hey Beatrice, no hard feelings, okay? Not on *my* side." Ron nudged her forward, whispered something in her ear she didn't catch. She saw her hand go out and she saw Eddie Farrell take it, as if they were characters in a movie. Was this happening? Was she doing this? She didn't even know if, beneath her shock, she was surprised.

"No hard feelings, honey: not on *my* side," Eddie repeated.

He was cheery, expansive, his old self. Grateful to be out, he said, and to be *alive*.

The focus of attention, however, was Eddie's new Camaro. He demonstrated, along lower Tice, how powerfully it accelerated—from zero to forty miles an hour *in under twenty seconds*. Hell, these were only city streets, traffic lights and all that shit, he'd really cut loose when they got out on the highway.

Ron and Beatrice were sitting in the backseat of the speeding car but Ron and Eddie carried on a conversation in quick staccato exchanges. Iris shifted around to smile back at Beatrice. She was a redhead, petite, startlingly pretty, Beatrice's age though she looked younger. Her eyelids were dusted with something silvery and glittering and her long, beautifully shaped fingernails were painted frosty pink. To be friendly she asked Beatrice a few questions—about Beatrice's baby, about her parents—*not* about Tony—but with all the windows down and the wind rushing in it was impossible to talk.

Eddie drove out of town by the quickest route, using his brakes at the intersections, careful about running red lights: he wasn't going to take any chances ever again, he said. It was a warm muggy autumn night but Beatrice had begun to shiver and couldn't seem to stop. She wore stylish white nylon trousers that flared at the ankle, a light-textured maroon top, open-toed sandals with a two-inch heel, she looked good but the goddamned wind was whipping her hair like crazy and it seemed to be getting colder every minute. Ron Boci noticed her shivering finally and laid his arm warm and heavy and hard around her shoulders, pulling her against him in a gesture that was playful, but loving: "Hey honey," he said, "is this a little better?"

NAIROBI

⎯

EARLY SATURDAY AFTERNOON the man who had introduced himself as Oliver took Ginny to several shops on Madison Avenue above Seventieth Street to buy her what he called an appropriate outfit. For an hour and forty-five minutes she modeled clothes, watching with critical interest her image in the three-way mirrors, and unable to decide if this was one of her really good days or only a mediocre day. Judging by Oliver's expression she looked all right but it was difficult to tell. The salesclerks saw too many beautiful young women to be impressed, though one told Ginny she envied her her hair—not just that shade of chestnut red but the thickness too. In the changing room she told Ginny that her own hair was "coming out in handfuls" but Ginny told her it didn't show. It will begin to show one of these days, the salesgirl said.

Ginny modeled a green velvet jumpsuit with a brass zipper and oversized buckles, and an Italian knit dress with bunchy sleeves in a zigzag pattern of beige, brown, and cream, and a ruffled organdy "tea dress" in pale orange, and a navy blue blazer made of Irish linen, with a pleated white linen skirt and a pale blue silk blouse. Assuming she could only have one costume, which seemed to be the case, she would have preferred the jumpsuit, not just because it was the most expensive outfit (the price tag read $475) but because the green velvet reflected in her eyes. Oliver decided on the Irish linen blazer and the skirt and blouse, however, and told the salesclerk to remove the tags and to pack up Ginny's own clothes, since she intended to wear the new outfit.

Strolling uptown he told her that with her hair down like that, and her bangs combed low on her forehead, she looked like a "convent schoolgirl." In theory, that was. Tangentially.

It was a balmy windy day in early April. Everyone was out. Ginny kept seeing people she almost knew, Oliver waved hello to several acquaintances. There were baby buggies, dogs being walked, sports cars with their tops down. In shop windows—particularly in the broad windows of galleries—Ginny's reflection in the navy blue blazer struck her as unfamiliar and quirky but not bad: the blazer with its built-up shoulders and wide lapels was more stylish than she'd thought at first. Oliver too was pleased. He had slipped on steel-frame tinted glasses. He said they had plenty of time. A pair of good shoes—really good shoes—might be an idea.

But first they went into a jewelry boutique at Seventy-sixth Street, where Oliver bought her four narrow silver bracelets, engraved in bird and animal heads, and a pair of conch-shaped silver earrings from Mexico. Ginny slipped her gold studs out and put on the new earrings as Oliver watched. "Doesn't it hurt to force those wires through your flesh?" he said. He was standing rather close.

"No," Ginny said. "My earlobes are numb, I don't feel a thing. It's easy."

"When did you get your ears pierced?" Oliver asked.

Ginny felt her cheeks color slightly—as if he were asking a favor of her and her instinct wasn't clear enough, whether to acquiesce or draw away just perceptibly. She drew away, still adjusting the earrings, but said, "I don't have any idea, maybe I was thirteen, maybe twelve, it was a long time ago. We all went out and had our ears pierced."

In a salon called Michel's she exchanged her chunky-heeled red shoes for a pair of kidskin sandals that might have been the most beautiful shoes she'd ever seen. Oliver laughed quizzically over them: they were hardly anything but a few straps and a price tag, he told the salesman, but they looked like the real thing, they were what he wanted. The salesman told Oliver that his taste was "unerring."

"Do you want to keep your old shoes?" Oliver asked Ginny.

"Of course," Ginny said, slightly hurt, but as the salesman was packing them she changed her mind. "No, the hell with them," she said. "They're too much trouble to take along." Which she might regret afterward: but it was the right thing to say at that particular moment.

IN THE CAB headed west and then north along the park, Oliver gave her instructions in a low casual voice. The main thing was that she should say very little. She shouldn't smile unless it was absolutely necessary. While he and his friends spoke—if they spoke at any length; he couldn't predict Marguerite's attitude—Ginny might even drift away, pick up a magazine and leaf through it if something appropriate was available, not nervously, just idly, for something to do, as if she were bored; better yet, she might look out the window or even step out on the terrace since the afternoon was so warm. "Don't even look at me," Oliver said. "Don't give the impression that anything I say—anything the three of us say—matters very much to you."

"Yes," said Ginny.

"The important thing," Oliver said, squeezing her hand and releasing it, "is that you're basically not concerned. I mean with the three of us. With Marguerite. With anyone. Do you understand?"

"Yes," said Ginny. She was studying her new shoes. Kidskin in a shade called "vanilla," eight straps on each shoe, certainly the most beautiful shoes she'd ever owned. The price had taken her breath away too. She hadn't any questions to ask Oliver.

When Ginny had been much younger—which is to say a few years ago when she'd been new to the city—she might have had some questions to ask. In fact she'd had a number of questions to ask, then. But the answers had not been forthcoming. Or they'd been disappointing. The answers had contained so much less substance than her own questions she had learned by degrees it was wiser to ask nothing.

So she told Oliver a second time, to assure *him*, "Of course I understand."

THE APARTMENT BUILDING they entered at Fifth and Eighty-eighth Street was older than Ginny might have guessed from the exterior—the mosaic murals in the lobby were in a quaint ethereal style unknown to her. Perhaps they were meant to be amusing but she didn't think so. It was impressive that the uniformed doorman knew Oliver, whom he called "Mr. Leahy," and that he was so gracious about keeping their package for them, while they visited upstairs; it was impressive that the black elevator operator nodded and murmured hello in a certain tone. Smiles were measured and respectful all around but Ginny didn't trouble to smile, she knew it wasn't expected of her.

In the elevator—which was almost uncomfortably small—Oliver looked at Ginny critically, standing back to examine her from her toes upward and finding nothing wrong except a strand or two of hair out of place. "The Irish linen blazer was an excellent choice," he said. "The earrings too. The bracelets. The shoes." He spoke with assurance, though Ginny had the idea he was nervous, or excited. He turned to study his own reflection in the bronze-frosted mirror on the elevator wall, facing it with a queer childlike squint. This was his "mirror face," Ginny supposed, the way he had of confronting himself in the mirror so that it wasn't *really* himself but a certain habitual expression that protected him. Ginny hadn't any mirror face herself. She had gone beyond that, she knew better, those childish frowns and half smiles and narrowed eyes and heads turned coyly or hopefully to one side—ways of protecting her from seeing "Ginny" when the truth of "Ginny" was that she required being seen head-on. But it would have been difficult to explain to another person.

Oliver adjusted his handsome blue-striped cotton tie and ran his fingers deftly through his hair. It was pale, fine, airily colorless hair, blond perhaps, shading into premature silver, rather thin, Ginny thought, for a man his age. (She estimated his age at thirty-four, which seemed old to her in certain respects, but she knew it was reasonably young in others.) Oliver's skin was slightly coarse; his nose wide at the bridge, and the nostrils disfigured by a few dark hairs that should have been snipped off; his lower jaw was somewhat heavy. But he was a handsome man. In his steel-rimmed blue-tinted glasses he was a handsome man and Ginny saw for the first time that they made an attractive couple.

"Don't trouble to answer any questions they might ask," Oliver said. "In any case the questions won't be serious—just conversation."

"I understand," Ginny said.

A Hispanic maid answered the door. The elevator and the corridor had been so dimly lit, Ginny wasn't prepared for the flood of sunlight in the apartment. They were on the eighteenth floor overlooking the park and the day was still cloudless.

Oliver introduced Ginny to his friends Marguerite and Herbert—the last name sounded like Crews—and Ginny shook hands with them unhesitatingly, as if it were a customary gesture with her. The first exchanges were about the weather. Marguerite was vehement in her gratitude since the past winter, January in particular, had been uncommonly long and dark and depressing. Ginny assented without actually agreeing. For the first minute or two she felt thrown off balance, she couldn't have said why, by the fact that Marguerite Crews was so tall a woman—taller even than Ginny. And she was, or had been, a very beautiful woman as well, with a pale olive complexion and severely black hair parted in the center of her head and fixed in a careless knot at the nape of her neck.

Oliver was explaining apologetically that they couldn't stay. Not even for a drink, really: they were in fact already late for another engagement in the Village. Both the Crewses expressed disappointment. And Oliver's plans for the weekend had been altered as well, unavoidably. At this announcement the disappointment was keener, and Ginny looked away before Marguerite's eyes could lock with hers.

But Oliver was working too hard, Marguerite protested.

But he *must* come out to the Point as they'd planned, Herbert said, and bring his friend along.

Ginny eased discreetly away. She was aloof, indifferent, just slightly bored, but unfailingly courteous: a mark of good breeding. And the Irish linen blazer and skirt were just right.

After a brief while Herbert Crews came over to comment on the view and Ginny thought it wouldn't be an error to agree: the view of Central Park was, after all, something quite real. He told her they'd lived here for eleven years "off and on." They traveled a good deal, he was required to travel almost more than he liked, being associated with an organization Ginny might have heard of?—the Zieboldt Foundation. He had just returned from Nairobi, he said. Two days ago. And still feeling the strain, the fatigue. Ginny thought that his affable talkative "social" manner showed not the least hint of fatigue but did not make this observation to Herbert Crews.

She felt a small pinprick of pity for the way Marguerite Crews's collarbones showed through her filmy muslin "Indian" blouse, and for the extreme thinness of her waist (cinched tight with a belt of silver coins or medallions), and for the faint scolding voice—so conspicuously a "voice"—with which she was speaking to Oliver. She saw that Oliver, though smiling nervously and standing in a self-conscious pose with the thumb of his right hand hooked in his sports coat pocket, was enjoying the episode very much; she noted for the first time something vehement and cruel though at the same time unmistakably boyish in his face. Herbert Crews was telling her about Nairobi but she couldn't concentrate on his words. She was wondering if it might be proper to ask where Nairobi was—she assumed it was a country somewhere in Africa—but Herbert Crews continued, speaking now with zest of the wild animals, including great herds of "the most exquisitely beautiful antelopes," in the Kenya preserves. Had she ever been there? he asked. No, Ginny said. "Well," said Herbert, nodding vigorously, "it really *is* worth it. Next time Marguerite has promised to come along."

Ginny heard Oliver explain again that they were already late for an appointment in the Village, unfortunately they couldn't stay for a drink, yet it was a pity but he hoped they might do it another time: with which Marguerite warmly agreed. Though it was clearly all right for Oliver and Ginny to leave now, Herbert Crews was telling her about the various animals he'd seen—elands, giraffes, gnus, hippopotami, crocodiles, zebras, "feathered monkeys," impala—he had actually eaten impala and found it fairly good. But the trip was fatiguing and his business in Nairobi disagreeable. He'd discovered—as in fact the Foundation had known from certain clumsily fudged reports—not only that the microbiological research being subsidized there had come to virtually nothing but that vast sums of money had disappeared into nowhere. Ginny professed to feel some sympathy though at the same time, as she said, she wasn't suprised. "Well," she said, easing away from Herbert Crews's side, "that seems to be human nature, doesn't it. All around the world."

"Americans and Swedes this time," Herbert Crews said, "equally taken in."

It couldn't be avoided that Herbert tell Oliver what he'd been saying—Oliver in fact seemed to be interested, he might have had some indirect connection with the Foundation himself—but unfortunately they were late for their engagement downtown, and within five minutes they were out of the apartment and back in the elevator going down.

Oliver withdrew a handkerchief from his breast pocket, unfolded it, and carefully wiped his forehead. Ginny was studying her reflection in the mirror and felt a pinprick of disappointment—her eyes looked shadowed and tired, and her hair wasn't really all that wonderful, falling straight to her shoulders. Though she'd shampooed it only that morning it was already getting dirty—the wind had been so strong on their walk up Madison.

On Fifth Avenue, in the gusty sunlight, they walked together for several blocks. Ginny slid her arm through Oliver's as if they were being watched but at an intersection they were forced to walk at different paces and her arm slipped free. It was time in any case to say goodbye: she sensed that he wasn't going to ask her, even out of courtesy, to have a drink with him: and she had made up her mind not to feel even tangentially insulted. After all, she hadn't been insulted.

He signaled a cab for her. He handed over the pink cardboard box with her denim jumper and sweater in it and shook her hand vigorously. "You were lovely up there," Oliver said, "just perfect. Look, I'll call you, all right?"

She felt the weight, the subtle dizzying blow, of the "were." But she

THE 1990S

HEAT

———

IT WAS MIDSUMMER, the heat rippling above the macadam roads, cicadas screaming out of the trees, and the sky like pewter, glaring.

The days were the same day, like the shallow mud-brown river moving always in the same direction but so slow you couldn't see it. Except for Sunday: church in the morning, then the fat Sunday newspaper, the color comics, and newsprint on your fingers.

Rhea and Rhoda Kunkel went flying on their rusted old bicycles, down the long hill toward the railroad yard, Whipple's Ice, the scrubby pastureland where dairy cows grazed. They'd stolen six dollars from their own grandmother who loved them. They were eleven years old; they were identical twins; they basked in their power.

Rhea and Rhoda Kunkel: it was always Rhea-and-Rhoda, never Rhoda-and-Rhea, I couldn't say why. You just wouldn't say the names that way. Not even the teachers at school would say them that way.

We went to see them in the funeral parlor where they were waked; we were made to. The twins in twin caskets, white, smooth, gleaming, perfect as plastic, with white satin lining puckered like the inside of a fancy candy box. And the waxy white lilies, and the smell of talcum powder and perfume. The room was crowded; there was only one way in and out.

Rhea and Rhoda were the same girl; they'd wanted it that way. Only looking from one to the other could you see they were two.

The heat was gauzy; you had to push your way through like swimming. On their bicycles Rhea and Rhoda flew through it hardly noticing, from their grandmother's place on Main Street to the end of South Main where the paved road turned to gravel leaving town. That was the summer before seventh grade, when they died. Death was coming for them, but they didn't know.

They thought the same thoughts sometimes at the same moment, had the same dream and went all day trying to remember it, bringing it back like something you'd be hauling out of the water on a tangled line. We watched them; we were jealous. None of us had a twin. Sometimes they were serious and sometimes, remembering, they shrieked and laughed like they were being killed. They stole things out of desks and lockers but if you caught them they'd hand them right back; it was like a game.

There were three floor fans in the funeral parlor that I could see, tall whirring fans with propeller blades turning fast to keep the warm air moving. Strange little gusts came from all directions, making your eyes water. By this time Roger Whipple was arrested, taken into police custody. No one had hurt him. He would never stand trial; he was ruled mentally unfit and would never be released from confinement.

He died there, in the state psychiatric hospital, years later, and was brought back home to be buried—the body of him, I mean. His earthly remains.

Rhea and Rhoda Kunkel were buried in the same cemetery, the First Methodist. The cemetery is just a field behind the church.

In the caskets the dead girls did not look like anyone we knew, really. They were placed on their backs with their eyes closed, and their mouths, the way you don't always look in life when you're sleeping. Their faces were too small. Every eyelash showed, too perfect. Like angels, everyone was saying, and it was strange it was *so*. I stared and stared.

What had been done to them, the lower parts of them, didn't show in the caskets.

Roger Whipple worked for his father at Whipple's Ice. In the newspaper it stated he was nineteen. He'd gone to DeWitt Clinton until he was sixteen; my mother's friend Sadie taught there and remembered him from the special education class. A big slow sweet-faced boy with these big hands and feet, thighs like hams. A shy gentle boy with good manners and a hushed voice.

He wasn't simpleminded exactly, like the others in that class. He was watchful, he held back.

Roger Whipple in overalls squatting in the rear of his father's truck, one of his older brothers driving. There would come the sound of the truck in the driveway, the heavy block of ice smelling of cold, ice tongs over his shoulder. He was strong, round-shouldered like an older man. Never staggered or grunted. Never dropped anything. Pale washed-looking eyes lifting out of a big face, a soft mouth wanting to smile. We giggled and looked away. They said he'd never been the kind to hurt even an animal; all the Whipples swore.

Sucking ice, the cold goes straight into your jaws and deep into the bone.

People spoke of them as the Kunkel twins. Mostly nobody tried to tell them apart: homely corkscrew-twisty girls you wouldn't know would turn up so quiet and solemn and almost beautiful, perfect little dolls' faces with the freckles powdered over, touches of rouge on the cheeks and mouths. I was tempted to whisper to them, kneeling by the coffins, *Hey, Rhea! Hey, Rhoda! Wake up!*

They had loud slip-sliding voices that were the same voice. They weren't shy. They were always first in line. One behind you and one in front of you and you'd better be wary of some trick. Flamey-orange hair and the bleached-out skin that goes with it, freckles like dirty raindrops splashed on their faces. Sharp green eyes they'd bug out until you begged them to stop.

Places meant to be serious, Rhea and Rhoda had a hard time sitting still. In church, in school, a sideways glance between them could do it. Jamming their knuckles into their mouths, choking back giggles. Sometimes laughter escaped through their fingers like steam hissing. Sometimes it came out like snorting and then none of us could hold back. The worst time was in assembly, the principal up there telling us that Miss Flagler had died, we would all miss her. Tears shining in the woman's eyes behind her goggle glasses and one of the twins gave a breathless little snort; you could feel it like flames running down the whole row of girls, none of us could hold back.

Sometimes the word "tickle" was enough to get us going, just that word.

I never dreamt about Rhea and Rhoda so strange in their caskets sleeping out in the middle of a room where people could stare at them, shed tears, and pray over them. I never dream about actual things, only things I don't know. Places I've never been, people I've never seen. Sometimes the person I am in the dream isn't me. Who it is, I don't know.

Rhea and Rhoda bounced up the drive on their bicycles behind Whipple's Ice. They were laughing like crazy and didn't mind the potholes jarring their teeth or the clouds of dust. If they'd had the same dream the night before, the hot sunlight erased it entirely.

When death comes for you, you sometimes know and sometimes don't.

Roger Whipple was by himself in the barn, working. Kids went down there to beg him for ice to suck or throw around or they'd tease him, not out of meanness but for something to do. It was slow, the days not changing in the summer, heat sometimes all night long. He was happy with children that age, he was that age himself in his head—sixth-grade learning abilities, as the newspaper stated, though he could add and subtract quickly. Other kinds of arithmetic gave him trouble.

People were saying afterward he'd always been strange. Watchful like he was, those thick soft lips. The Whipples did wrong to let him run loose.

They said he'd always been a good gentle boy, went to Sunday school and sat still there and never gave anybody any trouble. He collected Bible cards; he hid them away under his mattress for safe-keeping. Mr. Whipple started in early disciplining him the way you might discipline a big dog or a horse. Not letting the creature know he has any power to be himself exactly. Not giving him the opportunity to test his will.

Neighbors said the Whipples worked him like a horse, in fact. The older brothers were the most merciless. And why they all wore coveralls, heavy denim and long legs on days so hot, nobody knew. The thermometer above the First Midland Bank read 98 degrees F. on noon of that day, my mother said.

Nights afterward my mother would hug me before I went to bed. Pressing my face hard against her breasts and whispering things I didn't hear, like praying to Jesus to love and protect her little girl and keep her from harm, but I didn't hear; I shut my eyes tight and endured it. Sometimes we prayed together, all of us or just my mother and me kneeling by my bed. Even then I knew she was a good mother, there was this girl she loved as her daughter that was me and loved more than that girl deserved. There was nothing I could do about it.

Mrs. Kunkel would laugh and roll her eyes over the twins. In that house they were "double trouble"—you'd hear it all the time like a joke on the radio that keeps coming back. I wonder did she pray with them too. I wonder would they let her.

In the long night you forget about the day; it's like the other side of the world. Then the sun is there, and the heat. You forget.

We were running through the field behind school, a place where people dumped things sometimes, and there was a dead dog there, a collie with beautiful fur, but his eyes were gone from the sockets and the maggots had got him where somebody tried to lift him with her foot, and when Rhea and Rhoda saw they screamed a single scream and hid their eyes.

They did nice things—gave their friends candy bars, nail polish, some novelty key chains they'd taken from somewhere, movie stars' pictures framed in plastic. In the movies they'd share a box of popcorn, not noticing where one or the other of them left off and a girl who wasn't any sister of theirs sat.

Once they made me strip off my clothes where we'd crawled under the Kunkels' veranda. This was a large hollowed-out space where the earth dropped away at one end and you could sit without bumping your head; it was cool and smelled of dirt and stone. Rhea said all of a sudden, *Strip!* and Rhoda said at once, *Strip! Come on!* So it happened. They wouldn't let me out unless I took off my clothes, my shirt and shorts, yes, and my panties too. *Come on,* they said, whispering and giggling, they were blocking the way out so I had no choice. I was scared but I was laughing too. This is to show our power over you, they said. But they stripped too just like me.

You have power over others you don't realize until you test it.

Under the Kunkels' veranda we stared at each other but we didn't touch each other. My teeth chattered, because what if somebody saw us, some boy, or Mrs. Kunkel herself? I was scared but I was happy too. Except for our faces, their face and mine, we could all be the same girl.

The Kunkel family lived in one side of a big old clapboard house by the river; you could hear the trucks rattling on the bridge, shifting their noisy gears on the hill. Mrs. Kunkel had eight children. Rhea and Rhoda were the youngest. Our mothers wondered why Mrs. Kunkel had let herself go: she had a moon-shaped pretty face but her hair was frizzed ratty; she must have weighed two hundred pounds, sweated and breathed so hard in the warm weather. They'd known her in school. Mr. Kunkel worked construction for the county. Summer evenings after work he'd be sitting on the veranda drinking beer, flicking cigarette butts out into the yard; you'd be fooled, almost thinking they were fireflies. He went bare-chested in the heat, his upper body dark like stained wood. Flat little purplish nipples inside his chest hair the girls giggled to see. Mr. Kunkel teased us all; he'd mix Rhea and Rhoda up the way he'd mix the rest of us up, like it was too much trouble to keep names straight.

Mr. Kunkel was in police custody; he didn't even come to the wake. Mrs. Kunkel was there in rolls of chin fat that glistened with sweat and tears, the makeup on her face so caked and discolored you were embarrassed to look. It scared me, the way she grabbed me as soon as my parents and I came in, hugging me against her big balloon breasts, sobbing. All the strength went out of me; I couldn't push away.

The police had Mr. Kunkel for his own good, they said. He'd gone to the Whipples, though the murderer had been taken away, saying he would kill anybody he could get his hands on: the old man, the brothers. They were all responsible, he said; his little girls were dead. Tear them apart with his bare hands, he said, but he had a tire iron.

Did it mean anything special, or was it just an accident Rhea and Rhoda had taken six dollars from their grandmother an hour before? Because death was coming for them; it had to happen one way or another.

If you believe in God you believe that. And if you don't believe in God it's obvious.

Their grandmother lived upstairs over a shoe store downtown, an apartment looking out on Main Street. They'd bicycle down there for something to do and she'd give them grape juice or lemonade and try to keep them awhile, a lonely old lady but she was nice, she was always nice to me; it was kind of nasty of Rhea and Rhoda to steal from her but they were like that. One was in the kitchen talking with her and without any plan or anything the other went to use the bathroom, then slipped into her bedroom, got the money out of her purse like it was something she did every day of the week, that easy. On the stairs going down to the street Rhoda whispered to Rhea, What did you *do*? knowing Rhea had done something she hadn't ought to have done but not knowing what it was or anyway how much money it was. They started in poking each other, trying to hold the giggles back until they were safe away.

On their bicycles they stood high on the pedals, coasting, going down the hill but not using their brakes. *What did you do! Oh, what did you do!*

Rhea and Rhoda always said they could never be apart. If one didn't know exactly where the other was that one could die. Or the other could die. Or both.

Once they'd gotten some money from somewhere, they wouldn't say where, and paid for us all to go to the movies. And ice cream afterward too.

You could read the newspaper articles twice through and still not know what he did. Adults talked about it for a long time but not so we could hear. I thought probably he'd used an ice pick. Or maybe I heard somebody guess who didn't know any more than me.

We liked it that Rhea and Rhoda had been killed, and all the stuff in the paper, and everybody talking about it, but we didn't like it that they were dead; we missed them.

Later, in tenth grade, the Kaufmann twins moved into our school district. Doris and Diane. But it wasn't the same thing.

Roger Whipple said he didn't remember any of it. Whatever he did, he didn't remember. At first everybody thought he was lying; then they had to accept it as true, or true in some way: doctors from the state hospital examined him. He said over and over he hadn't done anything and he didn't remember the twins there that afternoon, but he couldn't explain why their bicycles were at the foot of his stairway and he couldn't explain why he'd taken a bath in the middle of the day. The Whipples admitted that wasn't a practice of Roger's or of any of them, ever, a bath in the middle of the day.

Roger Whipple was a clean boy, though. His hands always scrubbed so you actually noticed, swinging the block of ice off the truck and, inside the kitchen, helping to set it in the icebox. They said he'd go crazy if he got bits of straw under his nails from the icehouse or inside his clothes. He'd been taught to shave and he shaved every morning without fail; they said the sight of the beard growing in, the scratchy feel of it, seemed to scare him.

A few years later his sister Linda told us how Roger was built like a horse. She was our age, a lot younger than him; she made a gesture toward her crotch so we'd know what she meant. She'd happened to see him a few times, she said, by accident.

There he was squatting in the dust laughing, his head lowered, watching Rhea and Rhoda circle him on their bicycles. It was a rough game where the twins saw how close they could come to hitting him, brushing him with their bike fenders, and he'd lunge out, not seeming to notice if his fingers hit the spokes; it was all happening so fast you maybe wouldn't feel pain. Out back of the icehouse, the yard blended in with the yard of the old railroad depot next door that wasn't used any more. It was burning hot in the sun; dust rose in clouds behind the girls. Pretty soon they got bored with the game, though Roger Whipple even in his heavy overalls wanted to keep going. He was red-faced with all the excitement; he was a boy who loved to laugh and didn't have much chance. Rhea said she was thirsty, she wanted some ice, so Roger Whipple scrambled right up and went to get a big bag of ice cubes! He hadn't any more sense than that.

They sucked on the ice cubes and fooled around with them. He was panting and lolling his tongue pretending to be a dog, and Rhea and Rhoda cried, Here, doggie! Here, doggie-doggie! tossing ice cubes at Roger Whipple he tried to catch in his mouth. That went on for a while. In the end the twins just dumped the rest of the ice onto the dirt, then Roger Whipple was saying he had some secret things that belonged to his brother Eamon he could show them, hidden under his bed mattress; would they like to see what the things were?

He wasn't one who could tell Rhea from Rhoda or Rhoda from Rhea. There was a way some of us knew: the freckles on Rhea's face were a little darker than Rhoda's, and Rhea's eyes were just a little darker than Rhoda's. But you'd have to see the two side by side with no clowning around to know.

Rhea said OK, she'd like to see the secret things. She let her bike fall where she was straddling it.

Roger Whipple said he could only take one of them upstairs to his room at a time, he didn't say why.

OK, said Rhea. Of the Kunkel twins, Rhea always had to be first.

She'd been born first, she said. Weighed a pound or two more.

Roger Whipple's room was in a strange place: on the second floor of the Whipple house above an unheated storage space that had been added after the main part of the house was built. There was a way of getting to the room from the outside, up a flight of rickety wooden stairs. That way Roger could get in and out of his room without going through the rest of the house. People said the Whipples had him live there like some animal, they didn't want him tramping through the house, but they denied it. The room had an inside door too.

Roger Whipple weighed about one hundred ninety pounds that day. In the hospital he swelled up like a balloon, people said, bloated from the drugs; his skin was soft and white as bread dough and his hair fell out. He was an old man when he died aged thirty-one.

Exactly why he died, the Whipples never knew. The hospital just told them his heart had stopped in his sleep.

Rhoda shaded her eyes, watching her sister running up the stairs with Roger Whipple behind her, and felt the first pinch of fear, that something was wrong or was going to be wrong. She called after them in a whining voice that she wanted to come along too, she didn't want to wait down there all alone, but Rhea just called back to her to be quiet and wait her turn, so Rhoda waited, kicking at the ice cubes melting in the dirt, and after a while she got restless and shouted up to them—the door was shut, the shade on the window was drawn—saying she was going home, damn them, she was sick of waiting, she said, and she was going home. But nobody came to the door or looked out the window; it was like the place was empty. Wasps had built one of those nests that look like mud in layers under the eaves, and the only sound was wasps.

Rhoda bicycled toward the road so anybody who was watching would think she was going home; she was thinking she hated Rhea! hated her damn twin sister! wished she was dead and gone, God damn her! She was going home, and the first thing she'd tell their mother was that Rhea had stolen six dollars from Grandma: she had it in her pocket right that moment.

The Whipple house was an old farmhouse they'd tried to modernize by putting on red asphalt siding meant to look like brick. Downstairs the rooms were big and drafty; upstairs they were small, some of them unfinished and with bare flootboards, like Roger Whipple's room, which people would afterward say based on what the police said was like an animal's pen, nothing in it but a bed shoved into a corner and some furniture and boxes and things Mrs. Whipple stored there.

Of the Whipples—there were seven in the family still living at home—only Mrs. Whipple and her daughter Iris were home that afternoon. They said they hadn't heard a sound except for kids playing in the back; they swore it.

Rhoda was bent on going home and leaving Rhea behind, but at the end of the driveway something made her turn her bicycle wheel back ... so if you were watching you'd think she was just cruising around for something to do, a red-haired girl with whitish skin and freckles, skinny little body, pedaling fast, then slow, then coasting, then fast again, turning and dipping and crisscrossing her path, talking to herself as if she was angry. She hated Rhea! She was furious at Rhea! But feeling sort of scared too and sickish in the pit of her belly, knowing that she and Rhea shouldn't be in two places; something might happen to one of them or to both. Some things you know.

So she pedaled back to the house. Laid her bike down in the dirt next to Rhea's. The bikes were old hand-me-downs, the kickstands were broken. But their daddy had put on new Goodyear tires for them at the start of the summer, and he'd oiled them too.

You never would see just one of the twins' bicycles anywhere, you always saw both of them laid down on the ground and facing in the same direction with the pedals in about the same position.

Rhoda peered up at the second floor of the house, the shade drawn over the window, the door still closed. She called out, Rhea? Hey, Rhea? starting up the stairs, making a lot of noise so they'd hear her, pulling on the railing as if to break it the way a boy would. Still she was scared. But making noise like that and feeling so disgusted and mad helped her get stronger, and there was Roger Whipple with the door open staring down at her flush-faced and sweaty as if he was scared too. He seemed to have forgotten her. He was wiping his hands on his overalls. He just stared, a lemony light coming up in his eyes.

Afterward he would say he didn't remember anything. Just didn't remember anything. The size of a grown man but round-shouldered so it was hard to judge how tall he was, or how old. His straw-colored hair falling in his eyes and his fingers twined together as if he was praying or trying with all the strength in him to keep his hands still. He didn't remember the twins in his room and couldn't explain the blood but he cried a lot, acted scared and guilty and sorry like a dog that's done bad, so they decided he shouldn't be made to stand trial; there was no point to it.

Afterward Mrs. Whipple kept to the house, never went out, not even to church or grocery shopping. She died of cancer just a few months before Roger died; she'd loved her boy, she always said; she said none of it was his fault in his heart, he wasn't the kind of boy to injure an animal; he loved kittens especially and was a good sweet obedient boy and religious too and Jesus was looking after him and whatever happened it must have been those girls teasing him; everybody knew what the Kunkel twins were like. Roger had had a lifetime of being teased and taunted by children, his heart broken by all the abuse, and something must have snapped that day, that was all.

The Whipples were the ones, though, who called the police. Mr. Whipple found the girls' bodies back in the icehouse hidden under some straw and canvas. Those two look-alike girls, side by side.

He found them around 9 P.M. that night. He knew, he said. Oh, he knew.

The way Roger was acting, and the fact that the Kunkel girls were missing: word had gotten around town. Roger taking a bath like that in the middle of the day and washing his hair too and not answering when anyone said his name, just sitting there staring at the floor. So they went up to his room and saw the blood. So they knew.

The hardest minute of his life, Mr. Whipple said, was in the icehouse lifting that canvas to see what was under it.

He took it hard too; he never recovered. He hadn't any choice but to think what a lot of people thought—it had been his fault. He was an old-time Methodist, he took all that seriously, but none of it helped him. Believed Jesus Christ was his personal savior and He never stopped loving Roger or turned His face from him, and if Roger did truly repent in his heart he would be saved and they would be reunited in Heaven, all the Whipples reunited. He believed, but none of it helped in his life.

The icehouse is still there but boarded up and derelict, the Whipples' ice business ended long ago. Strangers live in the house, and the yard is littered with rusting hulks of cars and pickup trucks. Some Whipples live scattered around the country but none in town. The old train depot is still there too.

After I'd been married some years I got involved with this man, I won't say his name, his name is not a name I say, but we would meet back there sometimes, back in that old lot that's all weeds and scrub trees. Wild as kids and on the edge of being drunk. I was crazy for this guy, I mean crazy like I could hardly think of anybody but him or anything but the two of us making love the way we did; with him deep inside me I wanted it never to stop. Just fuck and fuck and fuck, I'd whisper to him, and this went on for a long time, two or three years, then ended the way these things do and looking back on it I'm not able to recognize that woman, as if she was someone not even not-me but a crazy woman I would despise, making so much of such a thing, risking her marriage and her kids finding out and her life being ruined for such a thing, my God. The things people do.

It's like living out a story that has to go its own way.

Behind the icehouse in his car I'd think of Rhea and Rhoda and what happened that day upstairs in Roger Whipple's room. And the funeral parlor with the twins like dolls laid out and their eyes like dolls' eyes too that shut when you tilt them back. One night when I wasn't asleep but wasn't awake either I saw my parents standing in the doorway of my bedroom watching me and I knew their thoughts, how they were thinking of Rhea and Rhoda and of me their daughter wondering how they could keep me from harm, and there was no clear answer.

In his car in his arms I'd feel my mind drift, after we'd made love or at least after the first time. And I saw Rhoda Kunkel hesitating on the stairs a few steps down from Roger Whipple. I saw her white-faced and scared but deciding to keep going anyway, pushing by Roger Whipple to get inside the room, to find Rhea; she had to brush against him where he was standing as if he meant to block her but not having the nerve exactly to block her and he was smelling of his body and breathing hard but not in imitation of any dog now, not with his tongue flopping and lolling to make them laugh. Rhoda was asking where was Rhea? She couldn't see well at first in the dark little cubbyhole of a room because the sunshine had been so bright outside.

Roger Whipple said Rhea had gone home. His voice sounded scratchy as if it hadn't been used in some time. She'd gone home, he said, and Rhoda said right away that Rhea wouldn't go home without her and Roger Whipple came toward her saying, Yes she did, yes she *did*, as if he was getting angry she wouldn't believe him. Rhoda was calling, *Rhea,*

THE KNIFE

———

S HE WAS A RELIGIOUS WOMAN, mildly—the aftermath of a rural
Methodist upbringing. But that was some time ago and she rarely
gave a thought to religion now, or to what's called God. Certainly she
wasn't superstitious. If her dreams of the previous night had brought her
a premonition of disaster, she didn't recall it and would have discounted
it in any case; she was always edgy, though not necessarily unhappy,
when her husband was away. She rather liked, she said, spending a day
or two alone with her daughter. It was like old times, she said. Meaning
a few years ago when Bonnie was a baby.

The night before, Bonnie had showed Harriet a glossy reproduction
of a Chagall painting—the one in which a startled woman is being kissed
by a floating, sinuous lover, a dream transmuted into colors so auda-
cious you couldn't help smiling as if in recognition—and when Bonnie
said with her new skepticism, "Nobody can do *this*, can they!" Harriet
said, "Oh, people can do anything, sometimes." The answer was meant
to be fanciful: Bonnie was of an age now—eight, nearly nine—when the
most subtle intonations and nuances in adults' voices registered with

her, like music. Harriet sometimes wondered if she and her husband
were training their daughter in the ambiguities of life and not its stark
primary colorations.

That day, a day in late spring, had been unusually warm but by
evening the temperature had dropped twenty degrees. A sudden fierce
wind was blowing up so Harriet went about closing windows; she was
straining to close a window in the rear room—a handsome converted
porch, mostly glass, her husband used as his study at home—when she
saw a movement, the fleet afterimage of a movement, somewhere be-
hind her, reflected in the glass. And she knew. She knew: the height of
the figure, its peculiar swiftness, meant it wasn't Bonnie, and of course
it wasn't her husband, who was away at an academic conference. She
knew, she knew, yet she continued tugging at the window even as her
heart beat rapidly and a wave of terror washed over her. She thought, I
can get out the back door, I can run for help, but she knew she'd never
leave Bonnie behind; Bonnie was upstairs in her room.

She had left a door unlocked, the door leading into the garage. She
knew at once that was it. Everyone in the neighborhood kept doors
unlocked during the day, children were always trailing in and out of
houses, why had hers been singled out? She could have wept for the
mistake she'd made she could not now undo.

She saw by the digital clock on her husband's desk that it was 7:40.
She thought, I must remember that time.

She was behaving, still, as if nothing were wrong. Dreamy and shiv-
ering. Walking a little slower and more stiffly than usual. Even as she
reentered the house knowing how the air was disturbed by their pres-
ence, smelling them, something acrid and sweaty and excited, sensing
their very weight on the floorboards, she was consciously behaving as if
nothing were wrong. As if, observing her, taking pity on her, they might
yet relent and go away. She found herself staring at the dining room
clock, but this time the hour didn't register.

Someone said loudly, "Lady!" and she turned to see two youngish
men advancing toward her, two strangers, both in jeans, T-shirts: one
of them with a flattened nose and oddly appealing eyes, the other tall,

rangy, weedy, with long lank faded red hair, jutting ears, a light dusting of freckles on his face. He was the one carrying the knife.

They were high, nerved up, staring at her and grinning, both talking at once. "We're not going to hurt you, lady! Just stay cool! Stay cool!"—she would think afterward that they spoke like hoodlums on television or in the movies, for how otherwise would they speak?—"Got some cash in here? Find us some cash, lady! Where's your purse, lady? C'mon, lady, nobody's going to get hurt! Get your ass moving and nobody's going to get hurt!"

Her heartbeat was so hard and rapid she thought she was going to faint, and afterward she would realize with a stab of angry regret that had she fainted at that moment, had she simply fallen, limp and helpless, crashing to the floor, they would probably have fled the house: grabbed a few things, whatever was handy, and fled. But, no: she made an effort to keep from fainting as if out of courtesy! And it was pride too, for she thought of herself as a woman who took control of situations, a woman who was mature, responsible, not hysterical—a woman with a steady level gaze whom you could trust.

That was what she wanted the men to think, wasn't it—that they could trust her—for wasn't she cooperative, wasn't she calm and even in a way gracious, leading them into the kitchen where she'd left her purse (except it wasn't there: where was it?) and speaking quietly to them, saying, "You don't want to do this, really; my husband will be home in a few minutes—he'll be back before eight o'clock"; saying, "That knife makes me nervous, why don't you put it away, it isn't necessary, really"; not quite pleading: "My daughter is upstairs, she's only eight years old, please don't frighten her—please go away before you frighten her." But where was her purse? Why couldn't she find her purse? Her teeth had begun to chatter and her hands and knees were shaking uncontrollably.

They were her age, perhaps a year or two younger. Mature men in their early thirties but loud, loutish, deliberately clumsy, it almost seemed, like teenagers. Scared of what they were doing but exhilarated by it too—showing off, Harriet saw, for each other's benefit. And, seeing that she was an attractive woman, a small-boned terrified woman, no match for them, perhaps for her benefit as well.

They gave her orders in high breathless voices, telling her to get some cash and where's the silverware and nobody's going to get hurt if she did what they said. "Move your ass, lady! C'mon, lady!" the man with the knife said repeatedly in a boyish sniggering tone as if Harriet were a dumb creature in need of prodding. So naturally Bonnie heard them—how could the child have failed to hear them—and started downstairs, and Harriet, her hands shaking even more violently, pulling open a drawer to show the men her silverware in its worn chamois-lined tray—what remained of an elegant sterling set belonging to her grandmother, rarely used now and badly tarnished—thought she would never hear anything again in her life so wrenching, so unspeakably terrible, as her daughter's running footsteps on the stairs and her daughter's lifted voice, inquisitive rather than alarmed, "Mommy? Mommy?"

"Don't come in here, honey," Harriet called out. "Bonnie? Go back upstairs, please," keeping her voice level and taking pride in the fact: yes, her voice *is* level, Mommy *is* calm, Bonnie will remember when it's over.

For she was thinking, even then, even as Bonnie ran into the kitchen, that this wasn't happening to her alone, this was happening to Bonnie as well and she must behave in a way that reflected the fact. And she was thinking that the men would be yet more impressed, how could they not be impressed—a woman behaving so rationally so cooperatively you might even say so sweetly under these emergency circumstances; surely they would feel admiration for her? sympathy for her? Surely they would go away quickly with whatever she could give them and would not injure her or her daughter—wouldn't they?

HARRIET SAW that the men were nearly as frightened of Bonnie as Bonnie was frightened of them; they were so high, so stoned, they hadn't seemed to have counted on a child. She said calmly, "Let her go up to her room, please"—she didn't want to plead or beg, she hoped simply to sound reasonable—"she's just a little girl, let her go up to her room, please," as Bonnie, whimpering and sobbing, hid behind her, clutching at her legs. The child was small-boned like her mother, with her mother's pale silvery-blond hair, her wide-spaced brown eyes. Her cheeks were babyish, plump, streaked now with tears. How quickly, Harriet thought, children cry . . . as if the tears are always there, in readiness. "Let her go upstairs, please," Harriet told the men with as much an air of authority, maternal authority, as she could simulate. "Don't frighten her like this—have some compassion!" The man with the flattened nose seemed confused by her words and shrugged OK, but the one with the knife said no—"Hell, no, lady"—his mouth stretching like a rubber band in a fond leering smile as if he knew Harriet intended to trick him and he was too smart for her. When he smiled his cheeks dimpled.

"She'd call the police or something. You think we're assholes? She don't need to go anywhere."

They were examining the silverware, they were going to dump it into a grocery bag they'd found in one of the cupboards, but the man with the flattened nose said nervously he didn't think it looked like anything much and the man with the knife, the lanky red-haired grinning man, said in derision, "That's *tarnish*, asshole, that's how you know it's the real thing!"

Harriet said desperately, "Please take it. It's good silver, really. It's worth money."

"OK, lady, and where's your purse?" the man with the knife said. "Where's your purse you said was out here?"

"I think it must be in the bedroom—"

"You said it was out here, lady."

"I don't know where it is. I don't think there's much money in it—"

"Shut up! Find it! Get a move on!"

"My husband will be home in a few minutes. He—"

"Fuck 'my husband'! Fuck that shit! Who you think you're jiving? *Get a move on!*"

He was furious suddenly, shouting in her face. Bonnie began screaming "Mommy! Mommy! Mommy!" She was pawing at Harriet as if she were crazed and Harriet had all she could do to subdue her, pinion her arms, clutch her tight. She could feel her daughter's heart beating wildly inside her small rib cage. How fragile, she thought, how easily smashed. . . . "Bonnie," she whispered, "Bonnie—it's all right, it's all right, really," saying the same words over and over like an incantation. To the men she said, "Let me put her in the bathroom, at least—there's a bathroom downstairs. Let me get her out of the way, please." She was pleading now, her voice rising: "My daughter can't help you, she has nothing to do with this—*please!*"

The man with the knife was still suspicious but his friend said, "Yeah, OK—good idea," and that seemed to be it. Bonnie was making them both very nervous. Harriet half carried her daughter to the bathroom in the hall, whispering to her to be a good girl, to be quiet, it would all be over in a few minutes, please please be quiet, could she promise? Lock the door and don't unlock it until Mommy tells her to: promise? "What if the kid climbs out the fucking window?" the man with the knife was saying in an aggrieved voice. His friend said, "She ain't going to climb out no window, it's too high. Get cool."

So Harriet hugged Bonnie a final time and shut her up in the closet-sized prettily decorated guest bathroom that always smelled of lemon-scented soap no one, even guests, ever used, and she thought, Now it will be all right, telling herself, Now it will be all right, even as she turned back to the men and saw the light around their heads blotch and darken as if it were about to go out. She was panicked, swaying, on the verge of fainting again, and again she willed herself to recover: head lowered, blood rushing into the arteries with a terrible percussive force. One of the men grabbed her by the shoulder and gave her a furious shake. "C'mon, lady! Cut that shit! *C'mon!*"

They shoved Harriet forward. They carried the silverware loose in the paper bag, and in the dining room she showed them the brass candlesticks on the mantel and they took those too, "They're expensive, they're worth money," Harriet said, and she led them into her husband's study where his newly purchased German-made camera was kept on a shelf, "There—that's worth at least a thousand dollars," she said, absurdly gratified when the man with the flattened nose snatched the camera up like a prize, though she knew it wasn't worth $1,000 or half that much. "You can sell all these things," she said. "They're worth money."

She could hear Bonnie crying in the rear of the house.

She said, still in her reasonable voice, "Why don't you leave now? If you leave now I won't call the police. You can have those things. I promise I won't call the police."

They were in the living room, which ran nearly the length of the front of the house. Its pretensions of understated taste, elegance—nubby tweed sofa, matching chairs, glass-topped coffee table, wall-to-wall beige carpeting, above all the glossy-leafed plants in their earthenware pots—struck Harriet as comical. She wondered that the men, hands on their hips, staring, assessing, did not laugh aloud.

They asked where was the TV and when Harriet said it was kept in another room one of them said, "OK, show me," and the other said derisively, "Who's going to carry a TV?" so that was dropped. They were going to go upstairs but one of them changed his mind, suddenly gripping Harriet by the back of the neck—it was this gesture that made her understand she was in trouble, seriously in trouble: the abrupt contact, the hard canny fingers closing on her flesh stopping her cold as a dog is stopped by his collar—and said in a triumphant voice, "Just a minute lady, *take that down*"—indicating of all things an oil painting, an unframed abstract canvas done by one of Harriet's friends, on the wall behind the sofa.

"Take it down? Why?"

"Let's just see what's behind it!"

"Behind it?"

Then she realized: he thought there might be a wall safe hidden behind the painting.

She said, "I'm afraid you have the wrong idea about this household," actually trying to laugh, to make a sound like laughter, faint and breathless, incredulous. She said, "Do you think we're wealthy people? This isn't a wealthy neighborhood—can't you tell?" She added, not wanting to insult them, "I'm just trying to save you time."

One of the men pushed her forward, the flat of his hand between her shoulder blades in a rude shove. "Do what I *say*, lady!" It was the young man with the knife: his dull-red hair had fallen into his face; he gave off a fierce hot odor of sweat and indignation. "Do what I *say* and you won't get hurt."

THEY WERE on the stairs when for no reason Harriet could determine the man with the flattened nose changed his mind: he was leaving.

He'd had it, he said, he was getting the hell out, and he and his friend argued briefly on the stairway landing but he had his way and ran back downstairs. He was carrying the bulky grocery bag with its mismatched rattling contents.

Harriet felt her heart clench, knowing it would be worse now.

(It would turn out that the first man to leave the house left by the front door—bold, brash, stupid, unthinking—and no one in the neighborhood saw him, or reported having seen him. The second man was to leave, a half hour later, by the door to the garage, as he'd come in.)

He was angry now, angrier, because of his "asshole" friend and Harriet "wasting his time like she was"—pushing her along the darkened hall to the bedroom where her purse had to be; it couldn't be any other place, Harriet was thinking, biting her lower lip and praying; it can't be any other place: and when she switched on the bedroom light there it was, there, on the bureau where of course she'd left it. She could have wept with gratitude.

She would have handed her purse over to the man but he snatched it up eagerly, opened it, drew out the wallet, letting the purse fall to the floor, his own hands trembling as if with a faint palsy. Harriet saw that his knuckles were oddly big-boned, scraped-looking. His fingernails were edged with dirt.

She said apologetically, "I'm afraid there isn't much."

He was counting out bills, breathing hard. Harriet's eye darted about the bedroom hopeful of things—anything—she might offer. Her jewelry, of course, a few heirlooms but they were inexpensive; the rings she was wearing; and her watch—not really expensive items but could he tell the difference? She was thinking that the bedroom was so quietly attractive a room, neat, clean, the bed made (of course: Harriet had been trained from the age of nine to make any bed she slept in within a few seconds of rising from it), the mahogany furniture polished, lovely pale silky curtains, and the rest—the evidence of lives intelligently but not extravagantly lived. Surely the man with the knife could *see*? And would not want to hurt her, for so little reason?

(Bonnie had stopped crying. Or, more likely, Harriet couldn't hear her any longer. The house was unnaturally quiet: no radio, no television, no voices. Harriet would have liked to think that Bonnie had disobeyed her and left the bathroom—was now running, running for her life, next door to get help—but she knew this couldn't be: Bonnie would never have disobeyed her under these extreme circumstances. She would not unlock the door until Mommy gave her permission.)

The man with the knife counted out $73 and some change and didn't look very happy, and Harriet said quickly, "I just went shopping today, that's why there isn't—" He raised his eyes to hers: blood-threaded, glassy, the irises so dark they couldn't be distinguished from the pupils. The eyes seemed too loose in their sockets and Harriet could see, close up, scar tissue above each eye, tiny stitchlike marks in the skin.

He said, slyly, "OK, where's the rest?"

"The rest?"

"Hidden somewhere? In a drawer? Underneath something?"

"I don't have any more money," Harriet said. "This is all I have."

"Come off it!"

"Please, you promised—"

"Where's the money? Where's the *real* money?"

He was getting excited, waving the knife, gesturing with it, giving off a frantic hot scent like rancid grease. His facial skin was now the color and texture of curdled milk. The freckles stood out like dirty rain spots. "Just don't you lie to me, lady," he said, "nobody lies to me, lady." He stuffed the bills in his jeans pocket, taking no notice of the coins that fell to the floor. "Nobody lies to *me*."

Harriet said, stammering, "But we don't keep money in the house. We don't keep cash. I have a checkbook—"

"A checkbook! You going to write me a check, lady?"

"I have some jewelry—that's all I have—in this drawer here—"

He shoved her aside and yanked open the drawer, pawing through Harriet's things. She had costume jewelry mainly, dozens of pairs of earrings, glass beads, Indian necklaces, brooches she rarely wore, but in her little red jewelry box—a gift from her parents for her sixteenth birthday—there were a string of good cultured pearls and an old diamond-and-emerald bracelet of her grandmother's and several rings of varying degrees of worth, and these things the man with the knife scooped up, greedy yet embittered, as if knowing they were worth very little, really: he was being cheated.

"My watch," Harriet said, slipping it off, handing it over. "It might be worth something." He examined it skeptically (and he had a right to be skeptical; it was only a moderately priced watch classily styled, with miniature facets in the white gold framing the timepiece that winked and glittered in a simulation of diamonds). "That's all I have. I don't have anything else—please believe me," Harriet said.

He ignored her, didn't hear her, rifling through the bureau drawers in search of cash—and there was no cash—tossing clothing to the floor: Harriet's underwear, Harriet's panty hose, her husband's socks, shorts, undershirts. He found several pairs of cuff links and tried to stuff them in a pocket and when they slipped through his fingers he didn't trouble to pick them up. Next he went to the clothes closet and pawed furiously through Harriet's and her husband's clothes, cursing in a loud whining voice like a small child. His breath came so harshly now Harriet could hear him across the room.

Why was he staying on so long, risking so much? He should have been eager, like his friend, to escape.

Why was he talking to himself, behaving with such self-conscious bravado? Was it for Harriet's benefit?

Her initial shock had subsided. Like a powerful shot of adrenaline, it had been; now it was gone. She was left with a chill desperate calm, thinking, I am trapped, and Bonnie is trapped, until this is over.

"My husband—" she began, and broke down.

"If you leave now—" she began.

"I don't have anything more. We don't—"

The man with the knife approached her and stood with his hands on his hips, smiling his sly little smile. "OK, lady, cut the shit," he said flatly.

Harriet didn't want to think that she knew, even before he knew, what he would do. She didn't want to think that.

She would wonder afterward when it first occurred to him: after he'd counted out the money in her wallet, seen how little there was, how little the break-in was going to net him—so much energy expended, so much risk, for so little? Or had it been when he'd first glimpsed her, downstairs, tugging at the window in her husband's study? But perhaps it had been his plan, his intention, all along, before he'd ever stepped into her house: any woman, any female, helpless, and available to him . . . ?

He said, not meanly, "You think you're hot shit, don't you? People like you."

"What? Why?"

"Living up here. People like you."

"What do you mean?" Harriet asked, though she knew what he meant. Her voice sounded weak, guilty.

"What's your husband do?"

"He teaches history at the university."

He laughed to show he didn't think much of it, history at the university.

They were standing quite close together and might have been having an ordinary if rather intense conversation. Until this moment Harriet had not really looked at the knife. She had seen it, she'd known what it was but had not wanted to look. Now she saw that it was about eight inches long and there was something strange about it—a sporty, chunky look to it—a fat two-edged blade. Two-edged? The handle was unnaturally long, simulated carved wood, probably plastic, black. She thought, He won't really hurt me. He doesn't intend to hurt me.

She thought, I could run.

The knife held conspicuously, he brushed his long damp hair out of his face with both hands in a deft, practiced gesture. He liked himself and he liked her watching him, and Harriet thought of a mass murderer who'd been quoted in the newspaper the previous year, a man who'd killed forty women including a twelve-year-old girl, and he'd said arrogantly, rhetorically, "Who has seen the past? Who has touched the past?" He was an intelligent man, an educated man, a lawyer in fact;

he'd been eloquent enough, saying, "The past? The past is a mist. The past doesn't exist."

And a woman had consented to marry him, after his conviction: borne him a child, a little girl.

Harriet thought, These things can't be.

Harriet thought, How can God let such things happen?

The red-haired young man with the knife was pulling back the bedspread—an odd, even quaint, sense of decorum. He said, "Get down."

Harriet stood frozen. She said, "You promised you wouldn't hurt me."

"I'm not going to hurt you," he said. "Just get down."

"My daughter is downstairs—"

"C'mon. Now. Do it. Get *down*."

"I can't," Harriet said, her voice breaking. "I can't do it." She began to cry. She said, "My husband—"

"You're somebody's wife!" the man said. He spoke with an air of angry incredulity as if Harriet were trying to trick him again. "You fuck all the time! You had a kid! What the hell! It's nothing! Don't tell *me*!"

Harriet said desperately, "No. Please. You promised. You said you wouldn't—"

"Nobody's going to hurt you, for Christ's sake," the man said. "Just get down here," he said, shoving her onto the bed, "and shut *up*."

"My daughter—"

"You want to see her again? Your daughter? Do you? You want to see her again?" he said.

He rapped her across the mouth with his knuckles. Harriet drew breath to scream but knew she should not scream—should not scream—not now: he was standing over her, panting, big-eyed, the knife in his hand.

She said, "You promised you wouldn't hurt me. I'm afraid of the knife."

"I'm not going to use the knife."

"Yes, but I'm afraid of it."

He was fumbling with his pants, flush-faced, excited. Harriet shut her eyes to a flurry of lights, something hot and crackling behind her eyelids; she shut her eyes and forced herself to open them again, to speak clearly, coherently, even now. "I'm afraid of the knife. Please put away the knife."

"You want to hold it? You can hold it," he said, crouching over her. "Go ahead, hold it. *Take* it." He was smiling his hard tight clenched smile. Harriet thought, He's crazy. Then she thought, He's trying to be a gentleman—is that it?

He pressed the knife into her fingers and it fell onto the bed. He picked it up and pressed it again into her fingers, closed her fingers around it. He said, "You're nice. You're pretty. You owe me money. You owe me fucking *something*, and you know it. Just lay still."

Harriet held the knife; Harriet was holding it, her arm bent awkwardly at the elbow. Her wrist was so weak it might have snapped like dried kindling.

Is this rape? she thought. *This?*—as the man pried her legs apart, poked himself against her. Rivulets of sweat ran down his face; his tongue appeared between his teeth in a parody of intense childlike concentration. Again he said he wouldn't hurt her, "This won't hurt, lady, just lay still," and Harriet was pinned beneath him rigid and disbelieving, thinking even now, This can't be happening, this can't, can't be happening—her legs spread wide, sweat-slick and clumsy, knees high as if she were on an examination table, feet caught in stirrups. The knife had slipped again from her fingers and she could not keep from crying out, a series of high little screams, she could not keep from fighting, threshing—

"Just lay still."

AS A CHILD of four Harriet had fallen from a porch on the second floor of her parents' Cape Cod summer house; she'd leaned against a railing that was badly rotted and gave way beneath her weight. Very likely she would have been killed or severely injured if it hadn't been for an overgrown evergreen shrub that broke her fall.

But she wasn't killed, wasn't even injured except for scratches and bruises and the shock of the accident. And forever afterward it was a legend of the family, one of those happy legends that spring up and thrive and are never forgotten in families, that Harriet was blessed with luck: fool's luck, perhaps, but luck nonetheless.

So now, returning to consciousness, alone in her bed, alone in her bedroom, alive, throbbing with pain but alive, she thought only, It's over.

In that first instant, before the pain really hit, and the disbelief, the loathing, the nausea—before, even, she began to call her daughter's name—she thought only, It's over. We're safe.

SHE TELEPHONED THE POLICE FIRST, and then her husband who was in Chicago, and she spoke evenly and carefully, keeping her voice low, calm, modulated; she was determined to demonstrate that she wasn't all that upset, she certainly wasn't hysterical: only a robbery after all, and they hadn't taken very much.

The police arrived within minutes and questioned her for about an hour. They asked for descriptions of the men and they asked if she recognized either or both of the men and they asked were the men armed, and Harriet said hesitantly, "Well—yes. I think one of them had a knife."

Bonnie was upstairs in bed by this time, Bonnie would have no part in the interrogation, perhaps Bonnie had not even seen the knife? Harriet was saying carefully, "I think one of them had a knife he kept in his pocket, you know, sort of threatening, in his pocket—"

"A knife? Not a gun?"

"Oh, no, not a gun. A knife, I think—"

"Did you see it?"

"I think I did, yes, actually—"

"Did he threaten you with it?"

"He did, yes, in a way, but not—"

"He didn't touch you with it?"

"Oh, no. No, he didn't touch me with it," she said emphatically. "He wasn't the kind—I mean, he didn't do that."

"Did either of them touch you?"

"Yes, but not—"

"Not roughly?"

She began to speak quickly. "I don't know, really. It was all so frightening and confused and I was worried mainly about my daughter. I mean—as soon as I thought she'd be safe it was only a matter of time, giving them some money, not much but all I had: seventy-three dollars, it was, and some jewelry, and my husband's camera, and a few other things, I've forgotten exactly; we don't have much that's valuable and I offered them what we had, I didn't protest or try to resist, I didn't think it was worth it, after all—not with my daughter here."

Which was of course—wasn't it?—the wisest thing to have done.

As the police told her. And others were to tell her, admiringly: the wisest thing to have done—to save your and Bonnie's lives.

She told the police about the robbery in as much detail as she could recall—she was to remember more the next morning and more, by degrees, in the days following—but she did not tell them about the rape because perhaps it had not been a rape? She'd held the knife in her fingers, after all, and had not used it.

And he had not hurt her—much. Not so much as he might have.

I THINK HE LIKED ME, she thought.

He didn't really want to hurt me, she thought.

I left the door unlocked and wasn't that an invitation to—something?

AND THE SHAME. And the public humiliation.

And her husband. "I can't do that to him," she said aloud. She was angry, not despairing, as if she were arguing with someone.

THE POLICE BELIEVED HER, or seemed to. Her husband believed her. Or seemed to. (But she wasn't sure. Those much-repeated questions, questions: Did they threaten you physically? Did they touch you? What kind of knife was it—how close did he come to using it on you?) The men were to be apprehended within two weeks, but it was only a few days later that Harriet was standing at a window in Bonnie's room—headachy, groggy from a powerful dose of codeine—watching steamy air rise from grass, sidewalks, the roofs of neighboring houses. It was a prematurely warm day, the sun seemed unnaturally bright though the sky was massed with rain clouds, and Harriet glanced up and saw a human figure—an angel?—contorted and struggling like a swimmer in the clouds: angular, sculpted, purely white, beautiful as living marble. What was it? Was she going mad? She fell to her knees as her parents had done in the little Methodist church in the country long ago and she cried aloud, "God, don't let me turn into a religious lunatic!" and when she looked up again of course the figure was gone. Just oddly shaped clouds, rain-swollen, turbulent, an El Greco sky.

That evening she would tell her husband about the rape. And what would happen, as a consequence, would happen.

THE HAIR

———

THE COUPLES FELL IN LOVE but not at the same time, and not evenly.

There was perceived to be, from the start, an imbalance of power. The less dominant couple, the Carsons, feared social disadvantage. They feared being hopeful of a friendship that would dissolve before consummation. They feared seeming eager.

Said Charlotte Carson, hanging up the phone, "The Riegels have invited us for dinner on New Year's," her voice level, revealing none of the childlike exultation she felt, nor did she look up to see the expression on her husband's face as he murmured, "Who? The Riegels?" pausing before adding, "That's very nice of them."

Once or twice, the Carsons had invited the Riegels to their home, but for one or another reason the Riegels had declined the invitation.

New Year's Eve went very well indeed and shortly thereafter— though not too shortly—Charlotte Carson telephoned to invite the Riegels back.

The friendship between the couples blossomed. In a relatively small community like the one in which the couples lived, such a new, quick, galloping sort of alliance cannot go unnoticed.

So it was noted by mutual friends who felt some surprise, and perhaps some envy. For the Riegels were a golden couple, newcomers to the area who, not employed locally, had about them the glamour of temporary visitors.

In high school, Charlotte Carson thought with a stab of satisfaction, the Riegels would have snubbed me.

Old friends and acquaintances of the Carsons began to observe that Charlotte and Barry were often busy on Saturday evenings, their calendar seemingly marked for weeks in advance. And when a date did not appear to be explicitly set Charlotte would so clearly—insultingly—hesitate, not wanting to surrender a prime weekend evening only to discover belatedly that the Riegels would call them at the last minute and ask them over. Charlotte Carson, gentlest, most tactful of women, in her mid-thirties, shy at times as a schoolgirl of another era, was forced repeatedly to say, "I'm sorry—I'm afraid we can't." And insincerely.

Paul Riegel, whose name everyone knew, was in his early forties: he was a travel writer; he had adventures of a public sort. He published articles and books, he was often to be seen on television, he was tall, handsome, tanned, gregarious, his graying hair springy at the sides of his head and retreating rather wistfully at the crown of his head. "Your husband seems to bear the gift of happiness," Charlotte Carson told Ceci Riegel. Charlotte sometimes spoke too emotionally and wondered now if she had too clearly exposed her heart. But Ceci simply smiled one of her mysterious smiles. "Yes. He tries."

In any social gathering the Riegels were likely to be, without visible effort, the cynosure of attention. When Paul Riegel strode into a crowded room wearing one of his bright ties, or his familiar sports-coat-sports-shirt-open-collar with well-laundered jeans, people looked immediately to him and smiled. There's Paul Riegel! He bore his minor celebrity with grace and even a kind of aristocratic humility, shrugging off questions in pursuit of the public side of his life. If, from time to time, having had a few drinks, he told wildly amusing exaggerated tales, even, riskily, outrageous ethnic or dialect jokes, he told them with such zest and childlike self-delight his listeners were convulsed with laughter.

Never, or almost never, did he forget names.

And his wife, Ceci—petite, ash-blond, impeccably dressed, with a delicate classically proportioned face like an old-fashioned cameo—was surely his ideal mate. She was inclined at times to be fey but she was really very smart. She had a lovely whitely glistening smile as dazzling as her husband's and as seemingly sincere. For years she had been an interior designer in New York City and since moving to the country was a consultant to her former firm; it was rumored that her family had money and that she had either inherited a small fortune or spurned a small fortune at about the time of her marriage to Paul Riegel.

It was rumored too that the Riegels ran through people quickly, used up friends. That they had affairs.

Or perhaps it was only Paul who had affairs.

Or Ceci.

Imperceptibly, it seemed, the Carsons and the Riegels passed from being friendly acquaintances who saw each other once or twice a month to being friends who saw each other every week, or more. There were formal dinners, and there were cocktail parties, and there were Sunday brunches—the social staples of suburban life. There were newly acquired favorite restaurants to patronize and, under Ceci's guidance, outings to New York City to see plays, ballet, opera. There were even picnics from which bicycle rides and canoe excursions were launched—not without comical misadventures. In August when the Riegels rented a house on Nantucket Island they invited the Carsons to visit; when the Riegels had houseguests the Carsons were almost always invited to meet them; soon the men were playing squash together on a regular basis. (Paul won three games out of five, which seemed just right. But he did not win easily.) In time Charlotte Carson overcame her shyness about telephoning Ceci as if on the spur of the moment—"Just to say hello!"

Ceci Riegel had no such scruples, nor did Paul, who thought nothing of telephoning friends—everywhere in the world; he knew so many people—at virtually any time of the day or night, simply to say hello.

The confidence born of never having been rejected.

Late one evening the Carsons were delighted to hear from Paul in Bangkok, of all places, where he was on assignment with a *Life* photographer.

Another time, sounding dazed and not quite himself, he telephoned them at 7:30 A.M. from John F. Kennedy Airport, newly arrived in the States and homesick for the sound of "familiar" voices. He hadn't been able to get hold of Ceci, he complained, but they were next on his list.

Which was enormously flattering.

Sometimes when Paul was away on one of his extended trips, Ceci was, as she said, morbidly lonely, so the three of them went out for Chinese food and a movie or watched videos late into the night; or impulsively, rather recklessly, Ceci got on the phone and invited a dozen friends over, and neighbors too, though always, first, Charlotte and Barry—"Just to feel I *exist*."

The couples were each childless.

Barry had not had a male friend whom he saw so regularly since college, and the nature of his work—he was an executive with Bell Labs—seemed to preclude camaraderie. Charlotte was his closest friend but he rarely confided in her all that was in his heart: this wasn't his nature.

Unlike his friend Paul he preferred the ragged edges of gatherings, not their quicksilver centers. He was big-boned with heavy-lidded quizzical eyes, a shadowy beard like shot, deep in the pores of his skin, wide nostrils, a handsome sensual mouth. He'd been an all-A student once and carried still that air of tension and precariousness strung tight as a bow. Did he take himself too seriously? Or not seriously enough? Wild moods swung in him, rarely surfacing. When his wife asked him why was he so quiet, what was he thinking, he replied, smiling, "Nothing important, honey," though resenting the question, the intrusion. The implied assertion: *I have a right to your secrets*.

His heart pained him when Ceci Riegel greeted him with a hearty little spasm of an embrace and a perfumy kiss alongside his cheek, but he was not the kind of man to fall sentimentally in love with a friend's wife. Nor was he the kind of man, aged forty and wondering when his life would begin, to fall in love with his friend.

The men played squash daily when Paul was in town. Sometimes, afterward, they had lunch together, and a few beers, and talked about their families: their fathers, mainly. Barry drifted back to his office pale and shaken and that evening might complain vaguely to Charlotte that Paul Riegel came on a little too strong for him, "As if it's always the squash court, and he's always the star."

Charlotte said quickly, "He means well. And so does Ceci. But they're aggressive people." She paused, wondering what she was saying. "Not like us."

When Barry and Paul played doubles with other friends, other men, they nearly always won. Which pleased Barry more than he would have wished anyone to know.

And Paul's praise: it burned in his heart with a luminosity that endured for hours and days and all in secret.

The Carsons were childless but had two cats. The Riegels were childless but had a red setter bitch, no longer young.

The Carsons lived in a small mock-Georgian house in town; the Riegels lived in a glass, stone, and redwood house, custom-designed, three miles out in the country. The Carsons' house was one of many attractive houses of its kind in their quiet residential neighborhood and had no distinctive features except an aged enormous plane tree in the front which would probably have to be dismantled soon—"It will break our hearts," Charlotte said. The Carsons' house was fully exposed to the street; the Riegels' house was hidden from the narrow gravel road that ran past it by a seemingly untended meadow of juniper pines, weeping willows, grasses, wildflowers.

Early on in their friendship, a tall cool summer drink in hand, Barry Carson almost walked through a plate glass door at the Riegels'—beyond it was the redwood deck, Ceci in a silk floral-printed dress with numberless pleats.

Ceci was happy and buoyant and confident always. For a petite woman—size five, it was more than once announced—she had a shapely body, breasts, hips, strong-calved legs. When she and Charlotte Carson played tennis, Ceci was all over the court, laughing and exclaiming, while slow-moving premeditated Charlotte, poor Charlotte, who felt, in her friend's company, ostrich-tall and ungainly, missed all but the easy shots. "You need to be more aggressive, Char!" Paul Riegel called out. "Need to be *murderous!*"

The late-night drive back to town from the Riegels' along narrow twisty country roads, Barry behind the wheel, sleepy with drink yet excited too, vaguely sweetly aching, Charlotte yawning and sighing, and there was the danger of white-tailed deer so plentiful in this part of the state leaping in front of the car; but they returned home safely, suddenly they were home, and, inside, one of them would observe that their house was so lacking in imagination, wasn't it? So exposed to the neighbors? "Yes, but you wanted this house." "No, you were the one who wanted this house." "Not *this* house—but this was the most feasible." Though sometimes one would observe that the Riegels' house had flaws: so much glass and it's drafty in the winter, so many queer elevated decks and flights of stairs, wall-less rooms, sparsely furnished rooms like design-ers' showcases, and the cool chaste neutral colors that Ceci evidently favored: "It's beautiful, yes, but a bit sterile."

In bed exhausted they would drift to sleep, separately wandering the corridors of an unknown building, opening one door after another in dread and fascination. Charlotte, who should not have had more than two or three glasses of wine—but it was an anniversary of the Riegels: they'd uncorked bottles of champagne—slept fitfully, waking often dry-mouthed and frightened not knowing where she was. A flood of hypnagogic images raced in her brain; the faces of strangers never before glimpsed by her thrummed beneath her eyelids. In that state of consciousness that is neither sleep nor waking Charlotte had the volition to will, ah, how passionately, how despairingly, that Paul Riegel would comfort her: slip his arm around her shoulders, nudge his jaw against her cheek, whisper in her ear as he'd done once or twice that evening in play but now in seriousness. Beside her someone stirred and groaned in his sleep and kicked at the covers.

Paul Riegel entranced listeners with lurid tales of starving Cambo-dian refugees, starving Ethiopian children, starving Mexican beggars. His eyes shone with angry tears one moment and with mischief the next, for he could not resist mocking his own sobriety. The laughter he aroused at such times had an air of bafflement, shock.

Ceci came to him to slip an arm through his as if to comfort or to quiet, and there were times when quite perceptibly Paul shook off her arm, stepped away, stared down at her with a look as if he'd never seen the woman before.

When the Carsons did not see or hear from the Riegels for several days their loneliness was almost palpable: a thickness in the chest, a density of being, to which either might allude knowing the other would immediately understand. If the Riegels were actually away that made the separation oddly more bearable than if they were in fact in their house amid the trees but not seeing the Carsons that weekend or mysteriously incommunicado with their telephone answering tape switched on. When Charlotte called, got the tape, heard the familiar static-y overture, then Paul Riegel's cool almost hostile voice that did not identify itself but merely stated *No one is here right now; should you like to leave a message please wait for the sound of the bleep*, she felt a loss too profound to be named and often hung up in silence.

It had happened as the Carsons feared—the Riegels were dominant. So fully in control.

For there was a terrible period, several months in all, when for no reason the Carsons could discover—and they discussed the subject endlessly, obsessively—the Riegels seemed to have little time for them. Or saw them with batches of others in which their particular friendship could not be readily discerned. Paul was a man of quick enthusiasms, and Ceci was a woman of abrupt shifts of allegiance; thus there was logic of sorts to their cruelty in elevating for a while a new couple in the area who were both theoretical mathematicians, and a neighbor's houseguest who'd known Paul in college and was now in the diplomatic service, and a cousin of Ceci's, a male model in his late twenties who was staying with the Riegels for weeks and weeks and weeks, taking up every spare minute of their time, it seemed, so when Charlotte called, baffled and hurt, Ceci murmured in an undertone, "I can't talk now, can I call you back in the morning?" and failed to call for days, days, days.

One night when Charlotte would have thought Barry was asleep he shocked her by saying, "I never liked her, much. Hot-shit little Ceci." She had never heard her husband utter such words before and did not know how to reply.

They went away on a trip. Three weeks in the Caribbean, and only in the third week did Charlotte scribble a postcard for the Riegels—a quick scribbled little note as if one of many.

One night she said, "*He's* the dangerous one. He always tries to get people to drink too much, to keep him company."

They came back, and not long afterward Ceci called, and the friendship was resumed precisely as it had been—the same breathless pace, the same dazzling intensity—though now Paul had a new book coming out and there were parties in the city, book signings at bookstores, an interview on a morning news program. The Carsons gave a party for him, inviting virtually everyone they knew locally, and the party was a great success and in a corner of the house Paul Riegel hugged Charlotte Carson so hard she laughed, protesting her ribs would crack, but when she drew back to look at her friend's face she saw it was damp with tears.

Later, Paul told a joke about Reverend Jesse Jackson that was a masterpiece of mimicry though possibly in questionable taste. In the general hilarity no one noticed, or at least objected. In any case there were no blacks present.

The Riegels were childless but would not have defined their condition in those terms: as a lack, a loss, a negative. Before marrying they had discussed the subject of children thoroughly, Paul said, and came to the conclusion *no*.

The Carsons too were childless but would perhaps have defined their condition in those terms, in weak moods at least. Hearing Paul speak so indifferently of children, the Carsons exchanged a glance almost of embarrassment.

Each hoped the other would not disclose any intimacy.

Ceci sipped at her drink and said, "I'd have been willing."

Paul said, "*I* wouldn't."

There was a brief nervous pause. The couples were sitting on the Riegels' redwood deck in the gathering dusk.

Paul then astonished the Carsons by speaking in a bitter impassioned voice of families, children, parents, the "politics" of intimacy. In any intimate group, he said, the struggle to be independent, to define oneself as an individual, is so fierce it creates terrible waves of tension, a field of psychic warfare. He'd endured it as a child and young adolescent in his parents' home, and as an adult he didn't think he could bear to bring up a child—"especially a son"—knowing of the doubleness and secrecy of the child's life.

"There is the group life, which is presumably open and observable," he said, "and there is the secret inner real life no one can penetrate." He spoke with such uncharacteristic vehemence that neither of the Carsons would have dared to challenge him or even to question him in the usual conversational vein.

Ceci sat silent, drink in hand, staring impassively out into the shadows.

After a while conversation resumed again and they spoke softly, laughed softly. The handsome white wrought-iron furniture on which they were sitting took on an eerie solidity even as the human figures seemed to fade: losing outline and contour, blending into the night and into one another.

Charlotte Carson lifted her hand, registering a small chill spasm of fear that she was dissolving, but it was only a drunken notion of course.

For days afterward Paul Riegel's disquieting words echoed in her head. She tasted something black, and her heart beat in anger like a cheated child's. *Don't you love me then? Don't any of us love any of us?* To Barry she said, "That was certainly an awkward moment, wasn't it? When Paul started his monologue about family life, intimacy, all that. What did you make of it?"

Barry murmured something evasive and backed off.

The Carsons owned two beautiful Siamese cats, neutered male and neutered female, and the Riegels owned a skittish Irish setter named Rusty. When the Riegels came to visit Ceci always made a fuss over one or the other of the cats, insisting it sit in her lap, sometimes even at the dinner table, where she'd feed it on the sly. When the Carsons came to visit, the damned dog as Barry spoke of it went into a frenzy of barking and greeted them at the front door as if it had never seen them before. "Nice dog! Good dog! Sweet Rusty!" the Carsons would cry in unison.

The setter was rheumy-eyed and thick-bodied and arthritic. If every year of a dog's age is approximately seven years in human terms, poor Rusty was almost eighty years old. She managed to shuffle to the front door to bark at visitors but then lacked the strength or motor coordination to reverse herself and return to the interior of the house so Paul had to carry her, one arm under her bony chest and forelegs, the other firmly under her hindquarters, an expression of vexed tenderness in his face.

Dryly he said, "I hope someone will do as much for me someday."

One rainy May afternoon when Paul was in Berlin and Barry was in Virginia visiting his family, Ceci impulsively invited Charlotte to come for a drink and meet her friend Nils Larson—or was the name Lasson? Lawson?—an old old dear friend. Nils was short, squat-bodied, energetic, with a gnomish head and bright malicious eyes, linked to Ceci, it appeared, in a way that allowed him to be both slavish and condescending. He was a "theater person"; his bubbly talk was studded with names of the famous and near-famous. Never once did he mention Paul Riegel's name, though certain of his mannerisms—head thrown back in laughter, hands gesticulating as he spoke—reminded Charlotte of certain of Paul's mannerisms. The man was Paul's elder by perhaps a decade.

Charlotte stayed only an hour, then made her excuses and slipped away. She had seen Ceci's friend draw his pudgy forefinger across the nape of Ceci's neck in a gesture that signaled intimacy or the arrogant pretense of intimacy, and the sight offended her. But she never told Barry and resolved not to think of it and of whether Nils spent the night at the Riegels' and whether Paul knew anything of him or of the visit. Nor did Ceci ask Charlotte what she had thought of Nils Larson—Lasson? Lawson?—the next time the women spoke.

Barry returned from Virginia with droll tales of family squabbling: his brother and his sister-in-law, their children, the network of aunts, uncles, nieces, nephews, grandparents, ailing elderly relatives whose savings were being eaten up—invariably the expression was "eaten

up"—by hospital and nursing home expenses. Barry's father, severely
crippled from a stroke, was himself in a nursing home from which he
would never be discharged, and all his conversation turned upon this
fact, which others systematically denied, including, in the exigency of
the moment, Barry. He had not, he said, really recognized his father. It
was as if another man—aged, shrunken, querulous, sly—had taken his
place.

The elderly Mr. Carson had affixed to a wall of his room a small
white card on which he'd written some Greek symbols, an inscription he
claimed to have treasured all his life. Barry asked what the Greek meant
and was told, *When my ship sank, the others sailed on.*

Paul Riegel returned from Berlin exhausted and depressed despite
the fact, a happy one to his wife and friends, that a book of his was on
the paperback bestseller list published by *The New York Times*. When
Charlotte Carson suggested with uncharacteristic gaiety that they cel-
ebrate, Paul looked at her with a mild quizzical smile and asked, "Why,
exactly?"

The men played squash, the women played tennis.

The Carsons had other friends, of course. Older and more reliable
friends. They did not need the Riegels. Except they were in love with
the Riegels.

Did the Riegels love them? Ceci telephoned one evening and Barry
happened to answer and they talked together for an hour, and afterward,
when Charlotte asked Barry what they'd talked about, careful to keep all
signs of jealousy and excitement out of her voice, Barry said evasively,
"A friend of theirs is dying. Of AIDS. Ceci says he weighs only ninety
pounds and has withdrawn from everyone: 'slunk off to die like a sick
animal.' And Paul doesn't care. Or won't talk about it." Barry paused,
aware that Charlotte was looking at him closely. A light film of perspi-
ration covered his face; his nostrils appeared unusually dark, dilated.
"He's no one we know, honey. The dying man, I mean."

When Paul Riegel emerged from a sustained bout of writing the first
people he wanted to see were the Carsons of course, so the couples went
out for Chinese food—"a banquet, no less!"—at their favorite Chinese
restaurant in a shopping mall. The Dragon Inn had no liquor license so

they brought bottles of wine and six-packs of beer. They were the last
customers to leave, and by the end waiters and kitchen help were stand-
ing around or prowling restlessly at the rear of the restaurant. There was
a minor disagreement over the check, which Paul Riegel insisted had
not been added up "strictly correctly." He and the manager discussed
the problem and since the others were within earshot he couldn't resist
clowning for their amusement, slipping into a comical Chinese (unless it
was Japanese?) accent. In the parking lot the couples laughed helplessly,
gasping for breath and bent double, and in the car driving home—Barry
drove: they'd taken the Carsons' Honda Accord, and Barry was seem-
ingly the most sober of the four of them—they kept bursting into peals
of laughter like naughty children.

They never returned to the Dragon Inn.

The men played squash together but their most rewarding games
were doubles in which they played, and routed, another pair of men.

As if grudgingly, Paul Riegel would tell Barry Carson he was a
"damned good player." To Charlotte he would say, "Your husband is a
damned good player but if only he could be a bit more *murderous*!"

Barry Carson's handsome heavy face darkened with pleasure when
he heard such praise, exaggerated as it was. Though afterward, regard-
ing himself in a mirror, he felt shame: he was forty years old, he had a
very good job in a highly competitive field, he had a very good marriage
with a woman he both loved and respected, he believed he was leading,
on the whole, a very good life, yet none of this meant as much to him as
Paul Riegel carelessly complimenting him on his squash game.

How has my life come to this?

Rusty developed cataracts on both eyes and then tumorous growths
in her neck. The Riegels took her to the vet and had her put to sleep,
and Ceci had what was reported to the Carsons as a breakdown of a
kind: wept and wept and wept. Paul too was shaken by the ordeal but
managed to joke over the phone about the dog's ashes. When Charlotte
told Barry of the dog's death she saw Barry's eyes narrow as he resisted
saying Thank God! and said instead, gravely, as if it would be a problem
of his own, "Poor Ceci will be inconsolable."

For weeks it wasn't clear to the Carsons that they would be invited to visit the Riegels on Nantucket; then, shortly before the Riegels left, Ceci said as if casually, "We did set a date, didn't we? For you two to come visit?"

On their way up—it was a seven-hour drive to the ferry at Woods Hole—Charlotte said to Barry, "Promise you won't drink so much this year." Offended, Barry said, "I won't monitor your behavior, honey, if you won't monitor mine."

From the first, the Nantucket visit went awkwardly. Paul wasn't home and his whereabouts weren't explained, though Ceci chattered brightly and effusively, carrying her drink with her as she escorted the Carsons to their room and watched them unpack. Her shoulder-length hair was graying and disheveled; her face was heavily made up, especially about the eyes. Several times she said, "Paul will be so happy to see you," as if Paul had not known they were invited; or, knowing, like Ceci herself, had perhaps forgotten. An east wind fanned drizzle and soft gray mist against the windows.

Paul returned looking fit and tanned and startled about the eyes; in his walnut-brown face the whites glared. Toward dusk the sky lightened and the couples sat on the beach with their drinks. Ceci continued to chatter while Paul smiled, vague and distracted, looking out at the surf. The air was chilly and damp but wonderfully fresh. The Carsons drew deep breaths and spoke admiringly of the view. And the house. And the location. They were wondering had the Riegels been quarreling? Was something wrong? Had they themselves come on the wrong day or at the wrong time? Paul had been effusive too in his greetings but had not seemed to see them and had scarcely looked at them since.

Before they sat down to dinner the telephone began to ring. Ceci in the kitchen (with Charlotte who was helping her) and Paul in the living room (with Barry; the men were watching a televised tennis tournament) made no move to answer it. The ringing continued for what seemed like a long time, then stopped and resumed again while they were having dinner, and again neither of the Riegels made a move to answer it. Paul grinned, running both hands roughly through the bushy patches of hair at the sides of his head, and said, "When the world beats a path to your doorstep, beat it back, friends! *Beat it back for fuck's sake!*"

His extravagant words were meant to be funny of course but would have required another atmosphere altogether to be so. As it was, the Carsons could only stare and smile in embarrassment.

Ceci filled the silence by saying loudly, "Life's little ironies! You spend a lifetime making yourself famous, then you try to back off and dismantle it. But it won't dismantle! It's a mummy and you're inside it!"

"Not *in* a mummy," Paul said, staring smiling at the lobster on his plate, which he'd barely eaten, "you *are* a mummy." He had been drinking steadily, Scotch on the rocks and now wine, since arriving home.

Ceci laughed sharply. " 'In,' 'are,' what's the difference?" she said, appealing to the Carsons. She reached out to squeeze Barry's hand, hard. "In any case you're a goner, right?"

Paul said, "No, *you're* a goner."

The evening continued in this vein. The Carsons sent despairing glances at each other.

The telephone began to ring, and this time Paul rose to answer it. He walked stiffly and took his glass of wine with him. He took the call not in the kitchen but in another room at the rear of the house, and he was gone so long that Charlotte felt moved to ask if something was wrong. Ceci Riegel stared at her coldly. The whites of Ceci's eyes too showed above the rims of the iris, giving her a fey festive party look at odds with her carelessly combed hair and the tiredness deep in her face. "With the meal?" she asked. "With the house? With us? With *you?* I don't know of anything wrong."

Charlotte had never been so rebuffed in her adult life. Barry too felt the force of the insult. After a long stunned moment Charlotte murmured an apology, and Barry too murmured something vague, placating, embarrassed.

They sat in suspension, not speaking, scarcely moving, until at last Paul returned. His cheeks were ruddy as if they'd been heartily slapped and his eyes were bright. He carried a bottle of his favorite Napa Valley wine, which he'd been saving, he said, just for tonight. "This is a truly special occasion! We've really missed you guys!"

They were up until two, drinking. Repeatedly Paul used the odd expression "guys" as if its sound, its grating musicality, had imprinted itself in his brain. "OK, guys, how's about another drink?" he would say, rubbing his hands together. "OK, guys, how the hell have you been?"

Next morning, a brilliantly sunny morning, no one was up before eleven. Paul appeared in swimming trunks and T-shirt in the kitchen around noon, boisterous, swaggering, unshaven, in much the mood of the night before—remarkable! The Riegels had hired a local handyman to shore up some rotting steps and the handyman was an oldish gray-grizzled black and after the man was paid and departed Paul spoke in an exaggerated comical black accent, hugging Ceci and Charlotte around their waists until Charlotte pushed him away stiffly, saying, "I don't think you're being funny, Paul." There was a moment's startled silence; then she repeated, vehemently, *"I don't think that's funny, Paul."*

As if on cue Ceci turned on her heel and walked out of the room.

But Paul continued his clowning. He blundered about in the kitchen, pleading with "white missus": bowing, shuffling, tugging what remained of his forelock, kneeling to pluck at Charlotte's denim skirt. His flushed face seemed to have turned to rubber, his lips red, moist, turned obscenely inside out. "Beg pardon, white missus! Oh, white missus, beg pardon!"

Charlotte said, "I think we should leave."

Barry, who had been staring appalled at his friend, as if he'd never seen him before, said quickly, "Yes. I think we should leave."

They went to their room at the rear of the house, leaving Paul behind, and in a numbed stricken silence packed their things, each of them badly trembling. They anticipated one or both of the Riegels following them but neither did, and as Charlotte yanked sheets off the bed, towels off the towel rack in the bathroom, to fold and pile them neatly at the foot of the bed, she could not believe that their friends would allow them to leave without protest.

With a wad of toilet paper she cleaned the bathroom sink as Barry called to her to please hurry. She examined the claw-footed tub—she and Barry had each showered that morning—and saw near the drain a tiny curly dark hair, hers or Barry's, indistinguishable, and this hair she leaned over to snatch up but her fingers closed in air and she tried another time, still failing to grasp it, then finally she picked it up and flushed it down the toilet. Her face was burning and her heart knocking so hard in her chest she could scarcely breathe.

The Carsons left the Riegels' cottage in Nantucket shortly after noon of the day following their arrival.

They drove seven hours back to their home with a single stop, silent much of the time but excited, nervously elated. When he drove Barry kept glancing in the rearview mirror. One of his eyelids had developed a tic.

He said, "We should have done this long ago."

"Yes," Charlotte said, staring ahead at dry sunlit rushing pavement. "Long ago."

That night in their own bed they made love for the first time in weeks, or months. "I love you," Barry murmured, as if making a vow. "No one but you."

Tears started out of the corners of Charlotte's tightly shut eyes.

Afterward Barry slept heavily, sweating through the night. From time to time he kicked at the covers, but he never woke. Beside him Charlotte lay staring into the dark. What would become of them now? Something tickled her lips, a bit of lint, a hair, and though she brushed it irritably away the tingling sensation remained. What would become of them, now?

THE SWIMMERS

———

THERE ARE STORIES that go unaccountably wrong and become impermeable to the imagination. They lodge in the memory like an old wound never entirely healed. This story of my father's younger brother, Clyde Farrell, my uncle, and a woman named Joan Lunt with whom he fell in love, years ago, in 1959, is one of those stories.

Some of it I was a part of, aged thirteen. But much of it I have to imagine.

IT MUST HAVE BEEN A PALE, wintry, unflattering light he first saw her in, swimming laps in the early morning in the local YM-YWCA pool, but that initial sight of Joan Lunt—not her face, which was obscured from him, but the movement of her strong, supple, creamy-pale body through the water and the sureness of her strokes—never faded from Clyde Farrell's mind.

He'd been told of her, in fact he'd come to the pool that morning partly to observe her, but still you didn't expect to see such serious swimming, 7:45 A.M. of a weekday, in the antiquated white-tiled Y pool,

light slanting down from the wired glass skylight overhead, a sharp me-
dicinal smell of chlorine and disinfectant pinching your nostrils. There
were a few other swimmers in the pool, ordinary swimmers, one of them
an acquaintance of Clyde's who waved at him, called out his name, when
Clyde appeared in his swim trunks on the deck, climbed up onto the
diving board, then paused to watch Joan Lunt swimming toward the
far end of the pool . . . just stood watching her, not rudely but with a
frank childlike interest, smiling with the spontaneous pleasure of seeing
another person doing something well, with so little waste motion. Joan
Lunt in her yellow bathing suit with the crossed straps in back and her
white rubber cap that gleamed and sparked in the miniature waves: an
attractive woman in her mid-thirties, though she looked younger, with
an air of total absorption in the task at hand, swimming to the limit of
her capacity, maintaining a pace and a rhythm Clyde Farrell would have
been challenged to maintain himself, and Clyde was a good swimmer,
known locally as a very good swimmer, a winner, years before, when
he was in his teens, of county and state competitions. Joan Lunt wasn't
aware of him standing on the diving board watching her, or so it ap-
peared. Just swimming, counting laps. How many she'd done already,
he couldn't imagine. He saw that she knew to cup the water when she
stroked back, not to let it thread through her fingers like most people
do; she knew as if by instinct how to take advantage of the element she
was in, propelling herself forward like an otter or a seal, power in her
shoulder muscles and upper arms and the steady flutter kick of her legs,
feet flashing white through the chemical-turquoise glitter of the water.
When Joan Lunt reached the end of the pool she ducked immediately
down into the water in a well-practiced maneuver, turned, used the tiled
side to push off from, in a single graceful motion that took her a con-
siderable distance, and Clyde Farrell's heart contracted when, emerg-
ing from the water, head and shoulders and flashing arms, the woman
didn't miss a beat, just continued as if she hadn't been confronted with
any limit or impediment, any boundary. It was just water, and her in
it, water that might go on forever, and her in it, swimming, sealed off
and invulnerable.

Clyde Farrell dived into the pool and swam vigorously, keeping to his own lane, energetic and single-minded too, and when, after some minutes, he glanced around for the woman in the yellow bathing suit, the woman I'd told him of meeting, Joan Lunt, he saw to his disappointment she was gone.

His vanity was wounded. He thought, She never once looked at me.

MY FATHER and my Uncle Clyde were farm boys who left the farm as soon as they were of age: joined the U.S. Navy out of high school, went away, came back, and lived and worked in town, my father in a small sign shop and Clyde in a succession of jobs. He drove a truck for a gravel company; he was a foreman in a local tool factory; he managed a sporting goods store; he owned property at Wolf's Head Lake, twenty miles to the north, and spoke with vague enthusiasm of developing it some day. He wasn't a practical man, and he never saved money. He liked to gamble at cards and horses. In the navy he'd learned to box and for a while after being discharged he considered a professional career as a welterweight, but that meant signing contracts, traveling around the country, taking orders from other men. Not Clyde Farrell's temperament.

He was a good-looking man, not tall, about five feet nine, compact and quick on his feet, a natural athlete, with well-defined shoulder and arm muscles, strong sinewy legs. His hair was the color of damp sand, his eyes a warm liquid brown, all iris. There was a gap between his two front teeth that gave him a childlike look and was misleading.

No one ever expected Clyde Farrell to get married, or even to fall seriously in love. That capacity in him seemed missing, somehow: a small but self-proclaimed absence, like the gap between his teeth.

But Clyde was powerfully attracted to women, and after watching Joan Lunt swim that morning he drifted by later in the day to Kress's, Yewville's largest department store, where he knew she'd recently started work. Kress's was a store of some distinction: the merchandise was of high quality, the counters made of solid burnished oak; the overhead lighting was muted and flattering to women customers. Behind the counter displaying gloves and leather handbags, Joan Lunt struck the eye as an ordinarily pretty woman, composed, intelligent, feminine, brunette, with a brunette's waxy-pale skin, carefully made up, even glamorous, but not a woman Clyde Farrell would have noticed much. He was thirty-two years old, in many ways much younger. This woman was too mature for him, wasn't she—probably married or divorced, very likely with children. Clyde thought, In her clothes she's just another one of them.

So Clyde walked out of Kress's, a store he didn't like anyway, and wasn't going to think about Joan Lunt, but one morning a few days later there he was, unaccountably, back at the YM-YWCA, 7:30 A.M. of a weekday in March 1959, and there too was Joan Lunt in her satiny-yellow bathing suit and gleaming white cap. Swimming laps, arm over strong slender arm, stroke following stroke, oblivious of Clyde Farrell and of her surroundings so Clyde was forced to see how her presence in the old, tacky, harshly chlorinated pool made of the place something extraordinary that lifted his heart.

That morning Clyde swam in the pool, but only for about ten minutes, then left and hastily showered and dressed and was waiting for Joan Lunt out in the lobby. Clyde wasn't a shy man, but he could give that impression when it suited him. When Joan Lunt appeared he stepped forward, and smiled, and introduced himself, saying, "Miss Lunt? I guess you know my niece Sylvie? She told me about meeting you." Joan Lunt hesitated, then shook hands with Clyde and said, in that way of hers that suggested she was giving information meant to be clear and unequivocal, "My first name is Joan." She didn't smile but seemed prepared to smile.

Close up, Joan Lunt was a good-looking woman with shrewd dark eyes, straight dark eyebrows, an expertly reddened mouth. There was an inch-long white scar at the left corner of her mouth like a sliver of glass. Her thick shoulder-length dark brown hair was carefully waved, but the ends were damp; though her face was pale it appeared heated, invigorated by exercise.

Joan Lunt and Clyde Farrell were nearly of a height, and comfortable together.

Leaving the YM-YWCA, descending the old granite steps to Main

Street that were worn smooth in the centers, nearly hollow with decades
of feet, Clyde said to Joan, "You're a beautiful swimmer—I couldn't
help admiring you, in there," and Joan Lunt laughed and said, "And so
are you—I was admiring you too," and Clyde said, surprised, "Really?
You saw me?" and Joan Lunt said, "Both times."

It was Friday. They arranged to meet for drinks that afternoon, and
spent the next two days together.

IN YEWVILLE, no one knew who Joan Lunt was except as she pre-
sented herself: a woman in her mid-thirties, solitary, very private, seem-
ingly unattached, with no relatives or friends in the area. No one knew
where exactly she'd come from, or why; why here of all places, Yewville,
New York, a small city of less than thirty thousand people, built on the
banks of the Eden River, in the southwestern foothills of the Chautau-
qua Mountains. She had arrived in early February, in a dented rust-red
1956 Chevrolet with New York State license plates, the rear of the car
piled with suitcases, cartons, clothes. She spent two nights in Yewville's
single good hotel, the Mohawk, then moved into a tiny furnished apart-
ment on Chambers Street. She spent several days interviewing for jobs
downtown, all jobs you might call jobs for women specifically, and was
hired at Kress's and started work promptly on the first Monday morning
following her arrival. If it was sheerly good luck, the job at Kress's, the
most prestigious store in town, Joan Lunt seemed to take it in stride, the
way a person would who felt she deserved as much. Or better.

The other saleswomen at Kress's, other tenants in the Chambers
Street building, men who approached her—no one could get to know
her. It was impossible to get beyond the woman's quick, just slightly
edgy smile, her resolute cheeriness, her purposefully vague manner.
Asked where she was from she would say, "Nowhere you'd know."
Asked was she married, did she have a family, she would say, "Oh, I'm
an independent woman, I'm well over eighteen." She'd laugh to suggest
that this was a joke, of a kind—the thin scar beside her mouth white
with anger.

It was observed that her fingers were entirely ringless.

But the nails were perfectly manicured, polished an enamel-hard red.

It was observed that, for a solitary woman, Joan Lunt had curious habits.

For instance, swimming. Very few women swam in the YM-YWCA pool in those days. Sometimes Joan Lunt swam in the early morning, and sometimes, Saturdays, in the late morning; she swam only once in the afternoon, after work, but the pool was disagreeably crowded, and too many people approached her. A well-intentioned woman asked, "Who taught you to swim like that?" and Joan Lunt said quietly, "I taught myself." She didn't smile, and the conversation was not continued.

It was observed that, for a woman in her presumed circumstances, Joan Lunt was remarkably arrogant.

It seemed curious too that she went to the Methodist church Sunday mornings, sitting in a pew at the very rear, holding an opened hymn-book in her hand but not singing with the congregation, and that she slipped away afterward without speaking to anyone. Each time, she left a neatly folded dollar bill in the collection basket.

She wasn't explicitly unfriendly, but she wasn't friendly. At church, the minister and his wife tried to speak with her, tried to make her feel welcome, *did* make her feel welcome, but nothing came of it; she'd hurry off in her car, disappear. People began to murmur there was something strange about that woman, something not right, yes, maybe even something wrong; for instance, wasn't she behaving suspiciously? Like a runaway wife, for instance? A bad mother? A sinner fleeing Christ?

Another of Joan Lunt's curious habits was to drink, alone, in the early evening, in the Yewville Bar & Grill or the White Owl Tavern or the restaurant-bar adjoining the Greyhound bus station. If possible, she sat in a booth at the very rear of these taverns, where she could observe the front entrances without being seen herself. For an hour or more she'd drink bourbon and water, slowly, very slowly, with an elaborate slowness, her face perfectly composed but her eyes alert. In the Yewville Bar & Grill there was an enormous sectioned mirror stretching the length of the taproom and in this mirror, muted by arabesques of frosted glass, Joan Lunt was reflected as beautiful and mysterious. Now and then men approached her to ask was she alone? did she want company?

how's about another drink? but she responded coolly to them and never invited anyone to join her. Had my Uncle Clyde approached her in such a fashion she would very likely have been cool to him too, but my Uncle Clyde wasn't the kind of man to set himself up for any sort of public rejection.

One evening in March, before Joan Lunt met up with Clyde Farrell, patrons at the bar of the Yewville Bar & Grill, one of them my father, reported with amusement hearing an exchange between Joan Lunt and a local farmer who, mildly drunk, offered to sit with her and buy her a drink, which ended with Joan Lunt saying, in a loud, sharp voice, "You don't want trouble, mister. Believe me, you don't."

Rumors spread, delicious and censorious, that Joan Lunt was a man-hater. That she carried a razor in her purse. Or an ice pick. Or a lady's-sized revolver.

IT WAS AT the YM-YWCA pool that I became acquainted with Joan Lunt, on Saturday mornings. She saw that I was alone, that I was a good swimmer, might have mistaken me for younger than I was and befriended me, casually and cheerfully, the way an adult woman might befriend a young girl to whom she isn't related. Her remarks were often exclamations, called across the slapping little waves of the turquoise-tinted water, "*Isn't* it heavenly!"—meaning the pool, the prospect of swimming, the icy rain pelting the skylight overhead while we, in our bathing suits, were snug and safe below.

Another time, in the changing room, she said almost rapturously, "There's nothing like swimming is there? Your mind just *dissolves*."

She asked my name, and when I told her she stared at me and said, "Sylvie. I had a close friend once named Sylvie, a long time ago. I loved that name, and I loved *her*."

I was embarrassed but pleased. It astonished me that an adult woman, a woman my mother's age, might be so certain of her feelings and so direct in expressing them to a stranger. I fantasized that Joan Lunt came from a part of the world where people knew what they thought and announced their thoughts importantly to others. This struck me with the force of a radically new idea.

I watched Joan Lunt covertly and I didn't even envy her in the pool, she was so far beyond me; her face that seemed to me strong and rare and beautiful, and her body that was a fully developed woman's body—prominent breasts, shapely hips, long firm legs—all beyond me. I saw how the swiftness and skill with which Joan Lunt swam made other swimmers, especially the adults, appear slow by contrast: clumsy, ill-coordinated, without style.

One day Joan Lunt was waiting for me in the lobby, hair damp at the ends, face carefully made up, her lipstick seemingly brighter than usual. "Sylvie!" she said, smiling. "Let's walk out together."

So we walked outside into the snow-glaring windy sunshine, and she said, "Are you going in this direction? Good, let's walk together." She addressed me as if I were much younger than I was, and her manner was nervous, quick, alert. As we walked up Main Street she asked questions of me of a kind she'd never asked before, about my family, about my "interests," about school, not listening to the answers and offering no information about herself. At the corner of Chambers and Main she asked eagerly would I like to come back to her apartment to visit for a few minutes, and though out of shyness I wanted to say No, thank you, I said yes instead because it was clear that Joan Lunt was frightened about something, and I didn't want to leave her.

Her apartment building was shabby and weatherworn, as modest a place as even the poorest of my relatives lived in, but it had about it a sort of makeshift glamour, up the street from the White Owl Tavern and the Shamrock Diner, where motorcyclists hung out, close by the railroad yards on the river. I felt excited and pleased to enter the building and to climb with Joan Lunt—who was chatting briskly all the while—to the fourth floor. On each floor Joan would pause, breathless, glancing around, listening, and I wanted to ask if someone might be following her? waiting for her? but of course I didn't say a thing. When she unlocked the door to her apartment, stepped inside, and whispered, "Come in, Sylvie!" I seemed to understand that no one else had been invited in there before.

The apartment was really just one room with a tiny kitchen alcove, a tiny bathroom, a doorless closet, and a curtainless window with stained, injured-looking venetian blinds. Joan Lunt said with an apologetic little laugh, "Those blinds—I tried to wash them but the dirt turned to a sort of paste." I was standing at the window peering down into a weedy back yard of tilting clotheslines and windblown trash, curious to see what the view was from Joan Lunt's window, and she came over and drew the blinds, saying, "The sunshine is too bright, it hurts my eyes."

She hung up our coats and asked if I would like some coffee? Fresh-squeezed orange juice? "It's my half-day off from Kress's," she said. "I don't have to be there until one." It was shortly after eleven o'clock.

We sat at a worn dinette table, and Joan Lunt chatted animatedly and plied me with questions as I drank orange juice in a tall glass, and she drank black coffee, and an alarm clock on the windowsill ticked the minutes briskly by. Few rooms in which I've lived even for considerable periods of time are as vividly imprinted in my memory as that room of Joan Lunt's, with its spare, battered-looking furniture (including a sofa bed and a chest of drawers), its wanly wallpapered walls bare of any hangings, even a mirror, and its badly faded shag rug laid upon painted floorboards. There was a mixture of smells: talcum powder, perfume, cooking odors, insect spray, general mustiness. Two opened suitcases were on the floor beside the sofa bed, apparently unpacked, containing underwear, toiletries, neatly folded sweaters and blouses, several pairs of shoes. A single dress hung in the closet, and a shiny black raincoat, and our two coats Joan had hung on wire hangers. I stared at the suitcases, thinking, How strange; she'd been living here for weeks but hadn't had time yet to unpack.

So this was where the mysterious Joan Lunt lived, the woman of whom people in Yewville spoke with such suspicion and disapproval! She was far more interesting to me, and in a way more real, than I was to myself; shortly, the story of the lovers Clyde Farrell and Joan Lunt, as I imagined it, would be infinitely more interesting, and infinitely more real, than any story with Sylvie Farrell at its core. (I was a fiercely introspective child, in some ways perhaps a strange child, and the solace of my life would be to grow not away from but ever more deeply and fruitfully *into* my strangeness, the way a child with an idiosyncratic, homely face often grows into that face and emerges, in adulthood, as "striking," "distinctive," sometimes even "beautiful.") It turned out that Joan liked poetry, and so we talked about poetry, and about love, and Joan asked me in that searching way of hers if I was "happy in my life," if I was "loved and prized" by my family, and I said, "Yes, I guess so," though these were not issues I had ever considered before and would not have known to consider if she hadn't asked. For some reason my eyes filled with tears. Joan said, "The crucial thing, Sylvie, is to have precious memories." She spoke almost vehemently, laying her hand on mine. "That's even more important than Jesus Christ in your heart, do you know why? Because Jesus Christ can fade out of your heart, but precious memories never do."

We talked like that. Like I'd never talked with anyone before.

I was nervy enough to ask Joan how she'd gotten the little scar beside her mouth, and she touched it quickly and said, "In a way I'm not proud of, Sylvie." I sat staring, stupid. The scar wasn't disfiguring in my eyes but enhancing. "A man hit me once," Joan said. "Don't ever let a man hit you, Sylvie." Weakly I said, "No, I won't."

No man in our family had ever struck any woman that I knew of, but it happened sometimes in families we knew. I recalled how a ninth-grade girl had come to school that winter with a blackened eye, and she'd seemed proud of it, in a way, and everyone had stared—and the boys just drifted to her, staring. Like they couldn't wait to get their hands on her themselves. And she knew precisely what they were thinking.

I told Joan Lunt that I wished I lived in a place like hers, by myself, and she said, laughing, "No, you don't, Sylvie, you're too young." I asked where she was from and she shrugged—"Oh, nowhere"—and I persisted: "But is it north of here, or south? Is it the country? Or a city?" and she said, running her fingers nervously through her hair, fingering the damp ends, "My only home is *here*, *now*, in this room, and, sweetie, that's more than enough for me to think about."

It was time to leave. The danger had passed, or Joan had passed out of thinking there was danger.

She walked with me to the stairs, smiling, cheerful, and squeezed my hand when we said goodbye. She called down after me, "See you next Saturday at the pool, maybe," but it would be weeks before I saw Joan

Lunt again. She was to meet my Uncle Clyde the following week, and her life in Yewville that seemed to me so orderly and lonely and wonderful would be altered forever.

CLYDE HAD a bachelor's place (that was how the women in our family spoke of it) to which he brought his women friends. It was a row house made of brick and cheap stucco, on the west side of town, near the old now-defunct tanning factories on the river. With the money he made working for a small Yewville construction company, and his occasional gambling wins, Clyde could have afforded to live in a better place, but he hadn't much mind for his surroundings and spent most of his spare time out. He brought Joan Lunt home with him because, for all the slapdash clutter of his house, it was more private than her apartment on Chambers Street, and they wanted privacy badly.

The first time they were alone together Clyde laid his hands on Joan's shoulders and kissed her, and she held herself steady, rising to the kiss, putting pressure against the mouth of this man who was virtually a stranger to her so that it was like an exchange, a handshake, between equals. Then, stepping back from the kiss, they both laughed; they were breathless, like people caught short, taken by surprise. Joan Lunt said faintly, "I—I do things sometimes without meaning them," and Clyde said, "Good. So do I."

THROUGH THE SPRING they were often seen together in Yewville; and when, weekends, they weren't seen, it was supposed they were at Clyde's cabin at Wolf's Head Lake (where he was teaching Joan Lunt to fish) or at the Schoharie Downs racetrack (where Clyde gambled on the Standardbreds). They were an attractive, eye-catching couple. They were frequent patrons of local bars and restaurants, and they turned up regularly at parties given by friends of Clyde's and at all-night poker parties in the upstairs rear of the Iroquois Hotel. Joan Lunt didn't play cards but she took an interest in Clyde's playing, and, as Clyde told my father admiringly, she never criticized a move of his, never chided or teased or second-guessed him. "But the woman has me figured out completely," Clyde said. "Almost from the first, when she saw the way I was winning and the way I kept on, she said, 'Clyde, you're the kind of gambler who won't quit because, when he's losing, he has to get back to winning, and, when he's winning, he has to give his friends a chance to catch up.' "

In May, Clyde brought Joan to a Sunday gathering at our house, a large noisy affair, and we saw how when Clyde and Joan were separated, in different rooms, they'd drift back together until they were touching, literally touching, without seeming to know what they did, still less that they were being observed. So that was what love was! Always a quickness of a kind was passing between them, a glance, a hand squeeze, a light pinch, a caress, Clyde's lazy fingers on the nape of Joan's neck beneath her hair, Joan's arm slipped around Clyde's waist, fingers hooked through his belt loop. . . . I wasn't jealous but I watched them covertly. My heart yearned for them, though I didn't know what I wanted of them, or for them.

At thirteen I was more of a child still than an adolescent girl: thin, long-limbed, eyes too large and naked-seeming for my face, and an imagination that rarely flew off into unknown territory but turned, and turned, and turned upon what was close at hand and known, but not altogether known. Imagination, says Aristotle, begins in desire: but what *is* desire? I could not, nor did I want to, possess my Uncle Clyde and Joan Lunt. I wasn't jealous of them, I loved them both. I wanted them to *be*. For this too was a radically new idea to me, that a man and a woman might be nearly strangers to each other, yet lovers; lovers, yet nearly strangers; and the love passing between them, charged like electricity, might be visible, without their knowing. Could they know how I dreamt of them!

After Clyde and Joan left our house, my mother complained irritably that she couldn't get to know Joan Lunt. "She's sweet-seeming and friendly enough, but you know her mind isn't there for you," my mother said. "She's just plain *not-there*."

My father said, "As long as the woman's there for Clyde."

He didn't like anyone speaking critically of his younger brother apart from himself.

BUT SOMETIMES in fact Joan Lunt wasn't there for Clyde: he wouldn't speak of it, but she'd disappear in her car for a day or two or three, without explaining very satisfactorily where she'd gone or why. Clyde could see by her manner that wherever Joan had gone had perhaps not been a choice of hers, and that her disappearances, or flights, left her tired and depressed, but still he was annoyed; he felt betrayed. Clyde Farrell wasn't the kind of man to disguise his feelings. Once on a Friday afternoon in June before a weekend they'd planned at Wolf's Head Lake, Clyde returned to the construction office at 5:30 P.M. to be handed a message hastily telephoned in by Joan Lunt an hour before: *Can't make it this weekend. Sorry. Love, Joan.* Clyde believed himself humiliated in front of others, vowed he'd never forgive Joan Lunt; that very night, drunk and mean-spirited, he took up again with a former girlfriend . . . and so it went.

But in time they made up, as naturally they would, and Clyde said, "I'm thinking maybe we should get married, to stop this sort of thing," and Joan, surprised, said, "Oh, that isn't necessary, darling—I mean, for you to offer that."

Clyde believed, as others did, that Joan Lunt was having difficulties with a former man friend or husband, but Joan refused to speak of it, just acknowledged that, yes, there was a man, yes, of course he was an *ex*, but she resented so much as speaking of him; she refused to allow him reentry into her life. Clyde asked, "What's his name?" and Joan shook her head, mutely: just no; no, she would not say, would not utter that name. Clyde asked, "Is he threatening you? Now? Has he ever shown up in Yewville?" and Joan, as agitated as he'd ever seen her, said, "He does what he does, and I do what I do. And I don't talk about it."

BUT LATER THAT SUMMER, at Wolf's Head Lake, in Clyde's bed in Clyde's hand-hewn log cabin on the bluff above the lake, overlooking wooded land that was Clyde Farrell's property for a mile in either direction, Joan Lunt wept bitterly, weakened in the aftermath of love, and said, "If I tell you, Clyde, it will make you feel too bound to me. It will seem to be begging a favor of a kind, and I'm not begging."

Clyde said, "I know you're not."

"I don't beg favors from anyone."

"I know you don't."

"I went through a long spell in my life when I did beg favors, because I believed that was how women made their way, and I was hurt because of it, but not more hurt than I deserved. I'm older now. I know better. The meek don't inherit the earth, and they surely don't deserve to."

Clyde laughed sadly and said, "Nobody's likely to mistake you for meek, Joan honey."

MAKING LOVE they were like two swimmers deep in each other, plunging hard. Wherever they were when they made love, it wasn't the place they found themselves in when they returned, and whatever the time, it wasn't the same time.

THE TROUBLE CAME in September. A cousin of mine, another niece of Clyde's, was married, and the wedding party was held in the Nautauga Inn, on Lake Nautauga, about ten miles east of Yewville. Clyde knew the inn's owner, and it happened that he and Joan Lunt, handsomely dressed, were in the large public cocktail lounge adjacent to the banquet room reserved for our party, talking with the owner-bartender, when Clyde saw an expression on Joan's face of a kind he'd never seen on her face before—fear, and more than fear, a sudden sick terror—and he turned to see a stranger approaching them, not slowly, exactly, but with a restrained sort of haste: a man of about forty, unshaven, in a blue seersucker sports jacket now badly rumpled, tieless, a muscled but soft-looking man with a blunt, rough, ruined-handsome face, complexion like an emery board, and this man's eyes were too bleached a color for his skin, unless there was a strange light rising in them. And this same light rose in Clyde Farrell's eyes in that instant.

Joan Lunt was whispering, "Oh, no—*no,*" pulling at Clyde's arm to turn him away, but naturally Clyde Farrell wasn't going to step away from a confrontation, and the stranger, who would turn out to be named

Robert Waxman, Rob Waxman, Joan Lunt's former husband, divorced from her fifteen months before, co-owner of a failing meat supplying company in Kingston, advanced upon Clyde and Joan, smiling as if he knew them both, saying loudly, in a slurred but vibrating voice, "Hello, hello, hello!" and when Joan tried to escape Waxman leapt after her, cursing, and Clyde naturally intervened, and suddenly the two men were scuffling, and voices were raised, and before anyone could separate them there was the astonishing sight of Waxman with his gravelly face and hot eyes crouched holding a pistol in his hand, striking Clyde clumsily about the head and shoulders with the butt, and crying, enraged, "Didn't ask to be born! God damn you! I didn't ask to be born!" and, "I'm no different from you! Any of you! *You!* In my heart!" There were screams as Waxman fired the pistol point-blank at Clyde, a popping sound like a firecracker, and Waxman stepped back to get a better aim, he'd hit his man in the fleshy part of a shoulder, and Clyde Farrell, desperate, infuriated, scrambled forward in his wedding party finery, baboon-style, not on his hands and knees but on his hands and feet, bent double, face contorted, teeth bared, and managed to throw himself on Waxman, who outweighed him by perhaps forty pounds, and the men fell heavily to the floor, and there was Clyde Farrell straddling his man, striking him blow after blow in the face, even with his weakened left hand, until Waxman's nose was broken and his nostrils streamed blood, and his mouth too was broken and bloody, and someone risked being struck by Clyde's wild fists and pulled him away.

And there on the floor of the breezy screened-in barroom of the Nautauga Inn lay a man, unconscious, breathing erratically, bleeding from his face, whom no one except Joan Lunt knew was Joan Lunt's former husband; and there, panting, hot-eyed, stood Clyde Farrell over him, bleeding too, from a shoulder wound he was to claim he'd never felt.

SAID JOAN LUNT REPEATEDLY, "Clyde, I'm sorry. I'm so sorry."

Said Joan Lunt, carefully, "I just don't know if I can keep on seeing you. Or keep on living here in Yewville."

And my Uncle Clyde was trying hard, trying very hard, to understand.

"You don't love me, then?" he asked several times.

He was baffled, he wasn't angry. It was the following week and by this time he wasn't angry, nor was he proud of what he'd done, though everyone was speaking of it and would speak of it, in awe, for years. He wasn't proud because in fact he couldn't remember clearly what he'd done, what sort of lightning-swift action he'd performed, no conscious decision had been made that he could recall. Just the light dancing up in a stranger's eyes, and its immediate reflection in his own.

Now Joan Lunt was saying this strange unexpected thing, this thing he couldn't comprehend. Wiping her eyes, and, yes, her voice was shaky, but he recognized the steely stubbornness in it, the resolute will. She said, "I do love you. I've told you. But I can't live like that any longer."

"You're still in love with *him*."

"Of course I'm not in love with him. But I can't live like that any longer."

"Like what? What I did? I'm not *like* that."

"I'm thirty-six years old. I can't take it any longer."

"Joan, I was only protecting you."

"Men fighting each other, men trying to kill each other—I can't take it any longer."

"I was only protecting you. He might have killed you."

"I know. I know you were protecting me. I know you'd do it again if you had to."

Clyde said, suddenly furious, "You're damned right I would."

Waxman was out on bail and returned to Kingston. Like Clyde Farrell he'd been treated in the emergency room at Yewville General Hospital; then he'd been taken to the county sheriff's headquarters and booked on charges of assault with a deadly weapon and reckless endangerment of life. In time, Waxman would be sentenced to a year's probation: with no prior record except for traffic violations, he was to impress the judge with his air of sincere remorse and repentance. Clyde Farrell, after giving testimony and hearing the sentencing, would never see the man again.

Joan Lunt was saying, "I know I should thank you, Clyde. But I can't."

Clyde splashed more bourbon into Joan's glass and into his own.

They were sitting at Joan's dinette table beside a window whose grimy and cracked venetian blinds were tightly closed. Clyde smiled and said, "Never mind thanking me, honey, just let's forget it."

Joan said softly, "Yes, but I can't forget it."

"It's just something you're saying. Telling yourself. Maybe you'd better stop."

"I want to thank you, Clyde, and I can't. You risked your life for me. I know that. And I can't thank you."

So they discussed it, like this. For hours. For much of a night. Sharing a bottle of bourbon Clyde had brought over. And eventually they made love, in Joan Lunt's narrow sofa bed that smelled of talcum powder, perfume, and the ingrained dust of years, and their lovemaking was tentative and cautious but as sweet as ever, and driving back to his place early in the morning, at dawn, Clyde thought surely things were changed, yes, he was convinced that things were changed; hadn't he Joan's promise that she would think it all over, not make any decision, they'd see each other that evening and talk it over then? She'd kissed his lips in goodbye, and walked him to the stairs, and watched him descend to the street.

But Clyde never saw Joan Lunt again.

THAT EVENING she was gone, moved out of the apartment, like that, no warning, not even a telephone call, and she'd left only a brief letter behind with *Clyde Farrell* written on the envelope. Which Clyde never showed to anyone and probably, in fact, ripped up immediately.

It was believed that Clyde spent some time, days, then weeks, into the early winter of that year, looking for Joan Lunt; but no one, not even my father, knew exactly what he did, where he drove, whom he questioned, the depth of his desperation or his yearning or his rage, for Clyde wasn't of course the kind of man to speak of such things.

Joan Lunt's young friend Sylvie never saw her again either, or heard of her. And this hurt me too, more than I might have anticipated.

And over the years, once I left Yewville to go to college in another state, then to begin my own adult life, I saw less and less of my Uncle Clyde. He never married: for a few years he continued the life he'd been leading before meeting Joan Lunt, a typical bachelor life, of its place and time; then he began to spend more and more time at Wolf's Head Lake, developing his property, building small wood-frame summer cottages and renting them out to vacationers and acting as caretaker for them, an increasingly solitary life no one would have predicted for Clyde Farrell.

He stopped gambling too, abruptly. His luck had turned, he said.

I saw my Uncle Clyde only at family occasions, primarily weddings and funerals. The last time we spoke together in a way that might be called forthright was in 1971, at my grandmother's funeral. I looked up and saw through a haze of tears a man of youthful middle age moving in my general direction: Clyde, who seemed shorter than I recalled, not stocky but compact, with a look of furious compression, in a dark suit that fitted him tightly about the shoulders. His hair had turned not silver but an eerie metallic-blond, with faint tarnished streaks, and it was combed down flat and damp on his head, a look here too of furious constraint. Clyde's face was familiar to me as my own, yet altered: the skin had a grainy texture, roughened from years of outdoor living, like dried earth, and the creases and dents in it resembled animal tracks; his eyes were narrow, damp, restless; the eyelids looked swollen. He was walking with a slight limp he tried, in his vanity, to disguise; I learned later that he'd had knee surgery. And the gunshot wound to his left shoulder he'd insisted at the time had not given him much, or any, pain gave him pain now, an arthritic sort of pain, agonizing in cold weather. I stared at my uncle, thinking, *Oh, why? Why?* I didn't know if I was seeing the man Joan Lunt had fled from or the man her flight had made.

But Clyde sighted me and hurried over to embrace me, his favorite niece still. If he associated me with Joan Lunt—and I had the idea he did—he'd forgiven me long ago.

Death gives to life—to the survivors' shared life, that is—an insubstantial quality. It's like an image of absolute clarity reflected in water, then disturbed, shattered into ripples, revealed as mere surface. Its clarity, even its beauty, can resume, but you can't any longer trust in its reality.

So my Uncle Clyde and I regarded each other, stricken in that instant with grief. But, being a man, *he* didn't cry.

We drifted off to one side, away from the other mourners, and I saw it was all right between us, it was all right to ask, so I asked had he ever heard from Joan Lunt, after that day? Had he ever heard *of* her? He said, "I never go where I'm not welcome, honey," as if this were the answer to my question. Then added, seeing my look of distress, "I stopped thinking of her years ago. We don't need each other the way we think we do when we're younger."

I couldn't bear to look at my uncle. *Oh, why? Why?* Somehow I must have believed all along that there was a story, a story unknown to me, that had worked itself out without my knowing, like a stream tunneling its way underground. I would not have minded not knowing this story could I only know that it *was*.

Clyde said, roughtly, "*You* didn't hear from her, did you? The two of you were so close."

He wants me to lie, I thought. But I said only, sadly, "No, I never heard from her. And we weren't close."

Said Clyde, "Sure you were."

The last I saw of Clyde that day, it was after dark and he and my father were having a disagreement just outside the back door of our house. My father insisted that Clyde, who'd been drinking, wasn't in condition to drive his pickup truck back to the lake; and Clyde was insisting he was; and my father said maybe yes, Clyde, and maybe no, but he didn't want to take a chance: why didn't *he* drive Clyde home; and Clyde pointed out truculently that, if my father drove him home, how in hell would he get back here except by taking Clyde's only means of transportation? So the brothers discussed their predicament, as dark came on.

WILL YOU

ALWAYS LOVE ME?

———

"WHY DO I LIKE to act?—because I feel comforted by the stage."
She spoke with a curious bright impersonality, this strange
young woman, as if she were speaking of another person. Her deep-
socketed eyes, which seemed to him unnerving in their intensity, took on
a tawny light, the dark irises rimmed with hazel as she looked up at him.
She was a petite woman even in her sleek fashionable high-heeled shoes,
and Harry Steinhart was tall, so she had to crane her neck to look up at
him—which he liked. Within minutes of their shaking hands, exchang-
ing names, she began to speak, in reply to a question of his, making a
confession as if spontaneously, as night came rapidly up beyond the
building's paneled glass walls.

"I played Irina a few years ago, in Chekhov's *Three Sisters*. Irina is
the youngest of the sisters, the most naive and the most hopeful. I'm
too old for Irina now—I'd like to play Masha now. I feel so protected
by the stage. And, of course, I'm only an amateur, there's nothing really
at stake. But I have an ease and a grace and a purposefulness on stage
that I don't have anywhere else. Here, for instance"—indicating the

crowded reception, in the ground-floor atrium of Mercury House—"I haven't any real idea who I'm supposed to be, or why I'm here. I'm an 'employee'—an 'editor'—and I'm reasonably well paid—but the job is interchangeable with a thousand other jobs, I feel no special commitment to it, and the company has no special commitment to me. But when I'm acting, I'm in someone else's head and not in my own. I execute a script, with others. We're never alone. We're embarked upon an adventure, like a journey up the Amazon. On stage, my emotions aren't silly or excessive or inappropriate—they're justified. They're necessary. I can't shrink away in embarrassment, or shame; I can't say"—and here suddenly she began to act, with exaggerated feminine mannerisms, to make her listener smile—" 'Look, please, I'm not this important, that any of you should pay attention to me!—this is ridiculous!' No, I'm an integral part of the production. It's a family, and I'm a member. Without me, there's no family. Whatever a play *is*, it's a family."

She spoke so insistently, her eyes so intense, Harry was quick to agree. Though he knew relatively little about the theater, amateur or otherwise.

How moved he was, by the young woman's warm response, which he'd elicited with his guileless, instinctive, American-male directness: the ritual of seduction programmed in Harry Steinhart that seemed, to him, always unpremeditated, thus innocent. And always for the first time.

HE'D BEEN MARRIED, and he'd been divorced, and all of it—the hurt, the befuddlement, the anger—belonged to the eighties, as to another man, and was behind him now. When he studied his face in the mirror he was grateful to see how, at the age of thirty-six, he bore so little of what he'd experienced. *Am I sliding through? I'm a statistic!* His new friends and colleagues knew nothing of his past.

Harry was amused, or was he in fact disgusted, by the notion of love in the old, sentimental sense: pledging fidelity, channeling one's very soul into the soul of another. The grasping needs, the anxieties. He thought: Apart from the sexual attraction of the female for the male, which is certainly powerful, there is the attraction of the mysterious.

You fall in love with what is *not-known* in the other. And what is *not-known* becomes the identity of the other. Sexual intercourse is the miming of the desire to make the *not-known* into the known. The strongest desire in the species—and sometimes the most ephemeral.

When Harry Steinhart introduced himself to Andrea McClure that evening, he allowed her to believe she was encountering him for the first time. Yet in fact Harry had been aware of the young woman for months, since she'd come to work for the investment firm for which he was a market analyst. She was not a beautiful woman exactly, but rather odd-looking, with an asymmetrical face, pronounced cheekbones, large dark quick-darting eyes that nonetheless failed to take in much of their surroundings. Her hair was dark brown streaked with gray, she must have been in her early thirties and looked her age, with a perpetually crinkling forehead, a quizzical half-smile. Why Harry found her so interesting, he couldn't have said. Once he'd ridden alone with her in a swiftly rising elevator for twenty-two floors but she'd been distracted by a sheath of papers she was carrying and seemed quite genuinely unaware of him. Another time, sighting her by chance in a local park where she was running alone on a jogging trail, Harry followed her at a discreet distance and traversed a rocky strip where the trail doubled back upon itself and he knew she'd have to pass him, and so she did. He'd been excited, watching her. Watching her and not being seen. This small-boned woman with the prematurely graying hair, legs in loose-fitting white shorts slenderly muscular, small fists clenched. She wasn't a natural runner, her arms swung stiffly at her sides, not quite in rhythm. She was frowning and her mouth worked as if she were silently arguing with someone. How *interesting*, Harry thought her: Andrea whose last name, at that time, he hadn't known. How *mysterious*.

Harry Steinhart was not the kind of man to spy upon a lone woman in a deserted place. Not at all. In order not to be misunderstood, he climbed into full view on an outcropping of granite, in a blaze of warm sunshine—khaki shorts and dazzling white T-shirt, bronze-fuzzy arms and legs, affable smile. That is, Harry was prepared to smile. But the woman no more than lifted her eyes toward him than, running past, she glanced away. She seemed scarcely to have seen him, to have seen anyone, at all.

He'd stared after her, amazed. Not that he'd been rebuffed—he hadn't even been noticed. His *maleness* acknowledged, let alone absorbed. Yet he'd felt oddly amused. Not annoyed, nor even hurt, but rather amused. And protective.

He deliberately stayed away from that park, to put himself out of the temptation of seeking her out, watching her, again.

AND THEN they formally met, and began to see each other in the evenings and on weekends, and through that spring and early summer Andrea's *mysteriousness* in Harry's eyes deepened—that vexation, almost at times like a physical chaffing, of the *not-known*: the sexually provocative. Though confident at first that he would quickly become her lover, Harry was surprised that he did not; which left him hurt, baffled, vaguely resentful—though not at Andrea, exactly. For she seemed to him so strangely oblivious, innocent. Even when she spoke with apparent artlessness, carelessness, as if baring her soul.

In his embrace she often stiffened, as if hearing a sound in the next room. She kissed him, and drew back from him, staring up at him searchingly. Making a joke of it—"You really should find someone normal, Harry!" so that Harry was provoked to say, smiling, "Hell, Andy, I'm crazy about *you*."

She'd told him the first evening they'd met, "My name is Andrea McClure and no one ever calls me 'Andy' "—which Harry interpreted not as a warning but a request.

WHEN FINALLY, in late summer, they made love, it was in silence, in the semidarkness of Andrea's bedroom into which one night, impulsively, she'd led Harry by the hand as if declaring to herself *Now! now or never!* Andrea's bedroom was on the ninth floor of a white-brick apartment building overlooking a narrow strip of green, her window open to a curious humming-vibrating sound of traffic from the Interstate a mile away. Penetrating this wash of sound through the night (Harry stayed the night) were distant sirens, mysterious cries, wails. Harry whispered,

"You're so beautiful! I love you!"—the words torn from him, always for the first time.

It would be their custom, then, to make love in virtual silence, by night and not by day. By day, there was too much of the other to see and to respond to; by day, Harry felt himself too visible, and in lovemaking as opposed to mere sexual intercourse, it's preferable to be invisible. So Harry thought.

THEY WERE LOVERS, yet sporadically. They were not a couple.

So far as Harry knew, Andrea was not seeing other men; nor did she seem to have close women friends. Alone of the women he'd known intimately, including the woman who'd been, for six years, his wife, Andrea was the one who never inquired about his previous love affairs—how tactful she was, or how indifferent! *She doesn't want you to ask any questions of her*, Harry thought.

Harry told Andrea he'd been married and divorced and his ex-wife now lived in London and they were on "amicable" terms though they rarely communicated. He said, as if presenting her with a gift, the gift of himself, "It's over completely, emotionally, on both sides—luckily, we didn't have any children."

Andrea said, frowning, "That's too bad."

WHAT WAS *not-known* in her. Which not even love-making could penetrate, after all.

Once lifting her deep-socketed eyes swiftly to his, startled as if he'd asked a question—"I'll need to trust you." This was not a statement but a question of her own. Harry said quickly, "Of course, darling. Trust me how?" And she looked at him searchingly, her smooth forehead suddenly creased, her mouth working. There was something ugly about the way, Harry thought, Andrea's mouth worked in an anguished sort of silence. He repeated, "Trust me how? What is it?"

Andrea stood and walked out of the room. (That evening, they were in Harry's apartment. He'd prepared an elaborate Italian meal for the evening, chosen special Italian wines—preparing meals for women had long been a crucial part of his ritual of seduction which perhaps he'd come to love for its own sake.) He followed Andrea, concerned she might leave, for the expression in her face was not one he recognized, a drawn, sallow, embittered look, as of a young girl biting her lips to keep from crying, but there she stood in a doorway weakly pressing her forehead against the doorframe, her eyes tightly shut and her thin shoulders trembling. "Andy, what is it?" Harry took her in his arms. He felt a sharp, simple happiness as if he were taking the *not-known* into his arms—and how easy it was, after all.

I will protect you: trust me!

Later, when she'd recovered, calmed and softened and sleepy by several glasses of wine, Andrea confessed to Harry she'd thought he'd asked her something. She knew he hadn't, but she thought she'd heard the words. When Harry asked, what were the words, Andrea said she didn't know. Her forehead, no longer creased with worry, kept the trace of thin horizontal lines.

HARRY THOUGHT: We're drawn to the mystery of others' secrets, and not to those secrets. Do I really want to *know?*

IN FACT, Andrea would probably never have told him. For what would have been the occasion?—he could imagine none.

But: one day in March a telephone call came for Andrea which she took in her bedroom, where Harry overheard her raised voice, and her sudden crying—Andrea, whom he'd never heard cry before. He did not know what to do—to go comfort her, or to stay away. Hearing her cry tore at his heart. He felt he could not bear it. Thinking too, *Now I'll know!—now it will come out!* Yet he respected her privacy. In truth, he was a little frightened of her. (They were virtually living together now though hardly as a conventional couple. There was no sense of playing at marriage, domestic permanency as there usually is in such arrangements. Most of Harry's things remained in his apartment several miles away, and he retreated to his apartment frequently; sometimes, depending upon the needs of his work or Andrea's schedule or whether Harry might be booked for an early air flight in the morning, he spent the night in his own apartment, in his own bed.)

Harry entered Andrea's bedroom but stopped short seeing the look on her face which wasn't grief but fury, a knotted contorted fury, of a kind he's never seen in any woman's face before. And what are her incredulous, choked words into the receiver—"What do you mean? What are you saying? Who are you? I can't believe this! Parole hearing? He was sentenced to life! He was sentenced to life! That filthy *murderer was sentenced to life!*"

LATER, Harry came to see how the dead sister had been an invisible third party in his relationship with Andrea. He recalled certain curiously insistent remarks she'd made about having been lonely growing up as an "only child"—her remoteness from her mother even as, with an edge of anxiety, she telephoned her mother every Sunday evening. She refused to read newspaper articles about violent crimes and asked Harry please to alert her so she could skip those pages. She refused to watch television except for cultural programs and there were few movies she consented to see with Harry—"I distrust the things a camera might pick up."

In a way, it was a relief of sorts, for Harry to learn that the *not-known* in Andrea's life had nothing to do with a previous lover, a disastrous marriage, a lost child or, what was most likely of all, an abortion. He had no male rival to contend with!

This much, Harry learned: In the early evening of April 13, 1973, Andrea's nineteen-year-old sister Frannie, visiting their widowed grandmother in Wakulla Beach, Florida, was assaulted while walking in a deserted area of the beach—beaten, raped, strangled with her shorts. Her body was dragged into a culvert where it was discovered by a couple walking their dog within an hour, before the grandmother would have had reason to report her missing. Naked from the waist down, her face so badly battered with a rock that her left eye dangled from its socket, the cartilage of her nose was smashed, and teeth broken—Frannie McClure was hardly recognizable. It would be discovered that her vagina and anus had been viciously lacerated and much of her pubic hair torn out. Rape may have occurred after her death.

The victim had died about approximately eight o'clock. By eleven,

Wakulla Beach police had in custody a twenty-seven-year-old motorcyclist-drifter named Albert Jefferson Rooke, Caucasian, with a record of drug arrests, petty thefts, and misdemeanors in Tallahassee, Tampa, and his hometown Carbondale, Illinois, where he'd spent time in a facility for disturbed adolescent boys. When Rooke was arrested he was reported as drunk on malt liquor and high on amphetamines; he was disheveled, with long scraggly hair and filthy clothes, and violently resisted police officers. Several witnesses would report having seen a-man who resembled him in the vicinity of the beach where the murdered girl's body was found and a drug-addicted teenage girl traveling with Rooke gave damaging testimony about his ravings of having "committed evil." In the Wakulla Beach police station, with no lawyer present, Rooke confessed to the crime, his confession was taped, and by two o'clock of the morning of April 14, 1973, police had their man. Rooke had relinquished his right to an attorney. He was booked for first-degree murder, among other charges, held in detention, and placed on suicide watch.

Months later, Rooke would retract this confession, claiming it was coerced. Police had beaten him and threatened to kill him, he said. He was drugged-out, spaced-out, didn't know what he'd said. But he hadn't confessed voluntarily. He knew nothing of the rape and murder of Frannie McClure—he'd never seen Frannie McClure. His lawyer, a public defender, entered a plea of not guilty to all charges but at his trial Rooke did so poorly on the witness stand that the lawyer requested a recess and conferred with Rooke and convinced him that he should plead guilty, so the case wouldn't go to the jurors who were sure to convict him and send him to the electric chair; Rooke could then appeal to the state court of appeals, on the grounds that his confession had been coerced, and he was innocent.

So Rooke waived his right to a jury trial, pleaded guilty, and was sentenced to life in prison. But the strategy misfired when, reversing his plea another time to not guilty and claiming that his confession was invalid, his case was summarily rejected by the court of appeals. That was in 1975. Now, in spring 1993, Rooke was eligible for parole, and the county attorney who contacted Andrea's mother under the auspices of the Florida Victim/Witness Program, and was directed by Andrea's mother to contact her, reported that Rooke seemed to have been a "model prisoner" for the past twelve years—there was a bulging file of supportive letters from prison guards, therapists, counsellors, literacy volunteers, a Catholic chaplain. The Victim/Witness Program allowed for the testimony to parole boards of victims and family members related to victims, and so Andrea McClure was invited to address Rooke's parole board when his hearing came up in April. If she wanted to be involved, if she had anything to say.

Her mother was too upset to be involved. She'd broken down, just discussing it on the phone with Andrea.

Except for a representative from the Wakulla County Attorney's Office, everyone who gave testimony at Albert Jefferson Rooke's parole hearing, if Andrea didn't attend, would be speaking on behalf of the prisoner.

Andrea said, wiping at her eyes, "If that man is freed, I swear I will kill him myself."

ANDREA SAID, "I was fourteen years old at the time Frannie died. I was supposed to fly down with her to visit Grandma, at Easter, but I didn't want to go, and Frannie went alone, and if I'd gone with Frannie she'd be alive today, wouldn't she? I mean, it's a simple statement of fact. It isn't anything but a simple statement of fact."

Harry said, hesitantly, "Yes, but"—trying to think what to say in the face of knowing that Andrea had made this accusation against herself continuously over the past twenty years—"a fact can distort. Facts need to be interpreted in context."

Andrea smiled impatiently. She was looking, not at Harry, but at something beyond Harry's shoulder. "You're either alive, or you're not alive. That's the only context."

WHERE in the past Andrea had kept the secret of her murdered sister wholly to herself, now, suddenly, she began to talk openly, in a rapid nervous voice, about what had happened. Frannie, and how Frannie's death had affected the family, and how, after the trial, they'd assumed it was over—"He *was* sentenced to life in prison. Instead of the electric chair. Doesn't that mean anything?"

Harry said, "There's always the possibility of parole, unless the judge sets the sentence otherwise. You must have known that."

Andrea seemed not to hear. Or, hearing, not to absorb.

Now she brought a scrapbook out of a closet. Showing Harry snapshots of the dead girl—pretty, thin-faced, with large expressive dark eyes like Andrea's own. Sifting through family snapshots, Andrea would have skipped over her own and seemed surprised that Harry would want to look at them. There were postcards and letters of Frannie's; there were clippings from a Roanoke paper—Frances McClure the recipient of a scholarship to Middlebury, Frances McClure embarked upon a six-week work-study program in Peru. (No clippings—none—pertaining to the crime.) Andrea answered at length, with warmth and animation, Harry's questions; in the midst of other conversations, or silence, she'd begin suddenly to speak of Frannie as if, all along, she and Harry had been discussing her.

Harry thought, It must be like a dream. An underground stream. Never ceasing.

"For years," Andrea confessed, "I wouldn't think of Frannie. After the trial, we were exhausted and we never talked about her. I truly don't believe it's what psychiatry calls 'denial'—there was nothing more to say. The dead don't change, do they? The dead don't get any older, they don't get any less dead. It's funny how Frannie was so old to me, so mature, now I see these pictures and I see she was so young, only nineteen, and now I'm thirty-four and I'd be so old to *her*. I almost wish I could say that Frannie and I didn't get along but we did—I loved her, I loved her so. She was older than I was by just enough, five years, so we never competed in anything, *she* was the one, everybody loved her, you would have loved her, she had such a quick, warm way of laughing, she was so *alive*. Her roommate at Middlebury would say how weird it was, that Frannie wasn't *alive* because Frannie was the most *alive* person of anybody and that doesn't change. But we stopped talking about her because it was too awful. I was lonely for her but I stopped thinking about her. I went to a different high school, my parents moved to a different part of Roanoke, it was possible to think different thoughts. I dream about Frannie now and it's been twenty years but I really don't think I was dreaming about her then. Except sometimes when I was alone, especially if I was shopping, and this is true now, because Frannie used to take me shopping when I was young, I'd seem to be with another person, I'd sort of be talking to, listening to, another person—but not really. I mean, it wasn't Frannie. Sometimes I get scared and think I've forgotten what she looks like exactly—my memory is bleaching out. But I'll never forget. I'm all she has. The memory of her—it's in my trust. She had a boyfriend, actually, but he's long gone from my life—he's married, has kids. He's gone. If he walked up to me on the street, if he turned up at work, if he turned up as my supervisor some day—I wouldn't know him. I'd look right through him. I look through my mother sometimes, and I can see she looks through me. Because we're thinking of Frannie but we don't acknowledge it because we can't talk about it. But if she's thinking of Frannie, and at the moment I'm not, that's when she really *will* look through me. My father died of liver cancer and it was obviously from what Frannie's murderer did to us. We never said his name, and we never thought his name. We were at the trial and we saw him and I remember how relieved I was—I don't know about Mom and Dad, but I know *I* was—to see he truly was depraved. His face was all broken out in pimples. His eyes were bloodshot. He was always pretending to be trying to commit suicide, to get sympathy, or to make out he was crazy, so they had him drugged, and the drugs did something to his motor coordination. Also, he was pretending. *He* was an actor. But the act didn't work—he's in prison for life. I can't believe any parole board would take his case seriously. I know it's routine. The more I think about it, of course it's routine. They won't let him out. But I have to make sure of that because if I don't, and they let him out, I'll be to blame. It will all be on my head. I told you, didn't I?—I was supposed to go to Grandma's with Frannie, but I didn't. I was fourteen, I had my friends, I didn't want to go to Wakulla Beach exactly then. If I'd gone with Frannie, she'd be alive today. That's a simple, neutral fact. It isn't an accusation just a fact. My parents never blamed me, or anyway never spoke of it. They're good people, they're Christians I guess you could say. They must have wished I'd gone in Frannie's place but I can't say I blame them."

Harry wasn't sure he'd heard correctly. "Your parents must have—what? Wished you'd died in your sister's place? Are you serious?"

Andrea had been speaking breathlessly. Now she looked at Harry, the skin between her eyebrows puckered.

She said, "I didn't say that. You must have misunderstood."

Harry said, "I must have—all right."

"You must have heard wrong. What did I say?"

At such times Andrea would become agitated, running her hands through her hair so it stood in affrighted comical tufts; her mouth would tremble and twist. "It's all right, Andy," Harry would say, "—hey c'mon. It's fine." He would stop her hands and maybe kiss them, the moist palms. Or slide his arms around her playful and husbandly. How small Andrea was, how small an adult woman can be, bones you could fracture by squeezing, so be careful. Harry's heart seemed to hurt, in sympathy. "Don't think about it anymore today, Andy, okay? I love you."

And Andrea might say, vague, wondering, as if she were making this observation for the first time, which in fact she was not, "—The only other person who ever called me 'Andy' was Frannie. Did you know?"

HE'D BEEN TRAINED as a lawyer. Not criminal law but corporate law. But he came to wonder if possibly Andrea had been attracted to him originally, that evening, because he had a law degree. When he'd mentioned law school, at Yale, her attention had quickened.

Unless he was imagining this? Human memory is notoriously unreliable, like film fading in amnesiac patches.

MEMORY: Frannie McClure now exists only in memory.

That's what's so terrible about being dead, Harry thought wryly. You depend for your existence as a historic fact upon the memories of others. Failing, finite, mortal themselves.

Though they'd never discussed it in such abstract terms, for Andrea seemed to shrink from speaking of her sister in anything but the most particular way, Harry understood that her anxiety was not simply that Albert Jefferson Rooke might be released on parole after having served only twenty years of a life sentence but that, if he was, Frannie McClure's claim to permanent, tragic significance would be challenged.

Also: for Frannie McClure to continue to exist as a historic fact, the memories that preserve her as a specific individual, not a mere name, sexual assault statistic, court case must continue to exist. These were still, after twenty years, fairly numerous, for as an American girl who'd gone to a large public high school and had just about completed two years of college, she'd known, and been known by, hundreds of people; but the number was naturally decreasing year by year. Andrea could count them on the fingers of both hands—relatives, neighbors who'd known Frannie from the time of her birth to the time of her death. The grandmother who'd lived in a splendid beachfront condominium over-looking Apalachee Bay of the Gulf of Mexico had been dead since 1979. She'd never recovered from the shock and grief, of course. And there was Andrea's father, dead since 1981. And Andrea's mother, whom Harry had yet to meet, and whom Andrea spoke of with purposeful vagueness as a "difficult" woman, living now in a retirement community in Roanoke, never spoke of her murdered daughter to anyone. So it was impossible to gauge to what extent the mother's memory did in fact preserve the dead girl.

Sometimes, when Andrea was out of the apartment, Harry contemplated the snapshots of Frannie McClure by himself. There was one of her dated Christmas 1969, she'd been fifteen at the time, hugging her ten-year-old sister Andy and clowning for the camera, a beautiful girl, in an oversized sweater and jeans, her brown eyes given an eerie red-maroon glisten by the camera's flash. Behind the girls, a seven-foot Christmas tree, resplendent with useless ornamentation.

HARRY NOTED: When he and Andrea made love it was nearly always in complete silence except for Andrea's murmured incoherent words, her soft cries, muffled sobs. You could credit such sounds to love, passion. But essentially there was silence, a qualitatively different silence from what Harry recalled from their early nights together. Harry understood that Andrea was thinking of Frannie's struggling body as it, too, was penetrated by a man's penis; this excited Harry enormously but made him cautious about being gentle, not allowing his weight to rest too heavily upon Andrea. The challenge, too, for Harry as a lover was to shake Andrea free of her trance and force her into concentrating on *him*. If Harry could involve Andrea in physical sensation, in actual passion, he would have succeeded. At the same time Harry had to concentrate on Andrea, exclusively upon Andrea, and not allow his mind to swerve to the mysterious doomed girl of the snapshots.

THE CALL from the Victim/Witness Program advocate came for Andrea in late March. Giving her only twenty-six days to prepare, emotionally and otherwise, for the hearing on April 20 in Tallahassee. Andrea mentioned casually to Harry it's only a coincidence of course—this first parole hearing for Rooke is scheduled for the Tuesday that's a week and two days following Easter, and it was 12:10 A.M. of the Tuesday following Easter 1973 that the call came from Wakulla Beach notifying the McClures of Frannie's death.

Andrea went on, wiping at her eyes, "It wasn't clear from that first call just how Frannie had died. What he'd done to her. She was dead, that was the fact. They said it was an 'assault' and they'd arrested the man but they didn't go into details over the telephone—of course. Not that kind of details. I suppose it's procedure. Notifying families when someone's been killed—that requires procedure. When they called Grandma, to make the identification, that night, *that* must have been difficult. She'd collapsed, she didn't remember much about it afterward. My mother and father had to make the identification, too. I suppose it was only Frannie's face?—but her face was so damaged. I didn't see, and the casket was closed, so I don't know. I shouldn't be talking about something I don't know, should I? I shouldn't be involving you in this, should I? So I'll stop."

"Of course I want to be involved, honey," Harry said. "I'm going with you. I'll help you all I can."

"No, really, you don't have to. Please don't feel that you have to."

"Of course I'm going with you to that goddamned hearing," Harry said. "I wouldn't let you go through something so terrible alone."

"But I could do it," Andrea said. "Don't you think I could? I'm not fourteen years old now. I'm all grown up."

EXCEPT: Harry heard Andrea crying when he woke in the night and discovered she was gone from bed, several nights in succession hearing her in the bathroom with the fan running to muffle her sobs. Or was it Andrea talking to herself in a low, rapid voice in the night. Rehearsing her testimony for the parole board. She'd been told it was best not to read a prepared statement, nor give the impression that she was repeating a prepared statement. So in the night locked in the bathroom with the fan running to muffle her words which are punctuated with sobs, or curses, Andrea rehearsed her role as Harry lay sleepless wondering, *Am I strong enough? What is required of me?*

THIS, without telling Andrea: A few days before they were scheduled to fly to Tallahassee, Harry drove to the Georgetown Law School library and looked up the transcript of the December 1975 appeal of the verdict of guilty in the *People of the State of Florida* v. *Albert Jefferson Rooke* of September 1973. He'd only begun reading Rooke's confession when he realized there was something wrong with it.

   . . . That night I got a feeling I wanted to do it . . . hurt one of them real bad . . . so I went out to find her . . . a girl or a woman . . . I hate them . . . I really hate them . . . I get a kick out of hurting people . . . I get a kick out of putting something over on you guys . . . so I saw this girl on the beach . . . I'd never seen her before . . . I jumped her and she started to scream and that pissed me off and I got real mad . . . and so on through twenty-three pages of a rambling monologue Harry believed he'd read before, or something very like it; its Wakulla Beach, Florida, details specific but its essence, its tone familiar.

   What was Albert Jefferson Rooke's "confession" but standard boilerplate of the kind that used to be used (in some parts of the country still is used?) by police who've arrested a vulnerable, highly suspicious person? In a particularly repulsive crime? Someone not a local resident

so drunk or stoned or so marginal and despicable a human being wit-
nesses take one look at him and say *He's the one!* cops take one look at
him *He's the one!* and if the poor bastard hadn't committed this crime
you can assume he's committed any number of other crimes he's never
been caught for so let's help him remember, let's give him a little assis-
tance. Harry could imagine it: this straggly-haired hippie-punk brought
handcuffed to police headquarters raving and disoriented not knowing
where the hell he is, waives his right to call an attorney or maybe they
don't even read him the Miranda statement, he's eager to cooperate
with these cops so they stop beating his head against the wall and won't
"restrain" him with a choke-hold when he "resists" for it's self-evident
to these professionals as eventually to a jury that this is exactly the kind
of sick degenerate pervert who rapes, mutilates, murders. Sure we know
"Albert Jefferson Rooke," he's our man.

Harry sat in the law library for a long time staring into space. He felt
weak, sick. Can it be? *Is* it possible?

ANDREA SAID, "Please don't feel you should care about this—ob-
session of mine. You have your own work, and you have your own
life. It isn't"—and here she paused, her mouth working—"as if we're
married."

"What has that got to do with it?" Harry saw how the quickened
light in Andrea's eyes for him, at his approach, had gone dead; she was
shrinking from him. He'd come home from the law library and he'd told
her just that he'd been reading about the Rooke trial and would she like
to discuss it in strictly legal terms and she'd turned to him this waxy
dead-white face, these pinched eyes, as if he'd confessed being unfaithful
to her. "That isn't an issue."

"I shouldn't have told you about Frannie. It was selfish of me. You're
the only person in my life now who knows and it was a mistake for me
to tell you and I'm *sorry*."

She walked blindly out of the room. This was the kind of apology
that masks bitter resentment: Harry knew the tone, Harry had been
there before.

Still, Harry followed Andrea, into another room, and to a window where she stood trembling refusing to look at him saying in a low rapid voice as if to herself how she shouldn't have involved him, he had never known her sister, what a burden to place upon him, a stranger to the family, how short-sighted she'd been, that night the call had come for her she should have asked him please to go home, this was a private matter—and Harry listened, Harry couldn't bring himself to interrupt, he loved this woman didn't he, in any case he can't hurt her, not now. She was saying, "I'm not a vengeful person, it's justice I want for Frannie. Her memory is in my trust—I'm all she has, now."

Harry said, carefully, "Andy, it's all right. We can discuss it some other time." On the plane to Tallahassee, maybe? They were leaving in the morning.

Andrea said, "We don't have to discuss it at all! I'm not a vengeful person."

"No one has said you're a vengeful person. Who's said that?"

"You didn't know Frannie and maybe you don't know me. I'm not always sure who I am. But I know what I have to *do*."

"That's the important thing, then. That's the"—Harry was searching for the absolutely right, the perfect word, which eluded him, unless—"moral thing, then. Of course."

The moral thing, then. Of course. On the plane to Tallahassee, he'd tell her.

BUT THAT NIGHT Andrea slept poorly. And in the early morning, Harry believed he heard her being sick in the bathroom. And on their way to the airport and on the plane south Andrea's eyes were unnaturally bright, glistening and the pupils dilated and she was alternately silent and nervously loquacious gripping his hand much of the time and how could he tell her, for what did he *know*, he *knew* nothing, only suspected, it was up to Rooke's defense attorney to raise such issues, how could he interfere, he could not.

Andrea said, her forehead creased like a chamois cloth that's been crumpled, "It's so strange: I keep seeing *his* face, *he's* my audience. I'm brought into this room that's darkened and at the front the parole board is sitting and the lights are on them and *he's* there—he hasn't changed in twenty years. As soon as he sees me, he knows. He sees, not me, of course not me, he wouldn't remember me, but Frannie. He sees Frannie. I've been reading these documents they've sent me, you know, and the most outrageous, the really obscene thing is, Rooke claims he doesn't remember Frannie's name, even! He claims he never saw her and he never raped her and he never tortured her and he never strangled her, he never knew her, and now, after twenty years, he's saying he wouldn't even remember her name if he isn't told it!" Andrea looked at Harry, to see if he was sharing her outrage. "But when he sees me, he'll see Frannie, and he'll remember everything. And he'll know. He'll know he's going back to prison for the rest of his life. Because Frannie wouldn't want revenge, she wasn't that kind of person, but she *would* want justice."

Harry considered: Is the truth worth it?—even if we can know the truth.

IN THE END, in the State Justice Building in Tallahassee, it wasn't clear whether Albert Jefferson Rooke was even on the premises when Andrea spoke with the parole board; and Andrea made no inquiries. In a blind blinking daze she was escorted into a room by a young woman attorney from the Victim/Witness Program and Harry Steinhart was allowed to accompany her as a friend of the McClure family, though not a witness. *At last*, Harry thought. *It will be over, something will be decided.*

The interview lasted one hour and forty minutes during which time Andrea held the undivided attention of the seven middle-aged Caucasian men who constituted the board—she'd brought along her cherished snapshots of her murdered sister, she read from letters written to her by Frannie, and by former teachers, friends, and acquaintances mourning Frannie's death in such a way as to make you realize (even Harry, as if for the first time, his eyes brimming with tears) that a young woman named Frances McClure did live, and that her loss to the world is a tragedy. The room in which Andrea spoke was windowless, on the eleventh floor of a sleekly modern building, not at all the room Andrea seemed to have envisioned but one brightly lit by recessed fluorescent lighting. No shadows here. The positioning of the chair in which Andrea sat,

facing at an angle the long table at which the seven men sat, suggested a
minimal, stylized stage. Andrea wore a dark blue linen suit and a creamy
silk blouse and her slender legs were nearly hidden beneath the suit's
fashionably long, flared skirt. Her face was pale, and her forehead finely
crossed with the evidence of grief, her voice now and then trembling but
over all she remained composed, speaking calmly, looking each of the
parole board members in the eye, each in turn; answering their courte-
ous questions unhesitatingly, with feeling, as if they were all companions
involved in a single moral cause. *It's people like us against people like
him.* By the end of the interview Andrea was beginning to crack, her
voice not quite so composed and her eyes spilling tears but still she
managed to speak calmly, softly, each word enunciated with care. "No
one can ever undo what Albert Jefferson Rooke did to my sister—even
if the State of Florida imprisons him for all his life, as he'd been sen-
tenced. He escaped the electric chair by changing his plea and then he
changed his plea again so we know how he values the truth and he's
never expressed the slightest remorse for his crime so we know he's the
same man who killed my sister, he can't have changed in twenty years.
He hasn't come to terms with his crime, or his sickness. We know that
violent sex offenders rarely change even with therapy, and this man has
not had therapy relating to his sickness because he has always denied
his sickness. So he'll rape and kill again. He'll take his revenge on the
first young girl he can, the way he did with my sister—he can always
pretend he doesn't remember any of it afterward. He's claiming now
he doesn't even remember my sister's name but her name is Frances
McClure and others remember. He claims he wants to be free on parole
so he can 'begin again.' What is a man like that going to 'begin again'?
I see he's collected a file of letters from well-intentioned fair-minded
people he's deceived the way he hopes to deceive you gentlemen—you
know what prison inmates call this strategy, it's a vulgar word I hesitate
to say: 'bullshitting.' They learn to 'bullshit' the prison guards and the
therapists and the social workers and the chaplains and, yes, the parole
boards. Sometimes they claim they're sorry for their crimes and won't
ever do such things again—they're 'remorseful.' But in this killer's case,

there isn't even 'remorse.' He just wants to get out of prison to 'begin again.' I seem to know how he probably talked to you, tried to convince you it doesn't matter what he did twenty years ago this Easter because he's reformed *now*, no more drugs and no more crime *now*. He'll get a job, he's eager to work. I seem to know how you want to believe him, because we want to believe people when they speak like this. It's a Christian impulse. It's a humane impulse. It makes us feel good about ourselves—we can be 'charitable.' But a prisoner's word for this strategy is 'bullshitting' and that's what we need to keep in mind. This killer has appealed to you to release him on parole—to 'bullshit' you into believing him. But I've come to speak the truth. I'm here on my sister's behalf. She'd say, she'd plead—don't release this vicious, sick, murderous man back into society, to commit more crimes! Don't be the well-intentioned parties whose 'charity' will lead to another innocent girl being brutally raped and murdered. It's too late for me, Frannie would say, but potential victims—they can be spared."

ONLY A HALF-HOUR LATER, Andrea was informed that the parole board voted unanimously against releasing Albert Jefferson Rooke. She asked could she thank the board members and she was escorted back into the room and Harry waited for her smiling in relief as she thanked the men one by one, shook their hands. Now she did burst into tears but it was all right. Telling Harry afterward, in their hotel room, "Every one of those men thanked *me*. They thanked *me*. One of them said, 'If it wasn't for you, Miss McClure, we might've made a bad mistake.' "

Harry said, in a neutral voice, "It was a real triumph, then, wasn't it? You exerted your will, and you triumphed."

Andrea looked at him, puzzled. She was removing her linen jacket and hanging it carefully on a pink silk hanger. Her face was soft, that soft brimming of her eyes, soft curve of her mouth, the woman's most intimate look, the look Harry sees in her face after love. Yet there's a clarity to her voice, almost a sharpness. "Oh, no—it wasn't my will. It was Frannie's. I spoke for her and I told the truth for her and that was all. And now it's over."

THAT EVENING Andrea is too exhausted to eat anywhere except in their hotel room and midway through the dinner she's too exhausted to finish it and then too exhausted to undress herself, to take a bath, to climb into the enormous king-sized canopied bed without Harry's help. And he's exhausted, too. And he's been drinking, too. Since that afternoon foreseeing with calm, impersonal horror how, like clockwork, every several years Albert Jefferson Rooke will present himself to the parole board and Andrea will fly to Tallahassee to present herself in opposition to the man she believes to be her sister's murderer; and so it will go through the years, and Rooke might die one day in prison, and this would release them both, or Rooke might be freed on parole, finally—of that, Harry doesn't want to think. Not right now.

In the ridiculous elevated bed, the lights out; a murmurous indefinable sound that might be the air-conditioning, or someone in an adjacent room quietly and drunkenly arguing; the feverish damp warmth of Andrea's body, her mouth hungry against his, her slender arms around his neck. Naively, childishly, in a voice Harry has never heard before, as if this is, of all Andrea's voices, the one truly her own, she asks, "Do you love me, Harry? Will you always love me?" and he kisses her mouth, her breasts, bunching her nightgown in his fists, he whispers, "Yes."

LIFE AFTER HIGH SCHOOL

——

"SUNNY? SUN-NY?"

On that last night of March 1959, in soiled sheepskin parka, unbuckled overshoes, but bare-headed in the lightly falling snow, Zachary Graff, eighteen years old, six feet one and a half inches tall, weight 203 pounds, IQ 160, stood beneath Sunny Burhman's second-storey bedroom window, calling her name softly, urgently, as if his very life depended upon it. It was nearly midnight: Sunny had been in bed for a half hour, and woke from a thin dissolving sleep to hear her name rising mysteriously out of the dark, low, gravelly, repetitive as the surf. "Sunny—?" She had not spoken with Zachary Graff since the previous week, when she'd told him, quietly, tears shining in her eyes, that she did not love him; she could not accept his engagement ring, still less marry him. This was the first time in the twelve weeks of Zachary's pursuit of her that he'd dared to come to the rear of the Burhmans' house, by day or night; the first time, as Sunny would say afterward, he'd ever appealed to her in such a way.

They would ask, In what way?

Sunny would hesitate, and say, So—emotionally. In a way that scared me.

So you sent him away?

She did. She'd sent him away.

IT WAS MUCH TALKED-OF, at South Lebanon High School, how, in this spring of their senior year, Zachary Graff, who had never to anyone's recollection asked a girl out before, let alone pursued her so publicly and with such clumsy devotion, seemed to have fallen in love with Sunny Burhman.

Of all people—Sunny Burhman.

Odd too that Zachary should seem to have discovered Sunny, when the two had been classmates in the South Lebanon, New York, public schools since first grade, back in 1947.

Zachary, whose father was Homer Graff, the town's preeminent physician, had, since ninth grade, cultivated a clipped, mock-gallant manner when speaking with female classmates; his Clifton Webb style. He was unfailingly courteous, but unfailingly cool; measured; formal. He seemed impervious to the giddy rise and ebb of adolescent emotion, moving, clumsy but determined, like a grizzly bear on its hind legs, through the school corridors, rarely glancing to left or right: *his* gaze, its myopia corrected by lenses encased in chunky black plastic frames, was firmly fixed on the horizon. Dr. Graff's son was not unpopular so much as feared, thus disliked.

If Zachary's excellent academic record continued uninterrupted through final papers, final exams, and there was no reason to suspect it would not, Zachary would be valedictorian of the Class of 1959. Barbara ("Sunny") Burhman, later to distinguish herself at Cornell, would graduate only ninth, in a class of eighty-two.

Zachary's attentiveness to Sunny had begun, with no warning, immediately after Christmas recess, when classes resumed in January. Suddenly, a half-dozen times a day, in Sunny's vicinity, looming large, eyeglasses glittering, there Zachary *was*. His Clifton Webb pose had dissolved, he was shy, stammering, yet forceful, even bold, waiting for the advantageous moment (for Sunny was always surrounded by friends) to push forward and say, "Hi, Sunny!" The greeting, utterly commonplace in content, sounded, in Zachary's mouth, like a Latin phrase tortuously translated.

Sunny, so-named for her really quite astonishing smile, that dazzling white Sunny-smile that transformed a girl of conventional freckled snub-nosed prettiness to true beauty, might have been surprised, initially, but gave no sign, saying, "Hi, Zach!"

In those years, the corridors of South Lebanon High School were lyric crossfires of *Hi!* and *H'lo!* and *Good to see ya!* uttered hundreds of times daily by the golden girls, the popular, confident, good-looking girls, club officers, prom queens, cheerleaders like Sunny Burhman and her friends, tossed out indiscriminately, for that was the style.

Most of the students were in fact practicing Christians, of Lutheran, Presbyterian, Methodist stock.

Like Sunny Burhman, who was, or seemed, even at the time of this story, too good to be true.

That's to say—*good.*

So, though Sunny soon wondered why on earth Zachary Graff was hanging around her, why, again, at her elbow, or lying in wait for her at the foot of a stairs, why, for the nth time that week, *him*, she was too *good* to indicate impatience, or exasperation; too *good* to tell him, as her friends advised, to get lost.

He telephoned her too. Poor Zachary. Stammering over the phone, his voice lowered as if he were in terror of being overheard, "Is S-Sunny there, Mrs. B-Burhman? May I speak with her, please?" And Mrs. Burhman, who knew Dr. Graff and his wife, of course, since everyone in South Lebanon, population 3,800, knew everyone else or knew of them, including frequently their family histories and facts about them of which their children were entirely unaware, hesitated, and said, "Yes, I'll put her on, but I hope you won't talk long—Sunny has homework tonight." Or, apologetically but firmly: "No, I'm afraid she isn't here. May I take a message?"

"N-no message," Zachary would murmur, and hurriedly hang up.

Sunny, standing close by, thumbnail between her just perceptibly gat-toothed front teeth, expression crinkled in dismay, would whisper, "Oh Mom. I feel so *bad.* I just feel so—*bad.*"

Mrs. Burhman said briskly, "You don't have time for all of them, honey."

Still, Zachary was not discouraged, and with the swift passage of time it began to be observed that Sunny engaged in conversations with him—the two of them sitting, alone, in a corner of the cafeteria, or walking together after a meeting of the Debate Club, of which Zachary was president, and Sunny a member. They were both on the staff of the South Lebanon High Beacon, and the South Lebanon High Yearbook 1959, and the South Lebanon Torch (the literary magazine). They were both members of the National Honor Society and the Quill & Scroll Society. Though Zachary Graff in his aloofness and impatience with most of his peers would be remembered as antisocial, a "loner," in fact, as his record of activities suggested, printed beneath his photograph in the yearbook, he had time, or made time, for things that mattered to him.

He shunned sports, however. High school sports, at least.

His life's game, he informed Sunny Burhman, unaware of the solemn pomposity with which he spoke, would be *golf.* His father had been instructing him, informally, since his twelfth birthday.

Said Zachary, "I have no natural talent for it, and I find it profoundly boring, but golf will be my game." And he pushed his chunky black glasses roughly against the bridge of his nose, as he did countless times a day, as if they were in danger of sliding off.

Zachary Graff had such a physical presence, few of his contemporaries would have described him as unattractive, still less homely, ugly. His head appeared oversized, even for his massive body; his eyes were deep-set, with a look of watchfulness and secrecy; his skin was tallow-colored, and blemished, in wavering patches like topographical maps. His big teeth glinted with filaments of silver, and his breath, oddly for one whose father was a doctor, was stale, musty, cobwebby—not that Sunny Burhman ever alluded to this fact, to others.

Her friends began to ask of her, a bit jealously, reproachfully, "What do you two talk about so much?—you and *him?*" and Sunny replied, taking care not to hint, with the slightest movement of her eyebrows, or rolling of her eyes, that, yes, she found the situation peculiar too, "Oh— Zachary and I talk about all kinds of things. *He* talks, mainly. He's brilliant. He's"—pausing, her forehead delicately crinkling in thought, her lovely brown eyes for a moment clouded—"well, *brilliant.*"

In fact, at first, Zachary spoke, in his intense, obsessive way, of impersonal subjects: the meaning of life, the future of Earth, whether science or art best satisfies the human hunger for self-expression. He said, laughing nervously, fixing Sunny with his shyly bold stare, "Just to pose certain questions is, I guess, to show your hope they can be answered."

Early on, Zachary seemed to have understood that, if he expressed doubt, for instance about "whether God exists" and so forth, Sunny Burhman would listen seriously; and would talk with him earnestly, with the air of a nurse giving a transfusion to a patient in danger of expiring for loss of blood. She was not a religious fanatic, but she *was* a devout Christian—the Burhmans were members of the First Presbyterian Church of South Lebanon, and Sunny was president of her youth group, and, among other good deeds, did YWCA volunteer work on Saturday afternoons; she had not the slightest doubt that Jesus Christ, that's to say His spirit, dwelled in her heart, and that, simply by speaking the truth of what she believed, she could convince others.

Though one day, and soon, Sunny would examine her beliefs, and question the faith into which she'd been born; she had not done so by the age of seventeen and a half. She was a virgin, and virginal in all, or most, of her thoughts.

Sometimes, behind her back, even by friends, Sunny was laughed at, gently—never ridiculed, for no one would ridicule Sunny.

Once, when Sunny Burhman and her date and another couple were gazing up into the night sky, standing in the parking lot of the high school, following a prom, Sunny had said in a quavering voice, "It's so big it would be terrifying, wouldn't it?—except for Jesus, who makes us feel at home."

When popular Chuck Crueller, a quarterback for the South Lebanon varsity football team, was injured during a game, and carried off by ambulance to undergo emergency surgery, Sunny mobilized the other cheerleaders, tears fierce in her eyes, "We can do it for Chuck—we can *pray.*" And so the eight girls in their short-skirted crimson jumpers and starched white cotton blouses had gripped one another's hands tight, weeping, on the verge of hysteria, had prayed, prayed, *prayed*—hidden away in the depths of the girls' locker room for hours. Sunny had led the prayers, and Chuck Crueller recovered.

So you wouldn't ridicule Sunny Burhman, somehow it wouldn't have been appropriate.

As her classmate Tobias Shanks wrote of her, as one of his duties as literary editor of the 1959 South Lebanon yearbook: *"Sunny" Burhman!—an all-American girl too good to be true who is nonetheless TRUE!*

If there was a slyly mocking tone to Tobias Shanks's praise, a hint that such goodness was predictable, and superficial, and of no genuine merit, the caption, mere print, beneath Sunny's dazzlingly beautiful photograph, conveyed nothing of this.

Surprisingly, for all his pose of skepticism and superiority, Zachary Graff too was a Christian. He'd been baptized Lutheran, and never failed to attend Sunday services with his parents at the First Lutheran Church. Amid the congregation of somber, somnambulant worshippers, Zachary Graff's frowning young face, the very set of his beefy shoulders, drew the minister's uneasy eye; it would be murmured of Dr. Graff's precocious son, in retrospect, that he'd been perhaps too *serious.*

Before falling in love with Sunny Burhman, and discussing his religious doubts with her, Zachary had often discussed them with Tobias Shanks, who'd been his friend, you might say his only friend, since seventh grade. (But only sporadically since seventh grade, since the boys, each highly intelligent, inclined to impatience and sarcasm, got on each other's nerves.) Once, Zachary confided in Tobias that he prayed every morning of his life—immediately upon waking he scrambled out of bed, knelt, hid his face in his hands, and prayed. For his sinful soul, for his sinful thoughts, deeds, desires. He lacerated his soul the way he'd been taught by his mother to tug a fine-toothed steel comb through his coarse, oily hair, never less than once a day.

Tobias Shanks, a self-professed agnostic since the age of fourteen, laughed, and asked derisively, "Yes, but what do you pray *for*, exactly?" and Zachary had thought a bit, and said, not ironically, but altogether seriously, "To get through the day. Doesn't everyone?"

This melancholy reply, Tobias was never to reveal.

ZACHARY'S PARENTS were urging him to go to Muhlenberg College, which was church-affiliated; Zachary hoped to go elsewhere. He said, humbly, to Sunny Burhman, "If you go to Cornell, Sunny, I—maybe I'll go there too?"

Sunny hesitated, then smiled. "Oh. That would be nice."

"You wouldn't mind, Sunny?"

"Why would I *mind*, Zachary?" Sunny laughed, to hide her impatience. They were headed for Zachary's car, parked just up the hill from the YM-YWCA building. It was a gusty Saturday afternoon in early March. Leaving the YWCA, Sunny had seen Zachary Graff standing at the curb, hands in the pockets of his sheepskin parka, head lowered, but eyes nervously alert. Standing there, as if accidentally.

It was impossible to avoid him, she had to allow him to drive her home. Though she was beginning to feel panic, like darting tongues of flame, at the prospect of Zachary Graff always *there*.

Tell the creep to get lost, her friends counseled. Even her nice friends were without sentiment regarding Zachary Graff.

Until sixth grade, Sunny had been plain little Barbara Burhman. Then, one day, her teacher had said, to all the class, in one of those moments of inspiration that can alter, by whim, the course of an entire life, "Tell you what, boys and girls—let's call Barbara 'Sunny' from now on—that's what she *is*."

Ever afterward, in South Lebanon, she was "Sunny" Burhman. Plain little Barbara had been left behind, seemingly forever.

So, of course, Sunny could not tell Zachary Graff to get lost. Such words were not part of her vocabulary.

Zachary owned a plum-colored 1956 Plymouth which other boys envied—it seemed to them distinctly unfair that Zachary, of all people, had his own car, when so few of them, who loved cars, did. But Zachary was oblivious of their envy, as, in a way, he seemed oblivious of his own good fortune. He drove the car as if it were an adult duty, with middle-aged fussiness and worry. He drove the car as if he were its own chauffeur. Yet, driving Sunny home, he talked—chattered—continuously. Speaking of college, and of religious "obligations," and of his parents' expectations of him; speaking of medical school; the future; the life—"beyond South Lebanon."

He asked again, in that gravelly, irksomely humble voice, if Sunny would mind if he went to Cornell. And Sunny said, trying to sound merely reasonable, "Zachary, it's a *free world.*"

Zachary said, "Oh no it isn't, Sunny. For some of us, it isn't."

This enigmatic remark Sunny was determined not to follow up.

Braking to a careful stop in front of the Burhmans' house, Zachary said, with an almost boyish enthusiasm, "So—Cornell? In the fall? We'll both go to Cornell?"

Sunny was quickly out of the car before Zachary could put on the emergency brake and come around, ceremoniously, to open her door. Gaily, recklessly, infinitely relieved to be out of his company, she called back over her shoulder, "Why not?"

SUNNY'S SECRET VANITY must have been what linked them.

For several times, gravely, Zachary had said to her, "When I'm with you, Sunny, it's possible for me to believe."

He meant, she thought, in God. In Jesus. In the life hereafter.

THE NEXT TIME Zachary maneuvered Sunny into his car, under the pretext of driving her home, it was to present the startled girl with an engagement ring.

He'd bought the ring at Stern's Jewelers, South Lebanon's single good jewelry store, with money secretly withdrawn from his savings account; that account to which, over a period of more than a decade, he'd deposited modest sums with a painstaking devotion. This was his "college fund," or had been—out of the $3,245 saved, only $1,090 remained. How astonished, upset, furious his parents would be when they learned—Zachary hadn't allowed himself to contemplate.

The Graffs knew nothing about Sunny Burhman. So far as they might have surmised, their son's frequent absences from home were nothing out of the ordinary—he'd always spent time at the public library, where his preferred reading was reference books. He'd begin with Volume One of an encyclopedia, and make his diligent way through each successive volume, like a horse grazing a field, rarely glancing up, uninterested in his surroundings.

"Please—will you accept it?"

Sunny was staring incredulously at the diamond ring, which was presented to her, not in Zachary's big clumsy fingers, with the dirt-edged nails, but in the plush-lined little box, as if it might be more attractive that way, more like a gift. The ring was 24-karat gold and the diamond was small but distinctive, and coldly glittering. A beautiful ring, but Sunny did not see it that way.

She whispered, "Oh. Zachary. Oh *no*—there must be some misunderstanding."

Zachary seemed prepared for her reaction, for he said, quickly, "Will you just try it on?—see if it fits?"

Sunny shook her head. No she couldn't.

"They'll take it back to adjust it, if it's too big," Zachary said. "They promised."

"Zachary, no," Sunny said gently. "I'm so sorry."

Tears flooded her eyes and spilled over onto her cheeks.

Zachary was saying, eagerly, his lips flecked with spittle, "I realize you don't l-love me, Sunny, at least not yet, but—you could wear the ring, couldn't you? Just—wear it?" He continued to hold the little box out to her, his hand visibly shaking. "On your right hand, if you don't want to wear it on your left? Please?"

"Zachary, no. That's impossible."

"Just, you know, as a, a gift—? Oh Sunny—"

They were sitting in the plum-colored Plymouth, parked, in an awkwardly public place, on Upchurch Avenue three blocks from Sunny's house. It was 4:25 P.M., March 26, a Thursday: Zachary had lingered after school in order to drive Sunny home after choir practice. Sunny would afterward recall, with an odd haltingness, as if her memory of the episode were blurred with tears, that, as usual, Zachary had done most of the talking. He had not argued with her, nor exactly begged, but spoke almost formally, as if setting out the basic points of his debating strategy: If Sunny did not love him, he could love enough for both; and, If Sunny did not want to be "officially" engaged, she could wear his ring anyway, couldn't she?

It would mean so much to him, Zachary said.

Life or death, Zachary said

Sunny closed the lid of the little box, and pushed it from her, gently. She was crying, and her smooth pageboy was now disheveled. "Oh Zachary, I'm *sorry*. I *can't*."

SUNNY KNELT by her bed, hid her face in her hands, prayed.

Please help Zachary not to be in love with me. Please help me not to be cruel. Have mercy on us both O God.

O God help him to realize he doesn't love me—doesn't know *me*.

Days passed, and Zachary did not call. If he was absent from school, Sunny did not seem to notice.

Sunny Burhman and Zachary Graff had two classes together, English and physics; but, in the busyness of Sunny's high school life, surrounded by friends, mesmerized by her own rapid motion as if she were lashed to the prow of a boat bearing swiftly through the water, she did not seem to notice.

She was not a girl of secrets. She was not a girl of stealth. Still, though she had confided in her mother all her life, she did not tell her mother about Zachary's desperate proposal; perhaps, so flattered, she did not acknowledge it as desperate. She reasoned that if she told either of her parents they would have telephoned Zachary's parents immediately. I can't betray him, she thought.

Nor did she tell her closest girlfriends, or the boy she was seeing most frequently at the time, knowing that the account would turn comical in the telling, that she and her listeners would collapse into laughter, and this too would be a betrayal of Zachary.

She happened to see Tobias Shanks, one day, looking oddly at *her*.

That boy who might have been twelve years old, seen from a short distance. Sunny knew that he was, or had been, a friend of Zachary Graff's; she wondered if Zachary confided in him; yet made no effort to speak with him. He didn't like her, she sensed.

No, Sunny didn't tell anyone about Zachary and the engagement ring. Of all sins, she thought, betrayal is surely the worst.

"SUNNY? Sun-ny?"

She did not believe she had been sleeping but the low, persistent, gravelly sound of Zachary's voice penetrated her consciousness like a dream-voice—felt, not heard.

Quickly, she got out of bed. Crouched at her window without turning on the light. Saw, to her horror, Zachary down below, standing in the shrubbery, his large head uplifted, face round like the moon, and shadowed like the moon's face. There was a light, damp snowfall; blossomlike clumps fell on the boy's broad shoulders, in his matted hair. Sighting her, he began to wave excitedly, like an impatient child.

"Oh. Zachary. My God."

In haste, fumbling, she put on a bulky-knit ski sweater over her flannel nightgown, kicked on bedroom slippers, hurried downstairs. The house was already darkened; the Burhmans were in the habit of going to bed early. Sunny's only concern was that she could send Zachary away without her parents knowing he was there. Even in her distress she was not thinking of the trouble Zachary might make for her: she was thinking of the trouble he might make for himself.

Yet, as soon as she saw him close up, she realized that something was gravely wrong. Here was Zachary Graff—yet not Zachary.

He told her he had to talk with her, and he had to talk with her now. His car was parked in the alley, he said.

He made a gesture as if to take her hand, but Sunny drew back. He loomed over her, his breath steaming. She could not see his eyes.

She said no she couldn't go with him. She said he must go home, at once, before her parents woke up.

He said he couldn't leave without her, he had to talk with her. There was a raw urgency, a forcefulness, in him, that Sunny had never seen before, and that frightened her.

She said no. He said yes.

He reached again for her hand, this time taking hold of her wrist.

His fingers were strong.

"I told you—I can love enough for both!"

Sunny stared up at him, for an instant mute, paralyzed, seeing not Zachary Graff's eyes but the lenses of his glasses which appeared, in the semidark, opaque. Large snowflakes were falling languidly, there was no wind. Sunny saw Zachary Graff's face which was pale and clenched as a muscle, and she heard his voice which was the voice of a stranger, and she felt him tug at her so roughly her arm was strained in its very socket, and she cried, "No! no! go away! no!"—and the spell was broken, the boy gaped at her another moment, then released her, turned, and ran.

No more than two or three minutes had passed since Sunny unlocked the rear door and stepped outside, and Zachary fled. Yet, afterward, she would recall the encounter as if it had taken a very long time, like a scene in a protracted and repetitive nightmare.

It would be the last time Sunny Burhman saw Zachary Graff alive.

NEXT MORNING, all of South Lebanon talked of the death of Dr. Graff's son Zachary: he'd committed suicide by parking his car in a garage behind an unoccupied house on Upchurch Avenue, and letting the motor run until the gas tank was emptied. Death was diagnosed as the result of carbon monoxide poisoning, the time estimated at approximately 4:30 A.M. of April 1, 1959.

Was the date deliberate?—Zachary had left only a single note behind, printed in firm block letters and taped to the outside of the car windshield:

April Fool's Day 1959

To Whom It May (Or May Not) Concern:

I, Zachary A. Graff, being of sound mind & body, do hereby declare that I have taken my own life of my own free will &

I hereby declare all others guiltless as they are ignorant of the death of the aforementioned & the life.

(signed)
ZACHARY A. GRAFF

Police officers, called to the scene at 7:45 A.M., reported finding Zachary, lifeless, stripped to his underwear, in the rear seat of the car; the sheepskin parka was oddly draped over the steering wheel, and the interior of the car was, again oddly, for a boy known for his fastidious habits, littered with numerous items: a Bible, several high school textbooks, a pizza carton and some uneaten crusts of pizza, several empty Pepsi bottles, an empty bag of M&M's candies, a pair of new, unlaced gym shoes (size eleven), a ten-foot length of clothesline (in the glove compartment), and the diamond ring in its plush-lined little box from Stern's Jewelers (in a pocket of the parka).

Sunny Burhman heard the news of Zachary's suicide before leaving for school that morning, when a friend telephoned. Within earshot of both her astonished parents, Sunny burst into tears, and sobbed, "Oh my God—it's my fault."

So the consensus in South Lebanon would be, following the police investigation, and much public speculation, not that it was Sunny Burhman's fault, exactly, not that the girl was to blame, exactly, but, yes, poor Zachary Graff, the doctor's son, had killed himself in despondency over her: her refusal of his engagement ring, her rejection of his love.

THAT WAS the final season of her life as "Sunny" Burhman.

She was out of school for a full week following Zachary's death, and, when she returned, conspicuously paler, more subdued, in all ways less sunny, she did not speak, even with her closest friends, of the tragedy; nor did anyone bring up the subject with her. She withdrew her name from the balloting for the senior prom queen, she withdrew from her part in the senior play, she dropped out of the school choir, she did not participate in the annual statewide debating competition—in which, in previous years, Zachary Graff had excelled. Following her last class of the day she went home immediately, and rarely saw her friends on weekends. Was she in mourning?—or was she simply ashamed? Like the bearer of a deadly virus, herself unaffected, Sunny knew how, on all sides, her classmates and her teachers were regarding her: She was the girl for whose love a boy had thrown away his life, she was an unwitting agent of death.

Of course, her family told her that it wasn't her fault that Zachary Graff had been mentally unbalanced.

Even the Graffs did not blame her—or said they didn't.

Sunny said, "Yes. But it's my fault he's dead."

The Presbyterian minister, who counseled Sunny, and prayed with her, assured her that Jesus surely understood, and that there could be no sin in *her*—it wasn't her fault that Zachary Graff had been mentally unbalanced. And Sunny replied, not stubbornly, but matter-of-factly, sadly, as if stating a self-evident truth, "Yes. But it's my fault he's dead."

Her older sister, Helen, later that summer, meaning only well, said, in exasperation, "Sunny, when are you going to cheer *up?*" and Sunny turned on her with uncharacteristic fury, and said, "Don't call me that idiotic name ever again!—I want it *gone!*"

WHEN in the fall she enrolled at Cornell University, she was "Barbara Burhman."

She would remain "Barbara Burhman" for the rest of her life.

BARBARA BURHMAN EXCELLED as an undergraduate, concentrating on academic work almost exclusively; she went on to graduate school at Harvard, in American studies; she taught at several prestigious universities, rising rapidly through administrative ranks before accepting a position, both highly paid and politically visible, with a well-known research foundation based in Manhattan. She was the author of numerous books and articles; she was married, and the mother of three children; she lectured widely, she was frequently interviewed in the popular press, she lent her name to good causes. She would not have wished to think of herself as extraordinary—in the world she now inhabited, she was surrounded by similarly active, energetic, professionally engaged men and women—except in recalling as she sometimes did, with a mild pang of nostalgia, her old, lost self, sweet "Sunny" Burhman of South Lebanon, New York.

She hadn't been queen of the senior prom. She hadn't even continued to be a Christian.

The irony had not escaped Barbara Burhman that, in casting away his young life so recklessly, Zachary Graff had freed her for hers.

With the passage of time, grief had lessened. Perhaps in fact it had disappeared. After twenty, and then twenty-five, and now thirty-one years, it was difficult for Barbara, known in her adult life as an exemplar of practical sense, to feel a kinship with the adolescent girl she'd been, or that claustrophobic high school world of the late 1950s. She'd never returned for a single reunion. If she thought of Zachary Graff—about whom, incidentally, she'd never told her husband of twenty-eight years—it was with the regret we think of remote acquaintances, lost to us by accidents of fate. Forever, Zachary Graff, the most brilliant member of the class of 1959 of South Lebanon High, would remain a high school boy, trapped, aged eighteen.

Of that class, the only other person to have acquired what might be called a national reputation was Tobias Shanks, now known as T. R. Shanks, a playwright and director of experimental drama; Barbara Burhman had followed Tobias's career with interest, and had sent him a telegram congratulating him on his most recent play, which went on to win a number of awards, dealing, as it did, with the vicissitudes of gay life in the 1980s. In the winter of 1990 Barbara and Tobias began to encounter each other socially, when Tobias was playwright-in-residence at Bard College, close by Hazelton-on-Hudson where Barbara lived. At first they were strangely shy of each other; even guarded; as if, in even this neutral setting, their South Lebanon ghost-selves exerted a powerful influence. The golden girl, the loner. The splendidly normal, the defiantly "odd." One night Tobias Shanks, shaking Barbara Burhman's hand, had smiled wryly, and said, "It *is* Sunny, isn't it?" and Barbara Burhman, laughing nervously, hoping no one had overheard, said, "No, in fact it isn't. It's Barbara."

They looked at each other, mildly dazed. For one saw a small-boned but solidly built man of youthful middle-age, sweet-faced, yet with ironic, pouched eyes, thinning gray hair, and a close-trimmed gray beard; the other saw a woman of youthful middle-age, striking in appearance, impeccably well-groomed, with fading hair of no distinctive color and faint, white, puckering lines at the edges of her eyes. Their ghost-selves *were* there—not aged, or not aged merely, but transformed, as the genes of a previous generation are transformed by the next.

Tobias stared at Barbara for a long moment, as if unable to speak. Finally he said, "I have something to tell you, Barbara. When can we meet?"

TOBIAS SHANKS HANDED the much-folded letter across the table to Barbara Burhman, and watched as she opened it, and read it, with an expression of increasing astonishment and wonder.

"*He* wrote this? Zachary? To you?"

"He did."

"And you—? Did you—?"

Tobias shook his head.

His expression was carefully neutral, but his eyes swam suddenly with tears.

"We'd been friends, very close friends, for years. Each other's only friend, most of the time. The way kids that age can be, in certain restricted environments—kids who aren't what's called 'average' or 'normal.' We talked a good deal about religion—Zachary was afraid of hell. We both liked science fiction. We both had very strict parents. I suppose I might have been attracted to Zachary at times—I knew I was attracted to other guys—but of course I never acted upon it; I wouldn't have dared. Almost no one dared, in those days." He laughed, with a mild shudder. He passed a hand over his eyes. "I couldn't have *loved* Zachary Graff as he claimed he loved me, because—I couldn't. But I could have allowed him to know that he wasn't sick, crazy, 'perverted' as he called himself in that letter." He paused. For a long painful moment Barbara thought he wasn't going to continue. Then he said, with that same mirthless shuddering laugh, "I could have made him feel less lonely. But I didn't. I failed him. My only friend."

Barbara had taken out a tissue, and was dabbing at her eyes.

She felt as if she'd been dealt a blow so hard she could not gauge how she'd been hurt—if there was hurt at all.

She said, "Then it hadn't ever been 'Sunny'—she was an illusion."

Tobias said thoughtfully, "I don't know. I suppose so. There was the sense, at least as I saw it at the time, that, yes, he'd chosen you; decided upon you."

"As a symbol."

"Not just a symbol. We all adored you—we were all a little in love with you." Tobias laughed, embarrassed. "Even me."

"I wish you'd come to me and told me, back then. After—it happened."

"I was too cowardly. I was terrified of being exposed, and, maybe, doing to myself what he'd done to himself. Suicide is so very attractive to adolescents." Tobias paused, and reached over to touch Barbara's hand. His fingertips were cold. "I'm not proud of myself, Barbara, and I've tried to deal with it in my writing, but—that's how I was, back then." Again he paused. He pressed a little harder against Barbara's hand. "Another thing—after Zachary went to you, that night, he came to me."

"To you?"

"To me."

"And—?"

"And I refused to go with him too. I was furious with him for coming to the house like that, risking my parents discovering us. I guess I got a little hysterical. And he fled."

"He fled."

"Then, afterward, I just couldn't bring myself to come forward. Why I saved that letter, I don't know—I'd thrown away some others that were less incriminating. I suppose I figured—no one knew about me, everyone knew about you. 'Sunny' Burhman."

They were at lunch—they ordered two more drinks—they'd forgotten their surroundings—they talked.

After an hour or so Barbara Burhman leaned across the table, as at one of her professional meetings, to ask, in a tone of intellectual curiosity, "What do you think Zachary planned to do with the clothesline?"

MARK OF SATAN

———

A WOMAN HAD COME to save his soul and he wasn't sure he was ready.

It isn't every afternoon in the dead heat of summer, cicadas scream-ing out of the trees like lunatics, the sun a soft slow explosion in the sky, a husky young woman comes on foot rapping shyly at the screen door of a house not even yours, a house in which you are a begrudged guest, to save your soul. And she'd brought an angel-child with her, too.

Thelma McCord, or was it McCrae. And Magdalena who was a wisp of a child, perhaps four years old.

They were Church of the Holy Witness, headquarters Scranton, PA. They were God's own, and proud. Saved souls glowing like neon out of their identical eye sockets.

Thelma was an "ordained missionary" and this was her "first season of itinerary" and she apologized for disturbing his privacy but did he, would he, surrender but a few minutes of his time to the Teachings of the Holy Witness?

He'd been taken totally by surprise. He'd been dreaming a disagree-

able churning-sinking dream and suddenly he'd been wakened, sum-
moned, by a faint but persistent knocking at the front door. Tugging on
wrinkled khaki shorts and yanking up the zipper in angry haste—he was
already wearing a T-shirt frayed and tight in the shoulders—he'd pad-
ded barefoot to the screen door blinking the way a mollusk might blink
if it had eyes. In a house unfamiliar to you, it's like waking to somebody
else's dream. And there on the front stoop out of a shimmering-hot
August afternoon he'd wished to sleep through, this girlish-eager young
female missionary. An angel of God sent special delivery to *him*.

Quickly, before he could change his mind, before *no! no* intervened,
he invited Thelma and little Magdalena inside. Out of the wicked hot
sun—quick.

"Thank you," the young woman said, beaming with surprise and
gratitude, "—Isn't he a kind, thoughtful man, Magdalena!"

Mother and daughter were heat-dazed, clearly yearning for some
measure of coolness and simple human hospitality. Thelma was carrying
a bulky straw purse and a tote bag with a red plastic sheen that appeared
to be heavy with books and pamphlets. The child's face was pinkened
with sunburn and her gaze so downcast she stumbled on the threshold of
the door and her mother murmured *Tsk!* and clutched her hand tighter,
as if, already, before their visit had begun, Magdalena had brought them
both embarrassment.

He led them inside and shut the door. The living room opened
directly off the front door. The house was a small three-bedroom tract
ranch with simulated redwood siding; it was sparsely furnished, the
front room uncarpeted, with a beige-vinyl sofa, twin butterfly chairs in
fluorescent lime, and a coffee table that was a slab of weather-stained
granite set atop cinderblocks. (The granite slab was in fact a grave
marker, so old and worn by time that its name and dates were unintel-
ligible. His sister Gracie, whose rented house this was, had been given
the coffee table–slab by a former boyfriend.) A stain of the color of tea
and the shape of an octopus disfigured a corner of the ceiling but the
missionaries, seated with self-conscious murmurs of thanks on the sofa,
would not see it.

He needed a name to offer to Thelma McCord, or McCrae, who

had so freely offered her name to him. "Flash," he said, inspired, "—my name is Flashman."

He was a man no longer young yet by no means old; nor even, to the eye of a compassionate observer, middle-aged. His ravaged looks, his blood-veined eyes, appeared healable. He was a man given, however, to the habit of irony distasteful to him in execution but virtually impossible to resist. (Like masturbation, to which habit he was, out of irony too, given as well.) When he spoke to Thelma he heard a quaver in his voice that was his quickened, erratic pulse but might sound to another's ear like civility.

He indicated they should take the sofa, and he lowered himself into the nearest butterfly chair on shaky legs. When the damned contraption nearly overturned, the angel-child Magdalena, pale fluffy blond hair and delicate features, jammed her thumb into her mouth to keep from giggling. But her eyes were narrowed, alarmed.

"Mr. Flashman, so pleased to make your acquaintance," Thelma said uncertainly. Smiling at him with worried eyes possibly contemplating was he Jewish.

Contemplating the likelihood of a Jew, a descendant of God's chosen people, living in the scraggly foothills of southwestern Pennsylvania, in a derelict ranch house seven miles from Waynesburg with a front yard that looked as if motorcycles had torn it up. Would a Jew be three days' unshaven, jaws like sandpaper, knobbily barefoot and hairy-limbed as a gorilla. Would a Jew so readily welcome a Holy Witness into his house?

Offer them drinks, lemonade but no, he was thinking, *no.*

This, an opportunity for him to confront goodness, to look innocence direct in the eye, should not be violated.

Thelma promised that her visit would not take many minutes of Mr. Flashman's time. For time, she said, smiling breathlessly, is of the utmost—"That is one of the reasons I am here today."

Reaching deep into the tote bag to remove, he saw with a sinking heart, a hefty black Bible with gilt-edged pages and a stack of pamphlets printed on pulp paper—THE WITNESS. Then easing like a brisk mechanical doll into her recitation.

The man who called himself Flash was making every effort to listen. He knew this was important, there are no accidents. Hadn't he wakened in the night to a pounding heart and a taste of bile with the premonition that something, one of *his things*, was to happen soon; whether of his volition and calculation, or seemingly by accident (but there are no accidents), he could not know. Leaning forward gazing at the young woman with an elbow on his bare knee, the pose of Rodin's *Thinker*, listening hard. Except the woman was a dazzlement of sweaty-fragrant female flesh. Speaking passionately of the love of God and the passion of Jesus Christ and the Book of Revelation of St. John the Divine and the Testament of the Witness. Then eagerly opening her Bible on her knees and dipping her head toward it so that her sand-colored limp-curly hair fell into her face and she had to brush it away repeatedly—he was fascinated by the contrapuntal gestures, the authority of the Bible and the meek dipping of the head and the way in which, with childlike unconscious persistence, she pushed her hair out of her face. Unconscious too of her grating singsong voice, an absurd voice in which no profound truth could ever reside, and of her heavy young breasts straining against the filmy material of her lavender print dress, her fattish-muscular calves and good broad feet in what appeared to be white wicker ballerina slippers.

The grimy venetian blinds of the room were drawn against the glaring heat. It was above ninety degrees outside and there had been no soaking rains for weeks and in every visible tree hung ghostly bagworm nests. In his sister's bedroom a single window-unit air conditioner vibrated noisily and it had been in this room, on top of, not in, the bed, he'd been sleeping when the knocking came at the front door; the room that was his had no air conditioner. Hurrying out, he'd left the door to his sister's bedroom open and now a faint trail of cool-metallic air coiled out into the living room and so he fell to thinking that his visitors would notice the cool air and inquire about it and he would say yes there *is* air conditioning in this house, in one of the bedrooms, shall we go into that room and be more comfortable?

Now the Bible verses were concluded. Thelma's fair, fine skin glowed with excitement. Like a girl who has shared her most intimate secret and expects you now to share yours, Thelma lifted her eyes to Flash's and asked, almost boldly, was he aware of the fact that God loves him?—and he squirmed hearing such words, momentarily unable to respond, he laughed embarrassed, shook his head, ran his fingers over his sandpaper jaws, and mumbled no not really, he guessed that he was not aware of that fact, not really.

Thelma said that was why she was here, to bring the good news to him. That God loved him whether he knew of Him or acknowledged Him. And the Holy Witness their mediator.

Flashman mumbled is that so. A genuine blush darkening his face.

Thelma insisted yes it is so. A brimming in her close-set eyes which were the bluest eyes Flash had never glimpsed except in glamor photos of models, movie stars, naked centerfolds. He said apologetically that he wasn't one hundred percent sure how his credit stood with God these days. "God and me," he said, with a boyish tucked-in smile, "have sort of lost contact over the years."

Which was the answer the young female missionary was primed to expect. Turning to the little girl and whispering in her ear, "Tell Mr. Flashman the good, good news, Magdalena!" and like a wind-up doll the blond child began to recite in a breathy high-pitched voice, "We can lose God but God never loses us. We can despair of God but God never despairs of us. The Holy Witness records, 'He that overcometh shall not be hurt by the second death.' " Abruptly as she'd begun the child ceased, her mouth going slack on the word death.

It was an impressive performance. Yet there was something chilling about it. Flash grinned and winked at the child in his uneasiness and said, "Second death? Eh? What about the first?" But Magdalena just gaped at him. Her left eye losing its focus as if coming unmoored.

The more practiced Thelma quickly intervened. She took up both her daughter's hands in hers and in a brisk patty-cake rhythm chanted, "As the Witness records, 'God shall wipe away all tears from their eyes; and there will be no more death.' "

Maybe it was so? So simple? No more death.

Bemused by the simplicity of fate. In this house unknown to him as recently as last week in this rural no-man's-land where his older sister

Gracie had wound up a county social worker toiling long grueling hours five days a week and forced to be grateful for the shitty job, he'd heard a rapping like a summons to his secret blood padding barefoot to the dream doorway that's shimmering with light and there she *is*.

"Excuse me, Thelma—would you and Magdalena like some lemonade?"

Thelma immediately demurred out of country-bred politeness as he'd expected so he asked Magdalena who appeared to be parched with thirst, poor exploited child, but, annoyingly, she was too shy to even shake her head yes please. Flash, stimulated by challenge, apologized for not having fresh-squeezed lemonade calculating that Thelma would have to accept to prove she wasn't offended by his offer; adding to that he was about to get some lemonade for himself, icy-cold, and would they please join him so Thelma, lowering her eyes, said yes. As if he'd reached out to touch her and she hadn't dared draw back.

In the kitchen, out of sight, he moved swiftly—which was why his name was Flash. For a man distracted, a giant black-feathered eagle tearing out his liver, he moved with a surprising alacrity. But that had always been his way.

Opening the fridge, nostrils pinching against the stale stink inside, his sister Gracie's depressed housekeeping he tried his best to ignore, taking out the stained Tupperware pitcher of Bird's Eye lemonade—thank God, there was some. Tart chemical taste he'd have to mollify, in his own glass, with an ounce or two of Gordon's gin. For his missionary visitors he ducked into his bedroom and located his stash and returned to the kitchen counter crumbling swiftly between his palms several chalky-white pills, six milligrams each of barbiturate, enough to fell a healthy horse, reducing them to gritty powder to dissolve in the greenish lemonade he poured into two glasses: the taller for Thelma, the smaller for Magdalena. He wondered what the little girl weighed—forty pounds? Thirty? Fifty? He had no idea, children were mysteries to him. His own childhood was a mystery to him. But he wouldn't want Magdalena's heart to stop beating.

He'd seen a full-sized man go glassy-eyed and clutch at his heart and topple over stone dead overdosing on—what? Heroin. It was a clean death so far as deaths go but it came out of the corner of your eye, you couldn't prepare.

Carefully setting the three glasses of lemonade, two tall and slim for the adults, the other roly-poly for sweet little Magdalena, on a laminated tray. Returning then humming cheerfully to the airless living room where his visitors were sitting primly on the battered sofa as if, in his absence, they hadn't moved an inch. Shyly yet with trembling hands both reached for their glasses—"Say 'thank you, sir,' " Thelma whispered to Magdalena, who whispered, "Thank you, sir," and lifted her glass to her lips.

Thelma disappointed him by taking only a ladylike sip, then dabbing at her lips with a tissue. "Delicious," she murmured. But setting the glass down as if it was a temptation. Poor Magdalena was holding her glass in both hands taking quick swallows but at a sidelong glance from her mother she too set her glass down on the tray.

Flash said, as if hurt, "There's lots more sugar if it isn't sweet enough."

But Thelma insisted no, it was fine. Taking up, with the look of a woman choosing among several rare gems, one of the pulp-printed pamphlets. Now, Flash guessed, she'd be getting down to business. Enlisting him to join the Church of the Holy Ghost, or whatever it was—Holy Witness?

She named names and cited dates that flew past him—except for the date Easter Sunday 1899 when, apparently, there'd been a "shower from the heavens" north of Scranton, PA—and he nodded to encourage her though she hardly needed encouraging; taking deep thirsty sips from his lemonade to encourage her too. Out of politeness Thelma did lift her glass to take a chaste swallow but no more. Maybe there was a cult prescription against frozen foods, chemical drinks?—the way the Christian Scientists, unless it was the Seventh Day Adventists, forbade blood transfusions because such was "eating blood" which was outlawed by the Bible.

Minutes passed. The faint trickle of metallic-cool air touched the side of his feverish face. He tried not to show his impatience with Thelma fixing instead on the amazing fact of her: a woman not known to him an hour before, now sitting less than a yard away addressing him as if, out of all of the universe, *he mattered.* Loving how she sat wide-hipped and settled into the vinyl cushions like a partridge in a nest. Knees and ankles together, chunky farmgirl feet in the discount-mart wicker flats; half-moons of perspiration darkening the underarms of her floral-print dress. It was a Sunday school kind of dress, lavender rayon with a wide white collar and an awkward flared skirt and cloth-covered buttons the size of half-dollars. Beneath it the woman would be wearing a full slip, no half-slip for her. Damp from her warm pulsing body. No doubt, white brassiere, D-cups, and white cotton panties the waist and legs of which left red rings in her flesh. Undies damp, too. And the crotch of the panties, damp. Just possibly stained. She was bare-legged, no stockings, a concession to the heat: just raw female leg, reddish-blond transparent hairs on the calves for she was not a woman to shave her body hair. Nor did she wear makeup. No such vanity. Her cheeks were flushed as if rouged and her lips were naturally moist and rosy. Her skin would be hot to the touch. She was twenty-eight or -nine years old and probably Magdalena was not her first child, but her youngest. She had the sort of female body mature by early adolescence, beginning to go flaccid by thirty-five. That fair, thin skin that wears out from too much smiling and aiming to please. Suggestion of a double chin. Hips would be spongy and cellulite-puckered. Kneaded like white bread, squeezed banged and bruised. Moist heat of a big bush of curly pubic hair. Secret crevices of pearl-drops of moisture he'd lick away with his tongue.

Another woman would have been aware of Flash's calculating eyes on her like ants swarming over sugar but not this impassioned mission-ary for the Church of the Holy Witness. Had an adder risen quivering with desire before her she would have taken no heed. She was reading from one of THE WITNESS pamphlets and her gaze was shining and inward as she evoked in a hushed little-girl voice a vision of bearded prophets raving in the deserts of Smyrna and covenants made by Jesus Christ to generations of sinners up to this very hour. Jesus Christ was the most spectacular of the prophets, it seemed, for out of his mouth came a sharp two-edged sword casting terror into all who beheld. Yet he was a poet, his words had undeniable power, here was Flash the man squirming in his butterfly chair as Thelma recited tremulously, " 'And Jesus spake: I am he that liveth, and was dead; and, behold, I am alive for evermore; and have the keys of hell and death.' "

There was a pause. A short distance away a neighbor was running a chainsaw and out on the highway cars, trucks, thunderous diesel vehicles passed in an erratic whooshing stream and on all sides beyond the house's walls the air buzzed, quivered, vibrated, rang with the insects of late summer but otherwise it was quiet, it was silent. Like a vacuum waiting to be filled.

The child Magdalena, unobserved by her mother, had drained her glass of lemonade and licked her lips with a flicking pink tongue and was beginning to be drowsy. She wore a pink rayon dress like a nightie with a machine-stamped lace collar, tiny feet in white socks and shiny white plastic shoes. Flash saw, yes, the child's left eye had a cast in it. The right eye perceived you head-on but the left drifted outward like a sly wayward moon.

A defect in an eye of so beautiful a child would not dampen Flash's ardor. He was certain of that.

TEN MINUTES, fifteen. By now it was apparent that Thelma did not intend to drink her lemonade though Flash had drained his own glass and wiped his mouth with gusto. Did she suspect? Did she sense something wrong? But she'd taken no notice of Magdalena who had drifted off into a light doze, her angel-head drooping and a thread of saliva shining on her chin. Surely a suspicious Christian mother would not have allowed her little girl to drink spiked lemonade handed her by a barefoot bare-legged pervert possibly a Jew with eyes like the yanked-up roots of thistles—that was encouraging.

"Your lemonade, Thelma," Flash said, with a host's frown, "—it will be getting warm if you don't—"

Thelma seemed not to hear. With a bright smile she was asking, "Have you been baptized, Mr. Flashman?"

For a moment he could not think who Mr. Flashman was. The gin coursing through his veins which ordinarily buoyed him up like debris riding the crest of a flood and provided him with an acute clarity of mind had had a dulling, downward sort of effect. He was frightened of the possibility of one of *his things* veering out of his control for in the past when this had happened the consequences were always very bad. For him as for others.

His face burned. "I'm afraid that's my private business, Thelma. I don't bare my heart to any stranger who walks in off the road."

Thelma blinked, startled. Yet was immediately repentant. "Oh, I know! I have overstepped myself, please forgive me, Mr. Flashman!"

Such passion quickened the air between them. Flash felt a stab of excitement. But ducking his head, boyish-repentant too, murmuring, "No, it's okay, I'm just embarrassed I guess. I don't truly *know* if I was baptized. I was an orphan discarded at birth, set out with the trash. There's a multitude of us scorned by man and God. What happened to me before the age of twelve is lost to me. Just a whirlwind. A whirlpool of oblivion."

Should have left his sister's bedroom door shut, though. To keep the room cool. If he had to carry or drag this woman any distance—the child wouldn't be much trouble—he'd be miserable by the time he got to where he wanted to go.

Thelma all but exploded with solicitude, leaning forward as if about to gather him up in her arms.

"Oh that's the saddest thing I have ever heard, Mr. Flashman! I wish one of our elders was here right now to counsel you as I cannot! 'Set out with the trash'—can it be? Can any human mother have been so cruel?"

"If it was a cruel mother, which I don't contest, it was a cruel God guiding her hand, Thelma—wasn't it?"

Thelma blinked rapidly. This was a proposition not entirely new to her, Flash surmised, but one which required a moment's careful and conscious recollection. She said, uncertainly at first and then with gathering momentum, "The wickedness of the world is Satan's hand, and the ways of Satan as of the ways of God are not to be comprehended by man."

"What's Satan got to do with this? I thought we were talking about the good guys."

"Our Savior Jesus Christ—"

"*Our* Savior? Who says? On my trash heap I looked up, and He looked down, and He said, 'Fuck you, kid. Life *is* unfair.' "

Thelma's expression was one of absolute astonishment. Like a cow, Flash thought ungallantly, in the instant the sledgehammer comes crashing down on her head.

Flash added, quick to make amends, "I thought this was about me, Thelma, about my soul. I thought the Holy Witness or whoever had something special to say to *me.*"

Thelma was sitting stiff, her hands clasping her knees. One of THE WITNESS pamphlets had fallen to the floor and the hefty Bible too would have slipped had she not caught it. Her eyes now were alert and wary and she knew herself in the presence of an enemy yet did not know that more than theology was at stake. "The Holy Witness does have something special to say to you, Mr. Flashman. Which is why I am here. There is a growing pestilence in the land, flooding the Midwest with the waters of the wrathful Mississippi, last year razing the Sodom and Gomorrah of Florida, everywhere there are droughts and famines and earthquakes and volcanic eruptions and plagues—all signs that the old world is nearing its end. As the Witness proclaimed in the Book of Revelation that is our sacred scripture, 'There will be a new heaven and a new earth, as the first heaven and the first earth pass away. And the Father on His throne declaring, Behold I make all things new—' "

Flash interrupted, "None of this *is* new! It's been around for how many millennia, Thelma, and what good's it done for anybody?"

" '—I am Alpha and Omega, the beginning and the end,' " Thelma continued, unheeding, rising from the sofa like a fleshy angel of wrath in her lavender dress that stuck to her belly and legs, fumbling to gather up her Bible, her pamphlets, her dazed child, " '—I will give unto him that is athirst of the fountain of life freely but the fearful, and unbelieving, and the abominable, and murderers, and all liars, shall sink into the lake which burneth with fire and brimstone: which is the second death.' " Her voice rose jubilantly on the word *death.*

Flash struggled to disentangle himself from the butterfly chair.

The gin had done something weird to his legs—they were numb, and rubbery. Cursing, he fell to the floor, the rock-hard carpetless floor, as Thelma roused Magdalena and lifted her to her feet and half-carried her to the door. Flash tried to raise himself by gripping the granite marker coffee table but this too collapsed, the cinderblocks gave way and the heavy slab came crashing down on his right hand. Three fingers were broken at once but in the excitement he seemed not to notice. "Wait! You can't leave me now! I need you!"

At the door Thelma called back, panting, "Help *is* needed here. There is Satan in this house."

Flash stumbled to his feet, followed the woman to the door, calling after, "What do you mean, 'Satan in this house'—there is no Satan, there is no Devil, it's all in the heads of people like you. You're religious maniacs! You're mad! Wait—"

He could not believe the woman was escaping so easily. That *his thing* was nothing of *his* at all.

Hauling purse, bulky tote bag, sleep-dazed daughter on her hip, Thelma was striding in her white-wicker ballerina flats swiftly yet without apparent haste or panic out to the gravel driveway. There was a terrible quivering of the sun-struck air. Cicadas screamed like fire sirens. Flash tried to follow after, propelling himself on his rubbery legs which were remote from his head which was too small for his body and at the end of a swaying stalk. He was laughing, crying, "You're a joke, people like you! You're tragic victims of ignorance and superstition! You don't belong in the twentieth century with the rest of us! You're the losers of the world! You can't cope! *You* need salvation!"

Staring amazed at the rapidly departing young woman—the dignity in her body, the high-held head and the very arch of the backbone; her indignation that was not fear, an indignation possibly too primitive to concede to fear, like nothing in his experience nor even in his imagination. If this was a movie, he was thinking, panicked, the missionary would be *walking out of the frame* leaving him behind—just him.

"Help! Wait! Don't leave me here alone!"

He was screaming, terrified. He perceived that his life was of no more substance than a cicada's shriek. He'd stumbled as far as the driveway when a blinding light struck him like a sword piercing his eyes and brain.

FALLEN TO HIS KNEES then in the driveway amid sharp gravel and broken glass and bawling like a child beyond all pride, beyond all human shame. His head was bowed, sun beating down on the balding crown of his head. His very soul wept through his eyes for he knew he would die, and nothing would save him not even irony *Don't flatter yourself you matter enough even to grieve! Asshole!*—no, not even his wickedness would save him. Yet seeing him stricken the young Christian woman could not walk away. He cried, "Satan *is* here! In me! He speaks through me! It isn't me! Please help me, don't leave me to die!" His limbs shook as if palsied and his teeth chattered despite the heat. Where the young woman stood wavering there was a blurry shimmering figure of light and he pleaded with it, tore open his chest, belly to expose the putrescent tumor of Satan choking his entrails, he begged for mercy for help for Christ's love until at last the young woman cautiously approached him to a distance of about three feet kneeling too though not in the gravel driveway but in the grass and by degrees putting aside her distrust seeing the sickness in this sinner howling to be saved she bowed her head and clasped her hands to her breasts and began to pray loudly, triumphantly, "O Heavenly Father help this tormented sinner to repent of his sins and to be saved by Your Only Begotten Son that he might stand by the throne of Your righteousness, help all sinners to be saved by the Testament of the Holy Witness—"

How many minutes the missionary prayed over the man who had in jest called himself Flashman he would not afterward know. For there seemed to be a fissure in time itself. The two were locked in ecstasy as in the most intimate of embraces in the fierce heat of the sun, and in the impulsive generosity of her spirit the young woman reached out to clasp his trembling hands in hers and to squeeze them tight. Admonishing him, "Pray! Pray to Jesus Christ! Every hour of every day pray to Him in your heart!" She was weeping too and her face was flushed and swollen and shining with tears. He pleaded with her not to leave him for Satan was still with him, he feared Satan's grip in his soul, but there was a car at the end of the driveway toward which the child Magdalena had made her unsteady way and now a man's voice called, "Thelma! Thel-ma!" and at once the young woman rose to her full height brushing her damp hair out of her face and with a final admonition to him to love God and Christ and abhor Satan and all his ways she was gone, vanished into the light out of which she had come.

Alone he remained kneeling, too weak to stand. Rocking and swaying in the sun. His parched lips moved uttering babble. In a frenzy of self-abnegation he ground his bare knees in the gravel and shattered glass, deep and deeper into the pain so that he might bleed more freely bleeding all impurity from him or at least mutilating his flesh so that in the arid stretch of years before him that would constitute the remainder of his life he would possess a living memory of this hour, scars he might touch, read like Braille.

WHEN GRACIE SHUTTLE returned home hours later she found her brother Harvey in the bathroom dabbing at his wounded knees with a blood-soaked towel, picking bits of gravel and glass out of his flesh with a tweezers. And his hand—several fingers of his right hand were swollen as sausages, and grotesquely bruised. Gracie was a tall lank sardonic woman of forty-one with deep-socketed eyes that rarely acknowledged surprise; yet, seeing Harvey in this remarkable posture, sitting hunched on the toilet seat, a sink of blood-tinged water beside him, she let out a long high whistle. "What the hell happened to *you*?" she asked. Harvey raised his eyes to hers. He did not appear to be drunk, or drugged; his eyes were terribly bloodshot, as if he'd had one of his crying jags, but his manner was unnervingly composed. His face was ravaged and sunburnt in uneven splotches as if it had been baked. He said, "I've been on my knees to Gethsemane and back. It's too private to speak of." From years ago when by an accident of birth they'd shared a household with two hapless adults who were their parents, Gracie knew that her younger brother in such a state was probably telling the truth, or a kind of truth; she knew also that he would never reveal it to her. She waved in his face a pulp religious pamphlet she'd found on the living room floor beside the collapsed granite marker. "And what the hell is *this*?" she demanded. But again with that look of maddening calm Harvey said, "It's my private business, Gracie. Please shut the door on your way out."

Gracie slammed the door in Harvey's face and charged through the house to the rear where wild straggly bamboo was choking the yard. Since she'd moved in three years before the damned bamboo had spread everywhere, marching from the marshy part of the property where the cesspool was located too close to the surface of the soil. Just her luck! And her with a master's degree in social work from the University of Pennsylvania! She'd hoped, she'd expected more from her education, as from life. She lit a cigarette and rapidly smoked it exhaling luxuriant streams of smoke through her nostrils. "Well, fuck you," she said, laughing. She frequently laughed when she was angry, and she laughed a good deal these days.

It *was* funny. Whatever it was, it *was* funny—her parolee kid brother once an honors student now a balding middle-aged man picking tenderly at his knees that looked as if somebody had slashed them with a razor. That blasted-sober look in the poor guy's eyes she hadn't seen in him in twelve years—since one of his junkie buddies in Philly had dropped over dead mainlining heroin.

Some of the bamboo stalks were brown and desiccated but most of the goddamned stuff was still greenly erect, seven feet tall and healthy. Gracie flicked her cigarette butt out into it. Waiting bored to see if it caught fire, if there'd be a little excitement out here on Route 71 tonight, the Waynesburg Volunteer Firemen exercising their shiny red equipment and every yokel for miles hopping in his pickup to come gape—but it didn't, and there wasn't.

AFTERWORD

———

SELECTING A RELATIVELY few stories among so many written since the early 1960s was a project that stirred both anticipation and dread in the selector, for the endeavor has the unmistakable air of the posthumous, like the symmetrical dates 1966–2006. It was painful to leave out so many favorites among my own stories, but I had to abide by a principle of selection: no stories from my most recent collections *Faithless: Tales of Transgression* and *I Am No One You Know*, which are still in print; no "miniature narratives" from *The Assignation*, *Where Is Here?* and elsewhere, though this form, a variant of prose poetry, has long fascinated me; very few surreal or "gothic" tales, which are among the closest to my heart. I wasn't happy to give over so much space to stories like "Where Are You Going, Where Have You Been?" that are readily available in other anthologies, but including them seemed necessary. I think that I can speak for most short story writers in saying that each of our stories exacts from us the same approximate commitment and hope. Prose fiction is, in essence, the realization of an elusive abstract vision in elaborate and painstaking construction, sentence by sentence, word by word. The daunting task for the writer is: what to include? what to exclude? Through our lifetimes a Sargasso Sea of the discarded accumulates, far larger than what is called our "body" of work, for each story is an opening into the infinite, abruptly terminated and sealed in language.

In this endeavor, I was encouraged by my editor Daniel Halpern and my fellow short story writers Greg Johnson and Richard Bausch, to whom thanks and gratitude are due.

Joyce Carol Oates

ACKNOWLEDGMENTS

—

"Upon the Sweeping Flood" and "At the Seminary" are reprinted from *Upon the Sweeping Flood* (1966).

"In the Region of Ice," "Where Are You Going, Where Have You Been?," "How I Contemplated the World . . . ," and "Four Summers" are reprinted from *The Wheel of Love* (1970).

"The Dead" and "The Lady with the Pet Dog" are reprinted from *Marriages & Infidelities* (1962).

"Small Avalanches" and "Concerning the Case of Bobby T." are reprinted from *The Goddess and Other Women* (1974).

"The Tryst" is reprinted from *A Sentimental Education* (1980).

"Last Days," "My Warszawa: 1980," and "Our Wall" are reprinted from *Last Days* (1984).

"Raven's Wing," "Golden Gloves," and "Manslaughter" are reprinted from *Raven's Wing* (1986).

"Heat," "The Knife," "The Hair," and "The Swimmers" are reprinted from *Heat* (1991).

"Will You Always Love Me?," "Life After High School," and "Mark of Satan" are reprinted from *Will You Always Love Me?* (1996).

New Stories

New stories in this collection have originally appeared in the following magazines, in varying versions.

"Spider Boy" in *The New Yorker*.
"The Fish Factory" in *Salmagundi*.
"The Cousins" in *Harper's*; reprinted in *The Best American Short Stories 2005*, edited by Michael Chabon.
"Soft-Core" in *Granta*.
"The Gathering Squall" in *McSweeney's*.
"The Lost Brother" in *Zoëtrope*.
"In Hot May" in *Georgia Review*.
"High Lonesome" in *Zoëtrope*.
*BD*11 1 87" in *Atlantic Monthly*.
"Fat Man My Love" in *Conjunctions*.
"Objects in Mirror Are Closer Than They Appear" in *Boulevard*.